He ran on, ran on, stumbling forward, took another look.

A rider was bearing down on him; he could see the curve of his teeth in a tangled beard.

Wetterlant tried to run faster, tried desperately but he was so tired. Lungs burning, heart burning, breath whooping, the land jerking and see-sawing wildly with every step, the glittering hint of the shallows getting gradually closer, the thunder of hooves behind him—

And he was suddenly on his side, in the mud, an unspeakable agony burning out from his back. A crushing pressure on his chest as if there were rocks piled on it. He managed to move his head to look down. There was something glinting there. Something shining on his jacket in the midst of the dirt. Like a medal. But he hardly deserved a medal for running away.

"How silly," he wheezed, and the words tasted like blood. It had all happened so very, very fast. He found to his surprise, and then to his mounting horror, that he could not breathe.

Praise for

The Heroes

"Abercrombie never glosses over a moment of the madness, passion, and horror of war, nor the tribulations that turn ordinary people into the titular heroes." —*Publishers Weekly* (Starred Review)

"Brilliant." —*Guardian* (UK)

"Reminiscent of…Jim Butcher's Codex Alera novels in terms of scope and military action, this will appeal particularly to military fantasy buffs." —*Library Journal*

"Magnificent, richly entertaining." —*TIME*

"THE HEROES is as irresistibly inviting as a bowl of pistachios. After that first taste, you're going to find it almost impossible to stop until it's all gone." —*Philadelphia Inquirer*

"It's violent and full of treachery and horror, but it's delivered with Abercrombie's signature dark humor and a hint of cynicism." —*Sci Fi* magazine

"An outstanding novel." —Fantasy Book Critic

"This has been my favorite read of the past year and I cannot recommend THE HEROES highly enough." —www.graspingforthewind.com

"The book is gloriously funny. It's like an epic fantasy version of *All Quiet on the Western Front* spiked with some of the irreverence of Altman's *M*A*S*H*. The human tragedy has plenty of comedy to go around." —sff.net

"A blast to read." —sfsite.com

"Though I have loved the books before, for me this is Joe's highlight to date. This is an evolution from, and a distillation of, all that was great in his previous books... The man just keeps getting better and better. Damn him!"

— sffworld.com

Praise for

Best Served Cold

"Joe Abercrombie takes the grand tradition of high fantasy literature and drags it down into the gutter, in the best possible way."   —*TIME*

"Abercrombie is both fiendishly inventive and solidly convincing, especially when sprinkling his appallingly vivid combat scenes with humor so dark that it's almost ultraviolet."   —*Publishers Weekly*

"Joe Abercrombie's *Best Served Cold* is a bloody and relentless epic of vengeance and obsession in the grand tradition."   —George R.R. Martin

"A satisfyingly brutal fantasy quest. *Best Served Cold*? Modern fantasy doesn't get much hotter than this."   —Dave Bradley, *SFX*

"A rich, memorable tale, exciting and well structured."   —sffworld.com

Praise for

The Blade Itself

"Abercrombie has written the finest epic fantasy trilogy in recent memory. He's one writer that no one should miss."   —Junot Diaz

"There are great characters, sparky dialogue, an action-packed plot, and from the very first words ('The End') and an opening scene that is literally a cliffhanger, you know you are in for a cheeky, vivid, exhilarating ride."

—*Starburst*

"Delightfully twisted and evil." —*The Guardian* (UK)

"An admirably hard, fast, and unpretentious read." —*SFX*

"Abercrombie kicks off his series masterfully with a heroic fantasy without conventional heroes...Their dialogue is full of cynicism and wit, their lives full of intrigue, battles, and magic." —*Romantic Times*

"If you're fond of bloodless, turgid fantasy with characters as thin as newspaper and as boring as plaster saints, Joe Abercrombie is really going to ruin your day. A long career for this guy would be a gift to our genre."

—Scott Lynch, author of *The Lies of Locke Lamora*

"In addition to excellent characterizations and fascinating world-building, Abercrombie also writes the best fight scenes I have read in ages. I'm glad the whole package is good, but I could happily recommend *The Blade Itself* for the fight scenes alone." —sfsite.com

"Joe Abercrombie's *The Blade Itself* is sure to delight readers tired of the predictable machinations of standard fantasies...An author to watch."

— bn.com

Praise for

Before They Are Hanged

"Dark, deeply ironic, and full of character gems that will appeal to your cynical side, *Before They Are Hanged* is as brilliant as its predecessor."

—SF Revu

"*Before They Are Hanged* is an excellent sequel from an author writing compelling, character-driven, adult fantasy, for readers who want to be entertained as well as challenged."   — sffworld.com

"This grim and vivid sequel to 2007's *The Blade Itself* transcends its middle volume status, keeping the reader engaged with complicated plotting and intriguing character development."   — *Publishers Weekly*

Praise for

Last Argument of Kings

"You should always end with the best. Wow them in the final act, make the last chorus a belter, build to a climax, and then get them on their feet applauding when the curtain falls. *Last Argument of Kings* is the textbook example of this theory in practice."   — *SFX*

"A seminal work of modern fantasy."   — SF Revu

"Abercrombie is headed for superstar status."   — Jeff VanderMeer

"*Last Argument of Kings* concludes The First Law the way it began: with cynicism, blackly comic repartee, and nonstop, bloody action."
                                                          — *Starburst*

By Joe Abercrombie

THE FIRST LAW TRILOGY

The Blade Itself
Before They Are Hanged
Last Argument of Kings

Best Served Cold

The Heroes

THE
HEROES

JOE ABERCROMBIE

www.orbitbooks.net

Copyright © 2011 by Joe Abercrombie Limited
Excerpt from *The Dragon's Path* Copyright © 2011 by Daniel Abraham
Maps by Dave Senior

Orbit
Hachette Book Group
1290 Avenue of the Americas, New York, NY 10104
www.HachetteBookGroup.com

Originally published in Great Britain by Gollancz, January 2011
First North American Edition: February 2011
First Trade Edition: October 2011

Orbit is an imprint of Hachette Book Group, Inc.
The Orbit name and logo are trademarks of Little, Brown Book Group Limited.

The Library of Congress has cataloged the hardcover edition as follows:

Abercrombie, Joe.
  The heroes / by Joe Abercrombie. — 1st ed.
    p. cm.
  ISBN 978-0-316-04498-1
  1. Imaginary wars and battles—Fiction.   I. Title.
  PR6101.B49H47 2011
  823'.92—dc22

                              2010037868

10   9   8

Printed in the United States of America

ISBN 978-0-316-19356-6 (pbk.)

For Eve
One day you will read this
And say, "Dad, why all the swords?"

Order of Battle

THE UNION

High Command

Lord Marshal Kroy – commander-in-chief of his Majesty's armies in the North.
Colonel Felnigg – his chief of staff, a remarkably chinless man.

Colonel Bremer dan Gorst – royal observer of the Northern War and disgraced master swordsman, formerly the king's First Guard.
Rurgen and Younger – his faithful servants, one old, one…younger.

Bayaz, the First of the Magi – a bald wizard supposedly hundreds of years old and an influential representative of the Closed Council, the king's closest advisors.
Yoru Sulfur – his butler, bodyguard and chief bookkeeper.
Denka and Saurizin – two old Adepti of the University of Adua, academics conducting an experiment for Bayaz.

Jalenhorm's Division

General Jalenhorm – an old friend of the king, fantastically young for his position, described as brave yet prone to blunders.
Retter – his thirteen-year-old bugler.

Colonel Vallimir – ambitious commanding officer of the King's Own
First Regiment.
First Sergeant Forest – chief non-commissioned officer with the staff of
the First.
Corporal Tunny – long-serving profiteer, and standard-bearer of the First.
Troopers Yolk, Klige, Worth, and Lederlingen – clueless recruits
attached to Tunny as messengers.

Colonel Wetterlant – punctilious commanding officer of the Sixth
Regiment.
Major Culfer – his panicky second in command.
Sergeant Gaunt, Private Rose – soldiers with the Sixth.

Major Popol – commanding the first battalion of the Rostod Regiment.
Captain Lasmark – a poor captain with the Rostod Regiment.

Colonel Vinkler – courageous commanding officer of the Thirteenth
Regiment.

Mitterick's Division

General Mitterick – a professional soldier with much chin and little
loyalty, described as sharp but reckless.
Colonel Opker – his chief of staff.
Lieutenant Dimbik – an unconfident young officer on Mitterick's staff.

Meed's Division

Lord Governor Meed – an amateur soldier with a neck like a turtle, in
peacetime the governor of Angland, described as hating Northmen like
a pig hates butchers.
Colonel Harod dan Brock – an honest and hard-working member of
Meed's staff, the son of a notorious traitor.
Finree dan Brock – Colonel Brock's venomously ambitious wife, the
daughter of Lord Marshal Kroy.
Colonel Brint – senior on Meed's staff, an old friend of the king.
Aliz dan Brint – Colonel Brint's naive young wife.
Captain Hardrick – an officer on Meed's staff, affecting tight trousers.

The Dogman's Loyalists

The Dogman – Chief of those Northmen fighting with the Union. An old companion of the Bloody-Nine, once a close friend of Black Dow, now his bitter enemy.

Red-Hat – the Dogman's Second, who wears a red hood.

Hardbread – a Named Man of long experience, leading a dozen for the Dogman.

Redcrow – one of Hardbread's Carls.

THE NORTH

In and Around Skarling's Chair

Black Dow – the Protector of the North, or stealer of it, depending on who you ask.

Splitfoot – his Second, meaning chief bodyguard and arse-licker.

Ishri – his advisor, a sorceress from the desert South, and sworn enemy of Bayaz.

Caul Shivers – a scarred Named Man with a metal eye, who some call Black Dow's dog.

Curnden Craw – a Named Man thought of as a straight edge, once Second to Rudd Threetrees, then close to Bethod, now leading a dozen for Black Dow.

Wonderful – his long-suffering Second.

Whirrun of Bligh – a famous hero from the utmost North, who wields the Father of Swords. Also called Cracknut, on account of his nut being cracked.

Jolly Yon Cumber, Brack-i-Dayn, Scorry Tiptoe, Agrick, Athroc and Drofd – other members of Craw's dozen.

Scale's Men

Scale – Bethod's eldest son, now the least powerful of Dow's five War Chiefs, strong as a bull, brave as a bull, and with a bull's brain too.

Pale-as-Snow – once one of Bethod's War Chiefs, now Scale's Second.

White-Eye Hansul – a Named Man with a blind eye, once Bethod's herald.

"Prince" Calder – Bethod's younger son, an infamous coward and schemer, temporarily exiled for suggesting peace.

Seff – his pregnant wife, the daughter of Caul Reachey.

Deep and Shallow – a pair of killers, watching over Calder in the hope of riches.

Caul Reachey's Men

Caul Reachey – one of Dow's five War Chiefs, an elderly warrior, famously honourable, father to Seff, father-in-law to Calder.

Brydian Flood – a Named Man formerly a member of Craw's dozen.

Beck – a young farmer craving glory on the battlefield, the son of Shama Heartless.

Reft, Colving, Stodder and Brait – other young lads pressed into service with Beck.

Glama Golden's Men

Glama Golden – one of Dow's five War Chiefs, intolerably vain, locked in a feud with Cairm Ironhead.

Sutt Brittle – a famously greedy Named Man.

Lightsleep – a Carl in Golden's employ.

Cairm Ironhead's Men

Cairm Ironhead – one of Dow's five War Chiefs, notoriously stubborn, locked in a feud with Glama Golden.

Curly – a stout-hearted scout.

Irig – an ill-tempered axeman.

Temper – a foul-mouthed bowman.

Others

Brodd Tenways – the most loyal of Dow's five War Chiefs, ugly as incest.

Stranger-Come-Knocking – a giant savage obsessed with civilisation, Chief of all the lands east of the Crinna.

Back to the Mud (dead, thought dead, or long dead)

Bethod – the first King of the Northmen, father to Scale and Calder.

Skarling Hoodless – a legendary hero who once united the North against the Union.

The Bloody-Nine – once Bethod's champion, the most feared man in the North, and briefly King of the Northmen before being killed by Black Dow (supposedly).

Rudd Threetrees – a famously honourable Chief of Uffrith, who fought against Bethod and was beaten in a duel by the Bloody-Nine.

Forley the Weakest – a notoriously weak fighter, companion to Black Dow and the Dogman, ordered killed by Calder.

Shama Heartless – a famous champion killed by the Bloody-Nine. Beck's father.

BEFORE THE BATTLE

"Unhappy the land
that is in need
of heroes"

Bertolt Brecht

THE VALLEY OF OSRUNG

USTRED

YAWS

Holcum Farm

Bear Farm

Skarling's Finger

THE HEROES

The Chi

Moss Beck

Clail Farm

Clail's

Wall

Stole Farm

Old Bridge

Adwein

UFFRITH

TRICK GILL

Lock Fell

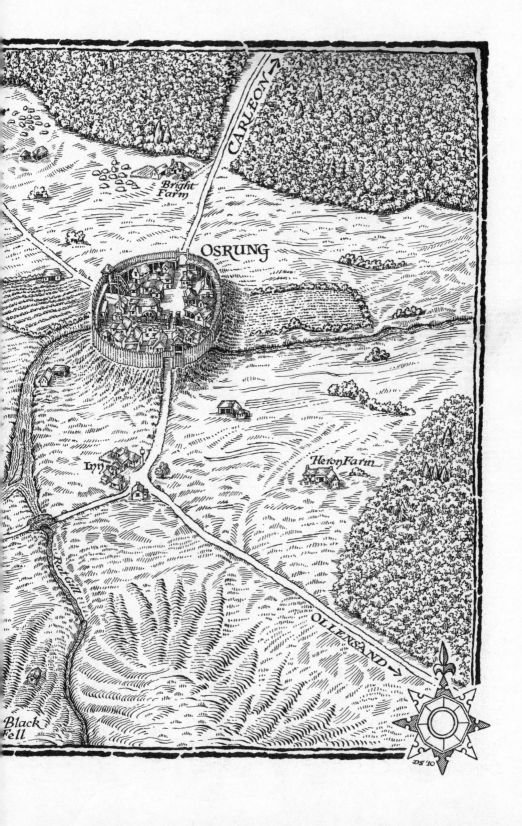

CARLEON →

Bright
Farm

OSRUNG

Lyn

Heron Farm

Red Gill

OLLENSAND →

Black
Fell

DS '10

The Times

Too old for this shit," muttered Craw, wincing at the pain in his dodgy knee with every other step. High time he retired. Long past high time. Sat on the porch behind his house with a pipe, smiling at the water as the sun sank down, a day's honest work behind him. Not that he had a house. But when he got one, it'd be a good one.

He found his way through a gap in the tumble-down wall, heart banging like a joiner's mallet. From the long climb up the steep slope, and the wild grass clutching at his boots, and the bullying wind trying to bundle him over. But mostly, if he was honest, from the fear he'd end up getting killed at the top. He'd never laid claim to being a brave man and he'd only got more cowardly with age. Strange thing, that – the fewer years you have to lose the more you fear the losing of 'em. Maybe a man just gets a stock of courage when he's born, and wears it down with each scrape he gets into.

Craw had been through a lot of scrapes. And it looked like he was about to snag himself on another.

He snatched a breather as he finally got to level ground, bent over, rubbing the wind-stung tears from his eyes. Trying to muffle his coughing which only made it louder. The Heroes loomed from the dark ahead, great holes in the night sky where no stars shone, four times man-height or more. Forgotten giants, marooned on their hilltop in the scouring wind. Standing stubborn guard over nothing.

Craw found himself wondering how much each of those great slabs of rock weighed. Only the dead knew how they'd dragged the bastard things up here. Or who had. Or why. The dead weren't telling, though, and Craw had no plans on joining 'em just to find out.

He saw the faintest glow of firelight now, at the stones' rough edges.

Heard the chatter of men's voices over the wind's low growl. That brought
back the risk he was taking, and a fresh wave of fear washed up with it. But
fear's a healthy thing, long as it makes you think. Rudd Threetrees told
him that, long time ago. He'd thought it through, and this was the right
thing to do. Or the least wrong thing, anyway. Sometimes that's the best
you can hope for.

So he took a deep breath, trying to remember how he'd felt when he
was young and had no dodgy joints and didn't care a shit for nothing,
picked out a likely gap between two of those big old rocks and strolled
through.

Maybe this had been a sacred place, once upon an ancient day, high
magic in these stones, the worst of crimes to wander into the circle unin-
vited. But if any old Gods took offence they'd no way of showing it. The
wind dropped away to a mournful sighing and that was all. Magic was in
scarce supply and there wasn't much sacred either. Those were the times.

The light shifted on the inside faces of the Heroes, faint orange on pitted
stone, splattered with moss, tangled with old bramble and nettle and seeding grass. One was broken off half way up, a couple more had toppled over
the centuries, left gaps like missing teeth in a skull's grin.

Craw counted eight men, huddled around their wind-whipped campfire
with patched cloaks and worn coats and tattered blankets wrapped tight.
Firelight flickered on gaunt, scarred, stubbled and bearded faces. Glinted
on the rims of their shields, the blades of their weapons. Lots of weapons.
Fair bit younger, in the main, but they didn't look much different to Craw's
own crew of a night. Probably they weren't much different. He even thought
for a moment one man with his face side-on was Jutlan. Felt that jolt of
recognition, the eager greeting ready on his lips. Then he remembered Jutlan was twelve years in the ground, and he'd said the words over his grave.

Maybe there are only so many faces in the world. You get old enough,
you start seeing 'em used again.

Craw lifted his open hands high, palms forward, doing his best to stop
'em shaking any. "Nice evening!"

The faces snapped around. Hands jerked to weapons. One man snatched
up a bow and Craw felt his guts drop, but before he got close to drawing the
string the man beside him stuck out an arm and pushed it down.

"Whoa there, Redcrow." The one who spoke was a big old lad, with a
heavy tangle of grey beard and a drawn sword sitting bright and ready

across his knees. Craw found a rare grin, 'cause he knew the face, and his chances were looking better.

Hardbread he was called, a Named Man from way back. Craw had been on the same side as him in a few battles down the years, and the other side from him in a few more. But he'd a solid reputation. A long-seasoned hand, likely to think things over, not kill then ask the questions, which was getting to be the more popular way of doing business. Looked like he was Chief of this lot too, 'cause the lad called Redcrow sulkily let his bow drop, much to Craw's relief. He didn't want anyone getting killed tonight, and wasn't ashamed to say that counted double for his self.

There were still a fair few hours of darkness to get through, though, and a lot of sharpened steel about.

"By the dead." Hardbread sat still as the Heroes themselves, but his mind was no doubt doing a sprint. "'Less I'm much mistaken, Curnden Craw just wandered out o' the night."

"You ain't." Craw took a few slow paces forwards, hands still high, doing his best to look light-hearted with eight sets of unfriendly eyes weighing him down.

"You're looking a little greyer, Craw."

"So are you, Hardbread."

"Well, you know. There's a war on." The old warrior patted his stomach. "Plays havoc with my nerves."

"All honesty, mine too."

"Who'd be a soldier?"

"Hell of a job. But they say old horses can't jump new fences."

"I try not to jump at all these days," said Hardbread. "Heard you was fighting for Black Dow. You and your dozen."

"Trying to keep the fighting to a minimum, but as far as who I'm doing it for, you're right. Dow buys my porridge."

"I love porridge." Hardbread's eyes rolled down to the fire and he poked thoughtfully at it with a twig. "The Union pays for mine now." His lads were twitchy – tongues licking at lips, fingers tickling at weapons, eyes shining in the firelight. Like the audience at a duel, watching the opening moves, trying to suss who had the upper hand. Hardbread's eyes came up again. "That seems to put us on opposite sides."

"We going to let a little thing like sides spoil a polite conversation?" asked Craw.

As though the very word "polite" was an insult, Redcrow had another rush of blood. "Let's just kill this fucker!"

Hardbread turned slowly to him, face squeezed up with scorn. "If the impossible happens and I feel the need for your contribution, I'll tell you what it is. 'Til then keep it shut, halfhead. Man o' Curnden Craw's experience don't just wander up here to get killed by the likes o' you." His eyes flicked around the stones, then back to Craw. "Why'd you come, all by your lone self? Don't want to fight for that bastard Black Dow no more, and you've come over to join the Dogman?"

"Can't say I have. Fighting for the Union ain't really my style, no disrespect to those that do. We all got our reasons."

"I try not to damn a man on his choice o' friends alone."

"There's always good men on both sides of a good question," said Craw. "Thing is, Black Dow asked me to stroll on down to the Heroes, stand a watch for a while, see if the Union are coming up this way. But maybe you can spare me the bother. Are the Union coming up this way?"

"Dunno."

"You're here, though."

"I wouldn't pay much mind to that." Hardbread glanced at the lads around the fire without great joy. "As you can see, they more or less sent me on my own. The Dogman asked me to stroll up to the Heroes, stand a watch, see if Black Dow or any of his lot showed up." He raised his brows. "You think they will?"

Craw grinned. "Dunno."

"You're here, though."

"Wouldn't pay much mind to that. It's just me and my dozen. 'Cept for Brydian Flood, he broke his leg a few months ago, had to leave him behind to mend."

Hardbread gave a rueful smile, prodded the fire with his twig and sent up a dusting of sparks. "Yours always was a tight crew. I daresay they're scattered around the Heroes now, bows to hand."

"Something like that." Hardbread's lads all twitched to the side, mouths gaping. Shocked at the voice coming from nowhere, shocked on top that it was a woman's. Wonderful stood with her arms crossed, sword sheathed and bow over her shoulder, leaning up against one of the Heroes as careless as she might lean on a tavern wall. "Hey, hey, Hardbread."

The old warrior winced. "Couldn't you even nock an arrow, make it look like you take us serious?"

She jerked her head into the darkness. "There's some boys back there, ready to put a shaft through your face if one o' you looks at us wrong. That make you feel better?"

Hardbread winced even more. "Yes and no," he said, his lads staring into the gaps between the stones, the night suddenly heavy with threat. "Still acting Second to this article, are you?"

Wonderful scratched at the long scar through her shaved-stubble hair. "No better offers. We've got to be like an old married couple who haven't fucked for years, just argue."

"Me and my wife were like that, 'til she died." Hardbread's finger tapped at his drawn sword. "Miss her now, though. Thought you'd have company from the first moment I saw you, Craw. But since you're still jawing and I'm still breathing, I reckon you're set on giving us a chance to talk this out."

"Then you've reckoned the shit out o' me," said Craw. "That's exactly the plan."

"My sentries alive?"

Wonderful turned her head and gave one of her whistles, and Scorry Tiptoe slid out from behind one of the stones. Had his arm around a man with a big pink birthmark on his cheek. Looked almost like two old mates, 'til you saw Scorry's hand had a blade in it, edge tickling at Birthmark's throat.

"Sorry, Chief," said the prisoner to Hardbread. "Caught me off guard."

"It happens."

A scrawny lad came stumbling into the firelight like he'd been shoved hard, tripped over his own feet and sprawled in the long grass with a squawk. Jolly Yon stalked from the darkness behind him, axe held loose in one fist, heavy blade gleaming down by his boot, heavy frown on his bearded face.

"Thank the dead for that." Hardbread waved his twig at the lad, just clambering up. "My sister's son. Promised I'd keep an eye out. If you'd killed him I'd never have heard the end of it."

"He was asleep," growled Yon. "Weren't looking out too careful, were you?"

Hardbread shrugged. "Weren't expecting anyone. If there's two things we've got too much of in the North it's hills and rocks. Didn't reckon a hill with rocks on it would be a big draw."

"It ain't to me," said Craw, "but Black Dow said come down here—"

"And when Black Dow says a thing…" Brack-i-Dayn half-sang the words, that way the hillmen tend to. He stepped into the wide circle of grass, tattooed side of his great big face turned towards the firelight, shadows gathered in the hollows of the other.

Redcrow made to jump up but Hardbread weighed him down with a pat on the shoulder. "My, my. You lot just keep popping up." His eyes slid from Jolly Yon's axe, to Wonderful's grin, to Brack's belly, to Scorry's knife still at his man's throat. Judging the odds, no doubt, just the way Craw would've done. "You got Whirrun of Bligh with you?"

Craw slowly nodded. "I don't know why, but he insists on following me around."

Right on cue, Whirrun's strange valley accent floated from the dark. "Shoglig said…I would be shown my destiny…by a man choking on a bone." It echoed off the stones, seeming to come from everywhere at once. He'd quite the sense of theatre, Whirrun. Every real hero needs one. "And Shoglig is old as these stones. Hell won't take her, some say. Blade won't cut her. Saw the world born, some say, and will see it die. That's a woman a man has to listen to, ain't it? Or so some say."

Whirrun strolled through the gap one of the missing Heroes had left and into the firelight, tall and lean, face in shadow from his hood, patient as winter. He had the Father of Swords across his shoulders like a milkmaid's yoke, dull grey metal of the hilt all agleam, arms slung over the sheathed blade and his long hands dangling. "Shoglig told me the time, and the place, and the manner of my death. She whispered it, and made me swear to keep it secret, for magic shared is no magic at all. So I cannot tell you where it will be, or when, but it is not here, and it is not now." He stopped a few paces from the fire. "You boys, on the other hand…" Whirrun's hooded head tipped to one side, only the end of his sharp nose, and the line of his sharp jaw, and his thin mouth showing. "Shoglig didn't say when you'd be going." He didn't move. He didn't have to. Wonderful looked at Craw, and rolled her eyes towards the starry sky.

But Hardbread's lads hadn't heard it all a hundred times before. "That Whirrun?" one muttered to his neighbour. "Cracknut Whirrun? That's him?"

His neighbour said nothing, just the lump on the front of his throat moving as he swallowed.

"Well, my old arse if I'm fighting my way out o' this," said Hardbread, brightly. "Any chance you'd let us clear out?"

"I've a mind to insist on it," said Craw.

"We can take our gear?"

"I'm not looking to embarrass you. I just want your hill."

"Or Black Dow does, at any rate."

"Same difference."

"Then you're welcome to it." Hardbread slowly got to his feet, wincing as he straightened his legs, no doubt cursed with some sticky joints of his own. "Windy as anything up here. Rather be down in Osrung, feet near a fire." Craw had to admit he'd a point there. Made him wonder who'd got the better end of the deal. Hardbread sheathed his sword, thoughtful, while his lads gathered their gear. "This is right decent o' you, Craw. You're a straight edge, just like they say. Nice that men on different sides can still talk things through, in the midst of all this. Decent behaviour . . . it's out o' fashion."

"Those are the times." Craw jerked his head at Scorry and he slipped his knife away from Birthmark's throat, gave this little bow and held his open hand out towards the fire. Birthmark backed off, rubbing at the new-shaved patch on his stubbly neck, and started rolling up a blanket. Craw hooked his thumbs in his sword-belt and kept his eyes on Hardbread's crew as they made ready to go, just in case anyone had a mind to play hero.

Redcrow looked most likely. He'd slung his bow over his shoulder and now he was standing there with a black look, an axe in one white-knuckled fist and a shield on his other arm, a red bird painted on it. If he'd been for killing Craw before, didn't seem the last few minutes had changed his mind. "A few old shits and some fucking woman," he snarled. "We're backing down to the likes o' these without a fight?"

"No, no." Hardbread slung his own scarred shield onto his back. "I'm backing down, and these fellows here. You're going to stay, and fight Whirrun of Bligh on your own."

"I'm what?" Redcrow frowned at Whirrun, twitchy, and Whirrun looked back, what showed of his face still stony as the Heroes themselves.

"That's right," said Hardbread, "since you're itching for a brawl. Then I'm going to cart your hacked-up corpse back to your mummy and tell her not to worry 'cause this is the way you wanted it. You loved this fucking hill so much you just had to die here."

Redcrow's hand worked nervously around his axe handle. "Eh?"

"Or maybe you'd rather come down with the rest of us, blessing the name o' Curnden Craw for giving us a fair warning and letting us go without any arrows in our arses."

"Right," said Redcrow, and turned away, sullen.

Hardbread puffed his cheeks at Craw. "Young ones these days, eh? Were we ever so stupid?"

Craw shrugged. "More'n likely."

"Can't say I felt the need for blood like they seem to, though."

Craw shrugged again. "Those are the times."

"True, true, and three times true. We'll leave you the fire, eh? Come on, boys." They made for the south side of the hill, still stowing the last of their gear, and one by one faded into the night between the stones.

Hardbread's nephew turned in the gap and gave Craw the fuck yourself finger. "We'll be back here, you sneaking bastards!" His uncle cuffed him across the top of his scratty head. "Ow! What?"

"Some respect."

"Ain't we fighting a war?"

Hardbread cuffed him again and made him squeal. "No reason to be rude, you little shit."

Craw stood there as the lad's complaints faded into the wind beyond the stones, swallowed sour spit, and eased his thumbs out from his belt. His hands were trembling, had to rub 'em together to hide it, pretending he was cold. But it was done, and everyone involved still drawing breath, so he guessed it had worked out as well as anyone could've hoped.

Jolly Yon didn't agree. He stepped up beside Craw frowning like thunder and spat into the fire. "Time might come we regret not killing those folks there."

"Not killing don't tend to weigh as heavy on my conscience as the alternative."

Brack tut-tutted from Craw's other side. "A warrior shouldn't carry too much conscience."

"A warrior shouldn't carry too much belly either." Whirrun had shrugged the Father of Swords off his shoulders and stood it on end, the pommel coming up to his neck, watching how the light moved on the crosspiece as he turned it round and round. "We all got our weights to heft."

"I've got just the right amount, you stringy bastard." And the hillman gave his great gut a proud pat like a father might give his son's head.

"Chief." Agrick strode into the firelight, bow loose in his hand and an arrow dangling between two fingers.

"They away?" asked Craw.

"Watched 'em down past the Children. They're crossing the river now, heading towards Osrung. Athroc's keeping a watch on 'em, though. We'll know if they double back."

"You reckon they will?" asked Wonderful. "Hardbread's cut from the old cloth. He might smile, but he won't have liked this any. You trust that old bastard?"

Craw frowned into the night. " 'Bout as much as I'd trust anyone these days."

"Little as that? Best post guards."

"Aye," said Brack. "And make sure ours stay awake."

Craw thumped his arm. "Nice o' you to volunteer for first shift."

"Your belly can keep you company," said Yon.

Craw thumped his arm next. "Glad you're in favour, you can go second."

"Shit!"

"Drofd!"

You could tell the curly lad was the newest of the crew 'cause he actually hurried up with some snap. "Aye, Chief?"

"Take the saddle horse and head back up the Yaws Road. Not sure whose lads you'll meet first – Ironhead's most likely, or maybe Tenways'. Let 'em know we ran into one of the Dogman's dozens at the Heroes. More'n likely just scouting, but…"

"Just scouting." Wonderful nibbled some scab off one knuckle and spat it from the tip of her tongue. "The Union are miles away, split up and spread out, trying to make straight lines out of a country with none."

"More'n likely. But hop on the horse and pass on the message anyway."

"Now?" Drofd's face was all dismay. "In the dark?"

"No, next summer'll be fine," snapped Wonderful. "Yes, now, fool, all you've got to do is follow a road."

Drofd heaved a sigh. "Hero's work."

"All war work is hero's work, boy," said Craw. He'd rather have sent someone else, but then they'd have been arguing 'til dawn over why the new lad wasn't going. There are right ways of doing things a man can't just step around.

"Right y'are, Chief. See you in a few days, I reckon. And with a sore arse, no doubt."

"Why?" And Wonderful gave a few thrusts of her hips. "Tenways a special friend o' yours is he?" That got some laughs. Brack's big rumble, Scorry's little chuckle, even Yon's frown got a touch softer which meant he had to be rightly tickled.

"Ha, bloody ha." And Drofd stalked off into the night to find the horse and make a start.

"I hear chicken fat can ease the passage!" Wonderful called after him, Whirrun's cackle echoing around the Heroes and off into the empty dark.

With the excitement over Craw was starting to feel all burned out. He dropped down beside the fire, wincing as his knees bent low, the earth still warm from Hardbread's rump. Scorry had found a place on the far side, sharpening his knife, the scraping of metal marking the rhythm to his soft, high singing. A song of Skarling Hoodless, greatest hero of the North, who brought the clans together long ago to drive the Union out. Craw sat and listened, chewed at the painful skin around his fingernails and thought about how he really had to stop doing it.

Whirrun set the Father of Swords down, squatted on his haunches and pulled out the old bag he kept his runes in. "Best do a reading, eh?"

"You have to?" muttered Yon.

"Why? Scared o' what the signs might tell you?"

"Scared you'll spout a stack of nonsense and I'll lie awake half the night trying to make sense of it."

"Guess we'll see." Whirrun emptied his runes into his cupped hand, spat on 'em then tossed 'em down by the fire.

Craw couldn't help craning over to see, though he couldn't read the damn things for any money. "What do the runes say, Cracknut?"

"The runes say..." Whirrun squinted down like he was trying to pick out something a long way off. "There's going to be blood."

Wonderful snorted. "They always say that."

"Aye." Whirrun wrapped himself in his coat, nuzzled up against the hilt of his sword like a lover, eyes already shut. "But lately they're right more often than not."

Craw frowned around at the Heroes, forgotten giants, standing stubborn guard over nothing. "Those are the times," he muttered.

The Peacemaker

He stood by the window, one hand up on the stone, fingertips drumming, drumming, drumming. Frowning off across Carleon. Across the maze of cobbled streets, the tangle of steep slate roofs, the looming city walls his father built, all turned shiny black by the drizzle. Into the hazy fields beyond, past the fork of the grey river and towards the streaky rumour of hills at the head of the valley. As if, by sulking hard enough, he could see further. Over two score miles of broken country to Black Dow's scattered army. Where the fate of the North was being decided.

Without him.

"All I want is just for everyone to do what I tell them. Is that too much to ask?"

Seff slid up behind him, belly pressing into his back. "I'd say it's no more than good sense on their part."

"I know what's best anyway, don't I?"

"I do, and I tell you what it is, so . . . yes."

"It seems there are a few pig-headed bastards in the North who don't realise we have all the answers."

Her hand slipped up his arm and trapped his restless fingers against the stone. "Men don't like to come out for peace, but they will. You'll see."

"And until then, like all visionaries, I find myself spurned. Scorned. Exiled."

"Until then, you find yourself locked in a room with your wife. Is that so bad?"

"There's nowhere I'd rather be," he lied.

"Liar," she whispered, lips tickling his ear. "You're almost as much of a liar as they say you are. You'd rather be out there, beside your brother, with your armour on." Her hands slid under his armpits and across his chest, giving him a ticklish shiver. "Hacking the heads from cartloads of Southerners."

"Murder is my favourite hobby, as you know."

"You've killed more men than Skarling."

"And I'd wear my armour to bed if I could."

"It's only concern for my soft, soft skin that stops you."

"But severed heads are prone to squirt." He wriggled around to face her and pushed one lazy fingertip into her breastbone. "I prefer a quick thrust through the heart."

"Just like you've skewered mine. Aren't you the swordsman."

He squeaked as he felt her hand between his legs and slid away sniggering across the wall, arms up to fend her off. "All right, I admit it! I'm more lover than fighter!"

"At last the truth. Only look what you've done to me." Putting one hand on her stomach and giving him a disapproving frown. It turned into a smile as he came close, slid his hand over hers, fingertips between hers, stroking her swollen belly.

"It's a boy," she whispered. "I feel it. An heir to the North. You'll be king, and then—"

"Shhhhh." And he stopped her mouth with a kiss. There was no way of knowing when someone might be listening, and anyway, "I've got an older brother, remember?"

"A pinhead of an older brother."

Calder winced, but didn't deny it. He sighed as he looked down at that strange, wonderful, frightening belly of hers. "My father always said there's nothing more important than family." Except power. "Besides, there's no point arguing over what we don't have. Black Dow's the one who wears my father's chain. Black Dow's the one we need to worry on."

"Black Dow's nothing but a one-eared thug."

"A thug with all the North under his boot and its mightiest War Chiefs taking his say-so."

"Mighty War Chiefs." She snorted in his face. "Dwarves with big men's names."

"Brodd Tenways."

"That rotten old maggot? Even the thought of him makes me sick."

"Cairm Ironhead."

"I hear he has a tiny little prick. That's why he frowns all the time."

"Glama Golden."

"Even tinier. Like a baby's finger. And you have allies."

"I do?"

"You know you do. My father likes you."

Calder screwed up his face. "Your father doesn't hate me, but I doubt he'll be leaping up to cut the rope if they hang me."

"He's an honourable man."

"Of course he is. Caul Reachey's a real straight edge, everyone knows it." For what that was worth. "But you and I were promised when I was the son of the King of the Northmen and the world was all different. He was getting a prince for a son-in-law, not just a well-known coward."

She patted his cheek, hard enough to make a gentle slapping sound. "A beautiful coward."

"Beautiful men are even less well liked in the North than cowardly ones. I'm not sure your father's happy with the way my luck's turned."

"Shit on your luck." She took a fistful of his shirt and dragged him closer, much stronger than she looked. "I wouldn't change a thing."

"Neither would I. I'm just saying your father might."

"And I'm saying you're wrong." She caught his hand in hers and pressed it against her bulging stomach again. "You're family."

"Family." He didn't bother saying that family could be as much a weakness as a strength. "So we have your honourable father and my pinhead brother. The North is ours."

"It will be. I know it." She was swaying backwards slowly, leading him away from the window and towards the bed. "Dow may be the man for war, but wars don't last forever. You're better than him."

"Few would agree." But it was nice to hear it, especially whispered in his ear in that soft, low, urgent voice.

"You're cleverer than him." Her cheek brushing his jaw. "Far cleverer." Her nose nuzzling his chin. "The cleverest man in the North." By the dead, how he loved flattery.

"Go on."

"You're certainly better looking than him." Squeezing his hand and sliding it down her belly. "The most handsome man in the North…"

He licked her lips with the tip of his tongue. "If the most beautiful ruled you'd be Queen of the Northmen already…"

Her fingers were busy with his belt. "You always know just what to say, don't you, Prince Calder…"

There was a thumping at the door and he froze, the blood suddenly pounding in his head and very much not in his cock. Nothing like the threat of sudden death for killing a romantic mood. The thumping came again, making the heavy door rattle. They broke apart, flushed and fussing with their clothes. More like a pair of child lovers caught by their parents than a man and woman five years married. So much for his dreams of being king. He didn't even command the lock on his own door.

"The damn bolt's on your side isn't it?" he snapped.

Metal scraped and the door creaked open. A man stood in the archway, shaggy head almost touching the keystone. The ruined side of his face was turned forwards, a mass of scar running from near the corner of his mouth, through his eyebrow and across his forehead, the dead metal ball in his blind socket glinting. If any trace of romance had been lingering in the corners, or in Calder's trousers, that eye and that scar were its grisly end. He felt Seff stiffen and, since she was a long stretch braver than he was, her fear did nothing for his own. Caul Shivers was about the worst omen a man could see. Folk called him Black Dow's dog, but never to his burned-out face. The man the Protector of the North sent to do his blackest work.

"Dow wants you." If the sight of Shivers' face had only got some hero half way horrified, his voice would have done the rest of the job. A broken whisper that made every word sound like it hurt.

"Why?" asked Calder, keeping his own voice sunny as a summer morning in spite of his hammering heart. "Can't he beat the Union without me?"

Shivers didn't laugh. He didn't frown. He stood there, in the doorway, a silent slab of menace.

Calder tried his best at a carefree shrug. "Well, I suppose everyone serves someone. What about my wife?"

Shivers' good eye flicked across to Seff. If he'd looked with leering lust, or sneering disgust, Calder would've been happier. But Shivers looked at a pregnant woman like a butcher at a carcass, only a job to be done. "Dow wants her to stay and stand hostage. Make sure everyone behaves. She'll be safe."

"As long as everyone behaves." Calder found he'd stepped in front of her, as if to shield her with his body. Not much of a shield against a man like Shivers.

"That's it."

"And if Black Dow misbehaves? Where's my hostage?"

Shivers' eye slid back to Calder, and stuck. "I'll be your hostage."

"And if Dow breaks his word I can kill you, can I?"

"You can try."

"Huh." Caul Shivers had one of the hardest names in the North. Calder, it hardly needed to be said, didn't. "Can you give us a moment to say our goodbyes?"

"Why not?" Shivers slid back until only the glint of his metal eye showed in the shadows. "I'm no monster."

"Back to the snake pit," muttered Calder.

Seff caught his hand, eyes wide as she looked up at him, fearful and eager at once. Almost as fearful and eager as he was. "Be patient, Calder. Tread carefully."

"I'll tiptoe all the way there." If he even made it. He reckoned there was about a one in four Shivers had been told to cut his throat on the way and toss his corpse in a bog.

She took his chin between her finger and thumb and shook it, hard. "I mean it. Dow fears you. My father says he'll take any excuse to kill you."

"Dow should fear me. Whatever else I am, I'm my father's son."

She squeezed his chin even harder, looking him right in the eye. "I love you."

He looked down at the floor, feeling the sudden pressure of tears at the back of his throat. "Why? Don't you realise what an evil shit I am?"

"You're better than you think."

When she said it he could almost believe it. "I love you too." And he didn't even have to lie. How he'd raged when his father announced the match. Marry that pig-nosed, dagger-tongued little bitch? Now she looked more beautiful every time he saw her. He loved her nose, and her tongue even more. It was almost enough to make him swear off other women. He drew her close, blinking back the wet, and kissed her once more. "Don't worry. No one's less keen to attend my hanging than I am. I'll be back in your bed before you know it."

"With your armour on?"

"If you like," as he backed away.

"And no lying while you're gone."

"I never lie."

"Liar," she mouthed at him before the guards closed the door and slid the bolt, leaving Calder in the shadowy hallway with only the sappy-sad thought that he might never see his wife again. That gave him a rare touch of bravery and he hurried after Shivers, catching up with him as he trudged away and slapping a hand down on his shoulder. He was more than a little unnerved by the wood-like solidity of it, but plunged on regardless.

"If anything happens to her, I promise you—"

"I hear your promises ain't up to much." Shivers' eye went to the offending hand and Calder carefully removed it. He might only rarely be brave, but he was never brave past the point of good sense.

"Who says so? Black Dow? If there's anyone in the North whose promises are worth less than mine it's that bastard's." Shivers stayed silent, but Calder wasn't a man to be easily put off. Good treachery takes effort. "Dow won't ever give you more than you can rip from him with both hands, you know. There'll be nothing for you, however loyal you are. In fact, the more loyal you are, the less there'll be. You'll see. Not enough meat and too many hungry dogs to feed."

Shivers' one eye narrowed just the slightest fraction. "I'm no dog."

That chink of anger would have been enough to scare most men silent, but to Calder it was only a crack to chisel at. "I see that," he whispered, as low and urgent as Seff had whispered to him. "Most men don't see past their fear of you, but I do. I see what you are. A fighter, of course, but a thinker too. An ambitious man. A proud man, and why not?" Calder brought them to a halt in a shadowy stretch of the hallway, leaned in to a conspiratorial distance, smothering his instinct to cringe away as that awful scar turned towards him. "If I had a man like you working for me I'd make better use of him than Black Dow does, that much I promise."

Shivers raised one beckoning hand, a big ruby on his little finger gleaming the colour of blood in the gloom. Giving Calder no choice but to come closer, closer, far too close for comfort. Close enough to feel Shivers' warm breath. Close enough almost to kiss. Close enough so all Calder could see was his own distorted, unconvincing grin reflected in that dead metal ball of an eye.

"Dow wants you."

The Best of Us

Your August Majesty,

We are entirely recovered from the reverse at Quiet Ford and the campaign proceeds. For all Black Dow's cunning, Lord Marshal Kroy is driving him steadily north towards his capital at Carleon. We are no more than two weeks' march from the city, now. He cannot fall back for ever. We will have him, your Majesty can depend upon it.

General Jalenhorm's division won a small engagement on a chain of hills to the northeast yesterday. Lord Governor Meed leads his division south towards Ollensand in the hope of forcing the Northmen to split their forces and give battle at a disadvantage. I travel with General Mitterick's division, close to Marshal Kroy's headquarters. Yesterday, near a village called Barden, Northmen ambushed our supply column as it was stretched out along the bad roads. Through the alertness and bravery of our rearguard they were beaten back with heavy losses. I recommend to your Majesty one Lieutenant Kerns who showed particular valour and lost his life in the engagement, leaving, I understand, a wife and young child behind him.

The columns are well ordered. The weather is fair. The army moves freely and the men are in the highest spirits.

I remain your Majesty's most faithful and unworthy servant,

Bremer dan Gorst,
Royal Observer of the Northern War

The column was in chaos. The rain poured down. The army was mired in the filth and the men were in the most rotten spirits. *And mine the most rotten in the whole putrefying swarm.*

Bremer dan Gorst forced his way through a mud-spattered crush of soldiers, all wriggling like maggots, their armour running with wet, their shouldered pikes poking lethally in all directions. They were stopped as solid as milk turned rank in a bottle but men still squelched up from behind, adding their own burdens of ill temper to the jostling mass, choking the thread of muck that passed for a road and forcing men cursing into the trees. Gorst was already late and had to assert himself as the press tightened, brushing men aside. Sometimes they would turn to argue as they stumbled in the slop, but they soon shut their mouths when they saw who he was. They knew him.

The adversary that had so confounded his Majesty's army proved to be one of its own wagons, slid from the ankle-deep mud of the track and into the considerably deeper bog beside. Following the universal law that the most frustrating thing will always happen, no matter how unlikely, it had somehow ended up almost sideways, back wheels mired to their axles. A snarling driver whipped two horses into a pointless lather of terror while a half-dozen bedraggled soldiers floundered ineffectually about the back. On both sides of the road men slithered through the sodden undergrowth, cursing as gear was torn by brambles, pole-arms were tangled by branches, eyes were whipped at by twigs.

Three young officers stood nearby, the shoulders of their scarlet uniforms turned soggy maroon by the downpour. Two were arguing, stabbing at the wagon with pointed fingers while the other stood and watched, one hand carelessly resting on the gilded hilt of his sword, idle as a mannequin in a military tailor's.

The enemy could scarcely have arranged a more effective blockage with a thousand picked men.

"What is this?" Gorst demanded, fighting and, of course, failing, to sound authoritative.

"Sir, the supply train should be nowhere near this track!"

"That's nonsense, sir! The infantry should be held up while—"

Because the blame is what matters, of course, not the solution. Gorst shouldered the officers aside and squelched into the quagmire, wedging himself between the muddy soldiers, delving into the muck for the wagon's back axle, boots twisting through the slime to find a solid footing. He took a few short breaths and braced himself.

"Go!" he squeaked at the driver, for once forgetting even to try to lower his voice.

Whip snapped. Men groaned. Horses snorted. Mud sucked. Gorst strained from his toes to his scalp, every muscle locked and vibrating with effort. The world faded and he was left alone with his task. He grunted, then growled, then hissed, the rage boiling up in him as if he had a bottomless tank of it instead of a heart and he only had to turn the tap to rip this wagon apart.

The wheels gave with a protesting shriek, lurched from the bog and forward. Suddenly straining at nothing Gorst stumbled despairingly then flopped face down in the mire, one of the soldiers falling beside him. He struggled up as the wagon rattled away, the driver fighting to bring his plunging horses under control.

"Thanks for the help, sir." The mud-caked soldier reached out with a clumsy paw and managed to smear the muck that now befouled Gorst's uniform even more widely. "Sorry, sir. Very sorry."

Keep your axles oiled you retarded scum. Keep your cart on the road you gawping halfwits. Do your damn jobs you lazy vermin. Is that too much to ask? "Good," muttered Gorst, brushing the man's hand away and making a futile attempt to straighten his jacket. "Thank you." He stalked off into the drizzle after the wagon, and could almost hear the mocking laughter of the men and their officers prickling at his back.

Lord Marshal Kroy, commander-in-chief of his Majesty's armies in the North, had requisitioned for his temporary headquarters the grandest building within a dozen miles, namely a squat cottage so riddled with moss it looked more like an abandoned dunghill. A toothless old woman and her even more ancient husband, presumably the dispossessed owners, sat in the doorway of the accompanying barn under a threadbare shawl, and watched Gorst squelch up towards their erstwhile front door. They did not look impressed. Neither did the four guards loitering about the porch in wet oilskins. Nor the collection of damp officers infesting the low living room, who all looked around expectantly when Gorst ducked through the door, and all looked equally crestfallen when they realised who it was.

"It's Gorst," sneered one, as if he had been expecting a king and got a pot-boy.

It was quite the concentration of martial splendour. Marshal Kroy was the centrepiece, sitting with unflinching discipline at the head of the table, impeccable as always in a freshly pressed black uniform, stiff collar encrusted with silver leaves, every iron grey hair on his skull positioned at rigid attention. His chief of staff Colonel Felnigg sat bolt upright beside him, small, nimble, with sparkling eyes that missed no detail, his chin lifted uncomfortably high. Or rather, since he was a remarkably chinless man, his neck formed an almost straight line from his collar to the nostrils of his beaked nose. *Like an over-haughty vulture waiting for a corpse to feast upon.*

General Mitterick would have made a considerable meal. He was a big man with a big face, oversized features positively stuffed into the available room on the front of his head. Where Felnigg had too little chin Mitterick had far too much, and with a big, reckless cleft down the middle. *As if he had an arse suspended from his magnificent moustache.* He had affected buff leather gauntlets reaching almost to the elbow, probably intended to give the impression of a man of action, but which put Gorst in mind of the gloves a farmer might wear to wind a troubled cow.

Mitterick cocked an eyebrow at Gorst's mud-crusted uniform. "More heroics, Colonel Gorst?" he asked, accompanied by some light sniggering.

Ram it up your chin-arse, you cow-winding bladder of vanity. The words tickled Gorst's lips. But in his falsetto, whatever he said the joke would be on him. He would rather have faced a thousand Northmen than this ordeal by conversation. So he turned the first sound into a queasy grin, and smiled along with his humiliation as he always did. He found the gloomiest corner, crossed his arms over his filthy jacket and dampened his fury by imagining the smirking heads of Mitterick's staff impaled on the pikes of Black Dow's army. Not the most patriotic pastime, perhaps, but among his most satisfying.

It's an upside-down sham of a world in which men like these, if they can be called men at all, can look down on a man like me. I am worth twice the lot of you. And this is the best the Union has to offer? We deserve to lose.

"Can't win a war without getting your hands dirty."

"What?" Gorst frowned sideways. The Dogman was leaning beside him in his battered coat, a look of world-weary resignation on his no less battered face.

The Northman let his head tip back until it bumped gently against the peeling wall. "Some folk would rather keep clean, though, eh? And lose."

Gorst could ill afford to strike up an alliance with the one man even more of an outsider than himself. He slipped into his accustomed silence like a well-worn suit of armour, and turned his attention to the nervous chatter of the officers.

"When are they getting here?"

"Soon."

"How many of them?"

"I heard three."

"Only one. It only takes one member of the Closed Council."

"The Closed Council?" squeaked Gorst, voice driven up almost beyond the range of human hearing by a surge of nerves. A nauseating after-taste of the horror he had felt the day those horrible old men had stripped him of his position. *Squashing my dreams as carelessly as a boy might squash a beetle.* "And next..." as he was ushered into the hallway and the black doors were shut on him like coffin lids. *No longer commander of the king's guards. No longer a Knight of the Body. No longer anything but a squealing joke, my name made a byword for failure and disgrace.* He could see that panel of creased and sagging sneers still. And at the head of the table the king's pale face, jaw clenched, refusing to meet Gorst's eye. *As though the ruin of his most loyal servant was no more than an unpleasant chore...*

"Which of them will it be?" Felnigg was asking. "Do we know?"

"It hardly matters." Kroy looked towards the window. Beyond the half-open shutters the rain was getting heavier. "We already know what they will say. The king demands a great victory, at twice the speed and half the cost."

"As always!" Mitterick crowed with the regularity of an overeager cockerel. "Damn politicians, sticking their noses into our business! I swear those swindlers on the Closed Council cost us more lives than the bloody enemy ever—"

The doorknob turned with a loud rattle and a heavy-set old man entered the room, entirely bald with a short grey beard. He gave no immediate impression of supreme power. His clothes were only slightly less rain-soaked and mud-spattered than Gorst's own. His staff was of plain wood shod with steel, more walking stick than rod of office. But still, though he and the single, unassuming servant who scraped in after him were outnumbered ten to one by some of the finest peacocks in the army, it was the officers who held their breath. The old man carried about him an air of untouchable confidence, disdainful ownership, masterful control. *The air of a slaughterman casting an eye over that morning's hogs.*

"Lord Bayaz." Kroy's face had paled, slightly. It might have been the very first time Gorst had seen the marshal surprised, and he was not alone. The crowded room could not have been more dumbstruck if the corpse of Harod the Great had been trundled in on a trolley to address them.

"Gentlemen." Bayaz tossed his staff carelessly to his curly-headed servant, wiped the beads of moisture from his bald pate with a faint hissing and flicked them from the edge of his hand. For a legendary figure, there was no ceremony to him. "Some weather we're having, eh? Sometimes I love the North and sometimes... less so."

"We were not expecting—"

"Why would you be?" Bayaz chuckled with a show of good humour that somehow managed to seem a threat. "I am retired! I had left my seat on the Closed Council empty once again and was seeing out my dotage at my library, far removed from the grind of politics. But since this war is taking place on my very doorstep, I thought it would be neglectful of me not to stop by. I have brought money with me – I understand pay is standing somewhat in arrears."

"A little," conceded Kroy.

"A little more and the soldier's veneer of honour and obedience might swiftly rub away, eh, gentlemen? Without its golden lubricant the great machine of his Majesty's army would soon stutter to a halt, would it not, as with so much in life?"

"Concern for the welfare of our men is always uppermost in our minds," said the marshal, uncertainly.

"And mine!" answered Bayaz. "I am here only to help. To keep the wheels oiled, if you will. To observe and perhaps, should the occasion call, offer some trifling guidance. Yours is the command, Lord Marshal, of course."

"Of course," echoed Kroy, but no one was convinced. This, after all, was the First of the Magi. A man supposedly hundreds of years old, supposedly possessed of magical powers, who had supposedly forged the Union, brought the king to his throne, driven out the Gurkish and laid a good section of Adua to waste doing it. Supposedly. *Hardly a man noted for a reluctance to interfere.* "Er... might I introduce General Mitterick, commander of his Majesty's second division?"

"General Mitterick, even sealed away with my books I have heard tales of your valour. An honour."

The general fluffed up with happiness. "No, no! The honour is mine!"

"Yes," said Bayaz, with casual brutality.

Kroy charged boldly into the ensuing silence. "This is my chief of staff, Colonel Felnigg, and this the leader of those Northmen who oppose Black Dow and fight alongside us, the Dogman."

"Ah, yes!" Bayaz raised his brows. "I believe we had a mutual friend in Logen Ninefingers."

The Dogman stared evenly back, the one man in the room who showed no sign of being overawed. "I'm a long way from sure he's dead."

"If anyone can cheat the Great Leveller it was – or is – he. Either way, he is a loss to the North. To the world. A great man, and much missed."

Dogman shrugged. "A man, anyway. Some good and some bad in him, like most. As for much missed, depends on who you ask, don't it?"

"True." Bayaz gave a rueful smile, and spoke a few words in fluent Northern: "You have to be realistic about these things."

"You do," replied the Dogman. Gorst doubted whether anyone else in the room had understood their little exchange. He was not entirely sure he had, for all he knew the language.

Kroy tried to usher things on. "And this is —"

"Bremer dan Gorst, of course!" Bayaz shocked Gorst to his boots by warmly shaking his hand. For a man of his years, he had quite the grip. "I saw you fence against the king, how long ago, now? Five years? Six?"

Gorst could have counted the hours since. *And it says a great deal for my shadow of a life that my proudest moment is still being humiliated in a fencing match.* "Nine."

"Nine, imagine that! The decades flit past me like leaves on the wind, I swear. No man ever deserved the title more."

"I was fairly beaten."

Bayaz leaned close. "You were beaten, anyway, which is all that really counts, eh?" And he slapped Gorst on the arm as if they had shared a private joke, though if they had it was private to Bayaz alone. "I thought you were with the Knights of the Body? Were you not guarding the king at the Battle of Adua?"

Gorst felt himself colouring. *I was, as everyone here well knows, but now*

*I am nothing but a wretched scapegoat, used and discarded like some stuttering
serving girl by his lordship's caddish youngest son. Now I am—*

"Colonel Gorst is here as the king's observer," ventured Kroy, seeing his
discomfort.

"Of course!" Bayaz snapped his fingers. "After that business in Sipani."

Gorst's face burned as though the city's very name was a slap. *Sipani.*
And as simply as that the best part of him was where he spent so much of
his time: four years ago, back in the madness of Cardotti's House of Leisure. Stumbling through the smoke, searching desperately for the king,
reaching the staircase, seeing that masked face – and then the long, bouncing trip down the stairs, into unjust disgrace. He saw smirks among the
over-bright smear of faces the room had suddenly become. He opened his
dry mouth but, as usual, nothing of any use emerged.

"Ah, well." The Magus gave Gorst's shoulder the kind of consoling pat
one might give to a guard dog long ago gone blind, and occasionally tossed
a bone for sentimental reasons. "Perhaps you can work your way back into
the king's good graces."

*Depend upon it, you arcane fuck-hole, if I must spill every drop of blood in
the North.* "Perhaps," Gorst managed to whisper.

But Bayaz had already drawn out a chair and was steepling his fingers
before him. "So! The situation, Lord Marshal?"

Kroy jerked the front of his jacket smooth as he advanced on the great
map, so large it had been folded at the edges to fit on the biggest wall of the
mean little building. "General Jalenhorm's division is here, to our west."
Paper crackled as Kroy's stick hissed over it. "He is pushing northwards, fir-
ing crops and villages in the hope of drawing the Northmen into battle."

Bayaz looked bored. "Mmmm."

"Meanwhile Lord Governor Meed's division, accompanied by the majority of the Dogman's loyalists, have marched southeast to take Ollensand
under siege. General Mitterick's division remains between the two." Tap,
tap, stick on paper, ruthlessly precise. "Ready to lend support to either one.
The route of supply runs south towards Uffrith over poor roads, no more
than tracks, really, but we are—"

"Of course." Bayaz rendered it all irrelevant with a wave of one meaty
hand. "I have not come to interfere in the details."

Kroy's stick hovered uselessly. "Then—"

"Imagine yourself a master mason, Lord Marshal, working upon one turret of a grand palace. A craftsman whose dedication, skill and attention to detail are disputed by no one."

"Mason?" Mitterick looked baffled.

"Then imagine the Closed Council as the architects. Our responsibility is not the fitting of one stone to another, it is the design of the building overall. The politics, rather than the tactics. An army is an instrument of government. It must be used in such a way that it furthers the interests of government. Otherwise what use is it? Only an extremely costly machine for... minting medals." The room shifted uncomfortably. *Hardly the sort of talk the toy soldiers appreciate.*

"The policies of government are subject to sudden change," grumbled Felnigg.

Bayaz looked upon him like a schoolmaster at the dunce ruining the standard of his class. "The world is fluid. We must be fluid also. And since these latest hostilities began, circumstances have not flowed for the better. At home the peasants are restless again. War taxes, and so on. Restless, restless, always restless." He drummed his thick fingers restlessly on the table-top. "And the new Lords' Round is finally completed, so the Open Council is in session and the nobles have somewhere to complain. They are doing so. At tremendous length. They are impatient with the lack of progress, apparently."

"Damn windbags," grunted Mitterick. *Lending considerable support to the maxim that men always hate in others what is most hateful in themselves.*

Bayaz sighed. "Sometimes I feel I am building sandcastles against the tide. The Gurkish are never idle, there is no end to their intrigues. But once they were the only real challenge to us abroad. Now there is the Snake of Talins, too. Murcatto." He frowned as if the name tasted foul, hard lines deepening across his face. "While our armies are entangled here that cursed woman continues to tighten her grip on Styria, emboldened by the knowledge that the Union can do little to oppose her." Some patriotic tutting stirred the assembly. "Put simply, gentlemen, the costs of this war, in treasure, in prestige, in lost opportunities, are becoming too high. The Closed Council require a swift conclusion. Naturally, as soldiers, you all are prone to be sentimental about warfare. But fighting is only any use when it's cheaper than the alternatives." He calmly picked a piece of fluff from his sleeve, frowned at it, and flicked it away. "This is the North, after all. I mean to say... what's it worth?"

There was a silence. Then Marshal Kroy cleared his throat. "The Closed Council require a swift conclusion...do they mean by the end of the campaigning season?"

"The end of the season? No, no." The officers blew out their cheeks with evident relief. It was short-lived. "Considerably sooner than that."

The noise slowly built. Shocked gasps, then horrified splutters, then whispered swear-words and grumbles of disbelief, the officers' professional affront scoring a rare victory over their usually unconquerable servility.

"But we cannot possibly—!" Mitterick burst out, striking the table with one gauntleted fist then hastily remembering himself. "I mean to say, I apologise, but we cannot—"

"Gentlemen, gentlemen." Kroy ushered down his unruly brood, and appealed to reason. *The lord marshal is nothing if not a reasonable man.* "Lord Bayaz...Black Dow continues to evade us. To manoeuvre and fall back." He gestured at the map as though it was covered in realities that simply could not be argued with. "He has staunch war leaders at his side. His men know the land, are sustained by its people. He is a master at swift movement and retreat, at swift concentration and surprise. He has already wrong-footed us once. If we rush to battle, there is every chance that—"

But he might as well have reasoned with the tide. The First of the Magi was not interested. "You stray onto the details again, Lord Marshal. Masons and architects and so forth, did I speak about that? The king sent you here to fight, not march around. I have no doubt you will find a way to bring the Northmen to a decisive battle, and if not, well...every war is only a prelude to talk, isn't it?" Bayaz stood, and the officers belatedly struggled up after him, chairs screeching and swords clattering in an ill-coordinated shambles.

"We are...delighted you could join us," Kroy managed, though the army's feelings were very clearly the precise opposite.

Bayaz appeared impervious to irony, however. "Good, because I will be staying to observe. Some gentlemen from the University of Adua accompanied me. They have an invention that I am curious to see tested."

"Anything we can do to assist."

"Excellent." Bayaz smiled broadly. *The only smile in the room.* "I will leave the shaping of the stones in your..." He raised an eyebrow at Mitterick's absurd gauntlets. "Capable hands. Gentlemen."

The officers kept their nervous silence, as the First of the Magi's worn boots and those of his single servant receded down the hallway, like children sent early to bed, preparing to throw back the covers as soon as their parents reached a safe distance.

Angry babbling broke out the moment they heard the front door close. "What the hell—"

"How dare he?"

"Before the end of the season?" frothed Mitterick. "He is quite mad!"

"Ridiculous!" snapped Felnigg. "Ridiculous!"

"Bloody politicians!"

But Gorst had a smile, and not just at the dismay of Mitterick and the rest. Now they would have to seek battle. *And whatever they came for, I came to fight.*

Kroy brought his fractious officers to order by banging at the table with his stick. "Gentlemen, please! The Closed Council have spoken, and so the king has spoken, and we can only strive to obey. We are but the masons, after all." He turned towards the map as the room quieted, eyes running over the roads, the hills, the rivers of the North. "I fear we must abandon caution and concentrate the army for a concerted push northwards. Dogman?"

The Northman stepped up to the table and snapped out a vibrating salute. "Marshal Kroy, sir!" A joke, of course, since he was an ally rather than an underling.

"If we march for Carleon in force, is it likely that Black Dow will finally offer battle?"

The Dogman rubbed a hand over his stubbled jaw. "Maybe. He ain't the most patient. Looks bad for him, letting you tramp all over his back yard these past few months. But he's always been an unpredictable bastard, Black Dow." He had a bitter look on his face for a moment, as if remembering something painful. "One thing I can tell you, if he decides on battle he won't offer nothing. He'll ram it right up your arse. Still, it's worth a try." Dogman grinned around the officers. "'Specially if you like it up your arse."

"Not my first choice, but they say a general should be prepared for anything." Kroy traced a road to its junction, then tapped at the paper. "What is this town?"

The Dogman leaned over the table to squint at the map, considerably inconveniencing a pair of unhappy staff officers and giving the impression

31

of not caring in the least. "That's Osrung. Old town, set in fields, with a bridge and a mill, might have, what…three or four hundred people in peacetime? Some stone buildings, more wood. High fence around the outside. Used to have a damn fine tavern but, you know, nothing's how it used to be."

"And this hill? Near where the roads from Ollensand and Uffrith meet?"

"The Heroes."

"Odd name for a hill," grunted Mitterick.

"Named after a ring of old stones on top. Some warriors of ancient days are buried beneath 'em, or that's one rumour, anyway. You get quite a view from up there. I sent a dozen to have a look-see the other day, in fact, check if any of Dow's boys have shown their faces."

"And?"

"Nothing yet, but no reason there should be. There's help nearby, if they get pressed."

"That's the spot, then." Kroy craned closer to the map, pressing the point of his stick into that hill as though he could will the army there. "The Heroes. Felnigg?"

"Sir?"

"Send word to Lord Governor Meed to abandon the siege of Ollensand and march with all haste to meet us near Osrung."

That got a few sharp in-breaths. "Meed will be furious," said Mitterick.

"He often is. That cannot be helped."

"I'll be heading back that way," said Dogman. "Meet up with the rest o' my boys and get 'em moving north. I can take the message."

"It might be better if Colonel Felnigg carries it personally. Lord Governor Meed is…not the greatest admirer of Northmen."

"Unlike the rest of you, eh?" The Dogman showed the Union's finest a mouthful of sharp yellow teeth. "I'll make a move, then. With any luck I'll see you up the Heroes in what…three days? Four?"

"Five, if this weather gets no better."

"This is the North. Let's call it five." And he followed Bayaz out of the low sitting room.

"Well, it might not be the way we wanted it." Mitterick smashed a meaty fist into a meaty palm. "But we can show them something, now, eh? Get those skulking bastards out in the open and *show* them something!" The legs of his chair shrieked as he stood. "I will hurry my division along. We should make a night march, Lord Marshal! Get at the enemy!"

"No." Kroy was already sitting at his desk and dipping pen in ink to write orders. "Halt them for the night. On these roads, in this weather, haste will do more harm than good."

"But, Lord Marshal, if we—"

"I intend to rush, General, but not headlong into a defeat. We must not push the men too hard. They need to be ready."

Mitterick jerked up his gloves. "Damn these damn roads!" Gorst stood aside to let him and his staff file from the room, silently wishing he was ushering them through into a bottomless pit.

Kroy raised his brows as he wrote. "Sensible men...run away...from battles." His pen scratched neatly across the paper. "Someone will need to take this order to General Jalenhorm. To move with all haste to the Heroes and secure the hill, the town of Osrung, and any other crossings of the river that—"

Gorst stepped forwards. "I will take it." If there was to be action, Jalenhorm's division would be first into it. *And I will be at the front of the front rank. I will not bury the ghosts of Sipani in a headquarters.*

"There is no one I would rather entrust it to." Gorst grasped the order but the marshal did not release it at once. He remained looking calmly up, the folded paper a bridge between them. "Remember, though, that you are the king's observer, not the king's champion."

I am neither. I am a glorified errand boy, here because nowhere else will have me. I am a secretary in a uniform. A filthy uniform, as it happens. I am a dead man still twitching. Ha ha! Look at the big idiot with the silly voice! Make him dance! "Yes, sir."

"Observe, then, by all means. But no more heroics, if you please. Not like the other day at Barden. A war is no place for heroics. Especially not this one."

"Yes, sir."

Kroy let go of the order and turned back to peer at his map, measuring distances between stretched-out thumb and forefinger. "The king would never forgive me if we were to lose you."

The king has abandoned me here, and no one will care a stray speck of piss if I am hacked apart and my brains splattered across the North. Least of all me.

"Yes, sir." And Gorst strode out, through the front door and back into the rain, where he was struck by lightning.

There she was, picking her way across the boggy front yard towards him. In the midst of all that sullen mud her smiling face burned like the sun, incandescent. Delight crushed him, made his skin sing and his breath catch. The months he had spent away from her had done not the slightest good. He was as desperately, hopelessly, helplessly in love as ever.

"Finree," he whispered, voice full of awe, as in some silly story a wizard might pronounce a word of power. "Why are you here?" Half-expecting she would fade into nothing, a figment of his overwrought imagination.

"To see my father. Is he in there?"

"Writing orders."

"As always." She looked down at Gorst's uniform and raised one eyebrow, darkened from brown to almost black and spiked to soft points by the rain. "Still playing in the mud, I see."

He could not even bring himself to be embarrassed. He was lost in her eyes. Some strands of hair were stuck across her wet face. He wished he was. *I thought nothing could be more beautiful than you used to be, but now you are more beautiful than ever.* He dared not look at her and he dared not look away. *You are the most beautiful woman in the world – no – in all of history – no – the most beautiful thing in all of history. Kill me, now, so that your face can be the last thing I see.* "You look well," he murmured.

She looked down at her sodden travelling coat, mud-spotted to the waist. "I suspect you're not being entirely honest with me."

"I never dissemble." *I love you I love you I love you I love you I love you I love you I love you...*

"And are you well, Bremer? I may call you Bremer, may I?"

You may crush my eyes out with your heels. Only say my name again. "Of course. I am..." *Ill in mind and body, ruined in fortune and reputation, hating of the world and everything in it, but none of that matters, as long as you are with me.* "Well."

She held out her hand and he bent to kiss it like a village priest who had been permitted to touch the hem of the Prophet's robe—

There was a golden ring on her finger with a small, sparkling blue stone.

Gorst's guts twisted so hard he nearly lost control of them entirely. It was only by a supreme effort that he stayed standing. He could scarcely whisper the words. "Is that..."

"A marriage band, yes!" Could she know he would rather she had dangled a butchered head in his face?

He gripped to his smile like a drowning man to the last stick of wood. He felt his mouth move, and heard his own squeak. His repugnant, womanly, pathetic little squeak. "Who is the gentleman?"

"Colonel Harod dan Brock." A hint of pride in her voice. Of love. *What would I give to hear her say my name like that? All I have. Which is nothing but other men's scorn.*

"Harod dan Brock," he whispered, and the name was sand in his mouth. He knew the man, of course. They were distantly related, fourth cousins or some such. They had sometimes spoken years ago, when Gorst had served with the guard of his father, Lord Brock. Then Lord Brock had made his bid for the crown, and failed, and been exiled for the worst of treasons. His eldest son had been granted the king's mercy, though. Stripped of his many lands, and his lofty titles, but left with his life. How Gorst wished the king was less merciful now.

"He is serving on Lord Governor Meed's staff."

"Yes." Brock was nauseatingly handsome, with an easy smile and a winning manner. *The bastard.* Well-spoken of and well-liked, in spite of his father's disgrace. *The snake.* Had earned his place by bravery and bonhomie. *The fucker.* He was everything Gorst was not.

He clenched his right fist trembling hard, and imagined it ripping the easy-smiling jaw out of Harod dan Brock's handsome head. "Yes."

"We are very happy," said Finree.

Good for you. I want to kill myself. She could not have given him sharper pain if she had crushed his cock in a vice. Could she be such a fool as to not see through him? Some part of her must have known, must have delighted in his humiliation. *Oh, how I love you. Oh, how I hate you. Oh, how I want you.*

"My congratulations to you both," he murmured.

"I will tell my husband."

"Yes." *Yes, yes, tell him to die, tell him to burn, and soon.* Gorst kept the rictus smile clinging to his face while vomit tickled at his throat. "Yes."

"I must go to my father. Perhaps we will see each other again, soon?"

Oh, yes. Very soon. Tonight, in fact, while I lie awake with my cock in my hand, pretending it's your mouth... "I hope so."

She was already walking past. *For her, a forgettable encounter with an old acquaintance.* For him, as she turned away it was as if night fell. *The soil is heaped upon me, the grit of burial in my mouth.* He watched the door rattle shut behind her, and stood there for a long moment, in the rain. He wanted to weep, and weep, and weep for all his ruined hopes. He wanted to kneel in the mud and tear out the hair he still had. He wanted to murder someone, and hardly cared who. *Myself, perhaps?*

Instead he took a sharp breath, squeaking slightly in one nostril, and squelched away through the mud, into the gathering dusk.

He had a message to carry, after all. With no heroics.

Black Dow

The stable doors shut with a bang like a headsman's axe, and it took all of Calder's famous arrogance not to jump clean in the air. War meetings had never been his favourite style of gathering, especially ones full of his enemies. Three of Dow's five War Chiefs were in attendance and, as Calder's ever-worsening luck would have it, they were the three that liked him least.

Glama Golden looked the hero from his scalp to his toes, big-knuckle brawny and heavy-jaw handsome, his long hair, his bristling moustache, his eyelashes to their tips all the colour of pale gold. He wore more yellow metal than a princess on her wedding day – golden torc around his thick neck, bracelets at his thick wrists and fistfuls of rings on his thick fingers, every part of him buffed to a pretty shine with bluster and self-love.

Cairm Ironhead was a very different prospect. His scar-crossed face was a fortress of frown you could've blunted an axe on, eyes like nails under a brow like an anvil, cropped hair and beard an uncompromising black. He was shorter than Golden but wider still, a slab of a man, chain mail glinting under a cloak of black bear-fur. The rumour was he'd strangled that bear.

Possibly for looking at him wrong. Neither Ironhead nor Golden had much beyond contempt for Calder, but luckily they'd always despised each other like night hates day and their feud left no hatred in the quiver for anyone else.

When it came to hatred, Brodd Tenways had a bottomless supply. He was one of those bastards who can't even breathe quietly, ugly as incest and always delighted to push it in your face, leering from the shadows like the village pervert at a passing milkmaid. Foul-mouthed, foul-toothed, foul-smelling, and with some kind of hideous rash patching his twisted face he gave every sign of taking great pride in. He'd made a bitter enemy of Calder's father, lost to him in battle twice, and been forced to kneel and give up everything he had. Getting it back only seemed to have worsened his mood, and he'd easily shifted all his years of bile from Bethod to his sons, and Calder in particular.

Then there was the head of this mismatched family of villains, the self-styled Protector of the North, Black Dow himself. He sat easy in Skarling's Chair, one leg folded under him while the other boot tapped gently at the ground. He had something like a smile on his deep-lined, hard-scarred face but his eyes were narrowed, sly as a hungry tomcat that just now spied a pigeon. He'd taken to wearing fine clothes, the sparkling chain that Calder's father used to wear around his shoulders. But he couldn't hide what he was, and didn't want to either. A killer to the tips of his ears. Or ear, since the left one was no more than a flap of gristle.

As if Black Dow's name and his grin weren't threats enough, he'd made sure they were shored up with plenty of steel. A long, grey sword leaned against Skarling's Chair on one side, an axe on the other, notched with long use, in easy reach of his dangling fingers. Killer's fingers – scuffed, and swollen, and scarred at the knuckles from a lifetime of the dead knew what dark work.

Splitfoot stood in the gloom at Dow's shoulder. His Second, meaning his closest bodyguard and chief arse-licker, stuck to his master tight as his shadow with thumbs hooked in his silver-buckled sword-belt. Two of his Carls lurked behind, armour, and shield-rims, and drawn swords all agleam, others dotted about the walls, flanking the door. There was a smell of old hay and old horses, but far stronger was the reek of ready violence, thick as the stink in a marsh.

And as if all that wasn't enough to make Calder shit his well-tailored trousers, Shivers still loomed at his shoulder, adding his own chill threat to the recipe.

"Well, if it ain't brave Prince Calder." Dow looked him up and down like the tomcat at the shrub it was about to piss on. "Welcome back to the good fight, lad. You going to do as you're fucking told this time around?"

Calder swept out a bow. "Your most obedient servant." He smirked as if the very words didn't burn his tongue. "Golden. Ironhead." He gave each a respectful nod. "My father always said there weren't two stouter hearts in all the North." His father always said there weren't two thicker heads in all the North, but his lies were no more use than money down a well in any case. Ironhead and Golden did nothing but glower at each other. Calder felt a burning need for someone who liked him. Or at least didn't want him dead. "Where's Scale?"

"Your brother's out west," said Dow. "Doing some fighting."

"You know what that is, do you, boy?" Tenways turned his head and spat through the gap in his brown front teeth.

"Is it…the thing with all the swords?" Calder took a hopeful look around the stable but no allies had crept in, and he ended up glancing at Shivers' ruined frown, which was even worse than Dow's smile. However often he saw that scar, it was always more hideous than he remembered. "How about Reachey?"

"Your wife's daddy's a day or so east," said Dow. "Putting on a weapontake."

Golden snorted. "I'd be surprised if there's a boy can grip a blade isn't pressed already."

"Well, he's scraping up what there is. Reckon we'll need every ready hand when it comes to a battle. Yours too, maybe."

"Oh, you'll have to hold me back!" Calder slapped the hilt of his sword. "Can't wait to get started!"

"You ever even drawn the fucking thing?" sneered Tenways, stretching his neck out to spit again.

"Just the once. I had to trim your daughter's hairy cunt before I could get at it."

Dow burst out laughing. Golden chuckled. Ironhead gave the faintest of grins. Tenways choked on his spit and left a string of glistening drool down his chin, but Calder didn't much care. He was better off scoring points with those who weren't quite a lost cause yet. Somehow he needed to win at least one of these unpromising bastards over to his side.

"Never thought I'd say this." Dow sighed and wiped one eye with a fin-ger, "but I've missed you, Calder."

"Likewise. I'd much rather be trading horseshit in a stable than back at Carleon kissing my wife. What's to do?"

"You know." Dow took the pommel of his sword between finger and thumb, turning it this way and that so the silver mark near the hilt glinted. "War. Skirmish here, raid there. We cut off some stragglers, they burn out some villages. War. Your brother's been hitting fast, giving the Southerners something to think about. Useful man your brother, got some sting in him."

"Shame your father didn't have more'n one son," growled Tenways.

"Keep talking, old man," said Calder, "I can make you look a prick all day."

Tenways bristled but Dow waved him down. "Enough cock-measuring. We've a war to fight."

"And how many victories, so far?"

A brief, unhappy pause. "No battle," grunted Ironhead.

"This Kroy," sneered Golden back across the stable, "the one in charge o' the Union."

"Marshal, they call him."

"Whatever they call him, he's a cautious bastard."

"Baby-stepping coward fuck," growled Tenways.

Dow shrugged. "Naught cowardly about stepping careful. Wouldn't be my style with his numbers, but . . ." And he turned his grin on Calder. "Your father always used to say, 'In war it's the winning counts. The rest is for fools to sing about.' So Kroy's going slow, hoping to wear out our patience. We Northmen ain't known for it, after all. He's split his army in three parts."

"Three big bloody parts," said Ironhead.

Golden agreed, for once. "Might be ten thousand fighting men each, not even counting all the fetchers and carriers."

Dow leaned forwards like a grandfather teaching a child about fish. "Jalenhorm to the west. Brave but sluggish and apt to blunder. Mitterick in the centre. Sharpest of the three by all accounts, but reckless. Loves his horses, I hear. Meed to the east. Not a soldier, and he hates Northmen like a pig hates butchers. Could make him short-sighted. Then Kroy's got some Northmen of his own, spread out scouting mostly, but a fair few fighters too, and some good ones among 'em."

"The Dogman's men," said Calder.

"Fucking traitor that he is," hissed Tenways, making ready to spit.

"Traitor?" Dow jerked forwards in Skarling's Chair, knuckles white on its arms. "You dumb old rashy *fuck!* He's the one man in the North who's always stuck to the same side!" Tenways looked up, slowly swallowed whatever scum he'd been about to spit and leaned back into the shadows. Dow slid down limp again. "Shame it's the wrong side, is all."

"Well, we're going to have to move soon," said Golden. "Meed may be no soldier, but he's put Ollensand under siege. Town's got good walls but I ain't sure how long they can—"

"Meed broke off the siege yesterday morning," said Dow. "He's heading back north and most o' the Dogman's lot are with him."

"Yesterday?" Golden frowned. "How d'you know—"

"I've got my ways."

"I didn't hear anything."

"That's why I give the orders and you listen to 'em." Ironhead smiled to see his rival cut down a peg. "Meed's turned back north, and in quite the hurry. My guess is he'll be joining up with Mitterick."

"Why?" asked Calder. "Slow and steady all these months, then they just decide to take a rush?"

"Maybe they got tired o' cautious. Or maybe someone who has the say-so did. Either way, they're coming."

"Might give us a chance to catch 'em off guard." Ironhead's eyes were sparkling like a starving man just saw the roast brought in.

"If they're set on looking for a fight," said Dow, "I'd hate not to give 'em one. We got someone down at the Heroes?"

"Curnden Craw's there with his dozen," said Splitfoot.

"Safe hands," muttered Calder. He almost wished he was down at the Heroes with Curnden Craw, rather than here with these bastards. No power, maybe, but a lot more laughs.

"Had word from him an hour or two back, as it goes," said Ironhead. "He ran into some o' the Dogman's scouts up there and seen 'em off."

Dow looked down at the ground for a moment, rubbing at his lips with one fingertip. "Shivers?"

"Chief?" Whispered so soft it was hardly more than a breath.

"Ride down to the Heroes and tell Craw I want that hill held on to. Just might be one or other o' these Union bastards try to come through that way. Cross the river at Osrung, maybe."

40

"Good ground for a fight," said Tenways.

Shivers paused a moment. Long enough for Calder to see he wasn't happy playing messenger boy. Calder gave him the barest look, just a reminder of what was said in the hallway at Carleon. Just to give whatever seeds were planted a little water.

"Right y'are, Chief." And Shivers slid out through the doorway.

Golden gave a shiver of his own. "That one gives me the worries."

Dow only grinned the wider. "That's the point of him. Ironhead?"

"Chief."

"You're leading off down the Yaws Road. Point o' the spear."

"We'll be in Yaws evening tomorrow."

"Make it sooner." That got a deeper frown from Ironhead and a matching grin from Golden. It was as if the two sat on a pair of scales. You couldn't nudge one down without hoisting the other up. "Golden, you take the Brottun Road and join up with Reachey. Get him on the way soon as his weapontake's done, that old boy sometimes needs the spur."

"Aye, Chief."

"Tenways, bring your foragers in and get your lot ready to move, you'll be bringing up the back with me."

"Done."

"And all of you march your lads hard, but keep your eyes open. Be nice to give the Southerners a shock and not the other way around." Dow showed even more of his teeth. "If your blades ain't sharpened already, I reckon now's the time."

"Aye," the three of them chimed in, competing to sound the most bloodthirsty.

"Oh, aye," said Calder on the end, and giving his best smirk to go with it. He might not be much with a sword, but there were few men in the North who could handle a smirk better. It was wasted this time, though. Splitfoot was leaning down to mutter something in Dow's ear.

The Protector of the North sat back frowning. "Send him in, then!"

The doors were hauled open, wind sighing through and whisking loose straw across the stable floor. Calder squinted into the evening outside. Had to be some trick of the fading light, because the figure in the doorway seemed to fill it almost to the beam above. Then he took the step up. Then he straightened. It was quite the entrance, the room silent as he strode slowly to its centre except for the floor groaning under his every step. But then it's easy to make the big entrance when you're the size of a cliff. You just walk in and stand there.

"I am Stranger-Come-Knocking."

Calder knew the name. Stranger-Come-Knocking called himself Chief of a Hundred Tribes, called everything east of the Crinna his land and all the people who lived on it his property. Calder had heard he was a giant but hadn't taken it too seriously. The North was full of swollen men with swollen opinions of themselves and even more swollen reputations. More often than not you found the man a good deal smaller than the name. So this came as a bit of a shock.

When you said the word "giant," Stranger-Come-Knocking was pretty much what you thought of, stepped straight out from the age of heroes and into this petty latter time. He towered over Dow and his mighty War Chiefs, head among the rafters, black hair streaked with grey hanging around his craggy, bearded face. Glama Golden looked a gaudy dwarf beside him, and Splitfoot and his Carls a set of toy soldiers.

"By the dead," Calder whispered under his breath. "That is a big one."

But Black Dow showed no awe. He sprawled in Skarling's Chair easily as ever, one boot still tapping the straw, killer's hands still dangling, wolf grin still curled around his face. "Wondered when you'd…come knocking. Didn't think you'd come all this way your own self, though."

"An alliance should be sealed face to face, man to man, iron to iron and blood to blood." Calder had been expecting the giant to roar every word like the monsters in children's stories, but he had a soft sort of voice. Slow, as if he was puzzling out every word.

"The personal touch," said Dow. "I'm all for it. We've a deal, then?"

"We have." Stranger-Come-Knocking spread one massive hand, put the web between thumb and forefinger in his mouth and bit into it, held it up, blood starting to seep from the marks.

Dow slid his palm down his sword, leaving the edge gleaming red. Then he was out of Skarling's Chair in a flash and caught the giant's hand with his own. The two men stood there as blood streaked their forearms and started to drip from their elbows. Calder felt a little fear and a lot of contempt at the level of manliness on display.

"Right y'are." Dow let go of the giant's hand and slowly sat back in Skarling's Chair, leaving a bloody palm-print on one arm. "Reckon you can bring your men over the Crinna."

"I already did."

Golden and Ironhead exchanged a glance, not much caring for the idea of a lot of savages crossing the Crinna and, presumably, their land. Dow narrowed his eyes. "Did you, indeed?"

"On this side of the water they can fight the Southerners." Stranger-Come-Knocking looked slowly about the stable, fixing each man with his black eyes. "I came to *fight*!" He roared the last word, echoes ringing from the roof. A ripple of fury passed through him from his feet to his head, making his fists clench, and his chest swell, and his monstrous shoulders rise, seeming in that moment more outsize than ever.

Calder found himself wondering what fighting this bastard would feel like. How the hell would you stop him, once he was moving? Just the sheer weight of meat. What weapon would put him down? He reckoned everyone else in the room was thinking the same thing, and not much enjoying the experience.

Except Black Dow. "Good! That's what I want you for."

"I want to fight the Union."

"There's plenty to go round."

"I want to fight Whirrun of Bligh."

"Can't promise you that, he's on our side and has some odd notions. But I can ask if he'll give you a bout."

"I want to fight the Bloody-Nine."

The hairs on the back of Calder's neck prickled. Strange, how that name still weighed heavy, even in company like this, even if the man was eight years dead. Dow wasn't grinning any more.

"You missed your chance. Ninefingers is back in the mud."

"I hear he is alive, and standing with the Union."

"You hear wrong."

"I hear he is alive, and I will kill him."

"Will you now?"

"I am the greatest warrior in the Circle of the World." Stranger-Come-Knocking didn't boast it, puffed up and pouting as Glama Golden might have. He didn't threaten it, fists clenched and glowering as Cairm Ironhead might have. He stated the fact.

Dow scratched absently at the scar where his ear used to be. "This is the North. Lot of hard men about. Couple of 'em in this room. So that's quite a claim you're making."

Stranger-Come-Knocking unhooked his great fur cloak and shrugged it off, stood there stripped to the waist like a man ready to wrestle. Scars had always been almost as popular in the North as blades. Every man who reckoned himself a man had to have a couple of both. But Stranger-Come-Knocking's great expanse of body, sinew-knotted like an ancient tree, was almost more scar than skin. He was ripped, pocked, gouged with wounds, enough to make a score of champions proud.

"At Yeweald I fought the Dog Tribe and was pierced with seven arrows." He pointed out some pink blobs scattered across his ribs with his club of a forefinger. "But I fought on, and made a hill of their dead, and made their land my land, and their women and children my people."

Dow sighed, as if he had a half-naked giant at most of his war meetings and was getting tired of it. "Maybe it's time to think about a shield."

"They are for cowards to hide behind. My wounds tell the story of my strength." The giant jerked his thumb at a star-shaped mass that covered one shoulder, and his back, and half his left arm with flesh lumped and mottled as oak-bark. "The dreaded witch Vanian sprayed me with a liquid fire, and I carried her into the lake and drowned her while I burned."

Dow picked a fingernail. "Reckon I'd have tried to put it out first."

The giant shrugged, the pink burn across his shoulder creasing like a ploughed field. "It went out when she died." He pointed to a ragged pink mark that left a bald streak through the pelt of black hair on his chest and appeared to have taken a nipple off. "The brothers Smirtu and Weorc challenged me to single combat. They said because they grew together in one womb they counted as one man."

Dow snorted. "You fell for that?"

"I do not look for reasons *not* to fight. I split Smirtu in half with an axe, then crushed his brother's skull in my hand." The giant slowly closed one massive fist and squeezed the fingers white, muscle squirming in his arm like a giant sausage being stuffed.

"Messy," said Dow.

"In my country, men are impressed by messy deaths."

"Honestly, they're much the same here. Tell you what – anyone I call my enemy you can kill when you please. Anyone I call my friend...let me know before you give 'em a messy death. I'd hate for you to slaughter Prince Calder by accident."

Stranger-Come-Knocking looked around. "You are Calder?"

That awkward moment wondering whether to deny it. "I am."

"Bethod's second son?"

"The same."

He slowly nodded his monstrous head, long hair swaying. "Bethod was a great man."

"A great man for getting other men to fight for him." Tenways sucked his rotten teeth and spat one more time. "Not much of a fighter himself."

The giant's voice had suddenly softened again. "Why is everyone so bloodthirsty this side of the Crinna? There is more to life than fighting." He leaned down and dragged up his cloak between two fingers. "I will be at the place agreed upon, Black Dow. Unless…any of the little men wish to wrestle?" Golden, and Ironhead, and Tenways all took their turns to peer off into the furthest corners of the stable.

Calder was used to being scared out of his wits, though, and met the giant's eye with a smile. "I would, but I make a point of never stripping unless there are women present. Which is a shame, actually, because I have an almighty spot on my back that I think would quite impress everyone."

"Oh, I cannot wrestle with you, son of Bethod." The giant might even have had a knowing smirk of his own as he turned away. "You are made for other things." And he threw his cloak over his scarred shoulder and stooped under the high lintel, the Carls swinging the doors shut on the gust of wind that blew in behind him.

"He seems a good sort," said Calder, brightly. "Nice of him not to show off the scars on his cock."

"Fucking savages!" cursed Tenways, which was rich coming from him.

"Greatest warrior in the world," scoffed Golden, though he hadn't done much scoffing while the giant was in the room.

Dow rubbed his jaw thoughtfully. "The dead know I'm no fucking diplomat, but I'll take the allies I can get. And a man that size'll stop a lot of arrows." Tenways and Golden had themselves an arse-licking chuckle, but Calder saw beyond the joke. If the Bloody-Nine was still alive, maybe a man that size might stop him too. "You all know your tasks, eh? Let's get to 'em."

Ironhead and Golden gave each other a deadly glare on the way out. Tenways spat at Calder's feet but he only grinned back, promising himself he'd get the last laugh as the ugly old bastard shambled into the evening.

Dow stood, blood still dotting the ground from the tip of his middle finger, watching the doors as they were closed. Then he gave a sigh. "Feuding, feuding, always bloody feuding. Why can no one just get on, eh, Calder?"

"My father used to say, 'Point three Northmen the same way, they'll be killing each other before you can order the charge.'"

"Hah! He was a clever bastard, Bethod, whatever else he was. Couldn't stop the warring, though, once he'd started." Dow frowned at his blood-daubed palm, working the fingers. "Once your hands get bloody it ain't so easy to get 'em clean. The Dogman told me that. My hands been bloody all my life." Calder flinched as Splitfoot tossed something into the air, but it was only a cloth. Dow snatched it out of the darkness and started winding it around his cut hand. "Guess it's a bit late to clean 'em now, eh?"

"It'll just have to be more blood," said Splitfoot.

"I reckon." Dow wandered into one of the empty stalls, tipped his head back, rolled his eyes to the ceiling and winced. A moment later Calder heard the sound of his piss spattering the straw. "There...we...go."

If the aim was to make him feel even more insignificant, it worked. He'd been half-expecting them to murder him. Now it seemed they couldn't be bothered, and that pricked at Calder's pride. "Got any orders for me?" he snapped.

Dow glanced over his shoulder. "Why? You'd only fuck 'em up or ignore 'em."

Probably true. "Why send for me, then?"

"The way your brother tells it, you've got the sharpest mind in the whole North. I got sick of him telling me he couldn't do without you."

"I thought Scale was up near Ustred?"

"Two days' ride away, and soon as I learned the Union were moving I sent to him to join up with us."

"Not much point me going, then."

"Wouldn't say so..." The sound of pissing stopped. "There it is!" And started up again.

Calder ground his teeth. "Maybe I'll go see Reachey. Watch this weap-ontake of his." Or talk him into helping Calder live out the month, even better.

"You're a free man, ain't you?" They both knew the answer to that one. Free as a pigeon already plucked and in the pot. "Things are just like they were in your father's day, really. Any man can do what he likes. Right, Splitfoot?"

"Right, Chief."

"Just as long as it's exactly what I fucking tell 'em to do." And Dow's Carls all chuckled away like they never heard finer wit. "Give Reachey my regards."

"I will." Calder turned for the door.

"And Calder!" Dow was just tapping off the drips. "You ain't going to make more trouble for me, are you?"

"Trouble? Wouldn't know how, Chief."

"'Cause what with all those Southerners to fight...and unknowable fucks like Whirrun of Bligh and this Crinna-Come-Boasting weirdness... and my own people treading all over each other...I've got about as much arse-ache as I need. Can't stand for anyone playing their own games. Some-one tries to dig my roots from under me at a time like this, well, I've got to tell you, things'll get *fucking ugly*!" He screamed the last two words, eyes suddenly bulging from his face, veins popping from his neck, fury boiling out of him with no warning and making every man in the room flinch. Then he was calm as a kitten again. "Get me?"

Calder swallowed, trying not to let his fear show even though his skin was all prickling. "I think I have the gist."

"Good lad." Dow worked his hips about as he finished lacing up, then grinned around like a fox grins at a chicken coop left open. "I'd hate to hurt your wife, she's a pretty little thing. Not so pretty as you, o' course."

Calder hid his fury under another smirk. "Who is?"

He strode between the grinning Carls and out into the evening, all the while thinking about how he was going to kill Black Dow, and take back what was stolen from his father.

What War?

Beautiful, ain't it?" said Agrick, big grin across his freckled face.

"Is it?" muttered Craw. He'd been thinking about the ground, and how he might use it, and how an enemy might do the same. An old habit. It had been the better half of Bethod's talk, when they were on campaign. The ground, and how to make a weapon of it.

The hill the Heroes stood on was ground an idiot could've seen the value of. It sprouted alone from the flat valley, so much alone and so oddly smooth a shape it seemed almost a thing man-made. Two spurs swelled from it – one pushing west with a single needle of rock raised up on end which folk had named Skarling's Finger, one to the southeast, a ring of smaller stones on top they called the Children.

The river wound through the valley's shallow bottom, skirting golden barley fields to the west, losing itself in a bog riddled with mirror-pools, then under the crumbling bridge Scorry Tiptoe was watching which was called, with a stubborn lack of imagination, the Old Bridge. The water flowed on fast around the foot of the hill, flaring out in sparkling shallows streaked with shingle. Somewhere down there among the scraggy brush and driftwood Brack was fishing. Or, more likely, sleeping.

On the far side of the river, off to the south, Black Fell rose up. A rough-heaped mass of yellow grass and brown bracken, stained with scree and creased with white-watered gills. To the east Osrung straddled the river, a cluster of houses around a bridge and a big mill, huddled inside a high fence. Smoke drifted from chimneys, into the bright blue and off to nowhere. All normal, and nothing to remark upon, and no sign whatever of the Union, or Hardbread, or any of the Dogman's boys.

Hard to believe there was any war at all.

But then in Craw's experience, and he'd plenty, wars were made from ninety-nine parts boredom, usually in the cold and damp, hungry and ill, often hauling a great weight of metal uphill, to one part arse-opening terror. Made him wonder yet again why the hell he ever got into the black

48

business, and why the hell he still hadn't got out. Talent for it, or a lack of talent for aught else. Or maybe he'd just gone with the wind and the wind had blown him here. He peered up, shreds of cloud shifting across the deep sky, now one memory, now another.

"Beautiful," said Agrick again.

"Everything looks prettier in the sun," said Craw. "If it was raining you'd be calling it the ugliest valley in the world."

"Maybe." Agrick closed his eyes and tipped his face back. "But it ain't raining."

That was a fact, and not necessarily a happy one. Craw had a long-established tendency to sunburn, and had spent most of yesterday edging around the tallest of the Heroes along with the shade. Only thing he liked less than the heat was the cold.

"Oh, for a roof," he muttered. "Damn fine invention for keeping the weather off."

"Bit o' rain don't bother me none," grunted Agrick.

"You're young. Wait 'til you're out in all weathers at my age."

Agrick shrugged. "By then I hope to have a roof, Chief."

"Good idea," said Craw. "You cheeky little bastard." He opened his battered eyeglass, the one he'd taken from a dead Union officer they found frozen in the winter, and peered towards the Old Bridge again. Nothing. Checked the shallows. Nothing. Eyed the Ollensand Road, jerked up at a moving spot there, then realised it was some tiny fly on the end of the glass and sank back. "Guess a man can see further in fine weather, at least."

"It's the Union we're watching for, ain't it? Those bastards couldn't creep up on a corpse. You worry too much, Chief."

"Someone has to." But Agrick had a point. Worrying too much or not enough is ever a fine balance, and Craw always found himself falling heavily on the worried side of it. Every hint of movement had him starting, ripe to call for weapons. Birds flapping lazily into the sky. Sheep grazing on the slopes of the fells. Farmers' wagons creeping along the roads. A little while ago Jolly Yon had started up axe practice with Athroc, and the sudden scrape of metal had damn near made him soak his trousers. Craw worried too much, all right. Shame is, a man can't just choose not to worry.

"Why are we here, Agrick?"

"Here? Well, you know. Sit on the Heroes, watch to see if the Union come, tell Black Dow if they do. Scouting, like always."

"I know that. It was me told it to you. I mean, *why* are we here?"

"What, like, meaning of life and that?"

"No, no." Craw grabbed at the air as though what he meant was something he couldn't quite get a hold of. "Why are we *here*?"

Agrick's face puckered up as he thought on it. "Well . . . The Bloody-Nine killed Bethod, and took his chain, and made himself King o' the Northmen."

"True." Craw remembered the day well enough, Bethod's corpse sprawled out bloody in the circle, the crowd roaring Ninefingers' name, and he shivered in spite of the sun. "And?"

"Black Dow turned on the Bloody-Nine and took the chain for his self." Agrick realised he might have used some risky phrasing there, started covering his tracks. "I mean, he had to do it. Who'd want a mad bastard like the Bloody-Nine for king? But the Dogman called Dow traitor, and oathbreaker, and most of the clans from down near Uffrith, they tended to his way of seeing things. The King of the Union, too, having been on some mad journey with Ninefingers and made a friend of him. So the Dogman and the Union decided to make war on Black Dow, and here we all are." Agrick slumped back on his elbows, closing his eyes and looking quite heavily pleased with himself.

"That's a fine understanding of the politics of the current conflict."

"Thanks, Chief."

"Why Black Dow and the Dogman got a feud. Why the Union's taken the Dogman's side in it, though I daresay that's got more to do with who owns what than who made a friend of who."

"All right. There you are then."

"But why are *we* here?"

Agrick sat up again, frowning. Behind them, metal clonked on wood as his brother took a swipe at Yon's shield and got knocked over for his pains.

"Sideways, I said, y'idiot!" came Yon's un-jolly growl.

"Well . . ." tried Agrick, "I guess we stand with Dow because Dow stands for the North, rough bastard or not."

"The North? What?" Craw patted the grass beside him. "The hills and the forests and the rivers and that, he stands for them, does he? Why would they want armies tramping all over 'em?"

"Well, not the land of it. The people in it, I mean. You know. The North."

"But there's all kinds of people in the North, ain't there? Lot of 'em don't care much for Black Dow, and he certainly don't care much for them. Most just want to keep their heads down low and scratch out a living."

"Aye, I suppose."

"So how can Black Dow be for everyone?"

"Well..." Agrick squirmed about a bit. "I don't know. I guess, just..." He squinted down into the valley as Wonderful walked up behind them. "Why are we here, then?"

She clipped him across the back of the head and made him grunt. "Sit on the Heroes, watch for the Union. Scouting, like always, idiot. Damn fool bloody question."

Agrick shook his head at the injustice of it all. "That's it. I'm never talking again."

"You promise?" asked Wonderful.

"Why are we bloody here..." Agrick muttered to himself as he walked off to watch Yon and Athroc training, rubbing the back of his head.

"I know why I'm here." Whirrun had slowly raised one long forefinger, stalk of grass between his teeth thrashing around as he spoke. Craw had thought he was asleep, sprawled out on his back with the hilt of his sword for a pillow. But then Whirrun always looked asleep, and he never was. "Because Shoglig told me a man with a bone caught in his throat would—"

"Lead you to your destiny." Wonderful planted her hands on her hips. "Aye, we've heard it before."

Craw puffed out his cheeks. "Like the care of eight lives weren't a heavy enough burden, I need a madman's destiny to weigh me down."

Whirrun sat up and pushed his hood back. "I object to that, I'm not mad in the least. I just...got my own way of seeing things."

"A mad way," muttered Wonderful under her breath as Whirrun stood, slapped the arse of his stained trousers and dragged his sheathed sword up and over his shoulder.

He frowned, shifted from one leg to the other, then rubbed at his fruits. "I'm needing a wee, though. Would you go in the river, or up against one o' these stones, do you reckon?"

Craw thought about it. "River. Up against the stones would seem... disrespectful."

"You think there are Gods watching?"

"How do you tell?"

"True." Whirrun chewed his grass stalk across to the other side of his mouth and started off down the hill. "River it is, then. Maybe I'll give Brack a hand with the fishing. Shoglig used to be able to just talk the fish out of the water and I've never quite been able to get the trick of it."

"You could hack 'em out with that tree-cutter of yours!" Wonderful shouted after him.

"Maybe I will!" He lifted the Father of Swords high over his head, not much shorter'n a man from pommel to point. "High time I killed something!"

Craw wouldn't have complained if he held off for a spell. Leaving the valley with nothing dead was the sum of his hopes, right then. Which was an odd ambition for a soldier, when you thought about it. Him and Wonderful stood there silent for a while, side by side. Behind them steel squealed as Yon brushed Athroc away and sent him stumbling. "Put some effort in, you limp-wristed fuck!"

Craw found himself coming over nostalgic, like he did more and more these days. "Colwen loved the sunshine."

"That so?" asked Wonderful, lifting one brow at him.

"Always mocked at me about sticking to the shade."

"That so?"

"I should've married her," he muttered.

"Aye, you should've. Why didn't you?"

"You told me not to, apart from aught else."

"True. She had a sharp old tongue on her. But you don't usually have trouble ignoring me."

"Fair point. Guess I was just too coward to ask." And he couldn't wait to leave. Win a big name with high deeds. He hardly even knew the man who'd thought that way. "Didn't really know what I wanted back then, just thought I didn't have it, and I could get it with a sword."

"Think about her, at all?" asked Wonderful.

"Not often."

"Liar."

Craw grinned. She knew him too bloody well. "Call it half a lie. I don't think about her, really. Can't hardly remember her face half the time. But I think about what my life might've been, if I'd taken that path 'stead o' this." Sitting with his pipe, under his porch, smiling at the sunset on the water. He gave a sigh. "But, you know, choices made, eh? What about your husband?"

Wonderful took a long breath. "Probably he's getting ready to bring the harvest in about now. The children too."

"Wish you were with 'em?"

"Sometimes."

"Liar. How often you been back this year? Twice, is it?"

Wonderful frowned down into the still valley. "I go when I can. They know that. They know what I am."

"And they still put up with you?"

She was silent a moment, then shrugged. "Choices made, eh?"

"Chief!" Agrick was hurrying over from the other side of the Heroes. "Drofd's back! And he ain't alone."

"No?" Craw winced as he worked some movement into his dodgy knee. "Who's he got with him?"

Agrick had a face like a man sat on a thistle. "Looked like Caul Shivers."

"Shivers?" growled Yon, head snapping sideways. Athroc seized his moment, stepped around Yon's drooping shield and kneed him in the fruits. "Awwww, you little bastard..." And Yon went down, eyes bulging.

Craw might've laughed half his teeth out any other time, but Shivers' name had chased the fun right out of him. He strode across the circle of grass, hoping all the way Agrick might've got it wrong but knowing it wasn't likely. Craw's hopes had a habit of coming out bloodstained, and Caul Shivers was a difficult man to mistake.

Up he came towards the Heroes now, riding up that steep track on the north side of the hill. Craw watched him all the way, feeling like a shepherd watching a storm-cloud blow in.

"Shit," muttered Wonderful.

"Aye," said Craw. "Shit."

Shivers left Drofd to hobble their horses down at the drystone wall and came the rest of the way on foot. He looked at Craw, and Wonderful, and Jolly Yon too, half-ruined face slack as a hanged man's, the left side not much more'n a great line of burn through that metal eye. A spookier-looking bastard you never did see.

"Craw." Said in his whispery croak.

"Shivers. What brings you down here?"

"Dow sent me."

"That much I guessed. It's the why I'm after."

"He says you're to keep hold o' this hill and watch for the Union."

"He told me that already." Bit more snappish than Craw had meant. There was a pause. "So why send you here?"

Shivers shrugged. "To make sure you do it."

"Many thanks for the support."

"Thank Dow."

"I will."

"He'll like that. Have you seen the Union?"

"Not since Hardbread was up here, four nights ago."

"I know Hardbread. Stubborn old prick. He might come back."

"If he does there's only three ways across the river, far as I know." Craw pointed 'em out. "The Old Bridge over west near the bogs, the new bridge in Osrung and the shallows at the bottom of the hill there. We got eyes on all of 'em, and the valley's open. We could see a sheep cross the river from here."

"Don't reckon we need to tell Black Dow about a sheep." Shivers brought the ruined side of his face close. "But we better if the Union come. Maybe we can sing some songs, while we wait?"

"Can you carry a tune?" asked Wonderful.

"Shit, no. Don't stop me trying, though." And he strolled off across the circle of grass, Athroc and Agrick backing away to give him room. Craw couldn't blame 'em. Shivers was one of those men seemed to have a space around him where you'd better not be.

Craw turned slowly to Drofd. "Great."

The lad held his hands up. "What was I supposed to do? Tell him I didn't want the company? Least you didn't have to spend two days riding with him, and two nights sleeping next to him at the fire. He never closes that eye, you know. It's like he's looking at you all night long. I swear I haven't slept a wink since we set out."

"He can't see out of it, fool," said Yon, "any more'n I can see out your belt buckle."

"I know that, but still." Drofd looked around at them all, voice dropping. "Do you really reckon the Union are coming this way?"

"No," said Wonderful. "I don't." She gave Drofd one of her looks, and his shoulders slumped, and he walked away muttering to himself on the theme of what else he could've done. Then she came up beside Craw, and leaned close. "Do you really reckon the Union are coming this way?"

"Doubt it. But I've got a bad feeling." He frowned across at Shivers' black outline, leaning against one of the Heroes, the valley drenched in sunlight beyond, and he put one hand on his stomach. "And I've learned to listen to my gut."

Wonderful snorted. "Hard to ignore something so bloody big, I guess."

Old Hands

"T unny."

"Uh?" He opened one eye and the sun stabbed him directly in the brains. "Uh!" He snapped it shut again, wormed his tongue around his sore mouth. It tasted like slow death and old rot. "Uh." He tried his other eye, just a crack, trained it on the dark shape hovering above him. It loomed closer, sun making glittering daggers down its edges.

"Tunny!"

"I hear you, damn it!" He tried to sit and the world tossed like a ship in a storm. "Gah!" He became aware he was in a hammock. He tried to rip his feet clear, got them tangled in the netting, almost tipped himself over in his efforts to get free, somehow ended up somewhere near sitting, swallowing the overwhelming urge to vomit. "First Sergeant Forest. What a delight. What time is it?"

"Past time you were working. Where did you get those boots?"

Tunny peered down, puzzled. He was wearing a pair of superbly polished black cavalry boots with gilded accoutrements. The reflection of the sun in the toes was so bright it was painful to look at. "Ah." He grinned through the agony, some of the details of last night starting to leak from the shadowy crannies of his mind. "Won 'em...from an officer...called..." He squinted up into the branches of the tree his hammock was tied to. "No. It's gone."

Forest shook his head in amazement. "There's still someone in the division stupid enough to play cards with you?"

"Well, this is one of the many fine things about wartime, Sergeant. Lots of folks leaving the division." Their regiment had left two score in sick tents over the last couple of weeks alone. "That means lots of new card-players arriving, don't it?"

"Yes it does, Tunny, yes it does." Forest had that mocking little grin on his scarred face.

"Oh no," said Tunny.

"Oh yes."

"No, no, no!"

"Yes. Up you come, lads!"

And up they came indeed. Four of them. New recruits, fresh off the boat from Midderland by their looks. Seen off at the docks with kisses from Mummy or sweetheart or both. New uniforms pressed, straps polished, buckles gleaming and ready for the noble soldiering life, indeed. Forest gestured towards Tunny like a showman towards his freak, and trotted out that same little address he always gave.

"Boys, this here is the famous Corporal Tunny, one of the longest serving non-commissioned officers in General Jalenhorm's division. A veteran of the Starikland Rebellion, the Gurkish War, the last Northern War, the Siege of Adua, this current unpleasantness and a quantity of peacetime soldiering that would have bored a keener mind to death. He has survived the runs, the rot, the grip, the autumn shudders, the caresses of Northern winds, the buffets of Southern women, thousands of miles of marching, many years of his Majesty's rations and even a tiny bit of actual fighting to stand – or sit – before you now. He has four times been Sergeant Tunny, once even Colour Sergeant Tunny, but always, like a homing pigeon to its humble cage, returned to his current station. He now holds the exalted post of standard-bearer of his August Majesty's indomitable First Regiment of cavalry. That gives him responsibility—" Tunny groaned at the mere mention of the word "—for the regimental riders, tasked with carrying messages to and from our much admired commanding officer, Colonel Vallimir. Which is where you boys come in."

"Oh, bloody hell, Forest."

"Oh, bloody hell, Tunny. Why don't you introduce yourselves to the corporal?"

"Klige." Chubby-faced, with a big sty that had closed one eye and his strapping on the wrong way round.

"Previous profession, Klige?" asked Forest.

"Was going to be a weaver, sir. But I hadn't been 'prenticed more than a month before my master sold me out to the recruiter."

Tunny gave a further grimace. The replacements they were getting lately were an insult to the bottom of the barrel.

"Worth." The next was gaunt and bony with an ill-looking grey sheen to his skin. "I was in the militia and they disbanded the company, so we all got drafted."

"Lederlingen." A tall, rangy specimen with big hands and a worried look. "I was a cobbler." He offered no further detail on the mechanics of his entry into the King's Own and Tunny's head was hurting too much for him to pry. The man was here now, unfortunately for everyone involved.

"Yolk." A short lad with a lot of freckles, dwarfed by his pack. He glanced guiltily about. "They called me a thief but I never done it. Judge said it was this or five year in prison."

"I rather think we may all come to regret that choice," grunted Tunny, though probably as a thief he was the only one with transferrable skills. "Why's your name Yolk?"

"Er...don't know. Was my father's name...I guess."

"Think you're the best part of the egg, do you, Yolk?"

"Well..." He looked doubtfully at his neighbours. "Not really."

Tunny squinted up at him. "I'll be watching you, boy." Yolk's bottom lip almost trembled at the injustice.

"You lads stick close to Corporal Tunny here. He'll keep you out of danger." Forest had a smile that was tough to define. "If there was ever a soldier for staying clear of danger, it's Corporal Tunny. Just don't play cards with him!" he shouted over his shoulder as he made off through the shambles of ill-kempt canvas that was their camp.

Tunny took a deep breath, and stood. The recruits snapped to ill-coordinated attention. Or three of them did. Yolk followed up a moment later. Tunny waved them down. "For pity's sake don't salute. I might be sick on you."

"Sorry, sir."

"I'm not sir, I'm Corporal Tunny."

"Sorry, Corporal Tunny."

"Now look. I don't want you here and you don't want to be here—"

"I want to be here," said Lederlingen.

"You do?"

"Volunteered." A trace of pride in his voice.

"Vol…un…teered?" Tunny wrestled with the word as if it belonged to a foreign language. "So they do exist. Just make damn sure you don't volunteer me for anything while you're here. Anyway…" He drew the lads into a conspiratorial huddle with a crooked finger. "You boys have landed right on your feet. I've done all kind of jobs in his Majesty's army and this right here," and he pointed an affectionate finger at the standard of the First, rolled up safe under his hammock in its canvas cover, "this is a sweet detail. Now I may be in charge, that's true. But I want you lads to think of me as, let's say…your kindly uncle. Anything you need. Anything *extra*. Anything to make this army life of ours worth living." He leaned in closer and gave the suggestive eyebrows. "*Anything*. You can come to me." Lederlingen held up a hesitant finger. "Yes?"

"We're cavalrymen, aren't we?"

"Yes, trooper, we are."

"Shouldn't we have horses?"

"That's an excellent question and a keen grasp of tactics. Due to an administrative error, our horses are currently with the Fifth, attached to Mitterick's division, which, as a regiment of infantry, is not in a position to make best use of them. I'm told they'll be catching up with us any day, though they've been telling me that a while. For the time being we are a regiment of…horseless horse."

"Foot?" offered Yolk.

"You might say that, except we still…" and Tunny tapped his skull, "think like cavalry. Other than horses, which is a deficiency common to every man in the unit, is there anything else you need?"

Klige was next to lift his arm. "Well, sir, Corporal Tunny, that is…I'd really like something to eat."

Tunny grinned. "Well, that's definitely extra."

"Don't we get food?" asked Yolk, horrified.

"Of course his Majesty provides his loyal soldiers with rations, Yolk, of course he does. But nothing anyone would actually *want* to eat. You get sick of eating things you don't want to eat, well, you come to me."

"At a price, I suppose." Lederlingen, sour of face.

"A *reasonable* price. Union coin, Northern coin, Styrian coin, Gurkish coin. Any kind of coin, in fact. But if you're short of currency I'm prepared to consider all manner of things in trade. Arms salvaged from dead Northmen, for example, are popular at present. Or perhaps we can work on the basis of favours. Everyone has something to trade, and we can always come to some—"

"Corporal?" An odd, high, strained voice, almost like a woman's, but it wasn't a woman who stood behind Tunny when he turned, to his great disappointment if not surprise. It was a very large man, black uniform mud-spotted from hard riding, colonel's markings at the sleeves, long and short steels of a businesslike design at his belt. His hair was shaved to stubble, dusted with grey at the ears and close to bald on top. Heavy-browed, broad-nosed and slab-jawed like a prizefighter, dark eyes fixed on Tunny. Perhaps it was his notable lack of neck, or the way the big knuckles stuck white from his clenched fists, or that his uniform looked as if it was stretched tight over rock, but even standing still he gave the impression of fearsome strength.

Tunny could salute with the very best when it seemed a wise idea, and now he snapped to vibrating attention. "Sir! Corporal Tunny, sir, standard-bearer of his Majesty's First Regiment!"

"General Jalenhorm's headquarters?" The newcomer's eyes flicked over the recruits, as if daring them to laugh at his piping voice.

Tunny knew when to laugh, and now was not the moment. He pointed across the rubbish and tent-strewn meadow towards the farmhouse, smudges of smoke rising from the chimney and staining the bright sky. "You'll find the general just there, sir! In the house, sir! Probably still in bed, sir!"

The officer nodded once then strode off, head down, in a way that suggested he'd simply walk through anything and anyone in his way.

"Who was that?" muttered one of the lads.

"I believe that..." Tunny let it hang in the air for a moment, "was Bremer dan Gorst."

"The one who fenced with the king?"

"That's right, and was his bodyguard until that mess in Sipani. Still has the king's ear, some say." Not a good thing, that such a notable personage should be here. Never stand near anyone notable.

"What's he doing here?"

"Couldn't say for sure. But I hear he's a hell of a *fighter*." And Tunny gave his front teeth a worried sucking.

59

"Ain't that a good thing in a soldier?" asked Yolk.

"Bloody hell, no! Take it from me, who's lived through more than one melee, wars are hard enough work without people *fighting* in the middle of 'em." Gorst stalked into the front yard of the house, pulling something from his jacket. A folded paper. An order, by the look of it. He saluted the guards and went in. Tunny rubbed at his rebelling stomach. Something didn't feel right, and not just last night's wine.

"Sir?"

"Corporal Tunny."

"I...I..." It was the one called Worth, and he was in a fix. Tunny knew the signs, of course. The shifting from one leg to another, the pale features, the slightly dewy eyes. No time to spare.

He jerked his thumb towards the latrine pits. "Go!" The lad took off like a scared rabbit, hopping bow-legged through the mud. "But make sure you crap in the proper place!" Tunny turned to wag one lecturing finger at the rest of the litter. "*Always* crap in the proper place. This is a principle of soldiering of far greater importance than any rubbish about marching, or weapons, or ground." Even at this distance Worth's long groan could be heard, followed by some explosive farting. "Trooper Worth is fighting his first engagement with our real enemy out here. An implacable, merciless, liquid foe." He slapped a hand down on the shoulder of the nearest trooper. Yolk, as it happened, who nearly collapsed under the added weight. "Sooner or later, I've no doubt, you will all be called upon to fight your own battle of the latrines. Courage, boys, courage. Now, while we wait for Worth to force out the enemy or die bravely in the attempt, would any of you boys care for a friendly game of cards?" He produced the deck from nowhere, fanning it out under the recruits' surprised eyes, or eye in Klige's case, the mesmerising effect only mildly damaged by Trooper Worth's ongoing arse music. "We'll just play for honour. To begin with. Nothing you can't afford to lose, eh? Nothing you can't... Uh-oh."

General Jalenhorm had emerged from his headquarters, jacket wide open, hair in disarray, face flushed beetroot red, and shouting. He was always shouting, but this time he appeared, for once, to have a purpose. Gorst came after him, hunched and silent.

"Uh-oh." Jalenhorm stomped one way, seemed to think better of it, swivelled, roared at nobody, struggled with a button, slapped an assisting hand angrily away. Staff officers began to scatter from the house in all directions like birds whacked from the brush, chaos spreading rapidly from the general and infecting the entire camp.

"Damn it," muttered Tunny, shouldering his way into his bracers. "We'd best get ready to move."

"We just got here, Corporal," grumbled Yolk, pack half way off.

Tunny took hold of the strap and tugged it back over Yolk's shoulder, turned him by it to face towards the general. Jalenhorm was trying to shake his fist at a well-presented officer and button his own jacket at the same time, and failing. "You have before you a perfect demonstration of the workings of the army – the chain of command, trooper, each man shitting on the head of the man below. The much-loved leader of our regiment, Colonel Vallimir, is just getting shat on by General Jalenhorm. Colonel Vallimir will shit on his own officers, and it won't take long to roll downhill, believe me. Within a minute or two, First Sergeant Forest will arrive to position his bared buttocks above my undeserving head. Guess what that means for you lot?" The lads stayed silent for a moment, then Klige raised a tentative hand. "The question was meant to be rhetorical, numbskull." He carefully lowered it again. "For that you get to carry my pack."

Klige's shoulders slumped.

"You. Ladderlugger."

"Lederlingen, Corporal Tunny."

"Whatever. Since you love volunteering so much, you just volunteered to take my other pack. Yolk?"

"Sir?" Plain to see he could hardly stand under the weight of his own gear.

Tunny sighed. "You carry the hammock."

New Hands

Beck raised the axe high and snarled as he brought it down, split that log in two and pretended all the while it was some Union soldier's head. Pretended there was blood spraying from it rather'n splinters. Pretended the babbling of the brook was the sound of men cheering for him and the leaves across the grass were women swooning at his feet. Pretended he was a great hero, like his father had been, won himself a high name on the battlefield and a high place at the fire and in the songs. He was the hardest bastard in the whole damn North, no doubt. Far as pretending went.

He tossed the split wood onto the pile, stooped down to drag up another log. Wiped his forehead on his sleeve and frowned across the valley, humming to himself from the Lay of Ripnir. Somewhere out there beyond the hills, Black Dow's army was fighting. Out there beyond the hills high deeds were being done and tomorrow's songs written. He spat into his palms, rough from wood-axe, and plough, and scythe, and shovel, and washboard even. He hated this valley and the people in it. Hated this farm and the work he did on it.

He was made to fight, not chop logs.

He heard footsteps slapping, saw his brother struggling up the steep path from the house, bent over. Back from the village already, and it looked like he'd run the whole way. Beck's axe went up into the bright sky and came down, and one more Southerner's skull was laid to waste. Festen made it to the top of the path and stood there, bent over, shaking hands on his wobbly knees, round cheeks blotchy pink, struggling for breath.

"What's the hurry?" asked Beck, bending for more wood.

"There's...there's..." Festen fought to talk and breathe and stand up all at once. "There's men in the village!" he got out in a rush.

"What sort o' men?"

"Carls! Reachey's Carls!"

"What?" The axe hovered over Beck's head, forgotten.

"Aye. And they got a weapontake on!"

Beck stood there for a moment longer, then tossed the axe down on the pile of split logs and strode for the house. Strode fast and hard, his skin all singing. So fast Festen had to trot along to keep up, asking, "What you going to do?" over and over and getting no reply.

Past the pen and the staring goats and the five big tree stumps all hacked and scarred from years of Beck's blade practice every morning. Into the smoke-smelling darkness of the house, slashes of sunlight through the ill-fitting shutters, across bare boards and bald old furs. Wood creaked under his boots as he strode to his chest, knelt, pushed back the lid, tore his clothes out of the way with small patience. Lifted it with fingers tender as a lover's. The only thing he cared for.

Gold glimmered in the gloom and he wrapped his fingers around the hilt, feeling the perfect balance of it, slid a foot-length of steel from the scabbard. Smiled at that sound, that scraping, singing sound that set his already jangling nerves to thrill. How often had he smiled down like this, polishing, sharpening, polishing, dreaming of this day, and now it was come. He slapped the sword back in its sheath, turned . . . and froze.

His mother stood in the doorway, watching. A black shadow with the white sky behind.

"I'm taking my father's sword," he snapped, shaking the hilt at her.

"He was killed with that sword."

"It's mine to take!"

"It is."

"You can't make me stay here no more." He stuffed a few things in the pack he kept ready. "You said this summer!"

"I did."

"You can't stop me going!"

"Do you see me trying?"

"By my age Shubal the Wheel had been seven years on campaign!"

"Lucky him."

"It's time. It's past time!"

"I know." She watched as he took his bow down, unstrung and wrapped up with a few shafts. "It'll be cold nights, next month or two. Best take my good cloak with you."

That caught him off guard. "I . . . no, you should keep it."

"I'd be happier knowing you had it."

63

He didn't want to argue in case he lost his nerve. Off all big and bold to face down a thousand thousand Southerners but scared of the one woman who'd birthed him. So he snatched her good green-dyed cloak down from the peg and over his shoulder as he stalked for the door. Treated it like nothing even though he knew it was the best thing she had.

Festen was standing outside, nervous, not really understanding what was happening. Beck ruffled his red hair for him. "You're the man here, now. Get them logs chopped and I'll bring you something back from the wars."

"They've got nothing there we need," said his mother, eyeing him from the shadows. Not angry, like she used to be. Just sad. He'd hardly realised 'til that moment how much bigger'n her he was now. The top of her head hardly came up to his neck, even.

"We'll see." He took the two steps down to the ground outside, under the mossy eaves of the house, couldn't help turning back. "Well, then."

"One last thing, Beck." She leaned down, and kissed him on his forehead. The softest of kisses, gentle as the rain. She touched his cheek, and she smiled. "My son."

He felt the tightness of tears in his throat, and he was guilty for what he'd said, and joyful to get his way at last, and angry for all the months he hadn't, and sad to go, and afraid, and excited all at once. He could hardly make his face show one thing or another for all the different ways it was pulled. He touched the back of her hand quickly, and he turned before he started weeping and strode away down the path, and off to war.

Strode the way he thought his father might've.

The weapontake weren't quite what Beck had hoped for.

Rain flitted down, not enough to make anyone wet, really, but enough to make everyone squint and hunch, to damp down the feel of the whole business. And the feel was pretty damn soggy already. Folk who'd come to join up, or been made to come, more likely, stood in things that might've started off as rows but had melted into squelching, jostling, grumbling tangles. Most of 'em were young lads, too young for this by Beck's reckoning. Lads who might never have seen the next valley let alone a battle. Most of the rest were grey with age. A few cripples of one kind or another rounded out the numbers. At the edge of the crowd some of Reachey's Carls stood leaning on spears or sat mounted, looking every bit as unimpressed by the new recruits as Beck was. All in all, it was a long, low way from the noble band of brothers he'd been hoping to play a hero's part in.

He shook his head, one fist holding his mother's cloak tight at his neck, the other underneath it, gripping the warm hilt of his father's sword. He didn't belong with this lot. Maybe Skarling Hoodless had started out with an unpromising crowd, and made an army of 'em that beat the Union, but Beck couldn't see anyone telling high tales about this gathering of the hopeless. At one point he'd seen a new-made crew shambling by and two little lads at the front only had one spear between 'em. A weapontake without enough weapons to go round, you don't hear much about that in the songs.

For some reason, most likely on account of daydreaming it so often, he'd been half-expecting old Caul Reachey himself to be looking on, a man who'd fought in every battle since whenever, a man who did everything the old way. Maybe catching Beck's eye or giving him a slap on the back. Here's the kind o' lad we need! Everyone look at this lad! Let's find us some more like him! But there was no sign of Reachey. Or anyone else who knew what they were doing. For a moment he looked at the muddy way he'd come, and gave some hard thought to heading back to the farm. He could be home before dawn—

"Come to join up?" A short man but heavy in the shoulder, hair and stubble full of grey, a mace at his belt looked like it had seen some action. He stood with his weight all on one leg, like the other might not take it.

Beck weren't about to look the fool. He packed away any thoughts of quitting. "I've come to fight."

"Good for you. My name's Flood, and I'll be taking charge o' this little crew when it's mustered." He pointed out an unpromising row of boys, some with worn bows or hatchets, most with nothing but the clothes they stood in and those in a sorry state. "You want to do more'n talk about fighting, get in line."

"Reckon I will." Flood looked like he might know a sword from a sow at least, and one line looked pretty much as bad as another. So Beck swaggered up, chest out, and pushed his way in among the lads at the back. He fair towered over 'em, young as they were. "I'm Beck," he said.

"Colving," muttered one. Couldn't have been more'n thirteen and tubby with it, staring about wide-eyed, looking scared of everything.

"Stodder," mumbled around a mouthful of some rotten-looking meat by a hangdog lad with a fat lower lip, wet and dangling like he was touched in the head.

"I'm Brait," piped a boy even smaller'n Colving, ragged as a beggar, dirty toes showing through the end of one split boot. Beck was getting ready to feel sorry for him until he realised how bad he smelled. Brait offered his skinny hand but Beck didn't take it. He was busy sizing up the last of the group, older'n the others with a bow over his shoulder and a scar through one dark eyebrow. Probably just fell off a wall, but it made him look more dangerous than he'd any right to. Beck wished he had a scar.

"What about you?"

"Reft." He'd this knowing little grin on his face Beck didn't much like the look of. Felt right away like he was being laughed at.

"Something funny?"

Reft waved a hand at the muddle all around 'em. "Something not funny?"

"You laughing at me?"

"Not everything's about you, friend."

Beck weren't sure if this lad was making him look a fool, or if he was doing it to himself, or if he was just hacked off 'cause none of this matched his hopes, but he was getting angry, and fast. "You might want to watch your fucking—"

But Reft weren't listening. He was looking over Beck's shoulder, and so were the rest of the lads. Beck turned to see what at, got a shock to find a rider looming over him on a high horse. A good horse with an even better saddle, metal on the harness polished to a neat twinkle. A man of maybe thirty years, by Beck's guess, clear-skinned and sharp-eyed. He wore a fine cloak with a stitched edge and a rich fur collar, might've made Beck shamed of the one his mother had given him if most of the others in the row hadn't been wearing little better'n rags.

"Evening." The rider's voice was soft and smooth, the word hardly even sounding like Northern.

"Evening," said Reft.

"Evening," said Beck, no chance he was going to let Reft play at being leader.

The rider smiled down from his fancy saddle, just like they were all old mates together. "I don't suppose you lads could point me to Reachey's fire?"

Reft stuck a finger into the gathering gloom. "Over yonder, I reckon, on that rise there, lee o' them trees." Black outlines against the evening sky, branches lit underneath by firelight.

"Much obliged to you." The man nodded to each of them, even Brait and Colving, then clicked his tongue and nudged his horse through the press, smirk still at the corner of his mouth. Like he'd said something funny. Beck didn't see what.

"Who was that bastard?" he snapped, once the rider was well out of earshot.

"Don't know," whispered Colving.

Beck curled his lip at the lad. "'Course you don't. Weren't asking you, was I?"

"Sorry." He flinched like he was expecting a slap. "Just saying…"

"Reckon that was the great Prince Calder," said Reft.

Beck's lip curled further. "What, Bethod's son? Ain't a prince no more, then, is he?"

"Reckon he thinks he is."

"Married to Reachey's daughter, ain't he?" said Brait in his high little voice. "Come to pay respects to his wife's father, maybe."

"Come to try and lie his way back into his father's chair, judging on his reputation," said Reft.

Beck snorted. "Don't reckon he'll get much change out o' Black Dow."

"Get the bloody cross cut in him for the effort, more'n likely," grunted Stodder, licking his fingers as he finished eating.

"Get hung and burned, I reckon," piped up Colving. "That's what he does, Black Dow, wi' cowards and schemers."

"Aye," said Brait, as though he was the great expert. "Puts the flame to 'em himself and watches 'em dance."

"Can't say I'll weep any." Beck threw a dark glance after Calder, still easing through the press, high above everyone else in his saddle. If there was an opposite of a straight edge it was that bastard. "He don't look much of a fighter."

"So?" Reft's grin dropped down to the hem of Beck's cloak where the blunt end of the sword's sheath showed. "You do look a fighter. Don't necessarily make it so."

Beck weren't having that. He twitched his mother's cloak back over his shoulder to give him room, fists clenched. "You calling me a fucking coward?" Stodder slid carefully out of his way. Colving turned his scared eyes to the ground. Brait just had this helpless little smile.

Reft shrugged, not quite rising to it, but not quite backing down either. "Don't know you well enough to say what y'are. Stood in the line, have you, in battle?"

"Not in the line," snapped Beck, hoping they might think he'd fought a few skirmishes when in fact aside from some bare-handed tussles with boys in the village he'd only fought trees.

"Then you don't know yourself, do you? Never can tell what a man'll do once the blades are drawn, shoulder to shoulder, waiting for the charge to come. Maybe you'll stand and fight like Skarling his self. Or maybe you'll run. Maybe you only talk a good fight."

"I'll show you a fight, you fucker!" Beck stepped forwards, one fist going up. Colving gave a whimper, covered his face like he was the one might get hit. Reft took a pace back, pulling his coat open with one hand. Beck saw the handle of a long knife there, and he realised when he pushed the cloak back he'd showed the hilt of his father's sword, and it was right by his hand, and it came to him of a sudden how high the stakes had climbed all out of nothing. It came to him in a flash this might not end up a tussle between boys in the village, and he saw the fear in Reft's eyes, and the willingness, and the guts dropped out of him, and he faltered for a moment, not knowing how he got here or what he should do—

"Oy!" Flood lurched out of the crowd, dragging his bad leg behind him. "Enough o' that!" Beck slowly let his fist drop, mightily glad of the interruption if he was honest. "Good to see you've some fire in you, but there'll be plenty of fight to go round with the Southerners, don't you worry about that. We got marching to do on the morrow, and you'll march better without smashed mouths." Flood held his big fist up between Beck and Reft, grey hairs on the back, knuckles scuffed from a hundred old scrapes. "And that's what you'll be getting 'less you behave yourselves, understand?"

"Aye, Chief," growled Beck, giving Reft the eye though his heart was going so hard in his ears he thought it might pop 'em right off.

"Aye, 'course," said Reft, letting his coat fall closed.

"First thing a fighter has to learn is when not to fight. Now get up there, the pair o' you."

Beck realised the row of lads had melted away in front of him and there was just a stretch of trampled mud between him and a table, an awning of dripping canvas over it to keep the rain off. An old greybeard sat there waiting for him, and looking somewhat sour about it. He'd lost an arm, coatsleeve folded up and stitched across his chest. In the other hand he'd got a pen. Seemed they were taking each man's name and marking it down in a big book. New ways of doing things, with writing and what have you. Beck didn't reckon his father would've cared much for that, and neither did he. What was the purpose to fighting the Southerners if you took their ways yourselves? He trudged up through the slop, frowning.

"Name?"

"My name?"

"Who the bloody hell else's?"

"Beck."

The greybeard scratched it on his paper. "From?"

"A farm just up the valley there."

"Age?"

"Seventeen year."

The man frowned up at him. "And a big one too. You're a few summers late, lad. Where you been at?"

"Helping my mother on the farm." Someone behind snorted and Beck whipped around to give him a proper glare. Brait's sorry little grin wilted, and he looked down at his knackered shoes. "She's two little 'uns to care for, so I stayed to help her. That's man's work too."

"Guess you're here now, anyway."

"That's right."

"Your father's name?"

"Shama Heartless."

His head jerked right back up at that. "Don't poke me, lad!"

"I won't, old man. Shama Heartless was my father. This here is his sword." And Beck drew it, metal hissing, the weight in his hand putting heart right back in him, and stood it point-down on the table.

The one-armed old man looked it up and down for a moment, gold glinting with the sunset, mirror-brightness of good steel. "Well, there's a turn-up. Let's hope you're forged from the same iron as your father."

"I am."

"Reckon we'll see. Here's your first staple, lad." And he pressed a tiny silver coin into Beck's palm and took up his pen again. "Next man."

And there you go, farmer no more. Joined up with Caul Reachey and ready to fight for Black Dow against the Union. Beck sheathed his sword and stood frowning in the thickening rain, in the gathering darkness. A girl with red hair turned brown by the damp was pouring out grog for those who'd given their names and Beck took his own measure and threw it burning down his gullet. He tossed the cup aside, watching Reft, and Colving, and Stodder give their answers, thinking how it didn't matter a shit what these fools thought. He'd win his name. He'd show 'em who was the coward.

And who was the hero.

Reachey

I f it ain't my daughter's husband!" called out Reachey, firelight shining on a gap-toothed grin. "No need to tiptoe, lad."

"Muddy going," said Calder.

"And you always did like to keep your boots clean."

"Styrian leather, shipped in from Talins." And he planted one on a stone by the fire so Reachey's old Named Men could get a better look.

"Shipping in boots," grumbled Reachey, as if bemoaning the loss of all that was good in the world. "By the dead. How did a clever girl like my daughter fall for a tailor's dummy like you?"

"How did a butcher's block like you father such a beauty as my wife?"

Reachey grinned, so his men did too, the rustling flames picking out every crease and crinkle on their leathery faces. "I've always wondered at it myself. Less'n you, though. I knew her mother." A couple of the older lads grunted, faraway looks in their eyes. "And I was quite the beauty myself before life's buffets wore down my looks." The self-same older lads chuckled. Old men's jokes, all about how fine things used to be.

"Buffets," said one, shaking his head.

"Could I have a word?" asked Calder.

"Anything for my son. Lads." Reachey's closest stood, some with evident effort, and made their way grunting off into the dark. Calder picked a spot by the fire and squatted down, hands out to the flames.

"You want the pipe?" Reachey offered it, smoke curling from the bowl.

"No, thanks." Calder had to keep a straight head, even among supposed friends. It was a damn narrow path he was always treading these days, and he couldn't afford to weave about. There was a long drop on both sides of it and nothing soft at the bottom.

Reachey took a suck himself, sent up a couple of little brown smoke rings and watched them drift apart. "How's my daughter?"

"She's the best woman in the world." And he didn't even have to lie.

"You always know what to say, don't you, Calder? I won't disagree. And my grandson?"

"Still a little small to help out against the Union this time around, but he's swelling. You can feel him kick."

"Can't believe it." Reachey looked into the flames and slowly shook his head, scrubbing at his white stubble with his fingernails. "Me, a grand-father. Hah! Seems like just yesterday I was a child myself. Just this morning I was watching Seff kick at her mother's belly. It all slips by so fast. Slips by and you hardly notice, like leaves on the water. Savour the little moments, son, that's my advice. They're what life is. All the things that happen while you're waiting for something else. I've heard Black Dow wants you dead."

Calder tried not to show he'd been thrown by the shift of subject and failed. "Who says?"

"Black Dow."

No great surprise, but hearing it laid out stark as that didn't help Calder's shredded spirits. "I reckon he'd know."

"I think he's brought you back out here so he can find an easy way to kill you, or so someone else can in hopes of earning favours from him. I think he thinks you'll start scheming, and turning men against him, and trying to steal his chair. Then he'll find out about it, and be able to hang you fair, and no one can complain over much."

"He thinks if he hands me the knife I'll stab myself."

"Something like that."

"Maybe I'm quicker fingered than he reckons."

"I hope y'are. All I'm saying is, if you're planning on hatching a scheme or two, be aware he's aware, and he's waiting for you to miss a step. Providing he don't tire of tiptoeing around the issue and tell Caul Shivers to sharpen his axe on your brains."

"There'd be a few folk unhappy about that."

"True, and half the North's unhappy as it is. Too much war. Too much tax. War's got a fine tradition round these parts, o' course, but tax has never been popular. Dow needs to tread careful on folks' feelings these days, and he knows it. But it'd be a fool presumed too far on Black Dow's patience. He ain't a man made for treading carefully."

"But I suppose I am?"

"There's no shame in a soft footfall, lad. We like big, stupid men in the North, men who wade about in blood and so on. We sing songs about 'em. But those men get nothing done alone, and that's a fact. We need the other kind. Thinkers. Like you. Like your father. And we don't make half way enough of 'em. You want my advice?"

Reachey could stick his advice up his arse as far as Calder was concerned. He'd come for men, and swords, and cold hearts ready to do treachery. But he'd long ago learned that most men love nothing better than to be listened to. Especially powerful men. And Reachey was one of Dow's five War Chiefs, about as powerful as it got these days. So Calder did what he was best at, and lied. "It's your advice I came for."

"Then leave things be. 'Stead o' swimming out against a fierce current, risking it all in the cold deep, sit on the beach awhile, take your ease. Who knows? Maybe in good time the sea'll just wash up what you want."

"You reckon?" As far as Calder could tell, the sea had been washing up nothing but shit ever since his father died.

Reachey shuffled a little closer, speaking low. "Black Dow ain't sat too firmly in Skarling's Chair, for all he carts it around with him. He's the best bet for most, still, but outside o' that rotten old fuck Tenways he ain't got much loyalty. Lot less than your father had, and men these days, the likes of Ironhead and Golden? Pah!" And he snorted his contempt into the fire. "They're fickle as the wind. Folk fear Black Dow, but that only works long as you're fearsome, and if things keep dragging on, and he don't fight… folk got better things to do than sit around here going hungry and shitting in holes. I've lost as many men wandering off home to the harvest the last month as I'll pick up at this weapontake here. Dow has to fight, and soon, and if he don't, or if he loses, well, everything could spin around in an instant." And Reachey took a long, self-satisfied suck at his pipe.

"And what if he fights the Union and wins?"

"Well..." The old man squinted up at the stars as he finished blowing out his latest plume. "That is a point you've got there. If he wins he'll be everyone's hero."

"Not mine, I daresay." It was Calder's turn to lean close and whisper. "And in the meantime, we're not on the beach. What if Dow tries to murder me, or gives me some task I can't but fail at, or puts me in the line somewhere I'm good as dead? Will I have any friends at my back?"

"You're my daughter's husband, better or worse. Me and your father agreed to it when you and Seff weren't much more'n babies. I was proud to take you when you had the world at your feet. What kind of a man would I be if I turned my back now you've got the world on your shoulders? No. You're family." And he showed that missing tooth again, slapping his heavy hand down on Calder's shoulder. "I do things the old way."

"Straight edge, eh?"

"That's right."

"So you'd draw your sword for me?"

"Shit, no." And he gave Calder's shoulder a parting squeeze and took his hand away. "I'm just saying I won't draw it against you. If I have to burn, I'll burn, but I ain't setting myself on fire." About what Calder had expected, but still a disappointment. However many life gives you, each new one still stings. "Where you going, lad?"

"I think I'll meet up with Scale, help him with what's left of my father's men."

"Good idea. Strong as a bull, your brother, and brave as one with it but, well, might be he's got a bull's brain, too."

"Might be."

"Word's come from Dow, he's calling the army together. We're all marching for Osrung tomorrow morning. Heading for the Heroes."

"Guess I'll catch up with Scale there, then."

"And a warming reunion, I don't doubt." Reachey waved a gnarled paw at him. "Watch your back, Calder."

"That I will," he muttered under his breath.

"And Calder?"

Everyone always had just one more thing to say, and it never seemed to be something nice. "Aye?"

"You get yourself killed, that's one thing. But my daughter's stood hostage for you. Done it willingly. I don't want you doing anything that's going to bring harm to her or to her child. I won't stand for that. I've told Black Dow and I'm telling you. I won't stand for it."

"You think I will?" Calder snapped back, with a heat he hadn't expected. "I'm not quite the bastard they say I am."

"I know you're not." And Reachey gave him a pointed look from under his craggy brows. "Not quite."

Calder left the fire with worry weighing on his shoulders like a coat of double mail. When the best you can get from your wife's father is that he won't help to kill you, it doesn't take a clever man to see you're in shit to your chin.

Music was coming from somewhere, old songs badly sung about men long dead and the men they'd killed. Drunken laughter too, figures around the fire-pits, drinking to nothing. A hammer rang from the darkness and Calder caught the shape of the smith, frozen against the sparks of his forge. They'd be working all night arming up Reachey's new recruits. Blades, axes, arrowheads. The business of destruction. He winced at the shriek of a whetstone. Something about that sound had always set his teeth on edge. He'd never understood what men saw in weapons. Probably a weapontake wasn't the best place for him, when you thought about it. He stopped, peering into the darkness. Somewhere around here he'd tied his horse—

A boot squelched and he frowned over his shoulder. The shapes of two men, shaggy in the dark, a hint of a stubbly face. Somehow, right away he knew. And right away he took off running.

"Shit!"

"Stop him!"

He pounded to nowhere, not thinking about anything, which was a strange relief for a moment, and then, as the first flush of action faded and he realised they were going to kill him... not.

"Help!" he screamed at no one. "Help me!"

Three men about a fire looked over, part-curious, part-annoyed at being disturbed. None of them so much as reached for weapons. They didn't care a shit. People don't, on the whole. They didn't know who he was, and even if they had he was widely hated, and even if he'd been widely loved, still, on the whole, no one cares a shit.

He left them behind, scared breath starting to burn, slithered down a bank and up another, crashed through a patch of bushes, twigs snatching at him, not caring much about the state of his Styrian boots now as the fear clawed up his throat. He saw a shape looming out of the murk, a pale face, startled.

"Help!" he screeched. "Help!"

Someone squatting, pinching off a turd. "What?"

And Calder was past, thumping through the mud, leaving the fires of Reachey's camp behind. He snatched a glance over his shoulder, couldn't see a thing beyond the wobbling black outline of the land. But he could hear them still, too close behind. Far too close. He caught water glimmering at the bottom of a slope, then his lovely Styrian boot toe caught something and he was in the air.

He came down mouth first, crumpled, tumbled, head filled with his own despairing whimpers as the earth battered at him. Slid to what might've been a stop though it felt like he was still going. Struggled up, arms clutching at him.

"Off me, bastards!" It was his own cloak, heavy with mud. He floundered a half-step, realised he was going up the bank as the killers came down it. He tried to turn and flopped over in the stream, gasping for air, cold water gripping him.

"Some runner, ain't he?" The voice boomed through the surging blood in Calder's head, a nasty kind of chuckle on the end. Why do they always have to laugh?

"Oh, aye. Come here." That scraping sound as one drew a blade. Calder remembered he had a sword himself, fished numbly for it, trying to struggle up out of the freezing water. He only got as far as his knees. The nearest killer came at him, then fell over sideways.

"What you doing?" said the other. Calder wondered if he'd drawn and stabbed him, then realised his sword was still all tangled up with his cloak. He couldn't have got it free even if he had the strength to move his arm – which, at that moment, he didn't.

"What?" His tongue felt twice its normal size.

A shape flashed from nowhere. Calder gave a kind of squeal, arms jerking pointlessly to cover his face. He felt the wind of something passing, it crashed into the second killer and he went down on his back. The first was trying to crawl away up the bank, making a wet groan. The outline of a man walked down to him, slinging a bow over his shoulder and drawing a sword, and stabbed him through the back without breaking stride. He strolled up close and stood there, a blacker shape in the darkness. Calder stared at him through the spread-out fingers over his face, cold water bubbling at his knees. Thinking of Seff. Waiting for his death.

"If it ain't Prince Calder. Wouldn't expect to chance on you in such surroundings."

Calder slowly prised his trembling hands away from his face. He knew that voice. "Foss Deep?"

"Yes."

Relief spouted up in Calder like a fountain, so much he almost wanted to laugh. Laugh or be sick. "My brother sent you?"

"No."

"Scale's busy...busy...busy these days," grunted Shallow, still stabbing the second killer, blade squelching in and out.

"Very busy." Deep watched his brother as if he was watching a man dig a ditch. "Fighting and so forth. War. The old swords-and-marching game. Loves him some war, Scale, can't get enough. If that's not dead yet, by the way, ain't never going to be."

"True." Shallow stabbed his man once more then rocked back on his haunches, his blade, and his hand, and his arm to the elbow all sticky black with blood in the moonlight.

Calder made himself not look at it, trying to keep his mind off his rising gorge. "Where the hell did you come from?"

Deep offered a hand and Calder took it. "We heard you were returned from exile and – aware what a popular boy you are – thought we'd come and stand lookout. Case someone tried something. And whatever do you know..."

Calder held Deep's forearm a moment longer as the dark world started to steady. "Good thing you came when you did. Moment longer I'd have had to kill those bastards myself." He stood, the blood rushed to his head, and he doubled up and puked all over his Styrian boots.

"Things were about to get ugly, all right," said Deep solemnly.

"If you could just've got your sword free from your fancy-arsed cloak you'd have cut those bastards up every which way." Shallow was coming down the slope and dragging something after him. "We caught this one. He was holding their horses." And he shoved a shape down in the mud in front of Calder. A young lad, pale face dirt-speckled in the half-light.

"That's some good work." Calder wiped his sour mouth on the back of his sleeve. "My father always said you were two of the best men he knew."

"Funny." He could see Shallow's teeth as he grinned. "He used to tell us we were the worst."

"Either way, don't know how I'll thank you."

"Gold," said Shallow.

"Aye," said Deep. "Gold will go most of the way."

"You'll have it."

"I know we will. That's why we love you, Calder."

"Well, that and the winning sense of humour," said Shallow.

"And that beautiful face, and those beautiful clothes, and the smirk that makes you want to punch it."

"And the bottomless respect we had for your father." Shallow gave a little bow. "But, yes, mostly it's the old goldy-woldy."

"What rites for the dead?" asked Deep, poking one of the corpses with the toe of his boot.

Now that Calder's head was settling, the surging of blood in his ears was quieting, the pounding in his face was dulling to a throb, he was starting to think. To wonder what could be gained. He could show these boys to Reachey, try and get him riled up. Murdering his daughter's husband in his own camp, it was an insult. Especially to an honourable man. Or he could have them dragged before Black Dow, fling them at his feet and demand justice. But both options held risks, especially when he didn't know for a fact who was behind it. When you're planning what to do, always think of doing nothing first, see where that gets you. It was better to let these bastards wash away, pretend it never happened, and keep his enemies guessing.

"In the river," he said.

"And this one?" Shallow waved his knife at the lad.

Calder stood over him, lips pursed. "Who sent you?"

"I just mind the horses," whispered the boy.

"Come on, now," said Deep, "we don't want to cut you up."

"I don't mind," said Shallow.

"No?"

"Not bothered." He grabbed the boy around the throat and stuck his knife up his nose.

"No! No!" he squeaked. "Tenways, they said! They said Brodd Tenways!" Shallow let him drop back in the mud, and Calder gave a sigh.

"That flaking old fuck." How toweringly unsurprising. Maybe Dow had asked him to get it done, or maybe he'd taken his own initiative. Either way, this lad wouldn't know enough to help.

Shallow spun his knife around, blade flashing moonlight as it turned. "And for young master I-just-mind-the-horsey-boy?"

Calder's instinct was just to say, "Kill him," and be done. Quicker, simpler, safer. But these days, he tried always to think about mercy. A long time ago when he'd been a young idiot, or perhaps a younger idiot, he'd ordered a man killed on a whim. Because he'd thought it would make him look strong. Because he'd thought it might make his father proud. It hadn't. "Before you make a man into mud," his father had told him afterwards in his disappointed voice, "make sure he's no use to you alive. Some men will smash a thing just because they can. They're too stupid to see that nothing shows more power than mercy."

The lad swallowed as he looked up, eyes big and hopeless, gleaming in the darkness with maybe a sorry tear or two. Power was what Calder wanted most, and so he thought about mercy. Thought all about it. Then he pressed his tongue into his split lip, and it really hurt a lot.

"Kill him," he said, and turned away, heard the lad make a surprised yelp, quickly cut off. It always catches people by surprise, the moment of their death, even when they should see it coming. They always think they're special, somehow expect a reprieve. But no one's special. He heard the splash as Shallow rolled the lad's body into the water, and that was that. He struggled back up the slope, cursing at his soaked-through, clinging cloak, and his mud-caked boots, and his battered mouth. Calder wondered if he'd be surprised, when his moment came. Probably.

The Right Thing

Is it true?" asked Drofd.

"Eh?"

"Is it true?" The lad nodded towards Skarling's Finger, standing proud on its own tump of hill, casting no more'n a stub of shadow since it was close to midday. "That Skarling Hoodless is buried under there?"

"Doubt it," said Craw. "Why would he be?"

"Ain't that why they call it Skarling's Finger, though?"

"What else would they call it?" asked Wonderful. "Skarling's Cock?"

Brack raised his thick brows. "Now you mention it, it does look a bit like a—"

Drofd cut him off. "No, I mean, why call it that if he ain't buried there?"

Wonderful looked at him like he was the biggest idiot in the North. He might've been in the running. "There's a stream near my husband's farm – my farm – they call Skarling's Beck. There's probably fifty others in the North. Most likely there's a legend he wet his manly thirst in their clear waters before some speech or charge or noble stand from the songs. Daresay he did no more'n piss in most of 'em if he ever even came within a day's ride. That's what it is to be a hero. Everyone wants a little bit of you." She nodded at Whirrun, kneeling before the Father of Swords with hands clasped and eyes closed. "In fifty years there'll more'n likely be a dozen Whirrun's Becks scattered across farms he never went to, and numbskulls will point at 'em, all dewy-eyed, and ask – 'Is it true Whirrun of Bligh's buried under that stream?'" She walked off, shaking her cropped head.

Drofd's shoulders slumped. "I only bloody asked, didn't I? I thought that was why they called 'em the Heroes, 'cause there are heroes buried under 'em."

"Who cares who's buried where?" muttered Craw, thinking about all the men he'd seen buried. "Once a man's in the ground he's just mud. Mud and stories. And the stories and the men don't often have much in common."

Brack nodded. "Less with every time the story's told."

"Eh?"

"Bethod, let's say," said Craw. "You'd think to hear the tales he was the most evil bastard ever set foot in the North."

"Weren't he?"

"All depends on who you ask. His enemies weren't keen on him, and the dead know he made a lot o' the bastards. But look at all he did. More'n Skarling Hoodless ever managed. Bound the North together. Built the roads we march on, half the towns. Put an end to the warring between the clans."

"By starting wars with the Southerners."

"Well, true. There's two sides to every coin, but there's my very point. People like simple stories." Craw frowned at the pink marks down the edges of his nails. "But people ain't simple."

Brack slapped Drofd on the back and near made him fall. "Except for you, eh, boy?"

"Craw!" Wonderful's voice had that note in it made everyone turn. Craw sprang up, or as close as he got to springing these days, and hurried over to her, wincing as his knee crunched like breaking twigs, sending stings right up into his back.

"What am I looking at?" He squinted at the Old Bridge, at the fields and pastures and hedgerows, at the river and the fells beyond, struggling to shield his watery eyes from the wind and make the blurry valley come sharp.

"Down there, at the ford."

Now he saw them and his guts hollowed out. Little more'n dots to his eyes, but men for sure. Wading through the shallows, picking their way over the shingle, dragging themselves up onto the bank. The north bank. Craw's bank.

"Shit," he said. Not enough of 'em to be Union men, but coming from the south, which meant they were the Dogman's boys. Which meant more'n likely—

"Hardbread's back." Shivers' whisper was the last thing Craw needed behind him. "And he's found himself some friends."

"Weapons!" shouted Wonderful.

"Eh?" Agrick stood staring with a cookpot in his hands.

"Weapons, idiot!"

"Shit!" Agrick and his brother started running around, shouting at each other, dragging their packs open and spilling gear about the trampled grass.

"How many do you count?" Craw patted his pocket but his eyeglass was missing. "Where the bloody hell —"

Brack had it pressed to his face. "Twenty-two," he grunted.

"You sure?"

"I'm sure."

Wonderful rubbed at the long scar down her scalp. "Twenty-two. *Twenty-two. Twenty ... two.*"

The more she said it the worse it sounded. A particularly shitty number. Too many to beat without taking a terrible chance, but few enough that – with the ground on their side and a happy fall of the runes – it might be done. Too few to just run away from, without having to tell Black Dow why. And fighting outnumbered might be the lighter risk than telling Black Dow why.

"Shit." Craw glanced across at Shivers and caught his good eye looking back. Knew he'd juggled the same sum and come up with the same answer, but that he didn't care how much blood got spilled along the way, how many of Craw's dozen went back to the mud for this hill. Craw did care. Maybe too much, these days. Hardbread and his boys were out of the river now, last of 'em disappearing into the browning apple trees between the shallows and the foot of the hill, heading for the Children.

Yon appeared between two of the Heroes, bundle of sticks in his arms, puffing away from the climb. "Took a while, but I found some — What?"

"Weapons!" bellowed Brack at him.

"Hardbread's back!" added Athroc.

"Shit!" Yon let his sticks fall in a tangle, near tripped over them as he ran for his gear.

It was a bastard of a call and Craw couldn't dither on it. But that's what it is to be Chief. If he'd wanted easy choices he could've stayed a carpenter, where you might on occasion have to toss out a botched joint but rarely risk a friend's life.

He'd stuck all his days to the notion there's a right way to do things, even as it seemed to be going out of fashion. You pick your Chief, you pick your side, you pick your crew and then you stand by 'em, whatever the wind blows up. He'd stood by Threetrees 'til he lost to the Bloody-Nine.

Stood by Bethod 'til the end. Now he stood with Black Dow and, whatever the rights and wrongs of it, Black Dow said hold this hill. They were fighters by trade. Time comes a fighter has to toss the runes and fight. It was the right thing to do.

"The right thing," he hissed to himself. Or maybe it was just that, deep under his worries and his grumbles and his blather about sunsets, there was still a jagged little splinter left in him of that man he'd been years ago. That dagger-eyed fucker who would've bled all the blood in the North before he backed down a stride. The one who stuck himself in everyone's craw.

"Weapons," he growled. "Full gear! Battle gear!" Hardly needed saying, really, but a good Chief should shout a lot. Yon was delving into the packhorse's bags for the mail, dragging Brack's big coat rattling free. Scorry pulling his spear from the other side, jerking the oilskin from the bright blade, humming to himself while he did it. Wonderful stringing her bow with quick hands, making it sing its own note as she tested it. All the while Whirrun knelt still, eyes closed, hands clasped before the Father of Swords.

"Chief." Scorry tossed Craw's blade over, stained belt wrapped around it.

"Thanks." Though he didn't feel too thankful as he snatched it out of the air. Started to buckle it on, memories of other bright, fierce times he'd done it flashing by. Memories of other company, long gone back to the mud. By the dead, but he was getting old.

Drofd stared around for a moment, hands opening and closing. Wonderful gave him a slap on the side of the head as she passed and he came round, started loosening the shafts in his quiver with twitchy fingers.

"Chief." She handed Craw his shield and he slid it onto his arm, strap fitting into his clenched fist snug as a foot into an old boot.

"Thanks." Craw looked over at Shivers, standing still with his arms folded, watching the dozen make ready. "How about you, lad? Front rank?"

Shivers tipped his face back, little grin on the side that wasn't stiff with scar. "Front and middle," he croaked. Then he ambled off towards the ashes of the fire.

"We could kill him," Wonderful muttered in Craw's ear. "Don't care how hard he is, arrow in the neck, job done."

"He's just passing the message."

"Shooting the messenger ain't always a bad idea." Joking, but only half. "Stops him taking messages back."

"Whether or not he's here we've the same job. Keep hold o' the Heroes. We're meant to be fighters. A little fight shouldn't get us shitting ourselves." He almost choked on the words, since he was mostly shitting himself from morning to night, and especially in fights.

"A little fight?" she muttered, loosening her sword in its sheath. "Near three to one? Do we really need this hill?"

"Closer to two to one." As if that made it good odds. "If the Union do come, this hill's the key to the whole valley." Giving himself reasons as much as her. "Better to fight for it now while we're up here than give it away so we can fight our way up it later. That and it's the right thing to do." She opened her mouth like she was going to argue. "The right thing!" snapped Craw, and held his hand out, not wanting to give her the chance to talk him round.

She took a breath. "All right." She gave his hand a squeeze, almost painful. "We fight." And she walked away, pulling her archery guard on with her teeth. "Arm up, you bastards! We fight!"

Athroc and Agrick were ready, helmets on, bashing their shields together and grunting in each other's faces, working themselves up to it. Scorry was holding his spear just under the blade, using it to shave bits of Shudder Root off a lump and into his mouth. Whirrun had finally stood up and now he was smiling into the blue sky with his eyes closed, sun on his face. His preparations didn't go much beyond taking his coat off.

"No armour." Yon was helping Brack into his mail, shaking his head as he frowned over at Whirrun. "What kind of a bloody hero don't wear bloody armour?"

"Armour..." mused Whirrun, licking a finger and scrubbing some speck of dirt from the pommel of his sword, "is part of a state of mind...in which you admit the possibility...of being hit."

"What the *fuck*?" Yon tugged hard at the straps and made Brack grunt. "What does that even mean?"

Wonderful clapped her hand down on Whirrun's shoulder and leaned against him, one foot propped on its boot-toe. "How many years and you're still expecting sense out o' this article? He's mad."

"We're all fucking mad, woman!" Brack was red in the face from holding his breath out while Yon struggled to get the buckles closed at his back. "Why else would we be fighting for a hill and some old rocks?"

"War and madness have a lot in common." Scorry, not very helpfully, talking around his cheekful of mush.

Yon finally got the last buckle shut and held his arms out so Brack could start getting him into his mail. "Being mad don't stop you wearing bloody armour, though, does it?"

Hardbread's crew had made it through the orchards, and two sets of three split from the rest – one heading west around the base of the hill, the other north. Getting around their flanks. Drofd's eyes were wide as he watched 'em moving, then the others getting their gear ready. "How can they make jokes? How can they make bloody jokes?"

"Because every man finds courage his own way." Craw didn't admit that giving advice was his. There's nothing better for a dose of terror than standing by someone even more terrified than yourself. He clasped Drofd's hand and gave it a squeeze. "Just breathe, lad."

Drofd took a shuddering breath in and forced it out. "Right y'are, Chief. Breathe."

Craw turned to face the rest of the crew. "Right, then! They've two parties of three trying to get on our flanks, then a few less than a score coming up front." He rushed through the numbers, maybe hoping no one would notice the odds. Maybe hoping he wouldn't. "Athroc, Agrick, Wonderful to skirmish, Drofd too, give 'em arrows while they climb, spread 'em out on the slope. When they get in close to the stones . . . we charge." He saw Drofd swallow, not much taken with the idea of charging. The dead knew Craw could think of other ways to spend an afternoon himself. "There aren't enough of 'em to get all around us, and we've got the ground. We can pick where we hit 'em, and hit 'em hard. Any luck we'll break 'em before they get set, then if the other six have a mind to fight we can mop up."

"Hit 'em hard!" growled Yon, clasping hands with the others one after another.

"Just wait for my word, and move together."

"Together." Wonderful slapped her right hand into Scorry's and punched him on the arm with her left.

"Me, Shivers, Brack, Yon, we're front and centre."

"Aye, Chief," said Brack, still struggling with Yon's mail.

"Fucking aye!" Yon took a practice swipe with his axe and jerked the buckles out of Brack's hands.

Shivers grinned and stuck his tongue out, not especially reassuring.

"Athroc and Agrick fall back to the wings."

"Aye," they chimed in together.

"Scorry, anyone tries to get around the side early on, give 'em a poke. Once we close up, you're the back rank."

Scorry just hummed to himself, but he'd heard.

"Whirrun. You're the nut in the shell."

"No." Whirrun took the Father of Swords from its place against the stone and lifted it high, pommel glinting with the sunlight. "This is. Which makes me...I guess...that kind of...flaky bit between the nut and the shell."

"You're flaky all right," muttered Wonderful, under her breath.

"You can be whatever bit of the nut you like," said Craw, "long as you're there when it cracks."

"Oh, I'm going nowhere until you show me my destiny." Whirrun pushed back his hood and scrubbed a hand through his flattened hair. "Just like Shoglig promised me you would."

Craw sighed. "Can't wait. Questions?" No sound except the wind fumbling across the grass, the clapping of palms as they all finished shaking hands, the grunt and jingle as Brack finally got Yon's armour buckled. "All right." Case I don't have the chance to say it again, been an honour fighting with you all. Or an honour slogging across the North in all weathers, anyway. Just keep in mind what Rudd Threetrees once told me. Let's us get them killed, and not the other way round."

Wonderful grinned. "Best damn advice about war I ever heard."

The rest of Hardbread's lads were coming now. The big group. Coming slowly, taking time, up the long slope towards the Children. More than dots now. A lot more'n dots. Men, with a purpose, the odd glint of sunlight on sharp metal. A heavy hand thumped down on his shoulder and Craw jumped, but it was only Yon behind him.

"A word, Chief?"

"What's to do?" Though he knew already.

"The usual. If I'm killed—"

Craw nodded, keen to cut it short. "I'll find your sons, and give 'em your share."

"And?"

"I'll tell 'em what you were."

"All of it."

"All of it."

"Good. And don't dress it up any, you old bastard."

Craw waved a hand at his stained coat. "When did you last see me dress anything up?"

Yon might've had a trace of a smile as they clasped hands. "Not lately, Chief, that's sure." Left Craw wondering who'd need telling when he went back to the mud. His family were all here.

"Talking time," said Wonderful.

Hardbread had left his men behind at the Children and was climbing the grassy slope with empty hands and open grin turned up towards the Heroes. Craw drew his sword, felt the frightening, reassuring weight of it in his hand. Knew the sharpness of it, worked at with whetstone every day for a dozen years. Life and death in a length of metal.

"Makes you feel big, don't it?" Shivers spun his own axe around in one fist. A brutal-looking article, studs through the heavy wooden shaft, bearded head notched and gleaming. "A man should always be armed. If only for the feel of it."

"An unarmed man is like an unroofed house," muttered Yon.

"They'll both end up leaking," Brack finished for him.

Hardbread stopped well within bowshot, long grass brushing at his calves. "Hey, hey, Craw! Still up there, then?"

"Sadly, yes."

"Sleeping well?"

"I'd rather have a feather pillow. You brought me one?"

"Wish I had one spare. That Caul Shivers up there with you?"

"Aye. And he brought two dozen Carls with him." It was worth a stab, but Hardbread only grinned.

"Good try. No he didn't. Haven't seen you in a while, Caul. How are things?"

Shivers gave the smallest shrug. Nothing more.

Hardbread raised his brows. "Like that, is it?"

Another shrug. Like the sky could fall in and it'd make no difference to him.

"Have it your way. How about it, then, Craw? Can I have my hill back?"

Craw worked his hand around the grip of his sword, raw skin at the corners of his chewed fingernails burning. "I've a mind to sit here a few days more."

Hardbread frowned. Not the answer he'd been hoping for. "Look, Craw, you gave me a chance the other night, so I'm giving you one. There's a right way o' doing things, and fair's fair. But you might've noticed I had some friends come up this morning." And he jerked his thumb over his shoulder towards the Children. "So I'll ask one more time. Can I have my hill back?"

Last chance. Craw gave a long sigh, and shouted it into the wind. "'Fraid not, Hardbread! 'Fraid you'll have to come up here and take it off me!"

"How many you got up there? Nine? Against my two dozen?"

"We've faced down worse odds!" Though he couldn't remember ever picking 'em willingly.

"Good for fucking you, I wouldn't fancy it!" Hardbread brought his voice back down from angry to reasonable. "Look, there ain't no need for this to get out of hand—"

"'Cept we're in a *war*!" And Craw found he'd roared the last word with a sight more venom than he'd planned on.

Far as he could tell over the distance, Hardbread had lost his grin. "Right y'are. Thought I'd give you the chance you gave me is all."

"That's good o' you. Appreciate it. Just can't move."

"That's a shame all round."

"Aye. But there 'tis."

Hardbread took a breath, like he was about to speak, but he didn't. He just stood still. So did Craw. So did all his crew behind him, looking down. So did all Hardbread's too, looking up. Silent on the Heroes, except for the wind sighing, a bird or two warbling somewhere, a few bees buzzing in the warm, tending to the flowers. A peaceful moment. Considering they had a war to be about.

Then Hardbread snapped his mouth shut, turned around and walked back down the steep slope towards the Children.

"I could shoot him," muttered Wonderful.

"I know you could," said Craw. "And you know you can't."

"I know. Just saying."

"Maybe he'll think it over, and decide against." But Brack didn't sound all that hopeful.

"No. He don't like this any more'n us, but he backed down once already. His odds are too good to do it again." Craw almost whispered the last words. "Wouldn't be right." Hardbread reached the Children and vanished among the stones. "Everyone without a bow, back inside the Heroes and wait for the moment."

The quiet stretched out. Niggling pain in Craw's knee as he shifted his weight. Raised voices behind, Yon and Brack arguing about nothing as they got their stub of a line ready. More quiet. War's ninety-nine parts boredom and, now and then, one part arse-opening terror. Craw had a powerful sense one of those was about to drop on him from a height.

Agrick had planted a few arrows in the earth, flights fluttering like the seed heads on the long grass. Now he rocked back on his heels, rubbing at his jaw. "Might be he'll wait for dark."

"No. If he's been sent more men, it's 'cause the Dogman wants this hill. The Union wants this hill. He won't risk us getting help by tonight."

"Then..." muttered Drofd.

"Aye. I reckon they'll be coming now."

By some unhappy chance, as Craw said the word "now," men started to ease out from the shadows of the Children. They formed up in an orderly row, at a steady pace. A shield wall perhaps a dozen men wide, spear-points of a second row glittering behind, archers on the flanks, staying in the cover of the shields.

"Old style," said Wonderful, nocking an arrow.

"Wouldn't expect nothing else from Hardbread. He's old style himself." A bit like Craw. Two old leftover fools lasted longer than they'd any right to, setting to knock chunks out of each other. The right way, at least. They'd do it the right bloody way. He looked to the sides, straining for some sign of the two little groups who'd broken off. Couldn't see no one. Crawling in the long grass, maybe, or just biding their time.

Agrick drew his bowstring back to his frown. "When d'you want me to shoot?"

"Soon as you can hit something."

"Anyone in particular?"

Craw scraped his tongue over his front teeth. "Anyone you can put down." Say it straight, why not, he ought to have the bones to say it, at least. "Anyone you can kill."

"I'll do my best."

"Do your worst and I'll be happier."

"Right y'are." Agrick let fly, just a ranging shot, flitting over the heads of Hardbread's lot and making 'em duck. Wonderful's first arrow stuck humming into a shield and the man behind it dropped back, dragging the shield wall apart. It was starting to break up anyway, for all Hardbread's shouting. Some men moving quicker, some tiring faster on that bastard of a slope.

Drofd shot too, his arrow going way high, lost somewhere short of the Children. "Shit!" he cursed, snatching at another arrow with a trembling hand.

"Easy, Drofd, easy. Breathe." But Craw was finding easy breathing a bit of a challenge himself. He'd never cared for arrows. 'Specially, it hardly needed saying, when they were falling out of the sky at him. They didn't look much but they could have your death on the end, all right. He remembered seeing the shower of 'em dropping down towards their line at Ineward, like a flock of angry birds. Nowhere to run to. Just had to hope.

One sailed up now and he stepped sideways, behind the nearest Hero, crouching in the cover of his shield. Not much fun watching that shaft spin down, wondering whether the wind would snatch it at the last moment and put it right through him. It glanced off the stone and spun harmlessly away. Not a lot of air between your death and an arrow in the grass.

The man who'd shot it paused on one knee, fiddling with his quiver as the safety of the shields crept up the slope away from him. Athroc's shaft took him in the stomach. Craw saw his mouth open wide, his own arrow flying from his hand, his scream coming a moment later, sputtering out into a long-drawn wail. Maybe it was the sound of their odds getting that little bit better, but Craw still didn't much like hearing it. Didn't like the notion that he might be making a sound like that himself before the hour was out.

The end of the shield wall got ragged as men looked over at the howling archer, wondering whether to help or press on, or just wondering whether they'd be next. Hardbread barked orders, straightened up his line, but Wonderful's next arrow flitted close over their heads and bent 'em out of shape again. Craw's people had the height as an ally, could shoot fast and flat. Hardbread's had to shoot high, where the wind was sure to drag their shafts around. Still, there was no call to take chances. They wouldn't be settling this with arrows.

Craw let Drofd loose one more, then grabbed his arm. "Back to the others."

The lad jerked around, looking like he was about to scream. Battle lust on him, maybe. You never could tell who'd get it. Mad fear and mad courage are two leaves on one nettle all right, and you wouldn't want to grab a hold of either one. Craw dug his fingers into the lad's shoulder and dragged him close. "Back to the others, I said!"

Drofd swallowed, Craw's hand squeezing the sense back into him. "Chief." And he stumbled back between the stones, bent double.

"Fall back when you have to!" Craw shouted at Wonderful. "Take no chances!"

"Too fucking right!" she hissed over her shoulder, nocking another shaft.

Craw crept backwards, keeping an eye out for arrows until he was past the stones, then hurrying across the circle of grass, stupidly happy to get another couple of moments safe and feeling a coward because of it. "They're on the—Gah!"

Something caught his foot and he twisted his ankle, pain stabbing up his leg. Limped the rest of the way, teeth bared, and fell into line in the centre.

"Evil, those rabbit holes," whispered Shivers.

Before Craw could gather the wits to answer, Wonderful came running between two of the Heroes, waving her bow. "They're past the wall! Got one more o' the bastards!"

Agrick was at her heels, swinging his shield off his back, an arrow looping over from behind and sticking into the turf by his boots as he ran. "The rest are coming!"

Craw could hear their shouting from down below, still the faint scream of the stuck archer, all turned strange by the wind. "Get back 'ere!" he heard Hardbread bellow, short on breath. Sounded like they were still losing shape on the run up, some eager, some the opposite, not used to fighting together. That favoured Craw's crew, most of 'em been together for what felt like centuries.

He stole a glance over his shoulder and Scorry winked back, chewing away. Old friends, old brothers. Whirrun had his sword out of its sheath, great length of dull grey metal with hardly a gleam to its edge even in the sun. Like the runes had said, there was going to be blood. The only question was whose. It passed between 'em as their eyes met, no words spoken and none needed.

Wonderful knelt at the end of their little line in the shadow of Athroc's shield, nocked an arrow, and Craw's dozen were ready as they'd ever get.

Someone crept around one of the stones. His shield might've had something painted on it once but so scuffed by war and weather there was no telling what. Sword bright in his hand, helmet on, but he hardly looked like anyone's enemy. He looked knackered, mouth hanging open, panting from the long climb.

He stood staring at 'em, and they stared back. Craw felt Yon straining next to him, bursting to go, heard Shivers' breath crackling through gritted teeth, heard Brack growling deep in his throat, everyone's jangling nerves setting everyone else's jangling even worse.

"Steady," Craw hissed, "steady." Knew the hardest thing at a time like that was just to stand. Men ain't made for it. You need to charge or you need to flee, but either way you're desperate to move, to run, to scream. Had to wait, though. Finding the right moment was everything.

Another of Hardbread's crew showed themselves, knees bent low, peering over his shield. It had a fish painted on it, and badly. Craw wondered if his name was Fishy, felt a stupid urge to laugh, quickly gone.

They had to go soon. Use the ground. Catch 'em on the slope. Break 'em fast. It was up to him to feel the moment. Like he knew. Time was stretched out, full of details. Breath in his sore throat. Breeze tickling the back of his hand. Blades of grass shifting with the wind. His mouth so dry he wasn't sure he'd be able to say the word even if he thought the time was right.

Drofd loosed an arrow and the two men ducked down. But the sound of the string loosed something in Craw and, before he'd even thought whether it was the right moment or not, he'd given a great roar. Hardly even a word but his crew got the gist, and like a pack of dogs suddenly slipped the leash, they were away. Too late now. Maybe one moment's good as another anyway.

Feet pounding the ground, jolting his teeth, jolting his sore knee. Wondering if he'd hit another rabbit hole, go sprawling. Wondering where the six men were who'd gone around 'em. Wondering whether they should've backed off. What those two idiots, three now, they were charging at were thinking. What lies he'd tell Yon's sons.

The others matched him step for step, rims of their shields scraping against his, jostling at his shoulders. Jolly Yon on one side and Caul Shivers on the other. Men who knew how to hold a line. It occurred to Craw he was probably the weak link in here. Then that he thought too much.

Hardbread's boys skipped and wobbled with each footfall, more of 'em up now, trying to get some shape between the stones. Yon let go his war cry, high and shrill, then Athroc and his brother too, then they were all giving it the screech and wail, boots hammering the old sod of the Heroes. Ground where men prayed once, maybe, long ago. Prayed for better times.

Craw felt the terror and joy of battle burning in his chest, burning up his throat, Hardbread's men a buckled line of shields, blurred weapons between, blades swaying, twinkling.

They were between the stones, they were on 'em.

"Break!" roared Craw.

Him and Yon went left, Shivers and Brack went right, and Whirrun came out of the gap they left, howling his devil shriek. Craw caught a glimpse of the nearest face, jaw dropping, eyes wide. Men ain't just brave or not. It all depends on how things stand. Who stands beside 'em. Whether they've just had to run up a great big fucking hill with arrows falling on 'em. He seemed to shrink, this lad, trying to get his whole body behind his shield as the Father of Swords fell on him like a mountain. A mountain sharpened to a razor-edge.

Metal screamed, wood and flesh burst apart. Blood roaring and men roaring in Craw's ears. He twisted himself sideways, missed a spear-thrust, crashed on, blade rattling off wood, turning him, went into someone shield-first with a bone-jarring crunch and sent him over backwards, sliding down the hillside.

He saw Hardbread, long grey hair tangled around his face. His sword went up quick but Whirrun was quicker, arm snaking out and ramming the pommel of the Father of Swords into Hardbread's mouth, snapping his head back and sending him toppling. Craw had other worries. Crushed against a snarling cave of a face, sour breath blasting him. Dragging at his snagged sword, trying to get space to swing. He shoved with his shield, had the slope on his side, drove his man back enough to make room.

Athroc whacked a shield with his axe, got his whacked in reply. Craw chopped, his elbow caught on the shaft of a spear, tangled with it, his sword just tapped someone with the flat. A friendly pat on the shoulder.

Whirrun was in the midst of 'em, Father of Swords making blurred circles, scattering men squealing. Someone got in the way. Hardbread's nephew. "Oh—" And he fell in half. His arm flew in the air, body turning over and around, legs toppling. The long blade pinged like ice shifting as the weather warms, spots of blood showering off it. Craw gasped as they pit-pattered on his face, hacked away at a shield, teeth squeezed together so hard seemed they'd crack. Still snarling something through 'em, didn't know what, splinters in his face. Movement at the corner of his eye, shield up on an instinct and something thudded into it, cracking the rim into his jaw, making him stumble sideways, arm numbed.

He saw a weapon black against bright sky, caught it on his own as it came down. Blades clashing, scraping, grunting in someone's face, looked like Jutlan but Jutlan was years in the ground. Staggering around, off-balance on the slope, fingers clutching. His knee burned, his lungs burned. Gleam of Shivers' eye, battle smile creasing his ruined face. His axe split Jutlan's head open wide, dark pulp smeared down Craw's shield. Shoved him off, corpse tumbling through the grass. Father of Swords ripped armour beside him, bent mail rings flying, stinging the back of Craw's hand.

Clash and clatter, scrape and rattle, scream and hiss, thump, crack, men swearing and bellowing like animals at the slaughterhouse. Was Scorry singing? Something across Craw's cheek, in his eye, snatched his head away. Blood, blade, dirt, no way of knowing, lurched sideways as something came at him and he slid onto his elbow. Spear, snarling face with a birth-mark behind, spear jabbing, flapped it away clumsily with his shield, trying to scramble up. Scorry stuck the man in the shoulder and he fumbled his spear, wound welling.

Wonderful with blood all over her face. Hers or someone else's or both. Shivers laughing, smashing the metal rim of his shield into someone's mouth as they lay. Crunch, crunch, die, die. Yon shouting, axe going up and clattering down. Drofd stumbling, holding his bloody arm, broken wreck of his bow all tangled around his back.

Someone jumped after him with a spear and Craw stepped in his way, head buzzing with his own hoarse roar, sword lashing across. Grip jolted in his fist, cloth and leather flapped, split, bloody. Man's spear dropping, mouth open, long shriek drooling out of it. Craw hacked him down on the backswing, body spinning as it fell, severed arm flopping in his sleeve, black blood frozen in white cloud.

Someone was running away down the hill. Arrow flitted past, missed. Craw leaped at him, missed. Tangled with Agrick's elbow. Slid and fell hard, dug himself with his sword hilt, left himself open. But the runner didn't care, bounding off, flinging his shield away bouncing on its edge.

Craw tore his sword up along with a handful of grass. Nearly swung at someone, stopped himself. Scorry, gripping to his spear. All of Hardbread's lot were running. The ones that were alive. When men break they break all at once, like a wall falling, like a cliff splitting off into the sea. Broken. Thought he saw Hardbread stumbling after, bloody-mouthed. Half wanted the old bastard to get away, half wanted to charge on and kill him.

"Behind! Behind!" He tottered around, fear dragging at his guts, saw men among the stones. There was no shape left to any of it. Sun twinkling bright, blinding. He heard screams, clashing metal. He was running back, back between the stones, shield clattering against rock, arm numb. Breath wheezing now, aching. Coughing and running on.

The packhorse was dead beside the fire, arrow poking from its ribs. Shield with a red bird on it, blade rising and falling. Wonderful loosed a shaft, missed. Redcrow turned and ran, a bowman behind shooting an arrow and it looped over towards Wonderful. Craw stepped in front of it, eyes rooted to it, caught it on his shield and it glanced away into the tall grass.

And they were gone.

Agrick was looking down at something, not far from the fire. Staring down, axe in one hand, helmet in the other. Craw didn't want to know what he was looking at, but he already knew.

One of Hardbread's lot was crawling away, making the grass thrash as he dragged bloody legs behind him. Shivers walked up and split his head with the back of his axe. Not that hard, but hard enough. Neat. Like a practised miner testing the ground. Someone was still screaming, somewhere. Or maybe it was just in Craw's head. Maybe just the sighing breath in his throat. He blinked around. Why the hell had they stayed? He shook his head like it might shake the answer out. Just made his jaw ache worse.

"The leg move?" Scorry was asking, squatting down over Brack, sitting on the ground gripping a bloody hand to one big thigh.

"Aye, it fucking moves! It just fucking hurts to fucking move it!"

Craw was sticky with sweat, scratchy, burning hot. His jaw was throbbing where his shield had cracked it, arm throbbing too. Dodgy knee and ankle doing their usual whining, but he didn't seem hurt. Not really. Not sure how he'd come out of that not hurt. The hot glow of battle was fading fast, his aching legs shaky as a new-born calf's, his sight swimming. Like he'd borrowed all the strength he'd used and had to pay it back with interest. He took a few steps towards the burned-out fire and the dead packhorse. No sign of the saddle horses. Run off or dead. He dropped down on his arse in the middle of the Heroes.

"You all right?" Whirrun was leaning over him, great long sword held below the crosspiece in one fist, blade all spattered and dashed. Blooded, the way it had to be. Once the Father of Swords is drawn, it has to be blooded. "You all right?"

"I reckon." Craw's fingers were so tight around the strap of his shield he could hardly remember how to make them unclench. Finally forced 'em open, let the shield drop into the grass, its face showing a few fresh gouges to go with a hundred old wounds, a new dent in the dull boss.

Wonderful's stubbly hair was matted with blood. "What happened?" Rubbing her eyes on the back of her arm. "Am I cut?"

"Scratch," Scorry said, prodding at her scalp with his thumbs.

Drofd was kneeling beside her, rocking back and forward, gripping tight to his arm, blood streaked to his fingertips.

The sun flashed in Craw's eyes, made his lids flicker. He could hear Yon screaming, over by the stones, roaring after Hardbread and his lads. "Come back 'ere, you fuckers! Come on you bastard cowards!" Couldn't make no difference. Every man's a coward. A coward and a hero, depending how things stand. They weren't coming back. Looked like they'd left eight corpses behind. They weren't coming back. Craw prayed to the old dead Gods of this place they weren't coming back.

Scorry was singing, soft and low and sad as he took needle and thread from his pouch to start the stitching. You get no happy songs after a battle. The jaunty tunes come beforehand and they usually do some injury to the truth.

Craw caught himself thinking they'd come out of it well. Very well. Just the one dead. Then he looked at Athroc's silly-slack face, eyes all crossed, jerkin all ripped up by Redcrow's axe and turned sloppy red with his insides, and was sick with himself for thinking it. He knew this would stay with him, along with all the others. We all got our weights to heft.

He lay back in the grass and watched the clouds move, shift. Now one memory, now another. A good leader can't dwell on the choices he's made, Threetrees used to tell him, and a good leader can't help dwelling on 'em.

He'd done the right thing. Maybe. Or maybe there's no such thing.

DAY ONE

"A rational army would run away"

Montesquieu

THE VALLEY OF OSRUNG

DOW   IRONHEAD   JAWS

TENWAYS

SCALE

USTRED

Holcum Farm

Bear Farm

Skarling's Finger

Clail Farm

Moss Beck

Wetterlant

Wall

Clail's

The C...

Stole Farm

Old Bridge

JALENHORM

Adwein

UFFRITH

Lock Fell

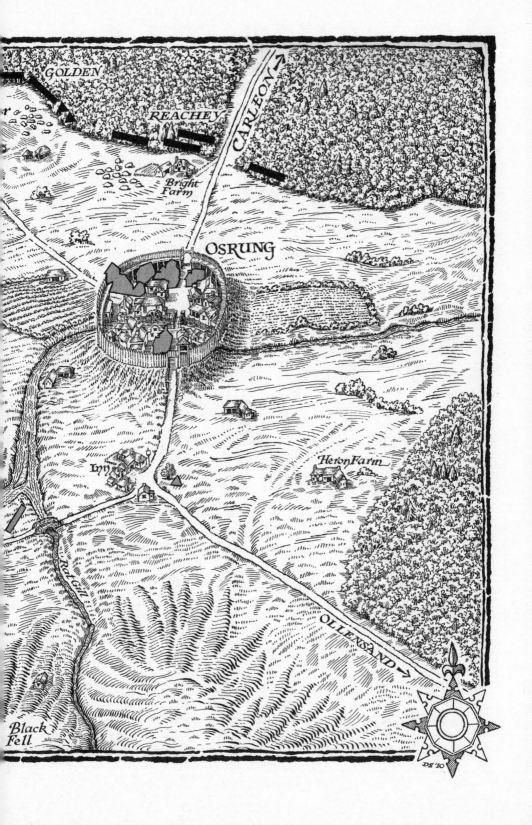

Silence

Your August Majesty,

Lord Bayaz, the First of the Magi, has conveyed to Marshal Kroy your urgent desire that the campaign be brought to a swift conclusion. The marshal has therefore devised a plan to bring Black Dow to a decisive battle with all despatch, and the entire army hums with gainful activity.

General Jalenhorm's division leads the way, marching from first light to last and with the vanguard of General Mitterick's but a few hours behind. One could almost say there is a friendly rivalry between the two to be first to grapple with the enemy. Lord Governor Meed, meanwhile, has been recalled from Ollensand. The three divisions will converge near a town called Osrung, then, united, drive north towards Carleon itself, and victory.

I accompany General Jalenhorm's staff, at the very spear-point of the army. We are somewhat hampered by the poor roads and changeable weather, which switches with little warning from sunshine to sharp downpours. The general is not a man to be stopped, however, either by the actions of the skies or the enemy. If we do come into contact with the Northmen I will, of course, observe, and immediately inform your Majesty of the outcome.

I remain your Majesty's most faithful and unworthy servant,

Bremer dan Gorst,
Royal Observer of the Northern War

You could barely have called it dawn. That funeral-grey light before the sun crawls up that has no colour in it. Few faces abroad, and those that were made ghosts. The empty country turned into the land of the dead. Gorst's favourite time of the day. *One could almost pretend no one will ever talk again.*

He had already been running for the best part of an hour, feet battering the rutted mud. Long slits of cartwheel puddle reflected the black tree branches and the washed-out sky. Happy mirror-worlds in which he had all he deserved, smashed apart as his heavy boots came down, spraying his steel-cased calves with dirty water.

It would have been madness to run in full armour, so Gorst wore only the essentials. Breast and back-plates with fauld to the hip and greaves at the shin. On the right arm, vambrace and fencing glove only to allow free movement of the sword. On the left, full-jointed steel of the thickest gauge, encasing the parrying arm from fingertips to weighty shoulder-plate. A padded jacket beneath, and thick leather trousers reinforced with metal strips, his wobbling window on the world the narrow slot in the visor of his sallet.

A piebald dog yapped wheezily at his heels for a while, its belly grotesquely bloated, but abandoned him to root through a great heap of refuse beside the track. *Is our rubbish the only lasting mark we will leave upon this country? Our rubbish and our graves?* He pounded through the camp of Jalenhorm's division, a sprawling maze of canvas all in blissful, sleeping silence. Fog clung to the flattened grass, wreathed the closest tents, turned distant ones to phantoms. A row of horses watched him glumly over their nosebags. A lone sentry stood with pale hands stretched out to a brazier, a bloom of crimson colour in the gloom, orange sparks drifting about him. He stared open-mouthed at Gorst as he laboured past, and away.

His servants were waiting for him in the clearing outside his tent. Rurgen brought a bucket and he drank deep, cold water running down his burning neck. Younger brought the case, straining under the weight, and Gorst slid his practice blades from inside. Great, blunt lengths of battered metal, their pommels big as half-bricks to lend some semblance of balance, three times the weight of his battle steels which were already of a particularly heavy design.

In wonderful silence they came for him, Rurgen with shield and stick, Younger jabbing away with the pole, Gorst struggling to parry with his unwieldy iron. They gave him no time and no chances, no mercy and no respect. He wanted none. He had been given chances before Sipani, and allowed himself to grow soft. To grow blunt. When the moment came he was found wanting. Never again. If another moment came, it would find him forged from steel, sharpened to a merciless, murderous razor's edge. And so, every morning for the last four years, every morning since Sipani, every morning without fail, in rain or heat or snow – this.

The clonk and scrape of wood on metal. The occasional thud and grunt as sticks bounced off armour or found their marks between. The rhythm of his ripping breath, his pounding heart, his savage effort. The sweat soaking his jacket, tickling his scalp, flying in drops from his visor. The burning in every muscle, worse and worse, better and better, as if he could burn away his disgrace and live again.

He stood there, mouth gaping, eyes closed, while they unbuckled his armour. When they lifted the breastplate off it felt as if he was floating away. Off into the sky never to come down. *What is that up there, above the army? Why, none other than famous scapegoat Bremer dan Gorst, freed from the clutching earth at last!*

He peeled off his clothes, soaked through and reeking, arms so swollen he could hardly bend them. He stood naked in the chill morning, blotched all over with chafe-marks, steaming like a pudding from the oven. He gasped with shock when they doused him with icy water, fresh from the stream. Younger tossed him a cloth and he rubbed himself dry, Rurgen brought fresh clothes and he dressed while they scrubbed his armour to its usual workmanlike dull sheen.

The sun was creeping over the ragged horizon, and through the gap in the trees Gorst could see the troopers of the King's Own First Regiment wriggling from their tents, breath smoking in the chilly dawn. Buckling on their own armour, poking hopefully at the embers of dead fires, preparing for the morning's march. One group had been drawn yawning up to see one of their fellows whipped for some infringement, the lash leaving faint red lines across his stripped back, its sharp crack reaching Gorst's ear a moment later followed by the soldier's whimper. *He does not realise his luck. If only my punishment had been so short, so sharp, and so deserved.*

Gorst's battle steels had been made by Calvez, greatest swordsmith of Styria. Gifts from the king, for saving his life at the Battle of Adua. Rurgen drew the long steel from the scabbard and displayed both sides, immaculately polished metal flashing with the dawn. Gorst nodded. His servant showed him the short steel next, edges coldly glittering. Gorst nodded, took the harness and buckled it on. Then he rested one hand on Younger's shoulder, one on Rurgen's, gave them a gentle squeeze and smiled.

Rurgen spoke softly, respecting the silence. "General Jalenhorm asked that you join him at the head of the column, sir, as soon as the division begins to march."

Younger squinted up into the brightening sky. "Only six miles from Osrung, sir. Do you think there'll be a battle today?"

"I hope not." *But by the Fates, I hope there is. Oh please, oh please, oh please, I beg you only for this one thing. Send me a battle.*

Ambition

"F in?"

"Mmmm?"

He propped himself up on his elbow, grinning down at her. "I love you."

"Mmmm."

A pause. She had long ago stopped expecting love to fall upon her like a bolt of lightning. Some people are prone to love of that kind. Others are harder-headed.

"Fin?"

"Mmmm?"

"Really. I love you."

She did love him, even if she somehow found it hard to say the words. Something very close to love. He looked magnificent in a uniform and even better without one, sometimes surprised her by making her laugh, and there was definite fire when they kissed. He was honourable, generous, diligent, respectful, good-smelling...no towering intellect, true, but probably that was just as well. There is rarely room for two of those in one marriage.

"Good boy," she murmured, patting him on his cheek. She had great affection for him, and only occasionally a little contempt, which was better than she could say for most men. They were well matched. Optimist and pessimist, idealist and pragmatist, dreamer and cynic. Not to mention his noble blood and her burning ambition.

He gave a disappointed sigh. "I swear every man in the whole damn army loves you."

"Your commanding officer, Lord Governor Meed?"

"Well…no, probably not him, but I expect even he'd warm to you if you stopped making such a bloody fool of him."

"If I stopped he'd only do it to himself."

"Probably, but men have a higher tolerance for that."

"There's only one officer whose opinion I give a damn about, anyway."

He smiled as he traced her ribs with a fingertip. "Really?"

"Captain Hardrick." She clicked her tongue. "I think it's those very, very tight cavalry trousers of his. I like to drop things so he'll pick them up for me. Ooops." She touched her finger to her lip, fluttering her lashes. "Curse my clumsiness, I've let fall my fan again! You couldn't just reach for it, could you, Captain? You've almost got it. Only bend a little lower, Captain. Only bend…a little… *lower*."

"Shameless. I don't think Hardrick would suit you at all, though. The man's dull as a plank. You'd be bored in minutes."

Finree puffed out her cheeks. "You're probably right. A good arse only goes so far. Something most men never realise. Maybe…" She thought through her acquaintance for the most ridiculous lover, smiled as she lighted on the perfect candidate. "Bremer dan Gorst, then? Can't really say he's got the looks…or the wit…or the standing, but I've a feeling there's a deep well of emotion beneath that lumpen exterior. The voice would take some getting used to, of course, if one could coax out more than two words together, but if you like the strong and silent type, I'd say he scores stupendously high on both counts—What?" Hal wasn't smiling any more. "I'm joking. I've known him for years. He's harmless."

"Harmless? Have you ever seen him fight?"

"I've seen him fence."

"Not quite the same."

There was something in the way he was holding back that made her want to know more. "Have you seen him fight?"

"Yes."

"And?"

"And...I'm glad he's on our side."

She brushed the tip of his nose with a finger. "Oh, my poor baby. Are you scared of him?"

He rolled away from her, onto his back. "A little. Everyone should be at least a little scared of Bremer dan Gorst." That surprised her. She hadn't thought Hal was afraid of anything. They lay there, for a moment, the canvas above them flapping gently with the wind outside.

Now she felt guilty. She did love Hal. She had marked down all the points the day he proposed. Considered all the pros and cons and categorically proved it to herself. He was a good man. One of the best. Excellent teeth. Honest, brave, loyal to a fault. But those things are not always enough. That was why he needed someone more practical to steer him through the rapids. That was why he needed her.

"Hal."

"Yes?"

She rolled towards him, pressing herself against his warm side, and whispered in his ear. "I love you."

She had to admit to enjoying the power she had over him. That was all it took to make him beam with happiness. "Good girl," he whispered, and he kissed her, and she kissed him back, tangling her fingers in his hair. What is love anyway, but finding someone who suits you? Someone who makes up for your shortcomings?

Someone you can work with. Work on.

Aliz dan Brint was pretty enough, clever enough and well-born enough not to constitute an embarrassment, but neither pretty enough, clever enough nor well-born enough to pose any threat. A comparatively narrow band in which Finree felt it was safe to cultivate a friend without danger of being overshadowed. She had never liked being overshadowed.

"I find it something of a difficult adjustment," murmured Aliz, glancing at the column of marching soldiers beside them from beneath her blonde lashes. "Being surrounded by men takes some getting used to—"

"I wouldn't know. The army has always been my home. My mother died when I was very young, and my father raised me."

"I'm...I'm sorry."

"Why? My father misses her, I think, but how can I? I never knew her."

An awkward silence, hardly surprising since, Finree realised, that had been the conversational equivalent of a mace to the head. "Your parents?"

"Both dead."

"Oh." That made Finree feel worse. She seemed to spend most conversations see-sawing between impatience and guilt. She resolved to be more tolerant, though she did that often and it never worked. Perhaps she should have resolved simply to keep her mouth shut, but she did that often too, with even more negligible results. Hooves clapped at the track, tramping boots rumbled in unison, punctuated by the occasional calls of officers annoyed by some break in the rhythm.

"We are heading…north?" asked Aliz.

"Yes, towards the town of Osrung to rendezvous with the other two divisions, under Generals Jalenhorm and Mitterick. They might be as little as ten miles from us now, on the other side of those hills," and she gestured towards the lowering fells on their left with her riding crop.

"What sort of men are they?"

"General Jalenhorm is…" Tact, tact. "A brave and honest man, an old friend of the king." And promoted far beyond his limited ability as a result. "Mitterick is a competent and experienced soldier." As well as a disobedient blowhard with his eyes firmly on her father's position.

"And each commanding as many men as our own Lord Governor Meed?"

"Seven regiments apiece, two of cavalry and five of foot." Finree could have reeled off their numbers, titles and senior officers, but Aliz looked as though she was reaching the limits of comprehension as it was. The limits of her comprehension never seemed to be far off, but Finree was determined to make a friend of her even so. Her husband, Colonel Brint, was said to be close to the king himself, which made him a very useful man to know. That was why she always made a point of laughing at his tiresome jokes.

"So many people," said Aliz. "Your father certainly carries a great responsibility."

"He does." The last time Finree had seen her father she had been shocked by how worn down he seemed. She had always thought of him as cast in iron, and the realisation that he might be soft in the middle was most disconcerting. Perhaps that was the moment you grew up, when you learned your parents were just as fallible as everyone else.

"How many soldiers on the other side?"

"The line between soldier and citizen is not sharply drawn in the North. They have a few thousand Carls, perhaps – professional fighters with their own mail and weapons, bred to a life of warfare, who form the spear-point of the charge and the front rank in the shield wall. But for each Carl there will be several Thralls – farmers or tradesmen pressed or paid to fight and labour, usually lightly armed with spear or bow but often hardened warriors even so. Then there are Named Men, veterans who have won a celebrated place through deeds on the battlefield and serve as officers, bodyguards or scouts in small groups called dozens. Like them." She pointed out a shabby set of the Dogman's men, shadowing the column on the ridge-line to their right. "I'm not sure anyone knows how many Black Dow has, altogether. Probably not even Black Dow does."

Aliz blinked. "You're so knowledgeable…"

Finree very much wanted to say, "yes, I am" but settled for a careless shrug. There was no magic to it. She simply listened, observed, and made sure she never spoke until she knew what she was speaking of. Knowledge is the root of power, after all.

Aliz sighed. "War is terrible, isn't it?"

"It blights the landscape, throttles commerce and industry, kills the innocent and rewards the guilty, thrusts honest men into poverty and lines the pockets of profiteers, and in the end produces nothing but corpses, monuments and tall tales." Finree neglected to mention that it also offered enormous opportunities, however.

"So many men injured," said Aliz. "So many dead."

"An awful thing." Though dead men leave spaces into which the nimble-footed can swiftly step. Or into which nimble wives can swiftly manoeuvre their husbands…

"And all these people. Losing their homes. Losing everything." Aliz was gazing moist-eyed at a miserable procession coming the other way, forced from the track by the soldiers and obliged to toil through their choking dust.

They were mostly women, though it was not easy to tell, they were so ragged. Some old men, and some children along with them. Northern, certainly. Poor, undoubtedly. Beyond poor, for they had virtually nothing, their faces pinched with hunger, jaws dangling with exhaustion, clutching at heartbreakingly meagre possessions. They did not look at the Union soldiers tramping the other way with hatred, or even with fear. They looked too desperate to register emotion of any kind.

Finree did not know who they were running from exactly, or where they were going. What horror had set them in motion or what others they might still face. Shaken from their homes by the blind tremors of war. Looking at them, Finree felt shamefully secure, revoltingly lucky. It is easy to forget how much you have, when your eyes are always fixed on what you have not.

"Something should be done," murmured Aliz, wistfully.

Finree clenched her teeth. "You're right." She gave her horse the spurs, possibly flicking a few specks of mud over Aliz' white dress, covered the ground in no time and slid her mount into the knot of officers that was the frequently misfiring brain of the division.

They spoke the language of war up here. Timing and supply. Weather and morale. Rates of march and orders of battle. It was no foreign tongue to Finree, and even as she slipped her horse between them she noticed mistakes, oversights, inefficiencies. She had been brought up in barracks, and mess halls, and headquarters, had spent longer in the army than most of the officers here and knew as much about strategy, tactics and logistics as any of them. Certainly a great deal more than Lord Governor Meed, who until last year had never presided over anything more dangerous than a formal banquet.

He rode at the very centre of the press, under a standard bearing the crossed hammers of Angland, and wearing a magnificent azure uniform rigged with gold braid, better suited to an actor in a tawdry production than a general on campaign. Despite all that money wasted on tailoring, his splendid collars never seemed quite to fit and his sinewy neck always stuck from them like a turtle's from its shell.

He had lost his three nephews years ago at the Battle of Black Well and his brother, the previous lord governor, not long after. He had nursed an insurmountable hatred for Northmen ever since and been such a keen advocate of war he had outfitted half his division at his own expense. Hatred of the enemy was no qualification for command, however. Quite the reverse.

"Lady Brock, how wonderful that you could join us," he said, with mild disdain.

"I was simply taking part in the advance and you all got in my way." The officers chuckled with, in Hal's case, a slightly desperate note. He gave her a pointed look sideways, and she gave him one back. "I and some of the other ladies noticed the refugees on our left. We were hoping you could be pre-vailed upon to spare them some food?"

Meed turned his watery eyes on the miserable file with the scorn one might have for a trail of ants. "I am afraid the welfare of my soldiers must come first."

"Surely these strapping fellows could afford to miss a meal in a good cause?" She thumped Colonel Brint's breastplate and made him give a nervous laugh.

"I have assured Marshal Kroy that we will be in position outside Osrung by midnight. We cannot stop."

"It could be done in—"

Meed turned rudely away from her. "Ladies and their charitable projects, mmm?" he tossed to his officers, provoking a round of sycophantic laughter.

Finree cut through it with a shrill titter of her own. "Men and their playing at war, mmm?" She slapped Captain Hardrick on the shoulder with her gloves, hard enough to make him wince. "What *silly, womanly nonsense,* to try to save a life or two. Now I see it! We should be letting them drop like flies by the roadside, spreading fire and pestilence wherever possible and leaving their country a blasted wasteland. That will teach them the proper respect for the Union and its ways, I am sure! *There's* soldiering!" She looked around at the officers, eyebrows raised. At least they had stopped laughing. Meed, in particular, had never looked more humourless, which took some doing.

"Colonel Brock," he forced through tight lips. "I think your wife might be more comfortable riding with the other ladies."

"I was about to suggest it," said Hal, pulling his horse in front of hers and bringing them both to a sharp halt while Meed's party carried on up the track. "What the *hell* are you doing?" he hissed under his breath.

"The man's a callous idiot! A farmer playing at soldiers!"

"We have to work with what we have, Fin! Please, don't bait him. For me! My bloody nerves won't stand it!"

"I'm sorry." Impatience back to guilt, yet again. Not for Meed, of course, but for Hal, who had to be twice as good, twice as brave and twice as hard-working as anyone else simply to stay free of his father's suffocating shadow. "But I hate to see things done badly on account of some old fool's pride when they could just as easily be done well."

"Did you consider that it's bad enough having an amateur general without having one who's a bloody laughing stock besides? Maybe with some support he'd do better."

"Maybe," she muttered, unconvinced.

"Can't you stay with the other wives?" he wheedled. "Please, just for now?"

"That prattling coven?" She screwed up her face. "All they talk about is who's barren, who's unfaithful, and what the queen's wearing. They're idiots."

"Have you ever noticed that everyone's an idiot but you?"

She opened her eyes wide. "You see it too?"

Hal took a hard breath. "I love you. You know I do. But think about who you're actually helping. You could have fed those people if you'd trodden softly." He rubbed at the bridge of his nose. "I'll talk to the quartermaster, try to arrange something."

"Aren't you a hero."

"I try, but bloody hell, you don't make it easy. Next time, for me, please, think about saying something bland. Talk about the weather, maybe!" As he rode off back towards the head of the column.

"Shit on the weather," she muttered at his back, "and Meed too." She had to admit Hal had a point, though. She wasn't doing herself, or her husband, or the Union cause, or even the refugees any good by irritating Lord Governor Meed.

She had to destroy him.

Give and Take

"Up you get, old man."

Craw was half in a dream still. At home, wherever that was. A young man, or retired. Was it Colwen smiling at him from the corner? Turning wood on the lathe, curled shavings scattering, crunching under his feet. He grunted, rolled over, pain flaring up his side, stinging him with panic. He tried to rip back his blanket.

"What's the—"

"It's all right." Wonderful had a hand on his shoulder. "Thought I'd let you sleep in." She had a long scab down the other side of her head now, stubble hair clumped with dried blood. "Thought you could use it."

"I could use a few hours yet." Craw gritted his teeth against ten different aches as he tried to sit up, first fast then very, very slow. "Bloody hell, but war's a young man's business."

"What's to do?"

"Not much." She handed him a flask and he sluiced water around his foul mouth and spat. "No sign of Hardbread. We buried Athroc." He paused, flask half way to his mouth, slowly let it drop. There was a heap of fresh dirt at the foot of one of the stones on the far side of the Heroes. Brack and Scorry stood in front of it, shovels in their hands. Agrick was between the two, looking down.

"You say the words yet?" asked Craw, knowing they wouldn't have but still hoping.

"Waiting for you."

"Good," he lied, and clambered up, gripping to her forearm. It was a grey morning with a nip in the wind, low clouds pawing at the craggy summits of the fells, mist still clinging to the creases in their sides, shrouding the bogs down in the valley's bottom.

Craw limped to the grave, shifting his hips, trying to wriggle away from the pain in his joints. He'd rather have gone anywhere else, but there are some things you can't wriggle away from. They were all drifting over there,

112

gathering in a half-circle. All sad and quiet. Drofd trying to cram down a whole crust of bread at once, wiping his hands on his shirt. Whirrun with hood drawn up, cuddling the Father of Swords like a man might cuddle his sick child. Yon with a face even grimmer'n usual, which took some doing. Craw found his place at the foot of the grave, between Agrick and Brack. The hillman's face had lost its usual ruddy glow, the bandage on his leg showing a big fresh stain.

"That leg all right?" he asked.

"Scratch," said Brack.

"Bleeding a lot for a scratch, ain't it?"

Brack smiled at him, tattoos on his face shifting. "Call that a lot?"

"Guess not." Not compared to Hardbread's nephew when Whirrun cut him in half, anyway. Craw glanced over his shoulder, towards where they'd piled the corpses in the lee of the crumbling wall. Out of sight, maybe, but not forgotten. The dead. Always the dead. Craw looked at the black earth, wondering what to say. Looked at the black earth like it had answers in it. But there's nothing in the earth but darkness.

"Strange thing." His voice came out a croak, he had to cough to clear it. "The other day Drofd was asking me whether they call these stones the Heroes 'cause there are Heroes buried here. I said not. But maybe there's one buried here now." Craw winced saying it, not out of sadness but 'cause he knew he was talking shit. Stupid shit wouldn't have fooled a child. But the dozen all nodded, Agrick with a tear-track down his cheek.

"Aye," said Yon.

You can say things at a grave would get you laughed out of a tavern, and be treated like you're brimming over with wisdom. Craw felt every word was a knife he had to stick in himself, but there was no stopping.

"Hadn't been with us long, Athroc, but he made his mark. Won't be forgot." Craw thought on all the other lads he'd buried, faces and names worn away by the years, and couldn't even guess the number of 'em. "He stood with his crew. Fought well." Died badly, hacked with an axe, on ground that meant nothing. "Did the right thing. All you can ask of a man, I reckon. If there's any—"

"Craw!" Shivers was standing maybe thirty strides away on the south side of the circle.

"Not now!" he hissed back.

"Aye," said Shivers. "Now."

113

Craw hurried over, the grey valley opening up between two of the stones. "What am I looking—Uh." Beyond the river, at the foot of Black Fell, there were horsemen on the brown strip of the Uffrith Road. Riding fast towards Osrung, smudges of dust rising behind. Could've been forty. Could've been more.

"And there."

"Shit." Another couple of score coming the other way, towards the Old Bridge. Taking the crossings. Getting around both sides of the Heroes. The surge of worry was almost a pain in Craw's chest. "Where's Scorry at?" Staring about like he'd put something down and couldn't remember where. Scorry was right behind him, holding up one finger. Craw breathed out slow, patting him on the shoulder. "There you are. There you are."

"Chief," muttered Drofd.

Craw followed his pointing finger. The road south from Adwein, sloping down into the valley from the fold between two fells, was busy with movement. He snapped his eyeglass open and peered towards it. "It's the Union."

"How many, d'you reckon?"

The wind swept some mist away and, for just a moment, Craw could see the column stretching back between the hills, men and metal, spears prickling and flags waving above. Stretching back far as he could see.

"Looks like all of 'em," breathed Wonderful.

Brack leaned over. "Tell me we ain't fighting this time."

Craw lowered his eyeglass. "Sometimes the right thing to do is run like fuck. Pack up!" he bellowed. "Right now! We're moving out!"

His crew always kept most of their gear stowed and they were busy packing the rest quick sharp, Scorry with a jaunty marching tune on the go. Jolly Yon was stomping the little fire out with one boot while Whirrun watched, already packed since all he owned was the Father of Swords and he had it in one hand.

"Why put it out?" asked Whirrun.

"I ain't leaving those bastards my fire," grunted Yon.

"Don't reckon they'll all be able to fit around it, do you?"

"Even so."

"We can't even all fit around it."

"Still."

"Who knows? You leave it, maybe one of those Union fellows burns himself and they all get scared and go home."

Yon looked up for a moment, then ground the last embers out under his boot. "I ain't leaving those bastards my fire."

"That's it then?" asked Agrick. Craw found it hard to look in his eye. There was something desperate in it. "That's all the words he gets?"

"We can say more later, maybe, but for now there's the living to think on."

"We're giving it up." Agrick glared at Shivers, fists clenched, like he was the one killed his brother. "He died for nothing. For a fucking hill we ain't even holding on to! If we hadn't fought he'd still be alive! You hear that!" He took a step, might've gone for Shivers if Brack hadn't grabbed him from behind, Craw from in front, holding him tight.

"I hear it." Shivers shrugged, bored. "And it ain't the first time. If I hadn't gone to Styria I'd still have both my eyes. I went. One eye. We fought. He died. Life only rolls one way and it ain't always the way we'd like. There it is." He turned and strolled off towards the north, axe over his shoulder.

"Forget about him," muttered Craw in Agrick's ear. He knew what it was to lose a brother. He'd buried all three of his in one morning. "You need a man to blame, blame me. I chose to fight."

"There was no choice," said Brack. "It was the right thing to do."

"Where'd Drofd get to?" asked Wonderful, slinging her bow over her shoulder as she walked past. "Drofd?"

"Over here! Just packing up!" He was down near the wall, where they'd left the bodies of Hardbread's lot. When Craw got there he was kneeling by one of 'em, going through his pockets. He grinned around, holding out a few coins. "Chief, this one had some…" He trailed off when he saw Craw's frown. "I was going to share it out—"

"Put it back."

Drofd blinked at him. "But it's no good to him now—"

"Ain't yours is it? Leave it there with Hardbread's lad and when Hardbread comes back he'll decide who gets it."

"More'n likely it'll be Hardbread gets it," muttered Yon, coming up behind with his mail draped over his shoulder.

"Maybe it will be. But it won't be any of us. There's a right way of doing things."

That got a couple of sharp breaths and something close to a groan. "No one thinks that way these days, Chief," said Scorry, leaning on his spear.

"Look how rich some no-mark like Sutt Brittle's made himself," said Brack.

"While we scrape by on a piss-pot staple and the odd gild," growled Yon.

"That's what you're due, and I'll see you get a gild for yesterday's work. But you'll leave the bodies be. You want to be Sutt Brittle you can beg a place with Glama Golden's lot and rob folk all day long." Craw wasn't sure what was making him so prickly. He'd let it pass before. Helped himself more'n once when he was younger. Even Threetrees used to overlook his boys picking a corpse or two. But prickly he was, and now he'd chosen to stand on it he couldn't back down. "What're we?" he snapped, "Named Men or pickers and thieves?"

"Poor is what we are, Chief," said Yon, "and starting to—"

"What the *fuck*?" Wonderful slapped the coins from Drofd's hand and sent 'em scattering into the grass. "When you're Chief, Jolly Yon Cumber, you can do it your way. 'Til then, we'll do it Craw's. We're Named Men. Or I am, at least – I ain't convinced about the rest of you. Now move your fat arses before you end up bitching to the Union about your poverty."

"We ain't in this for the coin," said Whirrun, ambling past with the Father of Swords over his shoulder.

Yon gave him a dark look. "You might not be, Cracknut. Some of us wouldn't mind a little from time to time." But he walked off shaking his head, mail jingling, and Brack and Scorry shrugged at each other, then followed.

Wonderful leaned close to Craw. "Sometimes I think the more other folk don't care a shit the more you think you've got to."

"Your point?"

"Can't make the world a certain way all on your own."

"There's a right way of doing things," he snapped.

"You sure the right way isn't just trying to keep everyone happy and alive?"

The worst thing was that she had a point. "Is that where we've come to now?"

"I thought that's about where we've always been."

Craw raised a brow at her. "You know what? That husband o' yours really should teach you some respect."

"That bitch? He's almost as scared o' me as you lot. Let's go!" She pulled Drofd up by his elbow, and the dozen made their way through the gap in the wall, moving fast. Or as fast as Craw's knees would go. They headed north down the ragged track the way they'd come and left the Heroes to the Union.

* * *

Craw worked his way through the trees, chewing at the fingernails of his sword hand. He'd already gnawed his shield hand down to his knuckles, more or less. Damn things never grew back fast enough. He'd felt less scared on the way up the Heroes at night than he did going to tell Black Dow he'd lost a hill. Can't be right when you're less scared of the enemy than your own Chief, can it? He wished he had some friendly company, but if there was going to be blame he wanted to shoulder it alone. He'd made the choices.

The woods were crawling with men thick as ants in the grass. Black Dow's own Carls – veterans, cold-headed and cold-hearted and with lots of cold steel to share out. Some had plate armour like the Union wore, others strange weapons, beaked, picked and hooked for punching through steel, all manner of savage inventions new to the world that the world was more'n likely better off without. He doubted any of these would be thinking twice before robbing a few coins off the dead, or the living either.

Craw had been most of his life a fighting man, but crowds of 'em still somehow made him nervous, and the older he got the less he felt he fit. Any day now they'd spot him for a fraud. Realise that keeping his threadbare courage stitched together was harder work every morning. He winced as his teeth bit into the quick and jerked his nails away.

"Can't be right," he muttered to himself, "for a Named Man to be scared all the time."

"What?" Craw had almost forgotten Shivers was there, he moved so silent.

"You get scared, Shivers?"

A pause, that eye of his glinting as the sun peeped through the branches. "Used to. All the time."

"What changed?"

"Got my eye burned out o' my head."

So much for calming small talk. "Reckon that could change your outlook."

"Halves it."

Some sheep were bleating away beside the track, pressed tight into a pen much too small. Foraged, no doubt, meaning stolen, some unlucky shepherd's livelihood vanished down the gullets and out the arses of Black

117

Dow's army. Behind a screen of hides, not two strides from the flock, a woman was slaughtering 'em and three more doing the skinning and gutting and hanging the carcasses, all soaked to the armpits in blood and not caring much about it either.

Two lads, probably just reached fighting age, were watching. Laughing at how stupid the sheep were, not to guess what was happening behind those hides. They didn't see that they were in the pen, and behind a screen of songs and stories and young men's dreams, war was waiting, soaked to the armpits and not caring. Craw saw it all well enough. So why was he still sitting meek in his pen? Might be old sheep can't jump new fences either.

The black standard of the Protector of the North was dug into the earth outside some ivy-wrapped ruin, long ago conquered by the forest. More men busy in the clearing before it, and stirring horses tethered in long rows. A grindstone being pedalled, metal shrieking, sparks spraying. A woman hammering at a cartwheel. A smith working at a hauberk with pincers and a mouthful of mail rings. Children hurrying about with armfuls of shafts, slopping buckets on yokes, sacks of the dead knew what. A complicated business, violence, once the scale gets big enough.

A man sprawled on a stone slab, oddly at ease in the midst of all this work that made nothing, on his elbows, head tipped back, eyes closed. Body all in shadow but a chink of sun from between the branches coming down across his smirk so it was bathed in double brightness.

"By the dead." Craw walked to him and stood looking down. "If it ain't the prince o' nothing much. Those women's boots you're wearing?"

"Styrian leather." Calder's lids drifted open a slit, that curl to his lip he'd had since a boy. "Curnden Craw. You still alive, you old shit?"

"Bit of a cough, as it goes." He hawked up and spat phlegm onto the old stone between Calder's fancy foot-leather. "Reckon I'll survive, though. Who made the mistake o' letting you crawl back from exile?"

Calder swung his legs off the slab. "None other than the great Protector himself. Guess he couldn't beat the Union without my mighty sword-arm."

"What's his plan? Cut it off and throw it at 'em?"

Calder spread his arms out wide. "How would I hold you then?" And they folded each other tight. "Good to see you, you stupid old fool."

"Likewise, you lying little fuck."

Shivers frowned from the shadows all the while. "You two seem tight," he muttered.

"Why, I practically raised this little bastard!" Craw scrubbed Calder's hair with his knuckles. "Fed him milk from a squeezed cloth, I did."

"Closest thing I ever had to a mother," said Calder.

Shivers nodded slowly. "Explains a lot."

"We should talk." Calder gave Craw's arm a squeeze. "I miss our talks."

"And me." Craw took a careful step back as a horse reared nearby, knocked its cart sideways and sent a tangle of spears clattering to the ground. "Almost as much as I miss a decent bed. Today might not be the day, though."

"Maybe not. I hear there's some sort of battle about to happen?" Calder backed off, throwing up his hands. "It's going to kill my whole afternoon!"

He passed a cage as he went, a couple of filthy Northmen squatting naked inside, one sticking an arm out through the bars in hopes of water, or mercy, or just so some part of him could be free. Deserters would've been hanged already which made these thieves or murderers. Waiting on Black Dow's pleasure, which was more'n likely going to be to hang 'em anyway, and probably burn 'em into the bargain. Strange, to lock men up for thieving when the whole army lived on robbery. To dangle men for murder when they were all at the business of killing. What makes a crime in a time when men take what they please from who they please?

"Dow wants you." Splitfoot stood frowning in the ruin's archway. He'd always been a dour bastard but he looked 'specially put upon today. "In there."

"You want my sword?" Craw was already sliding it out.

"No need."

"No? When did Black Dow start trusting people?"

"Not people. Just you."

Craw wasn't sure if that was a good sign. "All right, then."

Shivers made to follow but Splitfoot held him back with one hand. "Dow didn't ask for you."

Craw caught Shivers' narrowed eye for a moment, and shrugged, and ducked through the ivy-choked archway, feeling like he was sticking his head in a wolf's mouth and wondering when he'd hear the teeth snap. Down a passage hung with cobweb, echoing with dripping water. Into a wide stretch of brambly dirt, broken pillars scattered around its edge, some still holding up a crumbling vault, but the roof long gone and the clouds above starting to show some bright blue between. Dow sat in Skarling's

Chair at the far end of the ruined hall, toying with the pommel of his sword. Caul Reachey sat near him, scratching at his white stubble.

"When I give the word," Dow was saying, "you'll lead off alone. Move on Osrung with everything you've got. They're weak there."

"How d'you know that?"

Dow winked. "I've got my ways. They've too many men and not enough road, and they rushed to get here so they're stretched out thin. Just some horsemen in the town, and a few o' the Dogman's lads. Might've got some foot up there by the time we go, but not enough to stop you if you take a proper swing at it."

"Oh, I'll swing at it," said Reachey. "Don't worry on that score."

"I'm not. That's why you're leading off. I want your lads to carry my standard, nice and clear up at the front. And Golden's, and Ironhead's, and yours. Where everyone can see."

"Make 'em think it's our big effort."

"Any luck they'll pull some men off from the Heroes, leave the stones weaker held. Once they're in the open fields between hill and town, I'll let slip Golden's boys and he'll tear their arses out. Meantime me, and Ironhead, and Tenways'll make the proper effort on the Heroes."

"How d'you plan to work it?"

Dow flashed that hungry grin of his. "Run up that hill and kill everything living."

"They'll have had time to get set, and that's some tough ground to charge. It's where they'll be strongest. We could go around—"

"Strongest here." Dow dug his sword into the ground in front of Skarling's Chair. "Weakest here." And he tapped at his chest with a finger. "We've been going around the sides for months, they won't be expecting us front on. We break 'em at the Heroes, we break 'em here," and he thumped his chest again, "and the rest all crumbles. Then Golden can follow up, chase 'em right across the fords if need be. All the way to Adwein. Scale should be ready on the right by then, can take the Old Bridge. With you in Osrung in weight, when the rest o' the Union turn up tomorrow all the best ground'll be ours."

Reachey slowly stood. "Right y'are, Chief. We'll make it a red day. A day for the songs."

"Shit on the songs," said Dow, standing himself. "I'll take just victory."

They clasped hands a moment, then Reachey moved for the entrance, saw Craw and gave a big gap-toothed smile.

"Old Caul Reachey." And Craw held out his hand.

"Curnden Craw, as I live and breathe." Reachey folded it in one of his then slapped the other down on top. "Ain't enough of us good men left."

"Those are the times."

"How's the knee?"

"You know. It is how it is."

"Mine too. Yon Cumber?"

"Always with a joke ready. How's Flood getting on?"

Reachey grinned. "Got him looking after some new recruits. Right shower o' piss-water, in the main."

"Maybe they'll shape up."

"They better had, and fast. I hear we got a battle coming." Reachey clapped him on the arm as he passed. "Be waiting for your order, Chief!" And he left Craw and Black Dow watching each other over a few strides of rubble-strewn, weed-sprouting, nettle-waving old mud. Birds twittered, leaves rustled, the hint of distant metal serving notice there was bloody business due.

"Chief." Craw licked his lips, no idea how this was going to go.

Dow took a long breath in and screamed at the top of his voice. "Didn't I tell you to hold on to that *fucking* hill!"

Craw went cold as the echoes rang from the crumbling walls. Looked like it might not go well at all. He wondered if he might find himself stripped in a cage before sundown. "Well, I was holding on to it all right... until the Union showed up..."

Dow came closer, sheathed sword still in one fist, and Craw had to make himself not back off. Dow leaned forwards and Craw had to make himself not flinch. Dow raised one hand and put it gently down on Craw's sore shoulder, and he had to make himself not shudder. "Sorry 'bout this," said Dow quietly, "but I've a reputation to look to."

A wave of giddy relief. " 'Course, Chief. Let rip." He narrowed his eyes as Dow took another breath.

"You *useless* old limping *fuck*!" Spraying Craw with spit, then patting the bruised side of his face, none too gently. "You made a fight of it, then?"

"Aye. With Hardbread and a few of his lads."

"I remember that old bastard. How many did he have?"

"Twenty-two."

Dow bared his teeth somewhere between smile and scowl. "And you, what, ten?"

"Aye, with Shivers."

"And you saw 'em off?"

"Well—"

"Wish I'd fucking been there!" Dow twitched with violence, eyes fixed on nothing like he could see Hardbread and his boys coming up that slope and they couldn't come fast enough for him. "*Wish* I'd been there!" And he lashed out with the pommel of his sheathed sword and struck splinters from the nearest pillar, making Craw take a careful step back. "'Stead of sitting back here fucking *talking*. Talking, talking, fucking talking!" Dow spat, and took a breath, then seemed to remember Craw was there, eyes sliding back towards him. "You saw the Union come up?"

"At least a thousand on the road to Adwein and I got the feeling there were more behind."

"Jalenhorm's division," said Dow.

"How d'you know that?"

"He has his ways."

"By the—" Craw took a startled pace, got his feet caught in a bramble and nearly fell. There was a woman lying on one of the highest walls. Draped over it like a wet cloth, one arm and one leg dangling, head hanging over the side like she was resting on some garden bench 'stead of a tottering heap of masonry six strides above the dirt.

"Friend o' mine." Dow didn't even look up. "Well – when I say friend—"

"Enemy's enemy." She rolled off the back of the wall. Craw stared, waiting for the sound of her hitting the ground. "I am Ishri." The voice whispered in his ear.

This time he went right on his arse in the dirt. She stood over him, skin black, and smooth, and perfect, like the glazing on a good pot. She wore a long coat, tails dragging on the dirt, hanging open, body all bound in white bandages underneath. If anyone ever looked like a witch, she was it. Not that there was much more evidence of witchery needed past vanishing from one place and stepping out of another.

Dow barked with laughter. "You never can tell where she'll spring from. I'm always worried she'll pop out o' nowhere while I'm...you know." And he mimed a wanking action with one fist.

"You wish," said Ishri, looking down at Craw with eyes blacker than black, unblinking, like a jackdaw staring at a maggot.

"Where did you come from?" muttered Craw as he scrambled up, hopping a little on account of his stiff knee.

"South," she said, though that much was clear enough from her skin. "Or do you mean, why did I come?"

"I'll take why."

"To do the right thing." There was a faint smile on her face, at that. "To fight against evil. To strike mighty blows for righteousness. Or...do you mean who sent me?"

"All right, who sent you?"

"God." Her eyes rolled to the sky, framed by jutting weeds and saplings. "And how could it be otherwise? God puts us all where he wants us."

Craw rubbed at his knee. "Got a shitty sense o' humour, don't he?"

"You do not know the half of it. I came to fight against the Union, is that enough?"

"It's enough for me," said Dow.

Ishri's black eyes flicked away to him, and Craw felt greatly relieved. "They are moving onto the hill in numbers."

"Jalenhorm's lot?"

"I believe so." She stretched up tall, wriggling all over the place like she had no bones in her. Reminded Craw of the eels they used to catch from the lake near his workshop, spilling from the net, squirming in the children's hands and making them squeal. "You fat pink men all look the same to me."

"What about Mitterick?" asked Dow.

Her bony shoulders drifted up and down. "Some way behind, chomping at the bit, furious that Jalenhorm is in his way."

"Meed?"

"Where is the fun in knowing everything?" She pranced past Craw, up on her toes, almost brushing against him so he had to nervously step back and nearly trip again. "God must be so *bored*." She wedged one foot into a crack in the wall too narrow for a cat to squeeze through, twisting her leg, somehow working it in up to the hip. "To it, then, my heroes!" She writhed like a worm cut in half, wriggling into the ruined masonry, her coat dragging up the mossy stonework behind her. "Do you not have a battle to fight?" Her skull somehow slid into the gap, then her arms, she clapped her bandaged hands once and just a finger was left sticking from the crack.

Dow walked over to it, reached out, and snapped it off. It wasn't a finger at all, just a dead bit of twig.

"Magic," muttered Craw. "Can't say I care for the stuff." In his experience it did more harm than good. "I daresay a sorcerer's got their uses and all but, I mean, do they always have to act so bloody *strange*?"

Dow flicked the twig away with a wrinkled lip. "It's a war. I care for whatever gets the job done. Best not mention my black-skinned friend to anyone else though, eh? Folks might get the wrong idea."

"What's the right idea?"

"Whatever I fucking say it is!" snarled Dow, and he didn't look like he was faking the anger this time.

Craw held up his open hands. "You're the Chief."

"Damn right!" Dow frowned at that crack. "I'm the Chief." Almost like it was himself he was trying to convince. Just for a moment Craw wondered whether Black Dow ever felt like a fraud. Whether Black Dow's courage needed stitching together every morning.

He didn't like that thought much. "We're fighting, then?"

Dow's eyes swivelled sideways and his killing smile broke out fresh, no trace of doubt in it, or fear neither. "High fucking time, no? You hear what I was telling Reachey?"

"Most of it. He'll try and draw 'em off towards Osrung, then you'll go straight at the Heroes."

"Straight at 'em!" barked Dow, like he could make it work by shouting it. "The way Threetrees would've done it, eh?"

"Would he?"

Dow opened his mouth, then paused. "What does it matter? Threetrees is seven winters in the mud."

"True. Where do you want me and my dozen?"

"Right beside me when I charge up to the Heroes, o' course. Expect there's nothing in the world you'd like more'n to take that hill back from those Union bastards."

Craw gave a long sigh, wondering what his dozen would have to say about that. "Oh, aye. It's top o' my list."

The Very Model

An officer should command from horseback, eh, Gorst? The proper place for a headquarters is the saddle!" General Jalenhorm affectionately patted the neck of his magnificent grey, then leaned over without waiting for an answer to roar at a spotty-faced courier. "Tell the captain that he must simply clear the road by whatever means necessary! Clear the road and move them up! Haste, all haste, lad, Marshal Kroy wants the division moving north!" He swivelled to bellow over the other shoulder. "Speed, gentlemen, speed! Towards Carleon, and victory!"

Jalenhorm certainly looked a conquering hero. Fantastically young to command a division and with a smile that said he was prepared for anything, dressed with an admirable lack of pretension in a dusty trooper's uniform and as comfortable in the saddle as a favourite armchair. If he had been half as fine a tactician as he was a horseman, they would long ago have had Black Dow in chains and on public display in Adua. *But he is not, and we do not.*

A constantly shifting body of staff officers, adjutants, liaisons and even a scarcely pubescent bugler trailed eagerly along in the general's wake like wasps after a rotten apple, fighting to attract his fickle attention by snapping, jostling and shouting over one another with small dignity. Meanwhile Jalenhorm himself barked out a volley of confusing and contradictory replies, questions, orders and occasional musings on life.

"On the right, on the right, of course!" to one officer. "Tell him not to worry, worrying solves nothing!" to another. "Move them up, Marshal Kroy wants them all up by lunch!" A large body of infantry were obliged to shuffle exhausted from the road, watch the officers pass, then chew on their dust. "Beef, then," bellowed Jalenhorm with a regal wave, "or mutton, whichever, we have more important business! Will you come up the hill with me, Colonel Gorst? Apparently one gets quite the view from the Heroes. You are his Majesty's observer, are you not?"

I am his Majesty's fool. Almost as much his Majesty's fool as you are. "Yes, General."

Jalenhorm had already whisked his mount from the road and down the shingle towards the shallows, pebbles scattering. His hangers-on strained to follow, splashing out into the water and heedlessly showering a company of heavily loaded foot who were struggling across, up to their waists in the river. The hill rose out of the fields on the far side, a great green cone so regular as to seem artificial. The circle of standing stones that the Northmen called the Heroes jutted from its flat top, a much smaller circle on a spur to the right, a single tall needle of rock on another to the left.

Orchards grew on the far bank, the twisted trees heavy with reddening apples, thin grass underneath patched with shade and covered in half-rotten windfalls. Jalenhorm leaned out to pluck one from a low-hanging branch and happily bit into it. "Yuck." He shuddered and spat it out. "Cookers, I suppose."

"General Jalenhorm, sir!" A breathless messenger whipping his horse down one row of trees towards them.

"Speak, man!" Without slowing from a trot.

"Major Kalf is at the Old Bridge, sir, with two companies of the Fourteenth. He wonders whether he should push forward to a nearby farm and establish a perimeter—"

"Absolutely! Forward. We need to make room! Where are the rest of his companies?" The messenger had already saluted and galloped off westwards. Jalenhorm frowned around at his staff. "Major Kalf's other companies? Where's the rest of the Fourteenth?"

Dappled sunlight slid over baffled faces. An officer opened his mouth but said nothing. Another shrugged. "Perhaps held up in Adwein, sir, there is considerable confusion on the narrow roads—"

He was interrupted by another messenger, bringing a well-lathered horse from the opposite direction. "Sir! Colonel Vinkler wishes to know whether he should turn the residents of Osrung out of their houses and garrison—"

"No, no, turn them out? No!"

"Sir!" The young man pulled his horse about.

"Wait! Yes, turn them out. Garrison the houses. Wait! No. No. Hearts and minds, eh, Colonel Gorst? Hearts and mind, don't you think? What do you think?"

I think your close friendship with the king has caused you to be promoted far beyond the rank at which you were most effective. I think you would have made an excellent lieutenant, a passable captain, a mediocre major and a dismal col-

onel, *but as a general you are a liability. I think you know this, and have no confidence, which makes you behave, paradoxically, as if you have far too much. I think you make decisions with little thought, abandon some with none and stick furiously to others against all argument, thinking that to change your mind would be to show weakness. I think you fuss with details better left to subordinates, fearing to tackle the larger issues, and that makes your subordinates smother you with decisions on every trifle, which you then bungle. I think you are a decent, honest, courageous man. And I think you are a fool.* "Hearts and minds," said Gorst.

Jalenhorm beamed. The messenger tore off, presumably to win the people of Osrung to the Union cause by allowing them keep their own houses. The rest of the officers emerged from the shade of the apple trees and into the sun, the grassy slope stretching away above them.

"With me, boys, with me!" Jalenhorm urged his charger uphill, maintaining an effortless balance in the saddle while his retainers struggled to keep up, one balding captain almost torn from his seat as a low branch clubbed him in the head.

An old drystone wall ringed the hill not far from the top, sprouting with seeding weeds, no higher than a stride or two even on its outside face. One of the more impetuous young ensigns tried to show off by jumping it, but his horse shied and nearly dumped him. *A fitting metaphor for the Union involvement in the North so far – a lot of vainglory but it all ends in embarrassment.*

Jalenhorm and his officers passed in file through a narrow gap, the ancient stones on the summit looming larger with every hoofbeat, then rearing over Gorst and the rest as they crested the hill's flat top.

It was close to midday, the sun was high and hot, the morning mists were all burned off and, aside from some towers of white cloud casting ponderous shadows over the forests to the north, the valley was bathed in golden sunlight. The wind made waves through the crops, the shallows glittered, a Union flag snapped proudly over the tallest tower in the town of Osrung. To the south of the river the roads were obscured by the dust of thousands of marching men, the occasional twinkle of metal showing where bodies of soldiers moved: infantry, cavalry, supplies, rolling sluggishly from the south. Jalenhorm had drawn his horse up to take in the view, and with some displeasure.

"We aren't moving fast enough, damn it. Major!"

"Sir?"

"I want you to ride down to Adwein and see if you can hurry them along there! We need to get more men on this hill. More men into Osrung. We need to move them up!"

"Sir!"

"And Major?"

"Sir?"

Jalenhorm sat, open-mouthed, for a moment. "Never mind. Go!"

The man set off in the wrong direction, realised his error and was gone down the hill the way they had come.

Confusion reigned in the wide circle of grass within the Heroes. Horses had been tethered to two of the stones but one had got loose and was making a deafening racket, scaring the others and kicking out alarmingly while several terrified grooms tried desperately to snatch its bridle. The standard of the King's Own Sixth Regiment hung limp in the centre of the circle beside a burned out fire where, utterly dwarfed by the sullen slabs of rock that surrounded it on every side, it did little for morale. *Although, let us face the facts, my morale is beyond help.*

Two small wagons that had somehow been dragged up the hill had been turned over onto their sides and their eclectic contents – from tents to pans to smithing instruments to a shining new washboard – scattered across the grass while soldiers rooted through the remainder like plunderers after a rout.

"What the hell are you about, Sergeant?" demanded Jalenhorm, spurring his horse over.

The man looked up guiltily to see the attention of a general and two dozen staff officers all suddenly focused upon him, and swallowed. "Well, sir, we're a little short of flatbow bolts, General, sir."

"And?"

"It seems ammunition was considered very important by those that packed the supplies."

"Naturally."

"So it was packed first."

"First."

"Yes, sir. Meaning, on the bottom, sir."

"The bottom?"

"Sir!" A man with a pristine uniform hastened over, chin high, giving

Jalenhorm a salute so sharp that the snapping of his well-polished heels was almost painful to the ear.

The general swung from his saddle and shook him by the hand. "Colonel Wetterlant, good to see you! How do things stand?"

"Well enough, sir, most of the Sixth is up here now, though lacking a good deal of our equipment." Wetterlant led them across the grass, soldiers doing the best they could to make room amid the chaos. "One battalion of the Rostod Regiment too, though what happened to their commanding officer is anyone's guess."

"Laid up with the gout, I believe—" someone muttered.

"Is that a grave?" asked Jalenhorm, pointing out a patch of fresh-turned earth in the shadow of one of the stones, trampled with boot-prints.

The colonel frowned at it. "Well, I suppose—"

"Any sign of the Northmen?"

"A few of my men have seen movement in the woods to the north but nothing we could say for certain was the enemy. More likely than not it's sheep." Wetterlant led them between two of the towering stones. "Other than that, not a sniff of the buggers. Apart from what they left behind, that is."

"Ugh," said one of the staff officers, looking sharply away. Several blood-stained bodies were laid out in a row. One of them had been sliced in half and had lost his lower arm besides, flies busy on his exposed innards.

"Was there combat?" asked Jalenhorm, frowning at the corpses.

"No, those are yesterday's. And they were ours. Some of the Dogman's scouts, apparently." The colonel pointed out a small group of Northmen, a tall one with a red bird on his shield and a heavy set old man conspicuous among them, busy digging graves.

"What about the horse?" It lay on its side, an arrow poking from its bloated belly.

"I really couldn't say."

Gorst took in the defences, which were already considerable. Spearmen were manning the drystone wall on this side of the hill, packed shoulder to shoulder at a gap where a patchy track passed down the hillside. Behind them, higher up the slope, a wide double curve of archers fussed with bolts and flatbows or simply lazed about, chewing disconsolately at dried rations, a couple apparently arguing over winnings at dice.

"Good," said Jalenhorm, "good," without specifying exactly what met his approval. He frowned out across the patchwork of field and pasture, over the few farms and towards the woods that blanketed the north side of the valley. Thick forest, of the kind that covered so much of the country, the monotony of trees only relieved by the vague stripes of two roads leading north between the fells. One of them, presumably, to Carleon. *And victory.*

"There could be ten Northmen out there or ten thousand," muttered Jalenhorm. "We must be careful. Mustn't underestimate Black Dow. I was at the Cumnur, you know, Gorst, where Prince Ladisla was killed. Well, the day before the battle, in fact, but I was there. A dark day for Union arms. Can't be having another of those, eh?"

I strongly suggest that you resign your commission, then, and allow someone with better credentials to take command. "No, sir."

Jalenhorm had already turned away to speak to Wetterlant. Gorst could hardly blame him. *When did I last say anything worth hearing? Bland agreements and non-committal splutterings. The bleating of a goat would serve the same purpose.* He turned his back on the knot of staff officers and wandered over to where the Northmen were digging graves. The grey-haired one watched him come, leaning on his spade.

"My name is Gorst."

The older man raised his brows. *Surprise that a Union man should speak Northern, or surprise that a big man should speak like a little girl?* "Hardbread's mine. I fight for the Dogman." His words slightly mangled in a badly battered mouth.

Gorst nodded to the corpses. "These are your men?"

"Aye."

"You fought up here?"

"Against a dozen led by a man called Curnden Craw." He rubbed at his bruised jaw. "We had the numbers but we lost."

Gorst frowned around the circle of stones. "They had the ground."

"That and Whirrun of Bligh."

"Who?"

"Some fucking hero," scoffed the one with a red bird on his shield.

"From way up north in the valleys," said Hardbread, "where it snows every bloody day."

"Mad bastard," grunted one of Hardbread's men, nursing a bandaged arm. "They say he drinks his own piss."

"I heard he eats children."

"He has this sword they say fell out of the sky." Hardbread wiped his forehead on the back of one thick forearm. "They worship it, up there in the snows."

"They worship a sword?" asked Gorst.

"They think God dropped it or something. Who knows what they think up there? Either way, Cracknut Whirrun is one dangerous bastard." Hardbread licked at a gap in his teeth, and from his grimace it was a new one. "I can tell you that from my own experience."

Gorst frowned towards the forest, trees shining dark green in the sun. "Do you think Black Dow's men are near?"

"I reckon they are."

"Why?"

"Because Craw fought against the odds, and he ain't a man to fight over nothing. Black Dow wanted this hill." Hardbread shrugged as he bent back to his task. "We're burying these poor bastards then we're going down. I'll be leaving a tooth back there on the slope and a nephew in the mud and I don't plan on leaving aught else in this bloody place."

"Thank you." Gorst turned back towards Jalenhorm and his staff, now engaged in a heated debate about whether the latest company to arrive should be placed behind or in front of the ruined wall. "General!" he called. "The scouts think Black Dow might be nearby!"

"I hope he is!" shot back Jalenhorm, though it was obvious he was scarcely listening. "The crossings are in our hands! Take control of all three crossings, that's our first objective!"

"I thought there were four crossings." It was said quietly, one man murmuring to another, but the hubbub dropped away at that moment. Everyone turned to see a pale young lieutenant, somewhat surprised to have become the centre of attention.

"Four?" Jalenhorm rounded on the man. "There is the Old Bridge, to the west." He flung out one arm, almost knocking down a portly major. "The bridge in Osrung, to the east. And the shallows where we made the passage. Three crossings." The general waved three big fingers in the lieutenant's face. "All in our hands!"

The young man flushed. "One of the scouts told me there is a path through the bogs, sir, further west of the Old Bridge."

"A path through the bogs?" Jalenhorm squinted off to the west. "A secret way? I mean to say, Northmen could use that path and get right around us! Damn good work, boy!"

"Well, thank you, sir—"

The general spun one way, then back the other, heel twisting up the sod, casting around as though the right strategy was always just behind him. "Who hasn't crossed the river yet?"

His officers milled about in their efforts to stay in his line of sight.

"Are the Eighth up?"

"I thought the rest of the Thirteenth—"

"Colonel Vallimir's first cavalry are still deploying there!"

"I believe they have one battalion in order, just reunited with their horses—"

"Excellent! Send to Colonel Vallimir and ask him to take that battalion through the bogs."

A couple of officers grumbled their approval. Others glanced somewhat nervously at each other. "A whole battalion?" one muttered. "Is this path suitable for—"

Jalenhorm swatted them away. "Colonel Gorst! Would you ride back across the river and convey my wishes to Colonel Vallimir, make sure the enemy can't give us an unpleasant surprise."

Gorst paused for a moment. "General, I would prefer to remain where I can—"

"I understand entirely. You wish to be close to the action. But the king asked specifically in his last letter that I do everything possible to keep you out of danger. Don't worry, the front line will hold perfectly well without you. We friends of the king must stick together, mustn't we?"

All the king's fools, capering along in military motley to the same mad bugle music! Make the one with the silly voice turn another cartwheel, my sides are splitting! "Of course, sir." And Gorst trudged back towards his horse.

Scale

Calder nudged his horse down a path so vague he wasn't even sure it was one, smirk clamped tight to his face. If Deep and Shallow were keeping an eye on him – and since he was their best source of money it was a certainty – he couldn't tell. Admittedly, there wasn't much point to men like Deep and Shallow if a man like Calder could tell where they were, but by the dead he would've liked some company. Like a starving man tossed a crust, seeing Curnden Craw had only whetted Calder's appetite for friendly faces.

He'd ridden through Ironhead's men, soaking up their scorn, and Tenways', soaking up their hostility, and now he was getting into the woods at the west end of the valley, where Scale's men were gathered. His brother's men. His men, he supposed, though they didn't feel much like his. Tough-looking bastards, ragged from hard marching, bandaged from hard fighting. Worn down from being far from Black Dow's favour where they did the toughest jobs for the leanest rewards. They didn't look in a mood to celebrate anything, and for damn sure not the arrival of their Chief's coward brother.

It didn't help that he'd struggled into his chain mail shirt, hoping to at least look like a warrior prince for the occasion. It had been a gift from his father, years ago, made from Styrian steel, lighter than most Northern mixtures but still heavy as an anvil and hot as a sheepskin. Calder had no notion how men could wear these damn things for days at a time. Run in them. Sleep in them. Fight in them. Mad business, fighting in this. Mad business, fighting. He'd never understood what men saw in it.

And few men saw more in it than his own brother, Scale.

He was squatting in a clearing with a map spread out in front of him. Pale-as-Snow was at his left elbow and White-Eye Hansul at his right, old comrades of Calder's father from the time when he ruled the best part of the North. Men who'd fallen a long way when the Bloody-Nine threw Calder's father from his battlements. Almost as far as Calder had fallen himself.

Him and Scale were born to different mothers, and the joke always was that Scale's must've been a bull. He looked like a bull, and a particularly mean and muscular one at that. He was Calder's opposite in almost every way – blond where Calder was dark, blunt-featured where Calder was sharp, quick to anger and slow to think. Nothing like their father. Calder was the one who'd taken after Bethod, and everyone knew it. One reason why they hated him. That and he'd spent so much of his life acting like a prick.

Scale looked up when he heard the hooves of Calder's horse, gave a great smile as he strode over, still carrying that trace of a limp the Bloody-Nine had given him. He wore his chain mail lightly as a maiden wears a shift even so, a heavy black-forged double coat of it, plates of black steel strapped on top, all scratched and dented. "Always be armed," their father had told them, and Scale had taken it literally. He was criss-crossed with belting and bristling with weapons, two swords and a great mace at his belt, three knives in plain sight and probably others out of it. He had a bandage around his head stained brown on one side, and a new nick through his eyebrow to add to a rapidly growing collection of scars. It looked as if Calder's frequent attempts to persuade Scale to stay out of battle had been as wasted as Scale's frequent attempts to persuade Calder to charge into it.

Calder swung from his saddle, finding it a straining effort in his mail and trying to make it look like he was only stiff from a hard ride. "Scale, you thick bastard, how've you—"

Scale caught him in a crushing hug, lifted his feet clear of the ground and gave him a slobbery kiss on the forehead. Calder hugged him back the best he could with all the breath squeezed out of his body and a sword hilt poking him in the gut, so suddenly, pathetically happy to have someone on his side he wanted to cry.

"Get off!" he wheezed, hammering at Scale's back with the heel of his hand like a wrestler submitting. "Off!"

"Just good to see you back!" And Scale spun him helplessly around like a husband with his new bride, gave him a fleeting view of Pale-as-Snow and White-Eye Hansul. Neither of them looked like hugging Calder any time soon. The eyes on him from the Named Men scattered about the clearing were no more enthusiastic. Men he recognised from way back, kneeling to his father or sitting at the long table or cheering victory in the good old days. No doubt they were wondering whether they'd have to take Calder's orders now, and not much caring for the idea. Why would they? Scale was all those things warriors admire – loyal, strong and brave beyond the point of stupidity. Calder was none of them, and everyone knew it.

"What happened to your head?" he asked, once Scale had let his feet touch earth again.

"This? Bah. Nothing." Scale tore the bandage off and tossed it away. It didn't look like nothing, his yellow hair matted brown with dry blood on one side. "Seems you've a wound of your own though." Patting Calder's bruised lip none too gently. "Some woman bite you?"

"If only. Brodd Tenways tried to have me killed."

"What?"

"Really. He sent three men after me to Caul Reachey's camp. Luckily Deep and Shallow were looking out and...you know..."

Scale was moving fast from bafflement to fury, his two favourite emotions and never much of a gap between the two, little eyes opening wider and wider until the whites showed all the way around. "I'll kill the rotten old bastard!" He started to draw a sword, as if he was going to charge off through the woods to the ruin where Black Dow had their father's chair and slaughter Brodd Tenways on the spot.

"No, no, no!" Calder grabbed his wrist with both hands, managed to stop him getting his sword from the sheath and was nearly dragged off his feet doing it.

"Fuck him!" Scale shrugged Calder off, punched the nearest tree trunk with one gauntleted fist and tore a chunk of bark off it. "Fuck the shit out of him! Let's kill him! Let's just *kill* him!" He punched it again and brought a shower of seeds fluttering down. White-Eye Hansul looked on warily, Pale-as-Snow looked on wearily, both giving the strong impression this wasn't the first rage they'd had to deal with.

"We can't run around killing important people," coaxed Calder, palms up.

"He tried to kill you, didn't he?"

"I'm a special case. Half the North wants me dead." That was a lie, it was closer to three-quarters. "And we've no proof." Calder put his hand on Scale's shoulder and spoke softly, the way their father used to. "It's politics, brother. Remember? It's a delicate balance."

"Fuck politics and shit on the balance!" But the rage had flickered down now. Far enough that there was no danger of Scale's eyes popping out of his head. He rammed his sword back, hilt snapping against the scabbard. "Can't we just fight?"

Calder took a long breath. How could this unreasoning thug be his father's son? And his father's heir, besides? "There'll be a time to fight, but for now we need to tread carefully. We're short on allies, Scale. I spoke to Reachey, and he won't move against me but he won't move for."

"Creeping bloody coward!" Scale raised his fist to punch the tree again and Calder pushed it gently down with one finger.

"Just worried for his daughter." And he wasn't the only one. "Then there's Ironhead and Golden, neither too well disposed to us. If it weren't for their feud with each other I daresay they'd have been begging Dow for the chance to kill me."

Scale frowned. "You think Dow was behind it?"

"How could he not be?" Calder had to squeeze down his frustration and his voice with it. He'd forgotten how much talking to his brother could be like talking to a tree stump. "And anyway, Reachey had it from Dow's own mouth that he wants me dead."

Scale shook his head, worried. "I hadn't heard that."

"He's not likely to tell you, is he?"

"But he had you hostage." Scale's brow was wrinkled with the effort of thinking it out. "Why let you come back?"

"Because he's hoping I'll start plotting, and then he'll be able to bring it all out and hang me nice and fair."

"Don't plot, then, you should be right enough with everyone."

"Don't be an *idiot*." A couple of Carls looked up from their water cups, and he pushed his voice back down. Scale could afford to lose his temper, Calder couldn't. "We need to protect ourselves. We have enemies everywhere."

"True, and there's one you haven't talked about at all. Most dangerous of the lot, far as I can tell." Calder froze for a moment, wondering who he might have left out of his calculations. "The fucking Union!" Scale pointed through the trees towards the south with one thick finger. "Kroy, and the Dogman, and their forty thousand soldiers! The ones we've been fighting a war against! I've been, anyway."

"That's Black Dow's war, not mine."

Scale slowly shook his head. "Did you ever think it might be the easier, cheaper, safer path just to do what you're told?"

"Thought about it, decided against. What we need—"

"Listen to me." Scale came close, looking him right in the eye. "There's a battle coming, and we have to fight. Do you understand? This is the North. We have to fight."

"Scale—"

"You're the clever one. Far cleverer than me, everyone knows it. The dead know I know it." He leaned closer still. "But the men won't follow cleverness. Not without strength. You have to earn their respect."

"Huh." Calder glanced around at the hard eyes in the trees. "Can't I just borrow it from you?"

"One day I might not be here, and you'll need some respect of your own. You don't have to wade in blood. You just have to share the hardships and share the danger."

Calder gave a watery smile. "It's the danger that scares me." He wasn't over keen on the hardships either, if the truth be known.

"Fear is good." Easy for him to say whose skull was so thick fear couldn't get in. "Our father was scared every day of his life. Kept him sharp." Scale took Calder's shoulder in a grip that wasn't to be resisted and turned him to face south. Between the trunks of the trees at the edge of the woods he could see a long expanse of fields, gold, and green, and fallow brown. The western spur of the Heroes loomed up on the left, Skarling's finger sticking from the top, the grey streak of a road through the crops at its foot. "That track leads to the Old Bridge. Dow wants us to take it."

"Wants *you* to take it."

"Us. It's barely defended. Do you have a shield?"

"No." Nor the slightest wish to go where he might need one.

"Pale-as-Snow, lend me your shield there."

The waxy-faced old warrior handed it over to Calder. Painted white, appropriately enough. It had been a long time since he'd handled one, battered about a courtyard at sword practice, and he'd forgotten how much the damn things weighed. The feel of it on his arm brought back ugly memories of old humiliations, most of them at his brother's hands. But they'd probably be eclipsed by new ones before the day was out. If he lived through it.

Scale patted Calder on his sore cheek again. Unpleasantly firm, again. "Stay close to me and keep your shield up, you'll get through all right." He jerked his head towards the men scattered in the trees. "And they'll think more of you just for seeing you up front."

"Right." Calder hefted the shield with scant enthusiasm.

"Who knows?" His brother slapped him on the back and nearly knocked him over. "Maybe you will too."

Ours Not to Reason Why

"Y ou just love that bloody horse, don't you, Tunny?"

"She makes better conversation than you, Forest, that's for sure, and she's a damn sight better than walking. Aren't you, my darling?" He nuzzled at her long face and fed her an extra handful of grain. "My favourite animal in the whole bloody army."

He felt a tap on his arm. "Corporal?" It was Yolk, looking off towards the hill.

"No, Yolk, I'm afraid to say you're nowhere near. In fact you need to work hard at not being my least favourite animal—"

"No, Corporal. Ain't that that Gurts?"

Tunny frowned. "Gorst." The neckless swordsman was riding across the river from the direction of the orchards on the far bank, horse's hooves dashing up spray, armour glinting dully in what had turned out to be bright sunlight. He spurred up the bank and into the midst of the regiment's officers, almost knocking one young lieutenant down. Tunny might have been amused, except there was something about Gorst that drained all the laughs from the world. He swung from the saddle, nimbly for all his bulk, lumbered straight up to Colonel Vallimir and gave a stiff salute.

Tunny tossed his brush down and took a few steps towards them, watching closely. Long years in the military had given him a razor-keen sense of when he was about to get fucked, and he was having a painful premonition right now. Gorst spoke for a few moments, face a blank slab. Vallimir shook an arm at the hill, then off to the west. Gorst spoke again. Tunny edged closer, trying to catch the details. Vallimir flung up his hands in frustration, then stalked over, shouting.

"First Sergeant Forest!"

"Sir."

"Apparently there's a path through those bogs to our west."

"Sir?"

"General Jalenhorm wants us to send the First Battalion through it. Make sure the Northmen can't use it against us."

"The bog beyond the Old Bridge?"

"Yes."

"We won't be able to get horses through that—"

"I know."

"We only just got them back, sir."

"I know."

"But . . . what will we do with them in the meantime?"

"You'll just have to bloody well leave them here!" snapped Vallimir. "Do you think I like sending half my regiment across a bloody bog without their horses? Do you?"

Forest worked his jaw, scar down his cheek shifting. "No, sir."

Vallimir strode away, beckoning over some of the officers. Forest stood a moment, rubbing fiercely at the back of his head.

"Corporal?" whispered Yolk, in a small voice.

"Yes?"

"Is this another example of everyone shitting on the head of the man below?"

"Very good, Yolk. We may make a soldier of you yet."

Forest stopped in front of them, hands on hips, frowning off upriver. "Seems the First Battalion have a mission."

"Marvellous," said Tunny.

"We'll be leaving our horses here and heading west to cross that bog." A chorus of groans greeted him. "You think I like it? Get packed and get moving!" And Forest stomped off to break the happy news elsewhere.

"How many men in the battalion?" muttered Lederlingen.

Tunny took a long breath. "About five hundred when we left Adua. Currently four hundred, give or take a recruit or two."

"Four hundred men?" said Klige. "Across a bog?"

"What sort of a bog is it?" muttered Worth.

"A bog!" Yolk squealed, like a tiny, angry dog yapping at a bigger one. "A bloody bog! A massive load of mud! What other sort of bog would it be?"

"But . . ." Lederlingen stared after Forest, and then at his horse, onto which he'd just loaded most of his gear and some of Tunny's. "This is stupid."

Tunny rubbed at his tired eyes with finger and thumb. How often had he had to explain this to a set of recruits? "Look. You think how stupid people are most of the time. Old men drunk. Women at a village fair. Boys throwing stones at birds. Life. The foolishness and the vanity, the selfishness and the waste. The *pettiness,* the *silliness.* You think in a war it must be different. Must be better. With death around the corner, men united against hardship, the cunning of the enemy, people must think harder, faster, be... better. Be *heroic.*"

He started to heave his packages down from his horse's saddle. "Only it's just the same. In fact, do you know, because of all that pressure, and worry, and fear, it's worse. There aren't many men who think clearest when the stakes are highest. So people are even stupider in a war than the rest of the time. Thinking about how they'll dodge the blame, or grab the glory, or save their skins, rather than about what will actually *work.* There's no job that forgives stupidity more than soldiering. No job that encourages it more."

He looked at his recruits and found they were all staring back, horrified. Except for an oblivious Yolk, straining on tiptoe to get his spear down from his horse, perhaps the largest in the regiment. "Never mind," he snapped. "This bog won't cross itself." He turned his back on them, patted his horse gently on the neck and sighed. "Oh well, old girl. Guess you'll have to manage a little longer without me."

Cry Havoc and...

Scorry was cutting hair when Craw got back to his dozen, or the seven who were left, leastways. Eight including him. He wondered if there'd ever been a dozen that actually had the full twelve. Sure as hell his never had. Agrick sat on a fallen tree trunk all coated with ivy, frowning into nowhere as the shears snip-snipped around his face.

Whirrun was leaning against a tree, the Father of Swords stood up on its point and the hilt cradled in his folded arms. He'd stripped his shirt off for some reason and stood there in a leather vest, a big grey stain of old sweat down the front and his long, sinewy arms sticking out. Seemed as if the more dangerous things got the more clothes he liked to lose. Probably have his arse out by the time they were finished with this valley.

"Craw!" he shouted, lifting his sword and shaking it around.

"Hey, Chief." Drofd sitting on a branch above with back against trunk. Whittling a stick for an arrow shaft, shavings fluttering down.

"Black Dow didn't kill you, then?" asked Wonderful.

"Not right on the spot, anyway."

"Did he tell you what's to do?" Yon nodded towards the men crowding the woods all around. He had a lot less hair than when Craw left and it made him look older somehow, creases around his eyes and grey in his brows Craw never noticed before. "I get the feeling Dow's planning to go."

"That he is." Craw winced as he squatted down in the brush, peering south. Seemed a different world out there beyond the treeline. All dark and comforting under the leaves. Quiet, like being sunk in cool water. All bathed in harsh sunlight outside. Yellow-brown barley under the blue sky, the Heroes bulging up vivid green from the valley, the old stones on top, still standing their pointless watch.

Craw pointed over to their left, towards Osrung, the town no more'n a hint of a high fence and a couple of grey towers over the crops. "Reachey's going to move first, make a charge on Osrung." He found he was whispering, even though the Union were a good few hundred strides away on top of a hill and could hardly have heard him if he screamed. "He'll be carrying all the standards, make it look like that's the big push. Hope to draw some men down off the Heroes."

"Reckon they'll fall for that?" asked Yon. "Pretty thin, ain't it?"

Craw shrugged. "Any trick looks thin to them who know it's coming."

"Don't make too much difference whether they go or not, though." Whirrun was stretching now, hanging from a tree branch, sword slung over his back. "We still got the same hill to climb."

"Might help if there's half as many Union at the top when we get there," Drofd tossed down from his own perch.

"Let's hope they fall for it then, eh?" Craw moved his hand to the right, towards the field and pasture between Osrung and the Heroes. "If they do send men down from the hill, that's when Golden's going with his horse. Catch those boys trousers down in the open and spill 'em all the way back to the river."

"Drown those fuckers," grunted Agrick, with rare bloodthirstiness.

"Meantime Dow's going to make the main effort. Straight at the Heroes, Ironhead and Tenways alongside with all their lads."

"How's he going to work it?" asked Wonderful, rubbing at her new scar.

Craw gave her a look. "Black Dow, ain't it? He's going to run up there head on and make mud of everything ain't mud already."

"And us?"

Craw swallowed. "Aye. We'll be along."

"Front and centre, eh?"

"Up that bloody hill again?" growled Yon.

"Almost makes you wish we'd fought the Union for it last time," said Whirrun, swinging from one branch to another.

Craw pointed to their right. "Scale's over there in the woods under Salt Fell. Once Dow's made his move, he's going to charge his horsemen down the Ustred Road and snatch the Old Bridge. Him and Calder."

Amazing how much Yon could disapprove with just a shake of his head. "Your old mate Calder, eh?"

"That's right." Craw looked straight at him. "My old mate Calder."

"Then this lovely valley and all its nothing much shall be ours!" sang Whirrun. "Again."

"Dow's, at any rate," said Wonderful.

Drofd was counting the names off on his fingers. "Reachey, Golden, Ironhead, Tenways, Scale and Dow himself . . . that's a lot o' men."

Craw nodded. "Might be the most ever fought for the North in one spot."

"There's going to be quite a battle here," said Yon. "Quite the hell of a battle."

"One for the songs!" Whirrun had hooked his legs over the branch and was hanging upside down now, for some reason best known to his self.

"We're going to make a right mess o' those Southerners." Drofd didn't sound entirely convinced, though.

"By the dead, I hope so," mouthed Craw.

Yon edged forwards. "Did you get our gild, Chief?"

Craw winced. "Dow weren't in the mood to bring it up." There was a round of groans at that, just like he'd known there would be. "I'll get it later, don't worry. It's owed and you'll get it. I'll talk to Splitfoot."

Wonderful sucked her teeth. "You'd be better trying to get sense from Whirrun than coin out o' Splitfoot."

"I heard that!" called Whirrun.

"Think on this," said Craw, slapping Yon's chest with the back of his hand. "You get up that hill you'll be owed another gild. Two at once. Ain't going to be time to spend it now anyway, is there? We got a battle to fight."

That much no one could argue with. Men were moving through the woods now, all geared-up and ready. Rustling and rattling, whispering and clattering, forming a kneeling line stretching off both ways between the tree trunks. Sunlight came ragged through the branches, patching on frowning faces, glinting on helmet and drawn sword.

"When were we last in a proper battle, anyway?" muttered Wonderful.

"There was that skirmish down near Ollensand," said Craw.

Yon spat. "Don't hardly call that proper."

"Up in the High Places," said Scorry, finishing the cutting and brushing the hair from Agrick's shoulders. "Trying to prise Ninefingers out of that bloody crack of a valley."

"Seven years ago, was it? Eight?" Craw shuddered at the memory of that nightmare, scores of fighters crowded into a gap in the rock so tight no one could hardly breathe, so tight no one could swing, just prick at each other, knee at each other, bite at each other. Never thought he'd come through that little slice of horror alive. Why the hell would a man choose to risk it again?

He looked at that shallow bowl of crop-filled country between the woods and the Heroes. Looked a bloody long way for an old man with more'n one dodgy leg to run. Glorious charges came up a lot in the songs, but there was one advantage to the defensive no one could deny – the enemy come to you. He shifted from one leg to the other, trying to find the best spot for his knee, and his ankle, and his hip, but a variety of agony was the best he could manage. He snorted to himself. True of life in general, that was.

He looked around to check his dozen were all ready. Got quite the shock to see Black Dow himself down on one knee in the ferns not ten strides distant, axe in one hand, sword in the other, Splitfoot and Shivers and his closest Carls at his back. He'd put aside his furs and finery and looked about like any other man in the line. Except for his fierce grin, like he was looking forward to this as much as Craw was wondering if there was a way free of it.

"Nobody get killed, aye?" He looked around 'em all as he pressed Scorry's hand. They all shook their heads, gave frowns or nervous grins, said "no," or "aye," or "not me." All except Brack, sat staring out towards the trees like he was on his own, sweat beading his big, pale face.

"Don't get killed, eh, Brack?"

The hillman looked at Craw as if he'd only just realised he was there. "What?"

"You all right?"

"Aye." Taking Craw's hand and giving it a clammy press. "'Course."

"That leg good to run on?"

"I've had more pain taking a shit."

Craw raised his brows. "Well, a good shit can be quite punishing, can't it?"

"Chief." Drofd nodded over towards the light beyond the trees and Craw hunched a little lower. There were men moving out there. Mounted men, though only their heads and shoulders showed from where Craw was crouching.

"Union scouts," whispered Wonderful in his ear. Dogman's lads, maybe, worked their way through the fields and the farmhouses and were casting out towards the treeline. The forest the whole length of the valley was crawling with armed and armoured Northmen. It was a wonder they weren't seen yet.

Dow knew it, 'course. He coolly waved his axe over to the east, like he was asking for some beer to be brought over. "Best tell Reachey to go, 'fore they spoil our surprise." The word went out, that same gesture of Dow's arm copied down the line in a wave.

"Here we bloody go again, then," grunted Craw between chewing on his nails.

"Here we go," Wonderful forced through tight lips, sword drawn in her hand.

"I'm too old for this shit."

"Yep."

"Should've married Colwen."

"Aye."

"High time I retired."

"True."

"Could you stop fucking agreeing with me?"

"Ain't that the point of a Second? Support the Chief, no matter what! So I agree. You're too old and you should've married Colwen and retired."

Craw sighed as he offered his hand. "My thanks for your support."

She gave it a squeeze. "Always."

The deep, low blast of Reachey's horn throbbed out from the east. Seemed to make the earth buzz, tickle at the roots of Craw's hair. More horns, then came the feet, like distant thunder mixed with metal. He strained forwards, peering between the black tree trunks, trying to get a glimpse of Reachey's men. Could hardly see more than a few of Osrung's roofs across the sun-drenched fields. Then the war cries started, floating out over the valley, echoing through the trees like ghosts. Craw felt his skin tingling, part fear at what was coming and part wanting to spring up and add his own voice to the clamour.

"Soon enough," he whispered, licking his lips as he stood, hardly noticing the pain in his leg no more.

"I'd say so." Whirrun came up beside him, Father of Swords drawn and held under the crosspiece, his other hand pointing towards the Heroes. "Do you see that, Craw?" Looked like there might be men moving at the top of the green slopes. Gathering around a standard, maybe. "They're coming down. Going to be a happy meeting with Golden's lads out in those fields, ain't it?" He gave his soft, high chuckle. "A happy meeting."

Craw slowly shook his head. "Ain't you worried at all?"

"Why? Didn't I say? Shoglig told me the time and place of my death, and—"

"It's not here and it's not now, aye, only about ten thousand bloody times." Craw leaned in to whisper. "Did she tell you whether you'd get both your legs cut off here, though?"

"No, that she didn't," Whirrun had to admit. "But what difference would that make to my life, will you tell me? You can still sit around a fire and talk shit with no legs."

"Maybe they'll cut your arms off too."

"True. If that happens . . . I'll have to at least consider retirement. You're a good man, Curnden Craw." And Whirrun poked him in the ribs. "Maybe I'll pass the Father of Swords on to you, if you're still breathing when I cross to the distant shore."

Craw snorted. "I ain't carrying that bastard thing around."

"You think I *chose* to carry it? Daguf Col picked me out for the task, on his death-pyre after the Shanka tore out his innards. Purplish."

"What?"

"His innards. It has to go to someone, Craw. Ain't you the one always saying there's a right way to do things? Has to go to someone."

They stood in silence for a moment longer, peering into the brightness beyond the trees, the wind stirring the leaves and making them rustle, shaking a few dry bits of green down onto the spears, and helmets, and shoulders of all those men kneeling in the brush. Birds chirping in the branches, tweet bloody tweet, and even quieter the distant screaming of Reachey's charge.

Men were moving on the eastern flank of the Heroes. Union men, coming down. Craw rubbed his sweaty palms together, and drew his sword. "Whirrun."

"Aye?"

"You ever wonder if Shoglig might've been wrong?"

"Every bloody fight I get into."

Devoutly to be Wished

Your August Majesty,

General Jalenhorm's division has reached the town of Osrung, seized the crossings of the river with the usual focused competence, and the Sixth and Rostod Regiments have taken up a strong position on a hill the Northmen call the Heroes. From its summit one receives a commanding view of the country for miles around, including the all-important road north to Carleon, but, aside from a dead fire, we have seen no sign of the enemy.

The roads continue to be our most stubborn antagonists. The leading elements of General Mitterick's division have reached the valley, but become thoroughly entangled with the rearmost units of Jalenhorm's, making—

Gorst looked up sharply. He had caught the faintest hint of voices on the wind, and though he could not make out the words there was no mistaking a note of frantic excitement.

Probably deluding myself. I have a talent for it. There was no sign of excitement here behind the river. Men were scattered about the south bank, lazing in the sun while their horses grazed contentedly around them. One coughed on a chagga pipe. Another group were singing quietly as they passed around a flask. Not far away their commander, Colonel Vallimir, was arguing with a messenger over the precise meaning of General Jalenhorm's latest order.

"I see that, but the general asks you to hold your current position."

"Hold, by all means, but on the road? Did he not mean for us to cross the river? Or at least arrange ourselves on the bank? I have lost one battalion across a bog and now the other is in everyone's way!" Vallimir pointed out a dust-covered captain whose company was stalled in grumbling column further down the road. Possibly one of the companies the regiments on the hill were missing. *Or not.* The captain was not offering the information and no one was seeking it out. "The general cannot have meant for us to sit *here,* surely you see that!"

"I do see that," droned the messenger, "but the general asks you to hold your current position."

Only the usual random incompetence. A team of bearded diggers tramped past in perfect unison, shovels shouldered and faces stern. *The most organised body of men I've seen today, and probably his Majesty's most valuable soldiers too.* The army's appetite for holes was insatiable. Fire-pits, grave-pits, latrine-pits, dugouts and dig-ins, ramparts and revetments, ditches and trenches of every shape, depth and purpose imaginable and some that would never come to you in a month of thinking. *Truly the spade is mightier than the sword. Perhaps, instead of blades, generals should wear gilded trowels as the badge of their vocation. So much for excitement.*

Gorst turned his attention back to his letter, wrinkled his lip as he realised he had made an unsightly inkblot and crumpled it angrily in his fist.

Then the wind wafted up again and carried more shouts to his ear. *Do I truly hear it? Or do I only want to so badly that I am imagining it?* But a few of the troopers around him were frowning up towards the hill as well. Gorst's heart was suddenly thumping, his mouth dry. He stood and walked towards the water like a man under a spell, eyes fixed on the Heroes. He thought he could see men moving there now, tiny figures on the hill's grassy flank.

He crunched down the shingle to where Vallimir was standing, still arguing pointlessly over which side of the river his men should be doing nothing on. *I suspect that might soon be irrelevant.* He prayed it would be.

"... But surely the general does not—"

"Colonel Vallimir."

"What?"

"You should ready your men."

"I should?"

Gorst did not for a moment take his eyes from the Heroes. From the silhouettes of soldiers on the eastern slope. A considerable body of them. No messengers had crossed the shallows from Marshal Kroy. Which meant the only reason he could see for so many men to be leaving the hill was ... *an attack by the Northmen elsewhere. An attack, an attack, an attack...*

He realised he was still gripping his half-finished letter white-knuckle hard. He let the crumpled paper flutter down into the river, to be carried spinning away by the current. More voices came, even more shrill than before, no question now that they were real.

"That sounds like shouting," said Vallimir.

A fierce joy had begun to creep up Gorst's throat and made his voice rise higher than ever. He did not care. "Get them ready now."

"To do what?"

Gorst was already striding towards his horse. "Fight."

Casualties

Captain Lasmark thrashed through the barley at something between a brisk walk and a jog, the Ninth Company of the Rostod Regiment toiling after him as best they could, despatched towards Osrung with the ill-defined order to "get at the enemy!" still ringing in their ears.

The enemy were before them now, all right. Lasmark could see scaling ladders against the mossy logs of the town's fence. He could see missiles flitting up and down. He could see standards flapping in the breeze, a ragged black one over all the rest, the standard of Black Dow himself, the Northern scouts had said. That was when General Jalenhorm had given the order to advance, and made it abundantly clear nothing would change his mind.

Lasmark turned, hoping he wouldn't trip and catch a mouthful of barley, and urged his men forward with what was intended to be a soldierly jerk of the hand.

"On! On! To the town!"

It was no secret General Jalenhorm was prone to poorly considered orders, but saying so would have been terrible form. Usually officers quietly ignored him where possible and creatively interpreted him where not. But there was no room for interpretation in a direct order to attack.

"Steady, men, keep even!"

They kept even to no noticeable degree, indeed in the main they appeared rather ragged and reluctant, and Lasmark could hardly blame them. He didn't much care for charging unsupported into an empty mass of barley himself, especially since a good part of the regiment was still clogged up in the shambles of men and equipment on the bad roads south of the river. But an officer has his duty. He had made representations to Major Popol, and the major had made representations to Colonel Wetterlant of the Sixth, who was ranking officer on the hill. The colonel had appeared too busy to take much notice. The battlefield was no place for independent thought, Lasmark supposed, and perhaps his superiors simply knew better than he did.

Alas, experience did not support that conclusion.

"Careful! Watch the treeline!"

The treeline was some distance away to the north and seemed to Lasmark particularly gloomy and threatening. He did not care to imagine how many men could be concealed in its shadows. But then he thought that whenever he saw woods, and the North was bloody full of them. It was unclear what good watching them would do. Besides, there was no turning back now. On their right, Captain Vorna was urging his company ahead of the rest of the regiment, desperate to get into the action, as ever, so he could go home with a chestful of medals and spend the balance of his life boasting.

"That fool Vorna's going to pull us all out of formation," growled Sergeant Lock.

"The captain is simply obeying orders!" snapped Lasmark and then, under his breath, "The arsehole. Forward, men, at the double!" If the Northmen did come, the worst thing of all would be to leave gaps in the line.

They upped the pace, all tiring, men occasionally catching a boot and sprawling in the crops, their order fraying with every stride. They might have been half way between the hill and the town now, Major Popol in the lead on horseback, waving his sabre and bellowing inaudible encouragements.

"Sir!" roared Lock. "Sir!"

"I bloody know," gasped Lasmark, no breath to spare for moaning now, "I can't hear a word he's...oh."

He saw what Lock was desperately stabbing towards with his drawn sword and felt a horrible wave of cold surprise. There is a gulf of difference, after all, between expecting the worst and seeing it happen. Northmen had broken from the woods and were rushing across the pastures towards them. It was hard to tell how many from this angle – the dipping ground was cut up by ditches and patchy hedgerows – but Lasmark felt himself go colder yet as his eyes registered the width of their front, the glimmer of metal, the dots of colour that were their painted shields.

The Rostod Regiment was outnumbered. Several companies were still following Popol blithely off towards Osrung where even more Northmen waited. Others had stopped, aware of the approaching threat on their left and seeking desperately to form lines. The Rostod Regiment was heavily outnumbered, and out of formation, and caught unsupported in the open.

"Halt!" he screamed, rushing into the barley ahead of his company, spinning about and throwing his arms up at his men. "Form line! Facing north!"

That was the best thing to do, wasn't it? What else could they do? His soldiers began to perform a shambolic mockery of a wheel, some faces purposeful, others panicked as they scrambled into position.

Lasmark drew his sword. He'd picked it up cheap, an antique, really, the hilt was prone to rattle. He'd paid less for it than he had for his dress hat. That seemed a foolish decision now. But then one sword looked much like another and Major Popol had been very particular about the appearance of his officers on parade. They were not on parade now, more the pity. Lasmark glanced over his shoulder, found he was chewing so hard at his lip he could taste blood. The Northmen were closing swiftly. "Archers, ready your bows, spearmen to the—"

The words froze in his throat. Cavalry had emerged from behind a village even further to their left. A considerable body of cavalry, bearing down on their flank, hooves threshing up a pall of dust. He heard the gasps of alarm, felt the mood shift from worried resolve to horror.

"Steady!" he shouted, but his own voice quavered. When he turned, many of his men were already running. Even though there was nowhere to run to. Even though their chances running were even worse than they were fighting. A calm assessment of the odds was evidently not foremost in their minds. He saw the other companies falling apart, scattering. He caught a glimpse of Major Popol bouncing in his saddle as he rode full tilt for the river, no longer interested in presentation. Perhaps if captains had horses Lasmark would have been right beside him. But captains didn't get horses. Not in the Rostod Regiment. He really should have joined a regiment where the captains got horses, but then he could never have afforded one. He'd had to borrow the money to purchase his captaincy at an outrageous interest and had nothing to spare...

The Northmen were already horrifyingly close, breaking through the nearest hedgerow. He could pick out faces across their line. Snarling, screaming, grinning faces. Like animals, weapons raised high as they bounded on through the barley. Lasmark took a few steps backwards without thinking. Sergeant Lock stood beside him, his jaw muscles clenched.

"Shit, sir," he said.

Lasmark could only swallow and ready himself as his men flung down their weapons around him. As they turned and ran for the river or the hill, too far, far too far away. As the makeshift line of his company and the company beside them dissolved leaving only a few knots of the most stunned and hard-bitten to face the Northmen. He could see how many there were, now. Hundreds of them. Hundreds upon hundreds. A flung spear impaled a man beside him with a thud, and he fell screaming. Lasmark stared at him for a moment. Stelt. He'd been a baker.

He looked up at the tide of howling men, open-mouthed. You hear about this kind of thing, of course, but you assume it won't happen to you. You assume you're more important than that. He'd done none of the things he'd promised himself he'd do by the time he was thirty. He wanted to drop his sword and sit down. Caught sight of his ring and lifted his hand to look at it. Emlin's face carved into the stone. Didn't look likely he'd be coming back for her now. Probably she'd marry that cousin of hers after all. Marrying cousins, a deplorable business.

Sergeant Lock charged forward, wasted bravery, hacked a lump from the edge of a shield. The shield had a bridge painted on it. He chopped at it again, just as another Northman ran up and hit him with an axe. He was knocked sideways, then back the other way by a sword that left a long scratch across his helmet and a deep cut across his face. He spun, arms up like a dancer, then was barged over in the rush and lost in the barley.

Lasmark sprang at the shield with the bridge, for some reason barely taking note of the man behind it. Perhaps he wanted to pretend there was no man behind it. His sword instructor would have been livid with him. Before he got there a spear caught his breastplate, sent him stumbling. The point scraped past and he swung at the man who thrust it, an ugly-looking fellow with a badly broken nose. The sword split his skull open and brains flew out. It was surprisingly easy to do. Swords are heavy and sharp, he supposed, even cheap ones.

There was a clicking sound and everything turned over, mud thumped and barley tangled him. One of his eyes was dark. There was a ringing, stupidly loud, as if his head was the clapper in a great bell. He tried to get up but the world was spinning. None of the things he'd promised to do by the time he was thirty. Oh. Except join the army.

The Southerner tried to push himself up and Lightsleep knocked him on the back of the head with his mace and bonked his helmet in. One boot kicked a little and he was done.

"Lovely." The rest of the Union men were all surrounded and going down fast or scattering like a flock o' starlings, just like Golden said they would. Lightsleep knelt, tucked his mace under his arm and started trying to twist a nice-looking ring off the dead Southerner's finger. Couple of other lads were claiming their prizes, one was screaming with blood running down his face, but, you know, it's a battle, ain't it? If everyone came out smiling there'd be no point. Away south Golden's riders were mopping up, driving the fleeing Southerners to the river.

"Turn for the hill!" Scabna was bellowing, pointing at it with his axe, the smug arse. "To the hill, you bastards!"

"You turn for the hill," grunted Lightsleep, legs still sore from all that running, throat sore from all that screaming besides. "Hah!" Finally got the Union lad's ring off. Held it up to the light and frowned. Just some polished rock with a face cut into it, but he guessed it might fetch a couple of silvers. Tucked it into his jerkin. Took the lad's sword for good measure and stuck it through his belt, though it was a light little toothpick of a thing and the hilt rattled.

"Get on!" Scabna dragged one scavenger up and booted him in the arse to set him going. "Bloody get on!"

"All right, all right!" Lightsleep jogged on after the others, towards the hill. Upset at not getting the chance to go through the Southerners' pockets, maybe get his boots off. It'd all be swept by the pickers and the women following after now. Beggar bastards too cowardly to fight, turning a profit out of other men's work. A disgrace, but he guessed there was no stopping it. Facts of life, like flies and bad weather.

There were Union men up on the Heroes, he could see metal glinting round the drystone wall near the top, spears pricking the sky. He kept his shield up, peering over the rim. Didn't want to get stuck with one of those evil little arrows they used. Get stuck with one o' those, you won't never get yourself unstuck.

"Will you look at that," Scabna grunted.

Now they'd climbed a little higher they could see all the way to the woods up north, and the land between was full of men. Black Dow's Carls, and Tenways', and Ironhead's too. Thralls surging after. Thousands of 'em, all streaming across towards the Heroes. Lightsleep had never seen so many fighters in one place, not even when he fought with Bethod's army. Not at the Cumnur, or Dunbrec, or in the High Places. He'd half a mind to let 'em take the Heroes while he hung back, maybe pleading a twisted ankle, but he weren't going to raise a sharp dowry for his daughters on a cheap ring and a little sword, now, was he?

They hopped over a ditch patched with brown puddles and were out of the trampled crops at the foot of the slope. "Up the hill, you bastards!" screeched Scabna, waving his axe.

Lightsleep had swallowed about enough of that fool's carping, only Chief 'cause he was some friend to one of Golden's sons. He twisted sideways, snarling, "You get up the fucking hill, you—"

There was a thud and an arrowhead stuck out of his jerkin. He spent a silent moment just staring at it, then he took a great whooping breath in and screamed. "Ah, *fuck*!" He whimpered, shuddered, pain stabbing into his armpit as he tried to breathe again, coughed blood down his front, dropped on his knees.

Scabna stared at him, shield up to cover them both. "Lightsleep, what the hell?"

"Bloody...I'm stuck right...through." He had to spit blood out, gurgling with every word. He couldn't kneel any more, it was hurting him too much. He slumped over on his side. Seemed a shitty way to go back to the mud, but maybe they all are. Boots hammered around him as men started thumping up that hill, spraying spots of dirt in his face.

Scabna knelt, started to unbutton Lightsleep's jerkin. "Let's have a look here."

Lightsleep couldn't move hardly. Everything was going blurry. "By the... dead, it...hurts."

"Bet it does. Where did you put that ring?"

Gaunt lowered his bow, watched a few Northmen in the crowd topple over as the rest of the volley flickered down into them. From this height, the bolts from a heavy flatbow could split their shields and punch through chain mail easily as a lady's gown. One of them threw his weapons down and ran off hooting, clutching his stomach, left a gently curving trail through the crops. Gaunt had no way of knowing if his own bolt had found a mark or not, but it hardly mattered. It was all about quantity. Crank, load, level, shoot, crank, load...

"Come on, lads!" he shouted at the men around him. "Shoot! Shoot!"

"By the Fates," he heard Rose whisper, voice all choked off, pointing a wavering forefinger towards the north. The enemy were still pouring from the trees in fearsome numbers. The fields were crawling with them already, surging south towards the hill in a dully twinkling tide. But it took more than a pack of angry apes to make Sergeant Gaunt nervy. He'd watched the numberless Gurkish charge their little hill at Bishak and he'd cranked his flatbow just as hard as he could for the best part of an hour and in the end he'd watched them all run back again. Apart from those they left peppered in heaps. He grabbed Rose by the shoulder and steered him back to the wall.

"Never mind about that. The next bolt is all that matters."

"Sergeant." And Rose bent over his bow again, pale but set to his task.

"Crank, lads, crank!" Gaunt turned his own at a nice, measured pace, all oiled and clean and working smoothly. Not too fast, not too slow, making sure he did the job right. He fished out another bolt, frowning to himself. No more than ten left in his quiver. "What happened to that ammunition?" he roared over his shoulder, and then at his own people, "Pick your targets, nice and careful!" And he stood, levelled his bow, stock pressing into his shoulder.

The sight below gave a moment's pause, even to a man of his experience. The foremost Northmen had reached the hill and were charging up, slow-ing on the grassy slope but showing no sign of stopping. Their war cry got worryingly louder as he came up from behind the wall, the vague keening becoming a shrill howl.

He gritted his teeth, aiming low. Squeezed the trigger, felt the jolt, string humming. He saw where this one went, thudding straight into a shield and knocking the man who held it over backwards. Rattle and pop as a dozen or more bows went on his left, two or three Northmen dropping, one shot in the face, going over backwards and his axe spinning into the blue sky.

"That's the recipe, lads, keep shooting! Just load and—" There was a loud click beside him. Gaunt felt a searing pain in his neck, and all the strength went out of his legs.

It was an accident. Rose had been tinkering with the trigger of his flatbow for a week or longer, trying to stop it wobbling, worried it might go off at the wrong moment, but he'd never been any good with machines. Why they'd made him a bowman he'd no clue. Would have been better off with a spear. Sergeant Gaunt would have been a lot better off if they'd given Rose a spear, that was a fact most definite. It just went off as he was lifting it, the point of the metal lath leaving a long scratch down his arm. As he was cursing at that, he looked sideways, and Gaunt had the bolt through his neck.

They stared at each other for a moment, then Gaunt's eyes rolled down, crossed, towards the flights, and he dropped his own bow and reached up to his neck. His quivering fingers came away bloody. "Gurgh," he said. "Bwuthers." And his lids flickered, and he dropped all of a sudden, his skull smacking against the wall and knocking his helmet skewed across his face.

"Gaunt? Sergeant Gaunt?" Rose slapped his cheek as though trying to wake him from an unauthorised nap, smeared blood across his face. There was more and more blood welling out of him all the time. Out of his nose, out of the neat slit where the bolt entered his neck. Oily dark, almost black, and his skin so white.

"He's dead!" Rose felt himself dragged towards the wall. Someone shoved his empty flatbow back into his bloody hands. "Shoot, damn you! Shoot!" A young officer, one of the new ones, Rose couldn't remember his name. Could hardly remember his own name.

"What?"

"Shoot!"

Rose started cranking, aware of other men around him doing the same. Sweating, struggling, cursing, leaning over the wall to shoot. He could hear wounded men screaming, and above that a strange howl. He fumbled a bolt from his quiver, slotted it into the groove, cursing to himself at his trembling fingers, all smeared pink from Gaunt's blood.

He was crying. There were tears streaming down his face. His hands felt very cold, though it wasn't cold. His teeth were chattering. The man beside him threw down his bow and ran towards the top of the hill. There were a lot of men running, ignoring the desperate bellows of their officers.

Arrows flitted down. One went spinning from a steel cap just beside him. Others stuck into the hillside behind the wall. Silent, still, as if they'd suddenly sprung from the ground by magic rather than dropped from the sky. Someone else turned to run, but before he got a step the officer cut him down with his sword.

"For the king!" he squealed, his eyes gone all mad. "For the king!"

Rose had never seen the king. A Northman jumped up on the wall just to his left. He was stabbed with two spears right away, screamed and fell back. The man beside Rose stood, cursing as he raised his flatbow. The top of his head came off and he stumbled, shot his bolt high into the sky. A

Northman sprang over the wall into the gap he left, young-looking, face all twisted up with rage. A devil, screaming like a devil. A Union man came at him with a spear but he turned it away with his shield, swung as he dropped from the wall, axe blade thudding into the man's shoulder and sending blood flying in dark streaks. Northmen were coming over the wall all around. The gap to their left was choked with straining bodies, a tangle of spears, slipping boots ripping at the muddy grass.

Rose's head was full of mad noise, clash and clatter of weapons and armour, war cries and garbled orders and howls of pain all mingled with his own terrified, whimpering breath. He was just staring, bow forgotten. The young Northerner blocked the officer's sword and hit him in the side, twisted him up, chopped into his arm on the next blow, hand flying up bonelessly in its embroidered sleeve. The Northman kicked the officer's legs away and hacked at him on the ground, grin speckled with blood. Another was clambering over the wall beside him, a big face with a black and grey beard, shouting something in a gravelly voice.

A great tall one with long bare arms leaped clean over the jumble of stones, boots flicking at the grass that sprouted from the top, the biggest sword Rose had ever seen raised high. He didn't see how a man could swing a sword so big. The dull blade took an archer in the side, folded him up and sent him tumbling across the hillside in a mist of blood. It was as if Rose's limbs came suddenly unstuck and he turned and ran, was jostled by someone else doing the same, slipped, ankle twisting. He scrambled up, took one lurching stride, and was hit so hard on the back of his head he bit his tongue off.

Agrick hacked the archer between the shoulder-blades to make sure, haft jolting in his raw hand, sticky with blood. He saw Whirrun struggling with a big Union man, hit him in the back of the leg with his axe, made a mess of it and only caught him with the flat, still hard enough to bring him down where Scorry could spear him as he slipped over the wall.

Agrick never saw Union men in numbers before, and they all looked the same, like copies o' one man with the same armour, the same jackets, the same weapons. It was like killing one man over and over. Hardly like killing real people at all. They were running, now, up the slope, scattering from the wall, and he ran after like a wolf after sheep.

"Slow down Agrick, you mad bastard!" Jolly Yon, wheezing at his back, but Agrick couldn't stop. The charge was a great wave and all he could do was be carried along by it, forwards, upwards, get at them who'd killed his brother. On up the hill, Whirrun at the wall behind, the Father of Swords cutting into a knot of Southerners still standing, hacking 'em apart, armour or not. Brack near him, roaring as he swung his hammer.

"On! Fucking on!" Black Dow himself, lips curled from bloody teeth, shaking his axe at the summit, blade flashing red and steel in the sun. Lit a fire in Agrick knowing his leader was there, fighting beside him in the front rank. He came up level with a stumbling Union man, clawing at the slope, hit him in the face with his axe and knocked him shrieking back.

He burst between two of the great stones, head spinning like he was drunk. Blood-drunk, and needing more. Lots of corpses in the circle of grass inside the Heroes. Union men hacked in the back, Northmen stuck with arrows.

Someone shouted, and flatbows clattered, and a few dropped around him but Agrick ran right on, towards a flag in the middle of the Union line, voice hoarse from screaming. He chopped an archer down, broken bow tumbling. Swung at the big Southerner carrying the standard. He caught Agrick's first blow with the flagstaff, got it tangled with the blade. Agrick let go, pulled out his knife and stabbed the standard-bearer overhand though the open face of his helmet. He dropped like a hammered cow, mouth yawning all twisted and silent. Agrick tried to drag the standard from his dead-gripping fists, one hand on the pole, the other on the flag itself.

He heard himself make a weird whoop, sounded like someone else's voice. A half-bald man with grey hair round his ears pulled his arm back and his sword slid out of Agrick's side, scraping the bottom rim of his shield. It had been in him right to the hilt, the blade came out all bloody. Agrick tried to swing his axe but he'd dropped it just before and his knife was stuck in the standard-bearer's face, he just flapped his empty hand around. Something hit him in the shoulder and the world reeled.

He was lying in some dirt. A pile of trampled dirt, in the shadow of one of the stones. He had the torn flag in one hand.

He wriggled, but he couldn't get comfortable.

All numb.

Colonel Wetterlant was still having trouble believing it, but it appeared the King's Own Sixth Regiment was in a great deal of difficulty. The wall, he thought, was lost. Knots of resistance but basically overrun, and North-men were flooding into the circle of stones from the north. Where else would Northmen come from? It had all happened so damnably fast.

"We have to withdraw!" screamed Major Culfer over the din of combat. "There are too many of them!"

"No! General Jalenhorm will bring reinforcements! He promised us—"

"Then where the hell is he?" Culfer's eyes were bulging. Wetterlant would never have had him down as the panicky type. "He's left us here to die, he's—"

Wetterlant simply turned away. "We stand! We stand and fight!" He was a proud man of a proud family, and he would stand. He would stand until the bitter end, if necessary, and die fighting with sword in hand, as his grandfather was said to have done. He would die under the regimental colours. Well, he wouldn't, in fact, because that boy he ran through had torn them from the pole when he fell. But Wetterlant would stand, there was no question. He had often told himself so. Usually while admiring his reflection in the mirror after dressing for one official function or another. Straightening his sash.

These were very different circumstances, however, it had to be admitted. No one was wearing a sash, not even him. And there was the blood, the corpses, the spreading panic. The unearthly wailing of the Northmen, who were flooding through the gaps between the stones and into the trampled circle of grass at their centre. Virtually a constant press of them now, as far as Wetterlant could see. The difficulty with a ring of standing stones as a defensive position is undoubtedly the gaps between them. The Union line, if you could use the phrase about an improvised clump of soldiers and offi-cers fighting desperately wherever they stood, was bulging back under the pressure, in imminent danger of dissolving all together, and with nowhere defensible to dissolve back to.

Orders. He was in command, and had to give orders. "Er!" he shouted, brandishing his sword. "Er..." It had all happened so very, very fast. What orders would Lord Marshal Varuz have given at a time like this? He had always admired Varuz. Unflappable.

Culfer gave a thin scream. A narrow split had appeared in his shoulder, right down to his chest, splinters of white bone showing through it. Wet-terlant wanted to tell him not to scream in a manner so unbefitting of an officer in the King's Own. A scream like that might be good enough for one of the levy regiments, but in the Sixth he expected a manly roar. Culfer almost gracefully subsided to the ground, blood bubbling from the wound, and a large Northman stepped up with an axe in his fist and began to cleave him into pieces.

Wetterlant was vaguely conscious that he should have jumped to the aid of his second-in-command. But he found himself unable to move, fascinated by the Northman's expression of businesslike calm. As if he was a bricklayer getting a difficult stretch of wall to meet his high standards. Eventually satisfied by the number of pieces he had made of Culfer – who still, impossibly, seemed to be making a quiet squealing sound – the Northman turned to look at Wetterlant.

The far side of his face was crossed by a giant scar, a bright ball of dead metal in his eye socket.

Wetterlant ran. There was not the slightest thought involved. His mind was turned off like a candle snuffed out. He ran faster than he had in thirty years or more, faster than he thought a man of his years possibly could. He sprang between two of the ancient stones and jolted down the hillside, boots thrashing at the grass, vaguely conscious of other men running all around him, of screams and hisses and threats, of arrows whipping through the air about his head, shoulders itching with the inevitability of death at his back.

He passed the Children, then a column of dumbstruck soldiers who had been on their way up the hill and were just now scattering back down it. His foot found a small depression and the shock made his knee buckle. He bit his tongue, flew headlong, hit the ground and tumbled over and over, no way of stopping himself. He slid into shadow, finally coming to an ungainly stop in a shower of leaves, twigs, dirt.

He rolled stiffly over, groaning. His sword was gone, his right hand red raw. Twisted from his grip as he fell. The blade his father had given him the day he received his commission in the King's Own. So proud. He wondered if his father would have been proud now. He was in among trees. The orchard? He had abandoned his regiment. Or had they abandoned him? The rules of military behaviour, so unshakeable a foundation until a few moments ago, had vanished like smoke in a breeze. It had happened so fast.

His wonderful Sixth Regiment, his life's work, built out of copious polish, and rigorous drill, and unflinching discipline, utterly shattered in a few insane moments. If any survived it would be those who had chosen to run first. The rawest recruits and most craven cowards. And he was one of them. His first instinct was to ask Major Culfer for his opinion. He almost opened his mouth to do it, then realised the man had been butchered by a lunatic with a metal eye.

He heard voices, the sounds of men crashing through the trees, shrank against the nearest trunk, peering around it like a scared child over their bedclothes. Union soldiers. He shuddered with relief, stumbled from his hiding place, waving one arm.

"You! Men!"

They snapped around, but not at attention. In fact they stared at him as if he was a ghost risen from a grave. He thought he knew their faces, but it seemed they had turned suddenly from the most disciplined of soldiers into trembling, mud-smeared animals. Wetterlant had never been afraid of his own men before, had taken their obedience entirely for granted, but he had no choice but to blather on, his voice shrill with fear and exhaustion.

"Men of the Sixth! We must hold here! We must—"

"Hold?" one of them screeched, and hit Wetterlant with his sword. Not a full-blooded blow, only a jarring knock in the arm that sent him sliding onto his side, gasping more from shock than pain. He cringed as the soldier half-raised the sword again. Then one of the others squealed and scrambled away, and soon they were all running. Wetterlant looked over his shoulder, saw shapes moving through the trees. Heard shouting. A deep voice, and the words were in Northern.

Fear clutched him again and he whimpered, floundered through the slick of twigs and fallen leaves, the slime of rotten fruit smeared up his trouser leg, his own terrified breath echoing in his ears. He paused at the edge of the trees, the back of one sleeve pressed to his mouth. There was blood on his dangling hand. Seeing the torn cloth on his arm made him want to be sick. Was it torn cloth, or torn flesh?

He could not stay here. He would never make it to the river. But he could not stay here. It had to be now. He broke from the undergrowth, running for the shallows. There were other runners everywhere, most of them without weapons. Mad, desperate faces, eyes rolling. Wetterlant saw the cause of their terror. Horsemen. Spread out across the fields, converging on the shallows, herding the fleeing Union soldiers southwards. Cutting them down, trampling them, their howls echoing across the valley. He ran on, ran on, stumbling forwards, snatched another look. A rider was bearing down on him, he could see the curve of his teeth in a tangled beard.

Wetterlant tried to run faster but he was so tired. Lungs burning, heart burning, breath whooping, the land jerking and see-sawing wildly with every step, the glittering hint of the shallows getting gradually closer, the thunder of hooves behind him—

And he was suddenly on his side, in the mud, an unspeakable agony burning out from his back. A crushing pressure on his chest as if there were rocks piled on it. He managed to move his head to look down. There was something glinting there. Something shining on his jacket in the midst of the dirt. Like a medal. But he hardly deserved a medal for running away.

"How silly," he wheezed, and the words tasted like blood. He found to his surprise, and then to his mounting horror, that he could not breathe. It had all happened so very, very fast.

Sutt Brittle tossed the splintered shaft of his spear away. The rest was stuck in the back of that running fool. He'd run fast, for an old man, but not near as fast as Sutt's horse, which was no surprise. He hauled the old sword out, keeping the reins in his shield hand, and dug in his heels. Golden had promised a hundred gold coins to the first of his Named Men across the river, and Brittle wanted that money. Golden had showed it, in an iron box. Let 'em feel it, even, everyone's eyes on fire with looking at it. Strange coins, a head stamped on each side. Came from the desert, far away, someone had said. Sutt didn't know how Glama Golden came by desert coins, but he couldn't say he much cared either.

Gold was gold.

And this was almost too easy. The Union ran – knackered, stumbling, crying, and Sutt just leaned from the saddle and chopped 'em down, one side then t'other, whack, whack, whack. It was this Sutt got into the business for, not the skulking around and scouting they'd been doing, the pulling back over and over, trying to find the right spot and never getting there. He hadn't joined the grumblers, though, not him. He'd said Black Dow would bring 'em a red day afore too long, and here it was.

All the killing was slowing him down, though. Frowning over into the wind on his left he saw he weren't quite at the front of the pack no more.

Feathers had pulled ahead, bent low over his saddle, not bothering about the work and just riding straight through the rabbiting Southerners and down the bank into the shallows.

Sutt was damned if he was going to let a liar like Hengul Feathers steal his hundred coins. He dug his heels harder, wind and mane whipping at his eyes, tongue wedged into the big gap in his teeth. He plunged down into the river, water showering, Union men flailing up to their hips around him. He urged his horse on, eyes for nothing but Feathers' back as he trotted up onto the shingle and—

Went flying out of his saddle, war whoop cut off in a spray of blood.

Brittle weren't sure whether to be pleased or not as Feathers' corpse flopped over and over into the water. On the sunny side it looked like he was at the front of Golden's whole crew now. On the shady, there was a strange-looking bastard bearing down on him, well armoured and well horsed, short sword and the reins in one hand, long sword ready in the other, catching the sun and glistening with Feathers' blood. He had a plain round helmet with a slot in the front to see through and nothing but a big mouthful of gritted teeth showing below it. Riding at Golden's cavalry all on his own while the rest of the Union fled the other way.

In the midst of all Sutt's greed and bloodlust he felt this niggling moment of doubt made him check his horse to the right, get his shield between him and this steel-headed bastard. Just as well, 'cause a twinkling later his sword crashed into Sutt's shield and nearly ripped it off his arm. The shorter one came stabbing at him before the noise had faded, would've stuck him right in the chest if his own sword hadn't got in the way by blind chance.

By the dead he was fast, this bastard. Sutt couldn't believe how fast he was in all that armour. The swords came flickering out of nowhere. Sutt managed to block the short blade, the force of it near dumping him from the saddle. Tried to swing himself as he rocked back, screaming at the top of his lungs. "Die, you fucking—Uh?" His right hand wasn't there. He stared at the stump, blood squirting out of it. How had that happened? He saw something at the corner of his eye, felt a great crunching in his chest, and his howl of pain was cut off in a squawk of his own.

He was flung straight out of his saddle, no breath in him, and splashed down in the cold water where there was nothing but bubbles gurgling around his face.

* * *

Even before the gap-toothed Northman had toppled from his horse, Gorst had twisted in his saddle and brought his long steel blurring down on the other side. The next one had a patchy fur across his shoulders, managed to raise his axe to parry, but it was wasted effort. Gorst's blow splintered the haft and drove the pick on the back deep into him below the collarbone, the point of Gorst's long steel opening a gaping red wound in his neck. *A touch to me.*

The man was just opening his mouth, presumably to scream, when Gorst stabbed him through the side of the head with his short steel so the point came out of his cheek. *And another.* Gorst wrenched it free in time to deflect a sword with his buckler, shrug the blade harmlessly off his armoured shoulder. Someone clutched at him. Gorst smashed his nose apart with the pommel of his long steel. Smashed it again and drove it deep into his head.

They were all around him. The world was a strip of brightness through the slot in his helmet filled with plunging horses, and flailing men, and flashing weapons, his own swords darting by instinct to block, chop, stab, jerking the reins at the same time and dragging his panicked mount about in mindless circles. He swatted another man from his saddle, twisted chain mail rings flying like dust from a beaten carpet. He parried a sword and the tip glanced from his helmet and made his ears ring. Before its owner could swing again he was cut across the back and fell shrieking forward. Gorst caught him in a hug and bundled him down among the thrashing hooves.

Union cavalry were splashing through the shallows around him, meeting the Northmen as they charged in from the north bank and mingling in a clattering, shattering melee. Vallimir's men. *How nice that you could join us!* The river became a mass of stomping hooves and spray, flying metal and blood, and Gorst hacked his way through it, teeth ground together in a frozen smile. *I am home.*

He lost his short steel in the madness, stuck in someone's back and wrenched from his hand. It might have been a Union man. He was a long way from caring. He could scarcely hear a thing apart from his own breath, his own grunts, his own girlish squeaks as he swung, and swung, and swung, denting armour, smashing bone, splitting flesh, every jolting impact up his arm a burning thrill. Every blow like a swallow to a drunkard, better, and better, but never enough.

He chopped a horse's head half-off. The Northman riding it had a look of comical surprise, a clown in a cheap stage show, still pulling at the reins as his flopping mount collapsed under him. A rider squealed, hands full of his own guts. Gorst backhanded him across the head with his buckler and it tore from his fist with a crash of steel and flew into the air in a fountain of blood and bits of teeth, spinning like a flipped coin. *Heads or tails? Anyone?*

A big Northman sat on a black horse in the midst of the river, chopping around him with an axe. His horned helmet, his armour, his shield, all chased with whorls of gold. Gorst spurred straight through the combat at him, hacking a Northman across the back as he went and dumping another from the saddle by chopping into his horse's hind leg. His long steel was bright red with blood. Slathered with it, like an axle with grease.

It caught the golden shield with a shattering impact, left a deep dent through all that pretty craftsmanship. Gorst chopped at it again and crossed the one scar with another, sent the golden man lurching in his saddle. Gorst lifted his long steel for a finishing blow then felt it suddenly twisted from his hand.

A Northman with a shaggy red beard had knocked it away with a mace and now swung it at Gorst's head. *Bloody rude.* Gorst caught the shaft in one hand, pulled out his dagger in the other and rammed it up under the Northman's jaw to the crosspiece, left it stuck there as he toppled backwards. *Manners, manners.* The golden man had his balance back, standing in the stirrups with his axe raised high.

Gorst clutched hold of him, dragged him into an ungainly embrace between their two jostling horses. The axe came down but the shaft caught Gorst's shoulder and the blade only scraped harmlessly against his backplate. Gorst caught one of the absurd horns on the man's gilded helmet and twisted it, twisted it, twisting his head with it until it was pressed against Gorst's breastplate. The golden man snarled and spluttered, most of the way out of his saddle, one leg caught in his stirrup. He tried to drop his axe and wrestle but it was on a loop around his wrist, snagged on Gorst's armour, his other arm trapped by his battered shield.

Gorst bared his teeth, raised his fist and started punching the man in the face, his gauntlet crunching against one side of the golden helmet. Up and down, up and down, his fist was a hammer and gradually it marked, then dented, then twisted the helmet out of shape until one side of it dug into the man's face. *Even better than the sword.* Crunch, crunch, and it bent further, cutting into his cheek. *More personal.* No need for discussion or justification, for introductions or etiquette, for guilt or excuses. Only the incredible release of violence. So powerful that he felt this golden-armoured man must be his best friend in all the world. *I love you. I love you, and that is why I must smash your head apart.* He was laughing as he pounded his gauntleted knuckles into the man's bloody-blond moustache again. Laughing and crying at once.

Then something hit him in the backplate with a dull clang, his head snapped back and he was out of the saddle, jostled upside down between their two horses, gripped by cold and his helmet full of bubbling river. He came up coughing, water sprayed in his face by thrashing hooves.

The man in the golden armour had floundered to a riderless horse and was dragging himself drunkenly into the saddle. There were corpses everywhere: horses and men, Union and Northman, sprawled on the shingle, bobbing in the ford, carried gently by the soft current. He hardly saw any Union cavalry left. Only Northmen, weapons raised, nudging their horses cautiously towards him.

Gorst fumbled with the buckle on his helmet and dragged it off, the wind shockingly cold on his face. He clambered to his feet, armour leaden with river water. He held his arms out, as if to embrace a dear friend, and smiled as the nearest Northman raised his sword.

"I am ready," he whispered.

"Shoot!" There was a volley of clicks and rattles behind him. The Northman toppled from his saddle, stuck through with flatbow bolts. Another shrieked, axe tumbling as he clapped his hand to a bolt in his cheek. Gorst turned, stupidly, to look over his shoulder. The south bank of the shallows was one long row of kneeling flatbowmen. Another rank stepped between them as they started to reload, knelt and levelled their bows with mechanical precision.

A big man sat on a large grey at the far end of the line. General Jalenhorm. "Second rank!" he roared, slashing his hand down. "Shoot!" Gorst ducked on an instinct, head whipping around as he followed the bolts flickering overhead and into the Northmen, already turning their horses to flee, men and beasts screaming and snorting as they dropped in the shallows.

"Third rank! Shoot!" The hiss and twitter of another volley. A few more fell peppered, one horse rearing and going over backwards, crushing its rider. But most of the rest had made it up the bank and were away into the barley on the other side, tearing off to the north as quickly as they had arrived.

Gorst slowly let his arms drop as the sound of hooves faded and left, aside from the chattering of the water and the moaning of the wounded, an uncanny silence.

Apparently the engagement was over, and he was still alive.

How strangely disappointing.

The Better Part of Valour

By the time Calder pulled up his horse some fifty paces from the Old Bridge, the fighting was over. Not that he was shedding too many tears for having missed his part in it. That had been the point of hanging back.

The sun was starting to sink in the west and the shadows were stretching out towards the Heroes, insects floating lazily above the crops. Calder could almost have convinced himself he was out for an easy ride in the old days, son of the King of the Northmen and master of all he saw. Except for the few corpses of men and horses scattered on the track, one Union soldier spreadeagled on his face with a spear sticking straight up from his back, the dust underneath him stained dark.

It looked like the Old Bridge – a moss-crusted double span of ancient stone that looked as if it was about to collapse under its own weight – had been only lightly held, and when the Union men saw their fellows fleeing from the Heroes they'd pulled back to the other bank just as quickly as ever they could. Calder couldn't say he blamed them.

Pale-as-Snow had found a big rock to sit on, spear dug point first into the ground beside him, his grey horse nibbling at the grass and the grey fur around his shoulders blowing in the breeze. Whatever the weather, he never seemed warm. It took Calder a moment to find the end of his scabbard with the point of his sword – not usually a problem of his – before he sheathed it and sat down beside the old warrior.

"You took your time getting here," said Pale-as-Snow, without looking up.

"I think my horse might be lame."

"Something's lame, all right. You know your brother was right about one thing." He nodded towards Scale, striding about in the open ground at the north end of the bridge, shouting and waving his mace around. He still had his shield in the other fist, a flatbow bolt lodged near the rim. "Northmen won't follow a man reckoned a coward."

"What's that to me?"

"Oh, nothing." Pale-as-Snow's grey eyes showed no sign he was joking. "You're everyone's hero."

White-Eye Hansul was trying to argue with Scale, open hands up for calm. Scale shoved him over onto his back with an ill-tempered flick of his arm and started bellowing again. It looked as though there hadn't been enough fighting for his taste, and he was for pushing on across the river right away to find some more. It looked as though no one else thought that was a very good idea.

Pale-as-Snow gave a resigned sort of sigh, as if this had been happening a lot. "By the dead, but once your brother gets the fire under him it can be hard work putting it out. Maybe you can play at the voice of reason?"

Calder shrugged. "I've played at worse. Here's your shield back." And he tossed it at Pale-as-Snow's stomach so he almost fell off his rock catching it. "Oy! Pinhead!" Calder swaggered towards Scale with hands on his hips. "Pinhead Scale! Brave as a bull, strong as a bull, thick as a bull's arse." Scale's eyes bulged right out of his livid face as they followed him. So did everyone else's, but Calder didn't mind that. He liked nothing better than an audience.

"Good old stupid Scale! Great fighter but, you know...nothing but shit in his head." Calder tapped at his skull as he said it, then slowly stretched out his arm to point up towards the Heroes. "That's what they say about you." Scale's expression grew a touch less furious and a touch more thoughtful, but only a touch. "Up there, at Dow's little wank-parties. Tenways, and Golden, and Ironhead, and the rest. They think you're a fucking idiot." Calder didn't entirely disagree, if it came to that. He leaned in close to

Scale, well within punching range, he was painfully aware. "Why don't you ride on over that bridge, and prove them all right?"

"Fuck them!" barked Scale. "We could get over that bridge and into Adwein. Get astride the Uffrith Road! Cut those Union bastards off at the roots. Get in behind 'em!" He was punching at the air with his shield, trying to stoke his rage up again, but the moment he'd started talking instead of doing he'd lost and Calder had won. Calder knew it, and had to smother his contempt. That was no challenge, though. He'd been hiding contempt around his brother for years.

"Astride the Uffrith Road? Might be half the Union army coming up that road before sunset." Calder looked at Scale's horsemen, no more than ten score and most of their horses ridden out, the foot still hurrying through the fields far behind or stopped at a long wall that reached almost all the way to Skarling's Finger. "No offence to the valour of our father's proud Named Men here, but are you really going to take on countless thousands with this lot?"

Scale gave them a look himself, jaw muscles squirming in the side of his head as he ground his teeth. White-Eye Hansul, who'd picked himself up and was dusting his dented armour down, shrugged his shoulders. Scale flung his mace on the ground. "Shit!"

Calder risked a calming hand on his shoulder. "We were told to take the bridge. We took the bridge. If the Union want it back, they can cross over and fight us for it. On our ground. And we'll be waiting for them. Ready and rested, dug in and close to supplies. Honestly, brother, if Black Dow doesn't kill the pair of us through pure meanness you'll more than likely do it through pure rashness."

Scale took a long breath, and blew it out. He didn't look at all happy. But he didn't look like he was about to tear anyone's head off. "All right, damn it!" He frowned across the river, then back at Calder, then shook off his hand. "I swear, sometimes talking to you is like talking to our father."

"Thanks," said Calder. He wasn't sure it was meant as a compliment, but he took it as one anyway. One of their father's sons had to keep his temper.

Paths of Glory

Corporal Tunny tried to hop from one patch of yellow weed to another, the regimental standard held high above the filth in his left hand, his right already spattered to the shoulder from slips into the scum. The bog was pretty much what Tunny had been expecting. And that wasn't a good thing.

The place was a maze of sluggish channels of brown water, streaked on the surface with multicoloured oil, with rotten leaves, with smelly froth, ill-looking rushes scattered at random. If you put down your foot and it only squelched in to the ankle, you counted yourself lucky. Here and there some species of hell-tree had wormed its leathery roots deep enough to stay upright and hang out a few lank leaves, festooned with beards of brown creeper and sprouting with outsize mushrooms. There was a persistent croaking that seemed to come from everywhere and nowhere. Some cursed variety of bird, or frog, or insect, but Tunny couldn't see any of the three. Maybe it was just the bog itself, laughing at them.

"Forest of the fucking damned," he whispered. Getting a battalion across this was like driving a herd of sheep through a sewer. And, as usual, for reasons he could never understand, him and the four rawest recruits in the Union army were playing vanguard.

"Which way, Corporal Tunny?" asked Worth, doubled up around his guts.

"Stick to the grassy bits, the guide said!" Though there wasn't much around that an honest man could've called grass. Not that there were many honest men around either. "Have you got a rope, boy?" he asked Yolk, struggling through the mulch beside him, a long smear of mud down his freckled cheek.

"Left 'em with the horses, Corporal."

"Of course. Of course we bloody did." By the Fates, how Tunny wished he'd been left with the horses. He took one step and cold water rushed over the top of his boot like a clammy hand clamping around his foot. He was just setting up to have a proper curse at that when a shrill cry came from behind.

"Ah! My boot!"

Tunny spun round. "Keep quiet, idiot!" Totally failing to keep quiet himself. "The Northmen'll hear us in bloody Carleon!"

But Klige wasn't listening. He'd strayed well away from the rushes and left one of his boots behind, sucked off by the bog. He was wading out to get it, sliding in up to his thighs. Yolk snickered at him as he started delving into the slime.

"Leave it, Klige, you fool!" snapped Tunny, floundering back towards him.

"Got it!" The bog made a squelching suck as Klige dragged his boot free, looking like it was caked in black porridge. "Whoa!" He lurched one way, then the other. "Whoa!" And he was in up to his waist, face flipped from triumph to panic in an instant. Yolk snickered again, then suddenly realised what was happening.

"Who's got a rope?" shouted Lederlingen. "Someone get a rope!" He floundered out towards Klige, grabbing hold of the nearest piece of tree, a leafless twig thrust out over the mire. "Take my hand! Take my hand!"

But Klige was panicking, thrashing around and only working himself deeper. He went down with shocking speed, face tipped back, only just above the level of the filth, a big black leaf stuck across one cheek.

"Help me!" he squealed, stretching fingers still a good stride short of Lederlingen's. Tunny slopped up, shoving the flagstaff out towards Klige. "Help murghhh—" His bulging eyes rolled towards Tunny, then they were lost, his floating hair vanished, a few bubbles broke on the foetid surface, and that was it. Tunny poked at the mush uselessly, but Klige was gone. Aside from his rescued boot, floating slowly away, no trace he'd ever existed.

They struggled the rest of the way in silence, the other recruits looking stunned, Tunny with his jaw furiously clenched, all sticking to the tumps of yellow weed as close as new foals to their mothers. Soon enough the ground started to rise, the trees turned from twisted swamp monsters to firs and oaks. Tunny leaned the filthy standard against a trunk and stood, hands on hips. His magnificent boots were ruined.

"Shit!" he snarled. "Fucking *shit*!"

Yolk sank down in the muck, staring into nowhere, white hands trembling. Lederlingen licked his pale lips, breathing hard and saying nothing. Worth was nowhere to be seen, though Tunny thought he could hear someone groaning in the undergrowth. Even the drowning of a comrade couldn't delay the working of that lad's troublesome bowels. If anything it had made them accelerate. Forest walked up, caked to the knees in black mud. They all were caked, daubed, spattered with it, and Tunny in particular.

"I hear we lost one of our recruits." Forest had said it often enough that he could say it deadpan. That he had to.

"Klige," Tunny squeezed between gritted teeth. "Was going to be a weaver. We lost a man in a fucking *bog*. Why are we here, even?" The bottom half of his coat was heavy with oily filth and he peeled it off and flung it down.

"You did the best you could."

"I know," snapped Tunny.

"Nothing more you—"

"He had some of my bloody gear in his pack! Eight good bottles of brandy! You know how much that could've made me?"

There was a pause.

"Eight bottles." Forest slowly nodded. "Well, you're a piece of work, Corporal Tunny, you know that? Twenty-six years in his Majesty's army but you can always find a way to surprise me. I tell you what, you can get up that rise and find out where in the pit of hell we are while I try and get the rest of the battalion across without sinking any more bottles. Maybe that'll take your mind off the depth of your loss." And he stalked away, hissing to some men who were trying to heave a trembling mule out of the knee-deep muck.

Tunny stood fuming a moment longer, but fuming was going to do no good. "Yolk, Latherlister, Worth, get over here!"

Yolk stood up, wide-eyed. "Worth... Worth—"

"Still squirting," said Lederlingen, busy rooting through his pack and hanging various sodden items up on branches to dry.

"'Course he is. What else would he be doing? You wait for him, then. Yolk, follow me and try not to bloody die." He stalked off up the slope, sodden trousers chafing horribly, kicking bits of fallen wood out of his way.

"Shouldn't we be keeping quiet?" whispered Yolk. "What if we run into the enemy?"

"Enemy!" snorted Tunny. "Probably we'll run into the other bloody battalion, just trotted over the Old Bridge and up a path and got there ahead of us all nice and dry. That'll make a fine bloody picture, won't it?"

"Couldn't say, sir," muttered Yolk, dragging himself up the muddy slope almost on all fours.

"Corporal Tunny! And I wasn't soliciting an opinion. Some big bloody grins they'll have when they see the state of us. Some laugh they'll all have!" They were coming to the edge of the trees. Beyond the branches he could see the faint outline of the distant hill, the stones sticking from the top. "At least we're in the right bloody place," and then, under his breath, "to get wet, sore, hungry and poor, that is. General fucking Jalenhorm, I swear, a soldier expects to get shat on, but this…"

Beyond the trees the ground sloped down, studded with old stumps and new saplings where some woodcutters had once been busy, their slumping sheds abandoned and already rotting back to the earth. Beyond them a gentle river babbled, hardly more than a stream, really, flowing south to empty into the nightmare of swamp they'd just crossed. There was an earthy overhang on the far bank, then a grassy upslope on which some boundary-conscious farmer seemed to have built an irregular drystone wall. Above the wall Tunny saw movement. Spears, their tips glinting in the fading light. So he'd been right. The other battalion were there ahead of them. He just couldn't work out why they were on the north side of the wall…

"What is it, Corporal—"

"Didn't I tell you to stay bloody quiet?" Tunny dragged Yolk down into the bushes and pulled out his eyeglass, a good three-part brass one he won in a game of squares with an officer from the Sixth. He edged forwards, finding a gap in the undergrowth. The ground rose sharply on the other side of the stream then dipped away, but there were spears behind the whole length of wall that he could see. He glimpsed helmets too. Some smoke, perhaps from a cook-fire. Then he saw a man wading out into the stream, waving a fishing rod made from a spear and some twine, wild-haired and stripped to the waist, and very definitely not a Union soldier. Perhaps only two hundred strides from where they were squatting in the brush.

"Uh-oh," he breathed.

"Are those Northmen?" whispered Yolk.

"Those are a lot of bloody Northmen. And we're right on their flank." Tunny handed his eyeglass over, half-expecting the lad to look through the wrong end.

"Where did they come from?"

"I'd guess the North, wouldn't you?" He snatched back his eyeglass.

"Someone's going to have to go back. Let someone higher up the dunghill know the bother we're in here."

"They must know already, though. They'll have run into the Northmen themselves, won't they?" Yolk's voice, never particularly calm, had taken on a slightly hysterical note. "I mean, they must've! They must know!"

"Who knows what who knows, Yolk? It's a battle." As he said the words, Tunny realised with mounting worry they were true. If there were Northmen behind that wall, there must have been fighting. It was a battle, all right. Maybe the start of a big one. The Northman in the river had landed something, a flashing sliver of a fish flapping on the end of his line. Some of his mates stood up on the wall, shouting and waving. All bloody smiles. If there had been fighting, it looked pretty damn clear they won.

"Tunny!" Forest was creeping up through the brush behind them, bent double. "There are Northmen on the other side of that stream!"

"And fishing, would you believe. That wall's crawling with the bastards."

"One of the lads shinned up a tree. Said he could see horsemen at the Old Bridge."

"They took the bridge?" Tunny was starting to think that if he left this valley with no greater losses than eight bottles of brandy he might count himself lucky. "They cross it, we'll be cut off!"

"I'm aware of that, Tunny. I'm very bloody well aware of that. We need to take a message back to General Jalenhorm. Pick someone out. And stay out of bloody sight!" And he crawled away through the undergrowth.

"Someone's got to go back through the bog?" whispered Yolk.

"Unless you can fly there."

"Me?" The lad's face was grey. "I can't do it, Corporal Tunny, not after Klige...I just can't do it!"

Tunny shrugged. "Someone has to go. You made it across, you can make it back. Just stick to the grassy bits."

"Corporal!" Yolk had grabbed Tunny's dirty sleeve and come close, freckled face uncomfortably near. He let his voice drop down quiet. That intimate, urgent little tone that Tunny always liked to hear. The tone in which deals were made. "You told me, if I ever needed anything..." His wet eyes darted left and right, checking they were unobserved. He reached into his jacket and slid out a pewter flask, pressed it into Tunny's hand. Tunny raised a brow, unscrewed the cap, took a sniff, replaced the cap and slipped it into his own jacket. Then he nodded. Hardly made a dent in what he'd lost in the bog, but it was something.

"Leatherlicker!" he hissed as he crept back through the brush. "I need a volunteer!"

The Day's Work

B y the dead," grunted Craw, and there were enough of 'em.

They were scattered up the north slope of the hill as he limped past, a fair few wounded too, howling and whimpering as the wounded do, a sound that set Craw's teeth on edge more with every passing year. Made him want to scream at the poor bastards to shut up, then made him guilty that he wanted to, knowing he'd done plenty of his own squealing one time or another, and probably wasn't done with it yet.

Lots more dead around the drystone wall. Enough almost to climb the bloody hill without once stepping on the mangled grass. Ended men from both sides, all on the same side now – the pale and gaping, cold far side of the great divide. One young Union lad seemed to have died on his face, arse in the air, staring sideways at Craw with a look of baffled upset, like he was about to ask if someone could lay him out in a fashion more dignified.

Craw didn't bother. Dignity ain't much use to the living, it's none to the dead.

The slopes were just a build-up to the carnage inside the Heroes, though. The Great Leveller was a joker today, wending his long way up to the punchline. Craw wasn't sure he ever saw so many dead men all squeezed into one space. Heaps of 'em, all tangled up in the old grave-pit embrace. Hungry birds danced over the stones, waiting their chance. Flies already busy at the open mouths, open eyes, open wounds. Where do all the flies come from, on a sudden? The place had that hero's smell already. All those bodies bloating in the evening sun, emptying out their innards.

Should've been a sight to get anyone pondering his own mortality, but the dozens of Thralls picking over the wreckage seemed no more concerned than if they'd been picking daisies. Stripping off clothes and armour, stacking up weapons and shields good enough to be used. If they were upset it was 'cause the Carls who'd led the charge had snaffled the best booty.

"Too old for this shit," muttered Craw, leaning down to grip at his sore knee, a cold cord of pain running through it from ankle to hip.

"If it ain't Curnden Craw, at last!" Whirrun had been sitting against one of the Heroes and now he stood, brushing dirt from his arse. "I'd almost given up on waiting." He swung the Father of Swords up onto one shoulder, sheathed again, and pointed into the valley with it, the way they'd come. "Thought maybe you'd decided to settle down in one of those farms on the way over here."

"I wish I had."

"Aw, but then who'd show me my destiny?"

"Did you fight?"

"I did, yes, as it happens. Stuck into the midst of it. I'm quite a one for fighting, according to the songs. Lots of fighting here." Not that he had a scratch on him. Craw had never seen Whirrun come out of a fight with a single mark. He frowned around the circle of butchery, scrubbing at his hair, and the wind chose that moment to freshen, stirring the tattered clothes of the corpses. "Lot of dead men, ain't there."

"Aye," said Craw.

"Heaps and heaps."

"Aye."

"Union mostly, though."

"Aye."

Whirrun shrugged his sword off his shoulder and stood it on its tip, hilt in both hands, leaning forward so his chin rested on the pommel. "Still, even when it's enemies, a sight like this, well...makes you wonder whether war's really such a good thing after all."

"You joking?"

Whirrun paused, turning the hilt round and round so the end of the stained scabbard twisted into the stained grass. "I don't really know any more. Agrick's dead." Craw looked up, mouth open. "He charged off right at the head. Got killed in the circle. Stabbed, I think, with a sword, just about here," and he poked at his side, "under the ribs and went right through, probably—"

"Don't matter exactly how, does it?" snapped Craw.

"I guess not. Mud is mud. He had the shadow over him since his brother died, though. You could see it on him. I could, anyway. The boy wasn't going to last."

Some consolation, that. "The rest?"

"Jolly Yon got a nick or two. Brack's leg's still bothering him, though he won't say so. Other than that, they're all good. Good as before, leastways. Wonderful thought we could try and bury Agrick next to his brother."

"Aye."

"Let's get a hole dug, then, shall we, 'fore someone else digs there?"

Craw took a long breath as he looked around them. "If you can find a spare shovel. I'll come say the words." A fitting end to the day that'd be. Before he got more'n a couple of steps, though, he found Caul Shivers in his way.

"Dow wants you," he said, and with his whisper, and his scar, and his careless frown, he might've been the Great Leveller his self.

"Right." Craw fought the urge to start chewing his nails again. "Tell 'em I'll be back soon. I'll be back soon, will I?"

Shivers shrugged.

Craw might not much have cared for what they'd done with the place, but Black Dow looked happy enough with the day's work, leaning against one of the stones with a mostly eaten apple in one hand. "Craw, you old bastard!" As he turned, Craw saw one side of his grinning face was all dashed and speckled with blood. "Where the hell did you get to?"

"All honesty, limping along at the back." Splitfoot and a few of his Carls were scattered about, swords drawn and eyes peeled. A lot of bare steel, considering they'd won a victory.

"Thought maybe you got yourself killed," said Dow.

Craw winced as he worked his burning foot around, thinking there was still time. "I wish I could run fast enough to get myself killed. I'll stand wherever you tell me, but this charging business is a young man's game."

"I managed to keep up."

"Don't all have your taste for blood, Chief."

"It's been the making of me. Don't reckon I've done a better day's work than this, though." Dow put a hand on Craw's shoulder and drew him out between the stones, out to the edge of the hill where they could get a look south across the valley. The very spot Craw had stood when they first saw the Union come. Things had changed a lot in a few hours.

The tumbledown wall bristled with weapons, shining dully in the fading light. Men on the slope below as well, digging pits, whittling stakes, making the Heroes a fortress. Below them the south side of the hill was littered with bodies, all the way down to the orchards. Scavengers flitted from one to another, first men then crows, feathered undertakers croaking a happy chorus. Thralls were starting to drag the stripped shapes into heaps for burying. Strange constructions in which one corpse couldn't be told from another. When a man dies in peacetime it's all tears and processions, friends and neighbours offering each other comfort. A man dies in war and he's lucky to get enough mud on top to stop him stinking.

Dow crooked a finger. "Shivers."

"Chief."

"I hear tell they got a choice prisoner down in Osrung. A Union officer or some such. Why don't you bring him up here, see if we can prick anything out of him worth hearing?"

Shivers' eye twinkled orange with the setting sun each time he nodded. "Right." And he strode off, stepping over corpses as careless as autumn leaves.

Dow frowned after him. "Some men you have to keep busy, eh, Craw?"

"I guess." Wondering what the hell Dow planned to keep him busy with.

"Quite the day's work." He tossed his apple core away and patted his stomach like a man who'd had the best meal of his life and a few hundred dead men were the leftovers.

"Aye," muttered Craw. Probably he should've been celebrating himself. Doing a little jig. A one-legged one, anyway. Singing and clashing ale cups and all the rest. But he just felt sore. Sore and he wanted to go to sleep, and wake up in that house of his by the water, and never see another battlefield. Then he wouldn't have to say the lies over Agrick's mud.

"Pushed 'em back to the river. All across the line." Dow waved at the valley, blood dried black into the skin around his fingernails. "Reachey got over the fence and kicked the Union out of Osrung. Scale got a hold o' the Old Bridge. Golden drove this lot clean across the shallows. He got stopped there but...I'd worry if I started getting everything my way." Black Dow winked at him, and Craw wondered if he was about to get stabbed in the back. "Guess folk won't be carping that I ain't the fighter they thought I was, eh?"

"Guess not." As if that was all that mattered. "Shivers said you needed me for something."

"Can't a pair of old fighters have a chat after a battle?"

That gave Craw a much bigger surprise than the blade in the back might've. "I reckon they can. Just didn't reckon you'd be one of 'em."

Dow seemed to think about that for a moment. "Neither did I. Guess we're both surprised."

"Aye," said Craw, no idea what else to say.

"We can let the Union come to us tomorrow," said Dow. "Spare your old legs."

"You reckon they'll come on? After this?"

Dow's grin was wider'n ever. "We gave Jalenhorm a hell of a beating, but half his men never even got across the river. And that's only one division out of three." He pointed over towards Adwein, lights starting to twinkle in the dusk, bright dots marking the path of the road as marching men got torches lit. "And Mitterick's just bringing his men up over there. Fresh and ready. Meed on the other side, I hear." And his finger moved over to the left, towards the Ollensand Road. Craw picked out lights there too, further back, his heart sinking all the time. "There's still heaps more work here, don't worry about that." Dow leaned close, fingers squeezing at Craw's shoulder. "We're just getting started."

The Defeated

Your August Majesty,

I regret to inform you that today your army and interests in the North suf-
fered a most serious reverse. The foremost elements of General Jalenhorm's
division reached the town of Osrung this morning and took up a powerful

position on a hill surmounted by a ring of ancient stones called the Heroes. Reinforcements were held up on the bad roads, however, and before they could move across the river the Northmen attacked in great numbers. Although they fought with the greatest courage, the Sixth and Rostod Regiments were overwhelmed. The standard of the Sixth was lost. Casualties may well be close to a thousand dead, perhaps the same number of wounded, and many more in the hands of the enemy.

It was only by a valiant action of your Majesty's First Cavalry that further disaster was averted. The Northmen are now well entrenched around the Heroes. One can see the lights of their campfires on the slopes. One can almost hear their singing when the wind shifts northerly. But we yet hold the ground south of the river, and the divisions of General Mitterick on the western flank, and Lord Governor Meed on the eastern, have begun to arrive and are preparing to attack at first light.

Tomorrow, the Northmen will not be singing.

I remain your Majesty's most faithful and unworthy servant,

Bremer dan Gorst,
Royal Observer of the Northern War

The gathering darkness was full of shouts, clanks and squeals, sharp with the tang of woodsmoke, the even sharper sting of defeat. Fires rustled in the wind and torches sputtered in pale hands, illuminating faces haggard from a day of marching, waiting, worrying. *And perhaps, in a few cases, even fighting.*

The road up from Uffrith was an endless parade of overloaded wagons, mounted officers, marching men. Mitterick's division grinding through, seeing the wounded and the beaten, catching the contagion of fear before they even caught a whiff of the enemy. Things that might have been just objects before the rout on the Heroes had assumed a crushing significance. A dead mule, lamplight shining in its goggling eyes. A cart with a broken axle tipped off the road and stripped down for firewood. An abandoned tent, blown from its moorings, the yellow sun of the Union stitched into the trampled canvas. *All become emblems of doom.*

Fear had been a rarity over the past few months, as Gorst took his morning runs through the camps of one regiment or another. Boredom, exhaustion, hunger, illness, hopelessness and homesickness, all commonplace. *But not fear of the enemy.* Now it was everywhere, and the stink of it only grew stronger as the clouds rolled steadily in and the sun sank below the fells.

If victory makes men brave, defeat renders them cowards.

Progress through the village of Adwein had been entirely stalled by several enormous wagons, each drawn by a team of eight horses. An officer was bellowing red-faced at an old man huddled on the seat of the foremost one.

"I am Saurizin, Adeptus Chemical of the University of Adua!" he shouted back, waving a document smudged by the first spots of rain. "This equipment must be allowed through, by order of Lord Bayaz!"

Gorst left them arguing, strode past a quartermaster hammering on doors, searching for billets. A Northern woman stood in the street with three children pressed against her legs, staring at a handful of coins as the drizzle grew heavier. *Kicked out of their shack to make way for some sneering lieutenant, who'll be elbowed off to make way for some preening captain, who'll be shuffled on to make way for some bloated major. Where will this woman and her children be by then? Will they slumber peacefully in my tent while I doss heroically on the damp sod outside? I need only reach out my hand...* Instead he put his head down and trudged by them in silence.

Most of the village's mean buildings were already crowded with wounded, the less serious cases spilling out onto the doorsteps. They looked up at him, pain-twisted, dirt-smeared or bandaged faces slack, and Gorst looked back in silence. *My skills are for making casualties, not comforting them.* But he pulled the stopper from his canteen and offered it out, and each in turn they took a mouthful until it was empty. Apart from one who gripped his hand for a moment they did not thank him and he did not care.

A surgeon in a smeared apron appeared at a doorway, blowing out a long sigh. "General Jalenhorm?" Gorst asked. He was pointed down a rutted side-track and after a few strides heard the voice. That same voice he'd heard blathering orders for the last few days. Its tone was different now.

"Lay them down here, lay them here! Clear a space! You, bring bandages!" Jalenhorm was kneeling in the mud, clasping the hand of a man on a stretcher. He seemed to have shaken off his huge staff, finally, if he had not left them dead on the hill. "Don't worry, you'll have the best of care. You're a hero. You're all heroes!" His knees squelched into the muck beside the next man. "You did everything that could have been asked. Mine was the fault, my friends, mine were the mistakes." He squeezed the casualty's shoulder then stood, slowly, staring down. "Mine is the guilt."

Defeat, it seems, brings out the best in some men.

"General Jalenhorn."

He looked up, face tipping into the torchlight, looking suddenly very old for a man so young. "Colonel Gorst, how are you—"

"Marshal Kroy is here." The general visibly deflated, like a pillow with half the stuffing pulled out.

"Of course he is." He straightened his dirt-smudged jacket, twisted his sword-belt into the correct position. "How do I look?" Gorst opened his mouth to speak, but Jalenhorn cut him off. "Don't bother to humour me. I look defeated." *True.* "Please don't deny it." *I didn't.* "That's what I am." *It is.*

Gorst led the way back down the crowded alleys, through the steam of the army's kitchens and the glow from the stalls of enterprising pedlars, hoping for silence. He was disappointed. *As so very often.*

"Colonel Gorst, I need to thank you. That charge of yours saved my division."

Perhaps it will also have saved my career. Your division can all drown if I can be the king's First Guard again. "My motives were not selfless."

"Whose are? It's the results that go down in history. Our reasons are written in smoke. And the fact is I nearly destroyed my division. *My* division." Jalenhorn snorted bitterly. "The one the king had most foolishly lent me. I tried to turn it down, you know." *It seems you did not try hard enough.* "But you know the king." *All too well.* "He has romantic notions about his old friends." *He has romantic notions about everything.* "No doubt I will be laughed at when I return home. Humiliated. Shunned." *Welcome to my life.* "Probably I deserve it." *Probably you do. I don't.*

And yet, as Gorst frowned sideways at Jalenhorn's hanging head, hair plastered to his skull, a drop of rain clinging to the point of his nose, as thorough a picture of dejection as he could find without a mirror, he was swept up by a surprising wave of sympathy.

He found he had put his hand on the general's shoulder. "You did what you could," he said. "You should not blame yourself." *If my experience is anything to go by, there will soon be legions of self-righteous scum queuing up to do it for you.* "You must not blame yourself."

"Who should I blame, then?" Jalenhorn whispered into the rain. "Who?"

If Lord Marshal Kroy was infected by fear he showed no symptoms, and nor did anyone else in range of his iron frown. Within his sight soldiers marched in perfect step, officers spoke clearly but did not shout, and the wounded bit down on their howls and remained stoically silent. Within a circle perhaps fifty strides across, with Kroy bolt upright in his saddle at its centre, there was no lag in morale, there was no lapse in discipline, and there had certainly been no defeat.

Jalenhorm's bearing noticeably stiffened as he strode up and gave a rigid salute. "Lord Marshal Kroy."

"General Jalenhorm." The marshal glared down from on high. "I understand there was an engagement."

"There was. The Northmen came in very great numbers. Very great, and very quickly. A well-coordinated assault. They made a feint for Osrung and I sent a regiment to reinforce the town. I went to find more but, by that time...it was too late to do anything but try to keep them on the far side of the river. Too late to—"

"The condition of your division, General."

Jalenhorm paused. In one sense the condition of his division was painfully obvious. "Two of my five regiments of foot were held up on the bad roads and have yet to see action. The Thirteenth were holding Osrung and withdrew in good order when the Northmen breached the gate. Some casualties." Jalenhorm recited the butcher's bill in a dull monotone. "The majority of the Rostod Regiment, some nine companies, I believe, were caught in the open and routed. The Sixth were holding the hill when the Northmen attacked. They were comprehensively broken. Ridden down in the fields. The Sixth has..." Jalenhorm's mouth twitched silently. "Ceased to exist."

"Colonel Wetterlant?"

"Presumed among the dead on the far side of the river. There are very many dead there. Many wounded we cannot reach. You can hear them crying for water. They always want water, for some reason." Jalenhorm gave a horrifically inappropriate snort of nervous laughter. "I'd have thought they might want...spirits, or something."

Kroy kept his silence. Gorst was unlikely to break it.

Jalenhorm droned on, as if he could not bear the quiet. "One regiment of cavalry took losses near the Old Bridge and withdrew, but held the south bank. The First is split in two. One battalion made their way through the marshes to a position in the woods on our left flank."

"That could be useful. The other?"

"Fought valiantly alongside Colonel Gorst in the shallows, and turned back the enemy at great cost on both sides. Our one truly successful action of the day."

Kroy turned his frown on Gorst. "More heroics, eh, Colonel?"

Only the bare minimum of action necessary to prevent disaster turning into catastrophe. "Some action, sir. No heroics."

"I was mindful, Lord Marshal," cut in Jalenhorm, "of the urgency. You wrote to me of some urgency."

"I did."

"I was mindful that the king wished for quick results. And so I seized the chance to get at the enemy. Seized it... much too ardently. I made a terrible mistake. A most terrible mistake, and I alone bear the full responsibility."

"No." Kroy gave a heavy sigh. "You share it with me. And with others. The roads. The nature of the battlefield. The undue haste."

"Nonetheless, I have failed." Jalenhorm drew his sword and offered it up. "I humbly request that I be removed from command."

"The king would not hear of it. Neither will I."

Jalenhorm's sword drooped, the point scraping against the mud. "Of course, Lord Marshal. I should have scouted the trees more thoroughly—"

"You should have. But your orders were to push north and find the enemy." Kroy looked slowly around the torchlit chaos of the village. "You found the enemy. This is a war. Mistakes happen, and when they do... the stakes are high. But we are not finished. We have barely even begun. You will spend tonight and tomorrow behind the shallows where Colonel Gorst fought his unheroic action this afternoon. Regrouping in the centre, re-equipping your division, looking to the welfare of the wounded, restoring morale and," glowering balefully around at the decidedly unmilitary state of the place, "imposing *discipline*."

"Yes, Lord Marshal."

"I will be making my headquarters on the slopes of Black Fell, where there should be a good view of the battlefield tomorrow. Defeat is always painful, but I have a feeling you will get another chance to be involved in this particular battle."

Jalenhorm drew himself up, something of his old snap returning at being given a straightforward goal. "My division will be ready for action the day after tomorrow, you may depend upon it, Lord Marshal!"

"Good." And Kroy rode off, his indomitable aura fading into the night along with his staff. Jalenhorm stood frozen in a parting salute as the marshal clattered away, but Gorst looked back, when he had made it a few steps further down the road.

The general still stood beside the track, alone, hunched over as the rain grew heavier, white streaks through the fizzing torchlight.

Fair Treatment

At a pace no faster'n Flood's limping, which weren't that fast at all, they made their way down the road towards Osrung, in the flitting rain. They'd only the light of Reft's one guttering torch to see by, which showed just a few strides of rutted mud ahead, some flattened crops on either side, the scared little-boy faces of Brait and Colving and the clueless gawp of Stodder. All staring off towards the town, a cluster of lights up ahead in the black country, touching the weighty clouds above with the faintest glow. All holding tight to what passed for weapons in their little crew of beggars. As if they were going to be fighting now. Today's fighting was all long done with, and they'd missed it.

"Why the hell were we left at the back?" grumbled Beck.

"Because of my dodgy leg and your lack o' practice, fool," snapped Flood over his shoulder.

"How we going to get practice left at the back?"

"You'll get practice at not getting killed, which is a damn fine thing to have plenty o' practice at, if you're asking me."

Beck hadn't been asking. His respect for Flood was waning with every mile they marched together. All the old prick seemed to care about was keeping the lads he led out of the fight and set to idiot's tasks like digging, and carrying, and lighting fires. That and keeping his leg warm. If Beck had wanted to do women's work he could've stayed on the farm and spared his self a few nights out in the wind. He'd come to fight, and win a name, and do business fit for the singing of. He was about to say so too, when Brait tugged at his sleeve, pointing up ahead.

"There's someone there!" he squeaked. Beck saw shapes moving in the dark, felt a stab of nerves, hand fumbling for his sword. The torchlight fell across three somethings hanging from a tree by chains. All blackened up by fire, branch creaking gently as they turned.

"Deserters," said Flood, hardly breaking his limping stride. "Hanged and burned."

Beck stared at 'em as he passed. Didn't hardly look like men at all, just charred wood. The one in the middle might've had a sign hanging round his neck, but it was all scorched off and Beck couldn't read anyway.

"Why burn 'em?" asked Stodder.

"'Cause Black Dow got a taste for the smell o' men cooking long time ago and it hasn't worn off."

"It's a warning," Reft whispered.

"Warning what?"

"Don't desert," said Flood.

"Y'idiot," added Beck, though mostly 'cause looking at those strange man-shaped ashes was making him all kinds of jumpy. "No better'n a coward deserves, if you're asking—" Another squeak, Colving this time, and Beck went for his sword again.

"Just townsfolk." Reft lifted his torch higher and picked out a handful of worried faces.

"We ain't got nothing!" An old man at the front, waving bony hands. "We ain't got nothing!"

"We don't want nothing." Flood jerked his thumb over his shoulder. "Go your ways."

They trudged on past. Mostly old men, a few women too, a couple of children. Children even younger than Brait, which meant barely talking yet. They were all weighed down by packs and gear, one or two pushing creaking barrows of junk. Bald furs and old tools and cookpots. Just like the stuff might've come out of Beck's mother's house.

"Clearing out," piped Colving.

"They know what's coming," said Reft.

Osrung slunk out of the night, a fence of mossy logs whittled to points, a high stone tower looming up by the empty gateway with lights at slitted windows. Sullen men with spears kept watch, eyes narrowed against the rain. Some young lads were digging a big pit, working away in the light of a few guttering torches on poles, all streaked with mud in the drizzle.

"Shit," whispered Colving.

"By the dead," squeaked Brait.

"They's the dead all right." Stodder, his fat lip dangling.

Beck found he'd nothing to say. What he'd taken without thinking for some pile of pale clay or something was actually a pile of corpses. He'd seen Gelda from up the valley laid out waiting to be buried after he drowned in the river and not thought much about it, counted himself hard-blooded, but this was different. They looked all strange, stripped naked and thrown together, face up and face down, slippery with the rain. Men, these, he had to tell himself, and the thought made him dizzy. He could see faces in the mess, or bits of faces. Hands, arms, feet, mixed up like they was all one monstrous creature. He didn't want to guess at how many were there. He saw a leg sticking out, a wound in the thigh yawning black like a big mouth. Didn't look real. One of the lads doing the digging stopped a moment, shovel clutched in white hands as they trudged past. His mouth was all twisted like he was about to cry.

"Come on," snapped Flood, leading them in through the archway, broken doors leaning against the fence inside. A great tree trunk lay near, branches hacked off to easily held lengths, the heavy end filed to a point and capped with rough-forged black iron, covered with shiny scratches.

"You reckon that was the ram?" whispered Colving.

"I reckon," said Reft.

The town felt strange. Edgy. Some houses were shut up tight, others had windows and doorways wide and full of darkness. A set of bearded men sat in front of one, mean-eyed, passing round a flask. Some children hid in an alley mouth, eyes gleaming in the shadows as the torch passed 'em by. Odd sounds came from everywhere. Crashing and tinkling. Thumping and shouting. Groups of men darted between the buildings, torches in hands, blades glinting, all moving at a hungry half-jog.

"What's going on?" asked Stodder, in that stodgy-stupid voice of his.

"They're at a bit of sacking."

"But...ain't this our town?"

Flood shrugged. "They fought for it. Some of 'em died for it. They ain't leaving empty-handed."

A Carl with a long moustache sat under dripping eaves with a bottle in his hand, sneering as he watched 'em walk past. Beside him a corpse lay in the doorway, half-in, half-out, the back of its head a glistening mass. Beck couldn't tell if it was someone who'd lived in the house or someone who'd been fighting in it. Whether it was a man or a woman, even.

"You're quiet all of a sudden," said Reft.

Beck wanted to think of something sharp, but all he could manage was, "Aye."

"Wait here." And Flood limped up to a man in a red cloak, pointing Carls off this way and that. Some figures sat, slumped in an alleyway nearby, hands tied, shoulders hunched against the drizzle.

"Prisoners," said Reft.

"They don't look much different than our lot," said Colving.

"They ain't." Reft frowned at 'em. "Some o' the Dogman's boys, I guess."

"Apart from him," said Beck. "That's a Union man." He had a bandage round his head and a funny Union jacket, one red sleeve ripped and the skin underneath covered in grazes, the other with some kind of fancy gold thread all around the cuff.

"Right," said Flood as he walked back over. "You're going to look to these prisoners while I find out what the work'll be tomorrow. Just make sure none o' them, and none o' you, end up dead!" he shouted as he made off up the street.

"Looking to prisoners," grumbled Beck, some of his bitterness bubbling back as he looked down at their hangdog faces.

"Reckon you deserve better work, do you?" The one who spoke had a crazy look to him, a big bandage around his belly, stained through brown with some fresh red in the middle, ankles tied as well as wrists. "Bunch o' fucking boys, don't even have their Names yet!"

"Shut up, Crossfeet," grunted one of the other prisoners, not hardly looking up.

"*You* shut up, y'arsehole!" Crossfeet gave him a look like he might tear him with his teeth. "Whatever happens tonight, the Union'll be here tomorrow. More o' those bastards than ants in a hill. The Dogman too, and you know who the Dogman's got with him?" He grinned, eyes going huge as he whispered the name. "The Bloody-Nine." Beck felt his face go hot. The

Bloody-Nine had killed his father. Killed him in a duel with his own sword. The one he had sheathed beside him now.

"That's a lie," squeaked Brait, looking scared to his bones even though they had weapons and the prisoners were trussed up tight. "Black Dow killed Ninefingers, years ago!"

Crossfeet kept giving him that crazy grin. "We'll see. Tomorrow, you little bastard. We'll—"

"Let him alone," said Beck.

"Oh aye? And what's your name?"

Beck stepped up and booted Crossfeet in the fruits. "That's my name!" He kept on kicking him as he folded up, all his anger boiling out. "That's my name! That's my fucking name, you heard it enough?"

"Hate to interrupt."

"What?" snarled Beck, spinning round with his fists clenched.

A big man stood behind him, a half-head taller'n Beck, maybe, fur on his shoulders glistening with the rain. All across one side of his face, the biggest and most hideous scar Beck had ever seen, the eye on that side not an eye at all but a ball of dead metal.

"Name's Caul Shivers," voice a ground-down whisper.

"Aye," croaked Beck. He'd heard stories. Everyone had. They said Shivers did tasks for Black Dow too black for his own hands. They said he'd fought at Black Well, and the Cumnur, and Dunbrec, and the High Places, fought beside old Rudd Threetrees, and the Dogman. The Bloody-Nine too. They said he'd gone south across the sea and learned sorcery. That he'd traded his eye willingly for that silver one, and that a witch had made it, and through it he could see what a man was thinking.

"Black Dow sent me."

"Aye," whispered Beck, all his hairs standing up on end.

"To get one o' these. A Union officer."

"Reckon that's this one." Colving used his toe to poke at the man with the tattered sleeve and made him grunt.

"If it ain't Black Dow's bitch!" Crossfeet was smiling up, teeth shining red, bandages round him reddened too. "Why don't you bark, eh, Shivers? Bark, you bastard!" Beck could hardly believe it. None of 'em could. Maybe he knew that wound in his gut was death, and it'd sent him mad.

"Huh." Shivers jerked his trousers up so it was easy for him to squat down, boots grinding the dirt as he did it. When he got there he had a knife in his hand. Just a little one, blade no longer'n a man's finger, glinting red and orange and yellow. "You know who I am, then?"

"Caul Shivers, and I ain't fucking scared of a dog!"

Shivers raised one brow, the one above his good eye. The one above his metal eye didn't shift much. "Well, ain't you the hero?" And he poked Crossfeet in the calf with the blade. Not much weight behind it. Like Beck might've poked his brother with a finger to wake him up of a frosty morning. The knife stuck into his leg, silent, and back out, and Crossfeet snarled and wriggled.

"Black Dow's bitch, am I?" Shivers poked him in the other leg, knife going deeper into his thigh. "It's true I get some shitty jobs." Poked him again, somewhere around his hip. "Dog can't hold a knife, though, can it?" He didn't sound angry. Didn't look angry. Bored, almost. "I can." Poke, poke.

"Gah!" Crossfeet twisted and spat. "If I had a blade—"

"If?" Shivers poked him in the side, where his bandages were. "You don't, so there's the end o' that." Crossfeet had twisted over, so Shivers poked him in the back. "I've got one, though. Look." Poke, poke, poke. "Look at that, hero." Poked him in the backs of his legs, poked him in the arse, poked him all over, blood spreading out into his trousers in dark rings.

Crossfeet moaned and shuddered, and Shivers puffed out his cheeks, and wiped his knife on the Union man's sleeve, making the gold thread glint red. "Right, then." He made the Union man grunt as he jerked him to his feet, carefully sheathed his little knife somewhere at his belt. "I'll take this one off."

"What should we do with him?" Beck found he'd asked in a reedy little voice, pointing at Crossfeet, moaning softly in the mud, torn clothes all glistening sticky black.

Shivers looked straight at Beck, and it felt like he was looking into him. Right into his thoughts, like they said he could. "Do nothing. You can manage that, no?" He shrugged as he turned to go. "Let him bleed."

Tactics

The valley was spread out below them, a galaxy of twinkling points of orange light. The torches and campfires of both sides, occasionally smudged as a new curtain of drizzle swept across the hillside. One cluster must have been the village of Adwein, another the hill they called the Heroes, a third the town of Osrung.

Meed had made his headquarters at an abandoned inn south of the town and left his leading regiment digging in just out of bowshot of its fence, Hal with them, nobly wrestling to stamp some order on the darkness. More than half the division was still slogging up, ill-tempered and ill-disciplined, along a road that had begun the day as an uneven strip of dust and ended it churned to a river of mud. The rearmost elements would probably still not have arrived at first light tomorrow.

"I wanted to thank you," said Colonel Brint, rain dripping from the peak of his hat.

"Me?" asked Finree, all innocence. "Whatever for?"

"For looking after Aliz these past few days. I know she's not terribly worldly—"

"It's been my pleasure," she lied. "You've been such a good friend to Hal, after all." Just a gentle reminder that she damn well expected him to carry on being one.

"Hal's an easy man to like."

"Isn't he, though?"

They rode past a picket, four Union soldiers swaddled in sodden cloaks, spear-points glistening in the light of the lanterns of Meed's officers. There were more men beyond, unloading rain-spoiled gear from packhorses, struggling to pitch tents, wet canvas flapping in their faces. An unhappy queue of them were hunched beside a dripping awning clutching an assortment of tins, cups and boxes while rations were weighed out.

"There's no bread?" one was asking.

"Regulations say flour's an acceptable substitute," replied the quartermaster, measuring out a tiny quantity on his scales with frowning precision.

"Acceptable to who? What are we going to bake it on?"

"You can bake it on your fat arse far as I'm—Oh, begging your pardon, my lady," tugging his forelock as Finree rode past. As though seeing men go hungry for no good reason could cause no offence but the word "arse" might overcome her delicate sensibilities.

What looked at first to be a hump in the steep hillside turned out to be an ancient building, covered with wind-lashed creeper, somewhere between a cottage and a barn and probably serving as both. Meed dismounted with all the pomp of a queen at her coronation and led his staff in file through the narrow doorway, leaving Colonel Brint to hold back the queue so Finree could slip through near the front.

The bare-raftered room beyond smelled of damp and wool, wet-haired officers squeezed in tight. The briefing had the charged air of a royal funeral, every man vying to look the most solemn while they wondered eagerly whether there might be anything for them in the will. General Mitterick stood against one rough stone wall, frowning mightily into his moustache with one hand thrust between two buttons of his uniform, thumb sticking up, as if he was posing for a portrait, and an insufferably pretentious one at that. Not far from him Finree picked out Bremer dan Gorst's impassive slab of a face in the shadows, and smiled in acknowledgement. He scarcely tipped his head in return.

Finree's father stood before a great map, pointing out positions with expressive movements of one hand. She felt the warm glow of pride she always did when she saw her father at work. He was the very definition of a commander. When he saw them enter, he came over to shake Meed's hand, catching Finree's eye and giving her the slightest smile.

"Lord Governor Meed, I must thank you for moving north with such speed." Though if it had been left to his Grace to navigate they would still have been wondering which way was north.

"Lord Marshal Kroy," grated the governor, with little enthusiasm. Their relationship was a prickly one. In his own province of Angland, Meed was pre-eminent, but as a lord marshal carrying the king's commission, in time of war Finree's father outranked him.

"I realise it must have been a wrench to abandon Ollensand, but we need you here."

"So I see," said Meed, with characteristic bad grace. "I understand there was a serious—"

"Gentlemen!" The press of officers near the door parted to let someone through. "I must apologise for my late arrival, the roads are quite clogged." A stocky bald man emerged from the crowd, flapping the lapels of a travel-stained coat and heedlessly spraying water over everyone around him. He was attended by only one servant, a curly-haired fellow with a basket in one hand, but Finree had made it her business to know every person in his Majesty's government, every member of the Open Council and the Closed and the exact degrees of their influence, and the lack of pomp did not fool her for a moment. Put simply, whether he was said to be retired or not, Bayaz, the First of the Magi, outranked everyone.

"Lord Bayaz." Finree's father made the introductions. "This is Lord Governor Meed, of Angland, commanding his Majesty's third division."

The First of the Magi somehow managed to press his hand and ignore him simultaneously. "I knew your brother. A good man, much missed." Meed attempted to speak but Bayaz was distracted by his servant, who at that moment produced a cup from his basket. "Ah! Tea! Nothing seems quite so terrible once there is a cup of tea in your hand, eh? Would anyone else care for some?" There were no takers. Tea was generally considered an unpatriotic Gurkish fashion, synonymous with moustache-twiddling treachery. "Nobody?"

"I would love a cup." Finree slipped smoothly in front of the lord governor, obliging him to take a spluttering step back. "The perfect thing in this weather." She despised tea, but would happily have drunk an ocean of it for the chance to exchange words with one of the most powerful men in the Union.

Bayaz' eyes flickered briefly over her face like a pawnshop owner's asked for an estimate on some gaudy heirloom. Finree's father cleared his throat, somewhat reluctantly. "This is my daughter—"

"Finree dan Brock, of course. My congratulations on your marriage."

She smothered her surprise. "You are very well informed, Lord Bayaz. I would have thought myself beneath notice." She ignored a cough of agreement from Meed's direction.

"Nothing can be beneath the notice of a careful man," said the Magus. "Knowledge is the root of power, after all. Your husband must be a fine fellow indeed to outshine the shadow of his family's treason."

"He is," she said, unabashed. "He in no way takes after his father."

"Good." Bayaz still smiled, but his eyes were hard as flints. "I would hate to bring you pain by seeing him hanged."

An awkward silence. She glanced at Colonel Brint, then at Lord Governor Meed, wondering if either of them might offer some support for Hal in reward for his unstinting loyalty. Brint at least had the decency to look guilty. Meed looked positively delighted. "You will find no more loyal man in his Majesty's whole army," she managed to grate out.

"I am all delight. Loyalty is a fine thing in an army. Victory is another." Bayaz frowned about at the assembled officers. "Not the best of days, gentlemen. A long way from the best of days."

"General Jalenhorm overreached himself," said Mitterick, out of turn and with little empathy, behaviour entirely characteristic of the man. "He should never have been so damn spread out—"

"General Jalenhorm acted under my orders," snapped Marshal Kroy, leaving Mitterick to subside into a grumpy silence. "We overreached, yes, and the Northmen surprised us..."

"Your tea." A cup was insinuated into Finree's hand and the eyes of Bayaz' servant met hers. Odd-coloured eyes, one blue, one green. "I am sure your husband is as loyal, honest and hard-working as ever a man could be," he murmured, a most unservile curl to the corner of his mouth, as if they shared some private joke. She did not see what, but the man had already oozed back, pot in hand, to charge Bayaz' cup. Finree wrinkled her lip, checked she was unobserved and furtively tossed the contents of hers down the wall.

"...our choices were most limited," her father was saying, "given the great need for haste impressed upon us by the Closed Council—"

Bayaz cut him off. "The need for haste is a fact of our situation, Marshal Kroy, a fact no less compelling for being a political imperative rather than a physical." He slurped tea through pursed lips, but the room was held so silent for the duration one could have heard a flea jump. Finree wished she understood the trick, and could rely on her every facile utterance being given rapt attention, rather than endlessly chewing on her usual diet of sidelinings, humourings and brushings-off. "If a mason builds a wall upon a slope and it collapses, he can hardly complain that it would have stood a thousand years if only he had been given level ground to work with." Bayaz slurped again, again in utter silence. "In war, the ground is never level."

Finree felt an almost physical pressure to jump to her father's defence, as if there was a wasp down her back that had to be smashed, but she bit her tongue. Taunting Meed was one thing. Taunting the First of the Magi quite another.

"It was not my intention to offer excuses," said her father stiffly. "For the failure I take all the responsibility, for the losses I take all the blame."

"Your willingness to shoulder the blame does you much credit but us little good." Bayaz sighed as if reproving a naughty grandson. "But let us learn the lessons, gentlemen. Let us put yesterday's defeats behind us, and look to tomorrow's victories." Everyone nodded as though they had never heard anything so profound, even Finree's father. Here was power.

She could not remember ever coming to dislike anyone so much, or admire anyone so much, in so short a time.

Dow's meet was held around a big fire-pit in the centre of the Heroes, shimmering with heat, hissing and fizzing with the drizzle. There was an edgy feel about the gathering, somewhere between a wedding and a hanging. Firelight and shadow make men look like devils, and Craw had seen 'em make men act like devils more'n once. They all were there – Reachey, Tenways, Scale and Calder, Ironhead, Splitfoot and a couple score Named Men besides. The biggest names and the hardest faces in the North, less a few up in the hills and a few more with the other side.

Looked like Glama Golden had got in the fight. Looked like someone had used his face for an anvil. His left cheek was one big welt, mouth split and bloated, blooms of bruise already spreading. Ironhead smirked across the ring of leering faces like he'd never seen a thing so pretty as Golden's broken nose. They had bad blood between 'em, those two, so bad it poisoned everything around.

"What the hell are you doing here, old man?" murmured Calder as Craw jostled into place beside him.

"Damned if I know. My eyes ain't all they used to be." Craw took a hold on his belt buckle and squinted around. "Ain't this where we go to shit?"

Calder snorted. "It's where we go to talk it. Though if you want to drop your trousers and give Brodd Tenways some polish for his boots I won't complain."

Now Black Dow strolled out of the shadows, around the side of Skarling's

Chair, chewing at a bone. The chatter quieted then died altogether, leaving only the crackle and crunch of sagging embers, faint snatches of song floating from outside the circle. Dow stripped his bone to nothing and tossed it into the fire, licking his fingers one by one while he took in every shadow-pitted face. Drew out the silence. Made 'em all wait. Left no doubts who was the biggest bastard on the hill.

"So," he said in the end. "Good day's work, no?" And a great clatter went up, men shaking their sword hilts, thumping shields with gauntlets, beating their armour with their fists. Scale joined in, banging his helmet on one scratched thigh-plate. Craw rattled his sword in its sheath, somewhat guiltily, since he hadn't run fast enough to draw it. Calder stayed quiet, he noticed, just sourly sucked his teeth as the clamour of victory faded.

"A good day!" Tenways leered around the fire.

"Aye, a good day," said Reachey.

"Might've been better yet," said Ironhead, curling his lip at Golden, "if we'd only made it across the shallows."

Golden's eyes burned in their bruised sockets, jaw muscles squirming on the side of his head, but he kept his peace. Probably 'cause talking hurt too much.

"Men are always telling me the world ain't what it was." Dow held up his sword, grinning so the sharp point of his tongue stuck out between his teeth. "Some things don't change, eh?" Another clattering chorus of approval, so much steel thrust up it was a wonder no one got stabbed by accident. "For them who said the clans o' the North can't fight as one…" Dow curled his tongue and blew spit hissing into the fire. "For them who said the Union are too many to beat…" He sent another gob sailing neatly into the flames. Then he looked up, eyes shining orange. "And for them who say I'm not the man to do it…" And he rammed his sword point-first into the fire with a snarl, sparks whirling up around the hilt.

A hammering of approval loud as a busy smithy, loud enough to make Craw wince. "Dow!" shrieked Tenways, smashing the pommel of his sword with one scabby hand. "Black Dow!"

Others joined in, and found a rhythm with his name and with their fists on metal. "Black! Dow! Black! Dow!" Ironhead with it, and Golden mumbling through his battered mouth, and Reachey too. Craw kept his silence. Take victory quiet and careful, Rudd Threetrees used to say, 'cause you might soon be called on to take defeat the same way. Across the fire,

Craw caught the glint of Shivers' eye in the shadows. He wasn't chanting neither.

Dow settled back in Skarling's Chair just the way Bethod used to, basking in the love like a lizard in the sun then halting it with a kingly wave. "All right. We've got all the best ground in the valley. They've got to back off or come at us, and there ain't many places they can do it. So there's no need for anything clever. Clever'd be wasted on the likes o' you lot, anyway." A range of chuckles. "So I'll take blood, and bones, and steel, like today." More cheering. "Reachey?"

"Aye, Chief." The old warrior stepped into the firelight, mouth pressed into a hard line.

"I want your boys to hold Osrung. They'll come at you hard tomorrow, I reckon."

Reachey shrugged. "Only fair. We came at 'em pretty damn hard today."

"Don't let 'em get across that bridge, Reachey. Ironhead?"

"Aye, Chief."

"I'm giving you the shallows to mind. I want men in the orchard, I want men holding the Children, I want men ready to die but happier to kill. It's the one place they could come across in numbers, so if they try it we got to step on 'em hard."

"That's what I do." Ironhead sent a mocking look across the fire. "Won't nobody be turning me back."

"Whassat mean?" snarled Golden.

"You'll all get a stab at glory," said Dow, bringing the pair of 'em to heel. "Golden, you fought hard today so you'll be hanging back. Cover the ground between Ironhead and Reachey, ready to lend help to either one if they get pressed more'n they're comfortable with."

"Aye." Licking at his bloated lip with the point of his bloated tongue.

"Scale?"

"Chief."

"You took the Old Bridge. Hold the Old Bridge."

"Done."

"If you have to fall back—"

"I won't," said Scale, with all the confidence of youth and limited brains.

"—it'd be worth having a second line at that old wall. What do they call it?"

"Clail's Wall," said Splitfoot. "Some mad farmer built it."

"Might be a good thing for us he did," said Dow. "You won't be able to use all you've got in the space behind that bridge anyway, so plant some further back."

"I will," said Scale.

"Tenways?"

"Made for glory, Chief!"

"You've got the slope o' the Heroes and Skarling's Finger to look to, which means you shouldn't get into any scrapes right off. Scale or Ironhead need your help, maybe you can find 'em some."

Tenways sneered across the fire at Scale and Calder and, hopefully just 'cause he was standing with 'em, Craw. "I'll see what I can root out."

Dow leaned forward. "Splitfoot and me will be up here at the top, behind the drystone wall. Reckon I'll lead from the back tomorrow, like our friends in the Union do." Another round of harsh laughter. "So there it is. Anyone got any better ideas?" Dow slowly worked the gathering over with his grin. Craw had never felt less like speaking in his life, and it didn't seem likely anyone else would want to make a spectacle of themselves—

"I have." Calder held up a finger, always wanting to make a spectacle of himself.

Dow's eyes narrowed. "What a surprise. And what's your strategy, Prince Calder?"

"Put our backs to the Union and run?" asked Ironhead, a wave of chuckling following after.

"Put our backs to the Union and bend over?" asked Tenways, followed by another. Calder only smiled through it, and waited for the laughter to fade, and leave things silent.

"Peace," he said.

Craw winced. It was like getting up on a table and calling for chastity in a brothel. He felt a strong urge to step away, like you might from a man doused in oil when there are a lot of naked flames about. But what kind of man steps away from a friend just 'cause he isn't popular? Even if he is in danger of becoming a fireball. So Craw stayed shoulder to shoulder with him, wondering what the hell his game was, since sure as sure Calder always had some game in mind. The disbelieving silence stretched out long enough for a sudden gust to whip up, make cloaks flap and torch flames dance, throwing wild light across that circle of frowns.

"Why, you bastard fucking *coward*!" Brodd Tenways' rashy face was so twisted up with scorn it looked like it might split.

"Call my brother a coward?" snarled Scale, eyes bulging. "I'll twist your flaky fucking neck!"

"Now, now," said Dow. "If any necks need twisting I'll do the picking out. Prince Calder's known to have a way with words. I brought him out here to hear what he has to say, didn't I? So let's hear it, Calder. Why peace?"

"Careful, Calder," muttered Craw, trying not to move his lips. "Careful."

If Calder heard the warning, he chose to piss all over it. "Because war's a waste of men's time, and money, and lives."

"Fucking *coward*!" barked Tenways again, and this time even Scale didn't disagree, just stood staring at his brother. There was a chorus of disgust, and cursing, and spitting, almost as loud as the chorus of approval for Dow. But the louder it got the more Calder smiled. Like he thrived on their hatred like a flower on shit.

"War's a way of getting things," he said. "If it gets you nothing, what's the point? How long have we been marching around out here?"

"You've had a trip back home, bastard," someone called.

"Aye, and it was talk o' peace landed you there," said Ironhead.

"All right, how long have *you* been out here, then?" Pointing right in Ironhead's face. "Or you?" At Golden. "Or him?" Jerking a thumb sideways at Craw. Craw frowned, wishing he'd been left out of it. "Months? Years? Marching, and riding, and fearing, and lying out under the stars with your sickness and your wounds. In the wind, in the cold, while your fields, and your herds, and your workshops, and your wives go untended. For what? Eh? What plunder? What glory? If there are ten-score men in all this host who are richer because o' this I'll eat my own cock."

"Coward's fucking talk!" snarled Tenways, turning away, "I won't hear it!"

"Cowards run away from things. Scared of words, are you, Tenways? What a hero." Calder even got a ragged scatter of laughter for that. Made Tenways stop and turn back, bristling. "We won a victory here today! Legends, every man!" And Calder slapped at his sword hilt. "But it was just a little one." He jerked his head towards the south, where everyone knew the campfires of the enemy were lighting up the whole valley. "There's plenty more Union. There'll be harder fighting on the morrow, and heavier losses. Far heavier. And if we win it's to end up in the same spot, just with more dead men for company. No?" Some were still shaking their heads, but more were listening, thinking it over. "As for those who said the clans of the North can't fight as one, or the Union are too many to beat, well, I don't reckon those questions are quite settled yet." Calder curled his tongue, and sent a bit of his own spittle spinning into Dow's fire. "And any man can spit."

"Peace," snorted Tenways, who'd stuck around to listen after all. "We all know what a lover o' peace your father was! Didn't he take us to war with the Union in the first place?"

Didn't slow Calder down a step. "He did, and it was the end of him. Might be I learned from his mistake. Have you, is my question?" Looking every man in the eye. " 'Cause if you ask me, it'd be a damn fool who risked his life for what he could get just by the asking." There was silence for a while. A grudging, guilty silence. The wind flapped clothes some more, whipped sparks from the fire-pit in showers. Dow leaned forward, propping himself up on his sword.

"Well, you've done quite the job o' pissing on my cookfire, ain't you, Prince Calder?" Harsh chuckles all round, and the thoughtful moment was gone. "How about you, Scale? You want peace?"

The brothers eyed each other for a moment, while Craw tried to ease back gently from between the two. "No," said Scale. "I'm for fighting."

Dow clicked his tongue. "There we go. Seems you didn't even convince your own brother." More chuckling, and Calder laughed with the rest, if somewhat sickly. "Still, you've got quite the way with words, all right, Calder. Maybe the time'll come we need to talk peace with the Union. Then I'll be sure to give you the call." He showed his teeth. "Won't be tonight, though."

Calder swept out a fancy bow. "As you command, Protector of the North. You're the Chief."

"That's right," growled Dow, and most nodded along with him. "That's right." But Craw noticed a few had more thoughtful looks on their faces as they started to drift away into the night. Pondering their untilled fields, maybe, or their untilled wives. Could be Calder weren't so mad as he seemed. Northmen love battle, sure, but they love beer too. And like beer, there's only so much battle most can stomach.

* * *

We suffered a reverse today. But tomorrow will be different." Marshal Kroy's manner did not allow for the possibility of disagreement. It was stated as fact. "Tomorrow we will take the fight to our enemy, and we will be victorious." The room rustled, starched collars shifting as men nodded in unison.

"Victory," someone murmured.

"By tomorrow morning all three divisions will be in position." *Though one is ruined and the others will have marched all night.* "We have the weight of numbers." *We will crush them under our corpses!* "We have right on our side." *Good for you. I have a huge bruise on mine.* But the rest of the officers seemed cheered by the platitudes. *As idiots often are.*

Kroy turned to the map, pointing out the south bank of the shallows. The spot where Gorst had fought that very morning. "General Jalenhorm's division needs time to regroup, so they will stay out of action in the centre, demonstrating towards the shallows but not crossing them. We will attack instead on both flanks." He strode purposefully to the right side of the map, pushing his hand up the Ollensand Road towards Osrung. "Lord Governor Meed, you are our right fist. Your division will attack Osrung at first light, carry the palisade, occupy the southern half of the town, then aim to take the bridge. The northern half is the more built up, and the Northmen have had time to strengthen their positions there."

Meed's gaunt face was blotchy with intensity, eyes bright at the prospect of grappling with his hated enemy at last. "We will flush them out and put every one of them to the sword."

"Good. Be cautious, though, the woods to the east have not been thoroughly scouted. General Mitterick, you are the left hook. Your objective is to force your way across the Old Bridge and establish a presence on the far side."

"Oh, my men will take the bridge, don't concern yourself about that, Lord Marshal. We'll take the bridge and drive them all the way to bloody Carleon—"

"Taking the bridge will be adequate, for today."

"A battalion of the First Cavalry are being attached to your command." Felnigg glared down his beak of a nose as if he thought attaching anything to Mitterick deeply ill-advised. "They found a route through the marshes and a position in the woods beyond the enemy's right flank."

Mitterick did not deign even to look at Kroy's chief of staff. "I've asked for volunteers to lead the assault on the bridge, and my men have already built a number of sturdy rafts."

Felnigg's glare intensified. "I understand the current is strong."

"It's worth a try, isn't it?" snapped Mitterick. "They could hold us up all morning on that bridge!"

"Very well, but remember we are seeking victory, not glory." Kroy looked sternly around the room. "I will be sending written orders to each one of you. Are there any questions?"

"I have one, sir." Colonel Brint held up a finger. "Is it possible for Colonel Gorst to refrain from his heroics long enough for the rest of us to contribute?" There was a scattering of chuckles, utterly disproportionate to the humour displayed, the soldiers seizing on a rare chance to laugh. Gorst had been entirely occupied staring across the room at Finree and pretending not to. Now he found to his extreme discomfort that everyone was grinning at him. Someone started to clap. Soon there was a modest round of applause. He would have vastly preferred it if they had jeered at him. *That at least I could have joined in with.*

"I will observe," he grunted.

"As will I," said Bayaz, "and perhaps conduct my little experiment on the south bank."

The marshal bowed. "We stand entirely at your disposal, Lord Bayaz."

The First of the Magi slapped his thighs as he rose, his servant leaning forward to whisper something in his ear and, as though that was a call for the advance, the room began quickly to empty, officers hurrying back to their units to make preparations for the morning's attacks. *Make sure to pack plenty of coffins, you—*

"I hear you saved the army today."

He spun about with all the dignity of a startled baboon and found himself staring into Finree's face at paralysingly close quarters. News of her marriage should have allowed him to finally bury his feelings for her as he had buried all the others worth having. But it seemed they were stronger than ever. A vice in his guts clamped down whenever he saw her, screwed tighter the longer they spoke. If you could call it speaking.

"Er," he muttered. *I floundered around in a stream and killed seven men that I am sure of, but without doubt maimed several more. I hacked them apart in the hope that our fickle monarch would hear of it, and commute my unde-*

served sentence of undeath. I made myself guilty of mass murder so I could be proclaimed innocent of incompetence. Sometimes they hang men for this type of thing, and sometimes they applaud. "I am ... lucky to be alive."

She came closer and he felt a dizzy rush of blood, a lightness in his head not unlike serious illness. "I have a feeling we are all lucky you are alive."

I have a feeling in my trousers. If I was truly lucky you would put your hand down them. Is that too much to ask? After saving the army, and so on? "I ..." *I'm so sorry. I love you. Why am I sorry? I didn't say anything. Does a man need to feel sorry for what he thinks? Probably.*

She had already walked off to speak to her father, and he could hardly blame her. *If I was her, I wouldn't even look at me, let alone listen to me squeak my halting way through half a line of insipid drivel. And yet it hurts. It hurts so much when she goes.* He trudged for the door.

Fuck, I'm pathetic.

Calder slipped out of Dow's meet before he had to explain himself to his brother and hurried away between the fires, ignoring grumbled curses from the men gathered around them. He found a path between two of the torchlit Heroes, saw gold glinting on the slope and caught up with its owner as he strode angrily downhill.

"Golden! Golden, I need to talk to you!"

Glama Golden frowned over his shoulder. Perhaps the intention was fearsome fury, but the swellings on his cheek made him look like he was worried at the taste of something he was eating. Calder had to bite back a giggle. That smashed-up face was an opportunity for him, one he could ill afford to miss.

"What would I have to thay to you, Calder?" he snarled, three of his Named Men bristling behind him, hands tickling their many weapons.

"Quietly, we're watched!" Calder came close, huddling as though he had secrets to share. An attitude he'd noticed tended to make men do the same, however little they were inclined to. "I thought we could help each other, since we find ourselves in the same position—"

"The thame?" Golden's bloated, blotched and bloodied face loomed close. Calder shrank back, all fear and surprise, while on the inside he was a fisherman who feels the tug on his line. Talk was his battlefield, and most of these fools were as useless on it as he was on a real one. "How are we the thame, *peathemaker*?"

"Black Dow has his favourites, doesn't he? And the rest of us have to struggle over the scraps."

"Favourith?" Golden's battered mouth was giving him a trace of a lisp and every time he slurred a word he looked even more enraged.

"You led the charge today, while *others* lagged at the back. You put your life in the balance, were wounded fighting Dow's battle. And now *others* are getting the place of honour, in the front line, while you sit at the rear? Wait, in case you're needed?" He leaned even closer. "My father always admired you. Always told me you were a clever man, a righteous man, the kind who could be relied on." It's amazing how well the most pathetic flattery can work. On enormously vain people especially. Calder knew that well enough. He used to be one.

"He never told me," muttered Golden, though it was plain he wanted to believe it.

"How could he?" wheedled Calder. "He was King of the Northmen. He didn't have the luxury of telling men what he really thought." Which was just as well, because he'd thought Golden was a puffed-up halfhead, just as Calder did. "But I can." He just chose not to. "There's no reason you and I need to stand on different sides. That's what Dow wants, to divide us. So he can share all the power, and the gold, and the glory with the likes of Split-foot, and Tenways... and Ironhead." Golden twitched at the name as if it was a hook tugging at his battered face. Their feud was so big he couldn't see around it, the idiot. "We don't need to let that happen." Almost a lover's whisper, and Calder risked slipping his hand gently onto Golden's shoulder. "Together, you and I could do great things—"

"Enough!" mumbled Golden through his split lips, slapping away Calder's hand. "Peddle your lieth elthewhere!" But Calder could smell the doubt as Golden turned away, and a little doubt was all he was after. If you can't make your enemies trust you, you can at least make them mistrust each other. Patience, his father would have told him, patience. He allowed himself a smirk as Golden and his men stomped off into the night. He was just sowing seeds. Time would bring the harvest. If he lived long enough to swing the scythe.

Lord Governor Meed gave Finree one last disapproving frown before leaving her alone with her father. He clearly could not stand anyone being in a position of power over him, especially a woman. But if he supposed she would give him a lacklustre report behind his back, he had profoundly underestimated her.

"Meed is a primping dunce," she shot over her shoulder. "He'll be as much use on a battlefield as a two-copper whore." She thought about it a moment. "Actually, I'm not being fair. The whore at least might improve morale. Meed is about as inspiring as a mouldy flannel. Just as well for him you called off the siege of Ollensand before it turned into a complete fiasco."

She was surprised to see her father had dropped into a chair behind a travelling desk, head in his hands. He looked suddenly like a different man. Shrunken, and tired, and old. "I lost a thousand men today, Fin. And a thousand more wounded."

"Jalenhorm lost them."

"Every man in this army is my responsibility. I lost them. A *thousand* of them. A number, easily said. Now rank them up. Ten, by ten, by ten. See how many there are?" He grimaced into the corner as though it was stacked high with bodies. "Every one a father, a husband, a brother, a son. Every life lost a hole I can never fill, a debt I can never repay." He stared through his spread fingers at her with red-rimmed eyes. "Finree, I lost a thousand men."

She took a step or two closer to him. "Jalenhorm lost them."

"Jalenhorm is a good man."

"That's not enough."

"It's something."

"You should replace him."

"You have to put some trust in your officers, or they'll never be worthy of it."

"Is it possible for that advice to be as lame as it sounds?"

They frowned at each other for a moment, then her father waved it away. "Jalenhorm is an old friend of the king, and the king is most particular about his old friends. Only the Closed Council can replace him."

She was by no means out of suggestions. "Replace Meed, then. The man's a danger to everyone in the army and a good few who aren't. Leave him in charge for long and today's disaster will soon be forgotten. Buried under one much worse."

Her father sighed. "And who would I put in his place?"

"I have the perfect man in mind. A very fine young officer."

"Good teeth?"

"As it happens, and high born to a fault, and vigorous, brave, loyal and diligent."

"Such men often come with fearsomely ambitious wives."

"Especially this one."

He rubbed his eyes. "Finree, Finree, I've already done everything possible in getting him the position he has. In case you've forgotten, his father—"

"Hal is not his father. Some of us surpass our parents."

He let that go, though it looked as if it took some effort. "Be realistic, Fin. The Closed Council don't trust the nobility, and his family was the first among them, a heartbeat from the crown. Be patient."

"Huh," she snorted, at realism and patience both.

"If you want a higher place for your husband—" She opened her mouth but he raised his voice and talked over her. "—you'll need a more powerful patron than me. But if you want my advice – I know you don't, but still – you'll do without. I've sat on the Closed Council, at the very heart of government, and I can tell you power is a bloody mirage. The closer you seem to get the further away it is. So many demands to balance. So many pressures to endure. All the consequences of every decision weighing on you... small wonder the king never makes any. I never thought I would look forward to retirement, but perhaps without any power I can actually get something done."

She was not ready to retire. "Do we really have to wait for Meed to cause some catastrophe?"

He frowned up at her. "Yes. Really. And then for the Closed Council to write to me demanding his replacement and telling me who it will be. Providing they don't replace me first, of course."

"Who would they find to replace you?"

"I imagine General Mitterick would not turn down the appointment."

"Mitterick is a vainglorious backbiter with the loyalty of a cuckoo."

"He should suit the Closed Council perfectly, then."

"I don't know how you can stand him."

"I used to think I had all the answers myself, in my younger days. I maintain a guilty sympathy with those who still labour under the illusion." He gave her a significant look. "They are not few in number."

"And I suppose it's a woman's place to simper on the sidelines and cheer as idiots rack up the casualties?"

"We all find ourselves cheering for idiots from time to time, that's a fact of life. There really is no point heaping scorn on my subordinates. If a person is worthy of contempt, they'll bury themselves soon enough without help."

"Very well." She did not plan to wait that long, but it was plain she would do no more good here. Her father had enough to worry about, and she was supposed to be lifting his spirits rather than weighing them down. Her eye fell on the squares board, still set out in the midst of their last game.

"You still have the board set?"

"Of course."

"Then..." She had been planning her move ever since she last saw him, but made it as if it had only just occurred to her, brushing the piece forward with a shrug.

Her father looked up in that indulgent way he used to when she was a girl. "Are you entirely sure about that?"

She sighed. "It's as good as another."

He reached for a piece, and paused. His eyes darted around the board, hand hovering. His smile faded. He slowly withdrew the hand, touched one finger to his bottom lip. Then he started to smile. "Why, you—"

"Something to take your mind off the casualties."

"I have Black Dow for that. Not to mention the First of the Magi and his colleagues." He sourly shook his head. "Are you staying here tonight? I could find you a—"

"I should be with Hal."

"Of course. Of course you should." She bent and kissed him on the forehead, and he closed his eyes, held her shoulder for a moment. "Be careful tomorrow. I'd sooner lose ten thousand than lose you."

"You won't shake me off that easily." She headed for the door. "I mean to live to see you get out of that move!"

The rain had stopped for the time being and the officers had drifted back to their units. All except one.

It looked as if Bremer dan Gorst had been caught between leaning nonchalantly against the rail their horses were tied to or standing proudly straight, and had ended up posed awkwardly in no-man's-land between the two.

Even so, Finree could not think of him as quite the harmless figure she once had, when they used to share brief and laughably formal conversations in the sunny gardens of the Agriont. Only a graze down the side of his face gave any indication that he had been in action at all that day, and yet she had it from Captain Hardrick that he had charged alone into a legion of Northmen and killed six. When she heard the story from Colonel Brint it had become ten. Who knew what story the enlisted men were telling by now? The pommel of his steel glinted faintly as he straightened, and she realised with an odd cold thrill that he had killed men with that sword, only a few hours before. Several men, whichever story you believed. It should not have raised him in her estimation in the least, and yet it did, very considerably. He had acquired the glamour of violence.

"Bremer. Are you waiting for my father?"

"I thought…" in that strangely incongruous, piping voice of his, and then, slightly lower, "you might need an escort."

She smiled. "So there are still some heroes left in the world? Lead the way."

Calder sat in the damp darkness, a long spit from the shit-pits, listening to other men celebrate Black Dow's victory. He didn't like admitting it, but he missed Seff. He missed the warmth and safety of her bed. He certainly missed the scent of her as the breeze picked up and wafted the smell of dung under his nose. But in all this chaos of campfires, drunken singing, drunken boasting, drunken wrestling, there was only one place he could think of where you could be sure of catching a man alone. And treachery needs privacy.

He heard heavy footsteps thumping towards the pit. Their maker was no more than a black outline with orange firelight down the edges, the very faintest grey planes of a face, but even so Calder recognised him. There were few men, even in this company, who were quite so wide. Calder stood, stretching out his stiff legs, and walked up to the edge of the pit beside the newcomer, wrinkling his nose. Pits full of shit, and pits full of corpses. That's all war left behind, as far as he could see.

"Cairm Ironhead," he said quietly. "What are the chances?"

"My, my." The sound of spittle sucked from the back of a mouth, then sent spinning into the hole. "Prince Calder, this is an honour. Thought you were camped over to the west with your brother."

"I am."

"My pits smell sweeter than his, do they?"

"Not much."

"Come to measure cocks with me, then? It ain't how much you've got, you know, but what you do with it."

"You could say the same about strength."

"Or guile." Nothing else but silence. Calder didn't like a silent man. A boastful man like Golden, an angry man like Tenways, even a savage man like Black Dow, they give you something to work with. A quiet man like Ironhead gives nothing. Especially in the dark, where Calder couldn't even guess at his thoughts.

"I need your help," he tried.

"Think of running water."

"Not with that."

"With what, then?"

"I've heard it said Black Dow wants me dead."

"More'n I know. But if it's true, what's my interest? We don't all love you as much as you love yourself, Calder."

"You'll have need of allies of your own before too long, and you well know it."

"Do I?"

Calder snorted. "No fool gets where you are, Ironhead. Black Dow scarcely has more liking for you than me, I think."

"No liking? Has he not put me in the place of honour? Front and middle, boy!"

Calder got the unpleasant feeling there was a trace of mocking laughter in Ironhead's voice. But it was some kind of opening and he had no choice but to charge in with his most scornful chuckle. "The place of *honour?* Black Dow? He turned on the man who spared his life, and stole my father's chain for himself. The place of *honour?* He's done what I'd do to the man I fear most. Put you where you'll take the brunt of the enemy's fury. My father always said you were the toughest fighter in the North, and Black Dow knows it. Knows you'll never back down. He's put you where your own strength will work against you. And who's to benefit? Who's been left

209

out of the fight? Tenways and Golden." He'd been hoping for that name to work some magic, but Ironhead didn't move so much as a hair. "They hang back while you, and my brother, and my wife's father do the fighting. I hope your honour can stop a knife in the back, when it comes."

There was a grunt. "Finally."

"Finally what?"

The sound of piss spattering below them. "That. You know, Calder, you said it yourself."

"Said what?"

"No fool gets where I am. I'm a long way from convinced Black Dow's set on my doom or even on yours. But if he is, what help can you offer me? Your father's praise? That lost most of its worth when he got bested in the High Places, and all the rest when the Bloody-Nine smashed his skull to porridge. Oops." Calder felt piss spattering over his boots. "Sorry 'bout that. Guess we're not all as nimble with our cocks as you are. Reckon I'll stick with Dow, touched though I am by your offer of alliance."

"Black Dow's got nothing to offer but war and the fear men have of him. If he dies there's nothing left." Silence, while Calder wondered if he'd gone a step too far.

"Huh." There was a jingling as Ironhead fastened his belt. "Kill him, then. But until you do, find other ears for your lies. Find another piss-pit too, you wouldn't want to drown in this one." Calder was slapped on the back, hard enough to leave him teetering at the brink, waving his arms for balance. When he found it, Ironhead was gone.

Calder stood there for a moment. If talk sows seeds, he wasn't sure at all what harvest he could expect from this. But that didn't have to be a bad thing. He'd learned Cairm Ironhead was a subtler man than he appeared. That alone was worth some piss on his boots.

"One day I'll sit in Skarling's Chair," Calder whispered into the darkness. "And I'll make you eat my shit, and you'll tell me nothing ever tasted so sweet." That made him feel a little better.

He shook the wet from his boots as best he could, and strutted off into the night.

Rest and Recreation

Finree did not make much noise. Neither did Gorst. But that suited him well enough. Knobs of backbone showed through pale skin, thin muscles in her hunched shoulders tensing and relaxing, an unsightly ripple going through her arse with every thrust of his hips. He closed his eyes. In his head it was prettier.

They were in her husband's tent. *Or no.* That wasn't working. *My quarters in the palace.* The ones he used to have when he was the king's First Guard. *Yes.* That was better. Nice feel, they'd had. *Airy.* Or maybe her father's headquarters? *On his desk? In front of the other officers at a briefing?* Hell, no. *Urgh.* His quarters in the palace were easiest, familiar from a thousand well-worn fantasies in which the Closed Council had never stripped him of his position.

I love you, I love you, I love you. It hardly felt like love, though. It hardly felt like much of anything. Certainly nothing beautiful. A mechanical action. *Like winding a clock or peeling a carrot or milking a cow.* How long had he been at it now? His hips were aching, his stomach was aching, his back and his shoulder were bruised as a trampled apple from the fight in the shallows. Slap, slap, slap, skin on skin. He bared his teeth, gripping hard at her hips, forcing himself back to his airy quarters at the palace...

Getting there, getting there, getting there—

"Are you nearly done?"

Gorst stopped dead, snatched to reality with an icy shock. Nothing like Finree's voice. The side of her face turned towards him, gleaming damply in the light of the one candle, the dimple of an old acne scar inadequately covered by thick powder. Nothing like Finree's face. All his thrusting seemed to have made little impression. She might have been a baker asking his apprentice if the pies were done.

His rasping breath echoed back from the canvas. "I thought I told you not to talk."

"I've a queue."

So much for nearly there. His cock was already wilting. He struggled to his feet, sore head brushing against the ceiling of the tent. She was one of the cleaner ones, but still the air had a cloying feel. Too much sweat and breath, and other things, inadequately smothered by cheap flower-water. He wondered how many other men had already been through here tonight, how many more would come through. He wondered if they pretended they were somewhere else, she was someone else. *Does she pretend that we are someone else? Does she care? Does she hate us? Or are we a procession of clocks to be wound, carrots to be peeled, cows to be milked?*

She had her back to him, shrugging her dress on so she could shrug it off again. He felt as if he was suffocating. He dragged his trousers up and fumbled his belt shut. He tossed coins on a wooden box without counting, tore his way out through the flap into the night and stood there, eyes closed, breathing the damp air and swearing never to do this again. *Again.*

One of the pimps stood outside, apparently unbothered by the water gently dripping from the brim of his hat, with that knowing and slightly threatening smile they have to wear like uniforms. "Everything to your liking?"

My liking? I seem unable even to come in the allotted time. Most men are capable of that level of social interaction, at least, if no other, are they not? What am I, that I must debase and ruin even the one decent emotion I have? If one can call an entirely unhealthy obsession with another man's wife decent. I don't suppose one can. Well, probably he could.

Gorst looked at the man. Really looked, right in his eyes. Through that empty smile to the greed, and ruthlessness, and limitless boredom behind.

My liking? Shall I guffaw, and hug you like a brother? Hug you and hug you and twist your head all the way around, and your stupid fucking hat with it? If I beat your face until it has no bones in it, if I crush your scrawny throat with my hands, will that be a loss to the world, do you think? Will anyone even notice? Would I even notice? Would it be an evil deed, or a good? One less worm to get fat burrowing through the shit of the king's glorious army?

Gorst's mask must have slipped for a moment, or perhaps the man was more attuned by years of practice to hints of violence in a face than the cultured members of Jalenhorm's staff and Kroy's headquarters. His eyes narrowed and he took a cautious step back, one hand straying towards his belt.

Gorst found himself hoping the man would pull out a blade, excitement flaring briefly at the thought of seeing steel. *Is that all that excites me now?*

Death? Facing it and causing it? Did he even feel the slightest renewed stirring in his sore groin at the possibility of violence? But the pimp only stood there, watching.

"Everything is fine." And Gorst trudged past, boots squelching in the muck, away between the tents and into the mad carnival that sprang up behind the lines, as if by magic, whenever the army stopped for more than a couple of hours together. As full of bustle and variety as any market of the Thousand Isles, as full of blinding colour and choking fragrance as any Dagoskan bazaar, every need, taste or whim catered for a dozen times over.

Fawning merchants held swatches of bright cloth against officers too drunk to stand. Armourers battered out a shattering anvil music while salesmen demonstrated the strength, sharpness or beauty of wares nimbly replaced with trash when the money was handed over. A major with a bristling moustache sat frozen in double-chinned belligerence while a painter dashed off a shoddy representation by candlelight. Joyless laughter and meaningless babble hammered at Gorst's aching head. Everything the best, the finest, the bespoke and renowned.

"The new self-sharpening sheath!" someone roared. "Self-sharpening!"

"Advances to officers! Loans at first-rate rates!"

"Suljuk girls here! Best fuckery you'll ever get!"

"Flowers!" in a voice somewhere between song and scream. "For your wife! For your daughter! For your lover! For your whore!"

"For pet or pot!" a woman shrieked, thrusting up a bemused puppy. "For pet or pot!"

Children old long before their time darted through the crowd offering polishing or prophecy, sharpening or shaving, grooming or gravedigging. Offering anything and everything that could be bought or paid for. A girl whose age could not be reckoned slipped all around Gorst in a capering dance, bare feet mud-caked to the knee. Suljuk, Gurkish, Styrian, who knew of what mongrel derivation. "Like this?" she cooed, gesturing at a stick upon which samples of gold braid were stapled.

Gorst felt a sudden choking need to weep, and gave her a sad smile, and shook his head. She spat at his feet, and was gone. A pair of elderly ladies stood at the flap of a dripping tent, handing out printed papers extolling the virtues of temperance and sobriety to illiterate soldiers who had already left them trampled in the mud for a half-mile in every direction, worthy lessons gently erased by the rain.

A few more steps, each an unimaginable effort, and Gorst stopped in the track, alone in the midst of all that crowd. Cursing soldiers slopped through the mud around him, all stranded like him with their petty despairs, all shopping like him for what cannot be bought. He looked up, open-mouthed, rain tickling his tongue. Hoping for guidance, perhaps, but the stars were shrouded in cloud. *They light the happy way for better men. Harod dan Brock, and his like.* Shoulders and elbows knocked and jostled him. *Someone help me, please.*

But who?

DAY TWO

"You can't say that civilisation
don't advance, however,
for in every war they kill
you in a new way"

Will Rogers

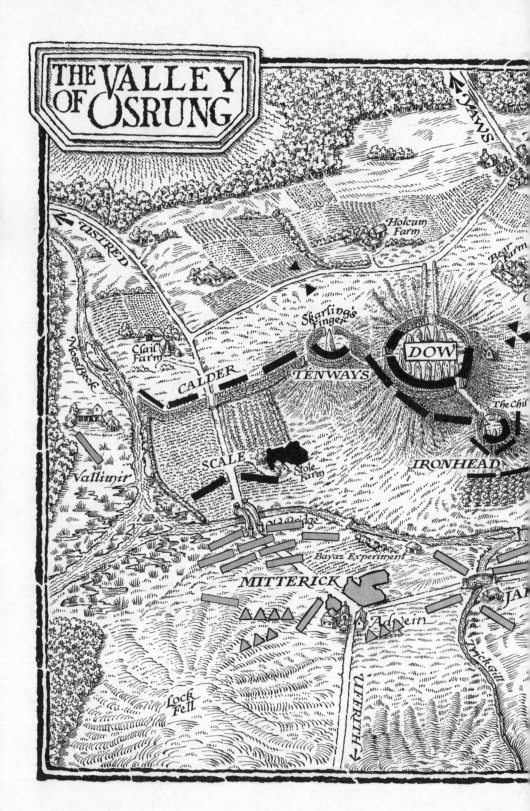

THE VALLEY OF OSRUNG

JAWS

USTRED

Holcum Farm

Bear Farm

Clail Farm

MossBeck

CALDER

Skarling's Finger

TENWAYS

DOW

The Chil

Vallimir

SCALE

Stole Farm

IRONHEAD

Old Bridge

Bayaz Experiment

JA

MITTERICK

Adwein

LIFERITH

Lock Fell

InchGill

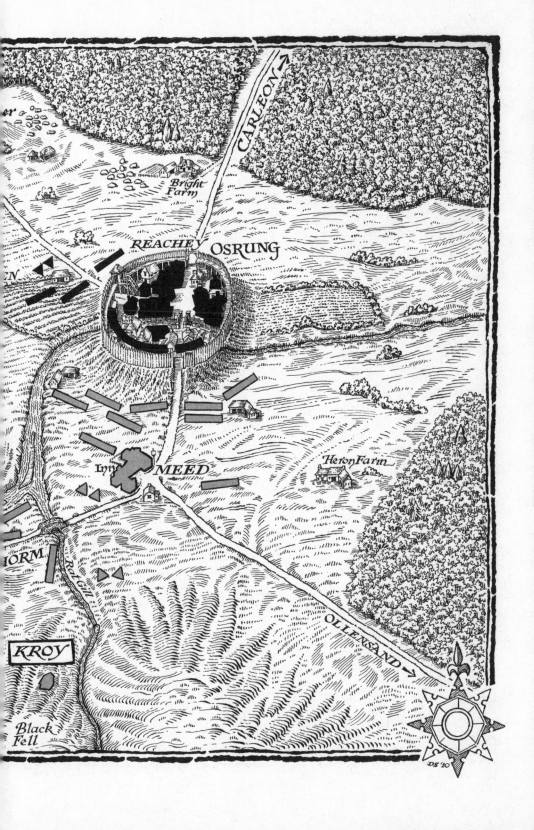

CARLEON

Bright
Farm

REACHEY OSRUNG

Inn MEED

Heron Farm

KROY

RatGill

IORM

OLLENSAND

Black
Fell

DS '10

Dawn

When Craw dragged himself from his bed, cold and clammy as a drowned man's grave, the sun was no more'n a smear of mud-brown in the blackness of the eastern sky. He fumbled his sword through the clasp at his belt then stretched, creaked and grunted through his morning routine of working out exactly how much everything hurt. His aching jaw he could blame on Hardbread and his lads, his aching legs on a lengthy jog across some fields and up a hill followed by a night huddled in the wind, but the bastard of a headache he'd have to take the blame for himself. He'd had a drink or two or even a few more last night, softening the loss of the fallen, toasting the luck of the living.

Most of the dozen were already gathered about the pile of damp wood that on a happier day would've been a fire. Drofd was bent over it, cursing softly while he failed to get it lit. Cold breakfast, then.

"Oh, for a roof," whispered Craw as he limped over.

"I slice the bread thin, d'you see?" Whirrun had the Father of Swords gripped between his knees with a hand's length drawn, and now he was rubbing loaf against blade with ludicrous care, like a carpenter chiselling at a vital joint.

"Sliced bread?" Wonderful turned away from the black valley to watch him. "Can't see it catching on, can you?"

Yon spat over his shoulder. "Either way, could you bloody get on with it? I'm hungry."

Whirrun ignored 'em. "Then, when I've got two cut," and he dropped a pale slab of cheese on one slice then slapped the other on top like he was catching a fly, "I trap the cheese between them, and there you have it!"

"Bread and cheese." Yon weighed the half-loaf in one hand and the cheese in the other. "Just the same as I've got." And he bit a lump off the cheese and tossed it to Scorry.

Whirrun sighed. "Have none of you no *vision?*" He held up his master-piece to such light as there was, which was almost none. "This is no more bread and cheese than a fine axe is wood and iron, or a live person is meat and hair."

"What is it, then?" asked Drofd, rocking back from his wet wood and tossing the flint aside in disgust.

"A whole new thing. A forging of the humble parts of bread and cheese into a greater whole. I call it . . . a cheese-trap." Whirrun took a dainty nib-ble from one corner. "Oh, yes, my friends. This tastes like . . . progress. Works with ham, too. Works with anything."

"You should try it with a turd," said Wonderful.

Drofd laughed up snot but Whirrun hardly seemed to notice. "This is the thing about war. Forces men to do new things with what they have. Forces them to think new ways. No war, no progress." He leaned back on one elbow. "War, d'you see, is like the plough that keeps the earth rich, like the fire that clears the fields, like—"

"The shit that makes the flowers grow?" asked Wonderful.

"Exactly!" Whirrun pointed at her sharply with his whole new thing and the cheese fell out into the unlit fire. Wonderful near fell over from laugh-ing. Yon snorted so hard he blew bread out of his nose. Even Scorry stopped his singing to have a high chuckle. Craw laughed along, and it felt good. Felt like too long since the last time. Whirrun frowned at his two flapping slices of bread. "Don't think I trapped it tight enough." And he shoved 'em in his mouth all at once and started rooting through the damp twigs for the cheese.

"Union showed any sign of moving?" asked Craw.

"None that we've seen." Yon squinted up at the stains of brightness in the east. "Dawn's on the march, though. Reckon we'll see more soon."

"Best get Brack up," said Craw. "He'll be pissy all day if he misses breakfast."

"Aye, Chief." And Drofd trotted off to where the hillman was sleeping.

Craw pointed down at the Father of Swords, short stretch of grey blade drawn. "Don't it have to be blooded now?"

"Maybe crumbs count," said Wonderful.

"Alas, they don't." Whirrun brushed the heel of his hand against its edge, then wiped it with his last bit of crust and slid the sword gently back into its scabbard. "Progress can be painful," he muttered, sucking the cut.

"Chief?" Far as Craw could tell in the gloom, and with Drofd's hair blown across his face by the wind, the lad looked worried. "Don't reckon Brack wants to get up."

"We'll see." Craw strode over to him, a big shape swaddled up on his side, shadow pooling in the folds of his blanket. "Brack." He poked him with the toe of his boot. "Brack?" The tattooed side of Brack's face was all beaded with dew. Craw put his hand on it. Cold. Didn't feel like a person at all. Meat and hair, like Whirrun said.

"Up you get, Brack, you fat hog," snapped Wonderful. "Before Yon eats all your—"

"Brack's dead," said Craw.

Finree could not have said how long she had been awake, sitting on her travelling chest at the window with her arms resting on the cold sill and her chin resting on her wrists. Long enough to watch the ragged line of the fells to the north become distinct from the sky, for the quick-flowing river to emerge glittering from the mist, for the forests to the east to take on the faintest texture. Now, if she squinted, she could pick out the jagged top of the fence around Osrung, a light twinkling at the window of a single tower. In the few hundred strides of black farmland between her and the town a ragged curve of flickering torches marked out the Union positions.

A little more light in the sky, a little more detail in the world, and Lord Governor Meed's men would be rushing from those trenches and towards the town. The strong right fist of her father's army. She bit down on the tip of her tongue, so hard it was painful. Excited and afraid at once.

She stretched, looking over her shoulder into the cobwebby little room. She had made a desultory effort at cleaning but had to admit she was pathetic as a homemaker. She wondered what had become of the owners of the inn. Wondered what its name was, even. She thought she had seen a pole over the gate, but the sign was gone. That's what war does. Strips people and places of their identities and turns them into enemies in a line, positions to be taken, resources to be foraged. Anonymous things that can be carelessly crushed, and stolen, and burned without guilt. War is hell, and all that. But full of opportunities.

She crossed to the bed, or the straw-filled mattress they were sharing, and leaned down over Hal, studying his face. He looked young, eyes closed and mouth open, cheek squashed against the sheet, breath whistling in his nose. Young, and innocent, and ever so slightly stupid.

"Hal," she whispered, and sucked gently at his top lip. His eyelids fluttered open and he stretched back, arms above his head, craned up to kiss her, then saw the window and the glimmer of light in the sky.

"Damn it!" He threw the blankets back and scrambled out of bed. "You should've woken me sooner." He splashed water from the cracked bowl onto his face and rubbed it with a cloth, started pulling yesterday's trousers on.

"You'll still be early," she said, leaning back on her elbows and watching him dress.

"I have to be twice as early. You know I do."

"You looked so peaceful. I didn't have the heart to wake you."

"I'm supposed to be helping coordinate the attack."

"I suppose someone has to."

He froze for a moment with his shirt over his head, then pulled it down. "Perhaps... you should stay at your father's headquarters today, up on the fell. Most of the other wives have already headed back to Uffrith."

"If we could only pack Meed off along with the rest of the clothes-obsessed old women, perhaps we'd have a chance of victory."

Hal soldiered on. "There's only you and Aliz dan Brint, now, and I worry about you—"

He was painfully transparent. "You worry that I'll make a scene with your incompetent commanding officer, you mean."

"That too. Where's my—"

She kicked his sword rattling across the boards and he had to stoop to retrieve it. "It's a shame, that a man like you should have to take orders from a man like Meed."

"The world is full of shameful things. That's a long way from the worst."

"Something really should be done about him."

Hal was still busy fumbling with his sword-belt. "There's nothing to be done but to make the best of it."

"Well... someone could mention the mess he's making to the king."

"You may not be aware of this, but my father and the king had a minor falling out. I don't stand very high in his Majesty's favour."

"Your good friend Colonel Brint does."

Hal looked up sharply. "Fin. That's low."

"Who cares how high it is if it helps you get what you deserve?"

"*I* care," he snapped, dragging the buckle closed. "You get on by doing the right thing. By hard work, and loyalty, and doing as you're told. You don't get on by...by..."

"By what?"

"Whatever it is you're doing."

She felt a sudden, powerful urge to hurt him. She wanted to say she could easily have married a man with a father who wasn't the most infamous traitor of his generation. She wanted to point out he only had the place he had now through her father's patronage and her constant wheedling, and that left to his own devices he'd have been demonstrating hard work and loyalty as a poor lieutenant in a provincial regiment. She wanted to tell him he was a good man, but the world was not the way good people thought it was. Fortunately, he got in first.

"Fin, I'm sorry. I know you want what's best for us. I know you've done a lot for me already. I don't deserve you. Just...let me do things my way. Please. Just promise me you won't do anything...rash."

"I promise." She'd make sure whatever she did was well thought out. That or she'd just break her promise. She didn't take them terribly seriously.

He smiled, somewhat relieved, and bent to kiss her. She returned it half-heartedly, but then, when she felt his shoulders slump, remembered he'd be in danger today, and she pinched his cheek and shook it about. "I love you." That was why she had come up here, no? Why she was slogging through the mud along with the soldiers? To be with him. To support him. To steer him in the right direction. The Fates knew, he needed it.

"I love you more," he said.

"It's not a competition."

"No?" And he went out, pulling on his jacket. She loved Hal. Really she did. But if she waited for him to get what they deserved through honesty and good nature she'd be waiting until the sky fell in.

And she did not plan to live out her days as some colonel's wife.

Corporal Tunny had long ago acquired a reputation as the fiercest sleeper in his Majesty's army. He could sleep on anything, in any situation, and wake in an instant ready for action or, better still, to avoid it. He'd slept through the whole assault at Ulrioch in the lead trench fifty strides from the breach, then woken just in time to hop between the corpses as the fighting petered out and snatch as fine a share of the booty as anyone who actually drew steel that day.

So a patch of waterlogged forest in the midst of a spotty drizzle with nothing but a smelly oilskin over his head was good as a feather bed to him. His recruits weren't anywhere near so tough in the eyelids, though. Tunny snapped awake in the chill gloom around dawn, back against a tree and the regimental standard in one fist, and nudged his oilskin up with one finger to see the two men he had left hunched over the damp ground.

"Like this?" Yolk was squeaking.

"No," whispered Worth. "Tinder under there, then strike it like—"

Tunny was up in a flash, stomped down hard on their pile of slimy sticks and crushed it flat. "No fires, idiots, if the enemy miss the flames they'll see the smoke for sure!" Not that Yolk would've got that pitiable collection of soaked rot lit in ten years of trying. He wasn't even holding the flint properly.

"How we going to cook our bacon, though, Corporal?" Worth held up his skillet, a pale and unappetising slice lying limp inside.

"You're not."

"We'll eat it raw?"

"Can't advise it," said Tunny, "especially not to you, Worth, given the sensitivity of your intestines."

"My what?"

"Your dodgy guts."

His shoulders slumped. "What do we eat, then?"

"What have you got?"

"Nothing."

"That's what you're eating, then. Unless you can find something better." Even considering he'd been woken before dawn, Tunny was unusually grumpy. He had a lurking sense he had something to be very annoyed about, but wasn't sure what. Until he remembered the dirty water closing over Klige's face, and kicked Yolk's embarrassment of a fire away into the dripping brush.

"Colonel Vallimir came up a while ago," murmured Yolk, as though that was the very thing Tunny needed to lift his spirits.

"Wonderful," he hissed. "Maybe we can eat him."

"Might be some food came up with him."

Tunny snorted. "All officers ever bring up is trouble, and our boy Valli-mir's the worst kind."

"Stupid?" muttered Worth.

"Clever," said Tunny. "And ambitious. The kind of officer climbs to a promotion over the bodies of the common man."

"Are we the common man?" asked Yolk.

Tunny stared at him. "You are the fucking definition." Yolk even looked pleased about it. "No sign of Latherliver yet?"

"Lederlingen, Corporal Tunny."

"I know his name, Worth. I choose to mispronounce it because it amuses me." He puffed out his cheeks. His standard for amusement really had plummeted since this campaign got underway.

"Haven't seen him," said Yolk, gazing sadly at that forlorn slice of bacon.

"That's something, at least." Then, when the two lads looked blankly at him. "Leperlover went to tell the tin-soldier pushers where we are. Chances are he'll be the one bringing the orders back."

"What orders?" asked Yolk.

"How the hell should I know what orders? But any orders is a bad thing." Tunny frowned off towards the treeline. He couldn't see much through the thicket of trunk, branch, shadow and mist, but he could just hear the sound of the distant stream, swollen with half the drizzle that had fallen last night. The other half felt like it was in his underwear. "Might even be an order to attack. Cross that stream and hit the Northmen in the flank."

Worth carefully set his pan down, pressing at his stomach. "Corporal, I think—"

"Well, I don't want you doing it here, do I?"

Worth dashed off into the shadowy brush, already fumbling with his belt. Tunny sat back against his trunk, slipped out Yolk's flask and took the smallest nip.

Yolk licked his pale lips. "Could I—"

"No." Tunny regarded the recruit through narrowed eyes as he took another. "Unless you've something to pay with." Silence. "There you go, then."

"A tent would be something," whispered Yolk in a voice almost too soft to hear.

"It would, but they're with the horses, and the king has seen fit to supply his loyal soldiers with a new and spectacularly inefficient type which leaks at every seam." Leading, as it happened, to a profitable market in the old type in which Tunny had already twice turned a handsome profit. "How would you pitch one here anyway?" And he wriggled back against his tree so the bark scratched his itchy shoulder blades.

"What should we do?" asked Yolk.

"Nothing whatsoever, trooper. Unless specifically and precisely instructed otherwise, a good soldier always does nothing." In a narrow triangle between black branches, the sky was starting to show the faintest sickly tinge of light. Tunny winced, and closed his eyes. "The thing folks at home never realise about war is just how bloody boring it is."

And like that he was asleep again.

Calder's dream was the same one as always.

Skarling's Hall in Carleon, dim with shadows, sound of the river outside the tall windows. Years ago, when his father was King of the Northmen. He was watching his younger self, sitting in Skarling's Chair and smirking. Smirking down at Forley the Weakest, all bound up, Bad-Enough standing over him with his axe out.

Calder knew it for a dream, but he felt the same freezing dread as ever. He was trying to shout, but his mouth was all stopped up. He was trying to move, but he was bound as tight as Forley. Bound by what he'd done, and what he hadn't.

"What shall we do?" asked Bad-Enough.

And Calder said, "Kill him."

He woke with a jolt as the axe came down, floundering with his blankets. The room was fizzing black. There was none of that warm wash of relief you get when you wake from a nightmare. It had happened. Calder swung from his bed, rubbing at his sweaty temples. He'd given up on being a good man long ago, hadn't he?

Then why did he still dream like one?

"Peace?" Calder looked up with a start, heart jumping at his ribs. There was a great shape in the chair in the corner. A blacker shape than the darkness. "It was talk of peace got you banished in the first place."

Calder breathed out. "And a good morning to you, brother." Scale was wearing his armour, but that was no surprise. Calder was starting to think he slept in it.

226

"I thought you were the clever one? At this rate you'll clever yourself right back into the mud, and me along with you, and so much for our father's legacy then. Peace? On a day of victory?"

"Did you see their faces, though? Plenty even at that meet are ready to stop fighting, day of victory or not. There'll be harder days coming, and when they come more and more will see it our way—"

"*Your* way," snapped Scale, "I've a battle to fight. A man doesn't get to be reckoned a hero by talking."

Calder could hardly keep the contempt out of his voice. "Maybe what the North needs is fewer heroes and more thinkers. More builders. Maybe our father's remembered for his battles, but his legacy is the roads he laid, the fields he cleared, the towns, and the forges, and the docks, and the—"

"He built the roads to march his armies on. He cleared the fields to feed them. The towns bred soldiers, the forges made swords, the docks brought in weapons."

"Our father fought because he had to, not because he—"

"This is the North!" bellowed Scale, voice making the little room ring. "Everyone has to fight!" Calder swallowed, suddenly unsure of himself and ever so slightly scared. "Whether they want to or not. Sooner or later, everyone has to fight."

Calder licked his lips, not ready to admit defeat. "Our father preferred to get what he wanted with words. Men listened to—"

"Men listened because they knew he had *iron in him*!" Scale smashed the arm of his chair with his fist, wood cracking, struck it again and broke it off, sent it clattering across the boards. "Do you know what I remember him telling me? 'Get what you can with words, because words are free, but the words of an armed man ring that much sweeter. So when you talk, bring your sword.'" He stood, and tossed something across the room. Calder squeaked, half-caught it, half-hit painfully in the chest by it. Heavy and hard, metal gleaming faintly. His sheathed sword. "Come outside." Scale loomed over him. "And bring your sword."

It was hardly any lighter outside the ramshackle farmhouse. Just the first smear of dawn in the heavy eastern sky, picking out the Heroes on their hilltop in solemn black. The wind was coming up keen, whipping drizzle in Calder's eyes, sweeping waves through the barley and making him hug himself tight. A scarecrow danced a mad jig on a pole near the house, torn gloves endlessly beckoning for a partner. Clail's Wall was a chest-high heap of moss running through the fields from beyond a rise on their right to a good way up the steep flank of the Heroes. Scale's men were huddled in its lee, most still swaddled in blankets, exactly where Calder wished he was. He couldn't remember the last time he'd seen the world this early and it was an even uglier place than usual.

Scale pointed south, through a gap in the wall and down a rough track scarred with puddles. "Half the men are hidden in sight of the Old Bridge. When the Union try to cross, we'll stop the bastards."

Calder didn't want to deny it, of course, but he had to ask. "How many Union on the other side of the river now?"

"A lot." Scale looked at him as if daring him to say something. Calder only scratched his head. "You're staying back here, with Pale-as-Snow and the rest of the men, behind Clail's Wall." Calder nodded. Staying behind a wall sounded like his kind of job. "Sooner or later, though, chances are I'll need your help. When I send for it, come forward. We'll fight together." Calder winced into the wind. That sounded less like his kind of job. "I can trust you to do that, right?"

Calder frowned sideways. "Of course." Prince Calder, a byword for trustiness. "I won't let you down." Brave, bold, good Prince Calder.

"Whatever we've lost, we've got each other still." Scale put his big hand on Calder's shoulder. "It's not easy, is it? Being a great man's son. You'd have thought it would come with all kinds of advantages – with borrowed admiration, and respect. But it's only as easy as it is for the seeds of a great tree, trying to grow in its choking shadow. Not many make it to the sunlight for themselves."

"Aye." Calder didn't mention that being a great man's younger son was twice the trial. Then you've two trees to take the axe to before you can spread your leaves in the sunshine.

Scale nodded up towards Skarling's Finger. A few fires still twinkled on the flanks of the hill where Tenways' men had their camps. "If we can't hold up, Brodd Tenways is meant to be helping."

Calder raised his brows. "I'll expect Skarling himself to ride to my aid before I count on that old bastard."

"Then it's you and me. We might not always agree, but we're family." Scale held out his hand, and Calder took it.

"Family." Half-family, anyway.

"Good luck, brother."

"And to you." Half-brother. Calder watched Scale swing up onto his horse and spur off sharply down that track towards the Old Bridge.

"Got a feeling you'll need more'n luck today, your Highness." Foss Deep was under the dripping ruins of a porch beside the house, his weathered clothes and his weathered face fading into the weathered wall behind.

"I don't know." Shallow sat wrapped in a grey blanket so only his grinning head showed, disembodied. "The biggest mountain of best luck ever might do it."

Calder turned away from them in sulky silence, frowning across the fields to the south. He'd a feeling they might have the truth of it.

Theirs wasn't the only bit of earth being turned over. Few other wounded men must've died in the night. You could see the little groups, hunched in the drizzle with sorrow, or more likely self-pity, which looks about the same and serves just as well at a funeral. You could hear the Chiefs trotting out their empty babble, all aiming at that same sorry tone. Splitfoot was one, standing over the grave of one of Dow's Named Men not twenty paces distant, giving it the moist eye. No sign of Dow himself, mind you. Moist eyes weren't really his style.

Meanwhile the ordinary business of the day got started like the burial parties were ghosts themselves, invisible. Men grumbling as they crawled from wet beds, cursing at damp clothes, rubbing down damp weapons and armour, searching out food, pissing, scratching, sucking the last drops from last night's bottles, comparing trophies stole from the Union, chuckling over one joke or another. Chuckling too loud because they all knew there'd be more dark work today and chuckles had to be grabbed where they could be.

Craw looked at the others, all with heads bowed. All except Whirrun, who was arching back, hugging the Father of Swords in his folded arms, letting the rain patter on his tongue. Craw was a little annoyed by that, and a little jealous of it. He wished he was known as a madman and didn't have to go through the empty routines. But there's a right way of doing things, and for him there was no dodging it.

"What makes a man a hero?" he asked the wet air. "Big deeds? Big name? Tall glory and tall songs? No. Standing by your crew, I reckon." Whirrun grunted his agreement, then stuck his tongue out again. "Brack-i-Dayn, come down from the hills fifteen years ago, fought beside me fourteen of 'em, and always thought of his crew 'fore himself. Lost count on the number o' times that big bastard saved my life. Always had a kind word, or a funny one. Think he even made Yon laugh one time."

"Twice," said Yon, face harder'n ever. Got any harder he'd be knocking lumps from the Heroes with it.

"He made no complaints. Except not enough to eat." Craw's voice went for a moment and he gave a kind of squeaky croak. Stupid bloody noise for a Chief to make, 'specially at a time like this. He cleared his throat and hammered on. "Never enough for Brack to eat. He died . . . peaceful. Reckon he'd have liked that, even if he loved a good fight. Dying in your sleep is a long stretch better'n dying with steel in your guts, whatever the songs say."

"Fuck the songs," said Wonderful.

"Aye. Fuck 'em. Don't know who's buried under here, really. But if it's Skarling his self he should be proud to share some earth with Brack-i-Dayn." Craw curled his lips back. "And if not, fuck him too. Back to the mud, Brack." He knelt, not having to try too hard to look in pain since his kneecap felt like it was going to pop off, clawed up a fistful of damp black soil and shook it out again over the rest.

"Back to the mud," muttered Yon.

"Back to the mud," came Wonderful's echo.

"Looking on the sunny side," said Whirrun, "it's where we're all headed, one way or another. No?" He looked about as though expecting that to lift spirits, and when it didn't, shrugged and turned away.

"Old Brack's all done." Scorry squatted by the grave, one hand on the wet ground, brow furrowed like at a puzzle he couldn't work out. "Can't believe it. Good words, though, Chief."

"You reckon?" Craw winced as he stood, slapping the dirt from his hands. "I'm not sure how many more o' these I can stand."

"Aye," murmured Scorry. "I guess those are the times."

Opening Remarks

"Get up."

Beck shoved the foot away, scowling. He didn't care for a boot in the ribs at any time, but 'specially not from Reft, and 'specially not when it felt like he only just got off to sleep. He'd lain awake in the darkness a long time, thinking on Caul Shivers stabbing that man, turning it over and over as he twisted about under his blanket. Not able to get comfortable. Not with his blanket or with the thought of that little knife poking away. "What?"

"The Union are coming, that's what."

Beck tore his blanket back and strode across the garret room, ducking under the low beam, sleep and anger forgotten both at once. He kicked the creaking door of the big cupboard closed, shouldered Brait and Stodder out of the way and stared through one of the narrow windows.

He'd half-expected to see men slaughtering each other outside in the lanes of Osrung, blood flying and flags waving and songs being sung right under his window. But the town was quiet at a first glance. Weren't much beyond dawn and the rain was flitting down, drawing a greasy haze over the huddled buildings.

Maybe forty strides away across a cobbled square the brown river was churning past, swollen with rain off the fells. The bridge didn't look much for all the fuss being made of it – a worn stone span barely wide enough for two riders to pass each other. A mill house stood on its right, a row of low houses on its left, shutters open with a few nervy faces at the windows, most looking off to the south, just like Beck. Beyond the bridge a rutted lane led between wattle shacks and up to the fence on the south side of town. He thought he could see men moving there on the walkways, dim through the drizzle. Maybe a couple with flatbows already shooting.

While he was looking, men started hurrying from an alley and into the square below, forming up a shield wall at the north end of the bridge while a man in a fine cloak bellowed at 'em. Carls to the front, ready to lock their painted shields together. Thralls behind, spears ready to bring down.

There was a battle on the way, all right.

"You should've told me sooner," he snapped, hurrying back to his blanket and dragging on his boots.

"Didn't know sooner," said Reft.

"Here." Colving offered Beck a hunk of black bread, his eyes scared circles in his chubby face.

Even the thought of eating made Beck feel sick. He snatched up his sword, then realised he'd nowhere to take it to. Weren't like he had a place at the fence, or in the shield wall, or anywhere else in particular. He looked towards the stairs, then towards the window, free hand opening and closing. "What do we do?"

"We wait." Flood dragged his stiff leg up the steps and into the attic. He'd got his mail on, glistening with drizzle across the shoulders. "Reachey's given us two houses to hold, this and one just across the street. I'll be in there."

"You will?" Beck realised he'd made himself sound scared, like a child asking his mummy if she was really going to leave him in the dark. "You know, some o' these boys could do with a man to look to—"

"That'll have to be you and Reft. You might not believe it, but the lads in the other house are even greener'n you lot."

"Right. 'Course." Beck had spent the past week chafing at Flood being always around, keeping him back. Now the thought of the old boy going only made him feel more jittery.

"There'll be you five and five more in this house. Some other lads from the weapontake. For the time being just set tight. Block up the windows downstairs best you can. Who's got a bow?"

"I have," said Beck.

"And me." Reft held his up.

"I've got my sling," said Colving, hopefully.

"You any good with it?" asked Reft.

The boy shook his head sadly. "Couldn't use it at a window, anyway."

"Why bring it up, then?" snapped Beck, fingering his own bow. His palm was all sweaty.

Flood walked to the two narrow windows and pointed towards the river. "Maybe we'll hold 'em at the fence, but if not we're forming up a shield wall at the bridge. If we don't hold 'em there, well, anyone with a bow start shooting. Careful, though, don't go hitting any of our boys in the back, eh? Better not to shoot at all than risk killing our own, and when the blood's up it can get hard to make out the difference. The rest of you downstairs, ready to keep 'em out of the house if they make it across." Stodder chewed at his big bottom lip. "Don't worry. They won't make it across, and even if they do they'll be in a right mess. Reachey'll be getting ready to hit back by then, you can bet on that. So if they try to get in, just keep 'em out 'til help gets here."

"Keep 'em out," piped Brait, jabbing happily at nothing with his twig of a spear. He didn't look like he could've kept a cat out of a chicken coop with that.

"Any questions?" Beck didn't feel he had a clue what to do, but it hardly seemed one question would plug the gap, so he kept quiet. "Right, then. I'll check back if I can." Flood limped to the stairway and was gone. They were on their own. Beck strode to a window again, thinking it was better'n doing nothing, but naught had changed that he could see.

"They over the fence yet?" Brait was up on tiptoe, trying to look over Beck's shoulder. He sounded all excited, eyes bright like a boy on his birthday, waiting to see what his present might be. He sounded a little bit like Beck always thought he'd feel facing battle. But he didn't feel that way. He felt sick and hot in spite of the damp breeze on his face.

"No. And ain't you supposed to be downstairs?"

"Not 'til they come, I'm not. Don't get to see this every day, do you?"

Beck brushed him off with an elbow. "Just get out of it! Your stink's making me sick!"

"All right, all right." Brait shambled away, looking hurt, but Beck couldn't bring up much sympathy. It was the best he could do not to bring up the breakfast he hadn't had.

Reft was stood at the other window, bow over his shoulder. "Thought you'd be happy. Looks like you'll get your chance to be a hero."

"I am happy," snapped Beck. And not shitting himself at all.

Meed had established his headquarters in the inn's common hall, which by the standards of the North was a palatial space, double height and with a gallery at first-floor level. Overnight it had been decorated like a palace too with gaudy hangings, inlaid cupboards, gilded candlesticks and all the pompous trappings one would expect in a lord governor's own residence, presumably carted half way across the North at monstrous expense. A pair of violinists had set up in the corner and were grinning smugly at each other as they sawed out jaunty chamber music. Three huge oil paintings had even been hoisted into position by Meed's industrious servants: two renderings of great battles from the Union's history and, incredibly, a portrait of Meed himself, glowering from on high in antique armour. Finree gaped at it for a moment, hardly knowing whether to laugh or cry.

Large windows faced south into the inn's weed-colonised courtyard, east across fields dotted with trees towards brooding woods, and north towards the town of Osrung. With all the shutters wide open a chilly breeze drifted through the room, ruffling hair and snatching at papers. Officers clustered about the northern windows, eager to catch a glimpse of the assault, Meed in their midst in a uniform of eye-searing crimson. He glanced sideways as Finree slipped up beside him and gave the slightest sneer of distaste, like a fastidious eater who has spied an insect in his salad. She returned it with a beaming smile.

"Might I borrow your eyeglass, your Grace?"

He worked his mouth sourly for a moment but was held prisoner by etiquette, and handed it stiffly over. "Of course."

The road curved off to the north, a muddy stripe through muddy fields overflowing with the sprawling camp, tents haphazardly scattered like monstrous fungi sprouted in the night. Beyond them were the earthworks Meed's men had thrown up in the darkness. Beyond them, through the haze of mist and drizzle, she could just make out the fence around Osrung, perhaps even the suggestion of scaling ladders against it.

Her imagination filled in the blanks. Ranks of marching men ordered forward to the palisade, grim-faced and determined as arrows showered down. The wounded dragged for the rear or left screaming where they lay. Rocks tumbling, ladders shoved from the fence, men butchered as they tried to climb over onto the walkways, thrust screaming back to be dashed on the ground below.

She wondered whether Hal was in the midst of that, playing the hero. For the first time she felt a stab of worry for him, a cold shiver through her shoulders. This was no game. She lowered Meed's eyeglass, chewing at her lip.

"Where the hell is the Dogman and his rabble?" the lord governor was demanding of Captain Hardrick.

"I believe they were behind us on the road, your Grace. His scouts came upon a burned-out village and the lord marshal gave him leave to investigate. They should be here within an hour or two—"

"Typical. You can rely on him for a knowing shrug but when the battle begins he is nowhere to be seen."

"Northmen are treacherous by nature," someone tossed out.

"Cowardly."

"Their presence would only slow us down, your Grace."

"That much is true," snorted Meed. "Order every unit into the attack. I want them overwhelmed. I want that town crushed into the dust and every Northman in it dead or running."

Finree could not help herself. "Surely it would be wise to leave at least one regiment behind? As I understand it, the woods to the east have not been thoroughly—"

"Do you seriously suppose you will hit upon some scheme by which you will replace me with your husband?"

There was a pause that seemed impossibly long, while Finree wondered if she might be dreaming. "I beg your—"

"He is a pleasant enough man, of course. Brave and honest and all those things housewives like to coo about. But he is a fool and, what is worse, the son of a notorious traitor and the husband of a shrew to boot. His only significant friend is your father, and your father's days in the sun are numbered in small digits." Meed spoke softly, but not so softly that he could not easily be overheard. One young captain's mouth fell open with surprise. It seemed Meed was not held quite so tightly by the bonds of etiquette as she had supposed.

"I frustrated an attempt by the Closed Council to prevent me taking my brother's place as lord governor, did you know that? The Closed Council. Do you really suppose some soldier's daughter might succeed where they failed? Address me only once again without the proper respect and I will crush you and your husband like the pretty, ambitious, irrelevant lice you are." He calmly plucked his eyeglass from her limp hand and looked through it towards Osrung, precisely as if he had never spoken and she did not exist.

Finree should have whipped out some acid rejoinder, but the only thing

in her mind was an overpowering urge to smash the front of Meed's eyeglass with her fist and drive the other end into his skull. The room seemed
uncomfortably bright. The violins ripped at her ears. Her face burned as if
she had been slapped. All she could do was blink, and meekly retreat. It was
as if she floated to the other side of the room without moving her feet. A
couple of the officers watched her get there, muttering among themselves,
evidently party to her one-sided humiliation and no doubt relishing it too.

"Are you all right?" asked Aliz. "You look pale."

"I am perfectly well." Or, in fact, seething with fury. Insulting her was
one thing, no doubt she deserved it. Insulting her husband and her father
were other things entirely. That she would make the old bastard pay for, she
swore it.

Aliz leaned close. "What do we do now?"

"Now? We sit here like good little girls and applaud while idiots stack up
the coffins."

"Oh."

"Don't worry. Later on they might let you weep over a wound or two
and, if the mood takes you, you can flutter your eyelashes at the awful futil-
ity of it all."

Aliz swallowed, and looked away. "Oh."

"That's right. Oh."

So this was battle. Beck and Reft had never had too much to say to each
other, but since the Union first started fighting their way over the fence
they hadn't said a word. Just stood silent at the windows. Beck wished he'd
got friends beside him. Or wished he'd tried harder to make friends of the
lads he'd found beside him. But it was too late now.

His bow was in his hand, an arrow nocked and the string ready to draw.
He'd had it ready the best part of an hour, but there was no one he could
shoot at. Nothing he could do but watch, and sweat, and lick his lips, and
watch. He'd started off wishing he could see more, but now the rain had
slacked off, and the sun was getting up, and Beck found he was seeing far
more than he wanted to.

The Union were over the fence in three or four places, into the town in
numbers. There was fighting all over, everything broken up into separate
little scraps facing every which way. No lines, just a mass of confusion and

mad noise. Shouts and howls mashed together, din of clashing metal and breaking wood.

Beck was no expert. He didn't know how anyone could be at this. But he could feel the balance shifting over there on the south side of the river. More and more Northmen were scurrying back across the bridge, some limping or holding wounds, some shouting and pointing off south, thread-ing their way through the shield wall at the north end of the span and into the square under Beck's window. Safety. He hoped. Felt a long bloody way from safe, though. Felt about as far from safe as Beck had in his whole life.

"I want to see!" Brait was dragging at Beck's shirt, trying to get a peek through the window. "What's going on?"

Beck didn't know what to say. Didn't know if he could find his voice, even. Right under them some wounded man was screaming. Gurgling, retching screams. Beck wished he'd stop. He felt dizzy with it.

The fence was mostly lost. He could see one tall Union man on the walk-way, pointing towards the bridge with a sword, clapping men on their backs as they flooded off the ladders to either side of him. There were still a few dozen Carls at the gate, clustered around a tattered standard, painted shields facing out in a half-circle but they were surrounded and well outnumbered, shafts hissing down into 'em from the walkways.

Some of the bigger buildings were still in Northern hands. Beck could see men at the windows, shooting arrows out, ducking back in. Doors nailed shut and barricaded, but Union men swarming around 'em like bees around a hive. They'd managed to set fires for a couple of the most stub-born holdouts, in spite of the damp. Now brown smoke billowed out and was carried off east by the wind, lit by the dull orange of flames flickering.

A Northman came charging from a burning building, swinging an axe around his head in both hands. Beck couldn't hear him shouting, could see he was, though. In the songs he'd have taken a load down with him and joined the dead proud. Couple of Union men scattered away before some others herded him back against the wall with spears. One stuck him in the arm and he dropped his axe, held his other hand up, shouting more. Giving up, maybe, or insults, didn't make much difference. They stuck him in the chest and he slumped down. Stuck him on the ground, spear shafts going up and down like a couple of men digging in the fields.

Beck's wide-open, watery eyes kept on darting across the buildings, mur-der in plain view all along the riverbank not a hundred strides from where he stood. They dragged someone struggling out from a hovel and bent him over. There was the twinkle of a knife, then they shoved him into the water and he floated away on his face while they wandered back inside the house. Cut his throat, Beck reckoned. Cut his throat, just like that.

"They've got the gate." Reft's voice sounded strangled. Like he'd never spoken before. Beck saw he was right, though. They'd cut down the last defenders, and were dragging the bars clear, and pulling the gates open, and daylight showed through the square archway.

"By the dead," whispered Beck, but it came out just a breath. Hundreds of the bastards started flowing into Osrung, pouring out into the smoke and the scattered buildings, flooding down the lane towards the bridge. The triple row of Northmen at its north end looked a pitiful barrier all of a sudden. A sand wall to hold back the ocean. Beck could see them stirring. Wilting, almost. Could feel their deep desire to join the men who were scattering back across the bridge and through their ranks, trying to escape the slaughter on the far bank.

Beck felt it too, that tickling need to run. To do something, and run was all he could think of. His eyes flickered over the burning buildings on the south side of the river, flames reaching higher now, smoke spreading over the town.

Beck wondered what it was like inside those houses. No way out. Thousands of Union bastards beating at the doors, at the walls, shooting arrows in. Low rooms filling up with smoke. Wounded men with small hopes of mercy. Counting their last shafts. Counting their dead friends. No way out. Time was Beck's blood would've run hot at thoughts like that. It was on the chilly side now, though. Those weren't no fortresses built for defending on the other side of the river, they were little wooden shacks.

Just like the one he was in.

The Infernal Contraptions

Your August Majesty,

Morning on the second day of battle, and the Northmen occupy strong positions on the north side of the river. They hold the Old Bridge, they hold Osrung, and they hold the Heroes. They hold the crossings and invite us to take them. The ground is theirs, but they have handed the initiative to Lord Marshal Kroy and, now that all our forces have reached the battlefield, he will not be slow to seize it.

On the eastern wing, Lord Governor Meed has already begun an attack in overwhelming force upon the town of Osrung. I find myself upon the western, observing General Mitterick's assault upon the Old Bridge.

The general delivered a rousing speech this morning as the first light touched the sky. When he asked for volunteers to lead the attack every man put up his hand without hesitation. Your Majesty would be most proud of the bravery, the honour, and the dedication of your soldiers. Truly, every man of them is a hero.

I remain your Majesty's most faithful and unworthy servant,

Bremer dan Gorst,
Royal Observer of the Northern War

Gorst blotted the letter, folded it and passed it to Younger, who sealed it with a blob of red wax and slid it into a courier's satchel with the golden sun of the Union worked into the leather in elaborate gilt.

"It will be on its way south within the hour," said the servant, turning to go.

"Excellent," said Gorst.

But is it? Does it truly matter whether it goes sooner, or later, or if Younger tosses it into the latrine pits along with the rest of the camp's ordure? Does it matter whether the king ever reads my pompous platitudes about General

Mitterick's pompous platitudes as the first light touched up the sky? When did I last get a letter back? A month ago? Two? Is just a note too much to ask? Thanks for the patriotic garbage, hope you're keeping well in ignominious exile?

He picked absently at the scabs on the back of his right hand, wanting to see if he could make them hurt. He winced as he made them hurt more than he had intended to. *Ever a fine line.* He was covered with grazes, cuts and bruises he could not even recall the causes of, but the worst pain came from the loss of his Calvez-made short steel, drowned somewhere in the shallows. One of the few relics remaining of a time when he was the king's exalted First Guard rather than an author of contemptible fantasies. *I am like a jilted lover too cowardly to move on, clinging tremble-lipped to the last feeble mementoes of the cad who abandoned her. Except sadder, and uglier, and with a higher voice. And I kill people for a hobby.*

He stepped from under the dripping awning outside his tent. The rain had slackened to a few flitting specks, and there was even some blue sky torn from the pall of cloud that smothered the valley. He surely should have felt some flicker of optimism at the simple pleasure of the sun on his face. But there was only the unbearable weight of his disgrace. The fool's tasks lined up in crushingly tedious procession. *Run. Practice. Shit a turd. Write a letter. Eat. Watch. Write a turd. Shit a letter. Eat. Bed. Pretend to sleep but actually lie awake all night trying to wank. Up. Run. Letter . . .*

Mitterick had already presided over one failed attempt on the bridge: a bold, rash effort by the Tenth Foot which had crossed unresisted to a lot of victorious whooping. The Northmen had met them with a hail of arrows as they attempted to find their order on the far side, then sprang from hidden trenches in the barley and charged with a blood-freezing wail. Whoever was in command of them knew his business. The Union soldiers fought hard but were surrounded on three sides and quickly cut down, forced back into the river to flounder helplessly in the water, or crushed into a hellish confusion on the bridge itself, mingled with those still striving mindlessly to cross from behind.

A great line of Mitterick's flatbowmen had then appeared from behind a hedgerow on the south bank and raked the Northmen with a savage volley, forcing them into a disorganised retreat back to their trenches, leaving the dead scattered in the trampled crops on their side of the bridge. The Tenth had been too mauled to take advantage of the opening, though, and now archers on both sides were busy with a desultory exchange of ammunition across the water while Mitterick and his officers marshalled their next wave. *And, one imagines, their next batch of coffins too.*

Gorst watched the whirling clouds of gnats that haunted the bank, and the corpses that floated past beneath them. *The bravery.* Turning with the current. *The honour.* Face up and face down. *The dedication of the soldiers.* One sodden Union hero wallowed to a halt in some rushes, bobbing for a moment on his side. A Northman drifted up, bumped gently into him and carried him from the bank and through a patch of frothy yellow scum in an awkward embrace. *Ah, young love. Perhaps someone will hug me after my death. I certainly haven't had many before.* Gorst had to stop himself snorting with spectacularly inappropriate laughter.

"Why, Colonel Gorst!" The First of the Magi strolled up with staff in one hand and teacup in the other. He took in the river and its floating cargo, heaved a long breath through his nose and exhaled satisfaction. "Well, you couldn't say they aren't giving it a good try, anyway. Successes are all very well, but there's something grand about a glorious failure, isn't there?"

I can't see what, and I should know.

"Lord Bayaz." The Magus' curly-headed servant snapped open a folding chair, brushed an imaginary speck of dust from its canvas seat and bowed low.

Bayaz tossed his staff on the wet grass without ceremony and sat, eyes closed, tipping his smiling face towards the strengthening sun. "Wonderful thing, a war. Done in the right way, of course, for the right reasons. Separates the fruit from the chaff. Cleans things up." He snapped his fingers with an almost impossibly loud crack. "Without them societies are apt to become soft. Flabby. Like a man who eats only cake." He reached up and punched Gorst playfully on the arm, then shook out his limp fingers in fake pain. "Ouch! I bet you don't eat only cake, do you?"

"No."

Like virtually everyone Gorst ever spoke to, Bayaz was hardly listening. "Things don't change just by the asking. You have to give them a damn good shake. Whoever said war never changes anything, well...they just haven't fought enough wars, have they? Glad to see this rain's clearing up, though. It's been playing hell with my experiment."

The experiment consisted of three giant tubes of dull, grey-black metal, seated upon huge wooden cradles, each closed at one end with the other pointed across the river in the vague direction of the Heroes. They had been set up with immense care and effort on a hump of ground a hundred strides from Gorst's tent. The ceaseless din of men, horses and tackle would have kept him awake all night had he not been half-awake anyway, as he always was. Lost in the smoke of Cardotti's House of Leisure, searching desperately for the king. Seeing a masked face in the gloom, at the stairway. Before the Closed Council as they stripped him of his position, the bottom dropping out of the world all over again. Twisted up with Finree, holding her. Holding smoke. Coughing smoke, as he stumbled through the twisted corridors of Cardotti's House of—

"Pitiful, isn't it?" asked Bayaz.

For a moment, Gorst wondered if the Magus had read his thoughts. *And yes, it certainly fucking is.* "Pardon?"

Bayaz spread his arms to encompass the scene of crawling activity. "All the doings of men, still at the mercy of the fickle skies. And war most of all." He sipped from his cup again, grimaced and flung the dregs out across the grass. "Once we can kill people at any time of day, in any season, in any weather, why, *then* we'll be civilised, eh?" And he chuckled away to himself.

The two old Adepti from the University of Adua scraped up like a pair of priests given a personal audience with God. The one called Denka was ghoul-pale and trembling. The one called Saurizin had a sheen of sweat across his wrinkled forehead which sprang back as fast as he could wipe it off.

"Lord Bayaz." He tried to bow and grin at once and couldn't manage either with any conviction. "I believe the weather has improved to the point where the devices can be tested."

"At last," snapped the Magus. "Then what are you waiting for, the Mid-winter Festival?"

The two old men fled, Saurizin snarling fiercely at his colleague. They had an ill-tempered discussion with the dozen aproned engineers about the nearest tube, including a deal of arm-waving, pointing at the skies and reference to some brass instruments. Finally one produced a long torch, flames licking at the tarred end. The Adepti and their minions hurried away, squatting behind boxes and barrels, covering their ears. The torch-bearer advanced with all the enthusiasm of a condemned man to the scaffold, touched the brand at arm's length to the top of the tube. A few sparks flew, a lick of smoke curled up, a faint pop and fizzle were heard.

Gorst frowned. "What is—"

There was a colossal explosion and he shrank to the ground, hands clasped over his head. He had heard nothing like it since the Siege of Adua, when the Gurkish put fire to a mine and blew a hundred strides of the walls to gravel. Guardsmen peeped terrified from behind their shields. Exhausted labourers scrambled gaping from their fires. Others struggled to control terrified horses, two of which had torn a rail free and were galloping away with it clattering behind them.

Gorst slowly, suspiciously, stood. Smoke was issuing gently from the end of one of the pipes, engineers swarming around it. Denka and Saurizin were arguing furiously with each other. What had been the effect of the device beyond the noise, Gorst had not the slightest idea.

"Well." Bayaz stuck a finger in one ear and waggled it around. "They're certainly loud enough."

A faint rumble echoed over the valley. Something like thunder, though it seemed to Craw the weather was just clearing up.

"You hear that?" asked Splitfoot.

Craw could only shrug up at the sky. Plenty of cloud still, even if there were a few blue patches showing. "More rain, maybe."

Dow had other things on his mind. "How are we doing at the Old Bridge?"

"They came just after first light but Scale held 'em," said Splitfoot. "Drove 'em back across."

"They'll be coming again, 'fore too long."

"Doubtless. Reckon he'll hold?"

"If he don't we got a problem."

"Half his men are across the valley with Calder."

Dow snorted. "Just the man I'd want at my back if I was fighting for my life."

Splitfoot and a couple of the others chuckled.

There was a right way of doing things, far as Craw was concerned, and it didn't include letting men laugh at your friends behind their backs, however laughable they may be. "That lad might surprise you," he said.

Splitfoot smirked wider. "Forgot you and him were tight."

"Practically raised the boy," said Craw, squaring up and giving him the eye.

"Explains a lot."

"Of what?"

Dow spoke over 'em, an edge to his voice. "The pair o' you can wank Calder off once the light's gone. In case you hadn't noticed we've got bigger business. What about Osrung?"

Splitfoot gave Craw a parting look, then turned back to his Chief. "Union are over the fence, fighting on the south side of town. Reachey'll hold 'em, though."

"He better," grunted Dow. "And the middle? Any sign of 'em crossing the shallows?"

"They keep marching around down there, but no —"

Splitfoot's head vanished and something went in Craw's eye.

There was a cracking sound then all he could hear was a long, shrill whine.

He got knocked in the back hard and he fell, rolled, scrambled up, bent over like a drunken man, the ground weaving.

Dow had his axe out, waving it at something, shouting, but Craw couldn't hear him. Just that mad ringing. There was dust everywhere. Choking clouds, like fog.

He nearly tripped over Splitfoot's headless corpse, blood welling out of it. Knew it was his from the collar of his mail coat. He was missing an arm as well. Splitfoot was. Not Craw. He had both his. He checked. Blood on his hands, though, not sure whose.

Probably he should've drawn his sword. He waved at the hilt but couldn't work out how far away it was. People ran about, shapes in the murk.

Craw rubbed at his ears. Still nothing but that whine.

A Carl was sitting on the ground, screaming silently, tearing at his bloody chain mail. Something was sticking out of it. Too fat to be an arrow. A splinter of stone.

Were they attacked? Where from? The dust was settling. People shambling about, knocking into each other, kneeling over wounded men, pointing every which way, cowering on their faces.

The top half of one of the Heroes was missing, the old stone sheared off jagged in a fresh, shiny edge. Dead men were scattered around its base. More'n dead. Smashed apart. Folded and twisted. Split open and gutted. Ruined like Craw had never seen before. Even after the Bloody-Nine did his black work up in the High Places.

A boy sat alive in the midst of the bodies and the chunks of rock, blood-sprayed, blinking at a drawn sword on his knees, a whetstone held frozen in one hand. No sign how he'd been saved, if he had been.

Whirrun's face loomed up. His mouth moved like he was talking but Craw could only hear a crackle.

"What? What?" Even his own words made no sound. Thumbs poked at his cheek. It hurt. A lot. Craw touched his face and his fingers were bloody. But his hands were bloody anyway. Everything was.

He tried to push Whirrun away, tripped over something and sat down heavily on the grass.

Probably best all round if he stayed there a bit.

A hit!" cackled Saurizin, shaking a mystifying arrangement of brass screws, rods and lenses at the sky like a geriatric warrior brandishing a sword in victory.

"A palpable hit with the second discharge, Lord Bayaz!" Denka could barely contain his delight. "One of the stones on the hill was struck directly and destroyed!"

The First of the Magi raised an eyebrow. "You talk as if destroying stones was the point of the exercise."

"I am sure considerable injury and confusion were inflicted upon the Northmen at the summit as well!"

"Considerable injury and confusion!" echoed Saurizin.

"Fine things to visit upon an enemy," said Bayaz. "Continue."

The mood of the two old Adepti sagged. Denka licked his lips. "It would be prudent to check the devices for evidence of damage. No one knows what the consequences of discharging them frequently might be—"

"Then let us find out," said Bayaz. "Continue."

The two old men clearly feared carrying on. *But a great deal less than they fear the First of the Magi.* They scraped their way back towards the tubes where they began to bully their helpless engineers as they themselves had been bullied. *And the engineers no doubt will harangue the labourers, and the labourers will whip the mules, and the mules will kick at the dogs, and the dogs will snap at the wasps, and with any luck one of the wasps will sting Bayaz on his fat arse, and thus the righteous wheel of life will be ready to turn once again...*

Away to the west a second attempt on the Old Bridge was just petering out, having achieved no more than the first. This time an ill-advised effort had been made to cross the river on rafts. A couple had broken up not long after pushing off, leaving their passengers floundering in the shallows or dragged under by their armour in deeper water. Others were swept off merrily downstream while the men on board flailed pointlessly with their paddles or their hands, arrows plopping around them.

"Rafts," murmured Bayaz, sticking out his chin and scratching absently at his short beard.

"Rafts," murmured Gorst, watching an officer on one furiously brandish his sword at the far bank, about as likely ever to reach it as he was the moon.

There was another thunderous explosion, followed almost immediately by a chorus of gasps, sighs and cheers of wonder from the swelling audience, gathered at the top of the rise in a curious crescent. This time Gorst scarcely flinched. *Amazing how quickly the unbearable becomes banal.* More smoke issued from the nearest tube, wandering gently up to join the acrid pall already hanging over the experiment.

That weird rumble rolled out again, smoke rising from somewhere across the river to the south. "What the hell are they up to?" muttered Calder. Even standing on the wall, he couldn't see a thing.

He'd been there all morning, waiting. Pacing up and down, in the drizzle, then the dry. Waiting, every minute an age, with his thoughts darting round and round like a lizard in a jar. Peering to the south and not being able to see a thing, the sounds of combat drifting across the fields in waves, sometimes sounding distant, sometimes worryingly near. But no call for help. Nothing but a few wounded carried past, scant reinforcement for Calder's wavering nerve.

"Here's news," said Pale-as-Snow.

Calder stretched up, shading his eyes. It was White-Eye Hansul, riding up hard from the Old Bridge. He had a smile on his wrinkled face as he reined in, though, which gave Calder a trace of hope. Right then putting off the fighting seemed almost as good as not doing it at all.

He wedged a boot up on the gate in what he hoped was a manly style, trying to sound cool as snow while his heart was burning. "Scale got himself in a pickle, has he?"

"It's the Southerners pickled so far, the stupid bastards." White-Eye pulled his helmet off and wiped his forehead on the back of his sleeve. "Twice Scale's driven them back. First time they came strolling across like they thought we'd just give the bridge over. Your brother soon cured them of that notion." He chuckled to himself and Pale-as-Snow joined him. Calder offered up his own, though it tasted somewhat sour. Everything did today.

"Second time they tried rafts as well." White-Eye turned his head and spat into the barley. "Could've told them the current's way too strong for that."

"Good thing they never asked you," said Pale-as-Snow.

"That it is. I reckon you lot can sit back here and take your boots off. We'll hold 'em all day at this rate."

"There's a lot of day still," Calder muttered. Something flashed by. His first thought was that it was a bird skimming the barley, but it was too fast and too big. It bounced once in the fields, sending up a puff of stalk and dust and leaving a long scar through the crop. A couple of hundred strides to the east, down at the grassy foot of the Heroes, it hit Clail's Wall.

Broken stones went spinning high, high into the air, showering out in a great cloud of dust and bits. Bits of tents. Bits of gear. Bits of men, Calder realised, because there were men camped behind the whole length of the wall.

"By—" said Hansul, gaping at the flying wreckage.

There was a sound like a whip cracking but a thousand times louder. White-Eye's horse reared up and he went sliding off the back, tumbling down into the barley, arms flailing. All around men gawped and shouted, drew weapons or flung themselves on the ground.

That last looked a good idea.

"Shit!" hissed Calder, scrambling from the gate and throwing himself in a ditch, his desire to look manly greatly outweighed by his desire to stay alive. Earth and stones rattled down around them like unseasonal hail, pinging from armour, bouncing in the track.

"Sticking to the sunny side," said Pale-as-Snow, utterly unmoved, "that's Tenways' stretch of wall."

Bayaz' servant lowered an eyeglass with a curl of mild disappointment to his mouth. "Wayward," he said.

A towering understatement. The devices had been discharged perhaps two dozen times and their ammunition, which appeared to be large balls of metal or stone, scattered variously across the slope of the hill ahead, the fields to each side, the orchard at the foot, the sky above and on one occasion straight into the river sending up an immense fountain of spray.

How much the cost of this little aside, so we could dig a few holes in the Northern landscape? How many hospitals could have been built with the money? How many alms-houses? Anything worthier? Burials for dead pauper children? Gorst struggled to care, but could not quite get there. *We probably could have paid the Northmen to kill Black Dow themselves and go home. But then what would I find to fill the blasted desert between getting out of bed and—*

There was an orange flash, and the vague perception of things flying. He thought he saw Bayaz' servant punch at nothing beside his master, his arm an impossible blur. A moment later Gorst's skull was set ringing by an explosion even more colossal than usual, accompanied by a note something like the tolling of a great bell. He felt the blast ripping at his hair, stumbled to keep his balance. The servant had a ragged chunk of curved metal the size of a dinner plate in his hand. He tossed it onto the ground where it smoked gently in the grass.

Bayaz raised his brows at it. "A malfunction."

The servant rubbed black dirt from his fingers. "The path of progress is ever a crooked one."

Pieces of metal had been flung in all directions. A particularly large one had bounced straight through a group of labourers leaving several dead and the rest spotted with blood. Other fragments had knocked little gaps in the stunned audience, or flicked over guardsmen like skittles. A great cloud of smoke was billowing from where one of the tubes had been. A blood and dirt-streaked engineer wandered out of it, his hair on fire, walking unsteadily at a diagonal. He didn't have any arms, and soon toppled over.

"Ever," as Bayaz sank unhappily into his folding chair, "a crooked one."

Some people sat blinking. Others screamed. Yet more rushed about, trying to help the many wounded. Gorst wondered whether he should do the same. *But what good could I do? Boost morale with jokes? Have you heard the one about the big idiot with the stupid voice whose life was ruined in Sipani?*

Denka and Saurizin were sidling towards them, black robes smudged with soot. "And here, the penitents," murmured Bayaz' servant. "With your leave, I should attend to some of our business on the other side of the river. I have a feeling the Prophet's little disciples are not idle over there."

"Then we cannot be idle either." The Magus waved his servant away with a careless hand. "There are more important things than pouring my tea."

"A very few." The servant gave Gorst a faint smile as he slipped away. "Truly, as the Kantic scriptures say, the righteous can afford no rest..."

"Lord Bayaz, er..." Denka looked across at Saurizin, who made a frantic get-on-with-it motion. "I regret to inform you that... one of the devices has exploded."

The Magus let them stand for a moment while, out of sight, a woman shrieked like a boiling kettle. "Do you suppose I missed that?"

"Another jumped from its carriage upon the last discharge, and I fear will take some considerable time to realign."

"The third," wheedled Denka, "is displaying a tiny crack which requires some attention. I am..." his face crumpling up as though he feared someone was going to stick a sword in it, "reluctant to risk charging it again."

"Reluctant?" Bayaz' displeasure was as a mighty weight. Even standing beside him Gorst felt a powerful urge to kneel.

"A defect in the casting of the metal," Saurizin managed to gasp, sending a poisonous glance at his colleague.

"My alloys are perfect," whined Denka, "it was an inconsistency in the explosive powders that was to—"

"Blame?" The voice of the Magus was almost as fearsome as the explosion had been. "Believe me, gentlemen, there is always plenty of that left over after a battle. Even on the winning side." The two old men positively grovelled. Then Bayaz waved a hand and the menace was gone. "But these things happen. Overall it has been... a most interesting demonstration."

"Why, Lord Bayaz, you are far too kind..."

Their servile mutterings faded as Gorst picked his way to where a guard had been standing a few moments before. He was lying in the long grass, arms out wide, a ragged chunk of curved metal embedded in his helmet. One eye could still be seen through the twisted visor, staring at the sky in a last moment of profound surprise. *Truly, every man of them is a hero.*

The guard's shield lay nearby, the golden sun on the face gleaming as its counterpart showed through the clouds. Gorst picked it up, slid his left hand into the straps and trudged off, upstream, towards the Old Bridge. As he passed, Bayaz was sitting back in his folding chair with one boot crossed over the other, his staff forgotten in the wet grass beside him.

"What should they be called? They are engines that produce fire, so... fire engines? No, silly. Death tubes? Names are so important, and I've never had the trick of them. Have you two any ideas?"

"I liked death tubes..." muttered Denka.

Bayaz was not listening. "I daresay someone will think up something suitable in due course. Something simple. I've a feeling we'll be seeing a great deal more of these devices..."

Reasoned Debate

Far as Beck could tell, things were coming apart.

The Union had a double row of archers on the south bank of the river. Squatting down behind a fence to load their evil little bows. Popping up every now and then to loose a clattering hail of bolts at the north end of the bridge. The Carls there were hunched behind their arrow-prickled shield wall, the Thralls huddling tight behind them, spears in a thoughtless tangle. A couple of men had ended up arrow-prickled too, been dragged squealing back through the ranks, doing nothing for the courage of the rest. Or for Beck's courage either. What there was of it left.

He was almost saying the words with every breath. Let's run. Plenty of others had. Grown men with names and everything, running for their lives from the fight across the river. Why the hell were Beck and the rest staying? Why should they care a shit whether Caul Reachey got to hold some town, or Black Dow got to keep wearing Bethod's old chain?

South of the river the fighting was done. The Union had broken into the last houses and slaughtered the defenders or burned 'em out with about the same results, the smoke of it still drifting across the water. Now they were getting ready to try the bridge, a wedge of soldiers coming together on the far side. Beck had never seen men so heavy armoured, cased head to toe in metal so they looked more like something forged than born. He thought of the lame weapons his half-arsed crew had. Dull knives and bent spears. It'd be like trying to bring down a bull with a pin.

Another hail of little arrows came hissing across the water and a great big Thrall leaped up, making a mad shriek, shoving men out of his way then toppling off the bridge and into the water. The shield wall loosened where he'd passed, the back rank drifting apart, going ragged. None of 'em wanted to just squat there and get peppered, and they wanted to face those armoured bastards close up even less. Maybe Black Dow liked the smell of burning cowards, but Black Dow was far away. The Union were awful near and fixing to get nearer. Beck could almost see the bones going out of 'em, all edging back together, shields coming unlocked, spears wobbling.

The Named Man who led the shield wall turned to shout, waving his axe, then fell on his knees, trying to reach over his back at something. He keeled over on his face, a bolt poking out of his fine cloak. Then someone gave a long shout on the other side of the bridge and the Union came on. All that polished metal tramping up together like some single angry beast. Not the wild charge of a crowd of Carls but a steady jog, full of purpose. Like that, without even a blow given, the shield wall broke apart and men ran. The next hail of arrows dropped a dozen or more as they showed their backs and scattered the rest across the square like Beck used to scatter starlings with a clap.

Beck watched a man drag himself over the cobbles with three bolts in him. Watched him wide-eyed, breath slithering in his throat. What did it feel like when the arrow went in you? Deep into your flesh? In your neck. In your chest. In your fruits. Or a blade? All that sharp metal, and a body so soft. What did it feel like to have a leg cut off? How much could something hurt? All the time he'd spent dreaming of battle, but somehow he'd never thought of it before.

Let's run. He turned to Reft to say it but he was letting an arrow fly, cursing and reaching for another. Beck should've been doing the same, like Flood told him, but his bow seemed to weigh a ton, his hand so weak he could hardly grip it. By the dead he was sick. They had to run, but he was too coward even to say it. Too coward to show his shitting, screaming, trembling fear to the lads downstairs. All he could do was stand there, with his bow out the window but the string not even drawn like a lad who's got his prick out to piss but found he couldn't manage it with someone watching.

He heard Reft's bow string go again. Heard him shout, "I'm going down!" Pulling out his long knife in one hand, his hatchet in the other and heading for the stairs. Beck watched him with his mouth half open but nothing to say. Trapped between his fear of staying here alone and his fear of going downstairs.

He had to force himself to look out of the window. Union men flooding across the square, the heavy armoured ones and more behind. Dozens. Hundreds. Arrows flitting from the buildings and down into them. Corpses all over. A rock came from the roof of the mill and stove in a Union helmet, sent the man toppling. But they were everywhere, charging through the streets, beating at the doors, hacking down the wounded as they tried to limp away. A Union officer stood near the bridge, waving his sword towards the buildings, dressed in a fancy jacket with gold thread like the prisoner Shivers had taken. Beck raised his bow, found his mark, finally drew the string back.

Couldn't do it. His ears were full of mad din, he couldn't think. He started trembling so bad he could hardly see, and in the end he squeezed his eyes shut and shot the arrow off at nothing. The only one he'd shot. Too late to run. They were all around the house. Trapped. He'd had his chance and now the Union was everywhere. Splinters flew in his face and he tumbled back inside the attic, slipped and fell on his arse, heels scraping at the boards. A flatbow bolt was buried in the window frame, splitting the timber, its gleaming point coming through into the room. He lay, propped on his elbows, staring at it.

He wanted his mother. By the dead, he wanted his mother. What kind of a thing was that for a man to want?

Beck scrambled up, could hear crashes and bangs everywhere, wails and roars sounding hardly human, downstairs, outside, inside, his head snapping round at every hint of a noise. Were they in the house already? Were they coming for him? All he could do was stand there and sweat. His legs were wet with it. Too wet. He'd pissed himself. Pissed himself like a child and hardly even known 'til it started going cold.

He drew his father's sword. Felt the weight of it. Should've made him feel strong, the way it always had before. But instead it made him feel homesick.

Sick for the smelly little room he'd always drawn it in, the brave dreams that
had hissed out of the sheath along with it. He could hardly believe he'd wished
for this. He edged to the stairs, head turned away, looking out of the corner of
one narrowed eye as if not seeing clearly might somehow keep him safe.

The room at the bottom was full of mad movement, shadows and darker
shadows and splashes of light through broken shutters, furniture scattered,
blades glinting. A regular splintering of wood, someone trying to break
their way in. Voices, mangled up and saying nothing, Union words or no
words at all. Screams and whimpers.

Two of Flood's Northern lads were lying on the floor. One was leaking
blood everywhere. The other was saying, "No, no, no," over and over. Colving had this wild, mad look on his chubby face, jabbing at a Union man
who'd squeezed in through the door. Reft came out of the shadows and hit
him in the back of the helmet with his hatchet, knocked him sprawling on
top of Colving, hacked away at his back-plate as he tried to get up, finally
found the gap between plate and helmet and put him down with his head
hanging off.

"Keep 'em out!" Reft screamed, jumping back to the door and heaving it
shut with his shoulder.

A Union man burst through the shutters not far from the bottom of the
steps. Beck could've stabbed him in the back. Probably without even being
seen. But he couldn't help thinking about what would happen if it went
wrong. What would happen after he did it. So he didn't do anything. Brait
squealed, spun around to poke at the Union man with his spear, but before
he could do it the soldier's sword thudded into Brait's shoulder and split
him open to his chest. He gave this breathy shriek, waving his spear about
while the Union man struggled to rip his sword out of him, blood squirting
out black over the pair of 'em.

"Help!" roared Stodder at no one, pressed against the wall with a cleaver
dangling from one hand. "Help!"

Beck didn't turn and run. He just backed softly up the stairs the way he
came, and he hurried to the open cupboard, ripped its single shelf out then
ducked into the cobwebby shadows inside. He worked his fingertips into a
gap between two planks of the door and he dragged it shut, bent over with
his back against the rafters. Pressed into the darkness, in a child's bad hiding place. Alone with his father's sword, and his own whimpering breath,
and the sounds of his crew being slaughtered downstairs.

* * *

Lord Governor Meed gazed imperiously out of the northern window of the common hall with hands clasped behind his back, nodding knowingly at scraps of information as if he understood them, his officers crowding about him and gabbling away like eager goslings around their mother. An apt metaphor, as the man had all the military expertise of a mother goose. Finree lurked at the back of the room, an ugly secret, desperately wanting to know what was going on but desperately not wanting to give anyone the satisfaction of asking, chewing at her nails, silently stewing and turning over various unlikely scenarios for her revenge.

Mostly, though, she was forced to admit, she was annoyed at herself. She saw now it would have been much better if she had pretended to be patient, and charming, and humble just as Hal had wanted, clapped her hands at Meed's pitiful soldiering and slid into his confidence like a cuckoo into an old pigeon's nest.

Still, the man was vain enough to haul an overblown portrait of himself around on campaign. It might not be too late to play the wayward lamb, and worm her way into his good graces through simpering contrition. Then, when the opportunity presented, she could stab him in the back from a nice, short distance. She'd stab him one way or another, that was a promise. She could hardly wait to see the look on Meed's papery old face when she finally—

Aliz let go a snort of laughter. "Why, who's that?"

"Who's what?" Finree glanced out of the eastern window, entirely ignored since the battle was happening to the north. A ragged man had emerged from the woods and was standing on a small outcropping of rock, staring towards the inn, long black hair twitched by the wind. Clearly, he was by no stretch of the imagination a Union soldier.

Finree frowned. Most of the Dogman's men were supposed to be well behind them, and in any case there was something about this lonely figure that just looked ... *wrong.*

"Captain Hardrick!" she called. "Is he one of the Dogman's men?"

"Who?" Hardrick strolled up beside them. "All honesty I couldn't say..."

The man on the rock lifted something to his mouth and bent his head back. A moment later a long, mournful note echoed out over the empty fields.

Aliz laughed. "A horn!"

Finree felt that note right in her stomach, and straight away she knew. She grabbed Hardrick's arm. "Captain, you need to ride to General Jalenhorm and tell him we are under attack."

"What? But there's..." His gormless grin slowly faded as he looked towards the east.

"Oh," said Aliz. The whole treeline was suddenly alive with men. Wild, they looked, even at this distance. Long-haired, rag-clothed, many half-naked. Now that he stood in the midst of hundreds of others and there was some sense of scale, Finree realised what had puzzled her about the man with the horn. He was a giant, in the truest sense of the word.

Hardrick stared, his mouth hanging open, and Finree dug her fingers into his arm and dragged him towards the door. "Now! Find General Jalenhorm. Find my father. Now!"

"I should have orders—" His eyes flickered over to Meed, still blithely observing his attack on Osrung, along with all the other officers except for a couple who had drifted over without much urgency to investigate the sound of the horn.

"Who are they?" one asked.

Finree had no time to argue her case. She gave vent to the shrillest, longest, most blood-curdling girlish scream she could manage. One of the musicians issued a screeching wrong note, the other played on for a moment before leaving the room in silence, every head snapping towards Finree, except Hardrick's. She was relieved to see she had shocked him into running for the door.

"What the hell—" Meed began.

"Northmen!" somebody wailed. "To the east!"

"What Northmen? Whatever are you—"

Then everyone was shouting. "There! There!"

"Bloody hell!"

"Man the walls!"

"Do we have walls?"

Men out in the fields – drivers, servants, smiths and cooks – were scattering wildly from tents and wagons, back towards the inn. There were already horsemen among them, mounted on shaggy ponies, without stirrups, even, but moving quickly nonetheless. She thought they might have bows, and a moment later arrows clattered against the north wall of the inn. One looped through a window and skittered across the floor. A black, jagged, ill-formed thing, but no less dangerous for that. Someone drew their sword with a faint ring of metal, and soon there were blades flashing out all around the hall.

"Get some archers on the roof!"

"Do we have archers?"

"Get the shutters!"

"Where is Colonel Brint?"

A folding table squealed in protest as it was dragged in front of one of the windows, papers sliding across the floor.

Finree snatched a look out as two officers struggled to get the rotten shutters closed. A great line of men was surging through the fields towards them, already half way between the trees and the inn and closing rapidly, spreading out as they charged. Torn standards flapped behind them, adorned with bones. At her first rough estimate there were at least two thousand, and no more than a hundred in the inn, most lightly armed. She swallowed at the simple horror of the arithmetic.

"Are the gates closed?"

"Prop them!"

"Recall the Fifteenth!"

"Is it too late to take—"

"By the Fates." Aliz' eyes had gone wide, white showing all the way around, darting about as if looking for some means of escape. There was none. "We're trapped!"

"Help will be coming," said Finree, trying to sound as calm as she could with her heart threatening to burst her ribs.

"From who?"

"From the Dogman," who had very reasonably made every effort to put as much ground between himself and Meed as possible, "or General Jalenhorm," whose men were in such a disorganised shambles after yesterday's disaster they were no help to themselves let alone anyone else, "or from our husbands," who were both thoroughly entangled with the attack on Osrung and probably had not the slightest idea that a new threat had emerged right behind them. "Help will be coming." It sounded pathetically unconvincing even to her.

Officers dashed to nowhere, pointed everywhere, screeched contradictory orders at each other, the room growing steadily darker and more confused as the windows were barricaded with whatever gaudy junk was to hand. Meed stood in the midst, suddenly ignored and alone, staring uncertainly about with his gilded sword in one hand and the other opening and closing powerlessly. Like a nervous father at a great wedding so carefully planned that he found himself entirely unwanted on the big day. Above him, his masterful portrait frowned scornfully down.

"What should we do?" he asked of no one in particular. His desperately wandering eyes lighted on Finree. "What should we do?"

It wasn't until she opened her mouth that she realised she had no answer.

Chains of Command

After a brief spell of fair weather the clouds had rolled back in and rain had begun to fall again, gently administering Marshal Kroy and his staff another dose of clammy misery and entirely obscuring both flanks of the battlefield.

"Damn this drizzle!" he snapped. "I might as well have a bucket on my head."

People often supposed that a lord marshal wielded supreme power on the battlefield, even beyond an emperor in his throne room. They did not appreciate the infinite constraints on his authority. The weather, in particular, was prone to ignore orders. Then there was the balance of politics to consider: the whims of the monarch, the mood of the public. There were a galaxy of logistical concerns: difficulties of supply and transport and signalling and discipline, and the larger the army the more staggeringly cumbersome it became. If one managed, by some miracle, to prod this unwieldy mass into a position to actually fight, a headquarters had to be well behind the lines and even with the opportunity to choose a good vantage point a commander could never see everything, if anything. Orders might take half an hour or longer to reach their intended recipients and so were often useless or positively dangerous by the time they got there, if they ever got there.

The higher you climbed up the chain of command, the more links between you and the naked steel, the more imperfect the communication became. The more men's cowardice, rashness, incompetence or, worst of all, good intentions might twist your purposes. The more chance could play a hand, and chance rarely played well. With every promotion, Marshal Kroy had looked forward to finally slipping the shackles and standing all powerful. And with every promotion he had found himself more helpless than before.

"I'm like a blind old idiot who's got himself into a duel," he murmured. Except there were thousands of lives hanging on his clueless flailing, rather than just his own.

"Would you care for your brandy and water, Lord—"

"No I would not bloody care for it!" he snapped at his orderly, then winced as the man backed nervously away with the bottle. How could he explain that he had been drinking it yesterday when he heard that he was responsible for the deaths of hundreds of his men, and now the very idea of brandy and water utterly sickened him?

It was no help that his daughter had placed herself so close to the front lines. He kept finding his eyeglass drawn towards the eastern side of the battle, trying to pick out the inn Meed was using as his headquarters through the drizzle. He scratched unhappily at his cheek. He had been interrupted while shaving by a worrying report sent from the Dogman, signs of savages from beyond the Crinna loose in the countryside to their east. Men the Dogman reckoned savage were savage indeed. Now Kroy was deeply distracted and, what was more, one side of his face was smooth and the other stubbly. Those sorts of details had always upset him. An army is made of details the way a house is made of bricks. One brick carelessly laid and the whole is compromised. But attend to the perfect mortaring of every—

"Huh," he muttered to himself. "I am a bloody mason."

"Latest report from Meed says things are going well on the right," said Felnigg, no doubt trying to allay his fears. His chief of staff knew him too well. "They've got most of southern Osrung occupied and are making an effort on the bridge."

"So things were going well half an hour ago?"

"Best one could say for them, sir."

"True." He looked for a moment longer, but could scarcely make out the inn, let alone Osrung itself. There was nothing to be gained by worrying. If his entire army had been as brave and resourceful as his daughter they would already have won and been on their way home. He almost pitied the Northman who ran across her in a bad mood. He turned to the west, following the line of the river with his eyeglass until he came to the Old Bridge.

Or thought he did. A faint, straight, light line across the faint, curved, dark line which he assumed was the water, all of it drifting in and out of existence as the rain thickened or slackened in the mile or two between him and the object. In truth he could have been looking at anything.

"Damn this drizzle! What about the left?"

"Last word from Mitterick was that his second assault had, how did he put it? Been blunted."

"By now it will have failed, then. Still, tough work, carrying a bridge against determined resistance."

"Huh," grunted Felnigg.

"Mitterick may lack many things—"

"Huh," grunted Felnigg.

"—but persistence is not one of them."

"No, sir, he is persistently an arse."

"Now, now, let us be generous." And then, under his breath, "Every man needs an arse, if only to sit on." If Mitterick's second assault had recently failed he would be preparing another. The Northmen facing him would be off balance. Kroy snapped his eyeglass closed and tapped it against his palm.

The general who waited to make a decision until he knew everything he needed to would never make one, and if he did it would be far too late. He had to feel out the moment. Anticipate the ebb and flow of battle. The shifting of morale, of pressure, of advantage. One had to trust one's instincts. And Marshal Kroy's instincts told him the crucial moment on the left wing was soon coming.

He strode through the door of his barn-cum-headquarters, making sure he ducked this time, as he had no need of another painful bruise on the crown of his head, and went straight to his desk. He dipped pen in ink without even sitting and wrote upon the nearest of several dozen slips of paper prepared for the purpose:

Colonel Vallimir

General Mitterick's troops are heavily engaged at the Old Bridge. Soon he will force the enemy to commit all his reserves. I wish you to begin your attack immediately, therefore, as discussed, and with every man at your disposal. Good luck.

Kroy

He signed it with a flourish. "Felnigg, I want you to take this to General Mitterick."

"He might take it better from a messenger."

"He can take it however he damn well pleases, but I don't want him to have any excuse to ignore it."

Felnigg was an officer of the old school and rarely betrayed his feelings; it was one of the things Kroy had always admired about the man. But his distaste for Mitterick was evidently more than he could suppress. "If I must, Lord Marshal." And he plucked the order sourly from Kroy's hand.

Colonel Felnigg stalked from the headquarters, nearly clubbing himself on the low lintel and only just managing to disguise his upset. He thrust the order inside his jacket pocket, checked that no one was looking and took a quick nip from his flask, then checked again and took another, pulled himself into the saddle and whipped his horse away down the narrow path, sending servants, guardsmen and junior officers scattering.

If it had been Felnigg put in command of the Siege of Ulrioch all those years ago and Kroy sent off on a fruitless ride to dusty nowhere, Felnigg who had reaped the glory and Kroy who had ridden thirsty back with his twenty captured wagons to find himself a forgotten man, things could so easily have been different. Felnigg might have been the lord marshal now, and Kroy his glorified messenger boy.

He clattered down from the hillside, spurring west towards Adwein along the puddle-pocked track. The ground sloping down to the river crawled with Jalenhorm's men, still struggling to find some semblance of organisation. Seeing things done in so slovenly a manner caused Felnigg something close to physical pain. It was the very most he could do not to pull up his horse, start screaming orders at all and sundry and put some damn purpose into them. *Purpose* – was that too much to ask in an army?

"Bloody Jalenhorm," Felnigg hissed. The man was a joke, and not even a funny one. He had neither the wit nor experience for a sergeant's place, let alone a general's, but apparently having been the king's old drinking partner was better qualification than years of competent and dedicated service. It would have been enough to make a lesser man quite bitter, but Felnigg it only drove to greater heights of excellence. He slowed for a moment to take another nip from his flask.

On the grassy slope to his right there had been some manner of accident. Aproned engineers fussed around two huge tubes of dark metal and a large patch of blackened grass. Bodies were laid out by the road, bloody sheets for shrouds. No doubt the First of the Magi's damn fool experiment blown up in everyone's faces. Whenever the Closed Council became directly involved in warfare there was sure to be some heavy loss of life and, in Felnigg's experience, rarely on the enemy's side.

"Out of the way!" he roared, forcing a path through a herd of foraged cattle that should never have been allowed on the road and making one of its handlers dive for the verge. He cantered through Adwein, as miserable a village as he had ever seen and packed today with miserable faces, injured men and filthy remnants of who-knew-what units. The useless, self-pitying flotsam of Mitterick's failed assaults, swept out the back of his division like dung from a stables.

At least Jalenhorm, fool that he was, could obey an order. Mitterick was forever squirming out from under his to do things his own way. Incompetence was unforgivable, but disobedience was . . . still less forgivable, damn it. If everyone simply did as they pleased, there would be no coordination, no command, no purpose. No army at all, just a great crowd of men indulging their own petty vanities. The very idea made him—

A servant carrying a bucket stepped suddenly from a doorway and right into Felnigg's path. His horse skittered to a stop, rearing up and nearly throwing him from the saddle.

"Out of the way!" Without thinking, Felnigg struck the man across the face with his riding crop. The servant cried out and went sprawling in the gutter, his bucket spraying water across the wall. Felnigg gave his horse the spurs and rode on, the heat of spirits in his stomach turned suddenly cold. He should not have done that. He had let anger get the better of him and the realisation only made him angrier than ever.

Mitterick's headquarters was the most unruly place in his unruly division. Officers dashed about, spraying mud and shouting over one another, the loudest voice obeyed and the finest ideas ignored. A commander set the tone for his entire command. A captain for his company, a major for his battalion, a colonel for his regiment and Mitterick for his entire division. Sloppy officers meant sloppy men, and sloppy soldiering meant defeat. Rules saved lives at times like these. What kind of officer allowed things to degenerate into chaos in his own headquarters? Felnigg reined his horse up and made a direct line for the flap of Mitterick's great tent, clearing excitable young adjutants from his path by sheer force of disapproval.

Inside the confusion was redoubled. Mitterick was leaning over a table in the midst of a clamouring press of crimson uniforms, an improvised map of the valley spread out upon it, holding forth at tremendous volume. Felnigg felt his revulsion for the man almost like a headwind. He was the worst kind of soldier, the kind that dresses his incompetence up as flair and, to make matters worse, he fooled people more often than not. But he did not fool Felnigg.

Felnigg stepped up and gave an impeccable salute. Mitterick gave the most peremptory movement of his hand, barely looking up from his map.

"I have an order for the King's Own First Regiment from Lord Marshal Kroy. I would be gratified if you could despatch it *at once*." He could not entirely keep the contempt out of his voice, and Mitterick evidently noticed.

"We're a little busy *soldiering* here, perhaps you could leave it—"

"I am afraid that will not be good enough, General." Felnigg only just prevented himself from slapping Mitterick across the face with his gloves. "The lord marshal was most specific, and I must insist on haste."

Mitterick straightened, the jaw muscles working on the side of his outsized head. "Must you?"

"Yes. I absolutely must." And Felnigg thrust the order at him as if he would throw it in his face, only by a last shred of restraint keeping it in his fingertips.

* * *

Mitterick snatched the paper from Felnigg's hand, only just preventing himself from punching him in the face with his other fist, and tore it open.

Felnigg. What an arse. What an arrogant, pedantic fool. A prickly stickler with no imagination, no initiative, none of what the Northmen called, with their gift for simplicity, "bones." He was lucky he had Marshal Kroy for a friend, lucky Kroy had dragged him up through the ranks behind him or he would most likely have remained all his career a tight-buttoned captain.

Felnigg. What an *arse*. Mitterick remembered him bringing in those six wretched wagons after Kroy won his great victory at Ulrioch. Remembered him demanding to have his contribution noted. His battalion ground down to a dusty stub for the sake of six bloody wagons. His contribution had been noted, all right. Mitterick had thought then, *what an arse,* and his opinion had not changed in all the years between.

Felnigg. What a suppurating arse. Look at him. Arse. Probably he thought he was better than everyone else, still, even though Mitterick knew for a fact he could barely get up without a drink. Probably he thought he could have done Mitterick's job better. Probably he thought he should have had Kroy's. Bloody arse. He was the worst kind of soldier, the kind that dresses his stupidity up as discipline, and to make matters worse he fooled people more often than not. But he did not fool Mitterick.

Already two of his assaults on the bridge had failed, he had a third to prepare and no time to waste on this pompous streak of bureaucracy. He turned to Opker, his own chief of staff, stabbing at the map with the crumpled order. "Tell them to get the Seventh ready, and I want the Second in place right behind. I want cavalry across that bridge as soon as we get a foothold, damn it, these fields are made for a charge! Get the Keln Regiment out of the way, clear out the wounded. Dump 'em in the river if we have to, we're giving the bloody Northmen time to get set. Time to have a bloody bath if they bloody want one! Tell them to get it done now or I'll go down there myself and lead the charge, whether I can fit my fat arse into my armour or not. Tell them to—"

A finger jabbed at his shoulder. "This order must be attended to at once, General Mitterick. *At once!*" Felnigg nearly shrieked the last words, blasting Mitterick with spit. He could hardly believe the man's obsession with proper form. Rules cost lives at times like these. What kind of an officer insisted on them in a headquarters while outside men were fighting? Dying? He ran a furious eye over the order:

Colonel Vallimir

General Mitterick's troops are heavily engaged at the Old Bridge. Soon he will force the enemy to commit all his reserves. I wish you to begin your attack immediately, therefore, as discussed, and with every man at your disposal. Good luck.

Kroy

The First had been attached to Mitterick's division and so, as their commander, it was his responsibility to clarify their instructions. Kroy's order was lean and efficient as the marshal himself, as always, and the timing was apt. But Mitterick was damned if he was going to miss an opportunity to frustrate the marshal's chinless stick-insect of a right hand man. If he wanted it by the book, he could have it by the book and bloody choke on it. So he spread the paper out on top of his map, snapped his fingers until someone thrust a pen into them, and added a scratchy line of his own at the bottom almost without considering the content.

Ensure that the enemy are fully engaged before crossing the stream, and in the meantime take care not to give away your position on their flank. My men and I are giving our all. I will not have them let down.

General Mitterick, Second Division

He took a route to his tent flap that enabled him to shoulder Felnigg rudely out of the way. "Where the hell is that boy from Vallimir's regiment?" he bellowed into the thinning drizzle. "What was his name? Leperlisper?"

"Lederlingen, sir!" A tall, pale, nervous-looking young man stepped forward, gave an uncertain salute and finished it off with an even more uncertain, "General Mitterick, sir." Mitterick would not have trusted him to convey his chamber pot safely to the stream, let alone to carry a vital order, but he supposed, as Bialoveld once said, "In battle one must often make the best of contrary conditions."

"Take this order to Colonel Vallimir at once. It's from the lord marshal, d'you understand? Highest importance." And Mitterick pressed the folded, creased and now slightly ink-blotted paper into his limp hand.

Lederlingen stood there for a moment, staring at the order.

"Well?" snapped the general.

"Er…" He saluted again. "Sir, yes—"

"Move!" roared Mitterick in his face. "Move!"

Lederlingen backed away, still at absurd attention, then hurried through the boot-mashed mud and over to his horse.

By the time he'd struggled into his wet saddle, a thin, chinless officer in a heavily starched uniform had emerged from Mitterick's tent and was hissing something incomprehensible at the general while a collection of guards and officers looked on, among them a large, sad-eyed man with virtually no neck who seemed vaguely familiar.

Lederlingen had no time to waste trying to place him. Finally, he had a job worth the doing. He turned his back on the unedifying spectacle of two of his Majesty's most senior officers bitterly arguing with one another and spurred off to the west. He couldn't honestly say he was sorry to be going. A headquarters appeared to be an even more frightening and disorientating place than the front line.

He rode through the tight-packed men before the tent, shouting for them to give him room, then through the looser mass making ready for another attack on the bridge, all the time with one hand on the reins and the order clutched in the other. He should have put it in his pocket, it was only making it harder for him to ride, but he was terrified of losing it. An order from Lord Marshal Kroy himself. This was exactly the kind of thing he'd been hoping for when he first signed up, bright-eyed, was it really only three months ago?

He'd cleared the main body of Mitterick's division now, their clamour fading behind him. He upped the pace, bending low over his horse's back, thumping down a patchy track away from the Old Bridge and towards the marshes. He'd have to leave his horse with the picket at the south bank, unfortunately, and cross the bogs on foot to take the order to Vallimir. If he didn't put a foot wrong and end up taking the order down to Klige instead.

That thought gave him a shudder. His cousin had warned him not to enlist. Had told him wars were upside-down places where good men did worse than bad. Had told him wars were all about rich men's ambitions and poor men's graves, and there hadn't been two honest fellows to strike a spark of decency in the whole company he served with. That officers were all arrogance, ignorance and incompetence. That soldiers were all cowards, braggarts, bullies or thieves. Lederlingen had supposed his cousin to be exaggerating for effect, but now had to admit that he seemed rather to have understated the case. Corporal Tunny, in particular, gave the strong impression of being coward, braggart, bully and thief all at once, as thorough a villain as Lederlingen had laid eyes upon in his life, but by some magic almost celebrated by the other men as a hero. All hail good old Corporal Tunny, the shabbiest cheat and shirker in the whole division!

The track had become a stony path, threading through a gully alongside a stream, or at any rate a wide ditch full of wet mud, trees heavy with red berries growing out over it. The place smelled of rot. It was impossible to ride at anything faster than a bumpy trot. Truly, the soldier's life took a man to some beautiful and exotic locations.

Lederlingen heaved out a sigh. War was an upside-down place, all right, and he was rapidly coming around to his cousin's opinion that it was no place for him at all. He would just have to keep his head low, stay out of trouble and follow Tunny's advice never to volunteer for anything—

"Ah!" A wasp had stung his leg. Or that was what he thought at first, though the pain was considerably worse. When he looked down, there was an arrow in his thigh. He stared at it. A long, straight stick with grey and white flights. An arrow. He wondered if someone was playing a joke on him for a moment. A fake arrow. It hurt so much less than he'd ever thought it might. But there was blood soaking into his trousers. It was a real arrow.

Someone was shooting at him!

He dug his heels into his horse's flanks and screamed. Now the arrow hurt. It hurt like a flaming brand rammed through his leg. His mount jerked forwards on the rocky path and he lost his grip on the reins, bounced once in the saddle, the hand clutching the order flailing at the air. Then he hit the ground, teeth rattling, head spinning, tumbling over and over.

He staggered up, sobbing at the pain in his leg, half-hopped about, trying to get his bearings. He managed to draw his sword. There were two men on the path behind. Northmen. One was walking towards him, purposeful, a knife in his hand. The other had a bow raised.

"Help!" shouted Lederlingen, but it was breathy, weak. He wasn't sure when he last passed a Union soldier. Before he came into the gully, maybe, he'd seen some scouts, but that had been a while back. "Help—"

The arrow stuck right through his jacket sleeve. Right through his arm inside it. This time it hurt from the start. He dropped his sword with a shriek. His weight went onto his right leg and it gave under him. He tumbled down the bank, jolts of agony shooting through his limbs whenever the ground caught at the broken shafts.

He was in the mud. Had the order in his fist still. He tried to get up. Heard the squelch of a boot beside him. Something hit him in the side of the neck and made his head jolt.

Foss Deep plucked the bit of paper out of the Southerner's hand, wiped his knife on the back of his jacket, then planted a boot on his head and pushed his face down into the bloody mud. Didn't want him screaming any. In part on account of stealth, but in part just because he found these days he didn't care for the sounds of persons dying. If it had to be done, so, so, but he didn't need to hear about it, thank you very much all the same.

Shallow was leading the Southerner's horse down the bank into the soggy stream bed. "She's a good one, no?" he asked, grinning up at it.

"Don't call her she. It's a horse, not your wife."

Shallow patted the horse on the side of its face. "She's better looking than your wife was."

"That's rude and uncalled for."

"Sorry. What shall we do with...it, then? It's a good one. Be worth a pretty—"

"How you going to get it back over the river? I ain't dragging that thing through a bog, and there's a fucking battle on the bridge, in case you forgot."

"I didn't forget."

"Kill it."

"Just a shame is all—"

"Just bloody kill it and let's get on." He pointed down at the Southerner under his boot. "I'm killing him, aren't I?"

"Well, he isn't bloody worth anything—"

"Just kill it!" Then, realising he shouldn't be raising his voice, since they was on the wrong side of the river and there might be Southerners any-where, whispered, "Just kill it and hide the bloody thing!"

Shallow gave him a sour look, but he dragged on the horse's bridle, put his weight across its neck and got it down, then gave it a quick stab in the neck, leaning on it while it poured blood into the muck.

"Shit on a shitty shit." Shallow shook his head. "There's no money in kill-ing horses. We're taking risksies enoughsies coming over here in the first—"

"Stop it."

"Stop what?" As he dragged a fallen tree branch over the horse's corpse.

Deep looked up at him. "Talking like a child, what do you think? It's odd, is what it is. It's like your head's trapped at four years old."

"My parts of speech upset you?" Chopping another branch free with his hatchet.

"They do, as it goes, yes."

Shallow got the horse hidden to his satisfaction. "Guess I'll have to stopsy wopsy, then."

Deep gave a long sigh through gritted teeth. One day he'd kill Shallow, or the other way around, he'd known it ever since he was ten years old. He unfolded the paper and held it up to the light.

"What's the matter of it?" asked Shallow, peering over his shoulder.

Deep turned slowly to look at him. He wouldn't have been surprised if today turned out to be the day. "What? Did I learn to read Southerner in my sleep and not realise? How in the land of the dead should I know what the bloody matter of it is?"

Shallow shrugged. "Fair point. It has the look of import, though."

"It do indeed have every appearance of significance."

"So?"

"I guess it becomes a question of who we know might find 'emselves tempted to fork out for it."

They looked at each other and said it together. "Calder."

This time White-Eye Hansul rode up fast, and with no hint of a smile. His shield had a broken arrow shaft in it and there was a cut across his forehead. He looked like a man who'd been in action. Calder felt sick just seeing him.

"Scale wants you to bring your men up." There was no laughter in his voice now. "The Southerners are coming across the bridge again and this time they've come hard. He can't hold out much longer."

"All right." Calder had known the moment would come, but that didn't make it any sweeter. "Get them ready."

"Aye." And Pale-as-Snow strode off barking orders.

Calder reached for his sword hilt and made a show of loosening it as he watched his brother's men – his men – stand up from behind Clail's Wall and prepare to join the battle. Time to write the first verse in the song of bold Prince Calder. And hope it wasn't the last.

"Your prince-li-ness!"

Calder looked round. "Foss Deep. You always come upon me at my brightest moments."

"I can smell desperation." Deep was dirty, and not just from a moral standpoint. Even dirtier than usual, as if he'd dived into a bog, which Calder didn't doubt he would have if he'd thought there was a coin at the bottom.

"What is it? I've a battle to die gloriously in."

"Oh, I wouldn't want to stop 'em strumming ballads in your honour."

"They already sing songs about him," said Shallow.

Deep grinned. "Not in his honour, though. We found something might be of interest."

"Look!" Shallow pointed off to the south, white teeth smiling in his mud-spattered face. "There's a rainbow!"

There was, in fact, a faint one, curving down towards the distant barley as the rain slackened and the sun showed itself again, but Calder was in no mood to appreciate it. "Did you just want to draw my attention to the endless beauty all around us, or is there something more to the point?"

Deep held out a piece of folded paper, creased and dirty. Calder reached for it and he whipped it theatrically away. "For a price."

"The price for paper isn't high."

"'Course not," said Deep. "It's what's written on that paper gives it value."

"And what's written on it?"

The brothers looked at each other. "Something. We found it on some Union lad."

"I've no time for this. Chances are high it's just some letter from Mother."

"Letter?" asked Shallow.

Calder snapped his fingers. "Give it me and I'll pay you what it's worth. Or you can peddle your rainbows elsewhere."

The brothers exchanged glances again. Shallow shrugged. Deep slapped the paper into Calder's hand. It didn't appear to be worth much at a glance, spotted with mud and what looked suspiciously like blood. Knowing these two, definitely blood. There was neat writing inside.

Colonel Vallimir,

General Mitterick's troops are heavily engaged at the Old Bridge. Soon he will force the enemy to commit all his reserves. I wish you to begin your attack immediately, therefore, as discussed, and with every man at your disposal. Good luck.

Then what might have been a name but it was right in the crease, the paper was all scuffed and Calder couldn't make sense of it. It looked like an order, but he'd never heard of any Vallimir. An attack on the Old Bridge. That was hardly news. He was about to throw it away when he caught the second block of writing in a wilder, slanting hand.

Ensure that the enemy are fully engaged before crossing the stream, and in the meantime take care not to give away your position on their flank. My men and I are giving our all. I will not have them let down.

General Mitterick,
Second Division

Mitterick. Dow had mentioned that name. One of the Union's generals. Something about him being sharp and reckless. My men and I are giving our all? He sounded a pompous idiot. Ordering an attack across a stream, though. On the flank. Calder frowned. Not the river. And not the bridge. He blinked around at the terrain, thinking about it. Wondering where soldiers could be for that order to make sense.

"By the dead," he whispered. There were Union men in the woods over to the west, ready to cross the beck and take them in their flank at any moment. There had to be!

"Worth something, then?" asked Shallow, smirking.

Calder hardly heard him. He pushed past the two killers and hurried up the rise to the west, shoving between the grim-faced men leaning against Clail's Wall so he could get a view across the stream.

"What is it?" asked White-Eye, bringing his horse up on the other side of the drystone.

Calder snapped open the battered eyeglass his father used to use and peered westwards, up that slope covered with old stumps, past the wood-cutters' sheds and towards the shadowy trees beyond. Were they crawling with Union soldiers, ready to charge across the shallow water as soon as they saw him move? There was no sign of men there. Not even a glint of steel among the trees. Could it be a trick?

Should he keep his promise, charge to his brother's aid and risk offering the whole army's bare arse to the enemy? Or stay behind the wall and leave Scale the one with his backside in the breeze? That was the safe thing, wasn't it? Hold the line. Prevent disaster. Or was he only telling himself what he wanted to hear? Was he relieved to have found a way to avoid fighting? A way to get rid of his idiot older brother? Liar, liar, he didn't even know when he was telling himself the truth any more.

He desperately wanted someone to tell him what to do. He wished Seff was with him, she always had bold ideas. She was brave. Calder wasn't made for riding to the rescue. Hanging back was more his style. Saving his own skin. Killing prisoners. Not doing it himself, of course, but ordering it done. Poking other men's wives while they were doing the fighting, maybe, if he was really feeling adventurous. But this was a long way outside his expertise. What the hell should he do?

"What's going on?" asked Pale-as-Snow. "The men are—"

"The Union are in the woods on the other side of that stream!"

There was a silence, in which Calder realised he'd spoken far louder than he needed to.

"The Union's over there? You sure?"

"Why haven't they come already?" White-Eye wanted to know.

Calder held up the paper. "Because I've got their orders. But they'll get more."

He could hear the Carls around him muttering. Knew they were passing the news from man to man. Probably that was no bad thing. Probably that was why he'd shouted it.

"What do we do, then?" hissed White-Eye. "Scale's waiting for help."

"I know that, don't I? No one knows that better than me!" Calder stood frowning towards the trees, his free hand opening and closing. "Tenways." By the dead, he was clutching at dust now, running for help to a man who'd tried to have him murdered a few days before. "Hansul, get up to Skarling's Finger and tell Brodd Tenways we've got the Union out there in the woods to the west. Tell him Scale needs him. Needs him now, or we'll lose the Old Bridge."

Hansul raised an eyebrow. "Tenways?"

"Dow said he should help, if we needed it! We need it."

"But—"

"Get up there!"

Pale-as-Snow and Hansul traded a glance. Then White-Eye clambered back up onto his horse and cantered off towards Skarling's Finger. Calder realised everyone was watching him. Wondering why he hadn't done the right thing already, and charged to his brother's rescue. Wondering whether they should stay loyal to this clueless idiot with the good hair.

"Tenways has to help," he muttered, though he wasn't sure who he was trying to convince. "We lose that bridge and we're all in the shit. This is about the whole North." As if he'd ever cared a damn about the whole North, or even anyone much further away than the end of his own foot.

His patriotic bluster carried no more weight with Pale-as-Snow than it did with him. "If the world worked that way," said the old warrior, "we'd have no need for swords in the first place. No offence, Calder, but Tenways hates you like the plague hates the living, and he doesn't feel a whole stretch warmer towards your brother. He won't put himself or his men on the line for your sakes, whatever Dow says. If you want your brother helped, I reckon you'll have to do it yourself. And soon." He raised his white brows. "So what do we do?"

Calder wanted very much to hit him, but he was right. He wanted to hit him because he was right. What should he do? He lifted his eyeglass again and scanned the treeline, slowly one way, then the other, then stopped dead.

Did he catch, just for a moment, the glint of another eyeglass trained on him?

Corporal Tunny peered through his eyeglass towards the drystone wall. He wondered if, just for an instant, he caught the glint of another trained on him? But probably he'd just imagined it. There certainly wasn't much sign of anything else going on.

"Movement?" squeaked Yolk.

"Nah." Tunny slapped the glass closed then scratched at his increasingly stubbly, greasy, itchy neck. He'd a strong feeling something other than him had taken up residence in his collar. A decision hard to understand, since he'd rather have been pretty much anywhere else himself. "They're just sitting there, far as I can tell."

"Like us."

"Welcome to the glory-fields, Trooper Yolk."

"Still no damn orders? Where the hell has bloody Lederlingen got to?"

"No way of knowing." Tunny had long ago given up feeling any surprise when the army didn't function quite as advertised. He glanced over his shoulder. Behind them, Colonel Vallimir was having another one of his rages, this time directed at Sergeant Forest.

Yolk leaned in to whisper, "Every man shitting on the man below, Corporal?"

"Oh, you're developing a keen sense of the mechanisms of his Majesty's forces. I do believe you'll make a fine general one day, Yolk."

"My ambition don't go past corporal, Corporal."

"I think that's very wise. As you can tell."

"Still no orders, sir," Forest was saying, face screwed up like a man looking into a stiff wind.

"Bloody hell!" snapped Vallimir. "It's the right time to go! Any fool can see that."

"But... we can't go without orders, sir."

"Of course we bloody can't! Dereliction of duty, that'd be! But now's the right time, so of course General bloody Mitterick will be demanding to know why I didn't act on my own initiative!"

"Very likely, sir."

"Initiative, eh, Forest? *Initiative*. What the bloody hell is that except an excuse to demote a man? It's like a card game they won't tell you the rules to, only the stakes!" And on, and on, and on he went, just like always.

Tunny gave a sigh, and handed his eyeglass to Yolk.

"Where you going, Corporal?"

"Nowhere, I reckon. Absolutely nowhere." He wedged himself back against his tree trunk and dragged his coat closed over him. "Wake me if that changes, eh?" He scratched his neck, then pulled his cap down over his eyes. "By some miracle."

Closing Arguments

It was the noise that was the most unexpected thing about battle. It was probably the loudest thing Finree had ever heard. Several dozen men roaring and shrieking at the very highest extent of their broken voices, crashing wood, stamping boots, clanging metal, all amplified and rendered meaningless by the enclosed space, the walls of the room ringing with mindless echoes of pain, and fury, and violence. If hell had a noise, it sounded like this. No one could have heard orders, but it hardly mattered.

Orders could have made no difference now.

The shutters of another window were bludgeoned open, a gilded cupboard that had been blocking them flattening an unfortunate lieutenant and spewing an avalanche of shattering dress crockery across the floor. Men swarmed through the square of brightness, ragged black outlines at first, gaining awful detail as they burst into the inn. Snarling faces smeared with paint, and dirt, and fury. Wild hair tangled with bones, with rough-carved wooden rings and rough-cast metal. They brandished jagged axes and clubs toothed with dull iron. They wept and gurgled a mad clamour, eyes bulging with battle-madness.

Aliz screamed again, but Finree felt oddly cold-headed. Perhaps it was some kind of beginner's luck at bravery. Or perhaps it had yet to really dawn on her how bad things were. They were very, very bad. Her eyes darted around as she struggled to take it all in, not daring to blink in case she missed something.

In the middle of the room an old sergeant was wrestling with a grey-haired primitive, each holding the other's wrist with weapons waggling at the ceiling, dragging each other this way and that as though through the steps of some drunken dance, unable to agree on who should be leading. Nearby one of the violinists was beating at someone with his shattered instrument, reduced now to a tangle of strings and splinters. Outside in the courtyard the gates were shuddering, splinters flying from their inside faces while guardsmen tried desperately to prop them shut with their halberds.

She found herself rather wishing that Bremer dan Gorst was beside her. Probably she should have wished for Hal instead, but she had a feeling courage, and duty, and honour would do no good here. Brute strength and rage were what was needed.

She saw a plump captain with a scratch down his face, who was rumoured to be the bastard son of someone-or-other important, stabbing at a man wearing a necklace of bones, both of them slick with red. She saw a pleasant major who used to tell her bad jokes when she was a girl clubbed on the back of the head. He tottered sideways, knees buckling like a clown's, one hand fishing at his empty scabbard. He was caught with a sword and flung to the floor in a shower of blood. Another officer's backswing, she realised.

"Above us!" someone screamed.

The savages had somehow got up onto the gallery, were shooting arrows down. An officer just next to Finree slumped over a table with a shaft in his back, dragging one of the hangings down on top of him, his long steel clattering from his dangling hand. She reached out nervously and slid his short steel from the sheath, backed away again towards the wall with it hidden beside her skirts. As though anyone would complain at a theft in the midst of this.

The door burst open and savages spilled into the common hall from the rest of the inn. They must have taken the courtyard, killed the guards. Men desperately trying to keep the attackers out from the windows spun about, their frozen faces pictures of horror.

"The lord governor!" someone screamed. "Protect his—" Cut off in a snivelling wail.

The melee had lost all shape. The officers were fighting hard for every inch of ground but they were losing, forced grimly back into a corner, cut down one by one. Finree was shoved against the wall, perhaps by some pointless act of chivalry, more likely by the random movement of the fight. Aliz was next to her, pale and blubbing, Lord Governor Meed on the other side, in a state little better. All three of them jostled by men's backs as they fought hopelessly for survival.

Finree could hardly see over the armoured shoulder of a guard, then he fell and a savage darted into the gap, a jagged iron sword in his fist. She got one quick, sharp look at his face. Lean, yellow-haired, splinters of bone pushed through the rim of one ear.

Meed held up a hand, breath whooshing in to speak, or scream, or beg.

The jagged sword chopped into him between neck and collarbone. He took a wobbling step, eyes rolled up to the ceiling so the whites showed huge, tongue sticking out and his fingers plucking at the ragged wound while blood welled up from between them and down the torn braid on the front of his uniform. Then he crashed over on his face, catching a table on the way and knocking it half in the air, a sheaf of papers spilling across his back.

Aliz let go another piercing shriek.

The thought flashed through Finree's mind as she stared at Meed's corpse that this might all have been her fault. That the Fates had despatched this as the method of her vengeance. It seemed disproportionate, to say the least. She would have been happy with something considerably less—

"Ah!" Someone grabbed her left arm, twisted it painfully around, and she was staring into a leering face, a mouthful of teeth filed to points, one pitted cheek marked with a blue handprint and speckled red.

She shoved him away, he gave a whooping squeal and she realised she had the short steel in her hand, had rammed it into his ribs. He pressed her against the wall, wrenching her head up. She managed to drag the steel free, slippery now, work it between them, grunting as she pushed the point up into his jaw, blade sliding into his head. She could see the skin on his blue cheek bulge from the metal behind it.

He tottered back, one hand fishing at the bloody hilt under his jaw, left her gasping against the wall, hardly able to stand her knees were shaking so badly. She felt her head suddenly yanked sideways, a stab of pain in her scalp, in her neck. She yelped, cut off as her skull smacked—

Everything was bright for a moment.

The floor thumped her in the side. Boots shuffled and crunched.

Fingers around her neck.

She couldn't breathe, plucked at the hand with her nails, ears throbbing with her own heartbeat.

A knee pressed into her stomach, crushing her against a table. Hot, foul breath blasted at her cheek. It felt as if her head was going to burst. She could hardly see, everything was so bright.

Then there was silence. The hand at her throat released a fraction, enough for her to draw in a shuddering breath. Cough, gag, cough again. She thought she was deaf, then realised the room had gone deathly quiet. Corpses of both sides were tangled up with broken furniture, scattered cut-

lery, torn papers, piles of fallen plaster. A few weak groans came from dying
men. Only three officers appeared to have survived, one holding his bloody
arm, the other two sitting with hands up. One was crying softly. The savages stood over them, still as statues. Nervous, almost, as if waiting for
something.

Finree heard a creaking footstep in the corridor outside. And then
another. As though some great weight was pressing on the boards. Another
groaning footstep. Her eyes rolled towards the doorway, straining to see.

A man came through. The shape of a man, at least, if not the size. He
had to duck under the lintel and then stayed suspiciously stooped, as if he
was below decks in a small ship, scared of catching his head on low beams.
Black hair streaked with grey stuck to his knobbly face with wet, black
beard jutting, tangled black fur across his great shoulders. He surveyed the
scene of wreckage with an expression strangely disappointed. Hurt even. As
if he had been invited to attend a tea party and found instead a slaughter-
yard at the venue.

"Why is everything broken?" he said in a voice oddly soft. He stooped to
pick up one of the fallen plates, no more than a saucer in his immense hand,
licked a fingertip and rubbed a few specks of blood from the maker's mark
on the back, frowning at it like a cautious shopper. His eyes lighted on
Meed's corpse, and his frown grew deeper. "Did I not ask for trophies?
Who killed this old man?"

The savages stared at each other, eyes bulging in their painted faces.
They were terrified, Finree realised. One raised a trembling arm to point at
the man who was holding her down. "Saluc did it!"

The giant's eyes slid across to Finree, then the man with his knee in her
stomach, then narrowed. He put the plate on a gouged table, so gently it
made no sound. "What are you doing with my woman, Saluc?"

"Nothing!" The hand around Finree's neck released and she dragged
herself back across the table, struggling to get a proper breath. "She killed
Bregga, I was just—"

"You were robbing me." The giant took a step forwards, his head on one
side.

Saluc stared desperately around but his friends were all scrambling away
from him as if he was infected with the plague. "But...I only wanted
to—"

"I know." The giant nodded sadly. "But rules are rules." He was across the space between them in an instant. With one great hand he caught the man's wrist while the other closed around his neck, fingers almost meeting thumb behind his head, lifting him squirming off his feet, smashing his skull crunching into the wall, once, twice, three times, blood spattering across the cracked plaster. It was over so quickly Finree did not have time to cower.

"You try to show them a better way..." The giant carefully set the dead man down in a sitting position against the wall, arranging his hands in his lap, resting his flattened head in a comfortable position, like a mother putting a child to sleep. "But some men will never be civilised. Take my women away. And do not tamper with them. Alive they are worth something. Dead they are..." He rolled Meed's corpse over with one huge boot. The lord governor flopped onto his back, eyes goggling at the ceiling. "Dirt."

Aliz screamed yet again. Finree wondered how she could still produce so high and true a note after all that screaming. She did not make a sound herself as they dragged her out. Partly that blow to her head seemed to have knocked all the voice out of her. Partly she was still having trouble getting a good breath after being throttled. But mostly she was occupied trying desperately to think of a way to live through this nightmare.

The battle was still going outside, Beck could hear it. But it was quiet downstairs. Maybe the Union men reckoned they'd got everyone killed. Maybe they'd missed the little stairway somehow. By the dead, he hoped they'd missed the—

One of the steps creaked and the breath stopped in Beck's throat. Maybe one creak sounds like another, but somehow he knew this was made by the foot of a man aiming to keep quiet. Sweat sprang out of his skin. Trickling, tickling down his neck. Didn't dare move to scratch it. He strained with every muscle to make no sound, wincing at every smallest wheeze in his throat, not daring even to swallow. His fruits, and his arse, and his guts all felt like they were a huge, cold weight he could hardly stop from dropping out of him.

Another stealthy, creaking step. Beck thought he could hear the bastard hissing something. Taunting him. Knew he was there, then. Couldn't make out the words, his heart was thumping so loud in his ears, so hard it felt like it might pop his eyes right out. Beck tried to shrink back into the cupboard, one eye fixed on the ragged slit between two planks of the door, the slice of attic beyond. The point of the man's sword slid into view, glinting murder, then the blade, dotted with red. Colving's blood, or Brait's, or Reft's. And Beck's too, soon enough. A Union sword, he could tell from the twisted metal around the hilt.

Another creaking step, and Beck spread his fingertips out against the rough wood, hardly touching it in case the rusted hinges gave him away. He gripped the hot hilt of his own sword, a narrow strip of light across the bright blade, the rest gleaming in the darkness. He had to fight. Had to, if he wanted to see his mother, and his brothers, and their farm again. And that was all he wanted, now.

One more creaking step. He took a long, cutting breath, chest swelling with it, frozen, frozen, time stretching. How long could a man need to take a pace?

One more footstep.

Beck burst out, screaming, flinging back the door. The loose corner caught on the boards and he stumbled over it, plunging off balance, no choice but to charge.

The Union man stood in the shadows, head turning. Beck thrust wild, felt the point bite, crosspiece digging at his knuckles as the blade slid through the Union man's chest. They spun in a growling hug and something whacked Beck hard on the head. The low beam. He came down on his back with the weight of the Union man full across him, breath driven out in a whoosh, hand squashed around the grip of his sword. Took a moment for Beck's eyes to adjust, but when they did he was staring straight up into a twisted, bulge-eyed face.

Only it weren't a Union man at all. It was Reft.

He took a long, slow, wheezing breath in, cheeks trembling. Then he coughed blood into Beck's face.

Beck whimpered, kicked, squirmed free, rolled Reft off and scrambled clear of him. Knelt there, staring.

Reft lay on his side. One hand scratched at the floor, one eye rolled up towards Beck. He was trying to say something but the words were gurgles. Blood bubbling out from mouth and nose. Blood creeping from underneath him and down the grain of the boards. Black in the shadows. Dark red where it crossed a patch of light.

Beck put one hand on his shoulder. Almost whispered his name, knew there was no point. His other hand closed around the grip of his sword, slick with blood. It was a lot harder to get it out than it had been to put it in. Made a faint sucking sound as it came clear. Almost said Reft's name again. Found he couldn't speak. Reft's fingers had stopped moving, his eyes wide open, red on his lips, on his neck. Beck put the back of one hand against his mouth. Realised it was all bloody. Realised he was bloody all over. Soaked with it. Red with it. Stood, stomach suddenly rolling. Reft's eyes were still on him. He tottered over to the stairs and down 'em, sword scraping a pink groove in the plaster. His father's sword.

No one moved downstairs. He could hear fighting out in the street, maybe. Mad shouting. There was a faint haze of smoke, tang of it tickling his throat. His mouth tasted of blood. Blood and metal and raw meat. All the lads were dead. Stodder was on his face near the steps, one hand reaching for 'em. The back of his head was neatly split, hair matted to dark curls. Colving was against the wall, head back, hands clamped to his chubby gut, shirt soaked with blood. Brait just looked like a pile of rags in the corner. Never had looked like much more'n a pile a rags, the poor bastard.

There were four Union men dead too, all near each other, like they'd decided to stick together. Beck stood in the midst of 'em. The enemy. Such good gear they all had. Breastplates, and greaves, and polished helmets, all the same. And boys like Brait had died with not much more'n a split stick and a knife blade stuck in it. Weren't fair, really. None of it was fair.

One of 'em was on his side and Beck rolled him over with his boot, head flopping. He was left squinting up at the ceiling, eyes looking off different ways. Apart from his gear, there didn't look to be much special about him. He was younger'n Beck had thought, a downy effort at a beard on his cheeks. The enemy.

There was a crash. The shattered door was kicked out of the way and someone took a lurching step into the room, shield in front of him and a mace up in the other hand. Beck just stood staring. Didn't even raise his sword. The man limped forward, and gave a long whistle.

"What happened, lad?" asked Flood.

"Don't know." He didn't know, really. Or at least, he knew what, but not how. Not why. "I killed..." He tried to point upstairs, but he couldn't raise his arm. Ended up pointing at the dead Union boys at his feet. "I killed..."

"You hurt?" Flood was pressing at his blood-soaked shirt, looking him over for a wound.

"Ain't mine."

"Got four o' the bastards, eh? Where's Reft?"

"Dead."

"Right. Well. You can't think about that. Least you made it." Flood slid one arm around his shoulders and led him out into the bright street.

The wind outside felt cold through Beck's blood-soaked shirt and his piss-soaked trousers, made him shiver. Cobbles coated with dust and blowing ash, with splintered wood, fallen weapons. Dead of both sides tossed around and wounded too. Saw a Union man on the ground, holding up a helpless arm while two Thralls hacked at him with axes. Smoke still shifting across the square, but Beck could see there was a new struggle on the bridge, shadows of men and weapons in the murk, the odd flitting arrow.

A big old-timer in dark mail and a battered helmet sat on horseback at the front of a wedge of others, pointing across the square with a broken length of wood, roaring at the top of his lungs in a voice husky from smoke. "Push 'em back over the bridge! Drive the bastards!" One of the men behind had a standard on a pole – white horse on green. Reachey's sign. Which he guessed made the old man Reachey his self.

Beck was only just starting to make sense of it. The Northmen had laid on an attack of their own, just the way Flood had said, and caught the Union as they got bogged down in the houses and the twisting lanes. Driven 'em back across the river. Looked like he might even not die today, and the thought made him want to cry. Maybe he would've, if his eyes hadn't been watering already from the smoke.

"Reachey!"

The old warrior looked over. "Flood! Still alive, y'old bastard?"

"Half way to it, Chief. Hard fighting hereabouts."

"I'll say. I broke my bloody axe! Union men got good helmets, eh? Not good enough, though." Reachey tossed the splintered haft clattering across the ruined square. "You did some decent work here."

"Lost about all my boys, though," said Flood. "Just this one left." And he clapped Beck on the shoulder. "Got four o' the bastards on his own, he did."

"Four? What's your name, lad?"

Beck gawped up at Reachey and his Named Men. All watching him. He should've put 'em all right. Told the truth. But even if he'd had the bones, and he didn't, he didn't have the breath in him to say that many words. So he just said, "Beck."

"Just Beck?"

"Aye."

Reachey grinned. "Man like you needs a bit more name than that, I reckon. We'll call you…" He looked Beck up and down for a moment, then nodded to himself like he had the answer. "Red Beck." He turned in his saddle and shouted to his Named Men. "How d'you like that, lads? Red Beck!" And they started banging their shields with their sword hilts, and their chests with their gauntlets, and sending up a right clatter.

"You see this?" shouted Reachey. "Here's the kind o' lad we need! Everyone look at this lad! Let's find us some more like him! Some more bloody little bastards!" Laughter, and cheering, and nods of approval all round. Mostly for the Union being driven back past the bridge, but partly for him, and his bloody day. He'd always wanted respect, and the company of fighting men, and above all a fearsome name. Now he had the lot, and all he'd had to do was hide in a cupboard and kill someone on his own side, then take the credit for his work.

"Red Beck." Flood grinned proudly like a father at his baby's first steps. "What d'you reckon to that, boy?"

Beck stared down at the ground. "Don't know."

Straight Edge

A h!" Craw jerked away from the needle on an instinct and only made the thread tug at his cheek and hurt him worse, "Ah!"

"Oftentimes," murmured Whirrun, "a man's better served embracing his pain than trying to escape it. Things are smaller when you face 'em."

"Easily said when you're the one with the needle." Craw sucked air through his teeth as the point nipped at his cheek again. Hardly the first stitches he ever had, but it's strange how quick you forget what a given kind of pain feels like. It was coming back to him now, and no mistake. "Best thing might be to get it over with quick, eh?"

"I'm right there with you on that, but the sorry fact is I'm a much better killer than I am a healer. Tragedy of my life. I can stitch all right and I know Crow's Foot from the Alomanter and how to rub each one on a bandage and I can hum a charm or two—"

"They any use?"

"The way I sing 'em? Only for scaring off cats."

"Ah!" grunted Craw as Whirrun pressed his cut closed between finger and thumb and pushed the needle through again. He really had to stop squawking, there were plenty about with far worse'n a scratch across the cheek.

"Sorry," grunted Whirrun. "You know, I've thought on it before, now and then, in the slow moments—"

"You get a lot o' those, don't you?"

"Well, you're taking your time about showing me this destiny of mine. Anyway, it seems to me a man can do an awful lot of evil in no time at all. Swing of a blade is all it takes. Doing good needs time. And all manner of complicated efforts. Most men don't have the patience for it. 'Specially not these days."

"Those are the times." Craw paused, chewing at a flap of loose skin on his bottom lip. "Do I say that too much? Am I turning into my father? Am I turning into a boring old fool?"

"All heroes do."

Craw snorted. "Those that live to hear their own songs."

"Terrible strain on a man, hearing his self sung about. Enough to make anyone a shit."

"Even if they weren't one in the first place."

"Which isn't likely. I guess hearing songs about warriors makes men feel brave their own selves, but a great warrior has to be at least half way mad."

"Oh, I've known a few great warriors weren't mad at all. Just heartless, careless, selfish bastards."

Whirrun bit off the thread with his teeth. "That is the other common option."

"Which are you, then, Whirrun? Mad or a heartless prick?"

"I try to bridge the gap between the two."

Craw chuckled in spite of the throbbing in his face. "That right there. That right there is a bloody hero's effort."

Whirrun settled back on his heels. "You're done. And not a bad job either, though I'm singing my own praises. Maybe I'll give up the killing and turn to healing after all."

A growling voice cut through the faint ringing still going in Craw's ears. "After the battle, though, eh?"

Whirrun blinked up. "Why, if it ain't the Protector of the North. I feel all... protected. Swaddled up, like in a good coat."

"Had that effect all my life." Dow looked down at Craw with his hands on his hips, the sun bright behind him.

"You going to bring me some fighting, Black Dow?" Whirrun slowly stood, pulling his sword up after him. "I came here to fill graves, and the Father of Swords is getting thirsty."

"I daresay I can scare you up something to kill before too long. In the meantime I need a private word with Curnden Craw, here."

Whirrun clapped a hand to his chest. "Wouldn't dream of putting myself in between two lovers." And he swanned off up the hill, sword over one shoulder.

"Strange bastard, that," said Dow as he watched Whirrun go.

Craw grunted as he unfolded his legs and slowly stood, shaking his aching joints out. "He plays up to it. You know how it is, having a reputation."

"Fame's a prison, no doubt. How's your face?"

"Lucky I've always been an ugly bastard. I'll look no worse'n before. Do we know what it was did the damage?"

Dow shook his head. "Who knows with the Southerners? Some new weapon. Some style o' sorcery."

"It's an evil one. That can just reach out and pluck men away like that."

"Is it? The Great Leveller's waiting for all of us, ain't he? There'll always be someone stronger, quicker, luckier'n you, and the more fighting you do the quicker he's going to find you. That's what life is for men like us. The time spent plummeting towards that moment."

Craw wasn't sure he cared for that notion. "At least in the line, or the charge, or the circle a man can fight. Pretend to have a hand in the outcome." He winced as he touched the fresh stitching with his fingertips. "How do you make a song about someone whose head got splattered while he was half way through saying nothing much?"

284

in fact, like a man who felt himself stepped in front of. Craw's wince became a full grimace. Seemed that was getting to be the normal shape to his face, one way and another. "A man's worst enemies are his own ambitions," Bethod used to tell him. "Mine have got me in all the shit I'm in today."

"Welcome to the shit," he muttered to himself through gritted teeth. That's the problem with mistakes. You can make 'em in an instant. Years upon years spent tiptoeing about like a fool, then you take your eye away for a moment and...

Bang.

Escape

Finree thought they were in some kind of shack. The floor was damp dirt, a chill draught across it making her shiver. The place smelled of fust and animals.

They had blindfolded her, and marched her lurching across the wet fields into the trees, crops tangling her feet, bushes clutching at her dress. It was a good thing she had been wearing her riding boots or she would probably have ended up barefoot. She had heard fighting behind them, she thought. Aliz had kept screaming for a while, her voice getting more and more hoarse, but eventually stopped. It changed nothing. They had crossed water on a creaking boat. Maybe over to the north side of the river. They had been shoved in here, heard a door wobble shut and the clattering of a bar on the outside.

And here they had been left, in the darkness. To wait for who knew what.

As Finree slowly got her breath back the pain began to creep up on her. Her scalp burned, her head thumped, her neck sent vicious stings down between her shoulders whenever she tried to turn her head. But no doubt she was a great deal better off than most who had been trapped in that inn.

"Like Splitfoot."

"Aye." Craw wasn't sure he'd ever seen anyone look deader than that bastard.

"I want you to take his place."

"Eh?" said Craw. "My ears are still whining. Not sure I heard you right."

Dow leaned closer. "I want you to be my Second. Lead my Carls. Watch my back."

Craw stared. "Me?"

"Aye, you, what did I fucking say?"

"But... why the hell *me?*"

"You got the experience, and the respect..." Dow looked at him for a moment, his jaw clenched tight. Then he waved a hand like he was swatting a fly. "You remind me o' Threetrees."

Craw blinked. It might've been one of the best things anyone had ever said to him, and not from a source prone to lazy compliments. Or any compliments at all, in fact. "Well... I don't know what to say. Thank you, Chief. That means a lot. A hell of a bloody lot. If I ever get to be a tenth of the man he was then I'll be more'n satisfied—"

"Shit on that. Just tell me you'll do it. I need someone I can count on, Craw, and you do things the old way. You're a straight edge, and there ain't many left. Just tell me you'll do it." He had a strange look to him, suddenly. An odd, weak twist to his mouth. If Craw hadn't known better, he'd have called it fear, and suddenly he saw it.

Dow had no one he could turn his back to. No friends but those he'd scared into serving him and a mountain of enemies. No choice but to trust to a man he hardly knew 'cause he reminded him of an old comrade long gone back to the mud. The cost of a great big name. The harvest of a lifetime in the black business.

"'Course I'll do it." And like that it was said. Maybe he felt for Dow in that moment, however mad it sounded. Maybe he understood the loneliness of being Chief. Or maybe the embers of his own ambitions, that he'd thought burned out beside his brothers' graves long ago, flared up one last time when Dow raked 'em over. Either way it was said, and there was no unsaying it. Without wondering if it was the right thing to do. For him, or for his dozen, or for anyone, and straight away Craw had a terrible feeling like he'd made a bastard of a mistake. "Just while the battle's on, though," he added, rowing back from the waterfall fast as he could. "I'll hold the gap 'til you find someone better."

"Good man." Dow held out his hand, and they shook, and when Craw looked up again it was into that wolf grin, not a trace of weakness or fear or anything even close. "You done the right thing, Craw."

Craw watched Dow walk back up the hillside towards the stones, wondering whether he'd really let his hard mask slip or if he'd just slipped a soft one on. The right thing? Had Craw just signed up as right hand to one of the most hated men in the world? A man with more enemies than any other in a land where everyone had too many? A man he didn't even particularly like, promised to guard with his life? He gave a groan.

What would his dozen have to say about this? Yon shaking his head with a face like thunder. Drofd looking all hurt and confused. Brack rubbing at his temples with his—Brack was back to the mud, he realised with a jolt. Wonderful? By the dead, what would she have to—

"Craw." And there she was, right at his elbow.

"Ah!" he said, taking a step away.

"How's the face?"

"Er...all right...I guess. Everyone else all right?"

"Yon got a splinter in his hand and it's made him pissier'n ever, but he'll live."

"Good. That's...good. That everyone's all right, that is, not...not the splinter."

Her brows drew in, guessing something was wrong, which wasn't too difficult since he was making a pitiful effort at hiding it. "What did our noble Protector want?"

"He wanted..." Craw worked his lips for a moment, wondering how to frame it, but a turd's a turd however it's framed. "He wanted to offer me Splitfoot's place."

He'd been expecting her to laugh her arse off, but she just narrowed her eyes. "You? Why?"

Good question, he was starting to wonder about it now. "He said I'm a straight edge."

"I see."

"He said...I remind him of Threetrees." Realising what a pompous cock he sounded even as the words came out.

He'd definitely been expecting her to laugh at that, but she just nar-

rowed her eyes more. "You're a man can be trusted. Everyone knows that. But I can see better reasons."

"Like what?"

"You were tight with Bethod and his crowd, and with Threetrees before him, and maybe Dow thinks you'll bring him a few friends he hasn't already got. Or at any rate a few less enemies." Craw frowned. Those were better reasons. "That and he knows Whirrun'll go wherever you go, and Whirrun's a damn good man to have standing behind you if things get ugly." Shit. She was double right. She'd sussed it all straight off. "And knowing Black Dow, things are sure to get ugly...What did you tell him?"

Craw winced. "I said yes," and hurried after with, "just while the battle's on."

"I see." Still no anger, and no surprise either. She just watched him. That was making him more nervy than if she'd punched him in the face. "And what about the dozen?"

"Well..." Ashamed to say he hadn't really considered it. "Guess you'll be coming along with me, if you'll have it. Unless you want to go back to your farm and your family and—"

"Retire?"

"Aye."

She snorted. "The pipe and the porch and the sunset on the water? That's you, not me."

"Then...I reckon it's your dozen for the time being."

"All right."

"You ain't going to give me a tongue-lashing?"

"About what?"

"Not taking my own advice, for a start. About how I should keep my head down, not stick my neck out, get everyone in the crew through alive, how old horses can't jump new fences and blah, blah, blah—"

"That's what you'd say. I'm not you, Craw."

He blinked. "Guess not. Then you think this is the right thing to do?"

"The right thing?" She turned away with a hint of a grin. "That's you an' all." And she strolled back up towards the Heroes, one hand resting slack on her sword hilt, and left him stood there in the wind.

"By the bloody dead." He looked off across the hillside, desperately searching for a finger that still had some nail left to chew at.

Shivers was standing not far off. Saying nothing. Just staring. Looking,

"Like Splitfoot."

"Aye." Craw wasn't sure he'd ever seen anyone look deader than that bastard.

"I want you to take his place."

"Eh?" said Craw. "My ears are still whining. Not sure I heard you right."

Dow leaned closer. "I want you to be my Second. Lead my Carls. Watch my back."

Craw stared. "Me?"

"Aye, you, what did I fucking say?"

"But . . . why the hell *me?*"

"You got the experience, and the respect . . ." Dow looked at him for a moment, his jaw clenched tight. Then he waved a hand like he was swatting a fly. "You remind me o' Threetrees."

Craw blinked. It might've been one of the best things anyone had ever said to him, and not from a source prone to lazy compliments. Or any compliments at all, in fact. "Well . . . I don't know what to say. Thank you, Chief. That means a lot. A hell of a bloody lot. If I ever get to be a tenth of the man he was then I'll be more'n satisfied—"

"Shit on that. Just tell me you'll do it. I need someone I can count on, Craw, and you do things the old way. You're a straight edge, and there ain't many left. Just tell me you'll do it." He had a strange look to him, suddenly. An odd, weak twist to his mouth. If Craw hadn't known better, he'd have called it fear, and suddenly he saw it.

Dow had no one he could turn his back to. No friends but those he'd scared into serving him and a mountain of enemies. No choice but to trust to a man he hardly knew 'cause he reminded him of an old comrade long gone back to the mud. The cost of a great big name. The harvest of a lifetime in the black business.

"'Course I'll do it." And like that it was said. Maybe he felt for Dow in that moment, however mad it sounded. Maybe he understood the loneliness of being Chief. Or maybe the embers of his own ambitions, that he'd thought burned out beside his brothers' graves long ago, flared up one last time when Dow raked 'em over. Either way it was said, and there was no unsaying it. Without wondering if it was the right thing to do. For him, or for his dozen, or for anyone, and straight away Craw had a terrible feeling like he'd made a bastard of a mistake. "Just while the battle's on, though," he added, rowing back from the waterfall fast as he could. "I'll hold the gap 'til you find someone better."

"Good man." Dow held out his hand, and they shook, and when Craw looked up again it was into that wolf grin, not a trace of weakness or fear or anything even close. "You done the right thing, Craw."

Craw watched Dow walk back up the hillside towards the stones, wondering whether he'd really let his hard mask slip or if he'd just slipped a soft one on. The right thing? Had Craw just signed up as right hand to one of the most hated men in the world? A man with more enemies than any other in a land where everyone had too many? A man he didn't even particularly like, promised to guard with his life? He gave a groan.

What would his dozen have to say about this? Yon shaking his head with a face like thunder. Drofd looking all hurt and confused. Brack rubbing at his temples with his—Brack was back to the mud, he realised with a jolt. Wonderful? By the dead, what would she have to—

"Craw." And there she was, right at his elbow.

"Ah!" he said, taking a step away.

"How's the face?"

"Er...all right...I guess. Everyone else all right?"

"Yon got a splinter in his hand and it's made him pissier'n ever, but he'll live."

"Good. That's...good. That everyone's all right, that is, not...not the splinter."

Her brows drew in, guessing something was wrong, which wasn't too difficult since he was making a pitiful effort at hiding it. "What did our noble Protector want?"

"He wanted..." Craw worked his lips for a moment, wondering how to frame it, but a turd's a turd however it's framed. "He wanted to offer me Splitfoot's place."

He'd been expecting her to laugh her arse off, but she just narrowed her eyes. "You? Why?"

Good question, he was starting to wonder about it now. "He said I'm a straight edge."

"I see."

"He said...I remind him of Threetrees." Realising what a pompous cock he sounded even as the words came out.

He'd definitely been expecting her to laugh at that, but she just narrowed her eyes more. "You're a man can be trusted. Everyone knows that. But I can see better reasons."

"Like what?"

"You were tight with Bethod and his crowd, and with Threetrees before him, and maybe Dow thinks you'll bring him a few friends he hasn't already got. Or at any rate a few less enemies." Craw frowned. Those were better reasons. "That and he knows Whirrun'll go wherever you go, and Whirrun's a damn good man to have standing behind you if things get ugly." Shit. She was double right. She'd sussed it all straight off. "And knowing Black Dow, things are sure to get ugly... What did you tell him?"

Craw winced. "I said yes," and hurried after with, "just while the battle's on."

"I see." Still no anger, and no surprise either. She just watched him. That was making him more nervy than if she'd punched him in the face. "And what about the dozen?"

"Well..." Ashamed to say he hadn't really considered it. "Guess you'll be coming along with me, if you'll have it. Unless you want to go back to your farm and your family and—"

"Retire?"

"Aye."

She snorted. "The pipe and the porch and the sunset on the water? That's you, not me."

"Then... I reckon it's your dozen for the time being."

"All right."

"You ain't going to give me a tongue-lashing?"

"About what?"

"Not taking my own advice, for a start. About how I should keep my head down, not stick my neck out, get everyone in the crew through alive, how old horses can't jump new fences and blah, blah, blah—"

"That's what you'd say. I'm not you, Craw."

He blinked. "Guess not. Then you think this is the right thing to do?"

"The right thing?" She turned away with a hint of a grin. "That's you an' all." And she strolled back up towards the Heroes, one hand resting slack on her sword hilt, and left him stood there in the wind.

"By the bloody dead." He looked off across the hillside, desperately searching for a finger that still had some nail left to chew at.

Shivers was standing not far off. Saying nothing. Just staring. Looking, in fact, like a man who felt himself stepped in front of. Craw's wince became a full grimace. Seemed that was getting to be the normal shape to his face, one way and another. "A man's worst enemies are his own ambitions," Bethod used to tell him. "Mine have got me in all the shit I'm in today."

"Welcome to the shit," he muttered to himself through gritted teeth. That's the problem with mistakes. You can make 'em in an instant. Years upon years spent tiptoeing about like a fool, then you take your eye away for a moment and...

Bang.

Escape

Finree thought they were in some kind of shack. The floor was damp dirt, a chill draught across it making her shiver. The place smelled of fust and animals.

They had blindfolded her, and marched her lurching across the wet fields into the trees, crops tangling her feet, bushes clutching at her dress. It was a good thing she had been wearing her riding boots or she would probably have ended up barefoot. She had heard fighting behind them, she thought. Aliz had kept screaming for a while, her voice getting more and more hoarse, but eventually stopped. It changed nothing. They had crossed water on a creaking boat. Maybe over to the north side of the river. They had been shoved in here, heard a door wobble shut and the clattering of a bar on the outside.

And here they had been left, in the darkness. To wait for who knew what.

As Finree slowly got her breath back the pain began to creep up on her. Her scalp burned, her head thumped, her neck sent vicious stings down between her shoulders whenever she tried to turn her head. But no doubt she was a great deal better off than most who had been trapped in that inn.

She wondered if Hardrick had made it to safety, or if they had ridden him down in the fields, his useless message never delivered. She kept seeing that major's face as he stumbled sideways with blood running from his broken head, so very surprised. Meed, fumbling at the bubbling wound in his neck. All dead. All of them.

She took a shuddering breath and forced the thought away. She could not think of it any more than a tightrope walker could think about the ground. "You have to look forward," she remembered her father telling her, as he plucked another of her pieces from the squares board. "Concentrate on what you can change."

Aliz had been sobbing ever since the door shut. Finree wanted quite badly to slap her, but her hands were tied. She was reasonably sure they would not get out of this by sobbing. Not that she had any better ideas.

"Quiet," Finree hissed. "Quiet, please, I need to think. Please. Please."

The sobbing stuttered back to ragged whimpering. That was worse, if anything.

"Will they kill us?" squeaked Aliz' voice, along with a slobbering snort. "Will they murder us?"

"No. They would have done it already."

"Then what will they do with us?"

The question sat between them like a bottomless abyss, with nothing but their echoing breath to fill it. Finree managed to twist herself up to sitting, gritting her teeth at the pain in her neck. "We have to think, do you understand? We have to look forward. We have to try and escape."

"How?" Aliz whimpered.

"Any way we can!" Silence. "We have to try. Are your hands free?"

"No."

Finree managed to worm her way across the floor, dress sliding over the dirt until her back hit the wall, grunting with the effort. She shifted herself along, fingertips brushing crumbling plaster, damp stone.

"Are you there?" squeaked Aliz.

"Where else would I be?"

"What are you doing?"

"Trying to get my hands free." Something tugged at Finree's waist, cloth ripped. She wormed her shoulder blades up the wall, following the caught material with her fingers. A rusted bracket. She rubbed away the flakes between finger and thumb, felt a jagged point underneath, a sudden surge of hope. She pulled her wrists apart, struggling to find the metal with the cords that held them.

"If you get your hands free, what then?" came Aliz' shrill voice.

"Get yours free," grunted Finree through gritted teeth. "Then feet."

"Then what? What about the door? There'll be guards, won't there? Where are we? What do we do if—"

"I don't know!" She forced her voice down. "I don't know. One battle at a time." Sawing away at the bracket. "One battle at a—" Her hand slipped and she lurched back, felt the metal leave a burning cut down her arm. "Ah!"

"What?"

"Cut myself. Nothing. Don't worry."

"Don't worry? We've been captured by the Northmen! Savages! Did you see—"

"Don't worry about the cut, I meant! And yes, I saw it all." And she had to concentrate on what she could change. Whether her hands were free or not was challenge enough. Her legs were burning from holding her up against the wall, she could feel the greasy wetness of blood on her fingers, of sweat on her face. Her head was pounding, agony in her neck with every movement of her shoulders. She wriggled the cord against that piece of rusted metal, back and forward, back and forward, grunting with frustration. "Damn, bloody—Ah!"

Like that it came free. She dragged her blindfold off and tossed it away. She could hardly see more without it. Chinks of light around the door, between the planks. Cracked walls glistening with damp, floor scattered with muddy straw. Aliz was kneeling a stride or two away, dress covered in dirt, bound hands limp in her lap.

Finree jumped over to her, since her ankles were still tied, and knelt down. She tugged off Aliz' blindfold, took both of her hands and pressed them in hers. Spoke slowly, looking her right in her pink-rimmed eyes. "We will escape. We must. We will." Aliz nodded, mouth twisting into a desperately hopeful smile for a moment. Finree peered down at her wrists, numb fingertips tugging at the knots, tongue pressed between her teeth as she prised at them with her broken nails—

"How does he know I have them?" Finree went cold. Or even colder. A voice, speaking Northern, and heavy footsteps, coming closer. She felt Aliz frozen in the dark, not even breathing.

"He has his ways, apparently."

THE HEROES

"His ways can sink in the dark places of the world for all I care." It was the voice of the giant. That soft, slow voice, but it had anger in it now. "The women are mine."

"He only wants one." The other sounded like his throat was full of grit, his voice a grinding whisper.

"Which one?"

"The brown-haired one."

An angry snort. "No. I had in mind she would give me children." Finree's eyes went wide. Her breath crawled in her throat. They were talking about her. She went at the knot on Aliz' wrists with twice the urgency, biting at her lip.

"How many children do you need?" came the whispering voice.

"Civilised children. After the Union fashion."

"What?"

"You heard me. Civilised children."

"Who eat with a fork and that? I been to Styria. I been to the Union. Civilisation ain't all it's made out to be, believe me."

A pause. "Is it true they have holes there in which a man can shit, and the turds are carried away?"

"So what? Shit is still shit. It all ends up somewhere."

"I want civilisation. I want civilised children."

"Use the yellow-haired one."

"She pleases my eye less. And she is a coward. She does nothing but cry. The brown-haired one killed one of my men. She has bones. Children get their courage from the mother. I will not have cowardly children."

The whispering voice dropped lower, too quiet for Finree to hear. She tugged desperately at the knots with her nails, mouthing curses.

"What are they saying?" came Aliz' whisper, croaky with terror.

"Nothing," Finree hissed back. "Nothing."

"Black Dow takes a high hand with me in this," came the giant's voice again.

"He takes a high hand with me and all. There it is. He's the one with the chain."

"I shit on his chain. Stranger-Come-Knocking has no masters but the sky and the earth. Black Dow does not command—"

"He ain't commanding nothing. He's asking nicely. You can tell me no. Then I'll tell him no. Then we can see."

There was a pause. Finree pressed her tongue into her teeth, the knot starting to give, starting to give—

The door swung open and they were left blinking into the light. A man stood in the doorway. One of his eyes was strangely bright. Too bright. He stepped under the lintel, and Finree realised that his eye was made of metal, and set in the midst of an enormous, mottled scar. She had never seen a more monstrous-looking man. Aliz gave a kind of stuttering wheeze. Too scared even to scream, for once.

"She got her hands free," he whispered over his shoulder.

"I said she had bones," came the giant's voice from outside. "Tell Black Dow there will be a price for this. A price for the woman and a price for the insult."

"I'll tell him." The metal-eyed man came forward, pulling something from his belt. A knife, she saw the flash of metal in the gloom. Aliz saw it too, whimpered, gripped hard at Finree's fingers and she gripped back. She was not sure what else she could do. He squatted down in front of them, forearms on his knees and his hands dangling, the knife loose in one. Finree's eyes flickered from the gleam of the blade to the gleam of his metal eye, not sure which was more awful. "There's a price for everything, ain't there?" he whispered to her.

The knife darted out and slit the cord between her ankles in one motion. He reached behind his back and pulled a canvas bag over her head with another, plunging her suddenly into fusty, onion-smelling darkness. She was dragged up by her armpit, hands slipping from Aliz' limp grip.

"Wait!" she heard Aliz shouting behind her. "What about me? What about—"

The door clattered shut.

The Bridge

Your August Majesty,

If this letter reaches you I have fallen in battle, fighting for your cause with my final breath. I write it only in the hope of letting you know what I could not in person: that the days I spent serving with the Knights of the Body, and as your Majesty's First Guard in particular, were the happiest of my life, and that the day when I lost that position was the saddest. If I failed you I hope you can forgive me, and think of me as I was before Sipani: dutiful, diligent, and always utterly loyal to your Majesty.

I bid you a fond farewell,

Bremer dan Gorst

He thought better of "a fond" and crossed it out, realised he should probably rewrite the whole thing without it, then decided he did not have the time. He tossed the pen away, folded the paper without bothering to blot it and tucked it down inside his breastplate.

Perhaps they will find it there, later, on my crap-stained corpse. Dramatically bloodied at the corner, maybe? A final letter! Why, to whom? Family? Sweetheart? Friends? No, the sad fool had none of those, it is addressed to the king! And borne upon a velvet pillow into his Majesty's throne room, there perhaps to wring out some wretched drip of guilt. A single sparkling tear spatters upon the marble tiles. Oh! Poor Gorst, how unfairly he was used! How unjustly stripped of his position! Alas, his blood has watered foreign fields, far from the warmth of my favour! Now what's for breakfast?

Down on the Old Bridge the third assault had reached its critical moment. The narrow double span was one heaving mass, rows of nervous soldiers waiting unenthusiastically to take their turn while the wounded, exhausted and otherwise spent staggered away in the opposite direction. The resolve of Mitterick's men was flickering, Gorst could see it in the pale faces of the officers, hear it in their nervous voices, in the sobs of the injured. Success or failure was balanced on a knife-edge.

"Where the hell is bloody Vallimir?" Mitterick was roaring at everyone and no one. "Bloody coward, I'll have him cashiered in disgrace! I'll go down there my bloody self! Where did Felnigg get to? Where…what… who…" His words were buried in the hubbub as Gorst walked down towards the river, his mood lifting with every jaunty step as if a great weight was floating from his shoulders piece by leaden piece.

A wounded man stumbled by, one arm around a fellow, clutching a bloody cloth to his eye. *Someone will be missing from next year's archery contest!* Another was hauled past on a stretcher, crying out piteously as he bounced, the stump of his leg bound tightly with red-soaked bandages. *No more walks in the park for you!* He grinned at the injured men laid groaning at the verges of the muddy track, gave them merry salutes. *Unlucky, my comrades! Life is not fair, is it?*

He strode through a scattered crowd, then threaded through a tighter mass, then shouldered through a breathless press, the fear building around him as the bodies squeezed tighter, and with it his excitement. Feelings ran high. Men shoved at each other, thrashed with their elbows, screamed pointless insults. Weapons waved dangerously. Stray arrows would occasionally putter down, no longer in volleys but in apologetic ones and twos. *Little gifts from our friends on the other side. No, really, you shouldn't have!*

The mud beneath Gorst's feet levelled off, then began to rise, then gave way to old stone slabs. Between twisted faces he caught glimpses of the river, the bridge's mossy parapet. He began to make out from the general din the metallic note of combat and the sound tugged at his heart like a lover's voice across a crowded room. *Like the whiff of the husk pipe to the addict. We all have our little vices. Our little obsessions. Drink, women, cards. And here is mine.*

Tactics and technique were useless here, it was a question of brute strength and fury, and very few men were Gorst's match in either. He put his head down and strained at the press as he had strained at the mired wagon a few days before. He began to grunt, then growl, then hiss, and he rammed his way through the soldiers like a ploughshare through soil, shoving heedlessly with shield and shoulder, tramping over the dead and wounded. *No small talk. No apologies. No petty embarrassments here.*

"Out of my fucking *way*!" he screeched, sending a soldier sprawling on his face and using him for a carpet. He caught a flash of metal and a spear-point raked his shield. For a moment he thought a Union man had taken objection, then he realised the spear had a Northman on the other end. *Greetings, my friend!* Gorst was trying to twist his sword free of the press and into a useful attitude when he was given an almighty shove from behind and found himself suddenly squashed up against the owner of the spear, their noses almost touching. A bearded face, with a scar on the top lip.

Gorst smashed his forehead into it, and again, and again, shoved him down and stomped on his head until it gave under his heel. He realised he was shouting at the falsetto top of his voice. He wasn't even sure of the words, if they were words. All around him men were doing the same, spitting curses in each other's faces that no one on the other side could possibly understand.

A glimpse of sky through a thicket of pole-arms and Gorst thrust his sword into it, another Northman bent sideways, breath wheezing silently through a mouth frozen in a drooling ring of surprise. Too tangled to swing, Gorst gritted his teeth and jabbed away, jabbed, jabbed, jabbed, point grating against armour, pricking at flesh, opening an arm up in a long red slit.

A growling face showed for a moment over the rim of Gorst's shield and he set his boots and drove the man back, battering at his chest, jaw, legs. Back he went, and back, and squealing over the parapet, his spear splashing into the fast-flowing water below. Somehow he managed to cling on with the other hand, desperate fingers white on stone, blood leaking from his bloated nose, looking up imploringly. *Mercy? Help? Forbearance, at least? Are we not all just men? Brothers eternal, on this crooked road of life? Could we be bosom friends, had we met in other circumstances?*

Gorst smashed his shield down on the hand, bones crunching under the metal edge, watched the man fall cartwheeling into the river. "The Union!" someone shrieked. "The Union!" Was it him? He felt soldiers pushing forward, their blood rising, surging across the bridge with an irresistible momentum, carrying him northwards, a stick on the crest of a wave. He cut someone down with his long steel, laid someone's else's head open with the corner of his shield, strap twisting in his hand, his face aching he was smiling so hard, every breath burning with joy. *This is living! This is living! Well, not for them, but—*

He tottered suddenly into empty space. Fields opened wide before him, crops shifting in the breeze, golden in the evening sun like the paradise the Prophet promises to the Gurkish righteous. Northmen ran. Some running away, and more running towards. A counter-attack, and leading it a huge warrior, clad in plates of black metal strapped over black chain mail, a long sword in one gauntleted fist, a heavy mace in the other, steel glinting warm and welcoming in the mellow afternoon. Carls followed in a mailed wedge, painted shields up and offering their bright-daubed devices, screaming a chant – "Scale! Scale!" in a thunder of voices.

The Union drive faltered, the vanguard still shuffling reluctantly forward from the weight of those behind. Gorst stood at their front and watched, smiling into the dropping sun, not daring to move a muscle in case the feeling ended. It was sublime. Like a scene from the tales he had read as a boy. Like that ridiculous painting in his father's library of Harod the Great facing Ardlic of Keln. *A meeting of champions! All gritted teeth and clenched buttocks! All glorious lives, glorious deaths and glorious . . . glory?*

The man in black hammered up onto the bridge, big boots thumping the stones. His blade came whistling at shoulder height and Gorst set himself to parry, the breathtaking shock humming up his arm. The mace came a moment later and he caught it on his shield, the heavy head leaving a dent just short of his nose.

Gorst gave two savage cuts in return, high and low, and the man in black ducked the first and blocked the second with the shaft of his mace, lashed at Gorst with his sword and made him spin away, using a Union soldier's shield as a backrest.

He was strong, this champion of the North, and brave, but strength and bravery are not always enough. He had not studied every significant text on swordsmanship ever committed to paper. Had not trained three hours a day every day since he was fourteen. Had run no ten thousand miles in his armour. Had endured no bitter, enraging years of humiliation. *And, worst of all, he cares whether he loses.*

Their blades met in the air with a deafening crash but Gorst's timing was perfect and it was the Northman who staggered off balance, favouring perhaps a weak left knee. Gorst was on him in a flash but someone else's stray weapon struck him on the shoulder-plate before he could swing, sent him stumbling into the man in black's arms.

They lumbered in an awkward embrace. The Northman tried to beat at him with the haft of his mace, trip him, shake him off. Gorst held tight. He was vaguely aware of fighting around them, of men locked in their own desperate struggles, of the screams of tortured flesh and tortured metal, but he was lost in the moment, eyes closed.

When was the last time I truly held someone? When I won the semi-final in the contest, did my father hug me? No. A firm shake of the hand. An awkward clap on the shoulder. Perhaps he would have hugged me if I'd won, but I failed, just as he said I would. When, then? Women paid to do it? Men I scarcely know in meaningless drunken camaraderie? But not like this. By an equal, who truly understands me. If only it could last...

He leaped back, jerking his head away from the whistling mace and letting the man in black stumble past. Gorst's steel flashed towards his head as he righted himself and he only just managed to deflect the blow, sword wrenched from his hand and sent skittering away among the pounding boots. The man in black bellowed, twisting to swing his mace at a vicious diagonal.

Too much brawn, not enough precision. Gorst saw it coming, let it glance harmlessly from his shield and slid around it into space, aimed a carefully gauged chop, little more than a fencer's flick, at that weak left knee. The blade of his steel caught the thigh-plate, found the chain mail on the joint and bit through. The man in black lurched sideways, only staying upright by clawing at the parapet, his mace scraping the mossy stone.

Gorst blew air from his nose as he brought the steel scything up and over, no fencer's movement this. It chopped cleanly through the man's thick forearm, armour, flesh and bone, and clanged against the old rock underneath, streaks of blood, rings of mail, splinters of stone flying.

The man in black gave an outraged snort as he struggled up, roared as he swung his mace at Gorst's head with a killing blow. Or would have, had his hand still been attached. Somewhat to the disappointment of them both, Gorst suspected, his gauntlet and half his forearm were hanging by a last shred of chain mail, the mace dangling puppet-like from the wrist by a leather thong. As far as Gorst could tell without seeing his face, the man was greatly confused.

Gorst smashed him in the head with his shield and snapped his helmet back, blood squirting from his severed arm in thick black drops. He was pawing clumsily for a dagger at his belt when Gorst's long steel clanged into his black faceplate and left a bright dent down the middle. He tottered, arms out wide, then toppled backwards like a great tree felled.

Gorst held up his shield and bloody sword, shaking them at the last few dismayed Northmen like a savage, and gave a great shrill scream. *I win, fuckers! I win! I win!*

As if that were an order, the lot of them turned and fled northwards, thrashing through the crops in their desperate haste to get away, weighed down by their flapping mail and their fatigue and their panic, and Gorst was among them, a lion among the goats.

Compared to his morning routine this was like dancing on air. A Northman slipped beside him, yelping in terror. Gorst charted the downward movement of his body, timed the downward movement of his arm to match and neatly cut the man's head off, felt it bounce from his knee as he plunged on up the track. A young lad tossed away a spear, face contorted with fear as he looked over his shoulder. Gorst chopped deep into his backside and he went down howling in the crops.

It was so easy it was faintly ridiculous. Gorst hacked the legs out from one man, gained on another and dropped him with a cut across the back, struck an arm from a third and let him stumble on for a few wobbling steps before he smashed him over backwards with his shield.

Is this still battle? Is this still the glorious matching of man against man? Or is this just murder? He did not care. *I cannot tell jokes, or make pretty conversation, but this I can do. This I am made for. Bremer dan Gorst, king of the world!*

He chopped them down on both sides, left their blubbing, leaking bodies wrecked in his wake. A couple turned stumbling to face him and he chopped them down as well. Made meat of them all, regardless. On he went, and on, hacking away like a mad butcher, the air whooping triumphantly in his throat. He passed a farm on his right, half way or more to a long wall up ahead. No Northmen within easy reach, he stole a glance over his shoulder, and slowed.

None of Mitterick's men were following. They had stopped near the bridge, a hundred strides behind him. He was entirely alone in the fields, a one-man assault on the Northmen's positions. He stopped, uncertainly, marooned in a sea of barley.

A lad he must have overtaken earlier jogged up. Shaggy-haired, wearing a leather jerkin with a bloody sleeve. No weapon. He spared Gorst a quick glance, then laboured on. He passed close enough that Gorst could have stabbed him without moving his feet, but suddenly he could not see the point.

The elation of combat was leaking out of him, the familiar weight gathering on his shoulders again. *So quickly I am sucked back into the bog of despond. The foetid waters close over my face. Only count three, and I am once again the very same sad bastard who all know and scorn.* He looked back towards his own lines. The trail of broken bodies no longer felt like anything to take pride in.

He stood, skin prickling with sweat, sucking air through gritted teeth. Frowning towards the wall through the crops to the north, and the spears bristling up behind it, and the beaten men still struggling back towards it. *Perhaps I should charge on, all alone. Glorious Gorst, there he goes! Falling upon the enemy like a shooting star! His body dies but his name shall live for ever!* He snorted. *Idiot Gorst, throwing his life away, the stupid, squeaking arse. Dropping into his pointless grave like a turd into a sewer, and just as quickly forgotten.*

He shook the ruined shield from his arm and let it drop to the track, pulled the folded letter from his breastplate between two fingers, crumpled it tightly in his fist, then tossed it into the barley. *It was a pathetic letter anyway. I should be ashamed of myself.*

Then he turned, head hanging, and trudged back towards the bridge.

One Union soldier, for some reason, had chased far down the track after Scale's fleeing troops. A big man wearing heavy armour and with a sword in his hand. He didn't look particularly triumphant as he stared up the road, standing oddly alone in that open field. He looked almost as defeated as Calder felt. After a while he turned and plodded back towards the bridge. Back towards the trenches Scale's men had dug the previous night, and where the Union were now taking up positions.

Not all dramas on the battlefield spring from glorious action. Some slink from everyone just sitting there, doing nothing. Tenways had sent no help. Calder hadn't moved. He hadn't even got as far as making his mind up not to move. He'd just stood, staring at nothing through his eyeglass, in a frozen agony of indecision, and then suddenly all of Scale's men who still could were running, and the Union had carried the bridge.

Thankfully, it looked as if they were satisfied for now. Probably they didn't want to risk pushing further with the light fading. They could push further tomorrow, after all, and everyone knew it. They had a good foothold on the north bank of the river, and no shortage of men in spite of the price Scale had made them pay. It looked as if the price Scale had paid had been heavier yet.

The last of his defeated Carls were still hobbling back, clambering over the wall to lie scattered in the crops behind, dirt and blood-smeared, broken and exhausted. Calder stopped a man with a hand on his shoulder.

"Where's Scale?"

"Dead!" he screamed, shaking him off. "Dead! Why didn't you come, you bastards? Why didn't you help us?"

"Union men over the stream there," Pale-as-Snow was explaining as he led him away, but Calder hardly heard. He stood at the gate, staring across the darkening fields towards the bridge.

He'd loved his brother. For being on his side when everyone else was against him. Because nothing's more important than family.

He'd hated his brother. For being too stupid. For being too strong. For being in his way. Because nothing's more important than power.

And now his brother was dead. Calder had let him die. Just by doing nothing. Was that the same as killing a man?

All he could think about was how it might make his life more difficult. All the extra tasks he'd have to do, the responsibilities he didn't feel ready for. He was the heir, now, to all his father's priceless legacy of feuds, hatred and bad blood. He felt annoyance rather than grief, and puzzled he didn't feel more. Everyone was looking at him. Watching him, to see what he'd do. To judge what kind of man he was. He was embarrassed, almost, that this was all his brother's death made him feel. Not guilty, not sad, just cold. And then angry.

And then very angry.

Strange Bedfellows

The hood was pulled from her head and Finree squinted into the light. Such as it was. The room was dim and dusty with two mean windows and a low ceiling, bowing in the middle, cobwebs drifting from the rafters.

A Northman stood a couple of paces in front of her, feet planted wide and hands on hips, head tipped slightly back in the stance of a man used to being obeyed, and quickly. His short hair was peppered with grey and his face was sharp as a chisel, notched with old scars, an appraising twist to his mouth. A chain of heavy golden links gleamed faintly around his shoulders. An important man. Or one who thought himself important, at least.

An older man stood behind him, thumbs in his belt near a battered sword hilt. He had a shaggy grey growth on his jaw somewhere between beard and stubble and a fresh cut on his cheek, dark red and rimmed with pink, closed with ugly stitches. He wore an expression somewhat sad, somewhat determined, as if he did not like what was coming but could see no way to avoid it, and now was fixed on seeing it through, whatever it cost him. A lieutenant of the first man.

As Finree's eyes adjusted she saw a third figure in the shadows against the wall. A woman, she was surprised to see, and with black skin. Tall and thin, a long coat hanging open to show a body wrapped in bandages. Where she stood in this, Finree could not tell.

She did not turn her head to look, in spite of the temptation, but she knew there was another man behind her, his gravelly breath at the edge of her hearing. The one with the metal eye. She wondered if he had that little knife in his hand, and how close the point was to her back. Her skin prickled inside her dirty dress at the thought.

"This is her?" sneered the man with the chain at the black-skinned woman, and when he turned his head Finree saw there was only a fold of old scar where his ear should have been.

"Yes."

"She don't look much like the answer to all my problems."

The woman stared at Finree, unblinking. "Probably she has looked better." Her eyes were like a lizard's, black and empty.

The man with the chain took a step forwards and Finree had to stop herself cringing. There was something in the set of him that made her feel he was teetering on the edge of violence. That his every smallest movement was the prelude to a punch, or a headbutt, or worse. That his natural instinct was to throttle her and it took a constant effort to stop himself doing it, and talk instead. "Do you know who I am?"

She lifted her chin, trying to look undaunted and almost certainly failing. Her heart was thumping so hard she was sure they must be able to hear it against her ribs. "No," she said in Northern.

"You understand me, then."

"Yes."

"I'm Black Dow."

"Oh." She hardly knew what to say. "I thought you'd be taller."

Dow raised one scar-nicked brow at the older man. The older man shrugged. "What can I say? You're shorter'n your reputation."

"Most of us are." Dow looked back at Finree, eyes narrowed, judging her response. "How 'bout your father? Taller'n me?"

They knew who she was. Who her father was. She had no idea how, but they knew. That was either a good thing or a very bad one. She looked at the older man and he gave her the faintest, apologetic smile, then winced since he must have stretched his stitches doing it. She felt the man with the metal eye shift his weight behind her, a floorboard creaking. This did not seem like a group from which she could expect good things.

"My father is about your height," she said, her voice whispery.

Dow grinned, but there was no humour in it. "Well, that's a damn good height to be."

"If you mean to gain some advantage over him through me, you will be disappointed."

"Will I?"

"Nothing will sway him from his duty."

"Won't be sorry to lose you, eh?"

"He'll be sorry. But he'll only fight you harder."

"Oh, I'm getting a fine sense for the man! Loyal, and strong, and bulging with righteousness. Like iron on the outside, but..." And he thumped at his chest with one fist and pushed out his bottom lip. "He feels it. *Feels* it all, right here. And weeps at the quiet times."

Finree looked right back. "You have him close enough."

Dow whipped out his grin like a killer might a knife. "Sounds like my fucking twin." The older man gave a snort of laughter. The woman smiled, showing a mouthful of impossibly perfect white teeth. The man with the metal eye made no sound. "Good thing you won't be relying on your father's tender mercies, then. I got no plans to bargain with you, or ransom you, or even send your head over the river in a box. Though we'll see how the conversation goes, you might yet change my mind on that score."

There was a long pause, while Dow watched her and she watched him. Like the accused waiting for the judge to pass sentence.

"I've a mind to let you go," he said. "I want you to take a message back to your father. Let him know I don't see the purpose shedding any more blood over this worthless fucking valley. Let him know I'm willing to talk." Dow gave a loud sniff, worked his mouth as if it tasted bad. "Talk about… *peace.*"

Finree blinked. "Talk."

"That's right."

"About peace."

"That's right."

She felt dizzy. Drunk on the sudden prospect of living to see her husband and her father again. But she had to put that to one side, think past it. She took a long breath through her nose and steadied herself. "That will not be good enough."

She was pleased to see Black Dow look quite surprised. "Won't it, now?"

"No." It was difficult to appear authoritative while bruised, beaten, dirt-spattered and surrounded by the most daunting enemies, but Finree did her very best. She would not get through this with meekness. Black Dow wished to deal with someone powerful. That would make him feel powerful. The more powerful she made herself, the safer she was. So she raised her chin and looked him full in the eye. "You need to make a gesture of goodwill. Something to let my father know you are serious. That you are willing to negotiate. Proof you are a reasonable man."

Black Dow snorted. "You hear that, Craw? Goodwill. Me."

The older man shrugged. "Proof you're reasonable."

"More proof than sending back his daughter without a hole in her head?"

grated Dow, looking her up and down. "Or her head in her hole, for that matter."

She floated over it. "After the battle yesterday, you must have prisoners." Unless they had all been murdered. Looking into Black Dow's eyes, it did not seem unlikely.

" 'Course we've got prisoners." Dow cocked his head on one side, drifting closer. "You think I'm some kind of an animal?"

Finree did, in fact. "I want them released."

"Do you, now? All of 'em?"

"Yes."

"For nothing?"

"A gesture of—"

He jerked forwards, nose almost touching hers, thick veins bulging from the side of his thick neck. "You're in no place to negotiate, you fucking little—"

"You aren't negotiating with me!" Finree barked back at him, showing her teeth. "You're negotiating with my father, and he is in every position! Otherwise you wouldn't be *fucking* asking!"

A ripple of twitches went through Dow's cheek, and for an instant she was sure he was going to beat her to a pulp. Or give the smallest signal to his metal-eyed henchman and she would be slit from her arse to the back of her head. Dow's arm jerked up, and for an instant she was sure her death was a breath away. But all he did was grin, and gently wag his finger in her face. "Oh, you're a sharp one. You didn't tell me she was so sharp."

"I am shocked to my very roots," intoned the black-skinned woman, looking about as shocked as the wall behind her.

"All right." Dow puffed out his scarred cheeks. "I'll let some of the wounded ones go. Don't need their sobbing keeping me awake tonight anyway. Let's say five dozen men."

"You have more?"

"A lot more, but my goodwill's a brittle little thing. Five dozen is all it'll stretch around."

An hour ago she had not seen any way to save herself. Her knees were almost buckling at the thought of coming out of this alive and saving sixty men besides. But she had to try one more thing. "There was another woman taken with me—"

"Can't do it."

"You don't know what I'm going to ask—"

"Yes I do, and I can't do it. Stranger-Come-Knocking, that big bastard who took you prisoner? Man's mad as a grass helmet. He don't answer to me. Don't answer to nothing. You've no idea what it's cost me getting you. I can't afford to buy anyone else."

"Then I won't help you."

Dow clicked his tongue. "Sharp is good, but you don't want to get so sharp you cut your own throat. You won't help me, you're no use to me at all. Might as well send you back to Stranger-Come-Fucking, eh? The way I see it, you got two choices. Back to your father and share in the peace, or back to your friend and share in...whatever she's got coming. Which appeals?"

Finree thought of Aliz' scared breath, in the darkness. Her whimper as Finree's hand slipped out of hers. She thought of that scarred giant, smashing his own man's head apart against the wall. She wished she was brave enough to have tried to call the bluff, at least. But who would be?

"My father," she whispered, and it was the most she could do to stop herself crying with relief.

"Don't feel bad about it." Black Dow drew his murderer's grin one more time. "That's the choice I'd have made. Happy fucking journey."

The bag came down over her head.

Craw waited until Shivers had bundled the hooded girl through the door before leaning forward, one finger up, and gently asking his question. "Er...what's going on, Chief?"

Dow frowned at him. "You're supposed to be my Second, old man. You should be the last one questioning me."

Craw held up his palms. "And I will be. I'm all for peace, believe me, just might help if I understood why you want it of a sudden."

"Want?" barked Dow, jerking towards him like a hound got the scent. "*Want?*" Closer still, making Craw back up against the wall. "I got what I want I'd hang the whole fucking Union and choke this valley with the smoke o' their cooking meat and sink Angland, Midderland and all their bloody other land in the bottom o' the Circle Sea, how's that for peace?"

"Right." Craw cleared his throat, rightly wishing he hadn't asked the question. "Right y'are."

"But that's being Chief, ain't it?" snarled Dow in his face. "A dancing fucking procession o' things you don't want to do! If I'd known what it meant when I took the chain I'd have tossed it in the river along with the Bloody-Nine. Threetrees warned me, but I didn't listen. There's no curse like getting what you want."

Craw winced. "So . . . why, then?"

"Because the dead know I'm no peacemaker but I'm no idiot either. Your little friend Calder may be a pissing coward but he's got a point. It's a damn fool risks his life for what he can get just by the asking. Not everyone's got my appetite for the fight. Men are getting tired, the Union are too many to beat and in case you hadn't noticed we're trousers down in a pit full of bloody snakes. Ironhead? Golden? Stranger-Come-Bragging? I don't trust those bastards further'n I can piss with no hands. Better finish this up now while we can call it a win."

"Fair point," croaked Craw.

"Got what I want there'd be no bloody talk at all." Dow's face twitched, and he looked over at Ishri, leaning in the shadows against the wall, face a blank, black mask. He ran his tongue around the inside of his sneering mouth and spat. "But calmer heads have prevailed. We'll try peace on, see whether it chafes. Now get that bitch back to her father 'fore I change my mind and cut the bloody cross in her for the fucking exercise."

Craw edged for the door sideways, like a crab. "On my way, Chief."

Hearts and Minds

How long should we spend out here, Corporal?"

"As short a time as is possible without disgrace, Yolk."

"How long's that?"

"Until it's too dark for me to see your gurning visage would be a start."

"And we patrol, do we?"

"No, Yolk, we'll just walk a few dozen strides and sit down for a while."

"Where will we find to sit that isn't wet as an otter's—"

"Shh," hissed Tunny, waving at Yolk to get down. There were men in the trees on the other side of the rise. Three men, and two of them in Union uniforms. "Huh." One was Lance Corporal Hedges. A squinty, mean-spirited rat of a man who'd been with the First for about three years and thought himself quite the rogue but was no better than a nasty idiot. The kind of bad soldier who gives proper bad soldiers a bad name. His gangly sidekick was unfamiliar, probably a new recruit. Hedges' version of Yolk, which was truly a concept too horrifying to entertain.

They both had swords drawn and pointed at a Northman, but Tunny could tell right off he was no fighter. Dressed in a dirty coat with a belt around it, a bow over one shoulder and some arrows in a quiver, no other weapon visible. A hunter, maybe, or a trapper, he looked somewhat baffled and somewhat scared. Hedges had a black fur in one hand. Didn't take a great mind to work it all out.

"Why, Lance Corporal Hedges!" Tunny grinned wide as he stood and strolled down the bank, his hand loose on the hilt of his sword, just to make sure everyone realised he had one.

Hedges squinted guiltily over at him. "Keep out o' this, Tunny. We found him, he's ours."

"Yours? Where in the rule book does it say prisoners are yours to abuse because you found them?"

"What do you care about the rules? What're you doing here, I'd like to know."

"As it happens, First Sergeant Forest sent me and Trooper Yolk on patrol to make sure none of our men were out beyond the picket causing mischief. And what should I find but you, out beyond the picket and in the process of robbing this civilian. I call that mischievous. Do you call that mischievous, Yolk?"

"Well, er..."

Tunny didn't wait for an answer. "You know what General Jalenhorm said. We're out to win hearts and minds as much as anything else. Can't have you robbing the locals, Hedges. Just can't have it. Contrary to our whole approach up here."

"General fucking Jalenhorm?" Hedges snorted. "Hearts and minds? You? Don't make me laugh!"

"Make you laugh?" Tunny frowned. "Make you *laugh*? Trooper Yolk, I want you to raise your loaded flatbow and point it at Lance Corporal Hedges."

Yolk stared. "What?"

"What?" grunted Hedges.

Tunny threw up an arm. "You heard me, point your bow!"

Yolk raised the bow so that the bolt was aimed uncertainly at Hedges' stomach. "Like this?"

"How else exactly? Lance Corporal Hedges, how's this for a laugh? I will count to three. If you haven't handed that Northman back his fur by the time I get there I will order Trooper Yolk to shoot. You never know, you're only five strides away, he might even hit you."

"Now, look—"

"One."

"Look!"

"Two."

"All right! All right." Hedges tossed the fur in the Northman's face then stomped angrily away through the trees. "But you'll fucking pay for this, Tunny, I can tell you that!"

Tunny turned, grinning, and strolled after him. Hedges was opening his mouth for another prize retort when Tunny coshed him across the side of the head with his canteen, which represented a considerable weight when full. It happened so fast Hedges didn't even try to duck, just went down hard in the mud.

"You'll fucking pay for this, *Corporal* Tunny," he hissed, and booted Hedges in the groin to underscore the point. Then he took Hedges' new canteen, and tucked his own badly dented one into his belt where it had been. "Something to keep me in your thoughts." He looked up at Hedges' lanky sidekick, fully occupied gawping. "Anything to add, pikestaff?"

"I...I—"

"I? What do you think that adds? Shoot him, Yolk."

"What?" squeaked Yolk.

"What?" squeaked the tall trooper.

"I'm joking, idiots! Bloody hell, does no one think at all but me? Drag your prick of a lance corporal back behind the lines, and if I see either one of you out here again I'll bloody shoot you myself." The lanky one helped Hedges up, whimpering, bow-legged and bloody-haired, and the two of them shuffled off into the trees. Tunny waited until they'd disappeared from sight. Then he turned to the Northman and held out his hand. "Fur, please."

To be fair to the man, in spite of any troubles with the language, he fully understood. His face sagged, and he slapped the fur down into Tunny's hand. It wasn't that good a one, even, now he got a close look at it, rough-cured and sour-smelling. "What else you got there?" Tunny came closer, one hand on the hilt of his sword, just in case, and started patting the man down.

"We're robbing him?" Yolk had his bow on the Northman now, which meant it was a good deal closer to Tunny than he'd have liked.

"That a problem? Didn't you tell me you were a convicted thief?"

"I told you I didn't do it."

"Exactly what a thief would say! This isn't robbery, Yolk, it's war." The Northman had some strips of dried meat, Tunny pocketed them. He had a flint and tinder, Tunny tossed them. No money, but that was far from surprising. Coinage hadn't fully caught on up here.

"He's got a blade!" squeaked Yolk, waving his bow about.

"A skinning knife, idiot!" Tunny took it and put it in his own belt. "We'll stick some rabbit blood on it, say it came off a Named Man dead in battle, and you can bet some fool will pay for it back in Adua." He took the Northman's bow and arrows too. Didn't want him trying a shot at them out of spite. He looked a bit on the spiteful side, but then Tunny probably would've looked spiteful himself if he'd just been robbed. Twice. He wondered about taking the trapper's coat, but it wasn't much more than rags, and he thought it might have been a Union one in the first place anyway. Tunny had stolen a score of new Union coats out of the quartermaster's stores back in Ostenhorm, and hadn't been able to shift them all yet.

"That's all," he grunted, stepping back. "Hardly worth the trouble."

"What do we do, then?" Yolk's big flatbow was wobbling all over the place. "You want me to shoot him?"

"You bloodthirsty little bastard! Why would you do that?"

"Well... won't he tell his friends across the stream we're over here?"

"We've had, what, four hundred men sitting around in a bog for over a day. Do you really think Hedges has been the only one wandering about? They know we're here by now, Yolk, you can bet on that."

"So... we just let him go?"

"You want to take him back to camp and keep him as a pet?"

"No."

"You want to shoot him?"

"No."

"Well, then?"

The three of them stood there for a moment in the fading light. Then Yolk lowered his bow, and waved with the other hand. "Piss off."

Tunny jerked his head into the trees. "Off you piss."

The Northman blinked for a moment. He scowled at Tunny, then at Yolk, then stalked off into the woods, muttering angrily.

"Hearts and minds," murmured Yolk.

Tunny tucked the Northman's knife inside his coat. "Exactly."

Good Deeds

The buildings of Osrung crowded in on Craw, all looking like they'd bloody stories to tell, each corner turned opening up a new stretch of disaster. A good few were all burned out, charred rafters still smouldering, air sharp with the tang of destruction. Windows gaped empty, shutters bristled with broken shafts, axe-scarred doors hung from hinges. The stained cobbles were scattered with rubbish and twisting shadows and corpses too, cold flesh that once was men, dragged by bare heels to their places in the earth.

Grim-faced Carls frowned at their strange procession. A full sixty wounded Union soldiers shambling along with Caul Shivers at the back like a wolf trailing a flock and Craw up front with his sore knees and the girl.

He found he kept glancing sideways at her. Didn't get a lot of chances to look at women. Wonderful, he guessed, but that wasn't the same, though she probably would've kicked him in the fruits for saying so. Which was just the point. This girl was a girl, and a pretty one too. Though probably she'd been prettier that morning, just like Osrung had. War makes nothing more beautiful. Looked as if she'd had a clump of hair torn from her head, the rest matted with clot on one side. A big bruise at the corner of her mouth. One sleeve of her dirty dress ripped and brown with dry blood. She shed no tears, though, not her.

"You all right?" asked Craw.

She glanced over her shoulder at the shambling column, and its crutches, and stretchers, and pain-screwed faces. "I could be worse."

"Guess so."

"Are you all right?"

"Eh?"

She pointed at his face and he touched the stitched cut on his cheek. He'd forgotten all about it until then. "What do you know, I could be worse myself."

"Just out of interest – if I wasn't all right, what could you do about it?"

Craw opened his mouth, then realised he didn't have much of an answer. "Don't know. A kind word, maybe?"

The girl looked around at the ruined square they were crossing, the wounded men propped against the wall of a house on the north side, the wounded men following them. "Kind words wouldn't seem to be worth much in the midst of this."

Craw slowly nodded. "What else have we got, though?"

He stopped maybe a dozen paces from the north end of the bridge, Shivers walking up beside him. That narrow path of stone flags stretched off ahead, a pair of torches burning at the far end. No sign of men, but Craw was sure as sure the black buildings beyond the far bank were crammed full of the bastards, all with flatbows and tickly trigger-hands. Wasn't that big a bridge, but it looked a hell of a march across right then. An awful lot of steps, and at every footfall he might get an arrow in his fruits. Still, waiting about wasn't going to make that any less likely. More, in fact, since it was getting darker every moment.

So he hawked up some snot, made ready to spit it, realised the girl was watching him and swallowed it instead. Then he shrugged his shield off his shoulder and set it down by the wall, dragged his sword out from his belt and handed it to Shivers. "You wait here with the rest, I'll go across and see if there's someone around with an ear for reason."

"All right."

"And if I get shot...weep for me."

Shivers gave a solemn nod. "A river."

Craw held his hands up high and started walking. Didn't seem that long ago he was doing more or less the same thing up the side of the Heroes. Walking into the wolf's den, armed with nothing but a nervy smile and an overwhelming need to shit.

"Doing the right thing," he muttered under his breath. Playing peacemaker. Threetrees would've been proud. Which was a great comfort, because when he got shot in the neck he could use a dead man's pride to pull the arrow out, couldn't he? "Too bloody old for this." By the dead, he should be retired. Smiling at the water with his pipe and his day's work behind him. "The right thing," he whispered again. Would've been nice if, just one time, the right thing could've been the safe thing too. But Craw guessed life wasn't really set up that way.

"That's far enough!" came a voice in Northern.

Craw stopped, all kinds of lonely out there in the gloom, water chattering away underneath him. "Couldn't agree more, friend! Just need to talk!"

"Last time we talked it didn't come out too well for anyone concerned." Someone was walking up from the other end of the bridge, a torch in his hand, orange light on a craggy cheek, a ragged beard, a hard-set mouth with a pair of split lips.

Craw found he was grinning as the man stopped an arm's length away. He reckoned his chances at living through the night just took a leap for the better. "Hardbread, 'less I'm mistook all over the place." In spite of the fact they'd been struggling to kill each other not a week before, it felt more like greeting an old friend than an old enemy. "What the hell are you doing over here?"

"Lot o' the Dogman's boys hereabouts. Stranger-Come-Knocking and his Crinna bastards showed up without an invite, and we been guiding 'em politely to the door. Some messed-up allies your Chief makes, don't he."

Craw looked over towards some Union soldiers who'd gathered in the torchlight at the south end of the bridge. "I could say the same o' yours."

"Aye, well. Those are the times. What can I do for you, Craw?"

"I got some prisoners Black Dow wants handed back."

Hardbread looked profoundly doubtful. "When did Dow start handing anything back?"

"He's starting now."

"Guess it ain't never too late to change, eh?" Hardbread called something in Union, over his shoulder.

"Guess not," muttered Craw, under his breath, though he was far from sure Dow had made that big a shift.

A man came warily up from the south side of the bridge. He wore a Union uniform, high up by the markings but young, and fine-looking too. He nodded to Craw and Craw nodded back, then he traded a few words with Hardbread, then he looked over at the wounded starting to come across the bridge and his jaw dropped.

Craw heard quick footsteps at his back, saw movement as he turned. "What the—" He made a tardy grab for his sword, realised it wasn't there, by which point someone had already flashed past. The girl, and straight into the young man's arms. He caught her, and they held each other tight, and they kissed, and Craw watched with his hand still fishing at the air where his hilt usually was and his eyebrows up high.

"That was unexpected," he said.

Hardbread's were no lower. "Maybe men and women always greet each other that way down in the Union."

"Reckon I'll have to move down there myself."

Craw leaned back against the pitted parapet of the bridge. Leaned back next to Hardbread and watched those two hold each other, eyes closed, swaying gently in the light of the torch like dancers to a slow music none could hear. He was whispering something in her ear. Comfort, or relief, or love. Words foreign to Craw, no doubt, and not just on account of the language. He watched the wounded shuffling across around the couple, a spark of hope lit in their worn-out faces. Going back to their own people. Hurt, maybe, but alive. Craw had to admit, the night might've been coming on cold but he'd a warmth inside. Not like that rush of winning a fight, maybe, not so strong nor so fierce as the thrill of victory.

But he reckoned it might last longer.

"Feels good." As he watched the soldier and the girl make their way across the bridge to the south bank, his arm around her. "Making a few folk happier, in the midst o' this. Feels damn good."

"It does."

"Makes you wonder why a man chooses to do what we do."

Hardbread took in a heavy breath. "Too coward to do aught else, maybe."

"You might be right." The woman and the officer faded into darkness, the last few wounded shambling after. Craw pushed himself away from the parapet and slapped the damp from his hands. "Right, then. Back to it, eh?"

"Back to it."

"Good to see you, Hardbread."

"Likewise." The old warrior turned away and followed the others back towards the south side of the town. "Don't get killed, eh?" he tossed over his shoulder.

"I'll try to avoid it."

Shivers was waiting at the north end of the bridge, offering out Craw's sword. The sight of his eye gleaming in his lopsided smile was enough to chase any soft feelings away sharp as a rabbit from a hunter.

"You ever thought about a patch?" asked Craw, as he took his sword and slid it through his belt.

"Tried one for a bit." Shivers waved a finger at the mass of scar around his eye. "Itched like a bastard. I thought, why wear it just to make other fuckers more comfortable? If I can live with having this face, they can live with looking at it. That or they can get fucked."

"You've a point." They walked on through the gathering gloom in silence for a moment. "Sorry to take the job."

Shivers said nothing.

"Leading Dow's Carls. More'n likely you should've had it."

Shivers shrugged. "I ain't greedy. I've seen greedy, and it's a sure way back to the mud. I just want what's owed. No more and no less. A little *respect*."

"Don't seem too much to ask. Anyway, I'll only be doing it while the battle's on, then I'm done. I daresay Dow'll want you for his Second then."

"Maybe." Another stretch of silence, then Shivers turned to look at him. "You're a decent man, aren't you, Craw? Folk say so. Say you're a straight edge. How d'you stick at it?"

Craw didn't feel like he'd stuck at it too well at all. "Just try to do the right thing, I reckon. That's all."

"Why? I tried it. Couldn't make it root. Couldn't see the profit in it."

"There's your problem. Anything good I done, and the dead know there ain't much, I done for its own sake. Got to do it because you want to."

"It ain't no kind o' sacrifice if you want to do it, though, is it? How does doing what you want make you a fucking hero? That's just what I do."

Craw could only shrug. "I haven't got the answers. Wish I did."

Shivers turned the ring on his little finger thoughtfully round and round, red stone glistening. "Guess it's just about getting through each day."

"Those are the times."

"You think other times'll be any different?"

"We can hope."

"Craw!" His own name echoed at him and Craw whipped around, frowning into the darkness, wondering who he'd upset recently. Pretty much everyone, was the answer. He'd made a shitpile of enemies the moment he said yes to Black Dow. His hand strayed to his sword again, which at least was in the sheath this time around. Then he smiled. "Flood! I seem to run into men I know all over the damn place."

"That's what it is to be an old bastard." Flood stepped over with a grin of his own, and a limp of his own too.

"Knew there had to be an upside to it. You know Caul Shivers, do you?"

"By reputation."

Shivers showed his teeth. "It's a fucking beauty, ain't it?"

"How's the day been over here with Reachey?" asked Craw.

"It's been bloody," was Flood's answer. "Had a few young lads calling me Chief. Too young. All but one back to the mud."

"Sorry to hear that."

"Me too. But it's a war. Thought I might come back over to your dozen, if you'll have me, and I thought I might bring this one with me." Flood jerked his thumb at someone else. A big lad, hanging back in the shadows, wrapped up in a stained green cloak. He was looking at the ground, dark hair across his forehead so Craw couldn't see much more'n the gleam of one eye in the dark. He'd a good sword at his belt, though, gold on the hilt. Craw saw the gleam of that quick enough. "He's a good hand. Earned his name today."

"Congratulations," said Craw.

The lad didn't speak. Not full of bragging and vinegar like some might be who'd won a name that day. Like Craw had been the day he won his, for that matter. Craw liked to see it. He didn't need any fiery tempers landing everyone in the shit. Like his had landed him in the shit, years ago.

"What about it then?" Flood asked. "You got room for us?"

"Room? I can't remember ever having more'n ten in the dozen, and there's not but six now."

315

"Six? What happened to 'em all?"

Craw winced. "About the same as happened to your lot. About what usually happens. Athroc got killed up at the Heroes day before yesterday. Agrick a day later. Brack died this morning."

There was a bit of a silence. "Brack died?"

"In his sleep," said Craw. "From a bad leg."

"Brack's back to the mud." Flood shook his head. "That's a tester. Didn't think he'd ever die."

"Nor me. The Great Leveller's lying in wait for all of us, no doubt, and he takes no excuses and makes no exceptions."

"None," whispered Shivers.

"'Til then, we could certainly use the pair o' you, if Reachey'll let you go."

Flood nodded. "He said he would."

"All right then. You ought to know Wonderful's running the dozen for now, though."

"She is?"

"Aye. Dow offered me charge of his Carls."

"You're Black Dow's Second?"

"Just 'til the battle's done."

Flood puffed out his cheeks. "What happened to never sticking your neck out?"

"Didn't take my own advice. Still want in?"

"Why not?"

"Happy to have you back, then. And your lad too, if you say he's up to it."

"Oh, he's up to it, ain't you boy?"

The boy didn't say a thing.

"What's your name?" asked Craw.

"Beck."

Flood thumped him on the arm. "*Red* Beck. Best get used to using the whole thing, eh?"

The lad looked a bit sick, Craw thought. Small wonder, given the state of the town. Must've been quite a scrap he'd been through. Quite an introduction to the bloody business. "Not much of a talker, eh? Just as well. We got more'n enough talk with Wonderful and Whirrun."

"Whirrun of Bligh?" asked the lad.

"That's right. He's one of the dozen. Or the half-dozen, leastways. Do you reckon I need to give him the big speech?" Craw asked Flood. "You know, the one I gave you when you joined up, 'bout looking out for your crew and your Chief, and not getting killed, and doing the right thing, and all that?"

Flood looked at the lad, and shook his head. "You know what, I think he learned today the hard way."

"Aye," said Craw. "Reckon we all did. Welcome to the dozen, then, Red Beck."

The lad just blinked.

One Day More

It was the same path she had ridden up the night before. The same winding route up the windswept hillside to the barn where her father had made his headquarters. The same view out over the darkened valley, filled with the pinprick lights of thousands of fires, lamps, torches, all glittering in the wet at the corners of her sore eyes. But everything felt different. Even though Hal was riding beside her, close enough to touch, jawing away to fill the silence, she felt alone.

"...good thing the Dogman turned up when he did, or the whole division might've come apart. As it is we lost the northern half of Osrung, but we managed to push the savages back into the woods. Colonel Brint was a rock. Couldn't have done it without him. He'll want to ask you...want to ask you about—"

"Later." There was no way she could face that. "I have to talk to my father."

"Should you wash first? Change your clothes? At least catch your breath for a—"

"My clothes can wait," she snapped at him. "I've a message from Black Dow, do you understand?"

"Of course. Stupid of me. I'm sorry." He kept flipping from fatherly stern to soppy soft, and she could not decide which was annoying her more. She felt as if he was angry, but lacked the courage to say so. At her for coming to the North when he had wanted her to stay behind. At himself for not being there to help her when the Northmen came. At both of them for not knowing how to help her now. Probably he was angry that he was angry, instead of revelling in her safe return.

They reined in their horses and he insisted on helping her down. They stood in awkward silence, with an awkward distance between them, he with an awkward hand on her shoulder that offered less than no comfort. She badly wanted him to find some words that might help her see some sense in what had happened that day. But there was no sense in it, and any words would fall pathetically short.

"I love you," he said lamely, in the end, and it seemed few words could have fallen as pathetically short as those did.

"I love you too." But all she felt was a creeping dread. A sense that there was an awful weight at the back of her mind she was forcing herself not to look at, but that at any moment it might fall and crush her utterly. "You should go back down."

"No! Of course not. I should stay with —"

She put a firm hand on his chest. She was surprised how firm it was. "I'm safe now." She nodded towards the valley, its fires prickling at the night. "They need you more than I do."

She could almost feel the relief coming off him. To no longer be taunted by his inability to make everything better. "Well, if you're sure —"

"I'm sure."

She watched him mount up, and he gave her a quick, uncertain, worried smile, and rode away into the gathering darkness. Part of her wished he had fought harder to stay. Part of her was glad to see the back of him.

She walked to the barn, pulling Hal's coat tight around her, past a staring guard and into the low-raftered room. It was a much more intimate gathering than last night's. Generals Mitterick and Jalenhorm, Colonel Felnigg, and her father. For a moment she felt an exhausting sense of relief to see him. Then she noticed Bayaz, sitting slightly removed from the others,

his servant occupying the shadows behind him with the faintest of smiles, and any relief died a quick death.

Mitterick was holding forth, as ever, and, as ever, Felnigg listening with the expression of a man forced to fish something from a latrine. "The bridge is in our hands and my men are crossing the river even as we speak. I'll have fresh regiments on the north bank well before dawn, including plenty of cavalry and the terrain to make use of it. The standards of the Second and Third are flying in the Northmen's trenches. And tomorrow I'll get Vallimir off his arse and into action if I have to kick him across that stream myself. I'll have those Northern bastards on the run by..."

His eyes drifted over to Finree, and he awkwardly cleared his throat and fell silent. One by one the other officers followed his gaze, and she saw in their faces what a state she must look. They could hardly have appeared more shocked if they had witnessed a corpse clamber from its grave. All except for Bayaz, whose stare was as calculating as ever.

"Finree." Her father started up, gathered her in his arms and held her tight. Probably she should have dissolved into grateful tears, but he was the one who ended up dashing something from his eye on one sleeve. "I thought maybe..." He winced as he touched her bloody hair, as though to finish the thought was more than he could bear. "Thank the Fates you're alive."

"Thank Black Dow. He's the one who sent me back."

"Black Dow?"

"Yes. I met him. I spoke to him. He wants to talk. He wants to talk about peace." There was a disbelieving silence. "I persuaded him to let some wounded men go, as a gesture of good faith. Sixty. It was the best I could do."

"You persuaded Black Dow to release prisoners?" Jalenhorm puffed out his cheeks. "That's quite a thing. Burning them is more his style."

"That's my girl," said her father, and the pride in his voice made her feel sick.

Bayaz sat forward. "Describe him."

"Tallish. Strong-built. Fierce-looking. He was missing his left ear."

"Who else was with him?"

"An older man called Craw, who led me back across the river. A big man with a scarred face and... a metal eye. And..." It seemed so strange now she was starting to wonder whether she had imagined the whole thing. "A black-skinned woman."

Bayaz' eyes narrowed, his mouth tightened, and Finree felt the hairs prickling on the back of her neck. "A thin, black-skinned woman, wrapped in bandages?"

She swallowed. "Yes."

The First of the Magi sat slowly back, and he and his servant exchanged a long glance. "They *are* here."

"I did say."

"Can nothing ever be straightforward?" snapped Bayaz.

"Rarely, sir," replied the servant, his different-coloured eyes shifting lazily from Finree, to her father, and back to his master.

"Who are here?" asked a baffled Mitterick.

Bayaz did not bother to answer. He was busy watching Finree's father, who had crossed to his desk and was starting to write. "What are you about, Lord Marshal?"

"It seems best that I should write to Black Dow and arrange a meeting so we can discuss the terms of an armistice —"

"No," said Bayaz.

"No?" There was a pregnant silence. "But... it sounds as if he is willing to be reasonable. Should we not at least —"

"Black Dow is not a reasonable man. His allies are..." Bayaz' lip curled and Finree drew Hal's coat tight around her shoulders. "Even less so. Besides, you have done so well today, Lord Marshal. Such fine work from you, and General Mitterick, and Colonel Brock, and the Dogman. Ground taken and sacrifices made and so on. I feel your men deserve another crack at it tomorrow. Just one more day, I think. What's one day?"

Finree found she was feeling awfully weak. Dizzy. Whatever force had been holding her up for the past few hours was ebbing fast.

"Lord Bayaz..." Her father looked trapped in no-man's-land between pain and bafflement. "A day is just a day. We will strive, of course, with every sinew if that is the king's pleasure, but there is a very good chance that we will not be able to secure a decisive victory in one day —"

"That would be a question for tomorrow. Every war is only a prelude to talk, Lord Marshal, but it's all about," and the Magus looked up at the ceiling, rubbing one thick thumb against one fingertip, "who you talk to. It would be best if we kept news of this among ourselves. Such things can be bad for morale. One more day, if you please."

Finree's father obediently bowed his head, but when he crumpled up his half-written letter in one fist his knuckles were white with force. "I serve at his Majesty's pleasure."

"So do we all," said Jalenhorn. "And my men are ready to do their duty! I humbly entreat the right to lead an assault upon the Heroes, and redeem myself on the battlefield." As though anyone was redeemed on the battlefield. They were only killed there, as far as Finree could see. Her legs seemed to weigh a ton a piece as she made for the door at the back of the room.

Mitterick was busy gushing his own military platitudes behind her. "My division is champing at the bloody bit, don't worry on that score, Marshal Kroy! Don't worry about that, Lord Bayaz!"

"I am not."

"We have a bridgehead. Tomorrow we'll drive the bastards, you'll see. Just one day more..."

Finree shut the door on their posturing, her back against the wood. Maybe whatever herder had built this barn had lived in this room. Now her father was sleeping there, his bed against one unplastered wall, travelling chests neatly organised against the others like soldiers around a parade ground.

Everything was painful, suddenly. She pulled the sleeve of Hal's coat back, grimacing at the long cut down her forearm, flesh angry pink along both sides. Probably it would need stitching, but she could not go back out there. Could not face their pitying expressions and their patriotic drivel. It felt as if her neck had ten strings of agony through it and however she moved her head it tugged at one or another. She touched her fingertips to her burning scalp. There was a mass of scab under her greasy hair. She could not stop her hand trembling as she took it away. She almost laughed it was shaking so badly, but it came out as an ugly snort. Would her hair grow back? She snorted again. What did it matter, compared to what she had seen? She found she could not stop snorting. Her breath came ragged, and shuddering, and in a moment her aching ribs were heaving with sobs, the quick breath whooping in her throat, her face crushed up and her mouth twisted, tugging at her split lip. She felt a fool, but her body would not let her stop. She slid down the door until her backside hit stone, and bit on her knuckle to smother her blubbering.

She felt absurd. Worse still, ungrateful. Treacherous. She should have been weeping with joy. She, after all, was the lucky one.

Bones

"**W**here's that scab-faced old cunt hiding?"

The man's eyes flickered about uncertainly, caught off balance with his cup frozen half way to the water butt. "Tenways is up on the Heroes with Dow and the rest, but if you're—"

"Get to *fuck*!" Calder shoved past him, striding on through Tenways' puzzled Carls, away from Skarling's Finger and towards the stones, picked out on their hilltop by the light of campfires behind.

"We won't be coming along up there," came Deep's voice in his ear. "Can't watch your arse if you're minded on sticking it in the wolf's mouth."

"No money's worth going back to the mud for," said Shallow. "Nothing is, in my humble opinion."

"That's an interesting point o' philosophy you've stumbled upon," said Deep, "what's worth dying for and what ain't. Not one we're likely to—"

"Stay and talk shit, then." Calder kept walking, uphill, the cold air nipping at his lungs and a few too many nips from Shallow's flask burning at his belly. The scabbard of his sword slapped against his calf, as if with every step it was gently reminding him it was there, and that it was far from the only blade about either.

"What're you going to do?" asked Pale-as-Snow, breathing hard from keeping up.

Calder didn't say anything. Partly because he was too angry to say anything worth hearing. Partly because he thought it made him look big. And partly because he hadn't a clue what he was going to do, and if he started thinking about it there was every chance his courage would wilt, and quick. He'd done enough nothing that day. He strode through the gap in the dry-stone wall that ringed the hill, a pair of Black Dow's Carls frowning as they watched him pass.

"Just keep calm!" Hansul shouted from further back. "Your father always kept calm!"

322

"Shit on what my father did," Calder snapped over his shoulder. He was enjoying not having to think and just letting the fury carry him. Sweep him up onto the hill's flat top and between two of the great stones. Fires burned inside the circle, flames tugged and snapped by the wind, sending up whirls of sparks into the black night. They lit up the inside faces of the Heroes in flickering orange, lit up the faces of the men clustered around them, catching the metal of their mail coats, the blades of their weapons. They clucked and grumbled as Calder strode heedless through them towards the centre of the circle, Pale-as-Snow and Hansul following in his wake.

"Calder. What are you about?" Curnden Craw, some staring lad Calder didn't know beside him. Jolly Yon Cumber and Wonderful were there too. Calder ignored the lot of them, brushed past Cairm Ironhead as he stood watching the flames with his thumbs in his belt.

Tenways was sitting on a log on the other side of the fire, and his flaking horror of a face broke out in a shining grin as he saw Calder coming. "If it ain't pretty little Calder! Help your brother out today, did you, you—" His eyes went wide for a moment and he tensed, shifting his weight to get up.

Then Calder's fist crunched into his nose. He squawked as he went over backwards, boots kicking, and Calder was on top of him, flailing away with both fists, bellowing he didn't even know what. Punching mindlessly at Tenways' head, and his arms, and his flapping hands. He got another good one on that scabby nose before someone grabbed his elbow and dragged him off.

"Whoa, Calder, whoa!" Craw's voice, he thought, and he let himself be pulled back, thrashing about and shouting like you're supposed to. As if all he wanted to do was keep fighting when in fact he was all relief to let it be stopped, as he'd run right out of ideas and his left hand was really hurting.

Tenways stumbled up, blood bubbling out of his nostrils as he snarled curses, slapping away a helping hand from one of his men. He drew his sword with that soft metal whisper that somehow sounds so loud, steel gleaming in the firelight. There was a silence, the crowd of curious men around them all heaving a nervous breath together. Ironhead raised his brows, and folded his arms, and took a pace out of the way.

"You little fucker!" growled Tenways, and he stepped over the log he'd been sitting on.

Craw dragged Calder behind him and suddenly his sword was out too.

Not a moment later a pair of Tenways' Named Men were beside their Chief, a big bearded bastard and a lean one with a lazy eye, weapons ready, though they looked like men who never had to reach too far for them. Calder felt Pale-as-Snow slide up beside him, blade held low. White-Eye Hansul on his other side, red-faced and puffing from his trek up the hillside but his sword steady. More of Tenways' boys sprang up, and Jolly Yon Cumber was there with his axe and his shield and his slab of frown.

It was then Calder realised things had gone a bit further than he'd planned on. Not that he'd planned at all. He thought it was probably bad form to leave his sword sheathed, what with everyone else drawing and him having stirred the pot in the first place. So he drew himself, smirking in Tenways' bloody face.

He'd felt grand when he'd seen his father put on the chain and sit in Skarling's Chair, three hundred Named Men on their knee to the first King of the Northmen. He'd felt grand when he put his hand on his wife's belly and felt his child kick for the first time. But he wasn't sure he'd ever felt such fierce pride as he did in the moment Brodd Tenways' nose-bone broke under his knuckles.

No way he would've said no to more of that feeling.

Ah, shit!" Drofd scrambled up, kicking embers over Beck's cloak and making him gasp and slap 'em off.

A right commotion had flared up, folk stomping, metal hissing, grunts and curses in the darkness. There was some sort of a fight, and Beck had no idea who'd started it or why or what side he was supposed to be on. But Craw's dozen were all piling in so he just went with the current, drew his father's sword and stood shoulder to shoulder with the rest, Wonderful on his left with her curved blade steady, Drofd on his right with a hatchet in his fist and his tongue stuck out between his teeth. Wasn't so difficult to do, what with everyone else doing it. Would've been damn near impossible not to, in fact.

Brodd Tenways and some of his boys were facing 'em across a wind-blown fire, and he had a lot of blood on his rashy face and maybe a broken nose too. Might be that Calder had been the one to do it, given how he'd come stomping past like that and now was standing next to Craw with sword in hand and smirk on face. Still, the whys didn't seem too important

right then. It was the what nexts that were looming large on everyone's minds.

"Put 'em away." Craw spoke slow but there was a kind of iron to his voice said he'd be backing down from nothing. It put iron in Beck's bones, made him feel like he'd be backing down from nothing neither.

Tenways didn't look like taking any backward steps himself, though. "You fucking put 'em away." And he spat blood into the fire.

Beck found his eyes had caught a lad's on the other side, maybe a year or two older'n him. Yellow-haired lad with a scar on one cheek. They turned a little to face each other. As if on an instinct they were all pairing off with the partner who suited 'em best, like folk at a harvest dance. Except this dance seemed likely to shed a lot of blood.

"Put 'em up," growled Craw, and his voice had more iron now. A warning, and the dozen all seemed to shift forwards around him at it, steel rattling.

Tenways showed his rotten teeth. "Fucking make me."

"I'll give it a try."

A man came strolling out of the dark, just his sharp jaw showing in the shadows of his hood, boots crunching heedless through the corner of the fire and sending a flurry of sparks up around his legs. Very tall, very lean and he looked like he was carved out of wood. He was chewing meat from a chicken bone in one greasy hand and in the other, held loose under the crosspiece, he had the biggest sword Beck had ever seen, shoulder-high maybe from point to pommel, its sheath scuffed as a beggar's boot but the wire on its hilt glinting with the colours of the fire-pit.

He sucked the last shred of meat off his bone with a noisy slurp, and he poked at all the drawn steel with the pommel of his sword, long grip clattering against all those blades. "Tell me you lot weren't working up to a fight without me. You know how much I love killing folk. I shouldn't, but a man has to stick to what he's good at. So how's this for a recipe..." He worked the bone around between finger and thumb, then flicked it at Tenways so it bounced off his chain mail coat. "You go back to fucking sheep and I'll fill the graves."

Tenways licked his bloody top lip. "My fight ain't with you, Whirrun."

And it all came together. Beck had heard songs enough about Whirrun of Bligh, and even hummed a few himself as he fought his way through the logpile. Cracknut Whirrun. How he'd been given the Father of Swords.

How he'd killed his five brothers. How he'd hunted the Shimbul Wolf in the endless winter of the utmost North, held a pass against the countless Shanka with only two boys and a woman for company, bested the sorcerer Daroum-ap-Yaught in a battle of wits and bound him to a rock for the eagles. How he'd done all the tasks worthy of a hero in the valleys, and so come south to seek his destiny on the battlefield. Songs to make the blood run hot, and cold too. Might be his was the hardest name in the whole North these days, and standing right there in front of Beck, close enough to lay a hand on. Though that probably weren't a good idea.

"Your fight ain't with me?" Whirrun glanced about like he was looking for who it might be with. "You sure? Fights are twisty little bastards, you draw steel it's always hard to say where they'll lead you. You drew on Calder, but when you drew on Calder you drew on Curnden Craw, and when you drew on Craw you drew on me, and Jolly Yon Cumber, and Wonderful there, and Flood – though he's gone for a wee, I think, and also this lad here whose name I've forgotten." Sticking his thumb over his shoulder at Beck. "You should've seen it coming. No excuse for it, a proper War Chief fumbling about in the dark like you've nothing in your head but shit. So my fight ain't with you either, Brodd Tenways, but I'll still kill you if it's called for, and add your name to my songs, and I'll still laugh afterwards. So?"

"So what?"

"So shall I draw? And you'd best keep always before you that if the Father of Swords is drawn it must be blooded. That's the way it's been since before the Old Time, and the way it must be still, and must always be."

They stood there for a moment longer, the lot of 'em, all still, all waiting, then Tenways' brows drew in, and his lips curled back, and Beck felt the guts dropping out of him, because he could feel what was coming, and—

"What the *fuck*?" Another man stalked up into the firelight, eyes slits and teeth bared, head forwards and shoulders up like a fighting dog, no want in it but killing. His scowl was crossed with old scars, one ear missing, and he wore a golden chain, a big jewel alive with orange sparks in the middle.

Beck swallowed. Black Dow, no question. Who beat Bethod's men six times in the long winter then burned Kyning to the ground with its people in the houses. Who fought the Bloody-Nine in the circle and nearly won, was left with his life and bound to serve. Fought alongside him then, and with Rudd Threetrees, and Tul Duru Thunderhead, and Harding Grim, as tough a crew as ever walked the North since the Age of Heroes and of which, aside from the Dogman, he was the last drawing breath. Then he betrayed the Bloody-Nine, and killed him who men said couldn't die, and took Skarling's Chair for himself. Black Dow, right before him now. Protector of the North, or stealer of it, depending on who you asked. He'd never dreamed of coming so close to the man.

Black Dow looked over at Craw, and he looked an awful long way from happy. Beck weren't sure how that pickaxe of a face ever could. "Ain't you supposed to be keeping the peace, old man?"

"That's what I'm doing." Craw's sword was still out but the point had dropped towards the ground now. Most of 'em had.

"Oh, aye. Here's a peaceful fucking picture." Dow swept the lot of 'em with his scowl. "No one draws steel up here without my say so. Now put 'em away, the lot o' you, you're embarrassing yourselves."

"Boneless little fucker broke my nose!" snarled Tenways.

"Spoil your looks, did he?" snapped Dow. "Want me to kiss it better? Let me frame this in terms you fucking halfheads can understand. Anyone still holding a blade by the time I get to five is stepping into the circle with me, and I'll do things like I used to 'fore old age softened me up. One."

He didn't even need to get to two. Craw put up right away, and Tenways just after, and all the rest of that steel was good and hidden almost as swift as it had come to light, leaving the two lines of men frowning somewhat sheepishly across the fire at each other.

Wonderful whispered in Beck's ear. "Might want to put that away."

He realised he still had his steel out, shoved it back so fast he damn near cut his leg. Only Whirrun was left there, between the two sides, one hand on the hilt of his sword and the other on the scabbard, still ready to draw, and looking at it with the smallest curl of a smile to his mouth. "You know, I'm just a little tempted."

"Another time," growled Dow, then threw one arm up. "Brave Prince Calder! I'm honoured all the way to fuck! I was about to send over an invitation but you've got in first. Come to tell me what happened at the Old Bridge today?"

Calder still had the fine cloak he'd been wearing when Beck first saw

327

him up at Reachey's camp, but he had mail underneath it now, and a scowl instead of a grin. "Scale got killed."

"I heard. Can't you tell? I'm weeping a sea o' tears. What happened at my bridge is what I'm asking."

"He fought as hard as he could. Hard as anyone could."

"Went down fighting. Good for Scale. What about you? Don't look like you fought that hard."

"I was ready to." Calder slid a piece of paper out from his collar and held it up between two fingers. "Then I got this. An order from Mitterick, the Union general." Dow snatched it from his hand and pulled it open, frowning down at it. "There are Union men in the woods to our west, ready to come across. It's lucky I found out, because if I'd gone to help Scale they'd have taken us in the flank and there's a good chance the lot of you would be dead now, rather than arguing the toss over whether I've got no bones."

"I don't think anyone's arguing you've got bones, Calder," said Dow. "Just sat there behind the wall, did you?"

"That, and sent to Tenways for help."

Dow's eyes slid sideways, glittering with the flames. "Well?"

Tenways rubbed blood from under his broken nose. "Well what?"

"Did he send for help?"

"Spoke to Tenways myself," piped up one of Calder's men. An old boy with a scar down his face and the eye on that side milky white. "Told him Scale needed help, but Calder couldn't go on account of the Southerners across the stream. Told him the whole thing."

"And?"

The half-blind old man shrugged. "Said he was busy."

"Busy?" whispered Dow, face getting harder'n ever if that was possible. "So you just sat there and all, did you?"

"I can't just move soon as that bastard tells me to—"

"You sat on the hill with Skarling's Finger up your arse and fucking *watched*?" Dow roared. "Sat and watched the Southerners have *my bridge*?" Stabbing at his chest with his thumb.

Tenways flinched back, one eye twitching. "There weren't no Southerners over the river, that's all lies! Lies like he always tells." He pointed across the fire with a shaking finger. "Always some fucking excuse, eh, Calder? Always some trick to keep your hands clean! Talk of peace, or talk of treachery, or some kind of bloody talk—"

"Enough." Black Dow's voice was quiet, but it cut Tenways off dead. "I don't care a runny shit whether there are Union men out west or if there aren't." He crumpled the paper up in his trembling fist and flung it at Calder. "I care whether you do as you're told." He took a step towards Tenways, and leaned in close.

"You won't be sitting watching tomorrow, no, no, no." And he sneered over at Calder. "And nor will you, prince of nothing fucking much. Your sitting days are over, the pair o' you. You two lovers'll be down there on that wall together. That's right. Side by side. Arm in arm from dawn to dusk. Making sure this shitcake you've cooked up between you don't start stinking any worse. Doing what I brought you idiots here for – which, in case anyone's started wondering, is *fighting the fucking Union*!"

"What if they are across that stream?" asked Calder. Dow turned towards him, brow furrowed like he couldn't believe what he was hearing. "We're stretched thin as it is, lost a lot of men today and we're well outnumbered—"

"It's a fucking *war*!" roared Dow, leaping over to him and making everyone shuffle back. "Fight the bastards!" He tore at the air as if he was only just stopping himself from tearing Calder's face apart with his hands. "Or you're the planner, ain't you? The great trickster? Trick 'em! You wanted your brother's place? Then deal with it, you little arsehole, or I'll find a man who will! And if anyone don't do his bit tomorrow, anyone with a taste for *sitting out*..." Black Dow closed his eyes and tipped his face back towards the sky. "By the dead, I'll cut the bloody cross in you. And I'll hang you. And I'll burn you. And I'll make such an end of you the very song of it will turn the bards white. Am I leaving room for doubts?"

"No," said Calder, sullen as a whipped mule.

"No," said Tenways, no happier.

Beck didn't get the feeling the bad blood between 'em was anywhere near settled, though.

"Then this is the fucking end o' this!" Dow turned, saw one of Tenways' lads was in his way, grabbed hold of his shirt and flung him cringing onto the ground, then stalked back into the night the way he came.

"With me," Craw hissed in Calder's ear, then took him under the armpit and marched him off.

Tenways and his boys found their way back to their seats, grumbling, the yellow-haired lad giving Beck a hard look as he went. Time was Beck would've given him one back, maybe even a hard word or two to go with it. After the day he'd had he just looked away quick as he could, heart thumping in his ears.

"Shame. I was enjoying that." Whirrun of Bligh pulled his hood back and scrubbed at his flattened hair with his fingernails. "What is your name, anyway?"

"Beck." He thought he'd best leave it at just that. "Is every day with you lot like this?"

"No, no, no, lad. Not every day." And Whirrun's pointed face broke into a mad grin. "Only a precious few."

Craw had always had rooted suspicions that one day Calder would land him in some right shit, and it seemed this was the day. He marched him down the hillside away from the Heroes, through the cutting wind, gripping him tight by the elbow. He'd spent a good twenty years trying to keep his enemies to a strict few. One afternoon as Dow's Second and they were sprouting up like saplings in a wet spring, and Brodd Tenways was one he could have very well done without. That man was as ugly inside as out and had a bastard of a memory for slights.

"What the hell was that?" He dragged Calder to a halt a good way from fires or prying ears. "You could've got us all killed!"

"Scale's dead. That's what that was. Because that rotting fucker did nothing, Scale's dead."

"Aye." Craw felt himself softening. Stood there for a moment while the wind lashed the long grass against his calves. "I'm sorry for that. But adding more corpses ain't going to help matters. 'Specially not mine." He stuck a hand on his ribs, heart thumping away behind 'em. "By the dead, I think I might die just o' the excitement."

"I'm going to kill him." Calder scowled up towards the fire, and he did seem to have a purpose in him Craw hadn't seen before. Something that made him put a warning hand on Calder's chest and gently steer him back.

"Keep it for tomorrow. Save it for the Union."

"Why? My enemies are here. Tenways sat there while Scale died. Sat there and laughed."

"And you're angry because he sat there, or because you did?" He put his other hand down on Calder's shoulder. "I loved your father, in the end. I love you, like the son I never had. But why the hell is it the pair o' you always had to take on every fight you were offered? There'll always be more. I'll stand by you if I can, you know I will, but there's other things to think about than just—"

"Yes, yes." Calder slapped Craw's hands away. "Keeping your crew alive, and not sticking your neck out, and doing the right thing, even when it's the wrong thing—"

Craw grabbed hold of his shoulders again and gave him a shake. "I have to keep the peace! I'm in charge o' Dow's Carls now, his Second, and I can't—"

"You're what? You're guarding him?" Calder's fingers dug into Craw's arms, his eyes suddenly wide and bright. Not anger. A kind of eagerness. "You're at his back, with your sword drawn? That's your job?" And Craw suddenly saw the pit he'd dug for himself opening under his feet.

"No, Calder!" snarled Craw, trying to wriggle free. "Shut your—"

Calder kept his grip, dragging him into an awkward hug, and Craw could smell the drink on his breath as he hissed in his ear. "You could do it! Put an end to this!"

"No!"

"Kill him!"

"No!" Craw tore free and shoved him off, hand tight around the grip of his sword. "No, you bloody fool!"

Calder looked like he couldn't understand what Craw was saying. "How many men have you killed? That's what you do for a living. You're a killer."

"I'm a Named Man."

"So you're better at it than most. What's killing one more? And this time for a purpose! You could stop all this. You don't even like the bastard!"

"Don't matter what I like, Calder! He's Chief."

"He's Chief now, but stick an axe in his head he's just mud. No one'll care a shit then."

"I will." They watched each other for what felt like a long while, still in the darkness, not much more to see but the gleam of Calder's eyes in his pale face. They slid down to Craw's hand, still on the hilt of his sword.

"Going to kill me?"

"'Course I'm not." Craw straightened, letting his hand drop. "But I'll have to tell Black Dow."

More silence. Then, "Tell him what, exactly?"

"That you asked me to kill him."

And another. "I don't think he'll like that very much."

"Nor do I."

"I think cutting the bloody cross in me, then hanging me, then burning me, is the least of what he'll do."

"Reckon so. Which is why you'd better run."

"Run where?"

"Wherever you like. I'll give you a start. I'll tell him tomorrow. I have to tell him. That's what Threetrees would've done." Though Calder hadn't asked for a reason, and that sounded a particularly lame one right then.

"Threetrees got killed, you know. For nothing, out in the middle of nowhere."

"Don't matter."

"Ever think you should be looking for another man to imitate?"

"I gave my word."

"Killer's honour, eh? Swear it, did you, on Skarling's cock, or whatever?"

"Didn't have to. I gave my word."

"To Black Dow? He tried to have me killed a few nights back, and I'm supposed to sit on my hands waiting for him to do it again? The man's more treacherous than winter!"

"Don't matter. I said yes." And by the dead how he wished he hadn't now.

Calder nodded, little smile at the corner of his mouth. "Oh, aye. Gave your word. And good old Craw's a straight edge, right? No matter who gets cut."

"I have to tell him."

"But tomorrow." Calder backed away, still with that smirk on his face. "You'll give me a start." One foot after another, down the hillside. "You won't tell him. I know you, Craw. Raised me from a babe, didn't you? You've got more bones than that. You're not Black Dow's dog. Not you."

"It ain't a question of bones, nor dogs neither. I gave my word, and I'll tell him tomorrow."

"No, you won't."

"Yes, I will."

"No." And Calder's smirk was gone into the darkness. "You won't."

Craw stood there for a moment, in the wind, frowning at nothing. Then he gritted his teeth, and pushed his fingers into his hair, bent over and gave a strangled roar of frustration. He hadn't felt this hollow since Wast Never sold him out and tried to kill him after eight years a friend. Would've done it too if it hadn't been for Whirrun. Wasn't clear who'd get him out of this particular scrape. Wasn't clear how anyone could. This time it was him doing the betraying. He'd be doing it to someone whatever he did.

Always do the right thing sounds an easy rule to stick to. But when's the right thing the wrong thing? That's the question.

The King's Last Hero

Your August Majesty,

Darkness has finally covered the battlefield. Great gains were made today. Great gains at great cost. I deeply regret to inform you that Lord Governor Meed was killed, fighting with the highest personal courage for your Majesty's cause alongside many of his staff.

There was bitter combat from dawn to dusk in the town of Osrung. The fence was carried in the morning and the Northmen driven across the river, but they launched a savage counterattack and retook the northern half of the town. Now the water separates the two sides once again.

On the western wing, General Mitterick had better fortune. Twice the Northmen resisted his assaults on the Old Bridge, but on the third attempt they were finally broken and fled to a low wall some distance away over open fields. Mitterick is moving his cavalry across the river, ready for an attack at first light tomorrow. From my tent I can see the standards of your Majesty's Second and Third Regiments, defiantly displayed on ground held by the Northmen only a few hours ago.

General Jalenhorm, meanwhile, has reorganised his division, augmented by reserves from the levy regiments, and is prepared for an attack upon the Heroes in overwhelming force. I mean to stay close to him tomorrow, witness his success at first hand, and inform your Majesty of Black Dow's defeat as soon as the stones are recaptured.

I remain your Majesty's most faithful and unworthy servant,

Bremer dan Gorst,
Royal Observer of the Northern War

Gorst held the letter out to Rurgen, clenching his teeth as pain flashed through his shoulder. Everything was hurting. His ribs were even worse than yesterday. His armpit was one great itching graze where the edge of his breastplate had been ground into it. For some reason there was a cut between his shoulder blades just where it was hardest to reach. *Though no doubt I deserve far worse, and probably will get it before we're done with this worthless valley.*

"Can Younger take this?" he grunted.

"Younger!" called Rurgen.

"What?" from outside.

"Letter!"

The younger man ducked his head through the tent flap, stretching for it. He winced, had to come a step closer, and Gorst saw that the right side of his face was covered by a large bandage, soaked through with a long brown mark of dried blood.

Gorst stared at him. "What happened?"

"Nothing."

"Huh," grunted Rurgen. "Tell him."

Younger frowned at his colleague. "It doesn't matter."

"Felnigg happened," said Rurgen. "Since you ask."

Gorst was out of his seat, pains forgotten. "Colonel Felnigg? Kroy's chief of staff?"

"I got in his way. That's all. That's the end of it."

"Whipped him," said Rurgen.

"Whipped...you?" whispered Gorst. He stood staring for a moment. Then he snatched up his long steel, cleaned, sharpened and sheathed just beside him on the table.

Younger blocked his way, hands up. "Don't do anything stupid." Gorst brushed him aside and was out through the tent flap, into the chilly night, striding across the trampled grass. "Don't do anything stupid!"

Gorst kept walking.

Felnigg's tent was pitched on the hillside not far from the decaying barn Marshal Kroy had taken for his headquarters. Lamplight leaked from the flap and into the night, illuminating a slit of muddy grass, a tuft of dishevelled sedge and the face of a guard, epically bored.

"Can I help you, sir?"

Help me, you bastard? Rather than giving him the opportunity to consider his position, the long walk up from the valley had only stoked Gorst's fury. He grabbed the guard's breastplate by one armhole and flung him tumbling down the hillside, ripping the tent flap wide. "Felnigg—!"

He came up short. The tent was crammed with officers. Senior members of Kroy's staff, some of them clutching cards, others drinks, most with uniforms unbuttoned to some degree, clustered around an inlaid table that looked as if it had been salvaged from a palace. One was smoking a chagga pipe. Another was sloshing wine from a green bottle. A third hunched over a heavy book, making interminable entries by candlelight in an utterly unreadable script.

"—that bloody captain wanted to charge fifteen for each cabin!" Kroy's chief quartermaster was braying as he clumsily sorted his hand. "Fifteen! I told him to be damned."

"What happened?"

"We settled on twelve, the bloody sea-leech..." He trailed off as, one by one, the officers turned to look at Gorst, the bookkeeper peering over thick spectacles that made his eyes appear grotesquely magnified.

Gorst was not good with crowds. Even worse than with individuals, which was saying something. *But witnesses will only add to Felnigg's humiliation. I will make him beg. I will make all of you bastards beg.* Yet Gorst had stopped dead, his cheeks prickling with heat.

Felnigg sprang up, looking slightly drunk. They all looked drunk. Gorst was not good with drunk. Even worse than with sober, which was saying something. "Colonel Gorst!" He lurched forwards, beaming. Gorst raised his open hand to slap the man across the face, but there was a strange delay in which Felnigg managed to grasp it with his own and give it a hearty shake. "I'm delighted to see you! Delighted!"

"I...What?"

"I was at the bridge today! Saw the whole thing!" Still pumping away at Gorst's hand like a demented washerwoman at a mangle. "Crashing through the crops after them, cutting them down!" And he slashed at the air with his glass, slopping wine about. "Like something out of a storybook!"

"Colonel Felnigg!" The guard from outside, shoving through the flap with mud smeared all down his side. "This man—"

"I know! Colonel Bremer dan Gorst! Never saw such personal courage! Such skill at arms! The man's worth a regiment to his Majesty's cause! Worth a division, I swear! How many of the bastards did you get, do you think? Must've been two dozen! Three dozen, if it was a single one!"

The guard scowled but, seeing that things were not running his way, was forced to retreat into the night. "No more than fifteen," Gorst found he had said. *And only a couple on our side! A heroic ratio if ever there was one!* "But thank you." He tried unsuccessfully to lower his voice to somewhere around a tenor. "Thank you."

"It's us who should be thanking you! That bloody idiot Mitterick certainly should be. His fiasco of an attack would have sunk in the river without you. No more than fifteen, did you hear that?" And he slapped one of his fellows on the arm and made him spill his wine. "I've already written to my friend Halleck on the Closed Council, told him what a bloody hero you are! Didn't think there was room for 'em in the modern age, but here you are, large as life." He clapped Gorst jauntily on the shoulder. "Larger! I've been telling everyone I could find all about it!"

"I'll say he has," grunted one of the officers, peering down at his cards.

"That is...most kind." *Most kind? Kill him! Hack his head off like you hacked the head from that Northman today. Throttle him. Murder him. Punch all his teeth out, at least. Hurt him. Hurt him now!* "Most...kind."

"I'd be bloody honoured if you'd consent to have a drink with me. We all would!" Felnigg spun about and snatched up the bottle. "What brings you up here onto the fell, anyway?"

Gorst took a heavy breath. *Now. Now is the time for courage. Now do it.* But he found each word was an immense effort, excruciatingly aware of how foolish his voice sounded. How singularly lacking in threat or authority, the nerve leaking out of him with every slobbering movement of his lips. "I am here...because I heard that earlier today...you whipped..." *My friend. One of my only friends. You whipped my friend, now prepare for your last moments.* "My servant."

Felnigg spun about, his jaw falling open. "That was your servant? By the ... you must accept my apologies!"

"You whipped someone?" asked one of the officers.

"And not even at cards?" muttered another, to scattered chuckles.

Felnigg blathered on. "So very sorry. No excuse for it. I was in a terrible rush with an order from the lord marshal. No excuse, of course." He grabbed Gorst by the arm, leaning close enough to blast him with a strong odour of spirits. "You must understand, I would never have ... never, had I known he was *your* servant ... of course I would never have done any such thing!"

But you did, you chinless satchel of shit, and now you will pay. There must be a reckoning, and it will be now. Must be now. Definitely, positively, absolutely bloody now. "I must ask—"

"Please say you'll drink with me!" And Felnigg thrust the overfull glass into Gorst's hand, wine slopping onto his fingers. "A cheer for Colonel Gorst! The last hero in his Majesty's army!" The other officers hurried to raise their own glasses, all grinning, one thumping at the table with his free hand and making the silverware jingle.

Gorst found he was sipping at the glass. And he was smiling. Worse yet, he was not even having to force himself. He was enjoying their adulation.

I slaughtered men today who had done me not the slightest grain of harm. No more than fifteen of them. And here I stand with a man who whipped one of my only friends. What horrors should I visit upon him? Why, to smile, and slurp up his cheap wine, and the congratulations of pandering strangers too, what else? What will I tell Younger? That he need not worry about his pain and humiliation because his tormentor warmly approved of my murderous rampage? The king's last hero? I want to be fucking sick. He became acutely aware that he was still clutching his sheathed long steel in one white knuckled fist. He attempted, unsuccessfully, to hide it behind his leg. *I want to vomit up my own liver.*

"It's certainly a hell of a story the way Felnigg tells it," one of the officers was droning while he rearranged his cards. "I daresay it's the second bravest thing I've heard about today."

"Risking his Majesty's rations hardly counts," someone frothed, to more drunken laughter.

"I was speaking of the lord marshal's daughter, in fact. I do prefer a heroine to a hero, they look much better in the paintings."

Gorst frowned. "Finree dan Kroy? I thought she was at her father's headquarters?"

"You didn't hear?" asked Felnigg, giving him another dose of foul breath. "The damndest thing! She was with Meed at the inn when the Northmen butchered him and his whole staff. Right there, in the room! She was taken prisoner, but she talked her way free, and negotiated the release of sixty wounded men besides! What do you make of that! More wine?"

Gorst did not know what to make of it, except that he felt suddenly hot and dizzy. He ignored the proffered bottle, turned without another word and pushed through the tent flap into the chill night air. The guard he had thrown was outside, making a futile effort to brush himself clean. He gave an accusing look and Gorst glanced guiltily away, unable to summon the courage even to apologise—

And there she was. Standing by a low stone wall before Marshal Kroy's headquarters and frowning down into the valley, a military coat wrapped tight around her, one pale hand holding it closed at her neck.

Gorst went to her. He had no choice. It was as if he was pulled by a rope. *A rope around my cock. Dragged by my infantile, self-destructive passions from one cringingly embarrassing episode to another.*

She looked up at him, and the sight of her red-rimmed eyes froze the breath in his throat. "Bremer dan Gorst." Her voice was flat. "What brings you up here?"

Oh, I came to murder your father's chief of staff but he offered me drunken praise so instead I drank a toast with him to my heroism. There is a joke there somewhere...

He found he was staring at the side of her darkened face. Staring and staring. A lantern beyond her picked out her profile in gold, made the downy hairs on her top lip glow. He was terrified that she would glance across, and catch him looking at her mouth. *No innocent reason, is there, to stare at a woman's mouth like this? A married woman? A beautiful, beautiful, married woman?* He wanted her to look. Wanted her to catch him looking. But of course she did not. *What possible reason would a woman have to look at me? I love you. I love you so much it hurts me. More than all the blows I took today. More even than all the blows I gave. I love you so much I want to shit.*

338

Say it. Well, not the part about shit, but the other part. What is there to lose? Say it and be damned!

"I heard that—" he almost whispered.

"Yes," she said.

An exquisitely uncomfortable pause. "Are you—"

"Yes. Go on, you can tell me. Tell me I shouldn't have been down there in the first place. Go on."

Another pause, more uncomfortable yet. For him there was a chasm between mind and mouth he could not see how to bridge. Did not dare to bridge. She did it so easily it quite took his breath away. "You brought men back," he managed to murmur in the end. "You saved lives. You should be proud of—"

"Oh, yes, I'm a real hero. Everyone's terribly proud. Do you know Aliz dan Brint?"

"No."

"Neither did I, really. Thought she was a fool, if I'm honest. She was with me. Down there." She jerked her head towards the dark valley. "She's still down there. What's happening to her now, do you think, while we stand here, talking?"

"Nothing good," said Gorst, before he had considered it.

She frowned sideways at him. "Well. At least you say what you really think." And she turned her back and walked away up the slope towards her father's headquarters, leaving him standing there as she always did, mouth half-open to say words he never could.

Oh yes, I always say what I really think. Would you like to suck my cock, by the way? Please? Or a tongue in the mouth? A hug would be something. She disappeared inside the low barn, and the door was closed, and the light shut in. *Hold hands? No? Anyone?*

The rain had started to come down again.

Anyone?

My Land

Calder took his time strolling up out of the night, towards the fires behind Clail's Wall, spitting and hissing in the drizzle. He'd been in danger for a long time, and never deeper than now, but the strange thing was he still had his smirk.

His father was dead. His brother was dead. He'd even managed to turn his old friend Craw against him. His scheming had got him nowhere. All his careful seeds had yielded not the slightest bitter little fruit. With the help of an impatient mood and a bit too much of Shallow's cheap booze he'd made a big, big mistake tonight, and there was a good chance it was going to kill him. Soon. Horribly.

And he felt strong. Free. No more the younger son, the younger brother. No more the cowardly one, the treacherous one, the lying one. He was even enjoying the throbbing pain in his left hand where he'd skinned his knuckles on Tenways' mail. For the first time in his life he felt... brave.

"What happened up there?" Deep's voice came out of the darkness behind him without warning, but Calder was hardly surprised.

He gave a sigh. "I made a mistake."

"Whatever you do, don't make another, then," came Shallow's whine from the other side.

Deep's voice again. "You ain't thinking of fighting tomorrow, are you?"

"I am, in fact."

A pair of sharp in-breaths. "Fighting?" said Deep.

"You?" said Shallow.

"Get moving now, we could be ten miles away before sun up. No reason to —"

"No," said Calder. There was nothing to think about. He couldn't run. The Calder of ten years ago, who'd ordered Forley the Weakest killed without a second thought, would already have been galloping off on the fastest horse he could steal. But now he had Seff, and an unborn child. If Calder stayed to pay for his own stupidity, Dow would probably stop at ripping

340

him apart in front of a laughing crowd but spare Seff so Reachey would be
left owing him. If Calder ran, Dow would see her hanged, and he couldn't
let that happen. It wasn't in him.

"Can't recommend this," said Deep. "Battles. Never a good idea."

Shallow clicked his tongue. "You want to kill a man, by the dead, you do
it while he's facing the other way."

"I heartily concur," said Deep. "I thought you did too."

"I did." Calder shrugged. "Things change."

Whatever else he might be, he was Bethod's last son. His father had been
a great man, and he wasn't about to put a cowardly joke on the end of his
memory. Scale might have been an idiot but at least he'd had the dignity to
die in battle. Better to follow his example than be hunted down in some
desolate corner of the North, begging for his worthless hide.

But more than that, Calder couldn't run because...fuck them. Fuck
Tenways, and Golden, and Ironhead. Fuck Black Dow. Fuck Curnden
Craw, too. He was sick of being laughed at. Sick of being called a coward.
Sick of being one.

"We don't do battles," said Shallow.

"Can't watch over you if you're fixed on fighting," said Deep.

"Wasn't expecting you to." And Calder left them in the darkness without
a backward glance and strolled on down the track to Clail's Wall, past men
darning shirts, and cleaning weapons, and discussing their chances on the
morrow. Not too good, the general opinion. He put one foot up on a crum-
bled patch of drystone and grinned over at the scarecrow, hanging sadly
limp. "Cheer up," he told it. "I'm going nowhere. These are my men. This is
my land."

"If it ain't Bare-Knuckle Calder, the punching prince!" Pale-as-Snow
came swaggering from the night. "Our noble leader returns! Thought
maybe we'd lost you." He didn't sound too upset at the possibility.

"I was giving some thought to running for the hills, in fact." Calder
worked his toes inside his boot, enjoying the feel of it. He was enjoying
little things a lot, tonight. Maybe that's what happened when you saw your
death coming at you fast. "But the hills are probably turning cold this time
of year."

"The weather's on our side, then."

"We'll see. Thanks for drawing your sword for me. I always had you
down as a man to back the favourite."

"So did I. But for a moment up there you reminded me of your father." Pale-as-Snow planted his own boot on the wall beside Calder's. "I remembered how it felt to follow a man I admire."

Calder snorted. "I wouldn't get used to that feeling."

"Don't worry, it's gone already."

"Then I'll spend every moment I've got left struggling to bring it back for you." Calder hopped up onto the wall, waving his arms for balance as a loose stone rocked under his feet, then stood, peering off across the black fields towards the Old Bridge. The torches of the Union pickets formed a dotted line, others moving about as soldiers poured across the river. Making ready to come flooding across the fields tomorrow morning, and over their tumbledown little wall, and murder the lot of them, and leave Bethod's memory a joke regardless.

Calder squinted, shading his eyes from the light of his own fires. It looked as if they'd stuck two tall flags right up at the front. He could see them shifting in the wind, gold thread faintly glinting. It seemed strange that they were so easy to see, until he realised they were lit up on purpose. Some sort of display. Some show of strength, maybe.

"By the dead," he muttered, and snorted with laughter. His father used to tell him it's easy to see the enemy one of two ways. As some implacable, terrifying, unstoppable force that can only be feared and never understood. Or some block of wood that doesn't think, doesn't move, a dumb target to shoot your plans at. But the enemy is neither one. Imagine he's you, that he's no more and no less of a fool, or a coward, or a hero than you are. If you can imagine that, you won't go too far wrong. The enemy is just a set of men. That's the realisation that makes war easy. And the one that makes it hard.

The chances were high that General Mitterick and the rest were just as big a set of idiots as Calder was himself. Which meant they were big ones. "Have you seen those bloody flags?" he called down.

Pale-as-Snow shrugged. "It's the Union."

"Where's White-Eye?"

"Touring the fires, trying to keep mens' spirits up."

"Not buoyed by having me in charge, then?"

Pale-as-Snow shrugged again. "They don't all know you like I do. Probably Hansul's busy singing the song of how you punched Brodd Tenways in the face. That'll do their love for you no harm."

Maybe not, but punching men on his own side wasn't going to be enough. Calder's men were beaten and demoralised. They'd lost a leader they loved and gained one nobody did. If he did any more nothing, the chances were high they'd fall apart in battle tomorrow morning, if they were even there when the sun rose.

Scale had said it. This is the North. Sometimes you have to fight.

He pressed his tongue into his teeth, the glimmers of an idea starting to take shape from the darkness. "Mitterick, is it, across the way?"

"The Union Chief? Aye, Mitterick, I think."

"Sharp, Dow told me, but reckless."

"He was reckless enough today."

"Worked for him, in the end. Men tend to stick to what works. He loves horses, I heard."

"What? Loves 'em?" Pale-as-Snow mimed a grabbing action and gave a couple of thrusts of his hips.

"Maybe that too. But I think fighting on them was more the point."

"That's good ground for horses." Pale-as-Snow nodded at the sweep of dark crops to the south. "Nice and flat. Maybe he thinks he'll ride all over us tomorrow."

"Maybe he will." Calder pursed his lips, thinking about it. Thinking about the order crumpled in his shirt pocket. *My men and I are giving our all.* "Reckless. Arrogant. Vain." Roughly what men said about Calder, as it went. Which maybe gave him a little insight into his opponent. His eyes shifted back to those idiot flags, thrust out front, lit up like a dance on mid-summer eve. His mouth found that familiar smirk, and stayed there. "I want you to get your best men together. No more than a few score. Enough to keep together and work quickly at night."

"What for?"

"We're not going to beat the Union moping back here." He kicked the bit of loose stone from the top of the wall. "And I don't think some farmer's boundary mark is going to keep them out either, do you?"

Pale-as-Snow showed his teeth. "Now you're reminding me of your father again. What about the rest of the lads?"

Calder hopped down from the wall. "Get White-Eye to round them up. They've got some digging to do."

DAY THREE

"I'm not sure how much violence and butchery
the readers will stand"

Robert E. Howard

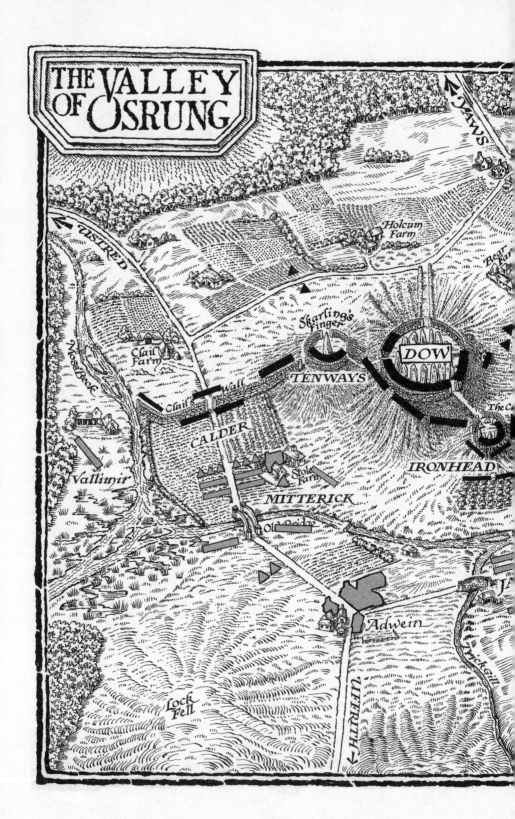

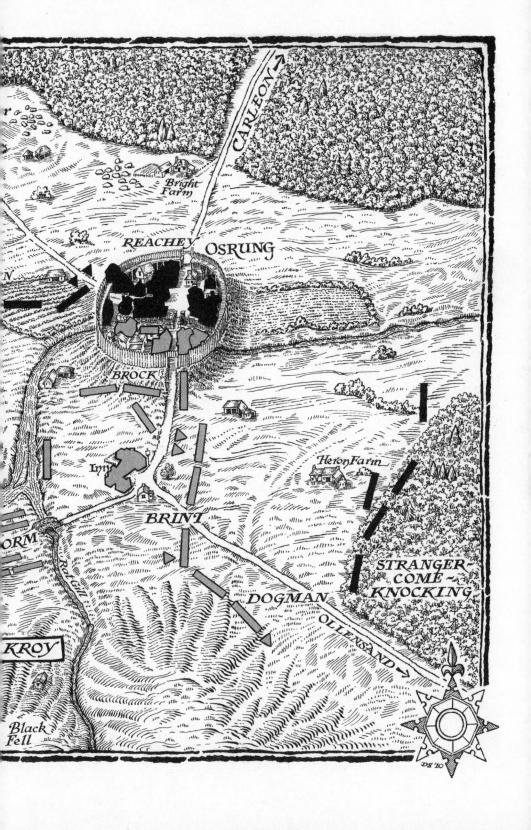

The Standard Issue

The light came and went as the clouds tore across the sky, showing a glimpse of the big full moon then hiding it away, like a clever whore might show a glimpse of tit once in a while, just to keep the punters eager. By the dead, Calder wished he was with a clever whore now, rather than crouching in the middle of a damp barley-field, peering through the thrashing stalks in the vain hope of seeing a whole pile of night-dark nothing. It was a sad fact, or perhaps a happy one, that he was a man better suited to brothels than battlefields.

Pale-as-Snow was rather the reverse. The only part of him that had moved in an hour or more was his jaw, slowly shifting as he ground a lump of chagga down to mush. His flinty calm only made Calder more jumpy. Everything did. The scraping of shovels dug at his nerves behind them, sounding just a few strides distant one moment then swallowed up by the wind the next. The same wind that was whipping Calder's hair in his face, blasting his eyes with grit and cutting through his clothes to the bone.

"Shit on this wind," he muttered.

"Wind's a good thing," grunted Pale-as-Snow. "Masks the sound. And if you're chill, brought up to the North, think how they feel over there, used to sunnier climes. All in our favour." Good points, maybe, and Calder was annoyed he hadn't thought of them, but they didn't make him feel any warmer. He clutched his cloak tight at his chest, other hand wedged into his armpit, and pressed one eye shut.

"I expected war to be terrifying but I never thought it'd be so bloody boring."

"Patience." Pale-as-Snow turned his head, softly spat and licked the juice from his bottom lip. "Patience is as fearsome a weapon as rage. More so, in fact, 'cause fewer men have it."

"Chief." Calder spun about, fumbling for his sword hilt. A man had slithered from the barley beside them, mud smeared on his face, eyes standing out strangely white in the midst of it. One of theirs. Calder wondered if he should've smeared some mud on his face too. It made a man look like he knew his business. He waited for Pale-as-Snow to answer for a while. Then he realised he was the Chief.

"Oh, right." Letting go of his sword and pretending he hadn't been surprised at all. "What?"

"We're in the trenches," whispered the newcomer. "Sent a few Union boys back to the mud."

"They seem ready?" asked Pale-as-Snow, who hadn't so much as looked round.

"Shit, no." The man's grin was a pale curve in his blacked-out face. "Most of 'em were sleeping."

"Best time to kill a man." Though Calder had to wonder whether the dead would agree. The old warrior held out one hand. "Shall we?"

"We shall." Calder winced as he set off crawling through the barley. It was far sharper, rougher, more painful stuff to sneak through than you could ever have expected. It didn't take long for his hands to chafe raw, and it hardly helped that he knew he was heading towards the enemy. He was a man better suited to the opposite direction. "Bloody barley." When he took his father's chain back he'd make a law against growing the bastard stuff. Only soft crops allowed, on pain of—He ripped two more bristly wedges out of his way and froze.

The standards were right ahead, no more than twenty strides off, flapping hard on their staves. Each was embroidered with a golden sun, glittering in the light of a dozen lanterns. Beyond them the stretch of bald, soggy ground Scale had died defending sloped down towards the river, crawling with Union horses. Hundreds of tons of big, glossy, dangerous-looking horseflesh and, as far as he could tell by the patchy torchlight, they were still coming across, hooves clattering on the flags of the bridge, panicked whinnies echoing out as they jostled each other in the darkness. There was no shortage of men either, shouting as they struggled to get their mounts into position, bellowed orders fading on the wind. All making good and ready to trample Calder and his boys into the mud in a few short hours.

Not a particularly comforting thought, it had to be said. Calder didn't mind the odd trampling but he much preferred being in the saddle to being under the hooves.

A pair of guards flanked the standards, one with his arms wrapped around him and a halberd hugged tight in the crook of his elbow, the other stamping his feet, sword sheathed and using his shield as a windbreak.

"Do we go?" whispered Pale-as-Snow.

Calder looked at those guards, and he thought about mercy. Neither one seemed the slightest bit ready for what was coming. They looked even more unhappy about being here than he was, which was quite the achievement. He wondered whether they had wives waiting for them too. Wives with children in their soft bellies, maybe, curled up asleep under the furs with a warm space beside them. He sighed. Damn shame they weren't all with their wives, but mercy wasn't going to drive the Union out of the North, or Black Dow out of his father's chair either.

"We go," he said.

Pale-as-Snow held up a hand and made a couple of gestures. Then he did the same on the other side and settled back onto his haunches. Calder wasn't sure who he was even waving at, let alone what the meaning was, but it worked like magic.

The guard with the shield suddenly went over backwards. The other turned his head to look then did the same. Calder realised they'd both had their throats cut. Two black shapes lowered them gently to the ground. A third had caught the halberd as it dropped and now he turned, hugging it in the crook of his own elbow, giving them a gap-toothed grin as he imitated the Union guard.

More Northmen had broken from the crops and were scurrying forwards, bent double, weapons gleaming faintly as the moon slipped from the clouds again. Not twenty strides away from them three Union soldiers were struggling with a wind-torn tent. Calder chewed at his lip, hardly able to believe they weren't seen as they crept across the open ground and into the lamplight, one of them taking a hold of the right-hand flag, starting to twist it free of the earth.

"You!" A Union soldier, a flatbow part-raised, a look of mild puzzlement on his face. There was a moment of awkward silence, everyone holding their breath.

"Ah," said Calder.

"Shit," said Pale-as-Snow.

The soldier frowned. "Who are—" Then he had an arrow in his chest. Calder didn't hear the bowstring but he could see the black line of the shaft. The soldier shot his flatbow into the ground, gave a high shriek and fell to his knees. Not far away some horses startled, one dragging its surprised handler over onto his face and bumping across the mud. The three soldiers with the tent all snapped around at the same moment, two of them letting go of the canvas so that it was blown straight into the face of the third. Calder felt a sucking feeling in his stomach.

More Union men spilled into the light with frightening suddenness, a dozen or more, a couple with torches, flames whipped out sideways by a new gust. High wails echoed on Calder's right and men darted from nowhere, steel glinting as swords were swung. Shadows flickered in the darkness, a weapon, or an arm, or the outline of a face caught for an instant against the orange glow of fire. Calder could hardly tell what was happening, then one of the torches guttered out and he couldn't tell at all. It sounded as if there was fighting over on the left now too, his head yanked about by every sound.

He nearly jumped into the sky when he felt Pale-as-Snow's hand on his shoulder. "Best be moving."

Calder needed no further encouragement, he was off through the barley like a rabbit. He could hear other men, whooping, laughing, cursing, no clue whether they were his or the enemy. Something hissed into the crops next to him. An arrow, or just the wind blowing stalks about. Crops tangled his ankles, thrashed at his calves. He tripped and fell on his face, tore his way back up with Pale-as-Snow's hand under his arm.

"Wait! Wait."

He stood frozen in the dark, bent over with his hands on his knees, rib-cage going like a bellows. Voices were gabbling over each other. Northern voices, he was greatly relieved to hear.

"They following?"

"Where's Hayl?"

"Did we get the bloody flags?"

"Those bastards wouldn't even know which way to go."

"Dead. Caught an arrow."

"We got 'em!"

"They were just dragging their bloody horses around!"

"Thought we'd have nothing to say about it."

"But Prince Calder had something to say," Calder looked up at his name and found Pale-as-Snow smiling at him, one of the standards in his fist. Something like the smile a smith might have when his favourite apprentice finally hammers out something worth selling on the anvil.

Calder felt a poke in his side, started, then realised it was the other standard, the flag rolled up tight. One of the men was offering it out to him, grin shining in the moonlight in the midst of his muddy face. There was a whole set of grins pointed at him. As if he'd said something funny. As if he'd done something great. It didn't feel that way to Calder. He'd just had the idea, which had been no effort at all, and set other men to work out how, and others still to take the risks. Hardly seemed possible that Calder's father had earned his great reputation like this. But maybe that's how the world works. Some men are made for doing violence. Some are meant for planning it. Then there are a special few whose talent is for taking the credit.

"Prince Calder?" And the grinning man offered him the flag again.

Well. If they wanted someone to admire, Calder wasn't about to disappoint them. "I'm no prince." He snatched the standard, swung one leg over the flagstaff and held it there, sticking up at an angle. He drew his sword, for the first time that night, and thrust it straight up into the dark sky. "I'm the king of the fucking Union!"

It wasn't much of a joke, but after the night they'd had, and the day they'd had yesterday, they were ready to celebrate. A gale of laughter went up, Calder's men chuckling away, slapping each other on the backs.

"All hail his fucking Majesty!" shouted Pale-as-Snow, holding up the other flag, gold thread sparkling as it snapped in the wind. "King bloody Calder!"

Calder just kept on grinning. He liked the sound of that.

Shadows

Your August Fuck-Hole,

The truth? Under the wilful mismanagement of the old villains on your Closed Council, your army is rotting. Frittered away with cavalier care-lessness, as a rake might fritter away his father's fortune. If they were the enemy's councillors they could scarcely do more to frustrate your Fuck-Hole's interests in the North. You could do better yourself, which is truly the most damning indictment of which I am capable. It would have been more honourable to load the men aboard in Adua, wave them off with a tear in the eye, then simply set fire to the ships and send them all to the bottom of the bay.

The truth? Marshal Kroy is competent, and cares for his soldiers, and I ardently desire to fuck his daughter, but there is only so much one man can do. His underlings, Jalenhorm, Mitterick and Meed, have been struggling manfully with each other for the place of worst general in his-tory. I hardly know which deserves the higher contempt – the pleasant but incompetent dullard, the treacherous, reckless careerist, or the indecisive, war-mongering pedant. At least the last has already paid for his folly with his life. With any luck the rest of us will follow.

The truth? Why would you care? Old friends like us need have no pre-tences. I know better than most you are a cringing cipher, a spineless fig-urehead, a self-pitying, self-loving, self-hating child-man, king of nothing but your own vanity. Bayaz rules here, and he is bereft of conscience, scruple or mercy. The man is a monster. The worst I have seen, in fact, since I last looked in the mirror.

The truth? I am rotting too. I am buried alive, and already rotting. If I was not such a coward I would kill myself, but I am, and so I must con-tent myself with killing others in the hope that one day, if I can only wade deep enough in blood, I will come out clean. While I wait breathlessly for rehabilitation that will never come, I will of course be delighted to con-

sume any shit you might deign to squeeze into my face from the royal buttocks.

I remain your Fuck-Hole's most betrayed and vilified scapegoat,

Bremer dan Gorst,
Royal Observer of the Northern Fiasco

Gorst put down his pen, frowning at a tiny cut he had somehow acquired on the very tip of his forefinger where it rendered every slightest task painful. He blew gently over the letter until every gleam of wet ink had turned dry black, then folded it, running his one unbroken nail slowly along it to make the sharpest of creases. He took up the stick of wax, tongue pressed into the roof of his mouth. His eyes found the candle flame, twinkling invitingly in the shadows. He looked at that spark of brightness as a man scared of heights looks at the parapet of a great tower. It called to him. Drew him. Made him dizzy with the delightful prospect of self-annihilation. *Like that, and this shameful unpleasantness that I laughingly call a life could all be over.* Only seal it, and send it, and wait for the storm to break.

Then he sighed, and slid the letter into the flame, watched it slowly blacken, crinkle, dropped the last smouldering corner on the floor of his tent and ground it under his boot. He wrote at least one of these a night, savage punctuation points between rambling sentences of trying to force himself to sleep. Sometimes he even felt better afterwards. *For a very short while.*

He frowned up at a clatter outside, then started at a louder crash, the gabble of raised voices, something in their tone making him reach for his boots. Many voices, then the sounds of horses too. He snatched up his sword and ripped aside his tent flap.

Younger had been sitting outside, tapping the day's dents out of Gorst's armour by lamplight. He was standing up now, craning to see, a greave in one hand and the little hammer in the other.

"What is it?" Gorst squeaked at him.

"I've no—Woah!" He shrank back as a horse thundered past, flicking mud all over both of them.

"Stay here." Gorst put a gentle hand on his shoulder. "Stay out of danger."

355

He strode from his tent and towards the Old Bridge, tucking his shirt in with one hand, sheathed long steel gripped firmly in the other. Shouts echoed from the darkness ahead, lantern beams twinkling, glimpses of figures and faces mixed up with the after-image of the candle flame still fizzing across Gorst's vision.

A messenger jogged from the night, breathing hard, one cheek and the side of his uniform caked with mud. "What's happening?" Gorst snapped at him.

"The Northmen have attacked in numbers!" he wheezed as he laboured past. "We're overrun! They're coming!" His terror was Gorst's joy, excitement flaring up his throat so hot it was almost painful, the petty inconveniences of his bruises and aching muscles all burned away as he strode on towards the river. *Will I have to fight my way across that bridge for the second time in twelve hours?* He was almost giggling at the stupidity of it. *I cannot wait.*

Some officers pleaded for calm while others ran for their lives. Some men searched feverishly for weapons while others threw them away. Every shadow was the first of a horde of marauding Northmen, Gorst's palm itching with the need to draw his sword, until the tricking shapes resolved themselves into baffled soldiers, half-dressed servants, squinting grooms.

"Colonel Gorst? Is that you, sir?"

He stalked on, thoughts elsewhere. Back in Sipani. Back in the smoke and the madness at Cardotti's House of Leisure. Searching for the king in the choking gloom. *But this time I will not fail.*

A servant with a bloody knife was staring at a crumpled shape on the ground. *Mistaken identity.* A man came blundering from a tent, hair sticking wildly from his head, struggling to undo the clasp on a dress sword. *Pray excuse me.* Gorst swept him out of his way with the back of one arm and squawking over into the mud. A plump captain sat, surprised face streaked with blood, clasping a bandage to his head. "What's happening? What's happening?" *Panic. Panic is happening. Amazing how quickly a steadfast army can dissolve. How quickly daylight heroes become night-time cowards. Become a herd, acting with the instincts of the animal.*

"This way!" someone shouted behind him. "He knows!" Footsteps slapped after him in the mud. *A little herd of my own.* He did not even look around. *But you should know I'm going wherever the killing is.*

A horse plunged out of nowhere, eyes rolling. Someone had been trampled, was howling, pawing at the muck. Gorst stepped over them, following an inexplicable trail of fashionable lady's dresses, lace and colourful silk crushed into the filth. The press grew tighter, pale faces smeared across the dark, mad eyes shining with reflected fire, water glimmering with reflected torches. The Old Bridge was as packed and wild as it had been the previous day when they drove the Northmen across it. More so. Voices shouted over each other.

"Have you seen my—"

"Is that Gorst?"

"They're coming!"

"Out of my way! Out of my—"

"They're gone already!"

"It's him! He'll know what to do!"

"Everyone back! Back!"

"Colonel Gorst, could I—"

"Have to find some order! Order! I beseech you!"

Beseeching will not work here. The crowd swelled, surged, opening out then crushing tight, fear flashing up like lightning as a drawn sword or a lit torch wafted in someone's face. An elbow caught Gorst in the darkness and he lashed out with his fist, scuffed his knuckles on armour. Something grabbed at his leg and he kicked at it, tore himself free and shoved on. There was a shriek as someone was pushed over the parapet, Gorst caught a glimpse of his boots kicking as he vanished, heard the splash as he hit the fast-flowing water below.

He ripped his way clear on the far side of the bridge. His shirt was torn, the wind blowing chill through the rip. A ruddy-faced sergeant held a torch high and bellowed in a broken voice for calm. There was more shouting up ahead, horses plunging, weapons waving. But Gorst could not hear the sweet note of steel. He gripped his sword tight and stomped grimly on.

"No!" General Mitterick stood in the midst of a group of staff officers, perhaps the best example Gorst had ever seen of a man incandescent with rage. "I want the Second and Third ready to charge at once!"

"But, sir," wheedled one of his aides, "it is still some time until dawn, the men are in disarray, we can't—"

Mitterick shook his sword in the young man's face. "I'll give the orders here!" *Though it is obviously too dark to mount a horse safely, let alone ride*

357

several hundred at a gallop towards an invisible enemy. "Put guards on the bridge! I want any man who tries to cross hanged for desertion! *Hanged!*"

Colonel Opker, Mitterick's second-in-command, stood just outside the radius of blame, watching the pantomime with grim resignation.

Gorst clapped a hand down on his shoulder. "Where are the Northmen?"

"Gone!" snapped Opker, shaking free. "There were no more than a few score of them! They stole the standards of the Second and Third and were off into the night."

"His Majesty will not countenance the loss of his standards, General!" someone was yelling. Felnigg. *Swooped down on Mitterick's embarrassment like a hawk on a rabbit.*

"I am well aware of what his Majesty will not countenance!" roared Mitterick back at him. "I'll damn well get those standards back and kill every one of those thieving bastards, you can tell the lord marshal that! I *demand* you tell him that!"

"Oh, I'll be telling him all about it, never fear!"

But Mitterick had turned his back and was bellowing into the night. "Where are the scouts? I told you to send scouts, didn't I? Dimbik? Where's Dimbik? The ground, man, the ground!"

"Me?" a white-faced young officer stammered out. "Well, er, yes, but—"

"Are they back yet? I want to be sure the ground's good! Tell me it's good, damn it!"

The man's eyes darted desperately about, then it seemed he steeled himself, and snapped to attention. "Yes, General, the scouts were sent, and have returned, in fact, very much returned, and the ground is...perfect. Like a card table, sir. A card table...with barley on it—"

"Excellent! I want no more bloody surprises!" Mitterick stomped off, loose shirt tails flapping. "Where the bloody hell is Major Hockelman? I want these horsemen ready to charge as soon as we have light to piss by! Do you understand me? To *piss* by!"

His voice faded into the wind along with Felnigg's grating complaints, and the lamps of his staff went with them, leaving Gorst frowning in the darkness, as choked with disappointment as a jilted groom.

A raid, then. An opportunistic little sally had caused all this, triggered by Mitterick's petty little display with his flags. *And there will be no glory and no redemption here. Only stupidity, cowardice and waste.* Gorst wondered idly how many had died in the chaos. *Ten times as many as the Northmen killed? Truly, the enemy are the least dangerous element of a war.*

How could we have been so ludicrously unready? Because we could not imagine they would have the gall to attack. If the Northmen had pushed harder they might have driven us back across the bridge, and captured two whole regiments of cavalry rather than just their standards. Five men and a dog could have done it. But they could not imagine we might be so ludicrously unready. A failure for everyone. Especially me.

He turned to find a small crowd of soldiers and servants with a mismatched assortment of equipment at his back. Those who had followed him down to the bridge, and beyond. A surprising number. *Sheep. Which makes me what? The sheep-dog? Woof, woof, you fools.*

"What should we do, sir?" asked the nearest of them.

Gorst could only shrug. Then he trudged slowly back towards the bridge, just as he had trudged back that afternoon, brushing through the deflated mob on the way. There was no sign of dawn yet, but it could not be far off.

Time to put on my armour.

Under the Wing

Craw picked his way down the hill, peering into the blackness for his footing, wincing at his sore knee with every other step. Wincing at his sore arm and his sore cheek and his sore jaw besides. Wincing most of all at the question he'd been asking himself most of a stiff, cold, wakeful night. A night full of worries and regrets, of the faint whimpering of the dying and the not-so-faint snoring of Whirrun of bloody Bligh.

Tell Black Dow what Calder had said, or not? Craw wondered whether Calder had already run. He'd known the lad since he was a child, and couldn't ever have accused him of courage, but there'd been something different about him when they talked last night. Something Craw hadn't recognised. Or rather something he had, but not from Calder, from his father. And Bethod hadn't been much of a runner. That was what had killed him. Well, that and the Bloody-Nine smashing his head apart. Which was probably better'n Calder could expect if Dow found out what had been said. Better'n Craw could expect himself, if Dow found out from someone else. He glanced over at Dow's frowning face, criss-cross scars picked out in black and orange by Shivers' torch.

Tell him or not?

"Fuck," he whispered.

"Aye," said Shivers. Craw almost took a tumble on the wet grass. 'Til he remembered there was an awful lot a man could be saying fuck about. That's the beauty of the word. It can mean just about anything, depending on how things stand. Horror, shock, pain, fear, worry. None were out of place. There was a battle on.

The little tumbledown house crept out of the dark, nettles sprouting from its crumbling walls, a piece of the roof fallen in and the rotten timbers sticking up like dead rib bones. Dow took Shivers' torch. "You wait here."

Shivers paused just a moment, then bowed his head and leaned back by the door, faintest gleam of moonlight settled on his metal eye.

Craw ducked through the low doorway, trying not to look worried. When he was alone with Black Dow, some part of him – and not a small one – always expected a knife in the back. Or maybe a sword in the front. But a blade, anyway. Then he was always the tiniest bit surprised when he lived out the meeting. He'd never felt that way with Threetrees, or even Bethod. Hardly seemed the mark of the right man to follow... He caught himself chewing at a fingernail, if you could even call it a fingernail there was that little left of the bastard thing, and made himself stop.

Dow took his torch over to the far side of the room, shadows creeping about the rough-sawn rafters as he moved. "Ain't heard back from the girl, then, or her father neither." Craw thought it best to stick to silence. Whenever he said a word these days it seemed to end up in some style of disaster. "Looks like I put myself in debt to the bloody giant for naught." Silence again. "Women, eh?"

Craw shrugged. "Don't reckon I'll be lending you any insights on that score."

"You had one for a Second, didn't you? How did you make that work?"

"She made it work. Couldn't ask for a better Second than Wonderful. The dead know I made some shitty choices but that's one I've never regretted. Not ever. She's tough as a thistle, tough as any man I know. Got more bones than me and sharper wits too. Always the first to see to the bottom o' things. And she's a straight edge. I'd trust her with anything. No one I'd trust more."

Dow raised his brows. "Toll the fucking bells. Maybe I should've picked her for your job."

"Probably," muttered Craw.

"Got to have someone you can trust for a Second." Dow crossed to the window, peering out into the windy night. "Got to have trust."

Craw snatched at another subject. "We waiting for your black-skinned friend?"

"Not sure I'd call her a friend. But yes."

"Who is she?"

"One o' those desert-dwellers. Don't the black give it away?"

"What's her interest in the North, is my question?"

"Couldn't tell you that for sure, but from what I've gathered she's got a war of her own to fight. An old war, and for now we've a battlefield in common."

Craw frowned. "A war between sorcerers? That something we want a part of?"

"We've a part of it already."

"Where did you find her?"

"She found me."

That was a long way from putting his fears to rest. "Magic. I don't know—"

"You were up on the Heroes yesterday, no? You saw Splitfoot."

Hardly a memory to lift the mood. "I did."

"The Union have magic, that's a fact, and they're happy to use it. We need to match fire with fire."

"What if we all get burned?"

"I daresay we will." Dow shrugged. "That's war."

"Can you trust her, though?"

"No." Ishri was leaning against the wall by the door, one foot crossed over the other and a look like she knew what Craw was thinking and wasn't much impressed. He wondered if she knew he'd been thinking about Calder and tried not to, which only brought him more to mind.

Dow, meanwhile, didn't even turn around. Just slid his torch into a rusted bracket on the wall, watching the flames crackle.

"Seems our little gesture of peace fell on stony ground," he tossed over his shoulder.

Ishri nodded.

Dow stuck his bottom lip out. "Nobody wants to be my friend."

Ishri made one thin eyebrow arch impossibly high.

"Well, who wants to shake hands with a man whose hands are bloody as mine?"

Ishri shrugged.

Dow looked down at his hand, made a fist of it and sighed. "Reckon I'll just have to get 'em bloodier. Any idea where they're coming from today?"

"Everywhere."

"Knew you'd say that."

"Why ask, then?"

"Least I got you to speak." There was a long silence, then Dow finally turned around, settling back with elbows on the narrow windowsill. "Go on, go for some more."

Ishri stepped away from the wall, letting her head drop back and roll in a slow circle. For some reason every movement of hers made Craw feel a little disgusted, like watching a snake slither. "In the east, a man called Brock has taken charge, and prepares to attack the bridge in Osrung."

"And what kind of man is he? Like Meed?"

"The opposite. He is young, pretty and brave."

"I love those young brave pretty men!" Dow glanced over at Craw. "It's why I picked one out for my Second."

"None out of three ain't bad." Craw realised he was chewing at his nail yet again, and whipped his hand away.

"In the centre," said Ishri, "Jalenhorm has a great number of foot ready to cross the shallows."

Dow gave his hungry grin. "Gives me something to look forward to today. I quite enjoy watching men try to climb hills I'm sat on top of." Craw couldn't say he was looking forward to it, however much the ground might have taken their side.

"In the west Mitterick strains at the leash, keen to make use of his pretty horses. He has men across the little river too, in the woods on your western flank."

Dow raised his brows. "Huh. Calder was right."

"Calder has been hard at work all night."

"Damned if it ain't the first hard work that bastard's ever done."

"He stole two standards from the Union in the darkness. Now he taunts them."

Black Dow chuckled to himself. "You'll not find a better hand at taunting. I've always liked that lad."

Craw frowned over at him. "You have?"

"Why else would I keep giving him chances? I got no shortage of men can kick a door down. I can use a couple who'll think to try the handle once in a while."

"Fair enough." Though Craw had to wonder what Dow would say if he knew Calder was trying the handle on his murder. When he knew. It was a case of when. Wasn't it?

"This new weapon they've got." Dow narrowed his eyes to lethal slits. "What is it?"

"Bayaz." Ishri did some fairly deadly eye-narrowing of her own. Craw wondered if there was a harder pair of eye-narrowers in the world than these two. "The First of the Magi. He is with them. And he has something new."

"That's the best you can do?"

She tipped her head back, looking down her nose. "Bayaz is not the only one who can produce surprises. I have one for him, later today."

"I knew there had to be a reason why I took you under my wing," said Dow.

"Your wing shelters all the North, oh mighty Protector." Ishri's eyes rolled slowly to the ceiling. "The Prophet shelters under the wing of God. I shelter under the wing of the Prophet. That thing that keeps the rain from your head?" And she held her arm up, long fingers wriggling, boneless as a jar of bait. Her face broke out in a grin too white and too wide. "Great or small, we all must find some shelter." Dow's torch popped, its light flickered for a moment, and she wasn't there.

"Think on it," came her voice, right in Craw's ear.

Names

B eck hunched his shoulders and stared at the fire. Not much more'n a tangle of blackened sticks, a few embers in the centre still with a glow to 'em and a little tongue of flame, whipped, and snatched, and torn about, helpless in the wind. Burned out. Almost as burned out as he was. He'd clutched at that dream of being a hero so long that now it was naught but ashes he didn't know what he wanted. He sat there under fading stars named for great men, great battles and great deeds, and didn't know who he was.

"Hard to sleep, eh?" Drofd shuffled up into the firelight cross-legged, blanket around his shoulders.

Beck gave the smallest grunt he could. Last thing he wanted to do was talk.

Drofd held out a piece of yesterday's meat to him, glistening with grease. "Hungry?"

Beck shook his head. He weren't sure when he last ate. Just before he last slept, most likely, but the smell alone was making him sick.

"Might keep it for later, then." Drofd stuck the meat into a pocket on the front of his jerkin, bone sticking out, rubbed his hands together and held 'em to the smear of fire, so dirty the lines on his palms were picked out black. He looked about of an age with Beck, but smaller and darker, some spare stubble on his jaw. Right then, in the darkness, he looked a little bit like Reft. Beck swallowed, and looked away. "So you got yourself a name, then, eh?"

A little nod.

"Red Beck." Drofd gave a chuckle. "It's a good 'un. Fierce-sounding. You must be pleased."

"Pleased?" Beck felt a stinging urge to say, "I hid in a cupboard and killed one o' my own," but instead he said, "I reckon."

"Wish I had a name. Guess it'll come in time."

Beck kept staring into the fire, hoping to head off any more chatter. Seemed Drofd was the chattering sort, though.

"You got family?"

All the most ordinary, obvious, lame bloody talk a lad could've thought of. Dragging the words out felt like a painful effort to begin with. "A mother. Two little brothers. One's 'prenticed to the smith in the valley." Lame, maybe, but once he'd started talking, thoughts drifting homewards, he found he couldn't stop. "More'n likely my mother's making ready to bring the harvest in. Was getting ripe when I left. She'll be sharpening the scythe and that. And Festen'll be gathering up after her..." And by the dead, how he wished he was with 'em. He wanted to smile and cry at once, didn't dare say more for fear of doing it.

"I got seven sisters," said Drofd, "and I'm the youngest. Like having eight mothers fussing over me, and putting me right all day long, and each with a tongue sharper'n the last. No man in the house, and no man's business ever talked of. Home was a special kind of hell, I can tell you that."

A warm house with eight women and no swords didn't sound so awful right then. Beck had thought his home was a special kind of hell once. Now he had a different notion of what hell looked like.

Drofd blathered on.

"But I got a new family now. Craw, and Wonderful, and Jolly Yon and the rest. Good fighters. Good names. Stick together, you know, mind their own. Lost a couple o' people the last few days. Couple of good people, but..." Seemed he ran out of words himself for a moment. Didn't take him long to find more, though. "Craw was Second to old Threetrees, you know, way back. Been in every battle since whenever. Does things the old way. Real straight edge. You fell on your feet to fall in with this lot, I reckon."

"Aye." Beck didn't feel like he'd fallen on his feet. He felt like he was still falling and, sooner or later but probably sooner, the ground would smash his brains out.

"Where did you get the sword?"

Beck blinked at the hilt, almost surprised to see it was still there beside him. "It was my father's."

"He was a fighter?"

"Named Man. Famous one, I guess." And how he'd loved to boast about it once. Now the name was sour on his tongue. "Shama Heartless."

"What? The one who fought a duel against the Bloody-Nine? The one who..."

Lost. "Aye. The Bloody-Nine brought an axe to the duel, and my father brought this blade, and they spun the shield, and the Bloody-Nine won, and he chose the sword." Beck slid it out, stupidly worried he might stab someone without meaning to. He'd a respect of sharp metal he hadn't had the night before. "They fought, and the Bloody-Nine split my father's belly wide open." Seemed mad now that he'd rushed to follow the man's footsteps. A man he'd never known, whose footsteps led all the way to his own spilled guts.

"You mean . . . the Bloody-Nine held that sword?"

"Guess he must've."

"Can I?"

Time was Beck would've told Drofd to fuck himself, but acting the loner hadn't worked out too well for anyone concerned. This time around maybe he'd try and coax out a friendship or two. So he handed the blade across, pommel first.

"By the dead, that's a damn good sword." Drofd stared at the hilt with big eyes. "There's still blood on it."

"Aye," Beck managed to croak.

"Well, well, well." Wonderful strutted up, hands on hips, tip of her tongue showing between her teeth. "Two young lads, handling each other's weapons by firelight? Don't worry, I see how it can happen. You think no one's watching, and there's a fight coming, and you might never get another chance to try it. Most natural thing in the world."

Drofd cleared his throat and gave the sword back quick. "Just talking about . . . you know. Names. How'd you come by yours?"

"Mine?" snapped Wonderful, narrowing her eyes at 'em. Beck didn't rightly know what to make of a woman fighting, let alone one who led a dozen. One who was his Chief, now, even. He had to admit she scared him a little, with that hard look and that knobbly head with an old scar down one side and a fresh one down the other. Being scared by a woman might've shamed him once, but it hardly seemed to matter now he was scared of everything. "I got it giving a pair of curious young lads a wonderful kicking."

"She got it off Threetrees." Jolly Yon rolled over in his blankets and propped himself on an elbow, peering at the fire through one hardly open eye, scratching at his black and grey thatch of a beard. "Her family had a farm just north of Uffrith. Stop me if I'm wrong."

"I will," she said, "don't worry."

"And when trouble started up with Bethod, some of his boys came down into that valley. So she shaved her hair."

"Shaved it a couple of months before. Always got in my way when I was following the plough."

"I stand corrected. You want to take over?"

"You're doing all right."

"No need for the shears, then, but she took up a sword, and she got a few others in the valley to do the same, and she laid an ambush for 'em."

Wonderful's eyes gleamed in the firelight. "Did I ever."

"And then Threetrees turned up, and me and Craw along with him, expecting to find the valley all burned out and the farmers scattered and instead he finds a dozen of Bethod's boys hanged and a dozen more prisoner and this bloody girl watching over 'em with quite the smile. What was it he said now?"

"Can't say I recall," she grunted.

"Wonderful strange to have a woman in charge," said Yon, putting on a gravelly bass. "We called her Wonderful Strange for a week or two, then the strange dropped off, and there you have it."

Wonderful nodded grimly at the fire. "And a month later Bethod came in earnest and the valley got all burned out anyway."

Yon shrugged. "Still a good ambush, though."

"And what about you, eh, Jolly Yon Cumber?"

Yon dragged his blankets off and sat up. "Ain't much to it."

"Don't be modest. Jolly was said straight in the old days, 'cause he used to be quite the joker, did Yon. Then his cock was tragically cut off in the battle at Ineward, a loss more mourned by the womenfolk of the North than all the husbands, sons and fathers killed there. Ever since then, not a single smile."

"A cruel lie." Yon pointed a thick finger across at Beck. "I never had a sense o' humour. And it was just a little nick out of my thigh at Ineward. Lot of blood but no damage. Everything still working down below, don't you worry."

Over his shoulder and out of his sight, Wonderful was pointing at her crotch. "Cock and fruits," she mouthed, miming a chopping action with one open hand. "Cock…and…" Then when Yon looked around peered at her fingernails like she'd done nothing.

"Up already?" Flood came limping between the sleepers and the fires along with a man Beck didn't know, lean with a mop of grey-streaked hair.

"Our youngest woke us," grunted Wonderful. "Drofd was having a feel of Beck's weapon."

"You can see how it can happen, though..." said Yon.

"You can check mine over if you like." Flood grabbed the mace at his belt and stuck it up at an angle. "It's got a big lump on the end!" Drofd gave a chuckle at that, but it seemed most of the rest weren't in a laughing mood. Beck surely weren't. "No?" Flood looked around at 'em expectantly. "It's 'cause I'm old, ain't it? You can say. It's 'cause I'm old."

"Old or not, I'm glad you're here," said Wonderful, one eyebrow up. "The Union won't dare attack now we've got you two."

"Never would have given 'em the chance but I had to go for a piss."

"Third of the night?" asked Yon.

Flood peered up at the sky. "Think it was the fourth."

"Which is why they call him Flood," murmured Wonderful under her breath. "'Case you were wondering."

"I ran into Scorry Tiptoe on the way." Flood jerked his thumb at the lean man beside him.

Tiptoe took a while weighing up the words, then spoke 'em soft. "I was taking a look around."

"Find anything out?" asked Wonderful.

He nodded, real slow, like he'd come upon the secret of life itself. "There's a battle on." He slid down next to Beck on crossed legs and held out a hand to him. "Scorry Tiptoe."

"On account of his gentle footfall," said Drofd. "Scouting, mostly. And back rank, with a spear, you know."

Beck gave it a limp shake. "Beck."

"Red Beck," threw in Drofd. "That's his name. Got it yesterday. Off Reachey. Down in the fight in Osrung. Now he's joined up...with us... you know..." He trailed off, Beck and Scorry both frowning at him, and huddled down into his blanket.

"Craw give you the talk?" asked Scorry.

"The talk?"

"About the right thing."

"He mentioned it."

"Wouldn't take it too seriously."

"No?"

Scorry shrugged. "Right thing's a different thing for every man." And he started pulling knives out and laying 'em on the ground in front of him, from a huge great thing with a bone handle only just this side of a short sword to a tiny little curved one without even a grip, just a pair of rings for two fingers to fit in.

"That for peeling apples?" asked Beck.

Wonderful drew a finger across her sinewy neck. "Slitting throats."

Beck thought she was probably having a laugh at him, then Scorry spat onto a whetstone and that little blade gleamed in the firelight and suddenly he weren't so sure. Scorry pressed it to the stone and gave it a lick both ways, snick, snick, and all of a sudden there was a thrashing of blankets.

"Steel!" Whirrun sprang up, reeling about, sword all tangled up with his bed. "I hear steel!"

"Shut up!" someone called.

Whirrun tore his sword free, jerking his hood out of his eyes. "I'm awake! Is it morning?" Seemed the stories about Whirrun of Bligh being always ready were a bit overdone. He let his sword drop, squinting up at the black sky, stars peeping between shreds of cloud. "Why is it dark? Have no fear, children, Whirrun is among you and ready to fight!"

"Thank the dead," grunted Wonderful. "We're saved."

"That you are, woman!" Whirrun pulled his hood back, scratched at his hair, plastered flat on one side and sticking out like a thistle on the other. He stared about the Heroes and, seeing nought but guttering fires, sleeping men and the same old stones as ever, crawled up close to the flames, yawning. "Saved from dull conversation. Did I hear some talk of names?"

"Aye," muttered Beck, not daring to say more. It was like having Skarling himself to talk to. He'd been raised on stories about Whirrun of Bligh's high deeds. Listened to old drunk Scavi tell 'em down in the village, and begged for more. Dreamed of standing beside him as an equal, claiming a place in his songs. Now here he was, sitting beside him as fraud, and coward, and friend-killer. He dragged his mother's cloak tight, felt something crusted under his fingers. Realised the cloth was still stiff with Reft's blood and had to stop a shiver. Red Beck. He'd blood on his hands, all right. But it didn't feel like he'd always dreamed it would.

"Names, is it?" Whirrun lifted his sword and stood it on end in the firelight, looking too long and too heavy ever to make much sense as a weapon. "This is the Father of Swords, and men have a hundred names for it." Yon closed his eyes and sank back, Wonderful rolled hers up towards the sky, but Whirrun droned on, deep and measured, like it was a speech he'd given often before. "Dawn Razor. Grave-Maker. Blood Harvest. Highest and

Lowest. Scac-ang-Gaioc in the valley tongue which means the Splitting of the World, the battle that was fought at the start of time and will be fought again at its end. This is my reward and my punishment both. My blessing and my curse. It was passed to me by Daguf Col as he lay dying, and he had it from Yorweel the Mountain who had it from Four-Faces who had it from Leef-reef-Ockang, and so on 'til the world was young. When Shoglig's words come to pass and I lie bleeding, face to face with the Great Leveller at last, I'll hand it on to whoever I think best deserves it, and will bring it fame, and the list of its names, and the list of the names of the great men who wielded it, and the great men who died by it, will grow, and lengthen, and stretch back into the dimness beyond memory. In the valleys where I was born they say it is God's sword, dropped from heaven."

"Don't you?" asked Flood.

Whirrun rubbed some dirt from the crosspiece with his thumb. "I used to."

"Now?"

"God makes things, no? God is a farmer. A craftsman. A midwife. God gives things life." He tipped his head back and looked up at the sky. "What would God want with a sword?"

Wonderful pressed one hand to her chest. "Oh, Whirrun, you're so fuck-ing *deep*. I could sit here for hours trying to work out everything you meant."

"Whirrun of Bligh don't seem so deep a name," said Beck, and regretted it straight away when everyone looked at him, Whirrun in particular.

"No?"

"Well... you're from Bligh, I guess. Ain't you?"

"Never been there."

"Then—"

"I couldn't honestly tell you how it came about. Maybe Bligh's the only place up there folk down here ever heard of." Whirrun shrugged. "Don't hardly matter. A name's got nothing in it by itself. It's what you make of it. Men don't brown their trousers when they hear the Bloody-Nine because of the name. They brown their trousers because of the man that had it."

"And Cracknut Whirrun?" asked Drofd.

"Straightforward. An old man up near Ustred taught me the trick of cracking a walnut in my fist. What you do is—"

Wonderful snorted. "That ain't why they call you Cracknut."

"Eh?"

"No," said Yon. "It ain't."

"They call you Cracknut for the same reason they gave Cracknut Leef the name," and Wonderful tapped at the side of her shaved head. "Because it's widely assumed your nut's cracked."

"They do?" Whirrun frowned. "Oh, that's less complimentary, the fuckers. I'll have to have words next time I hear that. You've completely bloody spoiled it for me!"

Wonderful spread her hands. "It's a gift."

"Morning, people." Curnden Craw walked slowly up to the fire with his cheeks puffed out and his grey hair twitching in the wind. He looked tired. Dark bags under his eyes, nostrils rimmed pink.

"Everyone on their knees!" snapped Wonderful. "It's Black Dow's right hand!"

Craw pretended to wave 'em down. "No need to grovel." Someone else came behind him. Caul Shivers, Beck realised with a sick lurch in his stomach.

"Y'all right, Chief?" asked Drofd, pulling the bit of meat out of his pocket and offering it over.

Craw winced as he bent his knees and squatted by the fire, put one finger on one nostril, then blew out through the other with a long wheeze like a dying duck. Then he took the meat and had a bite out of it. "The definition of all right changes with the passing winters, I find. I'm about all right by the standards of the last few days. Twenty years ago I'd have considered this close to death."

"We're on a battlefield, ain't we?" Whirrun was all grin. "The Great Leveller's pressed up tight against us all."

"Nice thought," said Craw, wriggling his shoulders like there was someone breathing on his neck. "Drofd."

"Aye, Chief?"

"If the Union come later, and I reckon it's a set thing they will... might be best if you stay out of it."

"Stay out?"

"It'll be a proper battle. I know you've got the bones but you don't have the gear. A hatchet and a bow? The Union got armour, and good steel and all the rest..." Craw shook his head. "I can find you a place behind somewhere—"

"Chief, no, I want to fight!" Drofd looked across at Beck, like he wanted support. Beck had none to give. He wished he could be left behind. "I want to win myself a name. Give me the chance!"

Craw winced. "Name or not, you'll just be the same man. No better. Maybe worse."

"Aye," Beck found he'd said.

"Easy for those to say who have one," snapped Drofd, staring surly at the fire.

"He wants to fight, let him fight," said Wonderful.

Craw looked up, surprised. Like he'd realised he wasn't quite where he'd thought he was. Then he leaned back on one elbow, stretching one boot out towards the fire. "Well. Guess it's your dozen now."

"That's a fact," said Wonderful, nudging that boot with hers. "And they'll all be fighting." Yon slapped Drofd on the shoulder, all flushed and grinning now at the thought of glory. Wonderful reached out and flicked the pommel of the Father of Swords with a fingernail. "Besides, you don't need a great weapon to win yourself a name. Got yours with your teeth, didn't you, Craw?"

"Bite someone's throat out, did you?" asked Drofd.

"Not quite." Craw had a faraway look for a moment, firelight picking out the lines at the corners of his eyes. "First full battle I was in we had a real red day, and I was in the midst. I had a thirst, back then. Wanted to be a hero. Wanted myself a name. We was all sat around the fire-pit after, and I was expecting something fearsome." He looked up from under his eyebrows. "Like Red Beck. Then when Threetrees was considering it, I took a big bite from a piece of meat. Drunk, I guess. Got a bone stuck in my throat. Spent a minute hardly able to breathe, everyone thumping me on the back. In the end a big lad had to hold me upside down 'fore it came loose. Could barely talk for a couple of days. So Threetrees called me Craw, on account of what I'd got stuck in it."

"Shoglig said…" sang Whirrun, arching back to look into the sky, "I would be shown my destiny…by a man choking on a bone."

"Lucky me," grunted Craw. "I was furious, when I got the name. Now I know the favour Threetrees was doing me. His way of trying to keep me level."

"Seems like it worked," croaked Shivers. "You're the straight edge, ain't you?"

"Aye." Craw licked unhappily at his teeth. "A real straight edge."

Scorry gave the straight edge of his latest knife one last flick with the whetstone and picked up the next. "You met our latest recruit, Shivers?" Sticking his thumb sideways. "Red Beck."

"I have." Shivers stared across the fire at him. "Down in Osrung. Yesterday."

Beck had that mad feeling Shivers could see right through him with that eye, and knew him for the liar he was. Made him wonder how none of the others could see it, writ across his face plain as a fresh tattoo. Cold prickled his back, and he pulled his blood-crusted cloak tight again.

"Quite a day yesterday," he muttered.

"And I reckon today'll be another." Whirrun stood and stretched up tall, lifting the Father of Swords high over his head. "If we're lucky."

Still Yesterday

The blue skin stretched as the steel slid underneath it, paint flaking like parched earth, stubbly hairs shifting, red threads of veins in the wide whites near the corners of his eyes. Her teeth ground together as she pushed it in, pushed it in, pushed it in, coloured patterns bursting on the blackness of her closed lids. She could not get that damned music out of her head. The music the violinists had been playing. Were playing still, faster and faster. The husk-pipe they had given her had blunted the pain just as they said it would, but they had lied about the sleep. She twisted the other way, huddling under the blankets. As though you can roll over and leave a day of murder on the other side of the bed.

Candlelight showed around the door, through the cracks between the slats. As the daylight had showed through the door of the cold room where they were kept prisoner. Kneeling in the darkness, plucking at the knots with her nails. Voices outside. Officers, coming and going, speaking with her father. Talking of strategy and logistics. Talking of civilisation. Talking of which one of them Black Dow wanted.

What had happened blurred with what might have, with what should have. The Dogman arrived an hour earlier with his Northmen, saw off the savages before they left the wood. She found out ahead of time, warned everyone, was given breathless thanks by Lord Governor Meed. Captain Hardrick brought help, instead of never being heard from again, and the Union cavalry arrived at the crucial moment like they did in the stories. Then she led the defence, standing atop a barricade with sword aloft and a blood-spattered breastplate, like a lurid painting of Monzcarro Murcatto at the battle of Sweet Pines she once saw on the wall of a tasteless merchant. All mad, and while she spun out the fantasies she knew they were mad, and she wondered if she was mad, but she did it all the same.

And then she would catch something at the edge of her sight, and she was there, as it had been, on her back with a knee crushing her in the stomach and a dirty hand around her neck, could not breathe, all the sick horror that she somehow had not felt at the time washing over her in a rotting tide, and she would rip back the blankets and spring up, and pace round and round the room, chewing at her lip, picking at the scabby bald patch on the side of her head, muttering to herself like a madwoman, doing the voices, doing all the voices.

If she'd argued harder with Black Dow. If she'd pushed, demanded, she could have brought Aliz with her, instead of... in the darkness, her blubbering wail as Finree's hand slipped out of hers, the door rattling shut. A blue cheek bulged as the steel slid underneath it, and she bared her teeth, and moaned, and clutched at her head, and squeezed her eyes shut.

"Fin."

"Hal." He was leaning over her, candlelight picking out the side of his head in gold. She sat up, rubbing her face. It felt numb. As if she was kneading dead dough.

"I brought you fresh clothes."

"Thank you." Laughably formal. The way one might address someone else's butler.

"Sorry to wake you."

"I wasn't asleep." Her mouth still had a strange taste, a swollen feeling from the husk. The darkness in the corners of the room fizzed with colours.

"I thought I should come…before dawn." Another pause. Probably he was waiting for her to say she was glad, but she could not face the petty politeness. "Your father has put me in charge of the assault on the bridge in Osrung."

She did not know what to say. Congratulations. Please, no! Be careful. Don't go! Stay here. Please. Please. "Will you be leading from the front?" Her voice sounded icy.

"Close enough to it, I suppose."

"Don't indulge in any heroics." Like Hardrick, charging out of the door for help that could never come in time.

"There'll be no heroics, I promise you that. It's just…the right thing to do."

"It won't help you get on."

"I don't do it to get on."

"Why, then?"

"Because someone has to." They were so little alike. The cynic and the idealist. Why had she married him? "Brint seems…all right. Under the circumstances." Finree found herself hoping that Aliz was all right, and made herself stop. That was a waste of hope, and she had none to spare.

"How should one feel when one's wife has been taken by the enemy?"

"Utterly desperate. I hope he will be all right."

"All right" was such a useless, stilted expression. It was a useless, stilted conversation. Hal felt like a stranger. He knew nothing about who she really was. How can two people ever really know each other? Everyone went through life alone, fighting their own battle.

He took her hand. "You seem—"

She could not bear his skin against hers, jerked her fingers away as though she was snatching them from a furnace. "Go. You should go."

His face twitched. "I love you."

Just words, really. They should have been easy to say. But she could not do it any more than she could fly to the moon. She turned away from him to face the wall, dragging the blanket over her hunched shoulder. She heard the door shut.

A moment later, or perhaps a while, she slid out of bed. She dressed. She splashed water on her face. She twitched her sleeves down over the scabbing chafe marks on her wrists, the ragged cut up her arm. She opened the door and went through. Her father was in the room on the other side, talking to the officer she saw crushed by a falling cupboard yesterday, plates spilling across the floor. No. A different man.

"You're awake." Her father was smiling but there was a wariness to him, as if he was expecting her to burst into flames and he was ready to grab for a bucket. Maybe she would burst into flames. She would not have been surprised. Or particularly sorry, right then. "How do you feel?"

"Well." Hands closed around her throat and she plucked at them with her nails, ears throbbing with her own heartbeat. "I killed a man yesterday."

He stood, put his hand on her shoulder. "It may feel that way, but—"

"It certainly does feel that way. I stabbed him, with a short steel I stole from an officer. I pushed the blade into his face. Into his face. So. I got one, I suppose."

"Finree—"

"Am I going mad?" She snorted up a laugh, it sounded so stupid. "Things could be so much worse. I should be glad. There was nothing I could do. What can anyone do? What should I have done?"

"After what you have been through, only a madman could feel normal. Try to act as though . . . it is just another day, like any other."

She took a long breath. "Of course." She gave him a smile which she hoped projected reassurance rather than insanity. "It is just another day."

There was a wooden bowl, on a table, with fruit in it. She took an apple. Half-green, half-blood-coloured. She should eat while she could. Keep her strength up. It was just another day, after all.

Still dark outside. Guards stood by torchlight. They fell silent as she passed, watching while pretending not to watch. She wanted to spew all over them, but she tried to smile as if it was just another day, and they did not look exactly like the men who had strained desperately to hold the gates of the inn closed, splinters bursting around them as the savages hacked down the doors.

She stepped from the path and out across the hillside, pulling her coat tight around her. Wind-lashed grass sloped away into the darkness. Patches of sedge tangled at her boots. A bald man stood, coat-tails flapping, looking out across the darkened valley. He had one fist clenched behind him, thumb rubbing constantly, worriedly at forefinger. The other daintily held a cup.

Above him, in the eastern sky, the first faint smudges of dawn were showing.

Perhaps it was the after-effects of the husk, or the sleeplessness, but after what she had seen yesterday the First of the Magi did not seem so terrible. "Another day!" she called, feeling as if she might take off from the hillside and float into the dark sky. "Another day's fighting. You must be pleased, Lord Bayaz!"

He gave her a curt bow. "I—"

"Is it 'Lord Bayaz' or is there a better term of address for the First of the Magi?" She pushed some hair out of her face but the wind soon whipped it back. "Your Grace, or your Wizardship, or your Magicosity?"

"I try not to stand on ceremony."

"How does one become First of the Magi, anyway?"

"I was the first apprentice of great Juvens."

"And did he teach you magic?"

"He taught me High Art."

"Why don't you do some then, instead of making men fight?"

"Because making men fight is easier. Magic is the art and science of forcing things to behave in ways that are not in their nature." Bayaz took a slow sip from his cup, watching her over the rim. "There is nothing more natural to men than to fight. You are recovered, I hope, from your ordeal yesterday?"

"Ordeal? I've almost forgotten about it already! My father suggested that I act as though this is just another day. Then, perhaps it will be one. Any other day I would spend feverishly trying to advance my husband's interests, and therefore my own." She grinned sideways. "I am venomously ambitious."

Bayaz' green eyes narrowed. "A characteristic I have always found most admirable."

"Meed was killed." His mouth opening and closing silently like a fish snatched from the river, plucking at the great rent in his crimson uniform, crashing over with papers sliding across his back. "I daresay you are in need of a new lord governor of Angland."

"His Majesty is." The Magus heaved up a sigh. "But making such a powerful appointment is a complicated business. No doubt some relative of Meed expects and demands the post, but we cannot allow it to become some family bauble. I daresay a score of other great magnates of the Open Council think it their due, but we cannot raise one man too close in power to the crown. The closer they come the less they can resist reaching for it, as your father-in-law could no doubt testify. We could elevate some bureau-crat but then the Open Council would rail about stoogery and they are troublesome enough as it is. So many balances to strike, so many rivalries, and jealousies, and dangers to navigate. It's enough to make one abandon politics altogether."

"Why not my husband?"

Bayaz cocked his head on one side. "You are very frank."

"I seem to be, this morning."

"Another characteristic I have always found most admirable."

"By the Fates, I'm admirable!" she said, hearing the door clatter shut on Aliz' sobs.

"I am not sure how much support I could raise for your husband, how-ever." Bayaz wrinkled his lip as he tossed the dregs from his cup into the dewy grass. "His father stands among the most infamous traitors in the his-tory of the Union."

"Too true. And the greatest of all the Union's noblemen, the first man on the Open Council, only a vote away from the crown." She spoke without considering the consequences any more than a spinning stone considers the water it skims across. "When his lands were seized, his power snuffed out as though it had never existed, I would have thought the nobles felt threat-ened. For all they delighted in his fall they saw in it the shadow of their own. I imagine restoring his son to some prudent fraction of his power might be made to play well with the Open Council. Asserting the rights of the ancient families, and so on."

Bayaz' chin went up a little, his brows drew down. "Perhaps. And?"

"And while the great Lord Brock had allies and enemies in abundance, his son has none. He has been scorned and ignored for eight years. He is part of no faction, has no agenda but faithfully to serve the crown. He has more than proved his honesty, bravery and unquestioning loyalty to his Majesty on the field of battle." She fixed Bayaz with her gaze. "It would be a fine story to tell. Instead of lowering himself to dabble in base politics, our monarch chooses to reward faithful service, merit and old-time heroism. The commoners would enjoy it, I think."

"Faithful service, merit and heroism. Fine qualities in a soldier." As though talking about fat on a pig. "But a lord governor is first a politician. Flexibility, ruthlessness and an eye for expediency are more his talents. How is your husband there?"

"Weak, but perhaps someone close to him could supply those qualities."

She fancied Bayaz had the ghost of a smile about his lips. "I am beginning to suspect they could. You make an interesting suggestion."

"You have not thought of everything, then?"

"Only the truly ignorant believe they have thought of everything. I might even mention it to my colleagues on the Closed Council when we next meet."

"I would have thought it would be best to make a choice swiftly, rather than to allow the whole thing to become... an issue. I cannot be considered impartial but, even so, I truly believe my husband to be the best man in the Union."

Bayaz gave a dry chuckle. "Who says I want the best man? It may be that a fool and a weakling as lord governor of Angland would suit everyone better. A fool and a weakling with a stupid, cowardly wife."

"That, I am afraid, I cannot offer you. Have an apple." And she tossed it at him, made him juggle it with one hand before catching it in the other, his cup tumbling into the sedge, his brows up in surprise. Before he could speak she was already walking away. She could hardly even remember what their conversation had been about. Her mind was entirely taken up with the way that blue cheek bulged as steel slid underneath it, pushing it in, pushing it in.

For What We Are About to Receive...

It's an awful fine line between being raised above folk like a leader and being raised above 'em like a hanged man on display. When Craw climbed up on an empty crate to give his little speech, he had to admit he felt closer to the latter. A sea of faces opened up in front of him, the

Heroes packed with men from one side of the circle to the other and plenty more pressing in outside. Didn't help that Black Dow's own Carls were the grimmest, darkest, toughest-looking crowd you'd find anywhere in the North. And you'll find a lot of tough crowds in the North. Probably these were a long stretch more interested in doing plunder, rape and murder than anyone's idea of the right thing, and didn't care much who got on the pointy end of it either.

Craw was glad he had Jolly Yon, and Flood, and Wonderful stood frowning around the crate. He was even gladder he had Whirrun just beside. The Father of Swords was enough metal to add some weight to anyone's words. He remembered what Threetrees told him when he made him his Second. He was trying to be their leader, not their lover, and a leader's best feared first, and liked afterward.

"Men o' the North!" he bellowed into the wind. "'Case you didn't hear, Splitfoot's dead, and Black Dow's put me in his place." He picked out the biggest, nastiest, most scornful-looking bastard in the whole crowd, a man looked like he shaved with an axe, and leaned towards him. "Do what I fucking tell you!" he snarled. "That's your job now." He lingered on him for long enough to make the point he feared nothing, even if the opposite was closer to the truth. "Keeping everyone alive, that's mine. There's a strong likelihood I ain't going to succeed in every case. That's war. Won't stop me trying, though. And by the dead it won't stop you lot trying either."

They milled about a little, a long way from won over. Time to list the pedigree. Bragging weren't his strong suit these days but there'd be no prize for modesty. "My name's Curnden Craw, and I'm thirty years a Named Man! I stood Second to Rudd Threetrees, back in the day." That name got a nodding rustle of approval. "The Rock of Uffrith himself. Held a shield for him when he fought his duel with the Bloody-Nine." That name got a bigger one. "Then I fought for Bethod, and now Black Dow. Every battle you pricks heard of I had a part in." He curled his lip. "So safe to say you needn't worry about whether I'm up to the task." Even if Craw was worrying his bowels loose over it himself. But his voice rang out gruff and deep still. Thank the dead for his hero's voice, even if time had given him a coward's guts.

"I want each man here to do the right thing today!" he roared. "And before you start sneering and I'm forced to stick my boot up your arse, I ain't talking about patting children on the head, or giving your last crust to a squirrel, or even being bolder'n Skarling once the blades are drawn. I ain't talking about acting the hero." He jerked his head towards the stones around them. "You can leave that to the rocks. They won't bleed for it. I'm talking about standing by your Chief! Standing with your crew! Standing with the man beside you! And above all I'm talking about not getting your-selves fucking killed!"

He picked Beck out with a pointed finger. "Look at this lad here. Red Beck, his name." Beck's eyes went wide as the whole front rank of killers turned to look at him. "He did the right thing yesterday. Stuck in a house in Osrung with the Union breaking down the door. Listened to his Chief. Stood with his kind. Kept his head. Put four o' the bastards in the mud and came through alive." Maybe Craw was flowering up the truth a little but that was the point of a speech, wasn't it? "If a lad o' seventeen years can keep the Union out of a shack, I reckon men o' your experience should have no trouble keeping 'em off a hill like this one here. And since everyone knows how rich the Union is ... no doubt they'll leave plenty behind 'em as they go running down that slope, eh?" That got a bit of a laugh at least. Nothing worked like tickling their greed.

"That's all!" he bellowed. "Find your places!" And he hopped down, little wobble as his knee jarred but at least he kept standing. No applause, but he reckoned he'd won enough of 'em over not to get stabbed in his back before the battle was done. And in this company that was about as much as he could've hoped for.

"Nice speech," said Wonderful.

"You reckon?"

"Not sure about the whole right thing bit, though. You have to say that?"

Craw shrugged. "Someone should."

You may have heard some commotion this morning." Colonel Vallimir gave the assembled officers and sergeants of his Majesty's First Regiment a stern glance. "That was the sound of a raid by the Northmen."

"That was the sound of someone fucking up," muttered Tunny. He'd known that as soon as he heard the clamour floating across from the east. There's no better recipe for fuck-ups than night-time, armies and surprises.

"There was some confusion on the front line..."

"Further fuck-ups," muttered Tunny.

"Panic spread in the darkness..."

"Several more," muttered Tunny.

"And..." Vallimir grimaced. "The Northmen made off with two standards."

Tunny opened his mouth a crack, but he lacked the words for that. A disbelieving murmur went through the gathering, clear in spite of the wind shaking the branches. Vallimir shouted them down.

"The standards of the Second and Third were captured by the enemy! General Mitterick is..." The colonel gave the impression of choosing his words with great care. "Not happy."

Tunny snorted. Mitterick wasn't happy at the best of times. What effect having two of his Majesty's standards stolen from under his nose might have on the man was anyone's guess. Probably if you stuck a pin in him right now he'd explode and take half the valley with him. Tunny realised he was clutching the standard of the First with extra-special care, and made his fists relax.

"To make matters a great deal worse," Vallimir went on, "apparently we were sent orders to attack yesterday afternoon and they never reached us." Forest gave Tunny a hard look sideways but he could only shrug. Of Lederlingen there was still no sign. Possibly he'd volunteered for desertion. "By the time the next set came it was dark. So Mitterick wants us to make up for it today. As soon as there's light, the general will launch an assault on Clail's Wall in overwhelming force."

"Huh." Tunny had heard a lot about overwhelming force the last few days and the Northmen were still decidedly underwhelmed.

"The wall at this far western end he's going to leave to us, though. The enemy cannot possibly spare enough men to hold it once the attack is underway. As soon as we see them leave the wall, we cross the river and take them in the flank." Vallimir slapped one hand with the other to illustrate the point. "And that'll be the end of them. Simple. As soon as they leave the wall, we attack. Any questions?"

What if they don't leave the wall? was the one that immediately occurred, but Tunny knew a great deal better than to make himself conspicuous in front of a crowd of officers.

"Good." Vallimir smiled as though silence meant the plan must be perfect, rather than just that his men were too thick, eager or cautious to point out its shortcomings. "We're missing half our men and all our horses, but that won't stop his Majesty's First, eh? If everyone does his duty today, there's still time for all of us to be heroes."

Tunny had to choke off his scornful laughter as the thick, eager, cautious officers broke up and began to drift into the trees to make their soldiers ready. "You hear that, Forest? We can all be heroes."

"I'll settle for living out the day. Tunny, I want you to get up to the tree-line and keep a watch on the wall. Need some experienced eyes up there."

"Oh, I've seen it all, Sergeant."

"And then some more, I don't doubt. The very instant you see the Northmen start to clear out, you give the signal. And Tunny?" He turned back. "You won't be the only one watching, so don't even think about pulling anything clever. I still remember what happened with that ambush outside Shricta. Or what didn't happen."

"No evidence of wrongdoing, and I'm quoting the tribunal there."

"Quoting the tribunal, you're a piece of work."

"First Sergeant Forest, I am crushed that a colleague would hold so low an opinion of my character."

"What character?" called Forest after him as he threaded his way uphill through the trees. Yolk was crouched in the bushes pretty much where they'd been crouching all night, peering across the stream through Tunny's eyeglass.

"Where's Worth?" Yolk opened his mouth. "On second thought, I can guess. Any signs of movement?" Yolk opened his mouth again. "Other than in Trooper Worth's bowels, that is?"

"None, Corporal Tunny."

"Hope you don't mind if I check." He snatched the eyeglass without waiting for an answer and scanned along the line of the wall, uphill from the stream, towards the east, where it disappeared over a hump in the land. "Not that I doubt your expertise…" There was no one in front of the dry-stone but he could see spears behind it, a whole lot of them, just starting to show against the dark sky.

"No movement, right, Corporal?"

"No, Yolk." Tunny lowered his eyeglass and gave his neck a scratch. "No movement."

* * *

General Jalenhorm's entire division, reinforced by two regiments from Mitterick's, was drawn up in parade-ground order on the gentle slope of grass and shingle that led down to the shallows. They faced north. Towards the Heroes. Towards the enemy. *So we got that much right, at least.*

Gorst had never seen so many arrayed for battle in one place and at one time, dwindling into darkness and distance on either side. Above their massed ranks a thicket of spears and barbed pole-arms jutted, the pennants of companies fluttered, and in one spot nearby the gilded standard of the King's Own Eighth Regiment snapped in the stiff breeze, proudly displaying several generations of battle honours. Lamps cast pools of light, picking out clutches of solemn faces, striking sparks from polished steel. Here and there mounted officers waited to hear orders and give them, swords shouldered. A ragged handful of the Dogman's Northmen stood near the water's edge, gawping up towards this military multitude.

For the occasion General Jalenhorm had donned a thing more work of art than piece of armour: a breastplate of mirror-bright steel engraved front and back with golden suns whose countless rays became swords, lances, arrows, entwined with wreaths of oak and laurel in the most exquisite craftsmanship.

"Wish me luck," he murmured, then gave his horse his heels and nudged it up the shingle towards the front rank.

"Good luck," whispered Gorst.

The men were quiet enough that one could hear the faint ringing as Jalenhorm drew his sword. "Men of the Union!" he thundered, holding it high. "Two days ago many of you were among those who suffered a defeat at the hands of the Northmen! Who were driven from the hill you see ahead of us. The fault that day was entirely mine!" Gorst could hear other voices echoing the general's words. Officers repeating the speech to those too far away to hear the original. "I hope, and I trust, that you will help me gain redemption today. Certainly I feel a great pride to be given the honour of leading men such as you. Brave men of Midderland, of Starikland, of Angland. Brave men of the Union!"

Staunch discipline prevented anyone from shouting out but a kind of murmur still went up from the ranks. Even Gorst felt a patriotic lifting of his chin. *A jingoistic misting of the eye. Even I, who should know so much better.*

"War is terrible!" Jalenhorm's horse pawed at the shingle and he brought it under control with a tug of the reins. "But war is wonderful! In war, a man can find out all he truly is. All he can be. War shows us the worst of men – their greed, their cowardice, their savagery! But it also shows us the best – our courage, our strength, our mercy! Show me your best today! And more than that, show it to the enemy!"

There was a brief pause as the distant voices relayed the last sentence, and as members of Jalenhorm's staff let it be known that the address was at an end, then the men lifted their arms as one and gave a thunderous cheer. Gorst realised after a moment that he was making his own piping contribution, and stopped. The general sat with his sword raised in acknowledgement, then turned his back on the men and rode towards Gorst, his smile fading.

"Good speech. Far as these things go." The Dogman was slouched in the battered saddle of a shaggy horse, blowing into his cupped palms.

"Thank you," answered the general as he reined in. "I tried simply to tell the truth."

"The truth is like salt. Men want to taste a little, but too much makes everyone sick." The Dogman grinned at them both. Neither replied. "Quite some piece of armour, too."

Jalenhorm looked down, somewhat uncomfortably, at his magnificent breastplate. "A gift from the king. It never seemed like quite the right occasion before…" *But if one shouldn't make an effort when charging to one's doom, then, really, when should one?*

"So what's the plan?" asked the Dogman.

Jalenhorm swept his arm towards his waiting division. "The Eighth and Thirteenth Foot and the Stariksa Regiment will lead off." *He makes it sound like a wedding dance. I suspect the casualties will be higher.* "The Twelfth and the Aduan Volunteers will form our second wave." *Waves break on a beach, and melt away into the sand, and are forgotten.* "The remnants of the Rostod Regiment and the Sixth will follow in reserve." *Remnants, remnants. We all will be remnants, in due course.*

The Dogman puffed his cheeks out as he looked at the massed ranks. "Well, you've no shortage of bodies, anyway." *Oh no, and no shortage of mud to bury them in either.*

"First we cross the shallows." Jalenhorm pointed towards the twisting channels and sandbars with his sword. "I expect they will have skirmishers hidden about the far bank."

"No doubt," said the Dogman.

The sword drifted up towards the rows of fruit trees, just becoming visible on the sloping ground between the glimmering water and the base of the hill. "We expect some resistance as we pass through the orchards." *More than some, I imagine.*

"We might be able to flush 'em out of the trees."

"But you have no more than a few score men over here."

The Dogman winked. "There's more to war than numbers. Few o' my boys are already across the river, lying low. Once you're over, just give us a chance. If we're able to shift 'em, fine, if not, you've lost nothing."

"Very well," said Jalenhorm. "I am willing to take any course that might save lives." *Ignoring the fact that the entire business is an exercise in slaughter.* "Once the orchards are in our hands…" His sword drifted implacably up the bare hillside, pointing out the smaller stones on the southern spur, then the larger ones on the summit, glowing faintly orange in the light of guttering fires. He shrugged, letting his sword drop. "We climb the hill."

"You climb that hill?" asked the Dogman, eyebrows high.

"Indeed."

"Fuck." Gorst could only silently concur. "They've been up there two days now. Black Dow's all kinds of things but he's no fool, he'll be ready. Stakes planted, and ditches dug, and men at the drystone walls, and arrows showering down, and—"

"Our purpose is not necessarily to drive them off," Jalenhorm interrupted, grimacing as though there were arrows showering on him already. "It is to fix them in place while General Mitterick on the left, and Colonel Brock on the right, force openings on the flanks."

"Aye," said the Dogman, somewhat uncertainly.

"But we hope we may achieve much more than that."

"Aye, but, I mean…" The Dogman took a deep breath as he frowned up towards the hill. "Fuck." *I'm not sure I could have said it better.* "You sure about this?"

"My opinion does not enter into the case. The plan is Marshal Kroy's, on the orders of the Closed Council and the wishes of the king. My responsibility is the timing."

"Well, if you're going to go, I wouldn't leave it too long." The Dogman nodded to them, then turned his shaggy horse away. "Reckon we'll have rain later. And lots of it!"

Jalenhorm peered up at the sullen sky, bright enough now to see the clouds flowing quickly across it, and sighed. "The timing is in my hands. Across the river, through the orchards, and straight up the hill. Just go north, basically. That should be within my capabilities, I would have thought." They sat in silence for a moment. "I wanted very much to do the right thing, but I have proved myself to be . . . not the greatest tactical mind in his Majesty's army." He sighed again. "At least I can still lead from the front."

"With the greatest respect, might I suggest you remain behind the lines?"

Jalenhorm's head jerked around, astonished. *At the words themselves or at hearing me speak more than three together? People talk to me as though they were talking to a wall, and they expect the same return.* "Your concern for my safety is touching, Colonel Gorst, but—"

"Bremer." *I might as well die with one person in the world who knows me by my first name.*

Jalenhorm's eyes went even wider. Then he gave a faint smile. "Truly touching, Bremer, but I am afraid I could not consider it. His Majesty expects—"

Fuck his Majesty. "You are a good man." *A floundering incompetent, but still.* "War is no place for good men."

"I respectfully disagree, on both counts. War is a wonderful thing for redemption." Jalenhorm narrowed his eyes at the Heroes, seeming so close now, just across the water. "If you smile in the face of danger, acquit yourself well, stand your ground, then, live or die, you are made new. Battle can make a man . . . clean, can't it?" *No. Wash yourself in blood and you come out bloody.* "Only look at you. I may or may not be a good man, but you are without doubt a hero."

"Me?"

"Who else? Two days ago, here at these very shallows, you charged the enemy alone and saved my division. An established fact, I witnessed part of the action myself. And yesterday you were at the Old Bridge?" Gorst frowned at nothing. "You forced a crossing when Mitterick's men were mired in the filth, a crossing that may very well win this battle for us today. You are an inspiration, Bremer. You prove that one man still can be worth something in the midst of . . . all this. You do not need to fight here today, and yet you stand ready to give your life for king and country." *To toss it away for a king who does not care and a country which cannot.* "Heroes are a great deal rarer than good men."

"Heroes are quickly fashioned from the basest materials. Quickly fashioned, and quickly replaced. If I qualify, they are worthless."

"I beg to differ."

"Differ, by all means, but please . . . remain behind the lines."

Jalenhorm gave a sad little smile, and he reached out, and tapped at Gorst's dented shoulder-plate with his fist. "Your concern for my safety really is touching, Bremer. But I'm afraid I cannot do it. I cannot do it any more than you can."

"No." Gorst frowned up towards the hill, a black mass against the stained sky. "A shame."

Calder squinted through his father's eyeglass. Beyond the circle of light cast by all the lamps, the fields faded into shifting blackness. Down towards the Old Bridge he could pick out spots of brightness, perhaps the odd glint of metal, but not much more. "Do you think they're ready?"

"I can see horses," said Pale-as-Snow. "A lot of horses."

"You can? I can't see a bloody thing."

"They're there."

"You think they're watching?"

"I reckon they are."

"Mitterick watching?"

"I would be."

Calder squinted up at the sky, starting to show grey between the fast-moving clouds. Only the most committed optimist could've called it dawn, and he wasn't one. "Guess it's time, then."

He took one more swig from the flask, rubbed at his aching bladder, then passed it over to Pale-as-Snow and clambered up the stack of crates, blinking into the lamplight, conspicuous as a shooting star. He took a look over his shoulder at the ranks of men ranged behind him, dark shapes in front of the long wall. He didn't really understand them, or like them, and they felt the same about him, but they had one powerful thing in common. They'd all basked in his father's glory. They'd been great men because of who they served. Because they'd sat at the big table in Skarling's Hall, in the places of honour. They'd all fallen a long way when Calder's father died.

It looked like none of them could stand to fall any further, which was a relief, since a Chief without soldiers is just a very lonely man in a big bloody field.

He was very much aware of all those eyes on him as he unlaced. The eyes of a couple of thousand of his boys behind, and a fair few of Tenways' too, and the eyes of a few thousand Union cavalry ahead, he hoped, General Mitterick among them, ready to pop his skull with anger.

Nothing. Try to relax or try to push? Bloody typical, that would be, all this effort and he found he couldn't go. To make matters worse the wind was keen and it was freezing the end of his prick. The man holding up the flag on his left, a grizzled old Carl with a great scar right across one cheek, was watching his efforts with a slightly puzzled expression.

"Can you not look?" snapped Calder.

"Sorry, Chief." And he cleared his throat and almost daintily averted his eyes.

Maybe it was being called Chief that got him over the hump. Calder felt that hint of pain down in his bladder, and he grinned, let it build, let his head drop back, looked up at the bruised sky.

"Hah." Piss showered out, drops shining in the lamplight, and spattered all over the first flag with a sound like rain on the daisies. Behind Calder, a wave of laughter swept down the lines. Easily pleased, maybe, but large bodies of fighting men don't tend to go for subtle jokes. They go for shit, and piss, and people falling over.

"And some for you too." He sent a neat arc across the other flag, and he smirked towards the Union as wide as he could. Behind him men started to jump up, and dance about, and jeer across the barley. He might not be much of a warrior, or a leader, but he knew how to make men laugh, and how to make them angry. With his free hand he pointed up at the sky, and he gave a great whoop, and he shook his hips around and sent piss shooting all over the place. "I'd shit on 'em too," he shouted over his shoulder, "but I'm all bound up from White-Eye's stew!"

"I'll shit on 'em!" someone shrieked, to a scattering of shrill chuckles.

"Save it for the Union, you can shit on them when they get here!"

And the men whooped and laughed, shook their weapons at the sky and clattered them against their shields and sent up quite the happy din. A couple had even climbed up on the wall and were pissing at the Union lines themselves. Maybe they found it a good deal funnier because they knew what was coming, just across the other side of the barley, but still Calder smiled to hear it. At least he'd stood up, and done one thing worth singing about. At least he'd given his father's men a laugh. His brother's men. His men.

Before they all got fucking murdered.

Beck thought he could hear laughter echoing on the wind, but he'd no idea what anyone might have to laugh about. It was getting light enough to see across the valley now. Light enough to get an idea of the Union's numbers. To begin with Beck hadn't believed those faint blocks on the other side of the shallows could be solid masses of men. Then he'd tried to make himself believe they weren't. Now there was no denying it.

"There are thousands of 'em," he breathed.

"I know!" Whirrun was nearly jumping with happiness. "And the more there are, the more our glory, right, Craw?"

Craw took a break from chewing his nails. "Oh, aye. I wish there were twice as many."

"By the dead, so do I!" Whirrun dragged in a long breath and blew it through a beaming smile. "But you never know, maybe they've got more out of sight!"

"We can hope," grunted Yon out of the corner of his mouth.

"I fucking love war!" squeaked Whirrun. "I fucking love it, though, don't you?"

Beck didn't say anything.

"The smell of it. The feel of it." He rubbed one hand up and down the stained sheath of his sword, making a faint swishing sound. "War is honest. There's no lying to it. You don't have to say sorry here. Don't have to hide. You cannot. If you die? So what? You die among friends. Among worthy foes. You die looking the Great Leveller in the eye. If you live? Well, lad, that's living, isn't it? A man isn't truly alive until he's facing death." Whirrun stamped his foot into the sod. "I love war! Just a shame Ironhead's down there on the Children. Do you reckon they'll even get all the way up here, Craw?"

"Couldn't say."

"I reckon they will. I hope they will. Better come before the rain starts, though. That sky looks like witch's work, eh?" It was true there was a strange colour to the first hint of sunrise, great towers of sullen-looking cloud marching in over the fells to the north. Whirrun bounced up and down on his toes. "Oh, bloody hell, I can't wait!"

"Ain't they people too, though?" muttered Beck, thinking of the face of that Union man lying dead in the shack yesterday. "Just like us?"

Whirrun squinted across at him. "More than likely they are. But if you start thinking like that, well . . . you'll get no one killed at all."

Beck opened his mouth, then closed it. Didn't seem much he could say to that. Made about as much sense as anything else had happened the last few days.

"It's easy enough for you," grunted Craw. "Shoglig told you the time and place of your death and it ain't here."

Whirrun's grin got bigger. "Well, that's true and I'll admit it's a help to my courage, but if she'd told me here and she'd told me now, do you really reckon that'd make any difference to me?"

Wonderful snorted. "You might not be yapping about it so bloody loud."

"Oh!" Whirrun wasn't even listening. "They're off already, look! That's early!" He pointed the Father of Swords at arm's length to the west, towards the Old Bridge, flinging his other arm around Beck's shoulders. The strength in it was fearsome, he nearly lifted Beck without even trying. "Look at the pretty horses!" Beck couldn't see much down there but dark land, the glimmer of the river and a speckling of lights. "That's fresh of 'em, isn't it, though? That's cheeky! Getting started and it's hardly dawn!"

"Too dark for riding," said Craw, shaking his head.

"They must be as bloody eager as I am. Reckon they mean business today, eh, Craw? Oh, by the dead," and he shook his sword towards the valley, dragging Beck back and forth and nearly right off his feet, "I reckon there'll be some songs sung about today!"

"I daresay," grunted Wonderful through gritted teeth. "Some folk'll sing about any old shit."

The Riddle of the Ground

Here they come," said Pale-as-Snow, utterly deadpan, as if there was nothing more worrying than a herd of sheep on its way. It hardly needed an announcement. Calder could hear them, however dark it was. First the long note of a trumpet, then the whispering rustle of horses through crops, far off but closing, sprinkled with calls, whinnies, jingles of harness that seemed to tickle at Calder's clammy skin. All faint, but all crushingly inevitable. They were coming, and Calder hardly knew whether to be smug or terrified. He settled on a bit of both.

"Can't believe they fell for it." He almost wanted to laugh it was so ridiculous. Laugh or be sick. "Those arrogant fucks."

"If you can rely on one thing in a battle, it's that men rarely do what's sensible." Good point. If Calder had any sense he'd have been on horseback himself, spurring hard for somewhere a long, long way away. "That's what made your father the great man. Always kept a cold head, even in the fire."

"Would you say we're in the fire now?"

Pale-as-Snow leaned forward and carefully spat. "I'd say we're about to be. Reckon you'll keep a cold head?"

"Can't see why." Calder's eyes darted nervously to either side, across the snaking line of torches before the wall. The line of his men, following the gentle rise and fall of the earth. "The ground is a puzzle to be solved," his father used to say, "the bigger your army, the harder the puzzle." He'd been a master at using it. One look and he'd known where to put every man, how to make each slope, and tree, and stream, and fence fight on his side. Calder had done what he could, used each tump and hummock and ranged his archers behind Clail's Wall, but he doubted that ribbon of waist-high farmer's drystone would give a warhorse anything more than a little light exercise.

The sad fact was a flat expanse of barley didn't offer much help. Except to the enemy, of course. No doubt they were delighted.

It was an irony Calder hadn't missed that his father was the one who'd smoothed off this ground. Who'd broken up the little farms in this valley and a lot of others. Pulled up the hedgerows and filled in the ditches so there could be more crops grown, and taxes paid, and soldiers fed. Rolled out a golden carpet of welcome to the matchless Union cavalry.

Calder could just make out, against the dim fells on the far side of the valley, a black wave through the black sea of barley, sharpened metal glimmering at the crest. He found himself thinking about Seff. Her face coming up so sharp it caught his breath. He wondered if he'd see that face again, if he'd live to kiss his child. Then the soft thoughts were crushed under the drumming of hooves as the enemy broke into a trot. The shrill calls of officers as they struggled to keep the ranks closed, to keep hundreds of tons of horseflesh lined up in one unstoppable mass.

Calder glanced over to the left. Not too far off the ground sloped up towards Skarling's Finger, the crops giving way to thin grass. Much better ground, but it belonged to that flaking bastard Tenways. He glanced over to the right. A gentler upward slope, Clail's Wall hugging the middle, then disappearing out of sight as the ground dropped away to the stream. Beyond the stream, he knew, were woods full of more Union troops, eager to charge into the flank of his threadbare little line and rip it to tatters. But enemies Calder couldn't see were far from his most pressing problem. It was the hundreds, if not thousands, of heavily armed horsemen bearing down from dead ahead, whose treasured flags he'd just pissed on, that were demanding his attention. His eyes flickered over that tide of cavalry, details starting from the darkness now, hints of faces, of shields, lances, polished armour.

"Arrows?" grunted White-Eye, leaning close beside him.

Best to look like he had some idea how far bowshot was, so he waited a moment longer before he snapped his fingers. "Arrows."

White-Eye roared the order and Calder heard the bowstrings behind him, shafts flickering overhead, flitting down into the crops between them and the enemy, into the enemy themselves. Could little bits of wood and metal really do any damage to all that armoured meat, though?

The sound of them was like a storm in his face, pressing him back as they closed and quickened, streaming north towards Clail's Wall and the feeble line of Calder's men. The hooves battered the shaking land, threshed crops flung high. Calder felt a sudden need to run. A shock through him. Found he was edging back despite himself. To stand against that was mad as standing under a falling mountain.

But he found he was less afraid with every moment, and more excited. All his life he'd been dodging this, ferreting out excuses. Now he was facing it, and finding it not so terrible as he'd always feared. He bared his teeth at the dawn. Almost smiling. Almost laughing. Him, leading Carls into battle. Him, facing death. And suddenly he was standing, and spreading his arms in welcome, and roaring nothing at the top of his lungs. Him, Calder, the liar, the coward, playing the hero. You never can tell who'll be called on to fill the role.

The closer the riders came the lower they leaned over their horses, lances swinging down. The faster they moved, stretching to a lethal gallop, the slower time seemed to crawl. Calder wished he'd listened to his father when he'd talked about the ground. Talked about it with a far-off look like a man remembering a lost love. Wished he'd learned to use it like a sculptor uses stone. But he'd been busy showing off, fucking and making enemies that would dog him for the rest of his life. So yesterday evening, when he'd looked at the ground and seen it thoroughly stacked against him, he'd done what he did best.

Cheat.

The horsemen had no chance of seeing the first pit, not in that darkness and those crops. It was only a shallow trench, no more than a foot deep and a foot wide, zigzagging through the barley. Most horses went clean over it without even noticing. But a couple of unlucky ones put a hoof right in, and they went down. They went down hard, a thrashing mass of limbs, tangled straps, breaking weapons, flying dust. And where one went down, more went down behind, caught up in the wreck.

The second pit was twice as wide and twice as deep. More horses fell, snatched away as the front rank ploughed into it, one flailing man flung high, lance still in his hand. The order of the rest, already crumbling in their eagerness to get at the enemy, started to come apart altogether. Some plunged onwards. Others tried to check as they realised something was wrong, spreading confusion as another flight of arrows fell among them. They became a milling mass, almost as much of a threat to each other as they were to Calder and his men. The terrible thunder of hooves became a sorry din of scrapes and stumbles, screams and whinnies, desperate shouting.

The third pit was the biggest of all. Two of them, in fact, about as straight as a Northman could dig by darkness and angling roughly inwards. Funnelling Mitterick's men on both sides towards a gap in the centre where the precious flags were set. Where Calder was standing. Made him wonder, as he gaped at the mob of plunging horses converging on him, whether he should have found somewhere else to stand, but it was a bit late for that.

"Spears!" roared Pale-as-Snow.

"Aye," muttered Calder, brandishing his sword as he took a few cautious steps back. "Good idea."

And Pale-as-Snow's picked men, who'd fought for Calder's brother and his father at Uffrith and Dunbrec, at the Cumnur and in the High Places, came up from behind the wind-blown barley five ranks deep, howling their high war cry, and their long spears made a deadly thicket, points glittering as the first sunlight crept into the valley.

Horses screamed and skidded, tumbled over, tossed their riders, driven onto the spears by the weight of those behind. A crazy chorus of shrieking steel and murdered men, tortured wood and tortured flesh. Spear shafts bent and shattered, splinters flying. A new gloom of kicked-up dirt and trampled barley dust and Calder coughing in the midst of it, sword dangling from his limp hand.

Wondering what strange convergence of mischances could have allowed this madness to happen. And what other one might allow him to get out of it alive.

Onwards and Upwards

D o you suppose we could call that dawn?" asked General Jalenhorm.

Colonel Gorst shrugged his great shoulders, battered armour rattling faintly.

The general looked down at Retter. "Would you call that dawn, boy?"

Retter blinked at the sky. Over in the east, where he imagined Osrung was though he'd never been there, the heavy clouds had the faintest ominous tinge of brightness about their edges. "Yes, General." His voice was a pathetic squeak and he cleared his throat, rather embarrassed.

General Jalenhorm leaned close and patted his shoulder. "There's no shame in being scared. Bravery is being scared, and doing it anyway."

"Yes, sir."

"Just stay close beside me. Do your duty, and everything will be well."

"Yes, sir." Though Retter was forced to wonder how doing his duty might stop an arrow. Or a spear. Or an axe. It seemed a mad thing to him to be climbing a hill as big as that one, with slavering Northmen waiting for them on the slopes. Everyone said they were slavering. But he was only thirteen, and had been in the army for six months, and didn't know much but polishing boots and how to sound the various manoeuvres. He wasn't even entirely sure what the word manoeuvres meant, just pretended. And there was nowhere safer to be than close by the general and a proper hero like Colonel Gorst, albeit he looked nothing like a hero and sounded like one less. There wasn't the slightest glitter about the man, but Retter supposed if you needed a battering ram at short notice he'd make a fair substitute.

"Very well, Retter." Jalenhorm drew his sword. "Sound the advance."

"Yes, sir." Retter carefully wet his lips with his tongue, took a deep breath and lifted his bugle, suddenly worried that he'd fumble it in his sweaty hand, that he'd blow a wrong note, that it would somehow be full of mud and produce only a miserable fart and a shower of dirty water. He had nightmares about that. Maybe this would be another. He very much hoped it would be.

But the advance rang out bright and true, tooting away as bravely as it ever had on the parade ground. "Forward!" the bugle sang, and forward went Jalenhorm's division, and forward went Jalenhorm himself, and Colonel Gorst, and a clump of the general's staff, pennants snapping. So, with some reluctance, Retter gave his pony his heels, and clicked his tongue, and forward he went himself, hooves crunching down the bank then slopping out into the sluggish water.

He supposed he was one of the lucky ones since he got to ride. At least he'd come out of this with dry trousers. Unless he wet himself. Or got wounded in the legs. Either one of which seemed quite likely, come to think of it.

A few arrows looped over from the far bank. Exactly from where, Retter couldn't say. He was more interested in where they were going. A couple plopped harmlessly into the channels ahead. Others were lost among the ranks where they caused no apparent damage. Retter flinched as one pinged off a helmet and spun in among the marching soldiers. Everyone else had armour. General Jalenhorm had what looked like the most expensive armour in the world. It hardly seemed fair that Retter didn't have any, but the army wasn't the place for fair, he supposed.

He snatched a look back as his pony scrambled from the water and up onto a little island of sand, driftwood gathered in a pale tangle at one end. The shallows were filled with soldiers, marching up to ankles, or knees, or even waists in places. Behind them the whole long bank was covered by ranks of men waiting to follow, still more appearing over the brow behind them. It made Retter feel brave, to be one among so many. If the Northmen killed a hundred, if they killed a thousand, there would still be thousands more. He wasn't honestly sure how many a thousand was, but it was a lot.

Then it occurred to him that was all very well unless you were one of the thousand flung in a pit, in which case it wasn't very good at all, especially since he'd heard only officers got coffins, and he really didn't want to lie pressed up cold against the mud. He looked nervously towards the orchards, flinched again as an arrow clattered from a shield a dozen strides away.

"Keep up, lad!" called Jalenhorm, spurring his horse onto the next bar of shingle. They were half way across the shallows now, the great hill looming up ever steeper beyond the trees ahead.

"Sir!" Retter realised he was hunching his shoulders, pressing himself down into his saddle to make a smaller target, realised he looked a coward and forced himself straight. Over on the far bank he saw men scurrying from a patch of scrubby bushes. Ragged men with bows. The enemy, he realised. Northern skirmishers. Close enough to shout at, and be heard. So close it seemed a little silly. Like the games of chase he used to play behind the barn. He sat up taller, forced his shoulders back. They looked every bit as scared as he was. One with a shock of blond hair knelt to shoot an arrow which came down harmlessly in the sand just ahead of the front rank. Then he turned and hurried off towards the orchards.

Curly ducked into the trees along with the rest, rushed through the apple-smelling darkness bent low, heading uphill. He hopped over the felled logs and came up kneeling on the other side, peering off to the south. The sun was barely risen and the orchards were thick with shadows. He could see the metal gleaming to either side, men hidden in a long line through the trees.

"They coming?" someone asked. "They here?"

"They're coming," said Curly. Maybe he'd been the last to run but that was nothing much to take pride in. They'd been rattled by the sheer number of the bastards. It was like the land was made of men. Seething with 'em. Hardly seemed worth sitting there on the bank, no cover but a scraggy bush or two, just a few dozen shooting arrows at all that lot. Pointless as going at a swarm of bees with a needle. Here in the orchard was a better place to give 'em a test. Ironhead would understand that. Curly hoped to hell he would.

They'd got all mixed up with some folks he didn't know on the way back. A tall old-timer with a red hood was squatting by him in the dappled shadows. Probably one of Golden's boys. There was no love lost between Golden's lot and Ironhead's most of the time. Not much more'n there was between Golden and Ironhead themselves, which was less than fuck all. But right now they had other worries.

"You see the number of 'em?" someone squeaked.

"Bloody hundreds."

"Hundreds and hundreds and hundreds and—"

"We ain't here to stop 'em," growled Curly. "We slow 'em, we put a couple down, we give 'em something to think about. Then, when we have to, we pull back to the Children."

"Pull back," someone said, sounding like it was the best idea he'd ever heard.

"When we have to!" snapped Curly over his shoulder.

"They got Northmen with 'em too," someone said, "some o' the Dogman's boys, I reckon."

"Bastards," someone grunted.

"Aye, bastards. Traitors." The man with the red hood spat over their log. "I heard the Bloody-Nine was with 'em."

There was a nervy silence. That name did no favours for anyone's courage.

"The Bloody-Nine's back to the mud!" Curly wriggled his shoulders. "Drowned. Black Dow killed him."

"Maybe." The man with the red hood looked grim as a gravedigger. "But I heard he's here."

A bowstring went right by Curly's ear and he spun around. "What the—"

"Sorry!" A young lad, bow trembling in his hand. "Didn't mean to, just—"

"The Bloody-Nine!" It came echoing out of the trees on their left, a mad yell, slobbering, terrified. "The Bloody—" It cut off in a shriek, long drawn out and guttering away into a sob. Then a burst of mad laughter in the orchard ahead, making the collar prickle at Curly's sweaty neck. An animal sound. A devil sound. They all crouched there for a stretched-out moment – staring, silent, disbelieving.

"Shit on this!" someone shouted, and Curly turned just in time to see one of the lads running off through the trees.

"I ain't fighting the Bloody-Nine! I ain't!" A boy scrambling back, kicking up fallen leaves.

"Get back here, you bastards!" Curly snarled, waving his bow about, but it was too late. His head snapped around at another blubbering scream. Couldn't see where it came from but it sounded like hell, right enough.

"The Bloody-Nine!" came roaring again out of the gloom on the other side. He thought he could see shadows in the trees, flashes of steel, maybe. There were others running, right and left. Giving up good spots behind their logs without a shaft shot or a blade drawn. When he turned back, most of his lads were showing their backs. One even left his quiver behind, snagged on a bush.

"Cowards!" But there was naught Curly could do. A Chief can kick one or two boys into line, but when the lot of 'em just up and run he's helpless. Being in charge can seem like a thing iron-forged, but in the end it's just an idea everyone agrees to. By the time he ducked back behind the log everyone had stopped agreeing, and far as he could tell it was just him and the stranger with the red hood.

"There he is!" he hissed, stiffening up all of a sudden. "It's him!"

That madman's laughter echoed through the trees again, bouncing around, coming from everywhere and nowhere. Curly nocked an arrow, his hands sticky, his bow sticky in 'em. Eyes jerking around, catching one slice of slashed-up shade then another, jagged branches and the shadows of jagged branches. The Bloody-Nine was dead, everyone knew that. What if he weren't, though?

"I don't see nothing!" His hands were shaking, but shit on it, the Bloody-Nine was just a man, and an arrow would kill him as dead as anyone else. Just a man is all he was, and Curly weren't running from one man no matter how fucking hard, no matter if the rest of 'em were running, no matter what. "Where is he?"

"There!" hissed the man with the red hood, catching him by the shoulder and pointing off into the trees. "There he is!"

Curly raised his bow, peering into the darkness. "I don't—Ah!" There was a searing pain in his ribs and he let go of the string, arrow spinning off harmless into the dirt. Another searing pain, and he looked down, and he saw the man with the red hood had stabbed him. Knife hilt right up against his chest, and the hand dark with blood.

Curly grabbed a fistful of the man's shirt, twisted it. "Wha..." But he didn't have the breath in him to finish, and he didn't seem to be able to take another.

"Sorry," said the man, wincing as he stabbed him again.

Red Hat took a quick look about, make sure no one was watching, but it looked like Ironhead's boys were all too busy legging it out of the orchards and uphill towards the Children, a lot of 'em with brown trousers, more'n likely. He'd have laughed to see it if it weren't for the job he'd just had to do. He laid down the man he'd killed, patting him gently on his bloody chest as his eyes went dull, still with that slightly puzzled, slightly upset look.

"Sorry 'bout that." A hard reckoning for a man who'd just been doing his job the best he could. Better'n most, since he'd chosen to stick when the rest had run. But that's how war is. Sometimes you're better off doing a worse job. This was the black business and there was no use crying about it. Tears'll wash no one clean, as Red Hat's old mum used to tell him.

"The Bloody-Nine!" he shrieked, broken and horror-struck as he could manage. "He's here! He's here!" Then he gave a scream as he wiped his knife on the lad's jerkin, still squinting into the shadows for signs of other holdouts, but signs there were none.

"The Bloody-Nine!" someone roared, no more'n a dozen strides behind. Red Hat turned and stood up.

"You can stop. They've gone."

The Dogman's grey face slid from the shadows, bow and arrows loose in one hand. "What, all of 'em?"

Red Hat pointed down at the corpse he'd just made. "All but a few."

"Who'd have thought it?" The Dogman squatted beside him, a few more of his lads creeping out from the trees behind. "The work you can get done with a dead man's name."

"That and a dead man's laugh."

"Colla, get back there and tell the Union the orchards are clear."

"Aye." And one of the others scurried off through the trees.

"How does it look up ahead?" Dogman slid over the logs and stole towards the treeline, keeping nice and low. Always careful, the Dogman, always sparing with men's lives. Sparing o' lives on both sides. Rare thing in a War Chief, and much to be applauded, for all the big songs tended to harp on spilled guts and what have you. They squatted there in the brush, in the shadows. Red Hat wondered how long the pair of 'em had spent squatting in the brush, in the shadows, in one damp corner of the North or another. Weeks on end, more'n likely. "Don't look great, does it?"

"Not great, no," said Red Hat.

Dogman eased his way closer to the edge of the trees and hunkered down again. "And it looks no better from here."

"Wasn't going to, really, was it?"

"Not really. But a man needs hope."

The ground weren't offering much. A couple more fruit trees, a scrubby bush or two, then the bare hillside sloped up sharp ahead. Some runners were still struggling up the grass and beyond them, as the sun started throwing some light onto events, the ragged line of some digging in. Above that the tumbledown wall that ringed the Children, and above that the Children themselves.

"All crawling with Ironhead's boys, no doubt," muttered the Dogman, speaking Red Hat's very thoughts.

"Aye, and Ironhead's a stubborn bastard. Always been tricky to shift, once he gets settled."

"Like the pox," said Dogman.

"And about as welcome."

"Reckon the Union'll need more'n dead heroes to get up there."

"Reckon they'll need a few living ones too."

"Aye."

"Aye." Red Hat shielded his eyes with one hand, realised too late he'd got blood stuck all over the side of his face. He thought he could see a big man standing up on the diggings below the Children, shouting at the stragglers as they fled. Could just hear his bellowing voice. Not quite the words, but the tone spoke plenty.

Dogman was grinning. "He don't sound happy."

"Nope," said Red Hat, grinning too. As his old mum used to say, there's no music so sweet as an enemy's despair.

You fucking coward bastards!" snarled Irig, and he kicked the last of 'em on the arse as he went past, bent over and gasping from the climb, knocked him on his face in the muck. Better'n he deserved. Lucky he only got Irig's boot, rather'n his axe.

"Fucking bastard cowards!" sneered Temper at a higher pitch, and kicked the coward in the arse again as he started to get up.

"Ironhead's boys don't run!" snarled Irig, and he kicked the coward in the side and rolled him over.

"Ironhead's boys never run!" And Temper kicked the lad in the fruits as he tried to scramble off and made him squeal.

"But the Bloody-Nine's down there!" shouted another, his face milk pale and his eyes wide as shit-pits, cringing like a babe. A worried muttering followed the name, rippling through the boys all waiting behind the ditch. "The Bloody-Nine. The Bloody-Nine? The Bloody-Nine. The—"

"*Fuck,*" snarled Irig, "the Bloody-Nine!"

"Aye," hissed Temper. "Fuck him. Fucking fuck him!"

"Did you even see him?"

"Well...no, I mean, not myself, but—"

"If he ain't dead, which he is, and if he's got the bones, which he don't, he can come up here." And Irig leaned close to the lad, and tickled him under the chin with the spike on the end of his axe. "And he can deal with me."

"Aye!" Temper was nearly shrieking it, veins popping out his head. "He can come up here and deal with...with him! With Irig! That's right! Ironhead's going to hang you bastards for running! Like he hung Crouch, and cut his guts out for treachery, he'll fucking do the same to you, he will, and we'll—"

"You think you're helping?" snapped Irig.

"Sorry, Chief."

"You want names? We got Cairm Ironhead up there at the Children. And at his back on the Heroes, we got Cracknut Whirrun, and Caul Shivers, and Black Dow his bloody self, for that matter—"

"Up there," someone muttered.

"Who said that?" shrieked Temper. "Who fucking well said—"

"Any man who stands now," Irig held up his axe and gave it a shake with each word, since he'd often found a shaken axe adds an edge to the bluntest of arguments, "and does his part, he'll get his place at the fire and his place in the songs. Any man runs from this spot here, well," and Irig spat onto the curled-up coward next to his boot. "I won't put Ironhead to the trouble o' passing judgement, I'll just give you to the axe, and there's an end on it."

"An end!" shrieked Temper.

"Chief." Someone was tugging at his arm.

"Can't you see I'm trying to—" snarled Irig, spinning around. "Shit."

Never mind the Bloody-Nine. The Union were coming.

Colonel, you must dismount."

Vinkler smiled. Even that was an effort. "Couldn't possibly."

"Sir, really, this is no time for heroics."

"Then…" Vinkler glanced across the massed ranks of men emerging from the fruit trees to either side. "When is the time, exactly?"

"Sir—"

"The bloody leg just won't manage it." Vinkler winced as he touched his thigh. Even the weight of his hand on it was agonising now.

"Is it bad, sir?"

"Yes, sergeant, I think it's quite bad." He was no surgeon, but he was twenty years a soldier and well knew the meaning of stinking dressings and a mottling of purple-red bruises about a wound. He had, in all honesty, been surprised to wake at all this morning.

"Perhaps you should retire and see the surgeon, sir—"

"I have a feeling the surgeons will be very busy today. No, Sergeant, thank you, but I'll press on." Vinkler turned his horse with a twitch of the reins, worried that the man's concern would cause his courage to weaken. He needed all the courage he had. "Men of his Majesty's Thirteenth!" He drew his sword and directed its point towards the scattering of stones high above them. "Forward!" And with his good heel he urged his horse up onto the slope.

He was the only mounted man in the whole division now, as far as he could tell. The rest of the officers, General Jalenhorm and Colonel Gorst among them, had left their horses in the orchard and were proceeding on foot. Only a complete fool would have chosen to ride up a hill as steep as this one, after all. Only a fool, or the hero from an unlikely storybook, or a dead man.

The irony was that it hadn't even been much of a wound. He'd been run through at Ulrioch, all those years ago, and Lord Marshal Varuz had visited him in the hospital tent, and pressed his sweaty hand with an expression of deep concern, and said something about bravery which Vinkler had often wished he could remember. But to everyone's surprise, his own most of all, he had lived. Perhaps that was why he had thought nothing of a little nick on the thigh. Now it gave every appearance of having killed him.

"Bloody appearances," he forced through gritted teeth. The only thing for it was to smile through the agony. That's what a soldier was meant to do. He had written all the necessary letters and supposed that was something. His wife had always worried there would be no goodbye.

Rain was starting to flit down. He could feel the odd spot against his face. His horse's hooves were slipping on the short grass and it tossed and snorted, making him grimace as his leg was jolted. Then a flight of arrows went up ahead. A great number of arrows. Then they began to curve gracefully downwards, falling from on high.

"Oh, bloody hell." He narrowed his eyes and hunched his shoulders instinctively as a man might stepping from a porch into a hailstorm. Some of them dropped down around him, sticking silently into the turf to either side. He heard clanks and rattles behind as they bounced from shields or armour. He heard a shriek, followed by another. Shouting. Men hit.

Damned if he was going to just sit there. "Yah!" And Vinkler gave his horse the spurs, wincing as it lurched up the hill, well ahead of his men. He stopped perhaps twenty strides from the enemy's earthworks. He could see the archers peering down, their bows picked out black against the sky, which was starting to darken again, drizzle prickling at Vinkler's helmet. He was terribly close. An absurdly easy target. More arrows whizzed past him. With a great effort he turned in his saddle and, lips curled back against the pain, stood in his stirrups, raising his sword.

"Men of the Thirteenth! At the double now! Have you somewhere else to be?"

A few soldiers fell as more arrows whipped past into the front rank, but the rest gave a hearty roar and broke into something close to a run, which was a damned fine testament to their spirit after the march they'd already had.

Vinkler became aware of an odd sensation in his throbbing leg, looked down, and was surprised to see an arrow poking from his dead thigh. He burst out laughing. "That's my least vulnerable spot, you bloody arseholes!" he roared at the Northmen on the earthworks. The foremost of his charging men were level with him now, pounding up the hill, yelling.

An arrow stuck deep into his horse's neck. It reared, and Vinkler bounced in his saddle, only just keeping hold of the reins, which proved a waste of time anyway as his mount tottered sideways, twisted, fell. There was an almighty thud.

Vinkler tried to shake the dizziness from his head. He tried to look about him but was trapped beneath his horse. Worse yet, it seemed he had crushed one of his soldiers and the man's spear had run him through as he fell. The bloody blade of it was poking through Vinkler's hip now, just under his breastplate. He gave a helpless sigh. It seemed that, wherever you put armour, you never had it where you needed it.

"Dear, dear," he said, looking down at the broken arrow-shaft protruding from his leg, the spear-point from his hip. "What a mess." It hardly hurt, that was the strange thing. Maybe that was a bad sign, though. Probably. Boots were thumping at the dirt all around him as his men charged up the hill. "On you go, boys," waving one hand weakly. They would have to make it the rest of the way without him. He looked towards the earthworks, not far off. Not far off at all. He saw a wild-haired man perched there, bow levelled at him.

"Oh, damn," he said.

Temper shot at the bastard who'd been on the horse. He was flattened under it, and no danger to no one, but a man acting that bloody fearless within shot of Temper's bow was an insult to his aim. As luck had it, luck being a fickle little shit, his elbow got jogged just as he was letting go the string and he shot his shaft off high into the air.

He snatched at another arrow, but by then things were getting a bit messy. A bit more'n a bit. The Union were up to the ditch they'd dug and the earth wall they'd thrown up, and Temper wished now they'd dug it a deal deeper and thrown it up a deal higher, 'cause there were a bloody lot of Southerners crowding round it, and plenty more on the way.

Irig's boys were packed in on the packed earth, jabbing down with spears, doing a lot of shouting. Temper saw a fair few spears jabbing the other way too. He went up on tiptoes trying to see, then lurched out the way of Irig's axe as it flashed past his nose. Once his blood was going that big bastard didn't care much who got caught on the backswing.

A Northman staggered past, tangling with Temper and nearly dragging him over, scrabbling at his chest as blood bubbled through his torn chain mail. A Union man sprang up onto the earth-wall in the gap he'd left like he was on a bloody spring. A neckless bastard with a great heavy jaw and hard brows wrinkled over hard little eyes. No helmet but thick plates of scuffed armour on the rest of him, shield in one hand, heavy sword in the other already dark with blood.

Temper stumbled away from him, since he only had his bow to hand and had always liked to keep fighting at a polite distance anyway, making way for a more willing Carl whose sword was already swinging. Neckless seemed off balance, the blade sure to take his head right off, but in one quick movement he blocked it with a clang of steel, and blood showered, and the Carl reeled back onto his face. Before he was still, Neckless had hit another man so hard he took him right off his feet, turned him over in the air and sent him tumbling down the hillside.

Temper scrambled back up the slope, mouth wide open and salty with someone's blood, sure he was looking the Great Leveller in the face at last, and an ugly face it was, too. Then Irig came rushing from the side, axe following close behind.

Neckless went down hard, a great dent smashed into his shield. Temper hooted with laughter but the Union man only went down as far as his knees would bend then burst straight back up, flinging Irig's great bulk away and slicing him across the guts all in one motion, sending him staggering, blood spraying from his chain mail coat, eyes popping more with shock than pain. Just couldn't believe he'd been done so easy, and neither could Temper. How could a man run up that hill and still move so hard and so fast at the top of it?

"It's the Bloody-Nine!" someone wailed, though it bloody obviously weren't the Bloody-Nine at all. He was causing quite a bloody panic all the same. Another Carl went at him with a spear and he slid around it, sword crashing down and leaving a mighty dent in the middle of the Carl's helmet, folding him on his face, arms and legs thrashing mindless in the mud.

Temper gritted his teeth, raised his bow, took a careful bead on the neckless bastard, but just as Temper let go the string Irig pushed himself up, clutching his bloody guts with one hand while he raised his axe in the other. Luck being luck, he got himself right in the way of the arrow and it took him in the shoulder, made him grunt.

The Union man's eyes flicked sideways, and his sword flicked out with 'em and took Irig's arm off just like that, and almost before the blood began to spurt from the stump the blade lashed back the other way and ripped a bloody gash in his chest, back the other way and laid Irig's head wide open between his mouth and his nose, top teeth snatched through the air and off down the hill.

Neckless crouched there still, dented shield up in front, sword up behind, big face all spotted with red and his eyes ahead, calm as a fisherman waiting for a tug on the line. Four carved Northmen dead as ever a man could be at his feet and Irig toppling gently sideways and into the ditch, even deader.

He might as well have been the Bloody-Nine, this neckless bastard, Carls falling over 'emselves to get away from him. More Union men started to pull themselves up to either side, over the earth wall in numbers, and the shift backwards became a run.

Temper went with 'em, as eager as any. He caught an elbow in the neck from someone, slipped over and slapped his chin on the grass, gave his tongue an awful bite, scrambled up and ran on, men shouting and shrieking all around. He snatched one desperate look back, saw Neckless hack down a running Carl calmly as you might swat a fly. Beside him a tall Union man in a bright breastplate was pointing towards Temper with a drawn blade, shouting at the top of his voice.

On!" roared Jalenhorm, waving his sword towards the Children. Bloody hell, he was out of breath. "Up! Up!" They had to keep the momentum. Gorst had opened the gate a crack, and they had to push through before it closed. "On! On!" He bent down, offering his hand to haul men over the ditch and slapping them on the back as they laboured off uphill again.

It looked as if the fleeing Northmen were causing chaos at the drystone wall above, tangling with the defenders there, spreading panic, letting the foremost of Jalenhorm's men clamber up after them without resistance. As soon as he had the breath to do it he followed himself, lurching up the steep slope. He had to push on.

Bodies. Bodies, and wounded men scattered on the grass. A Northman stared at him, bloody hands clapped to the top of his head. A Union soldier clutched dumbly at his oozing thigh. A soldier running just beside him made a hiccupping sound and fell on his back, and when Jalenhorm glanced over his shoulder he saw the man had an arrow in his face. He could not stop for him. Could only press on, swallowing a sudden wave of nausea. His own thudding heartbeat and his own whooshing breath damped the war cries and the clashes of metal down to an endless nagging rattle. The thickening drizzle was far from helping, turning the trampled grass slippery slick. The world jumped and wobbled, full of running men, slipping and sliding men, occasional whirring arrows, flying grass and mud.

"On," he grunted, "on." No one could have heard him. It was himself he was ordering. "On." This was his one chance at redemption. If they could only capture the summit. Break the Northmen where they were strongest. "Up. Up." Then nothing else would matter. He would be no longer the king's incompetent old drinking partner, who fumbled his command on the first day. He would have finally earned his place. "On," he wheezed, "up!"

He pushed on, bent over, clawing at the wet grass with his free hand, so intent on the ground that the wall caught him by surprise. He stood, waving his sword uncertainly, not sure whether it would be held by his men or the enemy, or what he should do about it in either case. Someone reached down with a gloved hand. Gorst. Jalenhorm found himself hauled up with shocking ease, scrambled over the damp stones and onto the flat top of the spur.

The Children stood just ahead. Much larger at close quarters than he had imagined, a circle of rough-hewn rocks a little higher than a man. There were more bodies here, but fewer than on the slopes below. It seemed resistance had been light and, for the moment at least, had disappeared altogether. Union soldiers stood about in various stages of exhausted confusion. Beyond them the hill sloped up towards the summit. Towards the

Heroes themselves. A gentler incline, and covered with retreating North-men. More of an organised withdrawal than a rout this time, from what Jalenhorm could gather at a glance.

A glance was all he could manage. With no immediate peril, his body sagged. He stood for a moment, hands on his knees, chest heaving, belly squeezing uncomfortably against the inside of his wondrous breastplate with every in-breath. Damn thing didn't bloody fit him any more. It had never bloody fit him.

"The Northmen are falling back!" Gorst's weird falsetto jangled in Jalen-horm's ears. "We must pursue!"

"General! We should regroup." One of Jalenhorm's staff, his armour beaded with wet. "We're well ahead of the second wave. Too far ahead." He gestured towards Osrung, shrouded now in the thickening rain. "And Northern cavalry have attacked the Stariksa Regiment, they're bogged down on our right—"

Jalenhorm managed to straighten up. "The Aduan Volunteers?"

"Still in the orchard, sir!"

"We're getting split up from our support—" chimed in another.

Gorst waved them angrily away, his piping voice making a ludicrous contrast with his blood-spotted aspect. He barely even looked out of breath. "Damn the support! We press on!"

"General, sir, Colonel Vinkler is dead, the men are exhausted, we must pause!"

Jalenhorm stared up at the summit, chewing at his lip. Seize the moment, or wait for support? He saw the spears of the Northmen against the darken-ing sky. Gorst's eager, red-speckled face. The clean, nervous ones of his staff. He winced, looked at the handful of men to hand, then shook his head. "We will hold here a little while for reinforcements. Secure this posi-tion and gather our strength."

Gorst had the expression of a boy who had been told he could not have a puppy this year. "But, General—"

Jalenhorm put a hand on his shoulder. "I share your eagerness, Bremer, believe me, but not everyone can run for ever. Black Dow is ready, and cun-ning, and this retreat might only be a ruse. I do not intend to be fooled by him a second time." He squinted up, the clouds getting steadily angrier above them. "The weather is against us. As soon as we have the numbers,

we must attack." They might not be resting long. Union soldiers were
flooding over the wall now, choking the stone circle.

"Where's Retter?"

"Here, sir," called the lad. He looked pale, and scared, but so did
they all.

Jalenhorm smiled to see him. There, indeed, was a hero. "Sound the
assembly, boy, and ready on the advance."

They could not be reckless, but nor could they afford to waste the initiative. This was their one chance at redemption. Jalenhorm stared yearningly
up at the Heroes, rain tinkling on his helmet. So very near. The last Northmen were swarming up the slopes towards the top. One stood, looking back
through the rain.

Ironhead frowned back towards the Children, already riddled with Union
soldiers.

"Shit," he hissed.

Hurt him to do this. He'd a hard-won name for never giving ground,
but he hadn't won it in fights he was sure to lose. He wasn't about to face
the might of the Union on his own just so men could blow their noses and
say Cairm Ironhead died bravely. He'd no plans to follow after Whitesides,
or Littlebone, or Old Man Yawl. They'd all died bravely, and who sang
about those bastards these days?

"Pull back!" he bellowed at the last of his men, urging 'em between the
planted stakes and up towards the Heroes. A shameful thing to show your
back to the enemy, but better their eyes on your back than their spears in
your front. If Black Dow wanted to fight for this worthless hill and these
worthless stones he could do it his worthless self.

He strode up frowning through the thickening rain, through the gap in
the mossy wall that ringed the Heroes. He walked slow, shoulders back and
head high, hoping folk would think this was all well planned and he'd done
nothing the least bit cowardly—

"Well, well, well. Who should I find running away from the Union but
Cairm Ironhead?" Who else but Glama Golden, the swollen prick, leaning
against one of the great stones with a big, fat smile on his big, bruised face.

By the dead, how Ironhead hated this bastard. Those big puffy cheeks.
That moustache, like a pair of yellow slugs on his fat top lip. Ironhead's

skin crawled at the sight of him. The sight of him smug made him want to tear his own eyes out. "Pulling back," he growled.

"Showing back, I'd call it."

That got a few laughs, but they sputtered out as Ironhead came forwards, baring his teeth. Golden took a careful step back, narrowed eyes flickering down to Ironhead's drawn sword, hand dropping to his own axe, making ready.

Then Ironhead stopped himself. He hadn't got his name by letting anger tug him about by the nose. There was a right time to settle this, and a right way, and it wasn't now, standing on even terms with all kinds of witnesses. No. He'd wait for his moment, and make sure he enjoyed it too. So he forced his face into a smile of his own. "We can't all have your record of bravery, Glama Golden. Takes some bones to batter a man's fist with your face the way you did."

"Least I fucking fought, didn't I?" snarled Golden, his Carls bristling up around him.

"If you can call it fighting when a man just falls off his horse then runs away."

Golden's turn to bare his teeth. "You dare talk to me about running away, you cowardly—"

"Enough." Black Dow had Curnden Craw on his left, Caul Shivers on his right and Cracknut Whirrun just behind. That and a whole crowd of heavy-armed, heavy-scarred, heavy-scowled Carls. A fearsome company, but the look on Dow's face was more fearsome still. He was rigid with rage, eyes bulging as if they might burst. "This what you call Named Men these days? A pair o' great big names with a pair o' sulking *children* hiding inside?" Dow curled his tongue and blew spit onto the mud between Ironhead and Golden. "Rudd Threetrees was a stubborn bastard, and Bethod a sly bastard, and the Bloody-Nine an evil bastard, the dead know that, but there are times I miss 'em. Those were *men!*" He roared the word in Ironhead's face, spraying spit and making everyone flinch. "They said a thing, they *did a fucking thing!*"

Ironhead thought it best to make a second quick retreat, eyes on Black Dow's ready weapons just in case an even quicker one was needful. He was no keener on that fight than he was on the one with the Union. Even less, if anything, but luckily Golden couldn't resist sticking his broken nose in.

"I'm with you, Chief!" he piped up. "With you all the way!"

"Is that right?" Dow turned to him, mouth curling with contempt. "Oh, lucky *fucking* me!" And he shouldered Golden out of his way and led his men towards the wall.

When Ironhead turned back he found Curnden Craw giving him a look from under his grey brows. "What?" he snapped.

Craw just kept giving him that look. "You know what."

He shook his head as he brushed between Ironhead and Golden. They were a sorry excuse for a pair of War Chiefs. For a pair of men, for that matter, but Craw had seen worse. Selfishness, cowardice and greed never surprised him these days. Those were the times.

"Pair o' fucking worms!" Dow hissed into the drizzle as Craw came up beside him. He clawed at the old drystone, tore loose a rock and stood, every muscle flexed, lips twisting and moving with no sound as if he didn't know whether to fling it down the slope or stave in someone's skull with it or smash his own face with it or what. In the end he just gave a frustrated snarl, and put it helplessly back on top of the wall. "I should kill 'em. Maybe I will. Maybe I will. Burn the fucking pair."

Craw winced. "Don't know they'd take a flame in this weather, Chief." He peered down through the shroud of rain towards the Children. "And I reckon there'll be killing enough for everyone soon." The Union had fearsome numbers down there and, from what he could tell, they were finding their order. Forming ranks. Lots and lots of close-packed ranks. "Looks like they're coming on."

"Why wouldn't they? Ironhead good as invited the bastards." Dow took a scowling breath and snorted it out like a bull ready to charge, breath smoking in the wet. "You'd think it'd be easy being Chief." He shifted his shoulders like the chain sat too heavy on 'em. "But it's like dragging a fucking mountain through the muck. Threetrees told me that. Told me every leader stands alone."

"Ground's still with us." Craw thought he should have a stab at building up the positive. "And this rain'll help too."

Dow only frowned down at his free hand, fingers spread. "Once they're bloody..."

"Chief!" Some lad was forcing his way through the crowd of sodden Carls, shoulders of his jerkin dark with damp. "Chief! Reachey's hard

pressed down in Osrung! They're over the bridge and fighting in the streets
and he needs someone to lend a—Gah!"

Dow grabbed him around the back of his neck, jerked him roughly forward and steered his face towards the Children and the Union men swarming over 'em like ants on a trodden nest. "Do I look like I've got fucking
men to spare? Well? What do you reckon?"

The lad swallowed. "No, Chief?"

Dow shoved him tottering back and Craw managed to stick out a hand
and catch him 'fore he fell. "Tell Reachey to hold on best he can," Dow
tossed over his shoulder. "Might be some help will come along."

"I'll tell him." And the lad backed off quick and was soon lost in the press.

The Heroes was left a strange, funeral quiet. Only the odd mutter, the
faint clatter of gear, the soft ping and patter of rain on metal. Down at the
Children, someone was tooting on a horn. Seemed a mournful little tune,
somehow, floating up out of the rain. Or maybe it was just a tune, and
Craw was the mournful one. Wondering who out of all these men around
him would kill before the sun was set, and who get killed. Wondering
which of them had the Great Leveller's cold hand on their shoulder. Wondering if he did. He closed his eyes, and made himself a promise that if he
got through this he'd retire. Just like he had a dozen times before.

"Looks like it's time." Wonderful was holding out her hand.

"Aye." Craw took it, and shook it, and looked her in the face, her jaw set
hard, her stubbly hair black in the wet, line of the long scar white down the
side. "Don't die, eh?"

"I'm not planning on it. Stick close and I'll try not to let you die either."

"Deal." And they were all grabbing each other's hands, and slapping each
other's shoulders, that last moment of comradeship before the blood, when
you feel bound together closer than with your own family. Craw clasped
hands with Flood, and with Scorry, and with Drofd, and Shivers, even, and
he found himself seeking among strangers for Brack's big paw to shake,
then realised he was under the sod behind 'em.

"Craw." Jolly Yon, and clear from his sorry look what he was after.

"Aye, Yon. I'll tell 'em. You know I will."

"I know." And they clasped hands, and Yon had a twitch to the corner of
his mouth might've been a smile for him. All the while Beck just stood
there, dark hair plastered to pale forehead, staring down towards the Children like he was staring at nothing.

Craw took the lad's hand and gave it a squeeze. "Just do what's right. Stand with your crew, stand with your Chief." He leaned a little closer. "Don't get killed."

Beck squeezed back. "Aye. Thanks, Chief."

"Where's Whirrun?"

"Never fear!" And he came shouldering through the wet and unhappy throng. "Whirrun of Bligh stands among you!"

For reasons known only to himself he'd taken his shirt off and was standing stripped to his waist, Father of Swords over one shoulder. "By the dead," muttered Craw. "Every time we fight you're bloody wearing less."

Whirrun tipped his head back and blinked into the rain. "I'm not wearing a shirt in this. A wet shirt only chafes my nipples."

Wonderful shook her head. "All part of the hero's mystery."

"That too." Whirrun grinned. "How about it, Wonderful? Does a wet shirt chafe your nipples? I need to know."

She shook his hand. "You worry about your nipples, Cracknut, I'll handle mine."

Everything was bright now, and still, and quiet. Water gleaming on armour, furs curled up with wet, bright painted shields beaded with dew. Faces flashed at Craw, known and unknown. Grinning, stern, crazy, afraid. He held out his hand, and Whirrun pressed it in his own, grinning with every tooth. "You ready?"

Craw always had his doubts. Ate 'em, breathed 'em, lived 'em twenty years or more. Hardly a moment free of the bastards. Every day since he buried his brothers.

But now was no time for doubts. "I'm ready." And he drew his sword, and looked down towards the Union men, hundreds upon hundreds, blurring in the rain to spots and splashes and glints of colour, and he smiled. Maybe Whirrun was right, and a man ain't really alive until he faces death. Craw raised his sword up high, and he gave a howl, and all around him men did the same.

And they waited for the Union to come.

More Tricks

The sun had to be up somewhere but you'd never have known it. The angry clouds had thickened and the light was still poor. Positively beggarly, in fact. As far as Corporal Tunny could tell, and somewhat to his surprise, no one had moved. The helmets and spears still showed above the stretch of wall that he could see, shifting a little from time to time but going nowhere fast. Mitterick's attack was well underway. That much they could hear. But on this forgotten far end of the battle, the Northmen waited.

"Are they still there?" asked Worth. Waiting for action like this got most men shitting themselves. Worth was unique, in that it seemed it was the one thing that could stop him.

"They're still there."

"Not moving?" squeaked Yolk.

"If they were moving we'd be moving, wouldn't we?" Tunny peered through his eyeglass once again. "No. They're not moving."

"Is that fighting I can hear?" muttered Worth, as a gust of wind brought the echoing of angry men, horses and metal across the stream.

"It's that or it's a serious disagreement in a stable. Do you think it's a disagreement in a stable?"

"No, Corporal Tunny."

"No. Neither do I."

"Then what's going on?" asked Yolk. A riderless horse appeared from over the rise, stirrups flapping at its flanks, trotted down towards the water, stopped and started nibbling at the grass.

Tunny lowered his eyeglass. "Honestly, I'm not sure." All around them, rain tapped at the leaves.

The trampled barley was scattered with dead and dying horses, dead and dying men. In front of Calder and his stolen standards they were heaped up in a bloody tangle. Only a few strides away, three Carls were arguing with each other as they tried to free their spears, all impaled in the same Union rider. A few boys had been sent scurrying out to gather spent arrows. A couple more had been unable to resist clambering into the third pit to get an early start at picking over the bodies there, and White-Eye was roaring at them to get back into line.

The Union cavalry were all done. A brave effort, but a stupid one. It seemed to Calder the two often went together. To make matters worse, having failed once they'd insisted on giving it another try, still more doomed. Three score or so had jumped the third pit on the right, managed to get over Clail's Wall and kill a few archers before they were shot or speared themselves. All pointless as mopping a beach. That was the trouble with pride, and courage, and all those clench-jawed virtues bards love to harp on. The more you have, the more likely you are to end up bottom in a pile of dead men. All the Union's bravest had achieved was to give Calder's men the biggest boost to their spirits they'd had since Bethod was King of the Northmen.

They were letting the Union know it, now, as the survivors rode, or limped, or crawled back towards their lines. They danced about, and clapped and whooped into the drizzle. They shook each others' hands, and thumped each other's backs, and clashed their shields together. They chanted Bethod's name, and Scale's, and even quite frequently Calder's, which was gratifying. The comradeship of warriors, who would've thought? He grinned around as men cheered and brandished their weapons at him, held up his sword and gave it a wave in return. He wondered whether it was too late to smear a bit of blood on the blade, since he hadn't quite got around to swinging it. There was plenty of blood about and he doubted its previous owners would miss it now.

"Chief?"

"Eh?"

Pale-as-Snow was pointing off to the south. "Might want to pull 'em back into position."

The rain was getting weightier, fat drops leaving the earth spattered with dark spots, pinging from the armour of the living and the dead. It had drawn a misty haze across the battlefield to the south, but beyond the riderless horses aimlessly wandering, and the horseless riders stumbling back towards the Old Bridge, Calder thought he could see shapes moving in the barley.

He shielded his eyes with one hand. More and more emerged from the rain, turning from ghosts to flesh and metal. Union foot. Vast blocks of them, trampling forward in carefully measured, well-ordered, dreadfully purposeful ranks, pole-arms held high, flags struck limp by the wet.

Calder's men had seen them too, and their triumphant jeering was already a memory. The barking voices of Named Men rang through the rain, bringing them grimly back to their places behind the third pit. White-Eye was marshalling some of the lightly wounded to fight as a reserve and plug any holes. Calder wondered if they'd be plugging holes in him before the day was out. It looked a good bet.

"Don't suppose you've got any more tricks?" asked Pale-as-Snow.

"Not really." Unless you counted running like hell. "You?"

"Just the one." And the old warrior carefully wiped the blood from his sword with a rag and held it up.

"Oh." Calder looked down at his own clean blade, glistening with beads of water. "That."

The Tyranny of Distance

I can't see a damn thing!" hissed Finree's father, taking a stride forwards and peering through his eyeglass again, presumably to no more effect than before. "Can you?"

"No, sir," grumbled one of his staff, unhelpfully.

They had witnessed Mitterick's premature charge in stunned silence. Then, as the first light crawled across the valley, the start of Jalenhorm's advance. Then the drizzle had begun. First Osrung had disappeared in the grey pall on the right, then Clail's Wall on the left, then the Old Bridge and the nameless inn where Finree had almost died yesterday. Now even the shallows were half-remembered ghosts. Everyone stood silent, paralysed with anxiety, straining for sounds that would occasionally tickle at the edge of hearing, over the damp whisper of the rain. For all that they could see now, there might as well have been no battle at all.

Finree's father paced back and forth, the fingers of one hand fussing at nothing. He came to stand beside her, staring off into the featureless grey. "I sometimes think there isn't a person in the world more powerless than a supreme commander on a battlefield," he muttered.

"How about his daughter?"

He gave her a tight smile. "Are you all right?"

She thought about smiling back but gave up on it. "I'm fine," she lied, and quite transparently too. Apart from the very real pain through her neck whenever she turned her head, down her arm whenever she used her hand, and across her scalp all the time, she still felt a constant, suffocating worry. Time and again she would startle, staring about like a miser for his lost purse, but with no idea what she was even looking for. "You have far more important things to worry about—"

As if to prove her point he was already striding away to meet a messenger, riding up towards the barn from the east. "News?"

"Colonel Brock reports that his men have begun their attack on the bridge in Osrung!" Hal was in the fight, then. Leading from the front, no doubt. She felt herself sweating more than ever under her clothes, the damp beneath Hal's coat meeting the damp leaking through from above in a crescendo of chafing discomfort. "Colonel Brint, meanwhile, is leading an assault against the savages who yesterday..." His eyes flickered nervously to Finree, and back. "Against the savages."

"And?" asked her father.

"That is all, Lord Marshal."

He grimaced. "My thanks. Please, bring further news when you are able."

The messenger saluted, turned his horse and galloped off through the rain.

"No doubt your husband is distinguishing himself enormously in the assault." Bayaz leaned beside her on his staff, bald pate glistening with moisture. "Leading from the front, in the style of Harod the Great. A latter-day hero! I've always had the greatest admiration for men of that stamp."

"Perhaps you should try it yourself."

"Oh, I have. I was quite the firebrand in my youth. But an unquenchable thirst for danger is unseemly in the old. Heroes have their uses, but someone has to point them the right way. And clean up afterwards. They always raise a cheer from the public, but they leave a hell of a mess." Bayaz thoughtfully patted his stomach. "No, a cup of tea at the rear is more my style. Men like your husband can gather the plaudits."

"You are far too generous."

"Few indeed would agree."

"But where is your tea now?"

Bayaz frowned at his empty hand. "My servant has . . . more important errands to run this morning."

"Can there be anything more important than attending to your whims?"

"Oh, my whims stretch beyond the kettle . . ."

Hoofbeats echoed out of the rain, a lone rider thumping up the track from the west, everyone straining breathlessly to see as a chinless frown emerged from the wet gloom.

"Felnigg!" snapped Finree's father. "What's happening on the left?"

"Mitterick bloody well went off half-drawn!" frothed Felnigg as he swung from the saddle. "Sent his cavalry across the barley in the dark! Pure bloody recklessness!"

Knowing the state of the relationship between the two men, Finree suspected Felnigg had made his own contribution to the fiasco.

"We saw," her father forced through tight lips, evidently coming to a similar conclusion.

"The man should be bloody drummed out!"

"Perhaps later. What was the outcome?"

"It was . . . still in doubt when I left."

"So you haven't the slightest idea what's going on over there?"

Felnigg opened his mouth, then closed it. "I thought it best to return at once—"

"And report Mitterick's mistake, rather than inform me of its consequences. My thanks, Colonel, but I am already amply supplied with ignorance." And her father turned his back before Felnigg had the chance to speak, striding across the hillside again to look fruitlessly to the north. "Shouldn't have sent them," she heard him mutter as he squelched past. "Should never have sent them."

Bayaz sighed, the sound niggling at her sweaty shoulders like a corkscrew. "I sympathise most deeply with your father."

Finree was finding that her admiration for the First of the Magi was steadily fading, while her dislike only sharpened with time. "Do you," she said, in the same way one would say, "Shut up," and with the same meaning.

If Bayaz took it he ignored it. "Such a shame we cannot see the little people struggle from afar. There is nothing quite like looking down upon a battle, and this is a large one, even in my experience. But the weather answers to no one." Bayaz grinned up into the increasingly solemn heavens. "A veritable storm! What drama, eh? What better accompaniment to a clash of arms?"

"Did you call it up yourself just for the atmosphere?"

"I wish I had the power. Only imagine, there could be thunder whenever I approached! In the Old Time my master, great Juvens, could call down lightning with a word, make a river flood with a gesture, summon a hoar frost with a thought. Such was the power of his Art." And he spread his hands wide, tipping his face into the rain and raising his staff towards the streaming heavens. "But that was long ago." He let his arms drop. "These days the winds blow their own way. Like battles. We who remain must work in a more...roundabout fashion."

More hoofbeats, and a dishevelled young officer cantered from the murk ahead.

"Report!" demanded Felnigg at great volume, making Finree wonder how he had lasted so long without being punched in the face.

"Jalenhorm's men have flushed the enemy from the orchards," answered the messenger breathlessly, "and are climbing the slope at the double!"

"How far have they gone?" asked Finree's father.

"When I last saw them they were well on the way up to the smaller stones. The Children. But whether or not they were able to take them—"

"Heavy resistance?"

"Becoming heavier."

"When did you leave them?"

"I rode here with all despatch, sir, so perhaps a quarter of an hour ago?"

Finree's father bared his teeth at the downpour. The outline of the hill the Heroes stood on was little more than a darker smudge in a curtain of grey. She could follow his thoughts. By now they might have captured the summit in glory, be engaged in furious combat, or have been bloodily driven off. Anyone or no one alive or dead, victorious or defeated. He spun on his heel. "Saddle my horse!"

Bayaz' smugness was snuffed out like a candle flame. "I would advise against it. There is nothing you can do down there, Marshal Kroy."

"There is certainly nothing I can do up here, Lord Bayaz," said her father curtly, stepping past him and towards the horses. His staff followed, along with several guards, Felnigg snapping out orders in every direction, the headquarters suddenly alive with rattling activity.

"Lord Marshal!" shouted Bayaz. "I deem this unwise!"

Her father did not even turn. "By all means remain here, then." And he planted one boot in the stirrup and pulled himself up.

"By the dead," hissed Bayaz under his breath.

Finree gave him a sickly smile. "It seems you may be called to the front after all. Perhaps you can see the little people struggle at first hand."

The First of the Magi did not appear amused.

Blood

hey're coming!"

That much Beck knew already, but men were packed so tight into the Heroes he didn't know much else. Wet furs, wet armour, weapons gleaming with rain, scowling faces running with water. The stones themselves were streaky shadows, ghosts beyond a forest of jagged spears. Spit and splattering whisper of drops on metal. Crash and clang of steel echoing from the slopes, shouts of battle muffled by the downpour.

A great surge went through the crowd and Beck was lifted right off his feet, kicking at nothing, dumped in a mass of punching, jostling, shouting men. Took him a moment to realise they weren't the enemy, but there were a lot of blades poking every which way even so and it didn't have to be a Union one to stick you in the fruits. Hadn't been a Union sword killed Reft, had it?

Someone elbowed him in the head and he staggered sideways, was knocked by someone else and onto his knees, a trampling boot squashed his hand into the mud. Dragged himself up by a shield with a dragon's head painted on it, owner not best pleased. Man with a beard roaring at him. Battle sounds were louder. Men struggling to get away or get towards. Men clutching at wounds, blood run pink in the rain, clutching at weapons, all dripping wet and mad on fear and anger.

By the dead, he wanted to run. He wasn't sure if he was crying. Just knew he couldn't fail again. Stand with his crew, that's what Craw said, weren't it? Stand with his Chief. He blinked into the storm, saw a flash of Black Dow's black standard flapping, soaked through. Knew Craw had to be near it. Pressed towards it between the jerking bodies, boots slithering in the churned-up slop. Thought he caught a glimpse of Drofd's snarling face. Heard a roar and a spear came at him. Not even fast. He moved his head to the side, far as he could, straining with everything he had, and the point slid past his ear. Someone squealed in the other one, dropped against him, warm on his shoulder. Grunting and gurgling. Hot and wet all down his arm. He gasped, wriggled his shoulders, shrugging the corpse off, working it down towards the mud.

Another surge in the crowd and Beck was dragged sliding to the left, mouth open as he fought to stay upright. Warm rain spattered his cheek, the man in front of him suddenly whisked away and he was left blinking at space. A strip of mud, covered with sprawled bodies, and rain-pocked puddles, and broken spears.

And on the other side of it, the enemy.

Dow roared something over his shoulder but Craw couldn't hear him. Could hardly hear anything over the hissing of the rain and the clamour of rough voices, loud as a storm themselves. Too late for orders. Time comes a man just has to stick with the orders he's given, trust in his men to do the right thing, and fight. He thought maybe he saw the hilt of the Father of Swords waving between the spears. Should've been with his dozen. Stood with his crew. Why had he said yes to being Dow's Second? Maybe 'cause he'd been Threetrees' Second once, and he'd somehow thought if he had the place he used to have the world would be like it used to be. An old fool, grabbing at ghosts. Way too late. Should've married Colwen when he had the chance. Asked her, anyway. Given her the chance to turn him down.

He closed his eyes for a moment, breathed in the wet, cold air. "Should've stayed a carpenter," he whispered. But the sword had been the easier choice. To work wood you need all manner of tools – chisels and saws, axes great and small, nails and hammers, awls and planes. To be a killer you just need two. A blade and the will. Only Craw wasn't sure he had the will any more. He squeezed his fist tight around his sword's wet grip, the roar of battle growing louder and louder, binding with the roar of his own breath in his ears, the roar of his own heart pumping. Choices made. And he gritted his teeth, and snapped his eyes open.

The crowd split apart like a timber down the grain and the Union boiled from the gap. One barrelled into Craw before he could swing, their shields locked together, boots slithering in the mud. A glimpse of a snarling face, managed to tip his shield forward so the metal rim dug up into a nose, and back, and up, gurgling, whimpering. Dragging at the shield strap with all his strength, jabbing with it, stabbing with it, growling and spitting with it, grinding it into the man's head. It caught the buckle on his helmet, half-tore it off. Craw tried to twist his sword free, a blade whipped past him and took a great chunk out of the man's face. Craw left sliding in the muck, nothing to push against.

Black Dow spun his axe around, brought the pick side down on someone's helmet, punching right through to the haft. Left it buried in the corpse's head as it toppled backwards, arms wide.

A mud-splattered Northman tangled with a spear, his arm twisted over it and his war-hammer wafting about uselessly, a clawing hand on his face, forcing his head up while he peered down at the fingers.

A Union soldier came at Craw. Someone tripped him and he went down on one knee in the muck. Craw hit him across the back of the head with a dull clonk and put a dent in his helmet. Hit him again and knocked him sprawling. Hit him again, and again, hammering his face into the mud, spitting curses.

Shivers smashed at someone with his shield, smiling, rain turned the great scar on his face bright red like a fresh wound. War tips everything upside down. Men who are a menace in peacetime become your best hope once the steel starts swinging.

A corpse kicked over from front to back, back to front again. Blood

curling out into dirty water, plopping rain. The Father of Swords swung down and split someone open like a chisel splitting a carving of a man. Craw ducked behind his shield again as blood showered across it, rain spattered against it, mist of drops.

Spears pushing every way, a random, rattling, slippery mass. The point of one slid slowly down wood and into a hand, and through it, skewering it into someone's chest and pushing him down into the muck, shaking his head, no, no, fumbling at the shaft with the other hand as the merciless boots thumped over him.

Craw prodded a spear-point away with his shield, stabbing back with his sword, caught someone under the jaw and sent his head jerking up, blood gushing as he fell, making a honking note like the first note of a song he used to know.

Behind him was a Union officer wearing the most beautiful armour Craw ever saw, carved all over with gleaming golden designs. He was beating away stupidly at Black Dow with a muddy sword, had managed to drive him to his knees. Stand by your Chief. Craw stepped up, roaring, boot hammering down in a puddle and showering muddy water. Cut mindlessly across that lovely breastplate, edge scoring a bright groove through all that craftsmanship and sending its owner lurching. Forward again, stabbing as the Union man turned, Craw's blade grating against the bottom edge of his armour, sliding right through him and carrying him backwards.

Craw struggled with the grip of his sword, hot blood sticky all over his hand, up his arm. Holding this bastard up as he wrestled to twist the blade out of him, staggering together in the muck in a mad hug. Face against Craw's cheek, stubble scratching, breath rasping in his ear, and Craw realised he never even got this close to Colwen. Choices made, eh? Choices—

Wanting is not always enough, and however much Gorst wanted to, he could not get there. Too many straining bodies in his way. By the time he had hacked the leg from the last of them and flung him aside, the old Northman had already run Jalenhorm right through the guts. Gorst could see the bloody point of the sword under the gilded rim of his rain-dewed breastplate. The general had the oddest expression as his killer struggled to pull the blade out of him. Almost a smile.

Redeemed.

The old Northman twisted around as he heard Gorst's howl, eyes going wide, bringing his shield up. The long steel chopped deep into it, splitting the timbers, wrenching it around on his arm, driving the metal rim into his head and tossing him tumbling sideways.

Gorst stepped up to finish the job but again there was someone in his way. *As always.* Hardly more than a boy, swinging a hatchet, shouting. *The usual stuff, probably, die, die, blah, blah, blah.* Gorst was happy to die, of course. *But not for this fool's convenience.* He jerked his head sideways, let the hatchet bounce harmlessly from his shoulder-plate, spun about, long steel curving after him through the wet air. The boy tried desperately to block it but the heavy blade snatched the hatchet from his hand and split his face wide open, spraying brains.

The point of a sword whispered at him and Gorst whipped back from the waist, felt the wind of it across his cheek, a niggling discomfort under his eye. A space had opened in the screaming crowd, the battle blooming from a single press to mindless clumps of sodden combat at the very centre of the Heroes. All concepts of lines, tactics, directions, orders, of sides even, vanished as though they had never been. *And good riddance, they only confuse things.*

For some reason a half-naked Northman stood facing him, with the biggest sword Gorst had ever seen. *And I have seen a lot.* Absurdly long, as if it had been forged for a giant's use, dull grey metal gleaming with rain, a single letter stamped near the hilt.

He looked like some lurid painting by an artist who never saw a battle-field, but silly-looking people can be just as deadly as silly-sounding ones, and Gorst had coughed out all his arrogance in the smoke of Cardotti's House of Leisure. *A man must treat every fight as though it is his last. Will this be my last? We can hope.*

He rocked back, cautious, as the man's elbow twitched up for a sideways blow, shifted his shield to meet it, steel ready to counter. But instead of swinging the Northman lunged, using the great blade like a spear, the point darting past the edge of Gorst's shield and squealing down his breastplate, sending him stumbling. *A feint.* The instinct to jump back was powerful but he forced himself to keep his eyes fixed on the blade, watched its path curve through the rain, an arc of glistening droplets following after.

Gorst wrenched himself sideways and the great sword hissed past, caught the armour on his elbow and ripped it flapping off. He was already thrusting but the point of his steel caught only falling water as his half-naked opponent slid away. Gorst switched back for a savage head-height cut but the man snaked under it, hefted the great sword up with shocking speed as Gorst's steel swept down, blades ringing together with a finger-numbing clang. They broke apart, watchful, the Northman's eyes calmly focused on Gorst in spite of the hammering rain.

His weapon might have looked like a prop from a bad comedy, but this man was no jester. The stance, the balance, the angle of the long blade gave him all manner of options both in defence and attack. The technique was hardly what one would find in Rubiari's *Forms of Swordsmanship*, but then neither was the sword itself. *We both are masters, nonetheless.*

A Union soldier came tottering between them before Gorst could move, bent over around a wound in his stomach, hands full of his own blood. Gorst smashed him impatiently out of the way with his shield, sprang at the half-naked Northman with a thrust and a slash, but he dodged the thrust and parried the cut faster than Gorst would have thought possible with that weight of metal. Gorst feinted right, switched left, swinging low. The Northman was ready, sprang out of the way, Gorst's steel feathering the mud then hacking a leg out from under a struggling man and bringing him down with a shriek. *Don't stand in the way, then, fool.*

Gorst recovered just in time to see the great sword coming, gasped as he ducked behind his shield. The blade crashed into it, leaving a huge dent in the already battered metal, bending it hard over Gorst's forearm and driving his fist into his mouth. But he kept his feet, drove back, tasting blood, crashed into the Northman's body shield-first and flung him away, lashed backhand and forehand with his steel, high and low. The Northman dodged the high but the low caught him across the leg with the very point, sent blood flying and made his knee buckle. *One to me. And now to finish it.*

Gorst whipped his steel across on the backhand, saw movement at the limit of his vision, changed the angle of his swing and let it go wide, roaring, opening his shoulder, hit a Carl in the side of the helmet so hard he was ripped off his feet and pitched upside down into a tangle of spears. Gorst snapped back, bringing the steel scything over, but the Northman rolled away as nimbly as a squirrel and came up ready even as Gorst's sword sent up a spray of dirty water beside them.

Gorst found he was smiling as they faced each other again, the battle a sodden nightmare around them. *When did I last live like this? Have I ever?* His heart was pumping fire, his skin singing as the rain trickled down it. *All the disappointments, the embarrassments, the failures are nothing now.* Every detail standing out like a flame in the blackness, every moment lasting an age, every tiniest movement of him or his opponent a story of its own. *There is only win or die.* The Northman smiled back as Gorst shook the ruined shield from his arm and into the mud, and nodded. *And we recognise each other, and understand each other, and meet as equals. As brothers.* There was respect, but there would be no mercy. The slightest hesitation on either side would be an insult to the skill of the other. So Gorst nodded back, but before he was done he was already springing forward.

The Northman caught the sword on his but Gorst still had his free hand, shrieking as he swung it, gloved fist thudding into bare ribs, the Northman twisted grunting sideways. Gorst aimed another lashing punch at his face but he jerked away, the pommel of the great sword shot out of nowhere and Gorst only just wrenched his chin back far enough, the lump of metal missing his nose by a whisker. He looked up to see the Northman leaping at him, sword raised high and already coming down. Gorst forced his aching legs to spring one more time, notched steel gripped in both hands, and caught the long blade with his own. Metal screeched, that grey edge biting into his Calvez-made steel and, with impossible keenness, peeling a bright shaving from the blade.

Gorst was sent sliding back by the force of it, the huge sword held just short of his face, his crossed eyes fixed on the rain-dewed edge. He got purchase as his heels hit a corpse and brought the two of them to a wobbling halt. He tried to kick the Northman's leg away but he blocked it with his knee, lurching closer, only getting them further tangled. They gasped and spat in each other's faces, locked together, blades scraping and squealing as they shifted their balance one way or another, twisted their grips one way or another, jerked with one muscle or another, both searching desperately for some tiniest advantage, neither one able to find it.

The perfect moment. Gorst knew nothing about this man, not even his name. *But we are still bound closer than lovers, because we share this one sublime splinter of time.* Facing each other. *And facing death, the ever-present third in our little party.* Knowing it might all be over in a bloody instant. *Victory and defeat, glory and oblivion, in absolute balance.*

The perfect moment. And though he strained with every sinew to bring it to an end, Gorst wished it would go on for ever. *And we will join the stones, two more Heroes to add to the circle, frozen in conflict, and the grass will grow up around us, a monument to the glory of war, to the dignity of single combat, an eternal meeting of champions on the noble field of—*

"Oh," said the Northman. The pressure released. The blades slid apart. He stumbled back through the rain, blinking at Gorst, and then down, mouth hanging stupidly open. He still held the great sword in one hand, its point dragging through the mud and leaving a watery groove behind. With the other he reached up and gently touched the spear stuck through his chest, the blood already running down the shaft.

"Wasn't expecting that," he said. Then he dropped like a stone.

Gorst stood, frowning down. It felt like a while, but probably it was only an instant. No telling from where the spear had come. *It is a battle. There is no shortage of them.* He heaved out a misty sigh. *Ah, well. The dance goes on.* The old man who had killed Jalenhorm was floundering in the muck just a step and a sword-swing away.

He took the step, raising his notched steel.

Then his head exploded with light.

Beck saw it all happen, through the straining bodies, barged and battered from all sides, his whole body numb with fear. Saw Craw go down, rolling in the mud. Saw Drofd step over him and be hacked down in turn. Saw Whirrun fight that mad bull of a Union soldier, a fight that only seemed to take a few savage moments, too fast for him to follow. Saw Whirrun fall.

He remembered Craw pointing him out in front of Dow's Carls. Pointing him out as an example of what to do. A man dropped screaming in front of him and a space opened. Just do what's right. Stand by your Chief. Keep your head. As the Union man stepped towards Craw, Beck stepped towards the Union man from his blind side.

Do what's right.

At the last moment he twisted his wrist, and it was the flat of Beck's sword that hit him on the side of his head and knocked him flopping in the muck. And that was the last Beck saw of him before the trampling boots, tangled weapons, snarling faces surged in again.

*   *   *

Craw blinked, shook his head, then, as puke burned the back of his throat, decided that wasn't helping. He rolled over, groaning like the dead in hell.

His shield was a shattered wreck, timbers splintered, bloody rim bent over his throbbing arm. He dragged it off. Scraped blood out of one eye.

Boom, boom, boom went his skull, like someone was hammering a great nail into it. Other'n that, it was oddly quiet. Seemed the Northmen had driven the Union off the hill, or the other way around, and Craw found he hardly cared which. The pounding feet had shuffled on, left the hilltop a sea of blood-sprinkled, rain-lashed, boot-churned filth, dead and wounded scattered tight as autumn leaves, the Heroes themselves standing their same useless watch over it all.

"Ah, shit." Drofd was lying just a stride or two off, pale face turned towards him. Craw tried to stand and nearly puked again. Chose to crawl instead, dragging himself through the muck. "Drofd, you all right? You —" The other side of the lad's head was all hacked away, Craw couldn't tell where the black mess inside met the black mess outside.

He patted Drofd on his chest. "Ah. Shit." He saw Whirrun. On his back, the Father of Swords half-buried in the mud beside him, pommel not far from his right hand. There was a spear through him, bloody shaft sticking straight up.

"Ah, shit," said Craw again. Didn't know what else to say.

Whirrun grinned up as he crawled close, teeth pink with blood. "Craw! Hey! I would get up, but..." He lifted his head to peer down at the spear-shaft. "I'm fucked." Craw had seen a lifetime of wounds, and he knew right off there was no help for this one.

"Aye." Craw slowly sat back, hands heavy as anvils in his lap. "I reckon."

"Shoglig was talking shit. That old bitch didn't know when I was going to die at all. If I'd known that I'd surely have worn more armour." Whirrun made a sound somewhere between a cough and a laugh, then winced, coughed, laughed again, winced again. "Fuck, it hurts. I mean, you know it will, but, fuck, it really does hurt. Guess you showed me my destiny anyway, eh, Craw?"

"Looks that way." Wasn't much of a destiny the way Craw saw it. Not one anyone would pick out from a set.

"Where's the Father of Swords?" grunted Whirrun, trying to twist around to look for it.

"Who cares?" Blood was tickling at Craw's eyelid, making it flicker.

"Got to pass it on. Those are the rules. Like Daguf Col passed it on to me, and Yorweel the Mountain to him, and I think it was Four-Faces before that? I'm getting sketchy on the details."

"All right." Craw leaned over him, head thumping, dug the hilt out of the muck and pressed it into Whirrun's hand. "Who do you want to give it to?"

"You'll make sure it's done?"

"I'll make sure."

"Good. There ain't many I'd trust it to, but you're a straight edge, Craw, like they say. A straight edge." Whirrun smiled up at him. "Put it in the ground."

"Eh?"

"Bury it with me. Time was I thought it was a blessing and a curse. But it's only a curse, and I ain't about to curse some other poor bastard with it. Time was I thought it was reward and punishment both. But this is the only reward for men like us." And Whirrun nodded down towards the bloody spear-shaft. "This or . . . just living long enough to become nothing worth talking of. Put it in the mud, Craw." And he winced as he heaved the grip into Craw's limp hand and pressed his dirty fingers around it.

"I will."

"Least I won't have to carry it no more. You see how bloody heavy it is?"

"Every sword's a weight to carry. Men don't see that when they pick 'em up. But they get heavier with time."

"Good words." Whirrun bared his bloody teeth for a moment. "I really should've thought out some good words for this. Words to get folk all damp about the eye. Something for the songs. Thought I had years still, though. Can you think of any?"

"What, words?"

"Aye."

Craw shook his head. "Never been any good with 'em. As for the songs . . . I daresay the bards just make up their own."

"Daresay they do at that, the bastards." Whirrun blinked up, past Craw's face into the sky. The rain was finally slacking off. "Sun's coming out, at least." He shook his head, still smiling. "What do you know? Shoglig was talking shit."

Then he was still.

Pointed Metal

The rain was hammering down and Calder could hardly see fifty paces. Ahead of him his men were in a mindless tangle with the Union's, spears and pole-arms locked together, arms, legs, faces all crushed up against each other. Roaring, howling, boots sliding in the puddled muck, hands slipping on slick grips, slick pikestaffs, bloody metal, the dead and wounded shoved up like corks in a flood or trampled into the mud beneath. From time to time shafts would flap down, no way of knowing from which side, bounce from helmets or spin from shields and into the slop.

The third pit, or what Calder could see of it, had become a nightmare bog in which filth-caked devils stabbed and wrestled at floundering half-speed. The Union were across it in quite a few places. More than once they'd made it through and over the wall, and only been pushed back by a desperate effort from White-Eye and his growing mob of fighting wounded.

Calder's throat was raw from shouting and still he couldn't make himself heard. Every man who could hold a weapon was fighting and still the Union kept coming, wave after wave, tramping on endlessly. He'd no idea where Pale-as-Snow had got to. Dead, maybe. A lot of men were. A hand-to-hand fight like this, the enemy close enough to spit in your face, couldn't last long. Men weren't made to stand it. Sooner or later one side would give and, like a dam crumbling, dissolve all at once. That moment wasn't far away now, Calder could feel it. He looked nervously behind him. A few wounded, and a few archers, and beyond them the faint shape of the farm. His horse was there. Probably not too late to —

Men were clambering out of the pit on his left and struggling towards him. For a moment he thought they were his own men, doing the sensible thing and running for their lives. Then, with a cold shock, he realised that under the muck they were Union soldiers, slipped through a gap in the shifting fight.

He stood open-mouthed as they lumbered at him. Too late to run. The leading man was on him, a Union officer who'd lost his helmet, tongue hanging out as he panted for breath. He swung a muddy blade and Calder lurched out of the way, splashing through a puddle. He managed to block the next swing, numbing impact twisting the sword in his grip, making his arm buzz to the shoulder.

He wanted to scream something manly, but what he shouted was, "Help! Fuck! Help!" All rough and throaty and nobody could hear him or cared a shit, they were all fighting for their own lives.

No one could have guessed that Calder had been dragged into the yard every morning as a boy to train with spear and blade. He remembered none of it. He poked away with both hands like some old matron poking at a spider with a broom, mouth hanging wide, eyes full of wet hair. Should've cut his damn—

He gasped as the officer's sword jabbed at him again, his ankle caught and he tottered, one arm grabbing at nothing, and went down on his arse. It was one of the stolen flags that had tripped him. Oh, the irony. His sodden Styrian boots kicked up mud as he tried to scramble back. The officer took a tired step, sword up, then gave a breathless squeal and fell onto his knees. His head flew off sideways and his body toppled into Calder's lap, squirting blood, leaving him gasping, spitting, blinking.

"Thought I might help you out." Who should be standing behind, sword in hand, but Brodd Tenways, nasty-looking grin on his rashy face and his chain mail gleaming with rainwater. An unlikely saviour if ever there was one. "Couldn't leave you to snatch all the glory on your own, could I?"

Calder kicked the leaking body away and floundered up. "I've half a mind to tell you to get fucked!"

"What about the other half?"

"Shitting itself." No joke. He wouldn't have been at all surprised if his was the next head Tenways' sword whipped off.

But Tenways only gave him a rotten smile. "Might be the first honest thing I've ever heard you say."

"Probably that's fair."

Tenways nodded towards the soaked melee. "You coming?"

"Damn right." Calder wondered for a moment whether he should charge in, roaring like a madman, and turn the tide of battle. That's what Scale would've done. But it would hardly have been playing to his strengths. The enthusiasm he'd felt when he saw the cavalry routed had long ago leached away leaving him wet, cold, sore and exhausted. He feigned a grimace as he took a step, clutching at his knee. "Ah! Shit! I'll have to catch you up."

Tenways grinned. "'Course. Why wouldn't you? With me, you bastards!" And he led a glowering wedge of his Carls towards the gap in the lines, more of them pouring over the wall on the left and adding their weight to the straining combat.

The rain was thinning. Calder could see a little further and, to his great relief, it looked as if Tenways' arrival might have shifted the balance back their way. Might have. A few more Union soldiers on the other side of the scales and it could all still come apart. The sun peeped through the clouds for a moment, brought out a faint rainbow that curved down above the heaving mass of wet metal on the right and gently touched the bare rise beyond, and the low wall on top of it.

Those bastards beyond the stream. How long would they just sit still?

Peace in Our Time

There were wounded men everywhere on the slopes of the hill. Dying men. Dead men. Finree thought she saw faces she knew among them, but could not be sure whether they really were dead friends, or dead acquaintances, or just corpses with familiar hair. More than once she saw Hal's slack face leering, gaping, grinning. It hardly seemed to matter. The truly frightening thing about the dead, once she realised it, was that she was used to them.

They passed through a gap in a low wall and into a circle of stones, casualties sprawled on every spare stretch of grass. A man was trying to hold a great wound in his leg together, but when he clamped one end shut the other sagged open, blood welling out. Her father climbed down from his horse, his officers following him, she following them, a pale lad with a bugle clutched in one muddy fist watching her in silence. They picked their way through the madness in a pale procession, virtually ignored, her father staring about him, jaw clenched tight.

A junior officer trampled heedlessly past, waving a bent sword. "Form up! Form *up*! You! Where the hell—"

"Lord Marshal." An unmistakable high voice. Gorst stood, somewhat unsteadily, from a group of tattered soldiers, and gave Finree's father a tired-looking salute. Without doubt he had seen a great deal of action. His armour was battered and stained. His scabbard was empty and drooped about his legs in a manner that might have been comical on another day. He had a long, black-scabbed cut under one eye, his cheek, his jaw, the side of his thick neck streaked and crusted with drying blood. When he turned his head Finree saw the white of the other eye was bruised a sickly red, bandages above it soaked through.

"Colonel Gorst, what happened?"

"We attacked." Gorst blinked, noticed Finree and seemed to falter, then silently raised his hands and let them fall. "We lost."

"The Northmen still hold the Heroes?"

He nodded slowly.

"Where is General Jalenhorm?" asked her father.

"Dead," piped Gorst.

"Colonel Vinkler?"

"Dead."

"Who is in command?"

Gorst stood in silence. Finree's father turned away, frowning towards the summit. The rain was slackening off, the long slope leading up to the Heroes starting to take shape out of the grey, and with each stride of trampled grass that became visible, so did more corpses. Dead of both sides, broken weapons and armour, shattered stakes, spent arrows. Then the wall that ringed the summit, rough stones turned black by the storm. More bodies below it, the spears of the Northmen above. Still holding. Still waiting.

"Marshal Kroy!" The First of the Magi had not bothered to dismount. He sat, wrists crossed over the saddle-bow and his thick fingers dangling. As he took in the carnage he had the discerning, slightly disappointed air of a man who has paid for his garden to be weeded but on inspecting the grounds finds there is still a nettle or two about. "A minor reverse, but reinforcements are arriving all the time and the weather is clearing. Might I suggest you reorganise and prepare your men for another attack? It would appear General Jalenhorm made it all the way up to the Heroes, so a second effort might—"

"No," said Finree's father.

Bayaz gave the slightest puzzled frown. As at a normally reliable hound who refused to come to heel today. "No?"

"No. Lieutenant, do you have a flag of parley with you?"

Her father's standard-bearer looked nervously over at Bayaz, then back, then swallowed. "Of course, Lord Marshal."

"I would like you to attach it to your flagstaff, ride carefully up towards the Heroes and see if the Northmen can be prevailed upon to talk."

A strange mutter went through the men within earshot. Gorst took a step forward. "Marshal Kroy, with another effort I think—"

"You are the king's observer. Observe."

Gorst stood frozen for a moment, glanced at Finree, then snapped his mouth shut and stepped back.

The First of the Magi watched the white flag raised, his frown growing ever more thunderous even as the skies cleared. He nudged his horse forwards, causing a couple of exhausted soldiers to scramble from his path.

"His Majesty will be greatly dismayed, Lord Marshal." He managed to project an aura of fearsomeness utterly disproportionate to a thickset old bald man in a soggy coat. "He expects every man to do his duty."

Finree's father stood before Bayaz' horse, chest out and chin raised, the overpowering weight of the Magus' displeasure on him. "My duty is to care for the lives of these men. I simply cannot countenance another attack. Not while I am in command."

"And how long do you suppose that will be?"

"Long enough. Go!" he snapped at his standard-bearer and the man spurred away, his white flag snapping.

"Lord Marshal." Bayaz leaned forward, each syllable dropping like a mighty stone. "I earnestly hope that you have weighed the consequences—"

"I have weighed them and I am content." Finree's father was leaning forward slightly himself, eyes narrowed as if he was facing into a great wind. She thought she could see his hand trembling, but his voice emerged calm and measured. "I suspect my great regret will be that I allowed things to go so far."

The Magus' brows drew in further, his hissing voice almost painful to the ear. "Oh, a man can have greater regrets than that, Lord Marshal—"

"If I may?" Bayaz' servant was striding jauntily through the chaos towards them. He was wet through, as though he had swum a river, dirt-caked as though he had waded a bog, but he showed not the slightest discomfort. Bayaz leaned down towards him and the servant whispered in his ear through a cupped hand. The Magus' frown slowly faded as he first listened, then sat slowly back in his saddle, considering, and finally shrugged.

"Very well, Marshal Kroy," he said. "Yours is the command."

Finree's father turned away. "I will need a translator. Who speaks the language?"

An officer with a heavily bandaged arm stepped up. "The Dogman and some of his Northmen were with us at the start of the attack, sir, but..." He squinted into the milling crowd of wounded and worn-out soldiery. Who could possibly know where anyone was now?

"I have a smattering," said Gorst.

"A smattering might cause misunderstandings. We cannot afford any."

"It should be me," said Finree.

Her father stared at her, as if astonished to find her there, let alone volunteering for duty. "Absolutely not. I cannot—"

"Afford to wait?" she finished for him. "I spoke with Black Dow only yesterday. He knows me. He offered me terms. I am the best suited. It should be me."

He looked at her for a moment longer, then gave the slightest smile. "Very well."

"I will accompany you," piped Gorst with a show of chivalry sickeningly inappropriate among so many dead men. "Might I borrow your sword, Colonel Felnigg? I left mine at the summit."

So they set off, the three of them, through the thinning drizzle, the Heroes jutting clearly now from the hilltop ahead. Not far up the slope her father slipped, gasped as he fell awkwardly, catching at the grass. Finree started forward to help him up. He smiled, and patted her hand, but he looked suddenly old. As if his confrontation with Bayaz had sucked ten years out of him. She had always been proud of her father, of course. But she did not think she had ever been so proud of him as she was at that moment. Proud and sad at once.

* * *

Wonderful slipped the needle through, pulled the thread after and tied it off. Normally it would've been Whirrun doing it, but Cracknut had sewed his last stitches, more was the pity. "Just as well you've got a thick head."

"Served me well my whole life." Craw made the joke without thinking, no laughter given or expected, just as shouting came up from the wall that faced the Children. Where shouting would come from if the Union came again. He stood, the world see-sawed wildly for a moment and his skull felt like it was going to burst.

Yon grabbed his elbow. "You all right?"

"Aye, all things considered." And Craw swallowed his urge to spew and pushed through the crowd, the valley opening out in front of him, sky stained strange colours as the storm passed off. "They coming again?" He wasn't sure they could stand another go. He was sure he couldn't.

Dow was all grin, though. "In a manner of speaking." He pointed out three figures making their way up the slope towards the Heroes. The very same route Hardbread had taken a few days before when he came to ask for his hill back. When Craw had still had the best part of a dozen, all looking to him to keep 'em safe. "Reckon they want to talk."

"Talk?"

"Let's go." And Dow tossed his blood-crusted axe to Shivers, straightened the chain about his shoulders and strode through the gap in the mossy wall and down the hillside.

"Not too fast," called Craw as he set off after. "Don't reckon my knees'll take it!"

The three figures came closer. Craw felt just the slightest bit happier when he realised one was the woman he'd taken across the bridge yesterday, wearing a soldier's coat. The relief leaked quick when he saw who the third was, though. The big Union man who'd nearly killed him, a bandage around his thick skull.

They met about half way between the Heroes and the Children. Where the first arrows were prickling the ground. The old man stood with shoulders back, one fist clasped behind him in the other. Clean-shaven, with short grey hair and a sharp look, like he missed nothing. He wore a black coat, stitched with leaves at the collar in silver thread, a sword at his side with a pommel made from some jewel, looked like it had never been drawn. The girl stood at his elbow, the neckless soldier a little further back, his eyes on Craw, the white of one turned all bloody red and a black cut under the other. Looked like he'd left his sword in the mud up on the hill, but he'd found another. You didn't have to look far for a blade around here. Those were the times.

Dow stopped a couple of paces above them and Craw stopped a pace behind that, hands crossed in front of him. Close enough to get at his sword quick, though he doubted he'd have had the strength to draw the damn thing. Standing up was enough of a challenge. Dow was chirpier.

"Well, well." Grinning down at the girl with every tooth and spreading his arms in greeting. "Never expected to be seeing you again so soon. Do you want to hold me?"

"No," she said. "This is my father, Lord Marshal Kroy, commander of his Majesty's—"

"I guessed. And you lied."

She frowned up at him. "Lied?"

"He's shorter'n me." Dow's grin spread even wider. "Or he looks it from where I'm standing, anyway. Quite the day we're having, ain't it? Quite the red day." He lifted a fallen Union spear with the toe of his boot, then nudged it away. "So what can I do for you?"

"My father would like to end the fighting."

Craw felt such a wave of relief his swollen knees almost went out from under him. Dow was cagier. "Could've done that yesterday when I offered, given us all a lot less bloody digging to do."

"He's offering now."

Dow looked across at Craw, and Craw just about managed to shrug. "Better tardy than not at all."

"Huh." Dow narrowed his eyes at the girl, and at the soldier, and at the marshal, like he was thinking of saying no. Then he put his hands on his hips, and sighed. "All right. Can't say I wanted any of this in the first place. There's people of my own I could've been killing, 'stead o' wasting my sweat on you bastards."

The girl said a few words to her father, he said a few back. "My father is greatly relieved."

"Then my life's worth living. I've a few things to tidy up before we hammer out the details." He cast an eye over the carnage on the Children.

438

"Probably you have too. We'll talk tomorrow. Let's say after lunch, I can't do business with a hollow belly."

The girl passed it on to her father in Union, and while she did it Craw looked down at the red-eyed soldier, and he looked back. He had a long smear of blood down his neck. His, or Craw's, or one of Craw's dead friends'? Not even an hour ago they'd struggled with every shred of strength and will to murder each other. Now there was no need. Made him wonder why there ever had been.

"He's a right fucking killer, your man there," said Dow, more or less summing up Craw's thoughts.

The girl looked over her shoulder. "He is..." searching for the right words. "The king's watcher."

Dow snorted. "He did a bit more'n fucking watch today. He's got a devil in him, and I mean that as a compliment. Man like him could do well over on our side o' the Whiteflow. He was a Northman he'd be in all the songs. Shit, might be he'd be a king instead o' just watching one." Dow smiled that killing smile he had. "Ask him if he wants to work for me."

The girl opened her mouth but the neckless one spoke first, with a thick accent and the strangest, high, girlish little voice Craw had ever heard on a man. "I am happy where I am."

Dow raised one brow. "'Course you are. Real happy. Must be why you're so damn good at killing men."

"What about my friend?" asked the girl. "The one who was captured with me—"

"Don't give up, do you?" Dow showed his teeth again. "You really think anyone'll want her back, now?"

She looked him right in the eye. "I want her back. Didn't I get what you asked for?"

"Too late for some." Dow ran a careless eye over the carnage scattered across the slope, took in a breath, and blew it out. "But that's war, eh? There have to be losers. Might be an idea to send some messengers, let everyone know they can all stop fighting and have a big sing-song instead. Be a shame to carry on butchering each other for nothing, wouldn't it?"

The woman blinked, then rendered it into Union again. "My father would like to recover our dead."

But the Protector of the North was already turning away. "Tomorrow. They won't run off."

* * *

Black Dow walked off up the slope, the older man giving her the faintest, apologetic grin before he followed.

Finree took a long breath, held it, then let it out. "I suppose that's it."

"Peace is always an anticlimax," said her father, "but no less desirable for that." He started stiffly back towards the Children and she walked beside him.

A throwaway conversation, a couple of bad jokes that half the gathering of five could not even have understood, and it was done. The battle was over. The war was over. Could they have had that conversation at the start, and would all those men – all these men – still be alive? Still have their arms, or legs? However she turned it around, she could not make it fit. Perhaps she should have been angry at the stupendous waste, but she was too tired, too irritated by the way her damp clothes were chafing her back. And at least it was over now after—

Thunder rolled across the battlefield. Terribly, frighteningly loud. For a moment she thought it must be lightning striking the Heroes. A last, petulant stroke of the storm. Then she saw the mighty ball of fire belching up from Osrung, so large she fancied she could feel the heat of it on her face. Specks flew about it, spun away from it, streaks and spirals of dust following them high into the sky. Pieces of buildings, she realised. Beams, blocks. Men. The flame vanished and a great cloud of black smoke shot up after it, spilling into the sky like a waterfall reversed.

"Hal," she muttered, and before she knew it, she was running.

"Finree!" shouted her father.

"I'll go." Gorst's voice.

She took no notice, charging on downhill as fast as she could with the tails of Hal's coat snatching at her legs.

What the hell—" muttered Craw, watching the column of smoke crawl up, the wind already dragging it billowing out towards them, the orange of fires flickering at its base, licking at the jagged wrecks that used to be buildings.

"Oops," said Dow. "That'll be Ishri's surprise. Shitty timing for all concerned."

Another day Craw might've been horror-struck, but today it was hard to get worked up. A man can only feel so sorry and he was way past his limit. He swallowed, and turned from the giant tree of dirt spreading its branches over the valley, and struggled back up the hillside after Dow.

"You couldn't call it a win, exactly," he was saying, "but not a bad result, all in all. Best send someone off to Reachey, tell him tools down. Tenways and Calder too, if they're still—"

"Chief." Craw stopped on the wet slope, next to the face-down corpse of a Union soldier. A man has to do the right thing. Has to stand by his Chief, whatever his feelings. He'd stuck to that all his life, and they say an old horse can't jump new fences.

"Aye?" Dow's grin faded as he looked into Craw's face. "What's to frown about?"

"There's something I need to tell you."

The Moment of Truth

The deluge had finally come to an end but the leaves were still dripping relentlessly on the soaked, sore, unhappy soldiers of his Majesty's First. Corporal Tunny was the most soaked, sore and unhappy of the lot. Still crouching in the bushes. Still staring towards that same stretch of wall he'd been staring at all day and much of the day before. His eye chafed raw from the brass end of his eyeglass, his neck chafed raw from his constant scratching, his arse and armpits chafed raw from his wet clothes. He'd had some shitty duties in his chequered career, but this was down there among the worst, somehow combining the two awful constants of the army life – terror and tedium. For some time the wall had been lost in the hammering rain but now had taken shape again. The same mossy pile slanting down towards the water. And the same spears bristling above it.

"Can we see yet?" hissed Colonel Vallimir.

"Yes, sir. They're still there."

"Give me that!" Vallimir snatched the eyeglass, peered towards the wall for a moment, then sulkily let it fall. "Damn it!" Tunny had mild sympathy. About as much as he could ever have for an officer. Going meant disobeying the letter of Mitterick's order. Staying meant disobeying the tone of it. Either way there was a good chance he'd suffer. Here, if one was needed, was a compelling argument against ever rising beyond corporal.

"We go anyway!" snapped Vallimir, desire for glory evidently having tipped the scales. "Get the men ready to charge!"

Forest saluted. "Sir."

So there it was. No stratagems for delay, no routes to light duty, no feigning of illness or injuries. It was time to fight, and Tunny had to admit he was almost relieved as he did up the buckle on his helmet. Anything but crouching in the bloody bushes any longer. There was a whispering as the order was passed down the line, a rattling and scraping as men stood, adjusted their armour, drew their weapons.

"That it, then?" asked Yolk, eyes wide.

"That's it." Tunny was strangely light-headed as he undid the ties and slid the canvas cover from the standard. He felt that old, familiar tightness in his throat as he gently unfurled the precious square of red material. Not fear. Not fear at all. That other, much more dangerous thing. The one Tunny had tried over and over to smother, but always sprouted up again as powerful as ever when he wanted it least.

"Oh, here we go," he whispered. The golden sun of the Union slipped out of hiding as the cloth unrolled. The number one embroidered on it. The standard of Corporal Tunny's regiment, which he'd served with since a boy. Served with in the desert and the snow. The names of a score of old battles stitched in gold thread, glittering in the shadows. The names of battles fought and won by better men than him.

"Oh, here we bloody go." His nose hurt. He looked up at the branches, at the black leaves and the bright cracks of sky between them, at the glittering beads of water at their edges. His eyelids fluttered, blinking back tears. He stepped forward to the very edge of the trees, trying to swallow the dull pain behind his breastbone as men gathered around him in a long line. His limbs were tingling. Yolk and Worth behind him, the last of his little flock of recruits, both pale as they faced towards the water, and the wall beyond it. As they faced—

"Charge!" roared Forest, and Tunny was away. He burst from the trees and down the long slope, threading between old tree stumps, bounding from one to another. He heard men shouting behind him, men running, but he was too busy holding the standard high in both hands, the wind taking the cloth and dragging it out straight above his head, tugging hard at his hands, his arms, his shoulders.

He splashed out into the stream, floundered through the slow water to the middle, no more than thigh deep. He turned, waving the standard back and forth, its golden sun flashing. "On, you bastards!" he roared at the crowd of running men behind him. "On, the First! Forward! Forward!" Something whipped past in the air, just seen out of the corner of his eye.

"I'm hit!" shrieked Worth, staggering in the stream, helmet twisted across his stricken face, clutching at his breastplate.

"By birdshit, idiot!" Tunny took the standard in one hand and wedged the other under Worth's armpit, dragged him along a few steps until he had his balance back then plunged on himself, lifting his knees up high, spraying water with every step.

He hauled himself up the mossy bank, free hand clutching at roots, wet boots wrestling at the loose earth, finally clambering onto the overhanging turf. He snatched a look back, all he could hear his own whooping breath echoing in his helmet. The whole regiment, or the few hundred who remained, at any rate, were flooding down the slope and across the stream after him, kicking up sparkling drops.

He shoved the snapping standard high into the air, gave a meaningless roar as he drew his sword and ran on, face locked into a snarling mask, thumping towards the wall, spear-tips showing above it. Two more great strides and he sprang up onto the drystone, screaming like a madman, swinging his sword wildly one way and the other to clatter against the spears and knock them toppling...

There was no one there.

Just old pole-arms leaning loose against the wall, and damp barley shifting in the wind, and the calm, wooded fells rising faint at the north side of the valley very much like they did at the south side.

No one to fight.

No doubt there had been fighting, and plenty of it too. Over to the right the crops were flattened, the ground before the wall trampled to a mass of mud, littered with the bodies of men and horses, the ugly rubbish of victory and defeat.

But the fighting was over now.

Tunny narrowed his eyes. A few hundred strides away, off to the north and east, figures were jogging across the fields, chinks of sunlight through the heavy clouds glinting on armour. The Northmen, presumably. And since no one appeared to be pursuing them, pulling back in their own time, and on their own terms.

"Yah!" shrieked Yolk as he ran up, a war cry that could hardly have made a duck nervous. "Yah!" Leaning over the wall to poke away wildly with his sword. "Yah?"

"No one here," said Tunny, letting his own blade slowly fall.

"No one here?" muttered Worth, trying to straighten his twisted helmet.

Tunny sat down on the wall, the standard between his knees. "Only him." Not far away a scarecrow had been planted, a spear nailed to each stick arm, a brightly polished helmet on its sack-head. "And I reckon the whole regiment can take him." It all looked a pathetic ruse now. But then ruses always do, once you've seen through them. Tunny ought to have known that. He'd played more than a few himself, though usually on his own officers rather than the enemy.

More soldiers were reaching the wall. Wet through, tired out, mixed up. One clambered over it, walked up to the scarecrow and levelled his sword.

"Lay down your arms in the name of his Majesty!" he roared. There was a smattering of laughter, quickly cut off as Colonel Vallimir clambered up onto the drystone with a face like fury, Sergeant Forest beside him.

A horseman was pounding over from the empty gap in the wall on their right. The gap where they'd been sure a furious battle was taking place. A battle they would gloriously turn the tide of. A battle that was already over. He reined in before them, he and his horse breathing hard, dashed with mud from a full gallop.

"Is General Mitterick here?" he managed to gasp.

"Afraid not," said Tunny.

"Do you know where he is?"

"Afraid not," said Tunny.

"What's the matter, man?" snapped Vallimir, getting tangled with his scabbard as he hopped down from the wall and nearly falling on his face.

The messenger snapped out a salute. "Sir. Lord Marshal Kroy orders all hostilities to cease at once." He smiled, teeth gleaming white in his muddy face. "We've made peace with the Northmen!" He turned his horse smartly and rode off, past a pair of stained and tattered flags drooping forgotten from leaning poles and south, towards a line of Union foot advancing across the ruined fields.

"Peace?" mumbled Yolk, soaked and shivering.

"Peace," grunted Worth, trying to rub the birdshit from his breastplate.

"Fuck!" snarled Vallimir, flinging down his sword.

Tunny raised his brows, and stuck his own blade point-first in the earth. He couldn't say he felt anywhere near as strongly as Vallimir about it, but he had to admit to feeling a mite disappointed at the way things had turned out.

"But that's war, eh, my beauty?" He started to roll up the standard of his Majesty's First, smoothing out the kinks with his thumb the way a woman might put away her wedding shawl when the big day was over.

"That was quite some standard-bearing, Corporal!" Forest was a stride or two away, foot up on the wall, a grin across his scarred face. "Up front, leading the men, in the place of most danger and most glory. 'Forward!' cried brave Corporal Tunny, hurling his courage in the teeth of the enemy! I mean, there was no enemy, as it turned out, but still, I always knew you'd come through. You always do. Can't help yourself, can you? Corporal Tunny, hero of the First!"

"Fuck yourself, Forest."

Tunny started to work the standard carefully back into its cover. Looking across the flat land to the north and east, watching the last of the Northmen hurrying away through the sunlit fields.

Luck. Some men have it. Some don't. Calder could not but conclude, as he bounded through the barley behind his men, exhausted and muddy but very much alive, that he had it. By the dead, he had it.

Mad luck, that Mitterick had done the apparently insane, chosen to charge without checking the ground or waiting for light and doomed his cavalry. Impossible luck, that Brodd Tenways, of all people, would have lent a helping hand, the worst of his many enemies saving his life at the last moment. Even the rain had fought on his side, swept over at just the time to ruin the order of the Union foot and turn their dream ground into a nightmare of mud.

Even then, the men in the woods could still have done for him, but they'd been put off by a bundle of dead men's spears, a scarecrow and a few boys each slipped a coin to wear a helmet twice too big and stick their heads up once in a while. Deal with them, Dow had said, and somehow bold Prince Calder had found a way.

When he thought of all the luck he'd had that day he felt dizzy. Felt as if the world must've chosen him for something. Must have great plans for him. How else could he have lurched through all this with his life? Him, Calder, who deserved it so bloody little?

There was an old ditch running through the fields up ahead with a low hedgerow behind. A boundary his father hadn't quite managed to tear up, and the perfect place to form a new line. Another little slice of luck. He found himself wishing that Scale had lived to see this. To hug him and thump his back and say how proud he was at last. He'd fought, and what was even more surprising, he'd won. Calder was laughing as he jumped the ditch, slid sideways through a gap in the bushes — And stopped.

A few of his lads were scattered around, most of them sitting or even lying, weapons tossed aside, all the way knackered from a day's hard fighting and a run across the fields. Pale-as-Snow was with them, but they weren't alone. A good score of Dow's Carls stood in a frowning crescent ahead. A grim-looking set of bastards, and the shitty jewel in the midst was Caul Shivers, his one eye fixed on Calder.

There was no reason for them to be there. Unless Curnden Craw had done what he said he would, and told Black Dow the truth. And Curnden Craw was a man famous for always doing what he said he would. Calder licked his lips. Seemed a bit of a foolish decision now, to have gambled against the inevitable. Seemed he was such a good liar he'd managed to trick himself on his chances.

"Prince Calder," whispered Shivers, taking a step forward.

Way too late to run. He'd only be running at the Union anyway. A mad hope tickled the back of his mind that his father's closest might leap to his defence. But they hadn't lasted as long as they had by pissing into the wind. He glanced at Pale-as-Snow and the old warrior offered him the tiniest shrug. Calder had given them a day to be proud of, but he'd get no suicidal gestures of loyalty and he deserved none. They weren't going to set themselves on fire for his benefit any more than Caul Reachey was. You have to be realistic, as the Bloody-Nine had been so bloody fond of saying.

So Calder could only give a hopeless smile, and stand there trying to get his breath as Shivers took another step towards him, then another. That terrible scar loomed close. Close enough almost to kiss. Close enough so all Calder could see was his own distorted, unconvincing grin reflected in that dead metal ball of an eye.

"Dow wants you."

Luck. Some men have it. Some don't.

Spoils

The smell, first. Of a kitchen mishap, perhaps. Then of a bonfire. Then more. An acrid note that niggled at the back of Gorst's throat. The smell of buildings aflame. Adua had smelled that way, during the siege. So had Cardotti's House of Leisure, as he reeled through the smoke-filled corridors.

Finree rode like a madwoman and, dizzy and aching as he was, she pulled away from him, sending men hopping from the road. Ash started to flutter down as they passed the inn, black snow falling. Rubbish was dotted about as the fence of Osrung loomed from the smoky murk. Scorched wood, broken slates, scraps of cloth raining from the sky.

More wounded here, dotted haphazardly about the town's south gate, burned as well as hacked, stained with soot as well as blood, but the sounds were the same as they had been on the Heroes. As they always were. Gorst gritted his teeth against it. *Help them or kill them, but someone please put an end to their damned bleating.*

Finree was already down from her horse and making for the town. He scrambled after, head pounding, face burning, and caught up with her just inside the gate. He thought the sun might be dropping in the sky, but it hardly mattered. In Osrung it was choking twilight. Fires burned among the wooden buildings. Flames rearing up, the heat of them drying the spit in Gorst's mouth, sucking the sweat out of his face, making the air shimmer. A house hung open like a man gutted, missing one of its walls, floorboards jutting into air, windows from nowhere to nowhere.

Here is war. Here it is, shorn of its fancy trappings. None of the polished buttons, the jaunty bands, the stiff salutes. None of the clenched jaws and clenched buttocks. None of the speeches, the bugles, the lofty ideals. Here it is, stripped bare.

Just ahead someone bent over a man, helping him. He glanced up, sooty-faced. Not helping. He had been trying to get his boots off. As Gorst came close he startled and dashed away into the strange dusk. Gorst looked down at the soldier he left behind, one bare foot pale against the mud. *Oh, flower of our manhood! Oh, the brave boys! Oh, send them to war no more until next time we need a fucking distraction.*

"Where should we look?" he croaked.

Finree stared at him for a moment, hair tangled across her face, soot stuck under her nose, eyes wild. *But still as beautiful as ever. More. More.* "Over there! Near the bridge. He'd have been at the front." *Such nobility! Such heroism! Lead on, my love, to the bridge!*

They went beneath a row of trees on fire, burning leaves fluttering down around them like confetti. *Sing! All sing for the happy couple!* People called out, voices muffled in the gloom. People looking for help, or looking for men to help, or men to rob. Figures shambled past, leaning on one another, carrying stretchers between them, casting about as though for something they had mislaid, digging at the wreckage with their hands. *How could you find one man in this? Where would you find one man? A whole one, anyway.*

There were bodies all about. There were parts of bodies. Strangely robbed of meaning. Bits of meat. *Someone scrape them up and pack them in gilt coffins back to Adua so the king can stand to attention as they pass and the queen can leave glistening tear-tracks through her powder and the people can tear their hair and ask why, why, while they wonder what to have for dinner or whether they need a new pair of shoes or whatever the fuck.*

"Over here!" shouted Finree, and he hurried to her, hauled a broken beam aside, two corpses underneath, neither one an officer. She shook her head, biting her lip, put one hand on his shoulder. He had to stop himself smiling. Could she know the thrill that touch sent through him? He was wanted. Needed. And by her.

Finree picked her way from one ruined shell to another, coughing, eyes watering, tearing at rubbish with her fingernails, turning over bodies, and he followed. Searching every bit as feverishly as she did. More, even. But for different reasons. *I will drag aside some fallen trash and there will be his ruined, gaping corpse, not half so fucking handsome now, and she will see it. Oh no! Oh yes. Cruel, vicious, lovely fate. And she will turn to me in her misery, and weep upon my uniform and perhaps thump my chest lightly with her fist, and I will hold her, and whisper insipid consolations, and be the rock for her to founder upon, and we will be together, as we should have been, and would have been had I had the courage to ask her.*

Gorst grinned to himself, teeth bared as he rolled over another body. Another dead officer, arm so broken it was wrapped right around his back. *Taken too soon with all his young life ahead of him and blah, blah, blah. Where is Brock? Show me Brock.*

A few splinters of stone and a great crater, flooded by churning river water, were all that remained to show where Osrung's bridge once stood. Most of the buildings around it were little more than heaps of rubbish, but one stone-built was largely intact, its roof stripped off and some of the bare rafters aflame. Gorst struggled towards it while Finree picked at some bodies, one arm over her face. A doorway with a heavy lintel, and in the doorway a thick door twisted from its hinges, and just showing beneath the door, a boot. Gorst reached down and heaved the door up like the lid of a coffin.

And there was Brock. He did not seem badly injured at a first glance. His face was streaked with blood, but not smashed to pulp as Gorst might have hoped. One leg was folded underneath him at an unnatural angle, but his limbs were all attached.

Gorst bent over him, placed a hand over his mouth. Breath. *Still alive.* He felt a surge of disappointment so strong that his knees nearly buckled, closely followed by a sobering rage. *Cheated. Gorst, the king's squeaking clown, why should he have what he wants? What he needs? What he deserves? Dangle it in his fat face and laugh! Cheated. Just as I was in Sipani. Just as I was at the Heroes. Just as I always am.*

Gorst raised one brow, and he blew out a long, soft breath, and he shifted his hand down, down to Brock's neck. He slid his thumb and his middle finger around it, feeling out the narrowest point, then gently, firmly squeezed.

What's the difference? Fill a hundred pits with dead Northmen, congratulations, have a parade! Kill one man in the same uniform as you? A crime. A murder. Worse than despicable. Are we not all men? All blood and bone and dreams?

He squeezed a little harder, impatient to be done. Brock did not complain. Did not so much as twitch. He was so nearly dead anyway. *Nothing more than nudging fate in the right direction.*

So much easier than all the others. No steel and screams and mess, just a little pressure and a little time. So much more point than all the others. They had nothing I needed, they simply faced the other way. I should be ashamed of their deaths. But this? This is justice. This is righteous. This is—

"Have you found anything?"

Gorst's hand sprang open and he shifted it slightly so two fingers were pressed up under Brock's jaw, as if feeling for a pulse. "He's alive," he croaked.

Finree leaned down beside him, touched Brock's face with a trembling hand, the other pressed to her mouth, gave a gasp of relief that might as well have been a dagger in Gorst's face. He slid one arm under Brock's knees, the other under his back, and scooped him up. *I have failed even at killing a man. It seems my only choice is to save him.*

A surgeon's tent stood near the south gate, canvas turned muddy grey by the falling ash. Wounded waited outside for attention, clutching at assorted injuries, moaning, or whimpering, or silent, eyes empty. Gorst stomped through them and up to the tent. *We can jump the queue, because I am the king's observer, and she is the marshal's daughter, and the wounded man is a colonel of the most noble blood, and so it is only fitting that any number of the rank and file can die before bastards like us are inconvenienced.*

Gorst pushed through the flap and set Brock down ever so gently on a stained table, and a tight-faced surgeon listened at his chest and proclaimed him alive. *And all my silly, pretty little hopes strangled. Again.* Gorst stepped back as the assistants crowded in, Finree bending over her husband, holding his sooty hand, looking eagerly down into his face, her eyes shining with hope, and fear, and love.

Gorst watched. *If it was me dying on that table, would anyone care? They would shrug and tip me out with the slops. And why shouldn't they? It would be better than I deserve.* He left them to it, trudged outside and stood there, frowning at the wounded, he did not know how long for.

"They say he is not too badly hurt."

He turned to look at her. Forcing the smile onto his face was harder work than climbing the Heroes had been. "I am . . . so glad."

"They say it is amazing luck."

"Too true."

They stood there in silence a moment longer. "I don't know how I can ever repay you . . ."

Easy. Abandon that pretty fool and be mine. That's all I want. That one little thing. Just kiss me, and hold me, and give yourself to me, utterly and completely. That's all. "It's nothing," he whispered.

But she had already turned and hurried into the tent, leaving him alone. He stood for a moment as the ash gently fluttered down, settled across the ground, settled across his shoulders. Beside him a boy lay on a stretcher. On the way to the tent, or while waiting for the surgeon, he had died.

Gorst frowned down at the body. *He is dead and I, self-serving coward that I am, still live.* He sucked in air through his sore nose, blew it out through his sore mouth. *Life is not fair. There is no pattern. People die at random.* Obvious, perhaps. Something that everyone knows. *Something that everyone knows, but no one truly believes. They think when it comes to them there will be a lesson, a meaning, a story worth telling. That death will come to them as a dread scholar, a fell knight, a terrible emperor.* He poked at the boy's corpse with a toe, rolled it onto its side, then let it flop back. *Death is a bored clerk, with too many orders to fill. There is no reckoning. No profound moment. It creeps up on us from behind, and snatches us away while we shit.*

He stepped over the corpse and walked back towards Osrung, past the shambling grey ghosts that clogged the road. He was no more than a dozen steps inside the gate when he heard a voice calling to him.

"Over here! Help!" Gorst saw an arm sticking from a heap of charred rubbish. Saw a desperate, ash-smeared face. He clambered carefully up, undid the buckle under the man's chin, removed his helmet and tossed it away. The lower half of his body was trapped under a splintered beam. Gorst took one end, heaved it up and swung it away, lifted the soldier as gently as a father might a sleeping child and carried him back towards the gate.

"Thank you," he croaked, one hand pawing at Gorst's soot-stained jacket. "You're a hero."

Gorst said nothing. *But if only you knew, my friend. If only you knew.*

Desperate Measures

Time to celebrate.

No doubt the Union would have their own way of looking at it, but Black Dow was calling this a victory and his Carls were minded to agree. So they'd dug new fire-pits, and cracked the kegs, and poured the beer, and every man was looking forward to a double gild, and most of 'em to heading home to plough their fields, or their wives, or both.

They chanted, laughed, staggered about in the gathering darkness, tripping through fires and sending sparks showering, drunker'n shit. All feeling twice as alive for facing death and coming through. They sang old songs, and made up new ones with the names of today's heroes where yesterday's used to be. Black Dow, and Caul Reachey, and Ironhead and Tenways and Golden raised up on high while the Bloody-Nine, and Bethod, and Threetrees and Littlebone and even Skarling Hoodless sank into the past like the sun sinking in the west, the midday glory of their deeds dimming just to washed-out memories, a last flare among the stringy clouds before night swallowed 'em. You didn't hear much about Whirrun of Bligh even. About Shama Heartless, not a peep. Names turned over by time, like the plough turning the soil. Bringing up the new while the old were buried in the mud.

"Beck." Craw lowered himself stiffly down beside the fire, a wooden ale cup in one hand, and gave Beck's knee an encouraging pat.

"Chief. How's your head?"

The old warrior touched a finger to the fresh stitches above his ear. "Sore. But I've had worse. Very nearly had a lot worse today, in fact, as you might've noticed. Scorry told me you saved my life. Most folk wouldn't place a high value on that particular article but I must admit I'm quite attached to it. So. Thanks, I guess. A lot of thanks."

"Just trying to do the right thing. Like you said."

"By the dead. Someone was listening. Drink?" And Craw offered out his wooden mug.

"Aye." Beck took it and a good swallow too. Taste of beer, sour on his tongue.

"You did good today. Bloody good, far as I'm concerned. Scorry told me it was you put that big bastard down. The one who killed Drofd."

"Did I kill him?"

"No. He's alive."

"Didn't kill no one today, then." Beck wasn't sure whether he should be disappointed by that or glad. He wasn't up to feeling much about anything either way. "I killed a man yesterday," he found he'd said.

"Flood said you killed four."

Beck licked his lips. Trying to lick away the sour taste, but it was going nowhere. "Flood got it wrong and I was too much the coward to put him right. Lad called Reft killed those men." He took another swallow, too fast, made his voice spill out breathless. "I hid in a cupboard while they were fighting. Hid in a cupboard and pissed my pants. There's Red Beck for you."

"Huh." Craw nodded, his lips pressed thoughtfully together. He didn't seem all that bothered. He didn't seem all that surprised. "Well, it don't change what you did today. There's far worse a man can do in a battle than hide in a cupboard."

"I know," muttered Beck, and his mouth hung open, ready to let it spill. It was like his body needed to say it, to spit out the rot like a sick man might need to puke. His mouth had to do it, however much he might want to keep it hid. "I need to tell you something, Chief," his dried-out tongue wrestling with the words.

"I'm listening," said Craw.

He cast about for the best way to put it, like the sick man casting about for the best thing to spew into. As though there were words pretty enough to make it less ugly. "The thing is—"

"Bastard!" someone shouted, knocked Beck so bad he spilled the dregs of the cup into the fire.

"Oy!" growled Craw, wincing as he got up, but whoever it was had already gone. There was a current through the crowd, of a sudden. A new mood, angry, jeering at someone being dragged through their midst. Craw followed on and Beck followed him, more relieved than upset at the distraction, like the sick man realising he don't have to puke into his wife's hat after all.

They shouldered through the crowd to the biggest fire-pit, in the centre of the Heroes, where the biggest men were. Black Dow sat in the midst of 'em in Skarling's Chair, one dangling hand twisting the pommel of his sword round and round. Shivers was there, on the far side of the fire, pushing someone down onto his knees.

"Shit," muttered Craw.

"Well, well, well." And Dow licked his teeth and sat back, grinning. "If it ain't Prince Calder."

Calder tried to look as comfortable as he could on his knees with his hands tied and Shivers looming over him. Which wasn't all that comfortable. "The invitation was hard to refuse," he said.

"I'll bet," answered Dow. "Can you guess why I made it?"

Calder took a look around the gathering. All the great men of the North were there. All the bloated fools. Glama Golden, sneering over from the far side of the fire. Cairm Ironhead, watching, one brow raised. Brodd Tenways, a bit less scornful than usual, but a long way from friendly. Caul Reachey, with a "my hands are tied" sort of a wince, and Curnden Craw, with a "why didn't you run?" sort of a one. Calder gave the pair of them a sheepish nod. "I've an inkling."

"For anyone who hasn't an inkling, Calder here tried to prevail on my new Second to kill me." Some muttering ran through the firelit crowd, but not that much. No one was overly surprised. "Ain't that right, Craw?"

Craw looked at the ground. "That's right."

"You going to deny it, even?" asked Dow.

"If I did, could we forget the whole thing?"

Dow grinned. "Still joking. I like that. Not that the faithlessness surprises me, you're known for a schemer. The stupidity does, though. Curnden Craw's a straight edge, everyone knows that." Craw winced even harder, and looked away. "Stabbing men in the back ain't his style."

"I'll admit it wasn't my brightest moment," said Calder. "How about we notch it up to youthful folly and let it slide?"

"Don't see how I can. You've pushed my patience too far, and it's got a spike on the end. Haven't I treated you like a son?" A few chuckles ran along both sides of the fire-pit. "I mean, not a favourite son. Not a firstborn or nothing. A runty one, down near the end o' the litter, but still. Didn't I let you take charge when your brother died, though you haven't the experience or the name for it? Didn't I let you have your say around the fire? And when you said too much didn't I clear you off to Carleon with your wife to cool your head rather than just cut your head off and worry later on the details? Your father weren't so forgiving to those who disagreed with him, as I recall."

"True," said Calder. "You've been generosity itself. Oh. Apart from trying to kill me, of course."

Dow's forehead wrinkled. "Eh?"

"Four nights past, at Caul Reachey's weapontake? Bringing anything back? No? Three men tried to murder me, and when I put one to the question he dropped Brodd Tenways' name. And everyone knows Brodd Tenways wouldn't do a thing without your say-so. You denying it?"

"I am, in fact." Dow looked over at Tenways and he gave a little shake of his rashy head. "And Tenways too. Might be he's lying, and has his own reasons, but I can tell you one thing for a fact – any man here can tell I had no part in it."

"How's that?"

Dow leaned forwards. "You're still fucking breathing, boy. You think if I'd a mind to kill you there's a man could stop me?" Calder narrowed his eyes. He had to admit there was something to that argument. He looked for Reachey, but the old warrior was steadfastly looking elsewhere.

"But it don't much matter who didn't die yesterday," said Dow. "I can tell you who'll die tomorrow." Silence stretched out, and never had the word to end it been so horribly clear. "You." Seemed like everyone was smiling. Everyone except Calder, and Craw, and maybe Caul Shivers, but that was probably just because his face was so scarred he couldn't get his mouth to curl. "Anyone got any objections to this?" Aside from the crackling of the fire, there wasn't a sound. Dow stood up on his seat and shouted it. "Anyone want to speak up for Calder?" None spoke.

How silly his whispers in the dark seemed now. All his seeds had fallen on stony ground all right. Dow was firmer set in Skarling's Chair than ever and Calder hadn't a friend to his name. His brother was dead and he'd somehow found a way to make Curnden Craw his enemy. Some spinner of webs he was.

"No one? No?" Slowly, Dow sat back down. "Anyone here not happy about this?"

"I'm not fucking delighted," said Calder.

Dow burst out laughing. "You got bones, lad, whatever they say. Bones of a rare kind. I'll miss you. You got a preference when it comes to method? We could hang you, or cut your head off, or your father was partial to the bloody cross though I couldn't advise it—"

Maybe the fighting today had gone to Calder's head, or maybe he was sick of treading softly, or maybe it was the cleverest thing to do right then. "Fuck yourself!" he snarled, and spat into the fire. "I'd sooner die with a sword in my hand! You and me, Black Dow, in the circle. A challenge."

Slow, scornful silence. "Challenge?" sneered Dow. "Over what? You make a challenge to decide an issue, boy. There's no issue here. Just you turning on your Chief and trying to talk his Second into stabbing him in the back. Would your father have taken a challenge?"

"You're not my father. You're not a fucking shadow of him! He made that chain you're wearing. Forged it link by link, like he forged the North new. You stole it from the Bloody-Nine, and you had to stab him in the back to get it." Calder smirked like his life depended on it. Which it did. "All you are is a thief, Black Dow, and a coward, and an oath-breaker, and a fucking idiot besides."

"That a fact?" Dow tried to smile himself, but it looked more like a scowl. Calder might be a beaten man, but that was just the point. Having a beaten man fling shit at him was souring his day of victory.

"Haven't you got the bones to face me, man to man?"

"Show me a man and we'll see."

"I was man enough for Tenways' daughter." Calder got a flutter of laughter of his own. "But what?" And he nodded up to Shivers. "You get harder men to do your black work now, do you, Black Dow? Lost your taste for it? Come on! Fight me! The circle!"

Dow had no real reason to say yes. He'd nothing to win. But sometimes it's more about how it looks than how it is. Calder was famous as the biggest coward and piss-poorest fighter in any given company. Dow's name was all built on being the very opposite. This was a challenge to everything he was, in front of all the great men of the North. He couldn't turn it down. Dow saw it, and he slouched back in Skarling's Chair like a man who'd argued with his wife over whose turn it was to muck out the pigpen, and lost.

"All right. You want it the hard way you can have it the fucking hard way. Tomorrow at dawn. And no pissing about spinning the shield and choosing weapons. Me and you. A sword each. To the death." He angrily waved his hand. "Take this bastard somewhere I don't have to look at him smirk."

Calder gasped as Shivers jerked him to his feet, twisted him around and marched him off. The crowd closed in behind them. Songs started up again, and laughter, and bragging, and all the business of victory and success. His imminent doom was a distraction hardly worth stopping the party for.

"I thought I told you to run." Craw's familiar voice in his ear, the old man pushing through the press beside him.

Calder snorted. "I thought I told you not to say anything. Seems neither of us can do as we're told."

"I'm sorry it had to be this way."

"It didn't have to be this way."

He saw Craw's grimace etched by firelight. "You're right. I'm sorry this is what I chose, then."

"Don't be. You're a straight edge, everyone knows it. And let's face the facts, I've been hurtling towards the grave ever since my father died. Just a surprise it's taken me this long to hit mud. Who knows, though?" he called as Shivers dragged him between two of the Heroes, giving Craw one last smirk over his shoulder. "Maybe I'll beat Dow in the circle!"

He could tell from Craw's sorry face he didn't think it likely. Neither did Calder, if he was honest for once. The very reasons for the success of his little plan were also its awful shortcomings. Calder was the biggest coward and piss-poorest fighter in any given company. Black Dow was the very opposite. They hadn't earned their reputations by accident.

He'd about as much chance in the circle as a side of ham, and everyone knew it.

Stuff Happens

I've a letter for General Mitterick," said Tunny, hooding his lantern as he walked up out of the dusk to the general's tent.

Even in the limited light, it was plain the guard was a man who nature had favoured better below the neck than above it. "He's with the lord marshal. You'll have to wait."

Tunny displayed his sleeve. "I'm a full corporal, you know. Don't I get precedence?"

The guard did not take the joke. "Press-a-what?"

"Never mind." Tunny sighed, and stood beside him, and waited. Voices burbled from the tent, gaining in volume.

"I demand the right to attack!" one boomed out. Mitterick. There weren't many soldiers in the army who had the good fortune not to recognise that voice. The guard frowned across at Tunny as though to say, you shouldn't be listening to this. Tunny held up the letter and shrugged. "We've forced them back! They're teetering, exhausted! They've no stomach left for it." Shadows moved on the side of the tent, perhaps a shaken fist. "The slightest push now...I have them just where I want them!"

"You thought you had them there yesterday and it turned out they had you." Marshal Kroy's more measured tones. "And the Northmen aren't the only ones who've run out of stomach."

"My men deserve the chance to finish what they've started! Lord Marshal, I deserve the—"

"No!" Harsh as a whip cracking.

"Then, sir, I demand the right to resign—"

"No to that too. No even more to that." Mitterick tried to say something but Kroy spoke over him. "No! Must you argue every point? You will swallow your damn pride and do your damn duty! You will stand down, you will bring your men back across the bridge and you will prepare your division for the journey south to Uffrith as soon as we have completed negotiations. Do you understand me, General?"

There was a long pause and then, very quietly, "We lost." Mitterick's voice, but hardly recognisable. Suddenly shrunk very small, and weak, sounding almost as if there were tears in it. As if some cord held vibrating taut had suddenly snapped, and all Mitterick's bluster had snapped with it. "We lost."

"We drew." Kroy's voice was quiet now, but the night was quiet, and few men could drop eaves like Tunny when there was something worth hearing. "Sometimes that's the most one can hope for. The irony of the soldier's profession. War can only ever pave the way for peace. And it should be no other way. I used to be like you, Mitterick. I thought there was but one right thing to do. One day, probably very soon, you will replace me, and you will learn the world is otherwise."

Another pause. "Replace you?"

"I suspect the great architect has tired of this particular mason. General Jalenhorm died at the Heroes. You are the only reasonable choice. One that I support in any case."

"I am speechless."

"If I had known I could achieve that simply by resigning I would have done it years ago."

A pause. "I would like Opker promoted to lead my division."

"I see no objection."

"And for General Jalenhorm's I thought—"

"Colonel Felnigg has been given the command," said Kroy. "General Felnigg, I should say."

"Felnigg?" came Mitterick's voice, with a tinge of horror.

"He has the seniority, and my recommendation to the king is already sent."

"I simply cannot work with that man—"

"You can and you will. Felnigg is sharp, and cautious, and he will balance you out, as you have balanced me. Though you were often, frankly, a pain in my arse, by and large it has been an honour." There was a sharp crack, as of polished boot heels snapping together.

Then another. "Lord Marshal Kroy, the honour has been entirely mine."

Tunny and the guard both flung themselves to the most rigid attention as the two biggest hats in the army suddenly strode from the tent. Kroy made sharply off into the gathering gloom. Mitterick stayed there, looking after him, one hand opening and closing by his side.

Tunny had a pressing appointment with a bottle and a bedroll. He cleared his throat. "General Mitterick, sir!"

Mitterick turned, very obviously wiping away a tear while pretending to be clearing dust from his eye. "Yes?"

"Corporal Tunny, sir, standard-bearer of his Majesty's First Regiment."

Mitterick frowned. "The same Tunny who was made colour sergeant after Ulrioch?"

Tunny puffed out his chest. "The same, sir."

"The same Tunny who was demoted after Dunbrec?"

Tunny's shoulders slumped. "The same, sir."

"The same Tunny who was court-martialled after that business at Shricta?"

And further yet. "The same, sir, though I hasten to point out that the tribunal found no evidence of wrongdoing, sir."

Mitterick snorted. "So much for tribunals. What brings you here, Tunny?"

He held out the letter. "I have come in my official capacity as standard-bearer, sir, with a letter from my commanding officer, Colonel Vallimir."

Mitterick looked down at it. "What does it say?"

"I wouldn't—"

"I do not believe a soldier with your experience of tribunals would carry a letter without a good idea of the contents. What does it say?"

Tunny conceded the point. "Sir, I believe the colonel lays out at some length the reasons behind his failure to attack today."

"Does he."

"He does, sir, and he furthermore apologises most profusely to you, sir, to Marshal Kroy, to his Majesty, and in fact to the people of the Union in general, and he offers his immediate resignation, sir, but also demands the right to explain himself before a court martial – he was rather vague on that point, sir – he goes on to praise the men and to shoulder the blame entirely himself, and—"

Mitterick took the letter from Tunny's hand, crumpled it up in his fist and tossed it into a puddle.

"Tell Colonel Vallimir not to worry." He watched the letter for a moment, drifting in the broken reflection of the evening sky, then shrugged. "It's a battle. We all made mistakes. Would it be pointless, Corporal Tunny, to tell you to stay out of trouble?"

"All advice gratefully considered, sir."

"What if I make it an order?"

"All orders considered too, sir."

"Huh. Dismissed."

Tunny snapped out his most sycophantic salute, turned and quick-marched off into the night before anyone decided to court martial him.

The moments after a battle are a profiteer's dream. Corpses to be picked over, or dug up and picked over, trophies to be traded, booze, and chagga, and husk to be sold to the celebrating or the commiserating at equally outrageous mark-ups. He'd seen men without a bit to their names in the year leading up to an engagement make their fortunes in the hour after. But most of Tunny's stock was still on his horse, which was who knew where, and, besides, his heart just wasn't in it.

So he kept his distance from the fires and the men around them, strolling along behind the lines, heading north across the trampled battlefield. He passed a pair of clerks booking the dead by lamplight, one making notes in a ledger while the other twitched up shrouds to look for corpses worth noting and shipping back to Midderland, men too noble to go in the Northern dirt. As though one dead man's any different from another. He clambered over the wall he'd spent all day watching, become again the unremarkable farmer's folly it had been before the battle, and picked his way through the dusk towards the far left of the line where the remains of the First were stationed.

"I didn't know, I just didn't know, I just didn't see him!"

Two men stood in barley patched with little white flowers, maybe thirty strides from the nearest fire, staring down at something. One was a nervous-looking young lad Tunny didn't recognise, holding an empty flatbow. A new recruit, maybe. The other was Yolk, a torch in one hand, stabbing at the lad with a pointed finger.

"What's to do?" growled Tunny as he walked up, already developing a bad feeling. It got worse when he saw what they were looking at. "Oh, no, no." Worth lay in a bald patch of earth, his eyes open and his tongue hanging out, a flatbow bolt right through his breastbone.

"I thought it was Northmen!" said the lad.

"The Northmen are on the north side of the lines, you fucking idiot!" snapped Yolk at him.

"I thought he had an axe!"

"A shovel." Tunny dug it out of the barley, just beyond the limp fingers of Worth's left hand. "Reckon he'd been off doing what he did best."

"I should fucking kill you!" snarled Yolk, reaching for his sword. The lad gave a helpless squeak, holding his flatbow up in front of him.

"Leave it." Tunny stepped between them, put a restraining palm on Yolk's chest and gave a long, painful sigh. "It's a battle. We all made mistakes. I'll go to Sergeant Forest, see what's to be done." He pulled the flatbow from the lad's limp hands and pushed the shovel into them. "In the meantime, you'd better get digging." For Worth, the Northern dirt would have to do.

AFTER THE BATTLE

"You never have to wait long, or look far,
to be reminded of how thin the line is
between being a hero or a goat"

Mickey Mantle

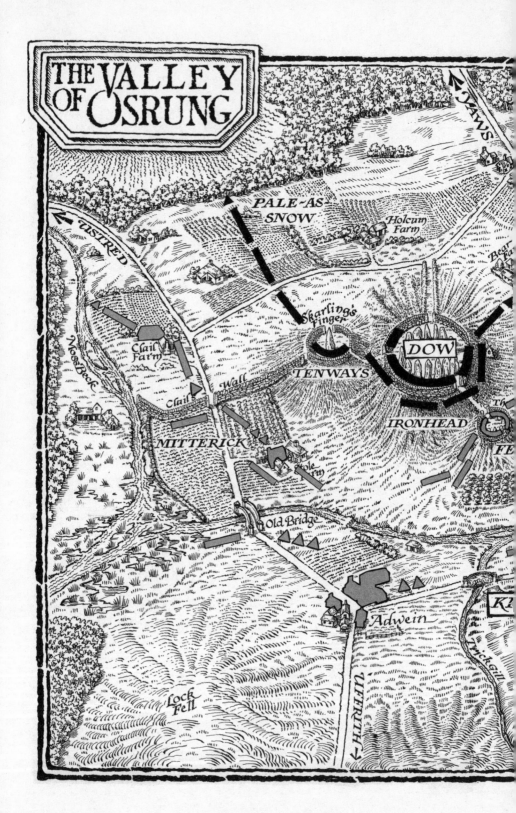

THE VALLEY
OF OSRUNG

USTRED

PALE-AS
SNOW

Holcum
Farm

Bear Fa

Skarling's
Finger

Clail
Farm

DOW

Moss Beck

Clail

Wall

TENWAYS

Th

IRONHEAD

FE

MITTERICK

ole
Inn

Old Bridge

K

Adwein

Lock
Fell

UFFRITH

Twic Gill

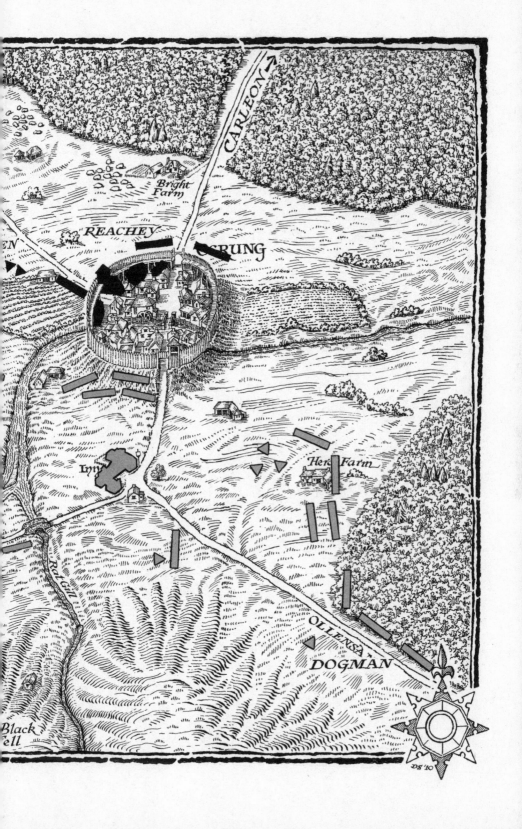

CARLEON

Bright
Farm

"REACHEY SPRUNG

Inn

Herl Farm

Rat Gill

OLLENSA
DOGMAN

Black
ell

DS '10

End of the Road

He in there?"

Shivers gave one slow nod. "He's there."

"Alone?" asked Craw, putting his hand on the rotten handle.

"He went in alone."

Meaning, more'n likely, he was with the witch. Craw wasn't keen to renew his acquaintance with her, especially after seeing her surprise yesterday, but dawn was on the way, and it was past time he was too. About ten years past time. He had to tell his Chief first. That was the right thing to do. He blew out through his puffed cheeks, grimaced at his stitched face, then turned the handle and went in.

Ishri stood in the middle of the dirt floor, hands on her hips, head hanging over on one side. Her long coat was scorched about the hem and up one sleeve, part of the collar burned away, the bandages underneath blackened. But her skin was still so perfect the torch flames were almost reflected in her cheek, like a black mirror.

"Why fight this fool?" she was sneering, one long finger pointing up towards the Heroes. "There is nothing you can win from him. If you step into the circle I cannot protect you."

"Protect me?" Dow slouched by the dark window, hard face all in shadow, his axe held loose just under the blade. "I've handled men ten times harder'n Prince bloody Calder in the circle." And he gave it a long, screeching lick with a whetstone.

"Calder." Ishri snorted. "There are other forces at work here. Ones beyond your understanding—"

"Ain't really beyond my understanding. You're in a feud with this First of the Magi, so you're using my feud with the Union as a way to fight each other. Am I close to it? Feuds I understand, believe me. You witches and whatever think you live in a world apart, but you've got both feet in this one, far as I can tell."

She lifted her chin. "Where there is sharp metal there are risks."

"'Course. It's the appeal o' the stuff." And the whetstone ground down the blade again.

Ishri narrowed her eyes, lip curling. "What is it with you damn pink men, and your damn fighting, and your damn pride?"

Dow only grinned, teeth shining as his face tipped out of the darkness. "Oh, you're a clever woman, no doubt, you know all kinds o' useful things." One more lick of the stone, and he held the axe up to the light, edge glittering. "But you know less'n naught about the North. I gave my pride up years ago. Didn't fit me. Chafed all over. This is about my name." He tested the edge, sliding his thumb-tip down it gently as you might down a lover's neck, then shrugged. "I'm Black Dow. I can't get out o' this any more'n I can fly to the moon."

Ishri shook her head in disgust. "After all the effort I have gone to—"

"If I get killed your wasted effort will be my great fucking regret, how's that?"

She scowled at Craw, and then at Dow as he set his axe down by the wall, and gave an angry hiss. "I will not miss your weather." And she took hold of her singed coat-tail and jerked it savagely in front of her face. There was a snapping of cloth and Ishri was gone, only a shred of blackened bandage fluttering down where she'd stood.

Dow caught it between finger and thumb. "She could just use the door, I guess, but it wouldn't have quite the...drama." He blew the scrap of cloth away and watched it twist through the air. "Ever wish you could just disappear, Craw?"

Only every day for the last twenty years. "Maybe she's got a point," he grunted. "You know. About the circle."

"You too?"

"There's naught to gain. Bethod always used to say there's nothing shows more power than—"

"*Fuck* mercy," growled Dow, sliding his sword from its sheath, fast enough to make it hiss. Craw swallowed, had to stop himself taking a step back. "I've given that boy all kinds o' chances and he's made me look a prick and a half. You know I've got to kill him." Dow started polishing the dull, grey blade with a rag, muscles working on the side of his head. "I got to kill him bad. I got to kill him so much no one'll think to make me look a prick for a hundred years. Got to teach a lesson. That's how this works." He looked up and Craw found he couldn't meet his eye. Found he was looking down at the dirt floor, and saying nothing. "Take it you won't be sticking about to hold a shield for me?"

"Said I'd stick 'til the battle's done."

"You did."

"The battle's done."

"The battle ain't ever done, Craw, you know that." Dow watched him, half his face in the light, the other eye just a gleam in the dark, and Craw started spilling reasons even though he hadn't been asked.

"There are better men for the task. Younger men. Men with better knees, and stronger arms, and harder names." Dow just kept watching. "Lost a lot o' my friends the last few days. Too many. Whirrun's dead. Brack's gone." Desperate not to say he'd no stomach for seeing Dow butcher Calder in the circle. Desperate not to say his loyalty might not stand it. "Times have changed. Men the likes o' Golden and Ironhead, they got no respect for me in particular, and I got less for them. All that, and... and..."

"And you've had enough," said Dow.

Craw's shoulders sagged. Hurt him to admit, but that summed it all up pretty well. "I've had enough." Had to clench his teeth and curl back his lips to stop the tears. As if saying it made it all catch up with him at once. Whirrun, and Drofd, and Brack and Athroc and Agrick and all those others. An accusing queue of the dead, stretching back into the gloom of memory. A queue of battles fought, and won, and lost. Of choices made, right and wrong, each one a weight to carry.

Dow just nodded as he slid his sword carefully back into its sheath. "We all got a limit. Man o' your experience needn't ever be shamed. Not ever."

Craw just gritted his teeth, and swallowed his tears, and managed to find some dry words to say. "Daresay you'll soon find someone else to do the job—"

"Already have." And Dow jerked his head towards the door. "Waiting outside."

"Good." Craw reckoned Shivers could handle it, probably better'n he had. He reckoned the man weren't as far past redemption as folk made out.

"Here." Dow tossed something across the room and Craw caught it, coins snapping inside. "A double gild and then some. Get you started, out there."

"Thanks, Chief," said Craw, and meant it. He'd expected a knife in his back before a purse in his hand.

Dow stood his sword up on its end. "What you going to do?"

"I was a carpenter. A thousand bloody years ago. Thought I might go back to it. Work some wood. You might shape a coffin or two, but you don't bury many friends in that trade."

"Huh." Dow twisted the pommel gently between finger and thumb, the end of the sheath twisting into the dirt. "Already buried all mine. Except the ones I made my enemies. Maybe that's where every fighter's road leads, eh?"

"If you follow it far enough." Craw stood there a moment longer but Dow didn't answer. So he took a breath, and he turned to go.

"It was pots for me."

Craw stopped, hand on the doorknob, hairs prickling all the way up his neck. But Black Dow was just stood there, looking down at his hand. His scarred, and scabbed, and calloused hand.

"I was apprentice to a potter." Dow snorted. "A thousand bloody years ago. Then the wars came, and I took up a sword instead. Always thought I'd go back to it, but... things happen." He narrowed his eyes, gently rubbing the tip of his thumb against the tips of his fingers. "The clay... used to make my hands... so soft. Imagine that." And he looked up, and he smiled. "Good luck, Craw."

"Aye," said Craw, and went outside, and shut the door behind him, and breathed out a long breath of relief. A few words and it was done. Sometimes a thing can seem an impossible leap, then when you do it you find it's just been a little step all along. Shivers was standing where he had been, arms folded, and Craw clapped him on the shoulder. "Reckon it's up to you, now."

"Is it?" Someone else came forward into the torchlight, a long scar through shaved-stubble hair.

"Wonderful," muttered Craw.

"Hey, hey," she said. Somewhat of a surprise to see her here, but it saved him some time. It was her he had to tell next.

"How's the dozen?" he asked.

"All four of 'em are great."

Craw winced. "Aye. Well. I need to tell you something." She raised one brow at him. Nothing for it but just to jump. "I'm done. I'm quitting."

"I know."

"You do?"

"How else would I be taking your place?"

"My place?"

"Dow's Second."

Craw's eyes opened up wide. He looked at Wonderful, then at Shivers, then back to her. "You?"

"Why not me?"

"Well, I just thought—"

"When you quit the sun would stop rising for the rest of us? Sorry to disappoint you."

"What about your husband, though? Your sons? Thought you were going to—"

"Last time I went to the farm was four years past." She tipped her head back, and there was a hardness in her eye Craw wasn't used to seeing. "They were gone. No sign o' where."

"But you went back not a month ago."

"Walked a day, sat by the river and fished. Then I came back to the dozen. Couldn't face telling you. Couldn't face the pity. This is all there is for the likes of us. You'll see." She took his hand, and squeezed it, but his stayed limp. "Been an honour fighting with you, Craw. Look after yourself." And she pushed her way through the door, and shut it with a clatter, and left him behind, blinking at the silent wood.

"You reckon you know someone, and then..." Shivers clicked his tongue. "No one knows anyone. Not really."

Craw swallowed. "Life's riddled with surprises all right." And he turned his back on the old shack and was off into the gloom.

He'd daydreamed often enough about the grand farewell. Walking down an aisle of well-wishing Named Men and off to his bright future, back sore from all the clapping on it. Striding through a passageway of drawn swords, twinkling in the sunlight. Riding away, fist held high in salute as Carls cheered for him and women wept over his leaving, though where the women might have sprung from was anyone's guess.

Sneaking away in the chill gloom as dawn crept up, unremarked and unremembered, not so much. But it's 'cause real life is what it is that a man needs daydreams.

Most anyone with a name worth knowing was up at the Heroes, waiting to see Calder get slaughtered. Only Jolly Yon, Scorry Tiptoe and Flood were left to see him off. The remains of Craw's dozen. And Beck, dark shadows under his eyes, the Father of Swords held in one pale fist. Craw could see the hurt in their faces, however they tried to plaster smiles over it. Like he was letting 'em down. Maybe he was.

He'd always prided himself on being well liked. Straight edge and that. Even so, his dead friends long ago got his living ones outnumbered, and they'd worked the advantage a good way further the last few days. Three of those that might've given him the warmest send-off were back to the mud at the top of the hill, and two more in the back of his cart.

He tried to drag the old blanket straight, but no tugging at the corners was going to make this square. Whirrun's chin, and Drofd's, and their noses, and their feet making sorry little tents of the threadbare old cloth. Some hero's shroud. But the living could use the good blankets. The dead there was no warming.

"Can't believe you're going," said Scorry.

"Been saying for years I would."

"Exactly. You never did."

Craw could only shrug. "Now I am."

In his head saying goodbye to his own crew had always been like pressing hands before a battle. That same fierce tide of comradeship. Only more, because they all knew it was the last time, rather than just fearing it might be. But aside from the feeling of squeezing flesh, it was nothing like that. They seemed strangers, almost. Maybe he was like the corpse of a dead comrade, now. They just wanted him buried, so they could get on. For him there wouldn't even be the worn-down ritual of heads bowed about the fresh-turned earth. There'd just be a goodbye that felt like a betrayal on both sides.

"Ain't staying for the show, then?" asked Flood.

"The duel?" Or the murder, as it might be better put. "I seen enough blood, I reckon. The dozen's yours, Yon."

Yon raised an eyebrow at Scorry, and at Flood, and at Beck. "All of 'em?"

"You'll find more. We always have. Few days time you won't even notice there's aught missing." Sad fact was it was more'n likely true. That's how it had always been, when they lost one man or another. Hard to imagine it'd be the same with yourself. That you'd be forgotten the way a pond forgets a stone tossed in. A few ripples and you're gone. It's in the nature of men to forget.

Yon was frowning at the blanket, and what was underneath. "If I die," he muttered, "who'll find my sons for me—"

"Maybe you should find 'em yourself, you thought o' that? Find 'em yourself, Yon, and tell 'em what you are, and make amends, while you've got breath still to do it."

Yon looked down at his boots. "Aye. Maybe." A silence comfortable as a spike up the arse. "Well, then. We got shields to hold, I reckon, up there with Wonderful."

"Right y'are," said Craw. Yon turned and walked off up the hill, shaking his head. Scorry gave a last nod then followed him.

"So long, Chief," said Flood.

"I guess I'm no one's Chief no more."

"You'll always be mine." And he limped off after the other two, leaving just Craw and Beck beside the cart. A lad he hadn't even known two days before to say the last goodbye.

Craw sighed, and he hauled himself up into the seat, wincing at all the bruises he'd gained the last few days. Beck stood below, Father of Swords in both hands, sheathed point on the dirt. "I've got to hold a shield for Black Dow," he said. "Me. You ever done that?"

"More'n once. There's nothing to it. Just hold the circle, make sure no one leaves it. Stand by your Chief. Do the right thing, like you did yesterday."

"Yesterday," muttered Beck, staring down at the wheel of the cart, like he was staring right through the ground and didn't like what he saw on the other side. "I didn't tell you everything, yesterday. I wanted to, but..."

Craw frowned over his shoulder at the two shapes under the blanket. He could've done without hearing anyone's confessions. He was carting enough weight around with his own mistakes. But Beck was already talking. Droning, flat, like a bee trapped in a hot room. "I killed a man, in Osrung. Not a Union one, though. One of ours. Lad called Reft. He stood, and fought, and I ran, and hid, and I killed him." Beck was still staring at the cartwheel, wet glistening in his eyes. "Stabbed him right through with my father's sword. Took him for a Union man."

Craw wanted just to snap those reins and go. But maybe he could help, and all his years wasted might be some use to someone. So he gritted his teeth, and leaned down, and put his hand on Beck's shoulder. "I know it burns at you. Probably it always will. But the sad fact is, I've heard a dozen stories just like it in my time. A score. Wouldn't raise much of an eyebrow from any man who's seen a battle. This is the black business. Bakers make bread, and carpenters make houses, and we make dead men. All you can do is take each day as it comes. Try and do the best you can with what you're given. You won't always do the right thing, but you can try. And you can try to do the right thing next time. That, and stay alive."

Beck shook his head. "I killed a man. Shouldn't I pay?"

"You killed a man?" Craw raised his arms, helplessly let them drop. "It's a battle. Everyone's at it. Some live, some die, some pay, some don't. If you've come through all right, be thankful. Try to earn it."

"I'm a fucking coward."

"Maybe." Craw jerked his thumb over his shoulder at Whirrun's corpse. "There's a hero. Tell me who's better off."

Beck took a shuddering breath. "Aye. I guess." He held up the Father of Swords and Craw took it under the crosspiece, hefted the great length of metal up and slid it carefully down in the back, next to Whirrun's body. "You taking it now, then? He left it to you?"

"He left it to the ground." Craw twitched the blanket across so it was out of sight. "Wanted it buried with him."

"Why?" asked Beck. "Ain't it God's sword, fell from the sky? I thought it had to be passed on. Is it cursed?"

Craw took up the reins and turned back to the north. "Every sword's a curse, boy." And he gave 'em a snap, and the wagon trundled off.

Away up the road.

Away from the Heroes.

By the Sword

Calder sat, and watched the guttering flames.

It was looking very much as if he'd used up all his cunning for the sake of another few hours alive. And cold, hungry, itchy, increasingly terrified hours at that. Sitting, staring across a fire at Shivers, bound wrists chafed and crossed legs aching and the damp working up through the seat of his trousers and making his arse clammy-cold.

But when a few hours is all you can get, you'll do anything for them. Probably he would've done anything for a few more. Had anyone been offering. They weren't. Like his brilliant ambitions the diamond-bright stars had slowly faded to nothing, crushed out as the first merciless signs of day slunk from the east, behind the Heroes. His last day.

"How long 'til dawn?"

"It'll come when it comes," said Shivers.

Calder stretched out his neck and wriggled his shoulders, sore from slumping into twisted half-sleep with his hands tied, twitching through nightmares which, when he jerked awake, he felt faintly nostalgic for. "Don't suppose you could see your way to untying my hands, at least?"

"When it comes."

How bloody disappointing it all was. What lofty hopes his father had held. "All for you," he used to say, a hand on Calder's shoulder and a hand on Scale's, "you'll rule the North." What an ending, for a man who'd spent his life dreaming of being king. He'd be remembered, all right. For dying the bloodiest death in the North's bloody history.

Calder sighed, ragged. "Things don't tend to work out the way we imagine, do they?"

With a faint clink, clink, Shivers tapped his ring against his metal eye. "Not often."

"Life is, basically, fucking shit."

"Best to keep your expectations low. Maybe you'll be pleasantly surprised."

Calder's expectations had plunged into an abyss but a pleasant surprise still didn't seem likely. He flinched at the memory of the duels the Bloody-Nine had fought for his father. The blood-mad shriek of the crowd. The ring of shields about the edge of the circle. The ring of grim Named Men holding them. Making sure no one could leave until enough blood was spilled. He'd never dreamed he'd end up fighting in one. Dying in one.

"Who's holding the shields for me?" he muttered, as much to fill the silence as anything.

"I heard Pale-as-Snow offered, and old White-Eye Hansul. Caul Reachey too."

"He can hardly get out of it, can he, since I'm married to his daughter?"

"He can hardly get out of it."

"Probably they've only asked for a shield so they don't get sprayed with too much of my gore."

"Probably."

"Funny thing, gore. A sour annoyance to those it goes on and a bitter loss to those it comes out of. Where's the upside, eh? Tell me that."

Shivers shrugged. Calder worked his wrists against the rope, trying to keep the blood flowing to his fingers. It would be nice if he could hold on to his sword long enough to get killed with it in his hand, at least. "Got any advice for me?"

"Advice?"

"Aye, you're some fighter."

"If you get a chance, don't hesitate." Shivers frowned down at the ruby on his little finger. "Mercy and cowardice are the same."

"My father always used to say that nothing shows greater power than mercy."

"Not in the circle." And Shivers stood.

Calder held up his wrists. "It's time?"

The knife glimmered pink with the dawn as it darted out and neatly slit the cord. "It's time."

We just wait?" grunted Beck.

Wonderful turned her frown on him. "Unless you fancy doing a little dance out there. Get everyone warmed up."

Beck didn't fancy it. The circle of raked-over mud in the very centre of the Heroes looked a lonely place to be right then. Very bare, and very empty, while all about its pebble-marked edge folk were packed in tight. It was in a circle like this one his father had fought the Bloody-Nine. Fought, and died, and bad.

A lot of the great names of the North were holding shields for this one. Beside the leftovers of Craw's dozen there was Brodd Tenways, Cairm Iron-head and Glama Golden on Dow's half of the circle, and plenty of their Named Men around 'em.

Caul Reachey stood on the opposite side of the case, a couple of other old boys, none of 'em looking happy to be there. Would've been a sorry lot compared to Dow's side if it hadn't been for the biggest bastard Beck had ever seen, towering over the rest like a mountain peak above the foothills.

"Who's the monster?" he muttered.

"Stranger-Come-Knocking," Flood whispered back. "Chief of all the lands east of the Crinna. Bloody savages out there, and I hear he's the worst."

It was a savage pack the giant had at his back. Men all wild hair and wild twitching, pierced with bone and prickled with paint, dressed in skulls and tatters. Men who looked like they'd sprung straight from an old song, maybe the one about how Shubal the Wheel stole the crag lord's daughter. How had it gone?

"Here they come," grunted Yon. A disapproving mutter, a few sharp words, but mostly thick silence. The men on the other side of the circle parted and Shivers came through, dragging Calder under the arm.

He looked a long stretch less smug than when Beck first saw him, riding up to Reachey's weapontake on his fine horse, but he was still grinning. A wonky, pale-faced, pink-eyed grin, but a grin still. Shivers let go of him, squelched heedless across the seven strides of empty muck leaving a trail of gently filling boot-prints, fell in beside Wonderful and took a shield from a man behind her.

Calder nodded across the circle at each man, like they were a set of old friends. He nodded to Beck. When Beck had first seen that smirk it'd looked full of pride, full of mockery, but maybe they'd both changed since. If Calder was laughing now it looked like he was only laughing at himself. Beck nodded back, solemn. He knew what it was to face your death, and he reckoned it took some bones to smile at a time like that. Some bones.

* * *

Calder was so scared the faces across the circle were just a dizzying smear. But he was set on meeting the Great Leveller as his father had, and his brother too. With some pride. He kept that in front of him, and he clung on to his smirk, nodding at faces too blurred to recognise as if they'd turned out for his wedding rather than his burial.

He had to talk. Fill the time with blather. Anything to stop him thinking. Calder grabbed Reachey's hand, the one without the battered shield on it. "You came!"

The old man hardly met his eye. "Least I could do."

"Most you could do, far as I'm concerned. Tell Seff for me...well, tell her I'm sorry."

"I will."

"And cheer up. This isn't a funeral." He nudged the old man in the ribs. "Yet." The scatter of chuckles he got for that made him feel a little less like shitting his trousers. There was a soft, low laugh among them, too. One that came from very high up. Stranger-Come-Knocking, and by all appearances on Calder's side. "You're holding a shield for me?"

The giant tapped the tiny-looking circle of wood with his club of a forefinger. "I am."

"What's your interest?"

"In the clash of vengeful steel and the blood watering the thirsty earth? In the roar of the victor and the scream of the slaughtered? What could interest me more than seeing men give all and take all, life and death balanced on the edge of a blade?"

Calder swallowed. "Why on my side, though?"

"There was room."

"Right." That was about all he had to offer now. A good spot to watch his own murder. "Did you come for the room?" he asked Pale-as-Snow.

"I came for you, and for Scale, and for your father."

"And me," said White-Eye Hansul.

After all the hate he'd shrugged off, that bit of loyalty almost cracked his smirk wide open. "Means a lot," he croaked. The really sad thing was that it was true. He thumped White-Eye's shield with his fist, squeezed Pale-as-Snow's shoulder. "Means a lot."

But the time for hugs and damp eyes was fading rapidly into the past.

There was noise in the crowd across the circle, then movement, then the shield-carriers stood aside. The Protector of the North strolled through the gap, easy as a gambler who'd already won the big bet, his black standard looming behind him like the shadow of death indeed. He'd stripped down to a leather vest, arms and shoulders heavy with branched vein and twisted sinew, the chain Calder's father used to wear hanging around his neck, diamond winking.

Hands clapped, weapons rattled, metal clanged on metal, everyone straining to get the faintest approving glance from the man who'd seen off the Union. Everyone cheering, even on Calder's side of the circle. He could hardly blame them. They'd still have to scratch a living when Dow had carved him into weeping chunks.

"You made it, then." Dow jerked his head towards Shivers. "I was worried my dog might've eaten you in the night." There was a good deal more laughter than the joke deserved but Shivers didn't so much as twitch, his scarred face a dead blank. Dow grinned around at the Heroes, their lichen-spotted tops peering over the heads of the crowd, and opened his arms, fingers spread. "Looks like we got a circle custom made for the purpose, don't it? Quite the venue!"

"Aye," said Calder. That was about all the bravado he could manage.

"Normally there's a form to follow." Dow turned one finger round and round. "Laying out the matter to decide, listing the pedigree of the champions and so on, but I reckon we can skip that. We all know the matter. We all know you got no pedigree." Another laugh, and Dow spread his arms again. "And if I start naming all the men I've put back in the mud we'll never get started!"

A flood of thigh-slapping manly amusement. Seemed Dow was intent on proving himself the better wit as well as the better fighter, and it was no fairer a contest. Winners always get the louder laughs and, for once, Calder was out of jokes. Dead men aren't that funny, maybe. So he just stood as the crowd quieted and left only the gentle wind over the muck, the flapping of the black standard, a bird chirruping from the top of one of the stones.

Dow heaved out a sigh. "Sorry to say I've had to send to Carleon for your wife. She stood hostage for you, didn't she?"

"Let her be, you bastard!" barked Calder, nearly choking on a surge of anger. "She's got no part in this!"

"You're in no place to tell me what's what, you little shit." Dow turned his head without taking his eyes off Calder, and spat into the mud. "I've half a mind to burn her. Give her the bloody cross, just for the fucking lesson. Wasn't that the way your father liked to do it, back in the old days?" Dow held up his open palm. "But I can afford to be generous. Reckon I'll let it pass. Out of respect to Caul Reachey, since he's the one man in the North who still does what he fucking says he will."

"I'm right grateful for it," grunted Reachey, still not meeting Calder's eye.

"'Spite of my reputation, I don't much care for hanging women. I get any softer they'll have to call me White Dow!" Another round of laughter, and Dow let go a flurry of punches at the air, so fast Calder could hardly count how many. "Reckon I'll just have to kill you twice as much to make up for it."

Something poked him in the ribs. The pommel of his sword, Pale-as-Snow handing it over with a look that said sorry, belt wrapped around the sheath.

"Oh, right. You got any advice?" asked Calder, hoping the old warrior would narrow his eyes and spout some razor observations about how Dow led with the point too much, or dipped his shoulder too low, or was awfully vulnerable to a middle cut.

All he did was puff out his cheeks. "It's fucking Black Dow," he muttered.

"Right." Calder swallowed sour spit. "Thanks for that." It was all so disappointing. He drew his sword, held the sheath uncertainly for a moment, then handed it back. Couldn't see why he'd have any need for it again. There was no talking his way out of this. Sometimes you have to fight. He took a long breath and a step forwards, his worn-out Styrian boot squelching into the muck. Only a little step over a ring of pebbles, but still the hardest he'd ever taken.

Dow stretched his head one way, then the other, then drew his own blade, taking his time about it, metal hissing softly. "This was the Bloody-Nine's sword. I beat him, man against man. You know. You were there. So what do you reckon your fucking chances are?" Looking at that long grey blade, Calder didn't reckon his chances were very good at all. "Didn't I warn you? If you tried to play your own games things'd get ugly." Dow swept the faces around the circle with his scowl. It was true, there were few pretty ones among them. "But you had to preach peace. Had to spread your little lies around. You had to—"

"Shut your fucking hole and get *on* with it!" screamed Calder. "You boring old cunt!"

A mutter went up, then some laughter, then another, bowel-loosening round of clattering metal. Dow shrugged, and took his own step forwards.

There was a rattle as men eased inwards, rims of their shields scraping, locking together. Locking them in. A round wall of bright painted wood. Green trees, dragon heads, rivers running, eagles flying, some scarred and beaten from the work of the last few days. A ring of hungry faces, teeth bared in snarls and grins, eyes bright with expectation. Just Calder, and Black Dow, and no way out but blood.

Calder probably should've been thinking about how he might beat the long, long odds, and get out of this alive. Opening gambits, thrust or feint, footwork, all the rest. Because he had a chance, didn't he? Two men fight, there's always a chance. But all he could think about was Seff's face, and how beautiful it was. He wished he'd been able to see it one more time. Tell her that he loved her, or not to worry, or to forget him and live her life or some other useless shit. His father always told him, "You find out what a man really is, when he's facing death." It seemed, after all, he was a sentimental little prick. Maybe we all are at the end.

Calder raised his sword, open hand out in front, the way he thought he remembered being taught. Had to attack. That's what Scale would've said. If you're not attacking you're losing. He realised too late his hand was trembling.

Dow looked him up and down, his own blade hanging carelessly at his side, and snorted a joyless chuckle. "I guess not every duel's worth singing about." And he darted forwards, lashing out underhand with a flick of his wrist.

Calder really shouldn't have been surprised to see a sword coming at him. That was what a duel was all about, after all. But even so he was pitifully unprepared. He lurched a pace back and Dow's sword crashed into his with numbing force, near ripping it from his hand, sending the blade flapping sideways and him stumbling, spare arm flailing for balance, all thought of attacking barged away by the overwhelming need to survive just one more moment.

Fortunately White-Eye Hansul's shield caught his back and spared him the indignity of sprawling in the mud, pushed him up straight in time to reel sideways as Dow sprang again, sword catching Calder's with a clang and wrenching his wrist the other way, a hearty cheer going up. Calder floundered back, cold with terror, trying to put as much space between them as he could, but the ring of shields was only so big. That was the point of it.

They slowly circled each other, Dow strutting with easy grace, sword swinging loose, as cocky and comfortable in a duel to the death as Calder might've been in his own bedchamber. Calder took the doddery, uncertain steps of a child just learning to walk, mouth hanging open, already breathing hard, cringing and stumbling at Dow's every tiniest taunting movement. The noise was deafening, breath going up in smoky puffs as the onlookers roared and hissed and hooted their support and their hatred and their —

Calder blinked, blinded for a moment. Dow had worked him around so the rising sun stabbed past the ragged edge of the standard and right in Calder's eyes. He saw metal glint, waved his sword helplessly, felt something thud into his left shoulder and spin him sideways, making a breathless squeal, waiting for the agony. He slid, righted himself, was shocked to see none of his own blood spraying. Dow had only slapped him with the flat. Toying with him. Making a show of it.

Laughter swept through the crowd, enough to sting some anger up in Calder. He gritted his teeth, hefting his sword. If he wasn't attacking he was losing. He lunged at Dow but it was so slippery underfoot he couldn't get any snap in it. Dow just turned sideways and caught Calder's wobbling sword as he laboured past, blades scraping together, hilts locking.

"Fucking weak," hissed Dow, and flung Calder away like a man might swat away a fly, heels kicking hopelessly at the slop as he reeled across the circle.

The men on Dow's side were less helpful than Hansul had been. A shield cracked Calder in the back of the skull and sent him sprawling. For a moment he couldn't see, couldn't breathe, skin fizzing all over. Then he was dragging himself up, limbs feeling like they weighed a ton a piece, the circle of mud tipping wildly about, jeering voices all booming and burbling.

He didn't have his sword. Reached for it. A boot came down and squashed his hand into the cold mud, spraying flecks of it in his face. He gave a gasp, more shock than pain. Then another, definitely pain as Dow twisted his heel, crushing Calder's fingers deeper.

"Prince of the North?" The point of Dow's sword pricked into Calder's neck, twisting his head towards the bright sky, making him slither helplessly up onto all fours. "You're a fucking embarrassment, boy." And Calder gasped as the point flicked his head back and left a burning cut up the middle of his chin.

Dow was trotting away, arms up, dragging out the show, a half-circle of leering, gurning, sneering faces showing above the shields behind him, all shouting. "Black...Dow...Black...Dow..." Tenways chanting gleefully along, and Golden, and Shivers just frowning, weapons thrusting at the air behind them in time.

Calder worked his hand trembling out of the mud. From what he could tell as red-black spots pattered onto it from his chin, not all of his finger-joints were where they used to be.

"Get up!" An urgent voice behind him. Pale-as-Snow, maybe. "Get up!"

"Why?" he whispered at the ground. The shame of it. Butchered by an old thug for the amusement of baying morons. He couldn't say it was undeserved, but that made it no more appealing, and no less painful either. His eyes flickered around the circle, desperately seeking a way out. But there was no way through the thicket of stomping boots, punching fists, twisted mouths, rattling shields. No way out but blood.

He took a few breaths until the world stopped spinning, then fished his sword from the mud with his left hand and got ever so slowly to his feet. Probably he should've been feigning weakness, but he didn't know how he could look any weaker than he felt. He tried to shake the fuzz from his head. He had a chance, didn't he? Had to attack. But by the dead, he was tired. Already. By the dead, his broken hand hurt, cold all the way to his shoulder.

Dow flicked his sword spinning into the air with a flourish. Left himself open for a moment in a show of warrior's arrogance. The moment for Calder to strike, and save himself, and earn a place in the songs besides. He tensed his leaden legs to spring, but by then Dow had already snatched the sword from the air with his left hand and was standing ready, his warrior's arrogance well deserved. They faced each other as the crowd slowly quieted, and the blood ran from Calder's slit chin and worked its way tickling down his neck.

"Your father died badly, as I remember," Dow called to him. "Head smashed to pulp in the circle." Calder stood in silence, saving his breath for another lunge, trying to judge the space between them. "Hardly had a face at all once the Bloody-Nine was done with him." A big step and a swing. Now, while Dow was busy boasting. Two men fight, there's always a chance. Dow grinned. "A bad death. Don't worry, though—"

Calder sprang, teeth rattling as his left boot thumped down and sprayed wet dirt, his sword going high and slicing hard towards Dow's skull. There was a slapping of skin as Dow caught Calder's left hand in his right, crushing Calder's fist around the hilt of his sword, blade wrenched up to waggle harmlessly at the sky.

"—I'll make sure yours is worse," Dow finished.

Calder pawed at Dow's shoulder with his broken hand, fingers flopping uselessly at his father's chain. The thumb still worked, though, and he scraped at Dow's pitted cheek with the nail, drawing a little bead of blood, growling as he tried to force it into the hole where Dow's ear used to be along with all his disappointment, and his desperation, and his anger, finding that flap of scar with the tip, baring his teeth as—

The pommel of Dow's sword drove into his ribs with a hollow thud and pain flashed through him to the roots of his hair. He probably would've screamed if he'd had any breath in him, but it was all gone in one ripping, vomiting wheeze. He tottered, bent over, bile washing into his frozen mouth and dangling in a string from his bloody lip.

"Thought you were the big *thinker*." Dow dragged him up by his left hand so he could hiss it right in his face. "Thought you could get the better o' me? In the *circle*? Don't look too clever now, do you?" The pommel crunched into Calder's ribs just as he was taking a shuddering breath and drove it whimpering out again, left him limp as a wet sheepskin. "Does he?" The crowd heckled and cackled and spat, rattled their shields and shrieked for blood. "Hold this." Dow tossed his sword through the air and Shivers caught it by the hilt.

"Stand up, fucker." Dow's hand thumped shut around Calder's throat, quick and final as a bear trap. "For once in your life, stand up." And Dow hauled Calder straight, not able to stand by himself, not able to move his one good hand or the sword still uselessly stuck in it, not able even to breathe. Singularly unpleasant, having your windpipe squeezed shut. Calder squirmed helplessly. His mouth tasted of sick. His face was burning, burning. It always catches people by surprise, the moment of their death, even when they should see it coming. They always think they're special, somehow expect a reprieve. But no one's special. Dow squeezed harder, making the bones in Calder's neck click. His eyes felt like they were going to pop. Everything was getting bright.

"You think this is the end?" Dow grinned as he lifted Calder higher, feet almost leaving the mud. "I'm just getting started, you fu—"

There was a sharp crack and blood sprayed up, dark streaks against the sky. Calder lurched back clumsily, gasping as his throat and his sword hand came free, near slipping over as Dow fell against him then flopped face down in the filth.

Blood gushed from his split skull, spattering Calder's ruined boots.

Time stopped.

Every voice sputtered out, coughed off, leaving the circle in sudden, breathless silence. Every eye fixed on the bubbling wound in the back of Black Dow's head. Caul Shivers stood glowering down in the midst of those gaping faces, the sword that had been the Bloody-Nine's in his fist, the grey blade dashed and speckled with Black Dow's blood.

"I'm no dog," he said.

Calder's eyes flicked to Tenways', just as his flicked to Calder's. Both their mouths open, both doing the sums. Tenways was Black Dow's man. But Black Dow was dead, and everything was changed. Tenways' left eye twitched, just a fraction.

You get a chance, don't hesitate. Calder flung himself forward, not much more than falling, his sword coming down as Tenways reached for the hilt of his, eyes going wide. He tried to bring his shield up, got it tangled with the man beside him, and Calder's blade split his rashy face open right down to his nose, blood showering out across the men beside him.

Just goes to show, a poor fighter can beat a great one easily, even with his left hand. As long as he's the one with the drawn sword.

Beck looked around as he felt Shivers move. Saw the blade flash over and stared, skin prickling, as Dow hit the muck. Then he went for his sword. Wonderful caught his wrist before it got there.

"No."

Beck flinched as Calder lurched at him, blade swinging. There was a hollow click and blood spattered around them, a spot on Beck's face. He tried to shake Wonderful off, get at his sword, but Scorry's hand was on his shield arm, dragging him back. "The right thing's a different thing for every man," hissed in his ear.

* * *

Calder stood swaying, his mouth wide open, his heart pounding so hard it was on the point of blowing his head apart, his eyes flickering from one stricken face to another. Tenways' blood-speckled Carls. Golden, and Ironhead, and their Named Men. Dow's own guards, Shivers in the midst of them, the sword that had split Dow's head still in his hand. Any moment now the circle would erupt into an orgy of carnage and it was anyone's guess who'd come out of it alive. Only certain thing seemed to be that he wouldn't.

"Come on!" he croaked, taking a wobbling step towards Tenways' men. Just to get it over with. Just to get it done.

But they stumbled back as if Calder was Skarling himself. He couldn't understand why. Until he felt a shadow fall across him, then a great weight on his shoulder. So heavy it almost made his knees buckle.

The huge hand of Stranger-Come-Knocking. "This was well done," said the giant, "and fairly done too, for anything that wins is fair in war, and the greatest victory is the one that takes the fewest blows. Bethod was King of the Northmen. So should his son be. I, Stranger-Come-Knocking, Chief of a Hundred Tribes, stand with Black Calder."

Whether the giant thought whoever was in charge stuck Black before his name, or whether he thought Calder claimed it having won, or whether he just thought it suited, who could say? Either way it stuck.

"And I." Reachey's hand slapped down on Calder's other shoulder, his grinning, grizzled face beside it. "I stand with my son. With Black Calder." Now the proud father, nothing but support. Dow was dead, and everything was changed.

"And I." Pale-as-Snow stepped up on the other side, and suddenly all those words Calder had thought wasted breath, all those seeds he'd thought dead and forgotten, sprouted forth and bore amazing blooms.

"And I." Ironhead was next, and as he stepped from his men he gave Calder the faintest nod.

"And I." Golden, desperate not to let his rival get ahead of him. "I'm for Black Calder!"

"Black Calder!" men were shouting all around, urged on by their Chiefs. "Black Calder!" All competing to shout it loudest, as though loyalty to this sudden new way of doing things could be proved through volume. "Black

Calder!" As though this had been what everyone wanted all along. What they'd expected.

Shivers squatted down and dragged the tangled chain over Dow's ruined head. He offered it to Calder, dangling from one finger, the diamond his father had worn swinging gently, made half a ruby by blood.

"Looks like you win," said Shivers.

In spite of the very great pain, Calder found it in himself to smirk. "Doesn't it, though?"

What was left of Craw's dozen slipped unnoticed back through the press even as most of the crowd were straining forwards.

Wonderful still had Beck's arm, Scorry at his shoulder. They bundled him away from the circle, past a set of wild-eyed men already busy tearing Dow's standard down and ripping it up between 'em, Yon and Flood behind. They weren't the only ones sloping off. Even as Black Dow's War Chiefs were stumbling over his corpse to kiss Black Calder's arse, other men were drifting away. Men who could feel which way the wind was blowing, and thought if they stuck about it might blow 'em right into the mud. Men who'd stood tight with Dow, or had scores with Bethod and didn't fancy testing his son's mercy.

They stopped in the long shadow of one of the stones, and Wonderful set her shield down against it and took a careful look around. Folk had their own worries though, and no one was paying 'em any mind.

She reached into her coat, pulled something out and slapped it into Yon's hand. "There's yours." Yon even had something like a grin as he closed his big fist around it, metal clicking inside. She slipped another into Scorry's hand, a third for Flood. Then she offered one to Beck. A purse. And with plenty in it too, by the way it was bulging. He stood, staring at it, until Wonderful shoved it under his nose. "You get a half-share."

"No," said Beck.

"You're new, boy. A half-share is more'n fair—"

"I don't want it."

They were all frowning at him now. "He don't want it," muttered Scorry.

"We should've done..." Beck weren't at all sure what they should've done. "The right thing," he finished, lamely.

"The *what*?" Yon's face screwed up with scorn. "I hoped to have heard the last of that shit! Spend twenty years in the black business and have naught to show for it but scars, then you can preach to me about the right fucking thing, you little bastard!" He took a step at Beck but Wonderful held her arm out to stop him.

"What kind of right ends up with more men dead than less?" Her voice was soft, no anger in it. "Well? D'you know how many friends I lost the last few days? What's right about that? Dow was done. One way or another, Dow was done. So we should've fought for him? Why? He's nothing to me. No better'n Calder or anyone else. You saying we should've died for that, Red Beck?"

Beck paused for a moment, mouth open. "I don't know. But I don't want the money. Whose is it, even?"

"Ours," she said, looking him right in the eye.

"This ain't right."

"Straight edge, eh?" She slowly nodded, and her eyes looked tired. "Well. Good luck with that. You'll need it."

Flood looked a patch guilty, but he wasn't giving aught back. Scorry had a little smile as he dropped his shield on the grass and sank cross-legged onto it, humming some tune in which noble deeds were done. Yon was frowning as he rooted through the purse, working out how much he'd got.

"What would Craw have made o' this?" muttered Beck.

Wonderful shrugged. "Who cares? Craw's gone. We got to make our own choices."

"Aye." Beck looked from one face to another. "Aye." And he walked off.

"Where you going?" Flood called after him.

He didn't answer.

He passed by one of the Heroes, shoulder brushing the ancient rock, and kept moving. He hopped over the drystone wall, heading north down the hillside, shook the shield off his arm and left it in the long grass. Men stood about, talking fast. Arguing. One pulled a knife, another backing off, hands up. Panic spreading along with the news. Panic and anger, fear and delight.

"What happened?" someone asked him, grabbing at his cloak. "Did Dow win?"

Beck shook his hand off. "I don't know." He strode on, almost breaking into a run, down the hill and away. He only knew one thing. This life weren't for him. The songs might be full of heroes, but the only ones here were stones.

The Currents of History

Finree had gone where the wounded lay, to do what women were supposed to do when a battle ended. To soothe parched throats with water tipped to desperate lips. To bind wounds with bandages torn from the hems of their dresses. To calm the dying with soft singing that reminded them of Mother.

Instead of which she stood staring. Appalled by the mindless chorus of weeping, whining, desperate slobbering. By the flies, and the shit, and the blood-soaked sheets. By the calmness of the nurses, floating among the human wreckage as serene as white ghosts. Appalled more than anything else by the numbers. Laid out in ranks on pallets or sheets or cold ground. Companies of them. Battalions.

"There are more than a dozen," a young surgeon told her.

"There are scores," she croaked back, struggling not to cover her mouth at the stink.

"No. More than a dozen of these tents. Do you know how to change a dressing?"

If there was such a thing as a romantic wound there was no room for them here. Every peeled-back bandage a grotesque striptease with some fresh oozing nightmare beneath. A hacked-open arse, a caved-in jaw with most of the teeth and half the tongue gone, a hand neatly split leaving only thumb and forefinger, a punctured belly leaking piss. One man had been cut across the back of the neck and could not move, only lie on his face, breath softly wheezing. His eyes followed her as she passed and the look in them made her cold all over. Bodies skinned, burned, ripped open at strange angles, their secret insides laid open to the world in awful violation. Wounds that would ruin men as long as they lived. Ruin those who loved them.

She tried to keep her eyes on her work, such as it was, chewing her tongue, trembling fingers fumbling with knots and pins. Trying not to listen to the whispers for help that she did not know how to give. That no one could give. Red spots appearing on the new bandages even before she finished, and growing, and growing, and she was forcing down tears, and forcing down sick, and on to the next, who was missing his left arm above the elbow, the left side of his face covered by bandages, and—

"Finree."

She looked up and realised, to her cold horror, that it was Colonel Brint. They stared at each other for what felt like for ever, in awful silence, in that awful place.

"I didn't know..." There was so much she did not know she hardly knew how to continue.

"Yesterday," he said, simply.

"Are you..." She almost asked him if he was all right, but managed to bite the words off. The answer was horribly obvious. "Do you need—"

"Have you heard anything? About Aliz?" The name alone was enough to make her guts cramp up even further. She shook her head. "You were with her. Where were you held?"

"I don't know. I was hooded. They took me away and sent me back." And oh, how glad she was that Aliz had been left behind in the dark, and not her. "I don't know where she'll be now..." Though she could guess. Perhaps Brint could too. Perhaps he was spending all his time guessing.

"Did she say anything?"

"She was...very brave." Finree managed to force her face into the sickly semblance of a smile. That was what you were supposed to do, wasn't it? Lie? "She said she loved you." She put a halting hand on his arm. The one he still had. "She said...not to worry."

"Not to worry," he muttered, staring at her with one bloodshot eye. Whether he was comforted, or outraged, or simply did not believe a word of her blame-shirking platitudes she could not tell. "If I could just *know*."

Finree did not think it would help him to know. It was not helping her. "I'm so sorry," she whispered, unable even to look at him any longer. "I tried...I did everything I could, but..." That, at least, was true. Wasn't it? She gave Brint's limp arm one last squeeze. "I have to...get some more bandages—"

"Will you come back?"

"Yes," she said, lurching up, not sure if she was still lying, "of course I will." And she almost tripped over her feet in her haste to escape that nightmare, thanking the Fates over and over and over that they had chosen her for saving.

Sick of penance, she wandered up the hillside path towards her father's headquarters. Past a pair of corporals dancing a drunken jig to the music of a squeaky fiddle. Past a row of women washing shirts in a brook. Past a row of soldiers queuing eagerly for the king's gold, gleaming metal in the paymaster's fingers glimpsed through the press of bodies. A small crowd of yammering salesmen, conmen and pimps had already gathered about the far end of the line like gulls about a patch of crumbs, realising, no doubt, that peace would soon put them out of business and give honest men the chance to thrive.

Not far from the barn she passed General Mitterick, chaperoned by a few of his staff, and he gave her a solemn nod. Right away she felt something was wrong. Usually his intolerable smugness was reliable as the dawn. Then she saw Bayaz step from the low doorway, and the feeling grew worse. He stood aside to let her pass with all the smugness Mitterick had been missing.

"Fin." Her father stood alone in the middle of the dim room. He gave her a puzzled smile. "Well, there it is." Then he sat down in a chair, gave a shuddering sigh and undid his top button. She had not seen him do that during the day in twenty years.

She strode back into the open air. Bayaz had made it no more than a few dozen strides, speaking softly to his curly-headed henchman.

"You! I want to speak to you!"

"And I to you, in fact. What a happy chance." The Magus turned to his servant. "Take him the money, then, as we agreed, and...send for the plumbers." The servant bowed and backed respectfully away. "Now, what can I—"

"You cannot replace him."

"And we are speaking of?"

"My father!" she snapped. "As you well know!"

"I did not replace him." Bayaz looked almost amused. "Your father had the good grace, and the good sense, to resign."

"He is the best man for the task!" It was an effort to stop herself from grabbing the Magus' bald head and biting it. "The one man who did a thing to limit this pointless bloody slaughter! That puffed-up fool Mitterick? He charged half his division to their deaths yesterday! The king needs men who—"

"The king needs men who obey."

"You do not have the authority!" Her voice was cracking. "My father is a lord marshal with a chair on the Closed Council, only the king himself can remove him!"

"Oh, the shame! Undone by the very rules of government I myself drafted!" Bayaz stuck out his bottom lip as he reached into his coat pocket and slid out a scroll with a heavy red seal. "Then I suppose this carries no weight either." He gently unrolled it, thick parchment crackling faintly. Finree found herself suddenly breathless as the Magus cleared his throat.

"By royal decree, Harod dan Brock is to be restored to his father's seat on the Open Council. Some of the family estates near Keln will be returned, along with lands near Ostenhorm from which, it will be hoped, your husband will attend to his new responsibilities as lord governor of Angland." Bayaz turned the paper around and brought it closer, her eyes darting over the blocks of masterful calligraphy like a miser's over a chest of jewels.

"How could the king not be moved by such loyalty, such bravery, such sacrifice as the young *Lord* Brock displayed?" Bayaz leaned close. "Not to mention the courage and tenacity of his wife who, captured by the Northmen, mark you, poked Black Dow in the eye and demanded the release of sixty prisoners! Why, his August Majesty would have to be made of *stone.* He is not, in case you were wondering. Few men less so, indeed. He wept when he read the despatch that described your husband's heroic assault upon the bridge. *Wept.* Then he ordered this paper drawn up, and signed it within the hour." The Magus leaned closer yet, so she could almost feel his breath upon her face. "I daresay...if one were closely to inspect this document...one could see the marks of his Majesty's earnest tears...staining the vellum."

For the first time since it had been produced, Finree shifted her eyes from the scroll. She was close enough to see each grey hair of Bayaz' beard, each brown liver spot on his bald pate, each deep, hard crease in his skin. "It would take a week for the despatch to reach him and another week for the edict to return. It has only been a day since—"

"Call it magic. His Majesty's carcass may be a week away in Adua, but his right hand?" Bayaz held his own up between them. "His right hand is a little closer by. But none of that matters now." He stepped back, sighing, and started to roll the parchment up. "Since you say I have not the authority. I shall burn this worthless paper, shall I?"

"No!" She had to stop herself snatching it from his hand. "No."

"You no longer object to your father's replacement?"

She bit her lip for a moment. War is hell, and all that, but it presents opportunities. "He resigned."

"Did he?" Bayaz smiled wide, but his green eyes stayed glittering hard. "You impress me once again. My earnest congratulations on your husband's meteoric rise to power. And your own, of course...Lady Governess." He held out the scroll by one handle. She took it by the other. He did not let go.

"Remember this, though. People love heroes, but new ones can always be found. With one finger of one hand I make you. With one finger of one hand..." He put his finger under her chin and pushed it up, sending a stab of pain through her stiff neck. "I can unmake you."

She swallowed. "I understand."

"Then I wish you good day!" And Bayaz released her and the scroll, all smiles again. "Please convey the happy news to your husband, though I must ask that you keep it between yourselves for the time being. People might not appreciate, as you do, quite how the magic works. I shall convey your husband's acceptance to his Majesty along with the news that he made the offer. Shall I?"

Finree cleared her throat. "By all means."

"My colleagues on the Closed Council will be delighted that the matter has been put to rest so swiftly. You must visit Adua when your husband is recovered. The formalities of his appointment. A parade, or some such. Hours of pomp in the Lords' Round. Breakfast with the queen." Bayaz raised one eyebrow as he turned away. "You really should procure some better clothes. Something with a heroic air."

The room was clean and bright, light streaming in through a window and across the bed. No sobbing. No blood. No missing limbs. No awful not knowing. The luck of it. One arm was bound under the covers, the other lying pale on the sheet, knuckles scabbed over, gently rising and falling with his breath.

"Hal." He grunted, eyelids flickering open. "Hal, it's me."

"Fin." He reached up and touched her cheek with his fingertips. "You came."

"Of course." She folded his hand in hers. "How are you?"

He shifted, winced, then gave a weak smile. "Bit stiff, honestly, but lucky.

Damn lucky to have you. I heard you dragged me out of the rubble. Shouldn't I be the one rushing to your rescue?"

"If it helps it was Bremer dan Gorst who found you and carried you back. I just ran around crying, really."

"You've always cried easily, it's one thing I love about you." His eyes started to drift shut. "I suppose I can live with Gorst...doing the saving..."

She squeezed his hand tighter. "Hal, listen to me, something has happened. Something wonderful."

"I heard." His eyelids moved lazily. "Peace."

She shrugged it off. "Not that. Well, yes, that, but..." She leaned over him, wrapping her other hand around his. "Hal, listen to me. You're getting your father's seat in the Open Council."

"What?"

"Some of his lands, too. They want us...you...the king wants you to take Meed's place."

Hal blinked. "As general of his division?"

"As lord governor of Angland."

For a moment he looked simply stunned then, as he studied her face, worried. "Why me?"

"Because you're a good man." And a good compromise. "A hero, apparently. Your deeds have come to the notice of the king."

"Hero?" He snorted. "How did you do it?" He tried to get up onto his elbows but she put a hand on his chest and held him gently down.

Now was the opportunity to tell him the truth. The idea barely crossed her mind. "You did it. You were right after all. Hard work and loyalty and all those things. Leading from the front. That's how you get on."

"But—"

"Shhhh." And she kissed him on one side of the lips, and on the other, and in the middle. His breath was foul, but she did not care. She was not about to let him ruin this. "We can talk about it later. You rest, now."

"I love you," he whispered.

"I love you too." Gently stroking his face as he slipped back into sleep. It was true. He was a good man. One of the best. Honest, brave, loyal to a fault. They were well matched. Optimist and pessimist, dreamer and cynic. And what is love anyway, but finding someone who suits you? Someone who makes up for your shortcomings?

Someone you can work with. Work on.

Terms

They're late," grumbled Mitterick.

The table had six chairs around it. His Majesty's new lord marshal occupied one, stuffed into a dress uniform swaddled with braid and too tight about his neck. Bayaz occupied another, drumming his thick fingers upon the tabletop. The Dogman slumped in the third, frowning up towards the Heroes, a muscle on the side of his head occasionally twitching.

Gorst stood a pace behind Mitterick's chair, arms folded. Beside him was Bayaz' servant, a map of the north rolled up in his hands. Behind them, posed stiffly within the ring of stones but out of earshot, were a handful of the most senior remaining officers of the army. *A sadly denuded complement. Meed, and Wetterlant, and Vinkler, and plenty more beside could not be with us. Jalenhorm too.* Gorst frowned up towards the Heroes. *Standing on first name terms with me is as good as a death sentence, it seems.* His Majesty's Twelfth Regiment were all in attendance, though, arrayed in parade ground order just outside the Children on the south side, their forest of shouldered halberds glittering in the chilly sun. *A little reminder that we seek peace today, but are more than prepared for the alternative.*

In spite of his battered head, burning cheek, a score of other cuts and scrapes and the countless bruises outside and in, Gorst was more than prepared for the alternative as well. Itching for it, in fact. *What employment would I find in peacetime, after all? Teach swordsmanship to sneering young officers? Lurk about the court like a lame dog, hoping for scraps? Sent as royal observer to the sewers of Keln? Or give up training, and run to fat, and become an embarrassing drunk trading on old stories of almost-glory. You know that's Bremer dan Gorst, who was once the king's First Guard? Let's buy the squeaking joke a drink! Let's buy him ten so we can watch him piss himself!*

Gorst felt his frown grow deeper. *Or... should I take up Black Dow's offer? Should I go where they sing songs about men like me instead of sniggering at their disgrace? Where peace need never come at all? Bremer dan Gorst, hero, champion, the most feared man in the North—*

"Finally," grunted Bayaz, bringing a sharp end to the fantasy.

There was the unmistakable sound of soldiers on the move and a body of Northmen began to tramp down the long slope from the Heroes, the rims of their painted shields catching the light. *It seems the enemy are prepared for the alternative, too.* Gorst gently loosened his spare long steel in its sheath, watchful for any sign of an ambush. Itching for it, in fact. A single Northern toe too close and he would draw. *And peace would simply be one more thing in my life that failed to happen.*

But to his disappointment the great majority halted on the gently sloping ground outside the Children, no nearer to the centre than the soldiers of the Twelfth. Several more stopped just inside the stones, balancing out the officers on the Union side. A truly vast man, black hair shifting in the breeze, was conspicuous among them. So was the one in gilded armour whose face Gorst had so enthusiastically beaten on the first day of the battle. He clenched his fist at the memory, fervently hoping for the chance to do it again.

Four men approached the table, but of Black Dow there was no sign. The foremost among them had a fine cloak, a very handsome face and the slightest mocking smile. In spite of a bandaged hand and a fresh scar down the middle of his chin, no one had ever looked more carelessly, confidently in charge. *And I hate him already.*

"Who is that?" muttered Mitterick.

"Calder." The Dogman's frown had grown deeper than ever. "Bethod's youngest son. And a snake."

"More of a worm," said Bayaz, "but it is Calder."

Two old warriors flanked him, one pale-skinned, pale-haired, a pale fur around his shoulders, the other heavyset with a broad, weathered face. A fourth followed, axe at his belt, terribly scarred on one cheek. His eye gleamed as if made of metal, but that was not what made Gorst blink. He felt a creeping sense of recognition. *Did I see him in the battle yesterday? Or the day before? Or was it somewhere before that...*

"You must be Marshal Kroy." Calder spoke the common tongue with only a trace of the North.

"Marshal Mitterick."

"Ah!" Calder's smile widened. "How nice to finally meet you! We faced each other yesterday, across the barley on the right of the battlefield." He waved his bandaged hand to the west. "Your left, I should say, I really am no soldier. That charge of yours was... magnificent."

496

Mitterick swallowed, his pink neck bulging over his stiff collar.

"In fact, do you know, I think…" Calder rooted through an inside pocket, then positively beamed as he produced a scrap of crumpled, muddied paper. "I have something of yours!" He tossed it across the table. Gorst saw writing over Mitterick's shoulder as he opened it up. An order, perhaps. Then Mitterick crumpled it again, so tightly his knuckles went white.

"And the First of the Magi! The last time we spoke was a humbling experience for me. Don't worry, though, I've had many others since. You won't find a more humbled man anywhere." Calder's smirk said otherwise, though, as he pointed out the grizzled old men at his back. "This is Caul Reachey, my wife's father. And Pale-as-Snow, my Second. Not forgetting my respected champion—"

"Caul Shivers." The Dogman gave the man with the metal eye a solemn nod. "It's been a while."

"Aye," he whispered back, simply.

"The Dogman, we all know, of course!" said Calder. "The Bloody-Nine's bosom companion, in all those songs along with him! Are you well?"

The Dogman ignored the question with a masterpiece of slouching disdain. "Where's Dow?"

"Ah." Calder grimaced, though it looked feigned. *Everything about him looks feigned.* "I'm sorry to say he won't be coming. Black Dow is…back to the mud."

There was a silence that Calder gave every indication of greatly enjoying. "Dead?" The Dogman slumped back in his chair. *As if he had been informed of the loss of a dear friend rather than a bitter enemy. Truly, the two can sometimes be hard to separate.*

"The Protector of the North and I had…a disagreement. We settled it in the traditional way. With a duel."

"And you won?" asked the Dogman.

Calder raised his brows and rubbed gently at the stitches on his chin with a fingertip, as if he could not quite believe it either. "Well, I'm alive and Dow's dead so…yes. It's been a strange morning. They've taken to calling me Black Calder."

"Is that a fucking fact?"

"Don't worry, it's just a name. I'm all for peace." Though Gorst fancied the Carls ranged on the long slope had different feelings. "This was Dow's battle, and a waste of everyone's time, money and lives as far as I'm concerned. Peace is the best part of any war, if you're asking me."

"I heartily concur." Mitterick might have had the new uniform, but it was Bayaz who did the talking now. "The settlement I propose is simple."

"My father always said that simple things stick best. You remember my father?"

The Magus hesitated for the slightest moment. "Of course." He snapped his fingers and his servant slipped forward, unrolling the map across the table with faultless dexterity. Bayaz pointed out the curl of a river. "The Whiteflow shall remain the northern boundary of Angland. The northern frontier of the Union, as it has for hundreds of years."

"Things change," said Calder.

"This one will not." The Magus' thick finger sketched another river, north of the first. "The land between the Whiteflow and the Cusk, including the city of Uffrith, shall come under the governorship of the Dogman. It shall become a protectorate of the Union, with six representatives on the Open Council."

"All the way to the Cusk?" Calder gave a sharp little in-breath. "Some of the best land in the North." He gave the Dogman a pointed look. "Sitting on the Open Council? Protected by the Union? What would Skarling Hoodless have said to that? What would my father have said?"

"Who cares a shit what dead men might have said?" The Dogman stared evenly back. "Things change."

"Stabbed with my own knife!" Calder clutched at his chest, then gave a resigned shrug. "But the North needs peace. I am content."

"Good." Bayaz beckoned to his servant. "Then we can sign the articles—"

"You misunderstand me." There was an uneasy pause as Calder shuffled forwards in his chair, as if they at the table were all friends together and the real enemy was at his back, and straining to hear their plans. "*I* am content, but I am not alone in this. Dow's War Chiefs are...a jealous set." Calder gave a helpless laugh. "And they have all the swords. I can't just agree to anything or..." He drew a finger across his bruised throat with a squelching of his tongue. "Next time you want to talk you might find some stubborn blowhard like Cairm Ironhead, or some tower of vanity like Glama Golden in this chair. Good luck finding terms then." He tapped the map with a fingertip. "I'm all for this myself. All for it. But let me take it away and convince my surly brood, then we can meet again to sign the whatevers."

Bayaz frowned, ever so sourly, at the Northmen standing just inside the Children. "Tomorrow, then."

"The day after would be better."

"Don't push me, Calder."

Calder was the picture of injured helplessness. "I don't want to push at all! But I'm not Black Dow. I'm more...spokesman than tyrant."

"Spokesman," muttered the Dogman, as though the word tasted of piss. "That will not be good enough."

But Calder's smirk was made of steel. Bayaz' every effort bounced right off. "If only you knew how hard I've worked for peace, all this time. The risks I've taken for it." Calder pressed his injured hand against his heart. "Help me! Help me to help us all." *Help you to help yourself, more likely.*

As Calder stood he reached across the map and offered his good hand to the Dogman. "I know we've been on different sides for a long time, one way or another, but if we're to be neighbours there should be no chill between us."

"Different sides. That happens. Time comes you got to bury it." The Dogman stood, looking Calder in the eye all the way. "But you killed Forley the Weakest. Never did no harm to no one, that lad. Came to give you a warning, and you killed him for it."

Calder's smile had turned, for the first time, slightly lopsided. "There isn't a morning comes I don't regret it."

"Then here's another." The Dogman leaned forward, extended his forefinger, pressed one nostril closed with it and blew snot out of the other straight into Calder's open palm. "Set foot south o' the Cusk, I'll cut the bloody cross in you. Then there'll be no chill." And he gave a scornful sniff, and stalked past Gorst and away.

Mitterick nervously cleared his throat. "We will reconvene soon, then?" Looking to Bayaz for support that did not arrive.

"Absolutely." Calder regained most of his grin as he wiped the Dogman's snot off on the edge of the table. "In three days." And he turned his back and went to talk to the man with the metal eye. The one called Shivers.

"This Calder seems a slippery bastard," Mitterick muttered to Bayaz as they left the table. "I'd rather have dealt with Black Dow. At least with him you knew what you were getting." Gorst was hardly listening. He was too busy staring at Calder and his scarred henchman. *I know him. I know that face. But from where...?*

"Dow was a fighter," Bayaz was murmuring. "Calder is a politician. He realises we are keen to leave, and that when the troops go home we will have nothing to bargain with. He knows he can win far more by sitting still and smirking than Dow ever did with all the steel and fury in the North..."

Shivers turned the ruined side of his face away as he spoke to Calder, the unburned side moving into the sun... and Gorst's skin prickled with recognition, and his mouth came open.

Sipani.

That face, in the smoke, before he was sent tumbling down the stairs. *That face.* How could it be the same man? And yet he was almost sure.

Bayaz' voice faded behind him as Gorst strode around the table, jaw clenched, and onto the Northmen's side of the Children. One of Calder's old retainers grunted as Gorst shouldered him out of the way. Probably this was extremely poor, if not potentially fatal, etiquette for peace negotiations. *And I could not care less.* Calder glanced up, and took a worried step back. Shivers turned to look. Not angry. Not afraid.

"Colonel Gorst!" someone shouted, but Gorst ignored it, his hand closing around Shivers' arm and pulling him close. The War Chiefs about the edge of the Children were all frowning. The giant took a huge step forwards. The man with the golden armour was calling out to the body of Carls. Another had put his hand to the hilt of his sword.

"Calm, everyone!" Calder shouted in Northern, one restraining palm up behind him. "Calm!" But he looked nervous. *As well he should. All our lives are balanced on a razor's edge. And I could not care less.*

Shivers did not look as if he cared overmuch himself. He glanced down at Gorst's gripping hand, then back up at his face, and raised the brow over his good eye.

"Can I help you?" His voice was the very opposite of Gorst's. A gravelly whisper, harsh as millstones grinding. Gorst looked at him. Really looked. As though he could drill into his head with his eyes. That face, in the smoke. He had glimpsed it only for a moment, and masked, and without the scar. *But still.* He had seen it every night since, in his dreams, and in his waking, and in the twisted space between, every detail stamped into his memory. *And I am almost sure.*

He could hear movement behind him. Excited voices. The officers and men of his Majesty's Twelfth. *Probably upset to have missed out on the battle. Probably almost as keen to become involved in a new chapter of it as I am myself.*

"Colonel Gorst!" came Bayaz' warning growl.

Gorst ignored him. "Have you ever been…" he hissed, "to Styria?" Every part of him tingling with the desire to do violence.

"Styria?"

"Yes," snarled Gorst, gripping even harder. Calder's two old men were creeping back in fighting crouches. "To Sipani."

"Sipani?"

"Yes." The giant had taken another immense step, looming taller than the tallest of the Children. *And I could not care less.* "To Cardotti's House of Leisure."

"Cardotti's?" Shivers' good eye narrowed as he studied Gorst's face. Time stretched out. All around them tongues licked nervously at lips, hands hovered ready to give their fatal signals, fingertips tickled at the grips of weapons. Then Shivers leaned close. Close enough almost for Gorst to kiss. Closer even than they had been to each other four years ago, in the smoke.

If they had been.

"Never heard of it." And he slipped his arm out of Gorst's slack grip and strode out of the Children without a backward glance. Calder swiftly followed, and the two old men, and the War Chiefs. All letting their hands drop from their weapons with some relief or, in the case of the giant, great reluctance.

They left Gorst standing there, in front of the table, alone. Frowning up towards the Heroes.

Almost sure.

Family

In many ways the Heroes hadn't changed since the previous night. The old stones were just as they had been, and the lichen crusted to them, and the trampled, muddied, bloodied grass inside their circle. The fires weren't much different, nor the darkness beyond them, nor the men who sat about them. But as far as Calder was concerned, there'd been some big-arsed changes.

Rather than dragging him in shame to his doom, Caul Shivers followed at a respectful distance, watching over his life. There was no scornful laughter as he strolled between the fires, no heckling and no hate. All changed the moment Black Dow's face hit the dirt. The great War Chiefs, and their fearsome Named Men, and their hard-handed, hard-hearted, hard-headed Carls all smiled upon him as if he was the sun rising after a bastard of a winter. How soon they'd adjusted. His father always said men rarely change, except in their loyalties. Those they'll shrug off like an old coat when it suits them.

In spite of his splinted hand and his stitched chin, Calder didn't have to work too hard to get the smirk onto his face now. He didn't have to work at all. He might not have been the tallest man about, but still he was the biggest in the valley. He was the next King of the Northmen, and anyone he told to eat his shit would be doing it with a smile. He'd already decided who'd be getting the first serving.

Caul Reachey's laughter echoed out of the night. He sat on a log beside a fire, pipe in his hand, spluttering smoke at something some woman beside him had said. She looked around as Calder walked up and he nearly tripped over his own feet.

"Husband." She stood, awkward from the weight of her belly, and held out one hand.

He took it in his and it felt small, and soft, and strong. He guided it over his shoulder, and slid his arms around her, hardly feeling the pain in his battered ribs as they held each other tight, tight. For a moment it seemed as if there was no one in the Heroes but them. "You're safe," he whispered.

"No thanks to you," rubbing her cheek against his.

His eyelids were stinging. "I... made some mistakes."

"Of course. I make all your good decisions."

"Don't leave me alone again, then."

"I think I can say it'll be the last time I stand hostage for you."

"So can I. That's a promise." He couldn't stop the tears coming. Some biggest man in the valley, stood weeping in front of Reachey and his Named Men. He would've felt a fool if he hadn't been so glad to see her he couldn't feel anything else. He broke away long enough to look at her face, light on one side, dark on the other, eyes with a gleam of firelight to them. Smiling at him, two little moles near the corner of her mouth he'd never noticed before. All he could think was that he didn't deserve this.

"Something wrong?" she asked.

"No. Just... wasn't long ago I thought I'd never see your face again."

"And are you disappointed?"

"I never saw anything so beautiful."

She bared her teeth at him. "Oh, they were right about you. You are a liar."

"A good liar tells as much truth as he can. That way you never know what you're getting."

She took his bandaged hand in hers, turning it over, stroking it with her fingertips. "Are you hurt?"

"Nothing to a famous champion like me."

She pressed his hand tighter. "I mean it. Are you hurt?"

Calder winced. "Doubt I'll be fighting any more duels for a while, but I'll heal. Scale's dead."

"I heard."

"You're all my family, now." And he laid his good hand on her swollen belly. "Still—"

"Like a sack of oats on my bladder all the way from Carleon in a lurching bloody cart? Yes."

He smiled through his tears. "The three of us."

"And my father too."

He looked over at Reachey, grinning at them from his log. "Aye. And him."

"You haven't put it on, then?"

"What?"

"Your father's chain."

He slid it from his inside pocket, warm from being pressed close to his heart, and the diamond dropped to one side, full of the colours of fire. "Waiting for the right moment, maybe. Once you put it on...you can't take it off." He remembered his father telling him what a weight it was. Near the end.

"Why would you take it off? You're king, now."

"Then you're queen." He slipped the chain over her head. "And it looks better on you." He let the diamond drop against her chest while she dragged her hair free.

"My husband goes away for a week and all he brings me is the North and everything in it?"

"That's just half your gift." He moved as if to kiss her and held back at the last moment, clicking his teeth together just short of her mouth. "I'll give you the rest later."

"Promises, promises."

"I need to talk to your father, just for a moment."

"Talk, then."

"Alone."

"Men and their bloody chatter. Don't keep me waiting too long." She leaned close, her lip tickling at his ear, her knee rubbing up against the inside of his leg, his father's chain brushing against his shoulder. "I've a mind to kneel before the King of the Northmen." One fingertip brushed the scab on his chin as she stepped away, keeping his face towards her, watching him over her shoulder, waddling just a little with the weight of her belly but none the worse for that. None the worse at all. All he could think was that he didn't deserve this.

He shook himself and clambered to the fire, somewhat bent over since his prick was pressing up hard against the inside of his trousers, and poking a tent in Reachey's face was no way to start a conversation. His wife's father had shooed his grey-bearded henchmen away and was sitting alone, pressing a fresh lump of chagga down into his pipe with one thick thumb. A private little chat. Just like the one they'd had a few nights before. Only now Dow was dead, and everything was changed.

Calder wiped the wet from his eyes as he sat beside the fire-pit. "She's one of a kind, your daughter."

"I've heard you called a liar, but there was never a truer word said than that."

"One of a kind." As Calder watched her disappear into the darkness.

"You're a lucky man to have her. Remember what I told you? Wait long enough by the sea, everything you want'll just wash up on the beach." Reachey tapped at the side of his head. "I've been around a while. You ought to listen to me."

"I'm listening now, aren't I?"

Reachey wriggled down the log, a little closer to him. "All right, then. A lot of my boys are restless. Had their swords drawn a long time. I could do with letting some of 'em get home to their own wives. You got a mind to take this wizard's offer?"

"Bayaz?" Calder snorted. "I've a mind to let the lying bastard simmer. He had a deal with my father, a long time ago, and betrayed him."

"So it's a question of revenge?"

"A little, but mostly it's good sense. If the Union had pushed on yesterday they might've finished us."

"Maybe. So?"

"So the only reason I can see for stopping is if they had to. The Union's a big place. Lots of borders. I reckon they've got other worries. I reckon every day I let that bald old fuck sit his terms'll get better."

"Huh." Reachey fished a burning stick from the fire, pressed it to the bowl of his pipe, starting to grin as he got it lit. "You're a clever one, Calder. A thinker. Like your father. Always said you'd make quite a leader."

Calder had never heard him say it. "Didn't help me get here, did you?"

"I told you I'd burn if I had to, but I wouldn't set myself on fire. What was it the Bloody-Nine used to say?"

"You have to be realistic."

"That's right. Realistic. Thought you'd know that better'n most." Reachey's cheeks went hollow as he sucked at his pipe, let the brown smoke curl from his mouth. "But now Dow's dead, and you've got the North at your feet."

"You must be almost as pleased as I am with how it's all come out."

"'Course," as Reachey handed the pipe over.

"Your grandchildren can rule the North," as Calder took it.

"Once you're finished with it."

"I plan not to finish for a while." Calder sucked, bruised ribs aching as he breathed deep and felt the smoke bite.

"Doubt I'll live to see it."

"Hope not." Calder grinned as he blew out, and they both chuckled, though there might've been the slightest edge on their laughter. "You know, I've been thinking about something Dow said. How if he'd wanted me dead I'd have been dead. The more I think on it, the more sense it makes."

Reachey shrugged. "Maybe Tenways tried it on his own."

Calder frowned at the bowl of the pipe as if thinking it over, though he'd already thought it over and decided it didn't add. "Tenways saved my life in the battle yesterday. If he hated me that much he could've let the Union kill me and no one would've grumbled."

"Who knows why anyone does anything? The world's a complicated bloody place."

"Everyone has their reasons, my father used to tell me. It's just a question of knowing what they are. Then the world's simple."

"Well, Black Dow's back to the mud. And from the look o' your sword in his head, Tenways too. I guess we'll never know now."

"Oh, I reckon I've worked it out." Calder handed the pipe back and the old man leaned to take it. "It was you said Dow wanted me dead." Reachey's eyes flicked up to his, just for an instant, but long enough for Calder to be sure. "That wasn't altogether true, was it? It was what you might call a lie."

Reachey slowly sat back, puffing out smoke rings. "Aye, a little bit, I'll admit. My daughter has a loving nature, Calder, and she loves you. I've tried explaining what a pain in the arse you are but she just ain't hearing it. There's naught she wouldn't do for you. But it was getting so you and Dow weren't seeing things at all the same way. All your talk of bloody peace making things hard for everyone. Then my daughter up and stands hostage for you? Just couldn't have my only child at risk like that. Out of you and Dow, one had to go." He looked evenly at Calder, through the smoke of his pipe. "I'm sorry, but there it is. If it was you, well, that's a shame, but Seff would've found a new man. Better still, there was always the chance you'd come out on top o' Dow. And I'm happy to say that's how it happened. All I wanted was the best for my blood. So I'm ashamed to admit it, but I stirred the pot between the two o' you."

"Hoping all along I'd get the better of Dow."

"Of course."

"So it wasn't you at all who sent those boys to kill me at your weapon-take?"

The pipe froze half way to Reachey's mouth. "Why would I do a thing like that?"

"Because Seff was standing hostage, and I was talking big about dealing with Dow, and you decided to stir the pot a bit harder."

Reachey pressed the end of his tongue between his teeth, lifted the pipe the rest of the way, sucked at it again, but it was dead. He tapped the ashes out on the stones by the fire. "If you're going to stir the pot, I've always believed in doing it . . . firmly."

Calder slowly shook his head. "Why not just get your old pricks to kill me when we were sat around the fire? Make sure of it?"

"I got a reputation to think on. When it comes to knives in the dark I hire out, keep my name free of it." Reachey didn't look guilty. He looked annoyed. Offended, even. "Don't sit there like you're disappointed. Don't pretend you haven't done worse. What about Forley the Weakest, eh? Killed him for nothing, didn't you?"

"I'm me!" said Calder. "Everyone knows me for a liar! I guess I just . . ." Sounded stupid now he said it. "Expected better from you. I thought you were a straight edge. Thought you did things the old way."

Reachey gave a scornful grunt. "The old way? Hah! People are apt to get all misty-eyed over how things used to be. Age o' Heroes, and all. Well, I remember the old way. I was there, and it was no different from the new." He leaned forward, stabbing at Calder with the stem of his pipe. "Grab what you can, however you can! Folk might like to harp on how your father changed everything. They like someone to blame. But he was just better at it than the rest. It's the winners sing the songs. And they can pick what tune they please."

"I'm just picking out what tune they'll play on you!" hissed Calder, the anger flaring up for a moment. But, "Anger's a luxury the man in the big chair can't afford." That's what his father used to say. Mercy, mercy, always think about mercy. Calder took in a long, sore breath, and heaved out resignation. "But maybe I'd have done no different, wearing your coat, and I've too few friends by far. The fact is I need your support."

Reachey grinned. "You'll have it. To the death, don't worry about that. You're family, lad. Family don't always get on but, in the end, they're the only ones you can trust."

"So my father used to tell me." Calder slowly stood and gave another aching sigh, right from his gut. "Family." And he made his way off through the fires, towards the tent that had been Black Dow's.

"And?" croaked Shivers, falling into step beside him.

"You were right. The old fuck tried to kill me."

"Shall I return the favour?"

"By the dead, no!" He forced his voice softer as they headed away. "Not until my child's born. I don't want my wife upset. Let things settle then do it quietly. Some way that'll point the finger at someone else. Glama Golden, maybe. Can you do that?"

"When it comes to killing, I can do it any way you want it."

"I always said Dow should've made better use of you. Now my wife's waiting. Go and have some fun."

"I just might."

"What do you do for fun, anyway?"

There was a glint in Shivers' eye as he turned away, but then there always was. "I sharpen my knives."

Calder wasn't quite sure if he was joking.

New Hands

Dear Mistress Worth,

With the greatest regret, I must inform you of the death of your son in action on the battlefield near Osrung.

It is usual for the commanding officer to write such letters, but I requested the honour as I knew your son personally, and have but rarely in a long career served with so willing, pleasant, able, and courageous a comrade. He embodied all those virtues that one looks for in a soldier. I do not know if it can provide you with any satisfaction in the face of a loss so great, but it is not stretching the truth to say that your son died a hero. I feel honoured to have known him.

With the deepest condolences,
Your obedient servant,

Corporal Tunny,
Standard-Bearer of His Majesty's First Regiment.

Tunny gave a sigh, folded the letter ever so carefully and pressed two neat creases into it with his thumbnail. Might be the worst letter the poor woman ever got, he owed it to her to put a decent crease in the damn thing. He tucked it inside his jacket next to Mistress Klige's, unscrewed the cap from Yolk's flask and took a nip, then dipped the pen in the ink bottle and started on the next.

Dear Mistress Lederlingen,

With the greatest regret, I must inform you of the death of your son in—

"Corporal Tunny!" Yolk was approaching with a cocky strut somewhere between a pimp and a labourer. His boots were caked with dirt, his stained jacket was hanging open showing a strip of sweaty chest, his sunburned face sported several days' worth of patchy stubble and instead of a spear over his shoulder he had a worn shovel. He looked, in short, like a proud veteran of his August Majesty's army. He came to a stop not far from Tunny's hammock, looking down at the papers. "Working out all the debts you're owed?"

"The ones I owe, as it goes." Tunny seriously doubted Yolk could read, but he pushed a sheet of paper over the unfinished letter even so. If this got out it could ruin his reputation. "Everything all right?"

"Everything's well enough," said Yolk as he set down his shovel, though under his good humour he looked, in fact, a little pensive. "The colonel's had us doing some burying."

"Uh." Tunny worked the stopper back into the ink bottle. He'd done a fair amount of burying himself and it was never a desirable duty. "Always some cleaning up to do after a battle. A lot to put right, here and at home. Might take years to clean up what takes a day or three to dirty." He cleaned off his pen on a bit of rag. "Might never happen."

"Why do it, then?" asked Yolk, frowning off across the sunlit barley towards the hazy hills. "I mean to say, all the effort, and all the men dead, and what've we got done here?"

Tunny scratched his head. Never had Yolk down as a philosopher, but he guessed every man has his thoughtful moments. "Wars don't often change much, in my considerable experience. Bit here, bit there, but overall there have to be better ways for men to settle their differences." He thought about it for a moment. "Kings, and nobles, and Closed Councils, and so forth, I never have quite understood why they keep at it, given how the lessons of history do seem to stack up powerfully against. War is damned uncomfortable work, for minimal rewards, and it's the soldiers who always bear the worst."

"Why be a soldier, then?"

Tunny found himself temporarily at a loss for words. Then he shrugged. "Best job in the world, isn't it."

A group of horses were being led without urgency up the track nearby, hooves clopping at the mud, a few soldiers trudging along with them. One detached himself and strolled over, chewing at an apple. Sergeant Forest, and grinning broadly.

"Oh, bloody hell," muttered Tunny under his breath, quickly clearing the last evidence of letter writing and tossing the shield he'd been leaning on under his hammock.

"What is it?" whispered Yolk.

"When First Sergeant Forest smiles there's rarely good news on the way."

"When is there good news on the way?"

Tunny had to admit Yolk had a point.

"Corporal Tunny!" Forest stripped his apple and flicked away the core. "You're awake."

"Sadly, Sergeant, yes. Any news from our esteemed commanders?"

"Some." Forest jerked a thumb towards the horses. "You'll be delighted to learn we're getting our mounts back."

"Marvellous," grunted Tunny. "Just in time to ride them back the way we came."

"Let it never be said that his August Majesty does not provide his loyal soldiers with everything needful. We're pulling out in the morning. Or the following morning, at the latest. Heading for Uffrith, and a nice warm boat."

Tunny found a smile of his own. He'd had about enough of the North. "Homewards, eh? My favourite direction."

Forest saw Tunny's grin and raised him a tooth on each side. "Sorry to disappoint you. We're shipping for Styria."

"Styria?" muttered Yolk, hands on hips.

"For beautiful Westport!" Forest flung an arm around Yolk's shoulders and pushed his other hand out in front of them, as if showing off a magnificent civic vista where there was, in fact, a stand of rotting trees. "Crossroads of the world! We're to stand alongside our bold allies in Sipani, and take righteous arms against that notorious she-devil Monzcarro Murcatto, the Snake of Talins. She is, by all reports, a fiend in human form, an enemy to freedom and the greatest threat ever to face the Union!"

"Since Black Dow." Tunny rubbed at the bridge of his nose, his smile a memory. "Who we made peace with yesterday."

Forest slapped Yolk on the shoulder. "The beauty of the soldier's profession, trooper. The world never runs out of villains. And Marshal Mitterick's just the man to make 'em quake!"

"Marshal...Mitterick?" Yolk looked baffled. "What happened to Kroy?"

"He's done," grunted Tunny.

"How many have you outlasted now?" asked Forest.

"I'm thinking...eight, at a quick guess." Tunny counted them off on his fingers. "Frengen, then Altmoyer, then that short one..."

"Krepsky."

"Krepsky. Then the other Frengen."

"The other Frengen," snorted Forest.

"A notable fool even for a commander-in-chief. Then there was Varuz, then Burr, then West—"

"He was a good man, West."

"Gone too early, like most good men. Then we had Kroy..."

"Lord marshals are temporary in nature," explained Forest, gesturing at Tunny, "but corporals? Corporals are eternal."

"Sipani, you say?" Tunny slid slowly back in his hammock, putting one boot up and rocking himself gently back and forth with the other. "Never been there myself." Now that he was thinking about it, he was starting to see the advantages. A good soldier always keeps an eye on the advantages. "Fine weather, I expect?"

"Excellent weather," said Forest.

"And I hear they have the best bloody whores in the world."

"The ladies of the city have been mentioned once or twice since the orders came down."

"Two things to look forward to."

"Which is two more than you get in the North." Forest was smiling bigger than ever. Bigger than seemed necessary. "And in the meantime, since your detail stands so sadly reduced, here's another."

"Oh, no," groaned Tunny, all hopes of whores and sunshine quickly wilting.

"Oh, yes! Up you come, lads!"

And up they came indeed. Four of them. New recruits, fresh off the boat from Midderland by their looks. Seen off at the docks with kisses from Mummy or sweetheart or both. New uniforms pressed, buckles gleaming, and ready for the noble soldiering life, indeed. They stared open-mouthed at Yolk, who could hardly have presented a greater contrast, his face pinched and rat-like, his jacket frayed and mud-smeared from grave-digging, one strap on his pack broken and repaired with string. Forest gestured towards Tunny like a showman towards his freak, and trotted out that same little speech he always gave.

"Boys, this here is the famous Corporal Tunny, one of the longest serving non-commissioned officers in General Felnigg's division." Tunny gave a long, hard sigh, right from his stomach. "A veteran of the Starikland Rebellion, the Gurkish War, the last Northern War, the Siege of Adua, the recent climactic Battle of Osrung and a quantity of peacetime soldiering that would have bored a keener mind to death." Tunny unscrewed the cap of Yolk's flask, took a pull, then handed it over to its original owner, who shrugged and had a swig of his own. "He has survived the runs, the rot, the grip, the autumn shudders, the caresses of Northern winds, the buffets of Southern women, thousands of miles of marching, many years of his Majesty's rations and even a tiny bit of actual fighting to stand – or sit – before you now..."

Tunny crossed one ruined boot over the other, sank slowly back into his hammock and closed his eyes, the sun glowing pink through his lids.

Old Hands

It was near sunset when he made it back. Midges swirling in clouds over the marshy little brook, yellowing leaves casting dappled shadows onto the path, boughs stirring in the breeze, low enough he had to duck.

The house looked smaller'n he remembered. It looked small, but it looked beautiful. Looked so beautiful it made him want to cry. The door creaked as he pushed it wide, almost as scared for some reason as he had been in Osrung. There was no one inside. Just the same old smoke-smelling dimness. His cot was packed away to make more space, slashes of pale sunlight across the boards where it had been.

No one here, and his mouth went sour. What if they were packed up and left? Or what if men had come when he was away, deserters turned bandit—

He heard the soft *clock* of an axe splitting logs. He ducked back out into the evening, hurrying past the pen and the staring goats and the five big tree stumps all hacked and scarred from years of his blade practice. Practice that hadn't helped much, as it went. He knew now stabbing a stump ain't much preparation for stabbing a man.

His mother was just over the rise, leaning on the axe by the old chopping block, arching her back while Festen gathered up the split halves and tossed 'em onto the pile. Beck stood there for a moment, watching 'em. Watching his mother's hair stirring in the breeze. Watching the boy struggling with the chunks of wood.

"Ma," he croaked.

She looked around, blinked at him for a moment. "You're back."

"I'm back."

He walked over to her, and she stuck one corner of the axe in the block for safe keeping and met him half way. Even though she was so much smaller than him she still held his head against her shoulder. Held it with one hand and pressed it to her, wrapped her other arm tight around him, strong enough to make it hard to breathe.

"My son," she whispered.

He broke away from her, sniffing back his tears, looking down. Saw his cloak, or her cloak, and how muddied, and bloodied, and torn it was. "I'm sorry. Reckon I got your cloak ruined."

She touched his face. "It's a bit of cloth."

"Guess it is at that." He squatted down, and ruffled Festen's hair. "You all right?" He could hardly keep his voice from cracking.

"I'm fine!" Slapping Beck's hand away from his head. "Did you get yourself a name?"

Beck paused. "I did."

"What is it?"

Beck shook his head. "Don't matter. How's Wenden?"

"Same," said Beck's mother. "You weren't gone more'n a few days."

He hadn't expected that. Felt like years since he was last here. "I guess I was gone long enough."

"What happened?"

"Can we . . . not talk about it?"

"Your father talked about nothing else."

He looked up at her. "If there's one thing I learned it's that I'm not my father."

"Good. That's good." She patted him gently on the side of the face, wet glimmering in her eyes. "I'm glad you're here. Don't have the words to tell you how glad I am. You hungry?"

He stood, straightening his legs feeling like quite the effort, and wiped away more tears on the back of his wrist. Realised he hadn't eaten since he left the Heroes, yesterday morning. "I could eat."

"I'll get the fire lit!" And Festen trotted off towards the house.

"You coming in?" asked Beck's mother.

Beck blinked out towards the valley. "Reckon I might stay out here a minute. Split a log or two."

"All right."

"Oh." And he slid his father's sword from his belt, held it for a moment, then offered it out to her. "Can you put this away?"

"Where?"

"Anywhere I don't have to look at it."

She took it from him, and it felt like a weight he didn't have to carry no more. "Seems like good things can come back from the wars," she said.

"Coming back's the only good thing I could see." He leaned down and set a log on the block, spat on one palm and took up the wood axe. The haft felt good in his hands. Familiar. It fitted 'em better than the sword ever had, that was sure. He swung it down and two neat halves went tumbling. He was no hero, and never would be.

He was made to chop logs, not to fight.

And that made him lucky. Luckier'n Reft, or Stodder, or Brait. Luckier'n Drofd or Whirrun of Bligh. Luckier'n Black Dow, even. He worked the axe clear of the block and stood back. They don't sing many songs about log-splitters, maybe, but the lambs were bleating, up on the fells out of sight, and that sounded like music. Sounded a sweeter song to him then than all the hero's lays he knew.

He closed his eyes and breathed in the smell of grass and woodsmoke. Then he opened 'em, and looked across the valley. Skin all tingling with the peace of that moment. Couldn't believe he used to hate this place.

Didn't seem so bad, now. Didn't seem so bad at all.

Everyone Serves

So you're standing with me?" asked Calder, breezy as a spring morning.

"If there's still room."

"Loyal as Rudd Threetrees, eh?"

Ironhead shrugged. "I won't take you for a fool and say yes. But I know where my best interest lies and it's at your heels. I'd also point out loyalty's a dangerous foundation. Tends to wash away in a storm. Self-interest stands in any weather."

Calder had to nod at that. "A sound principle." He glanced up at Foss Deep, lately returned to his service following the end of hostilities and an apt display of the power of self-interest in the flesh. Despite his stated distaste for battles he'd somehow acquired, gleaming beneath his shabby coat, a splendid Union breastplate engraved with a golden sun. "A man should have some, eh, Deep?"

"Some what?"

"Principles."

"Oh, I'm a big, big, big believer in 'em. My brother too."

Shallow took a quick break from furiously picking his fingernails with the point of his knife. "I like 'em with milk."

A slightly uncomfortable silence. Then Calder turned back to Ironhead. "Last time we spoke you told me you'd stick with Dow. Then you pissed on my boots." He lifted one up, even more battered, gouged and stained from the events of the past few days than Calder was himself. "Best bloody boots in the North a week ago. Styrian leather. Now look."

"I'll be more'n happy to buy you a new pair."

Calder winced at his aching ribs as he stood. "Make it two."

"Whatever you say. Maybe I'll get a pair myself and all."

"You sure something in steel wouldn't be more your style?"

Ironhead shrugged. "No call for steel boots in peacetime. Anything else?"

"Just keep your men handy, for now. We need to put a good show on 'til the Union get bored of waiting and slink off. Shouldn't be long."

"Right y'are."

Calder took a couple of steps away, then turned back. "Get a gift for my wife, too. Something beautiful, since my child's due soon."

"Chief."

"And don't feel too bad about it. Everyone serves someone."

"Very true." Ironhead didn't so much as twitch. A little disappointing, in fact – Calder had hoped to watch him sweat. But there'd be time for that later, once the Union were gone. There'd be time for all kinds of things. So he gave a lordly nod and smirked off, his two shadows trailing after.

He had Reachey on-side, and Pale-as-Snow. He'd had a little word with Wonderful, and she'd had the same little word with Dow's Carls, and their loyalty had washed with the rainwater, all right. Most of Tenways' men had drifted off, and White-Eye Hansul had made his own appeal to self-interest and argued the rest around. Ironhead and Golden still hated each other too much to pose a threat and Stranger-Come-Knocking, for reasons beyond Calder's ken, was treating him like an old and honoured friend.

Laughing stock to king of the world in the swing of a sword. Luck. Some men have it, some don't.

"Time to plumb the depth of Glama Golden's loyalty," said Calder happily. "Or his self-interest, anyway."

They walked down the hillside in the gathering darkness, stars starting to peep out from the inky skies, Calder smirking at the thought of how he'd make Golden squirm. How he'd have that puffed-up bastard tripping over his own tongue trying to ingratiate himself. How much he'd enjoy twisting the screw. They reached a fork in the path and Deep strolled off to the left, around the foot of the Heroes.

"Golden's camp is on the right," grunted Calder.

"True," said Deep, still walking. "You've an unchallenged grasp on your rights and lefts, which puts you a firm rung above my brother on the ladder of learning."

"They look the bloody same," snapped Shallow, and Calder felt something prick at his back. A cold and surprising something, not quite painful but certainly not pleasant. It took him a moment to realise what it was, but when he did all his smugness drained away as though that jabbing point had already made a hole.

How flimsy is arrogance. It only takes a bit of sharp metal to bring it all crashing down.

"We're going left." Shallow's point prodded again and Calder set off, hands up, his smirk abandoned in the gloom.

There were plenty of people about. Fires surrounded by half-lit faces. One set playing at dice, another making up ever more bloated lies about their high deeds in the battle, another slapping out stray embers on someone's cloak. A drunken group of Thralls lurched past but they barely even looked over. No one rushed to Calder's rescue. They saw nothing to comment on and even if they had, they didn't care a shit. People don't, on the whole.

"Where are we going?" Though the only real question was whether they'd dug his grave already, or were planning to argue over it after.

"You'll find out."

"Why?"

"Because we'll get there."

"No. Why are you doing this?"

They burst out laughing together, as though that was quite the joke. "Do you think we were watching you by accident, over at Caul Reachey's camp?"

"No, no, no," hummed Shallow. "No."

They were moving away from the Heroes, now. Fewer people, fewer fires. Hardly any light but the circle of crops picked out by Deep's torch. Any hope of help fading into the black behind them along with the bragging and the songs. If Calder was going to be saved he'd have to do it himself. They hadn't even bothered to take his sword away from him. But who was he fooling? Even if his right hand hadn't been useless, Shallow could've cut his throat a dozen times before he got it drawn. Across the darkened fields he could pick out the line of trees far to the north. Maybe if he ran—

"No." Shallow's knife pricked at Calder's side again. "No nee no no no."

"Really no," said Deep.

"Look, maybe we can come to an arrangement. I've got money—"

"There's no pockets deep enough to outbid our employer. Your best bet is just to follow along like a good boy." Calder rather doubted that but, clever as he liked to think he was, he had no better ideas. "We're sorry about this, you know. We've naught but respect for you just as we'd naught but respect for your father."

"What good is your sorry going to do me?"

Deep's shoulders shrugged. "A little less than none, but we always make a point of saying it."

"He thinks that lends us class," said Shallow.

"A noble air."

"Oh, aye," said Calder. "You're a right pair of fucking heroes."

"It's a pitiable fellow who ain't a hero to someone," said Deep. "Even if it's only himself."

"Or Mummy," said Shallow.

"Or his brother." Deep grinned over his shoulder. "How did your brother feel about you, my lordling?"

Calder thought about Scale, fighting against the odds on that bridge, waiting for help that never came. "I'm guessing he went off me at the end."

"Wouldn't cry too many tears about it. It's a rare fine fellow who ain't a villain to someone. Even if it's only himself."

"Or his brother," whispered Shallow.

"And here we are."

A ramshackle farmhouse had risen out of the darkness. Large and silent, stone covered with rustling creeper, flaking shutters slanting in the windows. Calder realised it was the same one he'd slept in for two nights, but it looked a lot more sinister now. Everything does with a knife at your back.

"This way, if you please." To the porch on the side of the house, lean-to roof missing slates, a rotten table under it, chairs lying on their sides. A lamp swung gently from a hook on one of the flaking columns, its light shifting across a yard scattered with weeds, a slumping fence beyond separating the farm from its fields.

There were a lot of tools leaning against the fence. Shovels, axes, pick-axes, caked in mud, as though they'd been hard used that day by a team of workmen and left there to be used again tomorrow. Tools for digging. Calder felt his fear, faded slightly on the walk, shoot up cold again. Through a gap in the fence and the light of Deep's torch flared out across trampled crops and fell on fresh-turned earth. A knee-high heap of it, big as the foundations of a barn. Calder opened his mouth, maybe to make some desperate plea, strike some last bargain, but he had no words any more.

"They been working hard," said Deep, as another mound crept from the night beside the first.

"Slaving away," said Shallow, as the torchlight fell on a third.

"They say war's an awful affliction, but you'll have a hard time finding a gravedigger to agree."

The last one hadn't been filled in yet. Calder's skin crawled as the torch found its edges, five strides across, maybe, its far end lost in the sliding shadows. Deep made it to the corner and peered over the edge. "Phew." He wedged his torch in the earth, turned and beckoned. "Up you come, then. Walking slow ain't going to make the difference."

Shallow gave him a nudge and Calder plodded on, throat tightening with each drawn-out breath, more and more of the sides of the pit crawling into view with each unsteady step.

Earth, and pebbles, and barley roots. Then a pale hand. Then a bare arm. Then corpses. Then more. The pit was full of them, heaped up in a grisly tangle. The refuse of battle.

Most were naked. Stripped of everything. Would some gravedigger end up with Calder's good cloak? The dirt and the blood looked the same in the torchlight. Black smears on dead white skin. Hard to say which twisted legs and arms belonged to which bodies.

Had these been men a couple of days before? Men with ambitions, and hopes, and things they cared for? A mass of stories, cut off in the midst, no ending. The hero's reward.

He felt a warmth down his leg and realised he'd pissed himself.

"Don't worry." Deep's voice was soft, like a father to a scared child. "That happens a lot."

"We've seen it all."

"And then a little more."

"You stand here." Shallow took him by the shoulders and turned him to face the pit, limp and helpless. You never think you'll just meekly do what you're told when you're facing your death. But everyone does. "A little to the left." Guiding him a step to the right. "That's left, right?"

"That's right, fool."

"Fuck!" Shallow gave him a harder yank and Calder slipped at the edge, boot heel sending a few lumps of earth down onto the bodies. Shallow pulled him back straight. "There?"

"There," said Deep. "All right, then."

Calder stood, looking down, silently starting to cry. Dignity no longer seemed to matter much. He'd have even less soon enough. He wondered how deep the pit was. How many bodies he'd share it with when they picked those tools up in the morning and heaped the earth on top. Five score? Ten score? More?

He stared at the nearest of them, right beneath him, a great black wound in the back of its head. *His* head, Calder supposed, though it was hard to think of it as a man. It was a thing, robbed of all identity. Robbed of all... unless...

The face had been Black Dow's. His mouth was open, half-full of dirt, but it was the Protector of the North, no doubt. He looked almost as if he was smiling, one arm flung out to welcome Calder, like an old friend, to the land of the dead. Back to the mud indeed. So quickly it can happen. Lord of all to meat in a hole.

Tears crept down Calder's hot face, glistened in the torchlight as they pattered into the pit, making fresh streaks through the grime on Black Dow's cold cheek. Death in the circle would've been a disappointment. How much worse was this? Tossed in a nameless hole, unmarked by those that loved or even those that hated him.

He was blubbing like a baby, sore ribs heaving, the pit and the corpses glistening through the salt water.

When would they do it? Surely, now, here it came. A breeze wafted up, chilling the tears on his face. He let his head drop back, squeezing his eyes shut, wincing, grunting, as if he could feel the knife sliding into his back. As if the metal was already in him. When would they do it? Surely now...

The wind dropped away, and he thought he heard clinking. Voices from behind him, from the direction of the house. He stood for a while longer, making a racking sob with every breath.

"Fish to start," someone said.

"Excellent."

Trembling, cringing, every movement a terrifying effort, Calder slowly turned.

Deep and Shallow had vanished, their torch flickering abandoned at the edge of the pit. Beyond the ramshackle fence, under the ramshackle porch, the old table had been covered with a cloth and set for dinner. A man was unpacking dishes from a large basket. Another sat in one of the chairs. Calder wiped his eyes on the back of his wildly trembling hand, not sure whether to believe the evidence of his senses. The man in the chair was the First of the Magi.

Bayaz smiled over. "Why, Prince Calder!" As if they'd run into each other by accident in the market. "Pray join me!"

Calder wiped snot from his top lip, still expecting a knife to dart from the darkness. Then ever so slowly, his knees wobbling so much he could hear them flapping against the inside of his wet trousers, he picked his way back through the gap in the fence and over to the porch.

The servant righted the fallen chair, dusted it off and held his open palm towards it. Calder sagged into it, numb, eyes still gently leaking by themselves, and watched Bayaz fork a piece of fish into his mouth and slowly, deliberately, thoroughly chew, and swallow.

"So. The Whiteflow shall remain the northern boundary of Angland."

Calder sat for a moment, aware of a faint snorting at the back of his nose with every quick breath but unable to stop it. Then he blinked, and finally nodded.

"The land between the Whiteflow and the Cusk, including the city of Uffrith, shall come under the governorship of the Dogman. It shall become a protectorate of the Union, with six representatives on the Open Council."

Calder nodded again.

"The rest of the North as far as the Crinna is yours." Bayaz popped the last piece of fish into his mouth and waved his fork around. "Beyond the Crinna it belongs to Stranger-Come-Knocking."

Yesterday's Calder might've snapped out some defiant jibe, but all he could think of now was how very lucky he felt not to be gushing blood into the mud, and how very much he wanted to carry on not gushing blood. "Yes," he croaked.

"You don't need time to...chew it over?"

Eternity in a pit full of corpses, perhaps? "No," whispered Calder.

"Pardon me?"

Calder took a shuddering breath. "No."

"Well." Bayaz dabbed his mouth with a cloth, and looked up. "This is much better."

"A very great improvement." The curly-headed servant had a pouty smile as he whisked Bayaz' plate away and replaced it with a clean one. Probably much the same as Calder's habitual smirk, but he enjoyed seeing it on another man about as much as he might have enjoyed seeing another man fuck his wife. The servant whipped the cover from a dish with a flourish.

"Ah, the meat, the meat!" Bayaz watched the knife flash and flicker as wafer slices were carved with blinding skill. "Fish is all very well, but dinner hasn't really started until you're served something that bleeds." The servant added vegetables with the dexterity of a conjuror, then turned his smirk on Calder.

There was something oddly, irritatingly familiar about him. Like a name at the tip of Calder's tongue. Had he seen him visit his father once, in a fine cloak? Or at Ironhead's fire with a Carl's helmet on? Or at the shoulder of Stranger-Come-Knocking, with paint on his face and splinters of bone through his ear? "Meat, sir?"

"No," whispered Calder. All he could think of was all the meat in the pits just a few strides away.

"You really should try it!" said Bayaz. "Go on, give him some! And help the prince, Yoru, he has an injured right hand."

The servant doled meat onto Calder's plate, bloody gravy gleaming in the gloom, then began to cut it up at frightening speed, making Calder flinch with each sweep of the knife.

Across the table, the Magus was already happily chewing. "I must admit, I did not entirely enjoy the tenor of our last conversation. It reminded me somewhat of your father." Bayaz paused as if expecting a response, but Calder had none to give. "That is meant as a very small compliment and a very large warning. For many years your father and I had...an understanding."

"Some good it did him."

The wizard's brows went up. "How short your family's memory! Indeed it did! Gifts he had of me, and all manner of help and wise counsel and oh, how he thrived! From piss-pot chieftain to King of the Northmen! Forged a nation where there were only squabbling peasants and pigshit before!" The edge of Bayaz' knife screeched against the plate and his voice sharpened with it. "But he became arrogant in his glory, and forgot the debts he owed, and sent his puffed-up sons to make demands of me. *Demands*," hissed the Magus, eyes glittering in the shadows of their sockets. "Of *me*."

Calder's throat felt uncomfortably tight as Bayaz sat back. "Bethod turned his back on our friendship, and his allies fell away, and all his great achievements withered, and he died in blood and was buried in an unmarked grave. There is a lesson there. Had your father paid his debts, perhaps he would be King of the Northmen still. I have high hopes you will learn from his mistake, and remember what you owe."

"I've taken nothing from you."

"Have...you...not?" Bayaz bit off each word with a curl of his lip. "You will never know, nor could you even understand, the many ways in which I have interceded on your behalf."

The servant arched one brow. "The account is lengthy."

"Do you suppose things run your way because you think yourself charming? Or cunning? Or uncommonly lucky?"

Calder had, in fact, thought exactly that.

"Was it charm that saved you from Reachey's assassins at his weapontake, or the two colourful Northmen I sent to watch over you?"

Calder had no answer.

"Was it cunning that saved you in the battle, or my instructions to Brodd Tenways that he should keep you from harm?"

Even less to that. "Tenways?" he whispered.

"Friends and enemies can sometimes be difficult to tell apart. I asked him to act like Black Dow's man. Perhaps he was too good an actor. I heard he died."

"It happens," croaked Calder.

"Not to you." The "yet" was unsaid, but still deafening. "Even though you faced Black Dow in a duel to the death! And was it luck that tipped the balance towards you when the Protector of the North lay dead at your feet, or was it my old friend Stranger-Come-Knocking?"

Calder felt as if he was up to his chest in quicksand, and had only just realised. "He's your man?"

Bayaz did not gloat or cackle. He looked almost bored. "I knew him when he was still called Pip. But big men need big names, eh, Black Calder?"

"Pip," he muttered, trying to square the giant with the name.

"I wouldn't use it to his face."

"I don't reach his face."

"Few do. He wants to bring civilisation to the fens."

"I wish him luck."

"Keep it for yourself. I gave it to you."

Calder was too busy trying to think his way through it. "But . . . Stranger-Come-Knocking fought for Dow. Why not have him fight for the Union? You could have won on the second morning and saved us all a—"

"He was not content with my first offer." Bayaz sourly speared some greens with his fork. "He demonstrated his value, and so I made a better one."

"This was all a disagreement over prices?"

The Magus let his head tip to one side. "Just what do you think a war is?" That sank slowly into the silence between them like a ship with all hands. "There are many others who have debts."

"Caul Shivers."

"No," said the servant. "His intervention was a happy accident."

Calder blinked. "Without him . . . Dow would've torn me apart."

"Good planning does not prevent accidents," said Bayaz, "it allows for them. It makes sure every accident is a happy one. I am not so careless a gambler as to make only one bet. But the North has ever been short of good material, and I admit you are my preference. You are no hero, Calder. I like that. You see what men are. You have your father's cunning, and ambition, and ruthlessness, but not his pride."

"Pride always struck me as a waste of effort," murmured Calder. "Everyone serves."

"Keep that in mind and you will prosper. Forget it, well . . ." Bayaz forked a slice of meat into his mouth and noisily chewed. "My advice would be to keep that pit of corpses always at your feet. The feeling as you stared down into it, waiting for death. The awful helplessness. Skin tickling with the expectation of the knife. The regret for everything left undone. The fear for those you leave behind." He gave a bright smile. "Start every morning and end every day at the brink of that pit. Remember, because forgetfulness is the curse of power. And you may find yourself once again staring into your own grave, this time with less happy results. You need only defy me."

"I've spent the last ten years kneeling to one man or another." Calder didn't have to lie. Black Dow had let him live, then demanded obedience, then made threats. Look how that turned out. "My knees bend very easily."

The Magus smacked his lips as he swallowed the last piece of carrot and tossed his cutlery on the plate. "That gladdens me. You cannot imagine how many similar conversations I have had with stiff-kneed men. I no longer have the slightest patience for them. But I can be generous to those who see reason. It may be that at some point I will send someone to you requesting . . . favours. When that day comes, I hope you will not disappoint me."

"What sort of favours?"

"The sort that will prevent you from ever again being taken down the wrong path by men with knives."

Calder cleared his throat. "Those kinds of favours I will always be willing to grant."

"Good. In return you will have gold from me."

"That's the generosity of Magi? Gold?"

"What were you expecting, a magic codpiece? This is no children's storybook. Gold is everything and anything. Power, love, safety. Sword and shield together. There is no greater gift. But I do, as it happens, have another." Bayaz paused like a jester about to deliver the joke. "Your brother's life."

Calder felt his face twitch. Hope? Or disappointment? "Scale's dead."

"No. He lost his right hand at the Old Bridge but he lives. The Union are releasing all prisoners. A gesture of goodwill, as part of the historic peace accord that you have so gratefully agreed to. You can collect the pinhead at midday tomorrow."

"What should I do with him?"

"Far be it from me to tell you what to do with your gift, but you do not get to be a king without making some sacrifices. You do want to be king, don't you?"

"Yes." Things had changed a great deal since the evening began, but of that Calder was more sure than ever.

The First of the Magi stood, taking up his staff as his servant began nimbly to clear away the dishes. "Then an elder brother is a dreadful encumbrance."

Calder watched him for a moment, looking calmly off across the darkened fields as though they were full of flowers rather than corpses. "Have you eaten here, within a long piss of a mass grave... just to show me how ruthless you are?"

"Must everything have some sinister motive? I have eaten here because I was hungry." Bayaz tipped his head to one side as he looked down at Calder. Like the bird looks at the worm. "Graves mean nothing to me either way."

"Knives," muttered Calder, "and threats, and bribes, and war?"

Bayaz' eyes shone with the lamplight. "Yes?"

"What kind of a fucking wizard are you?"

"The kind you obey."

The servant reached for his plate but Calder caught him by the wrist before he got there. "Leave it. I might get hungry later."

The Magus smiled at that. "What did I say, Yoru? He has a stronger stomach than you'd think." He waved over his shoulder as he walked away. "I believe, for now, the North is in safe hands."

Bayaz' servant took up the basket, took down the lamp, and followed his master.

"Where's dessert?" Calder shouted after them.

The servant gave him one last smirk. "Black Dow has it."

The glimmer of the lamp followed them around the side of the house and they were gone, leaving Calder to sink into his rickety chair in the darkness, eyes closed, breathing hard, with a mixture of crushing disappointment and even more crushing relief.

Just Deserts

My dear and trusted friend,

It gives me great pleasure to tell you that the circumstances have arisen in which I can invite you back to Adua, to once again take up your position among the Knights of the Body, and your rightful place as my First Guard.

You have been greatly missed. During your absence your letters have been a constant comfort and delight. For any wrong on your part, I long ago forgave you. For any wrong on mine, I earnestly hope that you can do the same. Please, let me know that we can continue as we were before Sipani.

Your sovereign,
The High King of Angland, Starikland, and Midderland,
Protector of Westport and Dagoska,
His August Majesty...

Gorst could read no further. He closed his eyes, tears stinging at the inside of the lids, and pressed the crumpled paper against his chest as one might embrace a lover. How often had poor, scorned, exiled Bremer dan Gorst dreamed of this moment? *Am I dreaming now?* He bit his sore tongue and the sweet taste of blood was a relief. Prised his eyelids open again, tears running freely, and stared at the letter through the shimmering water.

Dear and trusted friend... rightful place as First Guard... comfort and delight... as we were before Sipani. As we were before Sipani...

He frowned. Brushed his tears on the back of his wrist and peered down at the date. The letter had been despatched six days ago. *Before I fought at the fords, on the bridge, at the Heroes. Before the battle even began.* He hardly

527

knew whether to laugh or cry more and in the end did both, shuddering with weepy giggles, spraying the letter with happy specks of spit.

What did it matter why? *I have what I deserve.*

He burst from the tent and it was as if he had never felt the sunlight before. The simple joy of the life-giving warmth on his face, the caress of the breeze. He gazed about in damp-eyed wonder. The patch of ground sloping down to the river, a mud-churned, rubbish-strewn midden when he trudged inside, had become a charming garden, filled with colour. With hopeful faces and pleasing chatter. With laughter and birdsong.

"You all right?" Rurgen looked faintly concerned, as far as Gorst could tell through the wet.

"I have a letter from the king," he squeaked, no longer caring a damn how he sounded.

"What is it?" asked Younger. "Bad news?"

"Good news." And he grabbed Younger around the shoulders and made him groan as he hugged him tight. "The best." He gathered up Rurgen with the other arm, lifting their feet clear of the ground, squeezing the pair of them like a loving father might squeeze his sons. "We're going home."

Gorst walked with an unaccustomed bounce. Armour off, he felt so light he might suddenly spring into the sunny sky. The very air smelled sweeter, even if it did still carry the faint tang of latrines, and he dragged it in through both nostrils. All his injuries, all his aches and pains, all his petty disappointments, faded in the all-conquering glow.

I am born again.

The road to Osrung – or to the burned-out ruin that had been Osrung a few days before – brimmed with smiling faces. A set of whores blew kisses from the seat of a wagon and Gorst blew them back. A crippled boy gave excited hoots and Gorst jovially ruffled his hair. A column of walking wounded shuffled past, one on crutches at the front nodded and Gorst hugged him, kissed him on the forehead and walked on, smiling.

"Gorst! It's Gorst!" Some cheering went up, and Gorst grinned and shook one scabbed fist in the air. *Bremer dan Gorst, hero of the battlefield! Bremer dan Gorst, confidant of the monarch! Knight of the Body, First Guard to the High King of the Union, noble, righteous, loved by all!* He could do anything. He could have anything.

Joyous scenes were everywhere. A man with sergeant's stripes was being married by the colonel of his regiment to a pudding-faced woman with flowers in her hair while a gathering of his comrades gave suggestive whistles. A new ensign, absurdly young-looking, beamed in the sunlight as he carried the colours of his regiment by way of initiation, the golden sun of the Union snapping proudly. *Perhaps one of the very flags that Mitterick so carelessly lost only a day ago? How soon some trespasses are forgotten. The incompetent rewarded along with the wronged.*

As if to illustrate that very point, Gorst caught sight of Felnigg beside the road in his new uniform, staff officers in a crowing crowd around him, giving hell to a tearful young lieutenant beside a tipped-over cart, gear, weapons and for some reason a full-sized harp spilled from its torn awning like the guts from a dead sheep.

"General Felnigg!" called Gorst jauntily. "Congratulations on your promotion!" *It could not have happened to a less deserving drunken pedant.* He briefly considered the possibility of challenging the man to the duel he had been too cowardly to demand a few evenings before. Then to the possibility of backhanding him into the ditch as he passed. *But I have other business.*

"Thank you, Colonel Gorst. I wished to let you know how very much I admire your—"

Gorst could not even be bothered to make excuses. He simply barged past, scattering Felnigg's staff – most of whom had recently been Marshal Kroy's staff – like a plough through muck and left them clucking and puffing in his wake. *And away to fuck with the lot of you, I'm free. Free!* He sprang up and punched the air.

Even the wounded near the charred gates of Osrung looked happy as he passed, tapping shoulders with his fist, muttering banal encouragements. *Share my joy, you crippled and dying! I have plenty to spare!*

And there she stood, among them, giving out water. *Like the Goddess of mercy. Oh, soothe my pain.* He had no fear now. He knew what he had to do.

"Finree!" he called, then cleared his throat and tried again, a little deeper. "Finree."

"Bremer. You look…happy." She lifted one enquiring eyebrow, as though a smile on his face was as incongruous as on a horse, or a rock, or a corpse. *But get used to this smile, for it is here to stay!*

"I am, very happy. I wanted to say..." *I love you.* "Goodbye. I am return-ing to Adua this evening."

"Really? So am I." His heart leaped. "Well, as soon as my husband is well enough to be moved." And plummeted back down. "But they say that won't be long." She looked annoyingly delighted about it too.

"Good. Good." *Fuck him.* Gorst realised his fist was clenched, and forced it open. *No, no, forget him. He is nothing. I am the winner, and this is my moment.* "I received a letter from the king this morning."

"Really? So did we!" She blurted it out, seizing him by the arm, eyes bright. His heart leaped again, as though her touch was a second letter from his Majesty. "Hal is being restored to his seat on the Open Council." She looked furtively around, then whispered it in a husky rush. "They're mak-ing him lord governor of Angland!"

There was a long, uncomfortable pause while Gorst took that in. *Like a sponge soaking up a puddle of piss.* "Lord...governor?" It seemed a cloud had moved across the sun. It was no longer quite so warm upon his face as it had been.

"I know! There will be a parade, apparently."

"A parade." *Of cunts.* A chilly breeze blew up and flapped his loose shirt. "He deserves it." *He presided over a blown-up bridge and so he gets a parade?* "You deserve it." *Where's my fucking parade?*

"And your letter?"

My letter? My pathetic embarrassment of a letter? "Oh...the king has asked me to take up my old position as First Guard." Somehow he could no longer muster quite the enthusiasm he had when he opened it. *Not lord gov-ernor, oh no! Nothing like lord governor. The king's first hand-holder. The king's first cock-taster. Pray don't wipe your own arse your Majesty, let me!*

"That's wonderful news." Finree smiled as though everything had turned out just right. "War is full of opportunities, after all, however terrible it may be."

It is pedestrian news. My triumph is all spoiled. My garlands rotted. "I thought..." His face twitched. He could not cling on to his smile any lon-ger. "My success seems quite meagre now."

"Meagre? Well, of course not, I didn't mean—"

"I'll never have anything worth the having, will I?"

She blinked. "I—"

"I'll never have you."

Her eyes went wide. "You'll—What?"

"I'll never have you, or anyone like you." Colour burned up red under her freckled cheeks. "Then let me be honest. War is terrible, you say?" He hissed it right in her horrified face. "*Shit*, I say! I fucking *love* war." The unsaid words boiled out of him. He could not stop them, did not want to. "In the dreamy yards, and drawing rooms, and pretty parks of Adua, I am a squeaking fucking joke. A falsetto embarrassment. A ridiculous clown-man." He leaned even closer, enjoying it that she flinched. *Only this way will she know that I exist. Then let it be this way.* "But on the battlefield? On the battlefield I am a *god*. I love war. The steel, the smell, the corpses. I wish there were more. On the first day I drove the Northmen back alone at the ford. Alone! On the second I carried the bridge! Me! Yesterday I climbed the Heroes! I *love* war! I...I wish it wasn't over. I wish...I wish..."

But far sooner than he had expected, the well had run dry. He was left standing there, breathing hard, staring down at her. Like a man who has throttled his wife and come suddenly to his senses, he had no idea what to do next. He turned to make his escape, but Finree's hand was still on his arm and now her fingers dug into him, pulling him back.

The blush of shock was fading now, her face hard with growing anger, jaw muscles clenched. "What happened in Sipani?"

And now it was his cheeks that burned. As if the name was a slap. "I was betrayed." He tried to make the last word stab at her as it stabbed him, but his voice had lost all its edge. "I was made the scapegoat." A goat's plaintive bleating, indeed. "After all my loyalty, all my diligence..." He fumbled for more words but his voice was not used to making them, fading into a squeaky whine as she bared her teeth.

"I heard when they came for the king you were passed out drunk with a whore." Gorst swallowed. But he could hardly deny it. Stumbling from that room, head spinning, struggling to fasten his belt and draw his sword at once. "I heard it was not the first time you had disgraced yourself, and that the king had forgiven you before, and that the Closed Council would not let him do it again." She looked him up and down, and her lip curled. "God of the battlefield, eh? Gods and devils can look much alike to us little people. You went to a ford, and a bridge, and a hill, and what did you do there except kill? What have you made? Who have you helped?"

He stood there for a moment, all his bravado slithering out. *She is right. And no one knows it better than me.* "Nothing and no one," he whispered.

"So you love war. I used to think you were a decent man. But I see now I was mistaken." She stabbed at his chest with her forefinger. "You're a *hero*."

She turned with one last look of excruciating contempt and left him standing among the wounded. They no longer looked so happy for him as they had done. They looked, on the whole, to be in very great pain. The birdsong was half-dead crowing once more. His elation was a charming sandcastle, washed away by the pitiless tide of reality. He felt as if he was cast from lead.

Am I doomed always to feel like this? A most uncomfortable thought occurred. *Did I feel like this... before Sipani?* He frowned after Finree as she vanished back into the hospital tent. *Back to her pretty young dolt of a lord governor.* He realised far too late he should have pointed out that he had been the one to save her husband. *One never says the right things at the right time.* A stupendous understatement if ever there was one. He gave an epic, grinding sigh. *This is why I keep my fucking mouth shut.*

Gorst turned and trudged away into the gloomy afternoon, fists clenched, frowning up towards the Heroes, black teeth against the sky at the top of their solemn hill.

By the Fates, I need to fight someone. Anyone.

But the war was over.

Black Calder

"Just give me the nod."

"The nod?"

Shivers turned to look at him, and nodded. "The nod. And it's done."

"Simple as that," muttered Calder, hunching in his saddle.

"Simple as that."

Easy. Just nod, and you can be king. Just nod, and kill your brother.

It was hot, a few shreds of cloud hanging in the blue over the fells, bees floating about some yellow flowers at the edge of the barley, the river glittering silver. The last hot day, maybe, before autumn shooed the summer off and beckoned winter on. It should've been a day for lazy dreams and trailing hot toes in the shallows. Perhaps a hundred strides downstream a few Northmen had stripped off and were doing just that. A little further along the opposite bank and a dozen Union soldiers were doing the same. The laughter of both sets would occasionally drift to Calder's ear over the happy chattering of the water. Sworn enemies one day, now they played like children, close enough almost to splash.

Peace. And that had to be a good thing.

For months he'd been preaching for it, hoping for it, plotting for it, with few allies and fewer rewards, and here it was. If ever there was a day to smirk it was this one, but Calder could've lifted one of the Heroes more easily than the corners of his mouth. His meeting with the First of the Magi had been weighing them down all through a sleepless night. That and the thought of the meeting that was coming.

"Ain't that him?" asked Shivers.

"Where?" There was only one man on the bridge, and not one he recognised.

"It is. That's him."

Calder narrowed his eyes, then shaded them against the glare. "By the..."

Until last night he'd thought his brother killed. He hadn't been so far wrong. Scale was a ghost, crept from the land of the dead and ready to be snatched back by a breath of wind. Even at this distance he looked withered, shrunken, greasy hair plastered to one side of his head. He'd long had a limp but now he shuffled sideways, left boot dragging over the old stones. He had a threadbare blanket around his shoulders, left hand clutching two corners at his throat while the others flapped about his legs.

Calder slid from his saddle, tossing the reins over his horse's neck, bruised ribs burning as he hurried to help his brother.

"Just give me the nod," came Shivers' whisper.

Calder froze, guts clenching. Then he went on.

"Brother."

Scale squinted up like a man who hadn't seen the sun for days, sunken face covered with scabby grazes on one side, a black cut across the swollen bridge of his nose. "Calder?" He gave a weak grin and Calder saw he'd lost his two front teeth, blood dried to his cracked lips. He let go of his blanket to take Calder's hand and it slid off, left him hunched around the stump of his right arm like a beggar woman around her baby. Calder found his eyes drawn to that horrible absence of limb. Strangely, almost comically shortened, bound to the elbow with grubby bandages, spotted brown at the end.

"Here." He unclasped his cloak and slipped it around his brother's shoulders, his own broken hand tingling unpleasantly in sympathy.

Scale looked too pained and exhausted even to gesture at stopping him. "What happened to your face?"

"I took your advice about fighting."

"How did it work out?"

"Painfully for all concerned," said Calder, fumbling the clasp shut with one hand and one thumb.

Scale stood, swaying as if he might drop at any moment, blinking out across the shifting barley. "The battle's over, then?" he croaked.

"It's over."

"Who won?"

Calder paused. "We did."

"Dow did, you mean?"

"Dow's dead."

Scale's bloodshot eyes went wide. "In the battle?"

"After."

"Back to the mud." Scale wriggled his hunched shoulders under the cloak. "I guess it was coming."

All Calder could think of was the pit opening up at the toes of his boots. "It's always coming."

"Who's taken his place?"

Another pause. The swimming soldiers' laughter drifted over, then faded back into the rustling crops. "I have." Scale's scabbed mouth hung gormlessly open. "They've taken to calling me Black Calder, now."

"Black...Calder."

"Let's get you mounted." Calder led his brother over to the horses, Shivers watching them all the way.

"Are you two on the same side now?" asked Scale.

Shivers put a finger on his scarred cheek and pulled it down so his metal eye bulged from the socket. "Just keeping an eye out."

Scale reached for the saddle-bow with his right arm, stopped himself and took it awkwardly with his left. He found one stirrup with a fishing boot and started to drag himself up. Calder hooked a hand under his knee to help him. When Calder had been a child Scale used to lift him up into the saddle. Fling him up sometimes, none too gently. How things had changed.

The three of them set off up the track. Scale slumped in the saddle, reins dangling from his limp left hand and his head nodding with each hoof-beat. Calder rode grimly beside him. Shivers followed, like a shadow. The Great Leveller, waiting at their backs. Through the fields they went, at an interminable walk, towards the gap in Clail's Wall where Calder had faced the Union charge a few days before.

His heart was beating just as fast as it had then. The Union had pulled back behind the river that morning and Pale-as-Snow's boys were up north behind the Heroes, but there were still eyes around. A few nervous pickers combing through the trampled barley, searching for some trifle others might have missed. Scrounging up arrowheads or buckles or anything that could turn a copper. A couple of men thrashing through the crops off to the east, one with a fishing rod over his shoulder. Strange, how quickly a battle-field turned back to being just a stretch of ground. One day every finger's breadth of it is something men can die over. The next it's just a path from here to there. As he looked about Calder caught Shivers' eye and the killer lifted his chin, silently asking the question. Calder jerked his head away like a hand from a boiling pot.

He'd killed men before. He'd killed Brodd Tenways with his own sword hours after the man had saved his life. He'd ordered Forley the Weakest dead for nothing but his own vanity. Killing a man when Skarling's Chair was the prize shouldn't have made his hand shake on the reins, should it?

"Why didn't you help me, Calder?" Scale had eased his stump out from the gap in the cloak and was frowning down at it, jaw set hard. "At the bridge. Why didn't you come?"

"I wanted to." Liar, liar. "Found out there were Union men in the woods across that stream. Right on our flank. I wanted to go but I couldn't. I'm sorry." That much was true. He was sorry. For what good that did.

"Well." Scale's face was a grimacing mask as he slid the stump back under his cloak. "Looks like you were right. The world needs more thinkers and fewer heroes." He glanced over for an instant and the look in his eye made Calder wince. "You always were the clever one."

"No. It was you who was right. Sometimes you have to fight."

This was where he'd made his little stand and the land still bore the scars. Crops trodden, broken arrow shafts scattered, scraps of ruined gear around the remains of the trenches. Before Clail's Wall the ground had been churned to mud then baked hard again, smeared bootprints, hoofprints, handprints stamped into it, all that was left of the men who died there.

"Get what you can with words," muttered Calder, "but the words of an armed man ring that much sweeter. Like you said. Like our father said." And hadn't he said something about family, as well? How nothing is more important? And mercy? Always think about mercy?

"When you're young you think your father knows everything," said Scale. "Now I'm starting to realise he might've been wrong on more than one score. Look how he ended up, after all."

"True." Every word said was like lifting a great stone. How long had Calder lived with the frustration of having this thick-headed heap of brawn in his way? How many knocks, and mocks, and insults had he endured from him? His fist closed tight around the metal in his pocket. His father's chain. His chain. Is nothing more important than family? Or is family the lead that weighs you down?

They'd left the pickers behind, and the scene of the fighting too. Down the quiet track near the farmhouse where Scale had woken him a few mornings before. Where Bayaz had given him an even harsher awakening the previous night. Was this a test? To see whether Calder was ruthless enough for the wizard's tastes? He'd been accused of many things, but never too little ruthlessness.

How long had he dreamed of taking back his father's place? Even before his father lost it, and now there was only one last little fence to jump. All it would take was a nod. He looked sideways at Scale, wrung-out wreck that he was. Not much of a fence to trip a man with ambition. Calder had been accused of many things, but never too little ambition.

"You were the one took after our father," Scale was saying. "I tried, but... couldn't ever do it. Always thought you'd make a better king."

"Maybe," whispered Calder. Definitely.

Shivers was close behind, one hand on the reins, the other resting on his hip. He looked as relaxed as ever a man could, swaying gently with the movements of his horse. But his fingertips just so happened to be brushing the grip of his sword, sheathed beside the saddle in easy reach. The sword that had been Black Dow's. The sword that had been the Bloody-Nine's. Shivers raised one brow, asking the question.

The blood was surging behind Calder's eyes. Now was the time. He could have everything he wanted.

Bayaz had been right. You don't get to be a king without making some sacrifices.

Calder took an endless breath in, and held it. Now.

And he gently shook his head.

Shivers' hand slid away. His horse dropped ever so slowly back.

"Maybe I'm the better brother," said Calder, "but you're the elder." He brought his horse up close, and he pulled their father's chain from his pocket and slipped it over Scale's neck, arranged it carefully across his shoulders. Patted him on the back and left his hand there, wondering when he got to love this stupid bastard. When he got to love anyone besides himself. He lowered his head. "Let me be the first to bow before the new King of the Northmen."

Scale blinked down at the diamond on his grubby shirt. "Never thought things would end up this way."

Neither had Calder. But he found he was glad they had. "End?" He smirked across at his brother. "This is the beginning."

Retired

The house wasn't by the water. It didn't have a porch. It did have a bench outside with a view of the valley, but when he sat on it of an evening with his pipe he didn't tend to smile, just thought of all the men he'd buried. It leaked somewhat around the western eaves when the rain came down, which it had in quite some measure lately. It had just the one room, and a shelf up a ladder for sleeping on, and when it came to the great divide between sheds and houses, was only just on the right side of the issue. But it was a house, still, with good oak bones and a good stone chimney. And it was his. Dreams don't just spring up by themselves, they need tending to, and you've got to plant that first seed somewhere. Or so Craw told himself.

"Shit!" Hammer and nail clattered to the boards and he was off around the room, spitting and cursing and shaking his hand about.

Working wood was a tough way to earn a living. He might not have been chewing his nails so much, but he'd taken to hammering the bastards into his fingers instead. The sad fact was, now the wounds all over Craw's hands had forced him to face it, he wasn't much of a carpenter. In his dreams of retirement he'd always seen himself crafting things of beauty. Probably while light streamed in through coloured windows and sawdust went up in artful puffs. Gables carved with gilded dragon heads, so lifelike they'd be the wonder of the North, folk flocking from miles around to get a look. But it turned out wood was just as full of split, and warp, and splinters as people were.

"Bloody hell." Rubbing the life back into his thumb, nail already black from where he caught it yesterday.

They smiled at him in the village, brought him odd jobs, but he reckoned more'n one of the farmers was a good stretch better with a hammer than he was. Certainly they'd got that new barn up without calling on his skills and he had to admit it was likely a finer building for it. He'd started to think they wanted him in the valley more for his sword than his saw. While the war was on, the North's ready supply of scum had the Southerners to kill and rob. Now they just had their own kind, and were taking every chance at it. A Named Man to hand was no bad thing. Those were the times. Those were still the times, and maybe they always would be.

He squatted beside the stricken chair, latest casualty in his war against furniture. He'd split the joint he'd spent the last hour chiselling out and now the new leg stuck at an angle, an ugly gouge where he'd been hammering. Served him right for working as the light was going, but if he didn't get this done tonight he'd—

"Craw!"

His head jerked up. A man's voice, deep and rough.

"You in there, Craw?"

His skin went cold all over. Might be he'd played the straight edge most of his life, but you don't walk free of the black business without some scores however you play it.

He sprang up, or as close to springing as he could get these days, snatched his sword from the bracket above the door, fumbled it and nearly dropped it on his head, hissing more curses. If it was someone come to kill him it didn't seem likely they'd have given him a warning by calling his name. Not unless they were idiots. Idiots can be just as vengeful as anyone else, though, if not more so.

The shutters of the back window were open. He could slip out and off into the wood. But if they were serious they'd have thought of that, and with his knees he'd be outrunning no one. Better to come out the front way and look 'em in the eye. The way he would've done when he was young. He sidled up, swallowing as he drew his sword. Turned the knob, wedged the blade into the gap and gently levered the door open while he peered around the frame.

He'd go out the front way, but he wasn't painting a target on his shirt.

He counted eight at a glance, spread out in a crescent on the damp patch of dirt in front of his house. A couple had torches, light catching mail and helm and spear's tip and making 'em twinkle in the damp twilight. Carls, and battle-toughened by their looks, though there weren't many men left in the North you couldn't say that about. They all had plenty of weapons, but no blades drawn that he could see. That gave him some measure of comfort.

"That you, Craw?" He got a big measure more when he saw who was in charge, standing closest to the house with palms up.

"That it is." Craw let his sword point drop and poked his head out a bit further. "Here's a surprise."

"Pleasant one, I hope."

"I guess you'll tell me. What're you after, Hardbread?"

"Can I come in?"

Craw sniffed. "You can. Your crew might have to enjoy the night air for now."

"They're used to it." And Hardbread ambled up to the house alone. He looked prosperous. Beard trimmed back. New mail. Silver on the hilt of his sword. He climbed the steps and ducked past Craw, strolled to the centre of the one room, which didn't take long to get to, and cast an appraising eye around. Took in Craw's pallet on the shelf, his workbench and his tools, the half-finished chair, the broken wood and the shavings scattering the boards. "This what retirement looks like?" he asked.

"No, I've a fucking palace out back. Why you here?"

Hardbread took a breath. "Because mighty Scale Ironhand, King of the Northmen, has gone to war with Glama Golden."

Craw snorted. "Black Calder has, you mean. Why?"

"Golden killed Caul Reachey."

"Reachey's dead?"

"Poisoned. And Golden did the deed."

Craw narrowed his eyes. "That a fact?"

"Calder says it is, so Scale says it is, so it's close to a fact as anyone's going to get. All the North's lining up behind Bethod's sons, and I've come to see if you want to line up too."

"Since when did you fight for Calder and Scale?"

"Since the Dogman hung up his sword and stopped paying staples."

Craw frowned at him. "Calder would never take me."

"It was Calder sent me. He's got Pale-as-Snow, and Cairm Ironhead, and your old friend Wonderful as his War Chiefs."

"Wonderful?"

"Canny woman, that one. But Calder's lacking a Name to stand Second and lead his own Carls. He's in need of a straight edge, apparently." Hardbread cocked a brow at the chair. "So I don't reckon he'll be hiring you as a carpenter."

Craw stood there, trying to get his head around it. Offered a place, and a high one. Back among folk he understood, and admired him. Back to the black business, and trying to juggle the right thing, and finding words over graves.

"Sorry to bring you all this way for nothing, Hardbread, but the answer's no. Pass my apologies on to Calder. My apologies for this and... for whatever else. But tell him I'm done. Tell him I'm retired."

Hardbread gave a sigh. "All right. It's a shame, but I'll pass it on." He paused in the doorway, looking back. "Look after yourself, eh, Craw? Ain't many of us left know the difference between the right thing and the wrong."

"What difference?"

Hardbread snorted. "Aye. Look after yourself, anyway." And he stomped down the steps and out into the gathering dark.

Craw looked after him for a moment, wondering whether he was happy the thumping of his heart was softening or sad. Weighing his sword in his hand, remembering how it felt to hold it. Different from a hammer, that was sure. He remembered Threetrees giving it to him. The pride he'd felt, like a fire in him. Smiled in spite of himself to remember what he used to be. How prickly and wild and hungry for glory, not a straight edge on him anywhere.

He looked around at that one room, and the few things in it. He'd always thought retiring would be going back to his life after some nightmare pause. Some stretch of exile in the land of the dead. Now it came to him that all his life worth living had happened while he was holding a sword.

Standing alongside his dozen. Laughing with Whirrun, and Brack, and Wonderful. Clasping hands with his crew before the fight, knowing he'd die for them and they for him. The trust, the brotherhood, the love, knit closer than family. Standing by Threetrees on the walls of Uffrith, roaring their defiance at Bethod's great army. The day he charged at the Cumnur. And at Dunbrec. And in the High Places, even though they lost. Because they lost. The day he earned his name. Even the day he got his brothers killed. Even when he'd stood at the top of the Heroes as the rain came down, watching the Union come, knowing every dragged-out moment might be the last.

Like Whirrun had said – you can't live more'n that. Certainly not by fixing a chair.

"Ah, shit," he muttered, and he grabbed his sword-belt and his coat, threw 'em over his shoulder and strode out, slapping the door shut. Didn't even bother to lock it behind him.

"Hardbread! Wait up!"

Acknowledgements

As always, four people without whom:
Bren Abercrombie, whose eyes are sore from reading it.
Nick Abercrombie, whose ears are sore from hearing about it.
Rob Abercrombie, whose fingers are sore from turning the pages.
Lou Abercrombie, whose arms are sore from holding me up.

Then, my heartfelt thanks:
To all the lovely and talented folks at my UK Publisher, Gollancz, and their parent Orion, particularly Simon Spanton, Jo Fletcher, Jon Weir, Mark Stay and Jon Wood. Then, of course, all those who've helped make, publish, publicise, translate and above all *sell* my books wherever they may be around the world.

To the artists responsible for somehow making me look classy: Didier Graffet, Dave Senior and Laura Brett.

To editors across the Pond: Devi Pillai and Lou Anders.

To other hard-bitten professionals who've provided various mysterious services: Robert Kirby, Darren Turpin, Matthew Amos, Lionel Bolton.

To all the writers whose paths have crossed mine either electronically or in the actual flesh, and who've provided help, laughs and a few ideas worth stealing, including but by no means limited to: James Barclay, Mark Billingham, Peter V. Brett, Stephen Deas, Roger Levy, Tom Lloyd, Joe Mallozzi, George R. R. Martin, John Meaney, Richard Morgan, Mark Charan Newton, Garth Nix, Adam Roberts, Pat Rothfuss, Marcus Sakey, Wim Stolk and Chris Wooding.

And lastly, yet firstly:
She who wields the Father of Red Pens, which cannot be drawn without being blooded, a fearless champion on the battlefield of publishing, my editor, Gillian Redfearn. I mean, someone's got to do the actual *fighting*...

extras

orbit

meet the author

Lou Abercrombie

JOE ABERCROMBIE was born in Lancaster, England, on the last day of 1974. He studied psychology at Manchester University, then spent twelve years living in London, working as a film editor on documentaries and live music for bands from Iron Maiden to Coldplay. He is now a full-time writer, living in Bath with his wife and two daughters. Find out more about the author at www.joeabercrombie.com.

introducing

If you enjoyed
THE HEROES,
look out for

THE DRAGON'S PATH

Book 1 of The Dagger and the Coin

by Daniel Abraham

Marcus's hero days are behind him. He knows too well that even the smallest war still means somebody's death. When his men are impressed into a doomed army, staying out of a battle he wants no part of requires some unorthodox steps.

Cithrin is an orphan, ward of a banking house. Her job is to smuggle a nation's wealth across a war zone, hiding the gold from both sides. She knows the secret life of commerce like a second language, but the strategies of trade will not defend her from swords.

Geder, sole scion of a noble house, has more interest in philosophy than in swordplay. A poor excuse for a soldier, he is a pawn in these games. No one can predict what he will become.

Falling pebbles can start a landslide. A spat between the Free Cities and the Severed Throne is spiraling out of control. A new player rises from the depths of history, fanning the flames that will sweep the entire region onto the Dragon's Path—the path to war.

Prologue

The Apostate

The apostate pressed himself into the shadows of the rock and prayed to nothing in particular that the things riding mules in the pass below him would not look up. His hands ached, the muscles of his legs and back shuddered with exhaustion. The thin cloth of his ceremonial robes fluttered against him in the cold, dust-scented wind. He took the risk of looking down toward the trail.

The five mules had stopped, but the priests hadn't dismounted. Their robes were heavier, warmer. The ancient swords strapped across their backs caught the morning light and glittered a venomous green. Dragon-forged, those blades. They meant death to anyone whose skin they broke. In time, the poison would kill even the men who wielded them. All the more reason, the apostate thought, that his former brothers would kill him quickly and go home. No one wanted to carry those blades for long; they came out only in dire emergency or deadly anger.

Well. At least it was flattering to be taken seriously.

The priest leading the hunting party rose up in his saddle, squinting into the light. The apostate recognized the voice.

"Come out, my son," the high priest shouted. "There is no escape."

The apostate's belly sank. He shifted his weight, preparing to walk down. He stopped himself.

Probably, he told himself. *There is* probably *no escape. But perhaps there is.*

On the trail, the dark-robed figures shifted, turned, consulted among themselves. He couldn't hear their words. He waited, his body growing stiffer and colder. Like a corpse that hadn't had the grace to die. Half a day seemed to pass while the hunters below him conferred, though the sun barely changed its angle in the bare blue sky. And then, between one breath and the next, the mules moved forward again.

He didn't dare move for fear of setting a pebble rolling down the steep cliffs. He tried not to grin. Slowly, the things that had once been men rode their mules down the trail to the end of the valley, and then followed the wide bend to the south. When the last of them slipped out of sight, he stood, hands on his hips, and marveled. He still lived. They had not known where to find him after all.

Despite everything he'd been taught, everything he had until recently believed, the gifts of the spider goddess did not show the truth. It gave her servants something, yes, but not *truth*. More and more, it seemed his whole life had sprung from a webwork of plausible lies. He should have felt lost. Devastated. Instead, it was like he'd walked from a tomb into the free air. He found himself grinning.

The climb up the remaining western slope bruised him. His sandals slipped. He struggled for finger- and toeholds. But as the sun reached its height, he reached the ridge. To the west, mountain followed mountain, and great billowing clouds towered above them, thunderstorms a soft veil of grey. But in the farthest passes, he saw the land level. Flatten. Distance made the plains grey-blue, and the wind on the mountain's peak cut at his skin like claws. Lightning flashed on the horizon. As if in answer, a hawk shrieked.

It would take weeks alone and on foot. He had no food, and worse, no water. He'd slept the last five nights in caves and under bushes. His former brothers and friends—the men he had known and loved his whole life—were combing the trails and villages, intent on his death. Mountain lions and dire wolves hunted in the heights.

He ran a hand through his thick, wiry hair, sighed, and began the downward climb. He would probably die before he reached the Keshet and a city large enough to lose himself in.

But only *probably*.

In the last light of the falling sun, he found a stony overhang near a thin, muddy stream. He sacrificed a length of the strap from his right sandal to fashion a crude fire bow, and as the cruel chill came down from the sky, he squatted next to the high ring of stones that hid his small fire. The dry scrub burned hot and with little smoke, but quickly. He fell into a rhythm of feeding small twig after small twig into the flame, never letting it grow large enough to illuminate his shelter to those hunting and never letting it die. The warmth didn't seem to reach past his elbows.

Far off, something shrieked. He tried to ignore it. His body ached with exhaustion and spent effort, but his mind, freed now from the constant distraction of his journey, gained a dangerous speed. In the darkness, his memory sharpened. The sense of freedom and possibility gave way to loss, loneliness, and dislocation. Those, he believed, were more likely to kill him than a hunting cat.

He had been born in hills much like these. Passed his youth playing games of sword and whip using branches and woven bark. Had he ever felt the ambition to join the ranks of the monks in their great hidden temple? He must have, though from the biting cold of his poor stone shelter, it was hard to imagine it. He could remember looking up with awe at the high wall of stone. At the rock-carved sentries from all the thirteen races of humanity worn by wind and rain until all of them—Cinnae and Tralgu, Southling and Firstblood, Timzinae and Yemmu and Drowned—wore the same blank faces and clubbed fists. Indistinguishable. Only the wide wings and dagger teeth of the dragon arching above them all were still clear. And worked into the huge iron gate, black letters spelled out words in a language no one in the village knew.

When he became a novice, he learned what it said. BOUND IS NOT BROKEN. He had believed once that he knew what it meant.

The breeze shifted, raising the embers like fireflies. A bit of ash stung his eye, and he rubbed at it with the back of his hand. His blood shifted, currents in his body responding to something that was not him. The goddess, he'd thought. He had gone to the great gate with the other boys of his village. He had offered himself up—life and body—and in return...

In return the mysteries had been revealed. First, it had only been knowledge: letters enough to read the holy books, numbers enough to keep the temple's records. He had read the stories of the Dragon Empire and its fall. Of the spider goddess coming to bring justice to the world.

Deception, they said, had no power over her.

He'd tested it, of course. He believed them, and still he had tested. He would lie to the priests, just to see whether it could be done. He'd chosen things that only he could know: his father's clan name, his sister's favorite meals, his own dreams. The priests had whipped him when he spoke false, they had spared him when he was truthful, and they were never, *never* wrong. His certainty had grown. His faith. When the high priest had chosen him to rise to novice, he'd been certain that great things awaited him, because the priests had told him that they did.

After the nightmare of his initiation was over, he'd felt the power of the spider goddess in his own blood. The first time he'd felt someone lie, it had been like discovering a new sense. The first time he had spoken with the voice of the goddess, he'd felt his words commanding belief as if they had been made from fire.

And now he had fallen from grace, and none of it might be true. There might be no such place as the Keshet. He believed there was, so much so that he had risked his life on flight to it. But he had never been there. The marks on the maps could be lies. For that matter, there might have been no dragons, no empire, no great war. He had never seen the ocean; there might be no such thing. He knew only what he himself had seen and heard and felt.

He knew *nothing.*

On violent impulse, he sank his teeth into the flesh of his palm. His blood welled up, and he cupped it. In the faint firelight, it looked nearly black. Black, with small, darker knots. One of the knots unfurled tiny legs. The spider crawled mindlessly around the cup of his hand. Another one joined it. He watched them: the agents of the goddess in whom he no longer believed. Carefully, slowly, he tipped his hand over the small flame. One of the spiders fell into it, hair-thin legs shriveling instantly.

"Well," he said. "You can die. I know *that.*"

The mountains seemed to go on forever, each crest a new threat, each valley thick with danger. He skirted the small villages, venturing close only to steal a drink from the stone cisterns. He ate lizards and the tiny flesh-colored nuts of scrub pine. He avoided the places where wide, clawed paws marked paths in the dirt. One night, he found a circle of standing pillars with a small chamber beneath them that seemed to offer shelter and a place to recover his strength, but his sleep there had been troubled by dreams so violent and alien that he pushed on instead.

He lost weight, the woven leather of his belt hanging low around his waist. His sandals' soles thinned, and his fire bow wore out quickly. Time lost its meaning. Day followed day followed day. Every morning he thought, *This will probably be the last day of my life. Only probably.*

The *probably* was always enough. And then, late one morning, he pulled himself to the top of a boulder-strewn hill, and there wasn't another to follow it. The wide western plains spread out before him, a river shining in its cloak of green grass and trees. The view was deceptive. He guessed it would still be two days on foot before he reached it. Still, he sat on a wide, rough stone, looked out over the world, and let himself weep until almost midday.

As he came nearer to the river, he felt a new anxiety start to gnaw at his belly. On the day, weeks ago, when he had slipped over the temple's wall and fled, the idea of disappearing into a city had been a distant concern. Now he saw the smoke of a hundred cookfires rising from the trees. The marks of wild animals were scarce. Twice, he saw men riding huge horses in the distance. The dusty rags of his robe, the ruins of his sandals, and the reek of his own unwashed skin reminded him that this was as difficult and as dangerous as anything he'd done to now. How would the men and women of the Keshet greet a wild man from the mountains? Would they cut him down out of hand?

He circled the city by the river, astounded at the sheer size of the place. He had never seen anything so large. The long wooden buildings with their thatched roofs could have held a thousand people. The roads were paved in stone. He kept to the underbrush like a thief, watching.

It was the sight of a Yemmu woman that gave him courage. That and his hunger. At the fringe of the city, where the last of the houses sat between road and river, she labored in her garden. She was half again as tall as he was, and broad as a bull across the shoulders. Her tusks rose from her jaw until she seemed in danger of piercing her own cheeks if she laughed. Her breasts hung high above a peasant girdle not so different from the ones his own mother and sister had worn, only with three times the cloth and leather.

She was the first person he had ever seen who wasn't a Firstblood. The first real evidence that the thirteen races of humanity truly existed. Hiding behind the bushes, peeking at her as she leaned in the soft earth and plucked weeds between gigantic fingers, he felt something like wonder.

He stepped forward before he could talk himself back into cowardice. Her wide head rose sharply, her nostrils flaring. He raised a hand, almost in apology.

"Forgive me," he said. "I'm ... I'm in trouble. And I was hoping you might help me."

The woman's eyes narrowed to slits. She lowered her stance like a hunting cat preparing for battle. It occurred to him that it might have been wiser to discover if she spoke his language before he'd approached her.

"I've come from the mountains," he said, hearing the desperation in his own voice. And hearing something else besides. The inaudible thrumming of his blood. The gift of the spider goddess commanding the woman to believe him.

"We don't trade with Firstbloods," the Yemmu woman growled. "Not from those twice-shat mountains anyway. Get away from here, and take your men with you."

"I don't have any men," he said. The things in his blood roused themselves, excited to be used. The woman shifted her head as his stolen magic convinced her. "I'm alone. And unarmed. I've been walking for... weeks. I can work if you'd like. For a little food and a warm place to sleep. Just for the night."

"Alone and unarmed. Through the mountains?"

"Yes."

She snorted, and he had the sense he was being evaluated. Judged.

"You're an idiot," she said.

"Yes," he said. "I am. Friendly, though. Harmless."

It was a very long moment before she laughed.

She set him to hauling river water to her cistern while she finished her gardening. The bucket was fashioned for Yemmu hands, and he could only fill it half full before it became too heavy to lift. But he struggled manfully from the little house to the rough wooden platform and then back again. He was careful not to scrape himself, or at least not so badly as to draw blood. His welcome was uncertain enough without the spiders to explain.

At sunset, she made a place for him at her table. The fire in the pit seemed extravagant, and he had to remind himself that the things that had been his brothers weren't here, scanning for signs of him. She scooped a bowl of stew from the pot above the fire. It had the rich, deep, complex flavor of a constant pot; the stewpot never leaving the fire, and new hanks of meat and vegetables thrown in as they came to hand. Some of the bits of dark flesh swimming in the greasy broth might have been cooking since before he'd left the temple. It was the best meal he'd ever had.

"My man's at the caravanserai," she said. "One of the princes s'posed to be coming in, and they'll be hungry. Took all the pigs with. Sell 'em all if we're lucky. Get enough silver to see us through storm season."

He listened to her voice and also the stirring in his blood. The last part had been a lie. She *didn't* believe that the silver would last. He wondered if it worried her, and if there was some way he could see she had what she needed. He would try, at least. Before he left.

"What about you, you poor shit?" she asked, her voice soft and warm. "Whose sheep did you fuck that you're begging work from me?"

The apostate chuckled. The warm food in his belly, the fire at his side, and the knowledge that a pallet of straw and a thin wool blanket were waiting for him outside conspired to relax his shoulders and his belly. The Yemmu woman's huge gold-flecked eyes stayed on him. He shrugged.

"I discovered that believing something doesn't make it true," he said carefully. "There were things I'd accepted, that I believed to my bones, and I was...wrong."

"Misled?" she asked.

"Misled," he agreed, and then paused. "Or perhaps not. Not intentionally. No matter how wrong you are, it's not a lie if you believe it."

The Yemmu woman whistled—an impressive feat, considering her tusks—and flapped her hands in mock admiration.

"High philosophy from the water grunt," she said. "Next you'll be preaching and asking tithes."

"Not me," he said, laughing with her.

She took a long slurp from her own bowl. The fire crackled. Something—rats, perhaps, or insects—rattled in the thatch overhead.

"Fell out with a woman, did you?" she asked.

"A goddess," he said.

"Yeah. Always seems like that, dunit?" she said, staring into the fire. "Some new love comes on like there's something different about 'em. Like God himself talks whenever their lips flap. And then..."

She snorted again, part amusement, part bitterness.

"And what all went wrong with your goddess?" she asked.

The apostate lifted a scrap of something that might have been a potato to his mouth, chewed the soft flesh, the gritty skin. He struggled to put words to thoughts that had never been spoken aloud. His voice trembled.

"She is going to eat the world."